Fields of Gold

The Orchid and the Rose

Jim Stephens

PUBLISHED IN THE UNITED STATES BY JAY STAMPS

THIS NOVEL IS A WORK OF HISTORICAL FICTION. ALL
CHARACTERS ARE IMAGINARY OR ARE USED IN A FICTITIOUS
MANNER. ANY RESEMBLANCE TO REAL PEOPLE LIVING OR DEAD
IS PURELY COINCIDENTAL.

LIBRARY OF CONGRESS CONTROL NUMBER: 2013904762

FIELDS OF GOLD / JIM STEPHENS

ISBN-13 978-0-9890309-0-8

ISBN-10 0-9890309-0-3

TABLE OF CONTENTS

Chapter 1

"MATT THE RATT"

On that Sunday morning in late April 1939, the major American newspapers focused on three front page stories:

George Palmer Putnam, the famous son of an old American publishing dynasty and widowed husband of Amelia Earhart had been kidnapped from his California home. Most large American newspapers led with this as their primary headline.

Story number two was in smaller type and concerned Poland's warning to Germany that any attempt by the Nazi regime to take the free city of Danzig by force would be met by Poland's one and one third million man army. The story went on to say that Poland was completely prepared for war should it come. The papers stated it was a very "firm" warning to the Berlin Government of Adolph Hitler.

The last important story was printed "below the fold" and stated that the Japanese bombing of Chungking, China had reportedly resulted in the death or wounding of thousands of innocent civilians. United States Ambassador Joseph C. Grew in Tokyo had been instructed to protest. He was also instructed to protest the wide-spread Japanese destruction of American owned property in the city.

Only the story about George Putnam held any interest for the average American and none held any interest at all for Mathew Donnelly Weldon IV. Nineteen years of age, he was the scion of an old and established New York banking family which in 1812 had founded Empire National Bank.

Not the best year to start a bank, but it had survived that war as well as the Civil War and myriad economic ups and downs and political winds which had often blown the young Republic in unexpected directions. The Bank had been fortunate to always find itself with a firm hand on the tiller and that hand had always belonged to one of his forefathers. His father's hand was now steering it. He had brought it through the Depression intact and the skies were now becoming brighter.

Matt was intelligent, good-looking and completely spoiled. His mother had died when he was a few weeks short of one year old. During the passing years his father had remained a widower. Without the constant attention of a mother, the boy had been raised by housekeepers, a nanny and tutors who all treated him as the most precious, yet fragile child on earth. Not a sneeze or cough went unnoticed or untended. As he grew older it was easy for him to believe the entire solar system revolved around him and existed solely for his entertainment.

As Matt became a teenager, his father made the boy's self-centered lifestyle the norm by giving him everything he asked for. Mathew Donnelly Weldon III, known as "Trey" to people who knew him well, understood he shouldn't be indulging the boy as he did, but Matt was all that was left of his wife and he still loved her so much that he now found himself unable to deny their son anything, as he had never denied his wife anything.

He could be as steel in matters regarding the business of Empire National but when it came to Matt he seemed incapable of uttering the simple word, "NO!"

The one victory he had achieved in their non-arguments was convincing his son to go to Yale. Young Matt had heard UCLA was a party school and decided he was going to college in California, but on this one issue his father had not bent. The victory had, however, been an expensive one.

Yale was the University all the Weldons before his son attended and by heaven his boy was going there too. Whatever it took. In this case Trey won and all it took was a 1935 SJ LaGrande midnight blue Duesenberg convertible. The automobile was still brand new in the fall of 1937 when Matt started his first year at Yale. The Depression had prevented the sale of many things and this Duesy was one of its victims. Anyone who ever saw an SJ knew it was the most beautiful thing they had ever seen on four wheels.

Among the few who owned SJs were Gary Cooper and Clark Gable. The Duesy was the finest of all the automobiles produced in America. It had style, beauty and nearly 400 horsepower. Looks and speed. What more could a 19 year old want?

Well, in Matt's case, there was also the airplane. When he was twelve years old, his father had taken Matt with him to Washington when he was invited to a meeting with a group of other important bankers and the President of the United States, Franklin Delano Roosevelt.

The government was exploring ways to stabilize banks in the aftermath of the stock market collapse as most banks were under the shadow of absolute disaster. President Roosevelt was bringing together the still reasonably solvent banks for advice on saving the others, thereby salvaging the entire banking system.

4

His father had joked with him on the flight down, "Don't know why we are meeting in the Oval Office. A large phone booth would be adequate for the heads of the remaining solvent banks. Not many like us left."

At some point early in the flight, Matt had turned to his father and announced his intention to learn to fly. "Do you think you can flap your arms at the required speed?" his father had laughed.

Many times over the next few years he had raised the topic of wanting to become a pilot and his father always made light of it. Matt, however, was not joking. Matt was determined to become a pilot.

At sixteen, the five foot eleven inch young man began his flying lessons with an instructor who had flown bi-wing Spads in the Great War and was credited with shooting down seven German aircraft including two of the famed Red Barron's Flying Circus squadron. He told his father that the instructor was another of his tutors, which in a way was true enough.

The instructor, Thomas Devlin, found the young trainee to be a fast study and after the first few flights was convinced Matt would make a first rate pilot, if he lived long enough. Devlin worried that the young man insisted on attempting rolls, stall recoveries and maneuvers that could, or should, be done only by more experienced pilots. He taught the young man the best techniques only because he knew Matt would eventually do them anyway and during training he would be able to take over and correct any mistakes before they were fatal. He did worry about what might happen when he was no longer in the second cockpit.

Yet he found the young man so confident and enthusiastic that he was soon teaching him even more advanced maneuvers he had learned in the crucible of combat. The most effective was a quick barrel roll where you ended the maneuver behind the plane which had, moments earlier, been on your tail.

After a few months of instruction, Devlin announced that he had nothing left to teach Matt. Then he corrected himself, "Well, there's one thing that I can't somehow seem to get through your thick skull - caution. Flying skill, no matter how great, can be totally erased by foolhardiness. Try not to make that deadly mistake, my young friend. Too many have"

Matt had paid for the lessons out of his bank account and did not tell his father he was a fully qualified pilot until he received his license.

At first his father was angry that his son had misled him concerning Tom Devlin's tutoring subject, but in time relented and let him also become qualified on the Ford Tri-motor passenger aircraft owned by the

Bank. The company pilot, a man in his forties, had assured Matt's father that the young man was as good as much older pilots with years of experience. Matt convinced his father it was economical to allow him to fly as copilot. By handling the copilot's job on weekends and in the summer, it was not long before Matt completed the qualifications to fly multi-engine aircraft as a pilot.

As a prep school junior, Matt had wheedled a promise from his father to buy him a Waco biplane if he made perfect grades during his last year at Andover. Matt had an advantage his father wasn't aware of.

He already had nearly perfect grades in every class he had taken. His father, far too busy at the bank to sign report cards, had signed a form saying Mrs. Mulroney, manager of the Long Island Estate, could sign these in his place. The two of them had only discussed Matt's grades in the abstract. His father would enquire about Matt's progress and be told by her, "Really quite good," or "Excellent sir. He is quite a brilliant student." The only courses where he didn't have perfect scores were the ones which bored him. Those subjects were few and far between.

Matt won his wager with perfect grades and presented the report card to his father for his personal signature. The aircraft was a Royal Blue Waco F series biplane with a Wright 450 horse power R985 radial engine. It was painted light blue on the wings and tail surfaces and carried a silver lightning bolt down the fuselage. His father frowned as he wrote the check to pay for it.

Matt soon learned that taking girls for a flight and doing some mild acrobatics was a terrific seduction tool. And by now he had become an accomplished seducer. Between his good looks, easy, smooth style, the Duesenberg and the Waco, he was batting nearly 100% in bedding the young women who interested him, and there were many. All beautiful.

He never once considered how much his life differed from those of everyone else. Yet his privileged life was akin to the inside of a snow globe: small and perfect, but very fragile therefore highly breakable.

It was shattered by something as ordinary as a telephone message written on a simple piece of scratch paper. He found the note on a Monday morning in spring near the end of his second year at Yale. Taped to the door of his dorm room by his roommate Sean Fitzgerald, he couldn't miss it.

The note read: "Hey Ratt...Your Father called and wants you at his office today. Important you be there today. Called at 9:15 this morning. Sounded very stern and definite about your being there." - Fizz

Matt smiled at his nick-name "Ratt." It was given him several years back by the girls he had dated. Last night had been spent with his latest conquest, a little dark-haired beauty from Wellesley. After a night with her, he was expecting to get some sleep before his afternoon classes. That was now out of the question. The one person he did not want to anger was the 'old gentleman'; the fellow who controlled his check book. He liked his lifestyle too much to do anything that stupid. Besides, he was certain his Dad did not really approve of how he lived. Best to keep him mollified and arrive promptly.

The fastest way to reach New York was to fly. His Waco was at the small airport just outside New Haven's city limits. It was a lovely, clear day, perfect for flying. He was convinced the only thing as much fun as sex was flying. It would make up for his lack of sleep last night. To him, flying was always like a shot of adrenaline.

Football came in a close second. He played left end on the Yale team and his second roommate, big Adam Kowalski played center.

Matt was one of the few students at Yale who knew Kowalski's first name was Adam. The young man was so large everyone simply called him 'Kong.' Matt also knew something few people knew about him. Except on the football field, he was a very gentle, extremely intelligent 'Kong.'

It was 'Kong' who had once asked Matt a question which puzzled him.

"Hey Ratt, have you ever considered the effect your treatment of your Femme du Jours may be having on them?"

Matt looked at his big friend, at a loss how to answer. "I don't understand what you mean pal. Hey, it's just a little seduction. And hell, by now they all know my reputation. It's no secret what my interest is with the girls I take out. I mean... they all talk to each other. So we end up in bed for a few pleasant hours, where's the harm in that?

"Jesus, Kong, everyone calls me 'Ratt' by now anyway. At least those who don't refer to me as 'Matt the Ratt,'" he grinned.

"You think that's all there is to it, do you Matt? A little harmless fun? Do you ever consider how the girls might see it? They may not all be as 'sophisticated' about sex as you are. I'll bet you have also noticed it's the first time for more than a few of them. Girls don't do that lightly. Could it be they are expecting more than dancing, dinner and carnal pleasure from dating you for, what, two or three times before telling you goodbye and watching you move on to the next one? Ever occur to you they might be emotionally involved when they get in the sack with you? That it might be more than just a little sex in their mind?

"I only hope the way you treat them doesn't come back to haunt you. You know, like the spirits of Christmas past in 'A Christmas Carol.' I would hate to see that happen to you old pal. There is a nasty rumor our pasts tend to catch up with us sooner or later."

"Hell Kong!" Matt laughed, "Then I guess the answer is to have so much fun now, I'll be too worn out to care when it starts catching up with me. Besides, I never tell them I love them. And I have never *once* used the word 'marriage' in a conversation."

New Haven Airport was only four miles from Yale and it was only six minutes after Matt left his dorm when he parked beside the hanger which held his really fantastic Royal Blue Waco biplane. The plane and his Duesy were as close to understanding what love meant as he had ever come.

In a few minutes he performed the customary "walk around" to check her out and spent several additional minutes looking over her maintenance records to be sure everything was up-to-date. He then had two of the maintenance workers pull her out of the hanger onto the tarmac and "fire her up." While he waited, he donned his leather flight jacket and leather skull cap, a pair of flier's goggles and a white silk scarf as the open cockpit required elements of protection from the weather. More than once he had flown into perfectly clear sky only to be drenched an hour later by a thunderstorm.

Weather had recently ruined the seduction of a really spectacular girl from Radcliffe. She had transformed from a beautiful young woman into a drowned poodle in a few short minutes and seemed to blame him for the change. That ended their evening and when he phoned the next day her roommate informed him, "Judy has a really bad cold and will be unavailable into the foreseeable future." Matt understood the message and was back in the dorm disappointingly early that evening.

It took him only an hour to fly to New York City. The big buildings looked like children's toys to him from eight thousand feet. Even the Empire State building seemed small. He checked his altimeter and found he was flying almost six thousand feet above it.

Streets appeared as canyon floors cutting between the skyscrapers lining them. What would it feel like to fly between them? Matt had once seen a picture of a small biplane flying low through the Grand Canyon.

The Grand Canyon is in Arizona, he thought. But below me are certainly many grand canyons and I can make out Wall Street. Why waste an opportunity for a thrill like this? The space between the buildings is more than wide enough for the Waco to fly through. I will keep her up pretty high. No wires to contend with just clear air. I'll bet no one has ever flown down Wall Street. Dad's office is on the twenty-sixth floor so I will fly at that altitude or higher.

He smiled broadly as he pushed the plane's stick forward and felt her instantly respond as the nose angled gently downward. The white silk scarf trailed out behind Matt. In his imagination he felt a dashing adventurer off on a daring enterprise.

Chapter 2

APRIL 24, 1939

Marion Tompkins heard the heavy oak door to her boss' office open and turned to see him standing there red-faced and obviously upset. It was a condition she had seen only twice in the over two years since she had become his executive secretary. On both occasions she had been quite relieved to find that in neither case had his anger been directed at her. She treasured her job and worked with great diligence to maintain it. She understood of all the hundreds of secretaries and office girls at Empire National, she worked for the number one man in charge. Which made her, she supposed, the number one girl.

In reality she was not much *more* than a girl. She had fled her native Oklahoma during the hungry times making her way to New York with only a few dollars in her pocket, most of those a gift. Born with the name of Mary Smith, she had registered at the YWCA and signed the register with a name she thought sounded better. The name she chose was Marion Tompkins.

Her parents had told her years earlier that her dark skin, eyes and black hair came from a Cherokee ancestor in the distant past. She knew she was attractive because of the way men looked at her and constantly made passes; passes she always ignored.

Mary Smith had taken some secretarial courses in high school before she left home and more day classes as Marion Tompkins in New York while working two jobs, one early morning and one at night. About the time she was finishing her day classes, an event occurred which was certainly the best stroke of luck in her young life.

Mr. Mathew D. Weldon's previous secretary had become pregnant and left which had presented him a difficult decision. He knew he could pull a secretary from any of the officers below him and that some had perfectly capable assistants. He also knew these were relationships where both parties got used to working together. In reality each girl got used to her boss' quirks and learned to compensate for them. They made the officers they assisted stronger and better than they normally were. No.

What he needed was someone from outside the Bank that he could begin with from square one.

Empire National's personnel department contacted several nearby secretarial schools and nearly eighty girls applied. Mary, now Marion, was one of this group, and on arrival became convinced she had little or no chance to land such a prestigious position.

Most of the applicants were far better dressed and well spoken. She still had a touch of an Okie accent of which she had been unable to completely rid herself.

However at the end of the typing, spelling and personality tests she was surprised to find herself one of only four girls to be given a personal interview with Mr. Mathew Weldon III.

They were taken up to the twenty sixth floor one at a time. Marion was the last to be interviewed. When she walked into the huge office with dark paneling and oil paintings of old men covering the walls, her heart sank. She knew she would never find herself here again. It was like trying to imagine herself in heaven. She just couldn't do it. The distinguished gentleman who she knew must be Mr. Weldon rose from behind a large desk that looked to her the size of a small state, Rhode Island perhaps, shook her hand and led her to two leather chairs to see her comfortably seated. He then asked her name. "Marion Tompkins," she had answered. His blue eyes seemed to grow a bit colder. "Is that really your name?" he asked. At that instant she had known the game was over and her real name along with a lot of her story came tumbling out. She told him much of her short history almost from the day she was born and at the end of which she rose and said with a clearly embarrassed voice, "I am sorry Mr. Weldon. I realize your time is very valuable and I know I have wasted it to no good end. I'm sorry to admit I don't know how long I have been here. I don't even own a watch."

He rose and covered the few steps she already had taken toward the door. "If the time is truly important to you," he said smiling, "it has been a bit over forty-five minutes and I do not consider it time wasted at all."

She knew she was about to cry because he was being so very kind and understanding with her. She again thanked him and was opening the door when his voice stopped her once more. "Our test reports have determined your secretarial skills to be really quite superior. You have also proven yourself to be completely honest even in areas that are painful for you. Honesty and ability are both major qualifications for this job. They are my *only* qualifications. Now, it's true you may have to work very long hours on occasion. The Bank President's hours are not 'nine to four' like the Bank itself. If that is something you feel you could live with, could you begin tomorrow? Or will you need a later starting date?" He paused, and then added with emphasis, "Miss Tompkins."

She remembered, smiling to herself, how it had taken all of her resolve to keep from running to him and throwing her arms around his neck in gratitude. Instead she had simply turned toward him, smiled and told him that she would be in by eight o'clock if that was acceptable to him.

She arrived before eight o'clock the following morning and found a light blue box with Tiffany's name in white letters on it atop her desk. Inside the box was an 18 karat gold watch with her name engraved on the back. She loved the watch and, in time, came to secretly love the man who had gifted it to her.

She had been there by eight o'clock each morning since. They became the perfect team and their respect for each other was real, strong and mutual.

Brought back into the present when her boss stormed up to her desk, for a moment she was afraid she might have made a serious mistake even though she knew that when she had in the past, he had always told her that any error could be corrected.

Whenever she had made an error, his response was always a gentle, "I believe you meant to say," Or, "It might be better if." Occasionally he would comment, "Why don't we change this to...."

There had never been a single moment in the now two years when he had directed anything except gentleness toward her. Marion was convinced he was the kindest and finest boss she could have ever found.

"I assume you just heard an aircraft pass rather close by our building?" he stormed, his voice several decibels louder than she was used to hearing from this normally calm man.

"Yes sir. I have never heard one anything like that loud or close. I wondered if we were in peril."

"Well, Miss Tompkins," he huffed, "that pilot was a total idiot to pull that stunt and that total idiot, I am sorry to say, is my son. I got a good look at the aircraft flying by and it was unmistakably his; a royal blue Waco with a lightning bolt running down the side. I am sure there isn't another one like it and I should know. I bought it for him and I am seriously considering taking it away! At this moment I don't care if he has to walk all the way back to New Haven and Yale. He's going to have to return to pack, anyway: however he gets back."

Marion was quietly cheering while trying to keep her reaction bottled up. Thank heavens, she thought, it's high time this good man finally took that spoiled over-grown child of his to task. Try as she could the smile on her face managed to escape her control.

His next comment surprised and pleased her. "Yes Miss Tomkins, you are right to smile! I intend to not only read him the riot-act, but force him to do something he is not going to like. I had it in mind even before he pulled this stunt. That is why I had him come up; I intended to *ask* him to do something. Now I am determined to *tell* him to do it. It will *not* be framed as a request any longer. I believe the saying goes, 'better late than never.' Well, this is the 'late' preempting 'never.'

"Let's assume he lives to land at the airport and arrives here in one piece. I want you to toss him in my office and ignore anything you hear from then on. If you hear sounds of pain, don't worry. That will be my son in agony. If you hear begging, that too will be my son. If you hear shots being fired call both the hospital and the police, because that will be me shooting the spoiled brat and he will definitely need medical attention. He may need it even if I don't shoot him and at this moment that is a very real temptation."

By now she could no longer contain herself and she was smiling so broadly that her jaws had begun to ache.

A matching smile now slowly crept to his face while he continued with his instructions. "Before the battle of the twenty sixth floor begins, you need to make a few very important telephone calls for me in order to prevent my son's embarrassment of the Bank from becoming public knowledge.

"First, please call the mayor and tell him the flier along Wall Street was my son and assure him nothing like this will *ever* occur again. Further, near the end of the call, assure him of the Bank's support for his re-election campaign next year. We can be certain he will immediately contact the police department and strongly advise against any investigation of this incident. The department will comply with his request which, coming from him, is a demand.

"Please make your next call to the major newspapers. Call the publisher and give the least information you can. Tell them this is a personal embarrassment to me and I would certainly appreciate as little coverage as they can manage; perhaps they can call the pilot an "unknown showoff" trying to garner publicity. Naturally the paper will say it does not want to encourage behavior like this. Also let them know the Bank wants a series of advertisements in their paper."

He turned and started toward his office, but stopped at the open door. "The boy does not yet know it, but a new day has dawned."

Trey was near the end of his call with the Vice President in charge of the Commercial and Industrial Loan Department concerning a very large loan to Boeing aircraft for the expansion of two plants. They were going to produce long range, four engine heavy bombers for sale to the British Royal Air Force and American Army Air Corps. When his door opened, Marion looked in, nodded her head and gave him a wink. He understood the nod meant Matt had arrived and the wink that she had taken care of the phone calls for him and all had gone well. He gave a return nod and finished the call.

His son ambled in with his usual sense of self-assurance, totally unaware that anything was wrong and immediately said exactly what he should never have said, especially considering his father's dark mood. "Your secretary seems in an unusual mood today. She didn't even smile at me, Dad. I must say, however, I had never noticed before but she's really a looker, I'll bet she'd be really fine in b..."

He never finished the sentence. His father had come around his desk in a heartbeat, put his hand against Matt's chest and physically pushed him into a chair before his son had any chance to react.

"That, *Boy*, is a sentence you never want to finish as long as you live! And in the future you will always refer to her as *Miss Tompkins* and if you need a title attached, refer to her as my Executive Assistant and before your nasty little mind asks you, No! There is nothing going on between the two of us. **DO YOU UNDERSTAND?**"

Matt could only nod his head quietly in dismay. He had never in his nineteen years seen his father in such a dangerous mood. He knew this man, who he considered so reserved and dignified, had been near the point of hitting him and he had no idea what he would have done in reply. Though he was younger by twenty or more years, he realized he was not sure he could have won such a fight. He was faced with the certainty that his father was undoubtedly a very tough opponent. He also remembered seeing several trophies his dad had won boxing at Yale back in 1915 and '16.

Matt knew only that he was not anxious to find out. He was now ready to express his regret for his ill-chosen remark, but his father stopped him with a look and a slight shake of his head.

Trey turned his back on Matt, walked around his desk and seated himself facing his son. "Your little stunt with the Waco a short while ago," he began. "Neither that nor anything vaguely resembling it **WILL EVER**

OCCUR AGAIN," each of his last four words emphasized by his fist pounding the top of his desk. He continued eyes boring into his son, "Do you understand and will you comply?"

By now all Matt could do was dumbly nod his head in agreement. To him this was akin to being caught in a hurricane with no safe place to run.

"If I ever even get a hint that you have repeated that stunt or one like it your precious Wako is history. Remember it is in *my* name until you turn twenty one. I might add the same goes for the Duesenberg; though if you get the car airborne, the only worry will be a good funeral for you and who I will hire as mourners. Most of the people who have known you until now would, most probably, want to celebrate not mourn your passing. I know in that large contingent would be a number of girls who have been unfortunate enough to know you. Don't ask. Yes, I have had reports of your behavior in that area for some time now. I went to Yale too, remember? And I still know many people there.

"In actuality your stunt with the Waco was, more than likely, less dangerous than the way you have treated all those young ladies, but we will not at this particular moment linger on the less than stellar aspect of your moral character."

Matt felt his cheeks color knowing his father's opinion of his many brief affairs to be right. He always lied to himself that he was simply looking for the right one. The girl he could have the special feeling for, which his friends spoke of about their girlfriends; the feeling which was always shown in the romantic films. He never found it. Somehow, after having sex a few times with any girl, he always lost interest and moved on to the next. The magical feeling which was supposed to be so wonderful was never there.

He simply couldn't face the possibility that the problem lay within him. What Matt would never admit was that he simply didn't want to find the magic. It was the challenge of the seduction which was his magic. He had always considered the nickname the girls had hung on him "Matt the Ratt" a very high compliment. Even the guys used his nickname, but had shortened it to simply "Ratt."

His father continued in a coldly contemptuous tone, "I am pleasantly surprised by only two things regarding you. First, an irate father has neither shot and killed you, nor demanded your immediate marriage to his daughter. The latter probably in recognition of what a disaster you would be as a husband. Secondly, I have not had to put up bond to get you out of jail. But the week *is* still young.

16

"Of course, there is the oft repeated saying, 'God watches over children and idiots.' I am not certain which applies in your case; most probably both.

"I must reluctantly accept blame for many of your faults. Your mother passed away before you were a year old. If she had been alive your development would have followed a different path. She would have seen to it you grew up a better person entirely. I can attest your mother put up with no nonsense, not even from me. I know with her as your influence, you would have respected women. *Greatly*!

"Unfortunately she did not live and I had the Bank to run. I entrusted your care to others. I know now that was a grave mistake on my part. They said you were a bright child and a good student, both of which have proven completely true, but they pointed out that you were also willful and stubborn which has overshadowed your good points. Yes, you are a good student, you border on brilliance and you are an athlete of some merit, but I have enabled your faults past all conscience. I have given you any and everything you wanted and you have appreciated *none of it*.

"Well my son, a new day has dawned and I only hope you can endure the changes it will bring. If you can, you will become a man and it is past time that was happening. If not, I don't know what will become of you, but it will be far short of what your mother and I would have expected you to be. You have no idea what responsibility means, yet!" he said still red-faced with fury.

"Now, don't worry over much about the Waco. Whether I take it or not, I hope you know your pilot's license is gone. No one could get away with what you just did and hold on to that."

Matt interrupted his father, "Oh God, Dad! I didn't think. Can't you do something? Please! I would die if I lost that."

It was all his father could do to keep a smile from breaking through his grim visage. "That is one of the *major* flaws you suffer from Matt. You often don't think. You just do and then try to charm your way out of situations you have caused. From now on you are looking at one person who won't be charmed. But yes, I may be able to keep your ass out of a sling in this case. Perhaps I can help you keep your license, but it will require a 'quid pro quo.' On your part"

Matt's reply was instantaneous, "Anything Dad. Whatever you want. I promise."

"Are you sure Matt? Never make promises you don't intend to keep. This one will entail some big changes in your life. They will also make a man out of you if you stand up to the challenge. Are you completely sure?"

"If you can keep my pilot's license I will do anything in return. I will also never commit an act as dumb as what I just did. I will be more circumspect with the girls. I have been thoughtless there."

Matt had no idea the promise to do what his father wanted and the keeping of it would change the course the rest of his life would follow.

~ ~ ~ ~

Kong sat on the oversized travel trunk under the window of the room he shared with Matt and Fizz, a look of incomprehension plastered on his face like a Halloween mask. Fizz was snickering, sprawled across his bed at the end of the room. He spoke first, "Flew down Wall Street did you? Right past Daddy's Bank. And you're surprised he has you going away? Hell Matt, you are lucky he's not sending you to Russia or Nepal, some place like that. A location where word of your dumb stunts would at least take a very long time to get back here. I think maybe as a public service I should ring him up and suggest Nepal.

"Then all your disappointed conquests would want to bed me as a reward. No, *bad* idea. That many women in the two years I've got left before Med School would probably ruin me. I would flunk out."

Kong spoke up then with, "OK Fizz, I'll call his dad. I'm supposed to be nearly an animal anyway, so I could probably handle a sexual schedule that demanding. Besides, it would probably lower my disgraceful 3.8 average to one a *beast* should carry. No, that wouldn't work either. Amy would kill me and damned if I'll lose my girl for a few hundred rolls in the hay...but seriously Matt. England?"

Matt had promised his father he would treat his actual assignment as a confidential matter. Even though his two roommates were his best friends in the world, he had promised and he would live up to it.

"Yep old buddy that is where I am headed. I am enrolled in King's College in London, starting in the summer semester. Dad has it all arranged. If everything goes well, I could be back by next spring. Hell if I push it, I might be back by winter. He just needs me to do something for him and the Bank; sort of a confidential project. He has it all arranged here at Yale. They will hold a spot open for me. Besides, I think time away from you two dimwits will be good for me, though God knows how the team will win any games next fall without their star receiver. Namely me," he said with his best "it's great being me" smile.

Kong got up from the trunk, walked over to where Matt was standing, picked him up like a rag doll and casually tossed him atop the beat-up sofa near the door, laughingly saying, "Well Ratt, we will manage until you get back for your senior year. Hell, the question is how will the girls you haven't yet had a go with get along without you? Some will undoubtedly be cursed with that virginity thing until you return."

"Hey Kong," Matt replied, extracting himself from the sofa. "Just because you got snared by that pretty little Amy doesn't mean the rest of us have to settle for just one. You know though, you lucky devil, if I ever ran into another girl like her, I might consider it. It's a mystery to me what she sees in a big lug like you."

Kong settled back on the trunk with a smile. "Well Ratt, it's my dancing. She tells me I am very light on her feet."

Despite the three of them always throwing light hearted insults at each other, Matt knew he would miss his two roommates badly. The three had been together since arriving at Yale in the fall of 1937 on a Friday in early August within an hour of each other. Continually jostling one another trying to get settled into the small room while hauling their belongings up the stairs they arrived at the same conclusion at almost the same time. "Damn, I've got way too much stuff for this room." Once that was agreed upon, the disposal of unneeded possessions began.

Matt soon learned none of the three had been given admission to Yale on the basis of influence, though he knew *he* could have taken that path if required. All of his life he had been provided the best tutors and private schools money could buy. His grades had always been excellent. He enjoyed learning anything new and it was easy for him.

The first words out of his hulking new friend's mouth were, "Just call me Kong." There was an excellent reason for the big man's nickname. Kong had hands the size of catcher's mitts, stood over six feet five inches tall and, Matt was sure, weighed at least two hundred and sixty pounds. It was several weeks before Matt found out his given name. Joseph Adam Kowalski. He already knew that Kong was from Chicago and his family owed a large meat packing plant. He was at Yale to play football and even though Matt liked Kong, he at first, like everyone else, assumed him to be a big dumb jock that would be lucky to make it through four years.

Naturally Matt played on the same team, so he soon learned Kong was not simply a jock. He was a scholar who also played football. When grades were posted, two spaces above his near the very top of the listing was the name Joseph Kowalski. Matt was, at first, dumb-founded, but soon learned that Kong was one of the quickest minds on campus. One simply had to listen to what he said, not how he said it.

"Fizz" was Sean O'Riley Fitzgerald. Even if you didn't grasp it by his name, his red hair and attitude would have told you this was an Irish American. Lace curtain Irish. Third generation. Boston born and raised. Like Matt, his mother had died when he was less than three years old but unlike him; he had two older sisters to make sure he did not grow up spoiled.

Fizz said his father imported spirits from Ireland and Scotland before Prohibition started in 1920 and saw no reason to stop, so he was considered a bootlegger-gangster until the ban was repealed in 1933. Fizz was premed because he wanted to be a surgeon. He wanted to go to Harvard, but went to Yale instead to avoid being dogged by his father's reputation which was so well known in Boston.

When grades came out, at the very top of the list was Sean Fitzgerald. If Matt had not seen the list, he would never have known about either of them, because neither Kong nor Fizz ever said a word about it.

Matt hated to leave Yale because of these two friends. His Duesenberg and his Waco biplane, as much as he loved both, meant far less to him than these two roommates. Only being a pilot ranked as high.

The three went on triple dates every weekend. There were at least ten very good clubs which not only featured big band dance music but also turned a blind eye to drinking. All of the young men had flasks they smuggled into the dances. Matt's was sterling silver with the family crest and below that the motto, "Cum Fortitudine et Honore."

Matt always dated very attractive young women; none however, for very long. All were reputed to be excellent dancers and, after a few dates with Matt, very sexually proficient.

He carried rum in his flask. He was not crazy about it, but even girls that drank little of other liquors liked rum. It mixed well with Coke and other sweet drinks.

Matt changed girls so often and with such nonchalance that they had given him the nickname "Matt the Ratt." All of the girls knew his reputation. Yet, when he asked a 'new' girl out he was seldom refused. "So," Kong said from his seat atop the trunk, "when are you leaving for merry ole England?"

"Dad is arranging everything from his end. He is going to try and get my finals run up a couple of weeks; pulling some strings to get it done. He will probably be able to do it. Things seem a little easier when you have a building or two that carry your family's name over the door. He wants me in England at the earliest time it can be arranged. He plans to send me on the Queen Mary as the fastest, safest way to go. Four days New York to Southampton."

Kong interrupted him with a quick rejoinder, "Yeah...yeah, always talking about the name over the door business. Geez Matt, your family has been going to University here since there were teepees instead of buildings. I would hope they gave something back after all this time."

"Oh yeah," Matt returned. "Well at least we rode horses. We didn't come riding a cow like you did. Of course it was a damn big cow in your case."

From his bed Fizz gave a low long whistle, "The Queen huh? Boy, talk about roughing it. Or is he going to have you shoveling coal in the engine room all the way over?"

Matt smiled at him, "Well Fizz, funny you would say that. I offered to shovel coal. It would have been well worth it to get away from you two morons, but he insisted on getting me a nice state room. He said I deserved it after putting up with my impossible roommates for two years."

"Damn, Ratt," Kong interrupted him. "I hate to admit this, but you're like a bad case of hemorrhoids. A pain in the ass but we always know you are behind us. We are going to miss you, right Fizz?"

"Yeah Kong, my question is where we ever find a replacement as humble as 'the Ratt'? Plus, I will miss the written death threats from all the women he has humped and dumped. And the entertainment of watching him zigzag from class to class so the snipers can't get a clean shot. Guess that is why you made such a good receiver on the football field. Yeah buddy, I'm gonna miss you. Just get your job, whatever it is, done and get your butt back to this side of the Pond. Despite all the girls who would love to see you dead, they are amateur killers. The ones in Europe are professionals. Sure, right now the ones over there are only talking and threatening, but that can't last much longer. I am damn sure there is trouble coming on that side of the Atlantic and very soon."

Matt finished his finals with grades that were not as good as if he had been allowed to make his normal review of course material. But he had nothing below a B+ on any of them. It dropped his over-all average only slightly.

He said his final goodbyes to Kong and Fizz along with a few friends from the football team with a night of drinking and the next morning, more than a little fuzzy headed, drove to the Long Island Estate to pack for the trip.

Mrs. Mulroney, who ran everything on the Estate, was constantly refolding shirts so they wouldn't get wrinkled and repacking coats and ties which he was in the process of putting into two of his father's large leather-bound travel wardrobes. Almost as if his trip had been anticipated years before, the chests were imprinted only "M.D. Weldon" without the III. Packing took longer than if he had done it alone, but he was forced to admit that she was much better at it than he was. She also insisted that he carry a good waterproof trench coat. Matt acquiesced because he knew if he didn't, there would be one in one wardrobe or the other which probably wouldn't be a very good fit. He had learned long ago, she was a most determined woman and always arranged things the way she thought they should be. As much as he hated admitting it, she was usually right.

Matt had spent hours preparing his Duesenberg for a few months in storage inside the large garage behind the house. His father had promised to start it at least once a week to be sure the engine stayed well lubricated. The Waco he left in a hanger at the small airfield just outside New Haven. A pilot friend who flew a Granville Gee Bee Model Z had promised to look after her for him. Matt knew any man who owned and flew a Gee Bee could be trusted to do what he said. That is, assuming he didn't get killed flying such a hot little aircraft.

~ ~ ~ ~

The passenger ship terminals were huge, reaching five long fingers out into the Hudson River along Manhattan's West Side near 56th Street. Matt had driven by them numerous times but until this Friday had never gotten a true understanding of their gigantic size. They were not as much pier as multi-storied, covered buildings which allowed passengers comfortable access when boarding or disembarking their ship. The five terminals were impressive, but they were dwarfed by the overwhelming size and stunning beauty of a ship like the "Queen Mary." It towered over Pier 90 making it seem little more than a toy. Built by the British Cunard Line to be their showpiece liner, she was over one thousand feet long and well over one hundred feet across her beam.

The French Line had built the "S. S. Normandie" as an example of their entry into the field of luxury travel. Those two countries, along with Nazi Germany and its "S.S. Bremen" were competing to build the most luxurious steamship afloat. In reality, Matt understood, it was really about national prestige. Traveling in luxury was a secondary consideration.

The day of Matt's departure, two of these huge ocean-going hotels sat side by side. The "Queen Mary" docked at her normal location at Pier 90 and the "S.S. Normandie" at Pier 88. As nearly as he could decide, only a coin toss could determine which was more impressive. He knew the two companies were in a constant battle over which ship was faster; the trophy for the fastest crossing constantly changing hands.

Matt entered the terminal marked "Pier 90 – Passenger Terminal." It was bustling with people from several strata of society. He saw financiers, oil moguls and the son of J. D. Rockefeller Jr., Nelson.

Like the "Normandie," which carried the cream of American society going to France and the Continent, the "Queen Mary" carried those traveling to England, Scotland or Ireland.

It was not only the most luxurious way to make the crossing, but the safest. Pan Am's giant water-landing "Flying Clippers" built by Boeing Aircraft Company could make the trip in a single day, but were weather dependent and lacked the same level of comfort. Even considering those drawbacks, Matt would have taken one of them if the choice were his. It was not. His father had made that crystal clear.

Chapter 3

JOANNA BARTON

Joanna Barton's eyes were the green found only in the most perfect Columbian emeralds, yet with an intensity and vibrancy he had never seen in anyone's eyes before. Her hair, in the room's subdued lighting, shone the color of burnished bronze in moonlight. She was wearing a black silk evening dress with a lavender iris climbing up from the hem below her knees and reaching full bloom at her breasts. Matt had never seen a woman this sensual, while still fully dressed, in his life. She seemed to fit perfectly in the elegant London townhouse which belonged to her family. Even at her young age she was the impeccable hostess to her friends and a few professors from King's College.

When she extended her hand to him, Matt found it to be smooth, soft and warm. She was wearing a hint of perfume which reminded him of the large white gardenias in their gardens at the Long Island Estate.

"Ah yes," she said in a voice which reminded him of Greta Garbo, smoky and entrancing, "the young American. I have been hearing so much regarding you from many of the other girls. The young Lord-To-Be here, had mentioned he would be bringing you as a guest tonight and I had sooo been looking forward to finally meeting you. A pleasure, I am sure."

Matt instantly knew what she had heard from "the girls" had not been good and she was making it very clear to everyone within hearing, that it certainly was no "pleasure."

In spite of her allure, he found his hackles rising and his response would clearly show he was offended. He had learned years ago never to be on the defensive. His only uncertainty was if her displeasure was truly directed at him or, as she had put it, "the young Lord-To-Be." Larry Trusdale had been quite adamant that he really must introduce Matt to Joanna. He would never forgive himself if he did not. Matt could now see that his new "friend" Trusdale was hanging on every word between the two of them with a snide smile on his face. He was convinced there was far more between Trusdale and Joanna Barton than he yet understood, but how could this confrontation possibly be of benefit to anyone?

He was also aware that several of the people standing nearby had closely observed the meeting and were obviously awaiting his reaction to the clearly evident chill in her greeting.

"And you must be Joanna Barton. Yes, Larry told me about you also. Said you were the daughter of a very old, beer-making family. Informed me your father makes more beer than anyone in England. Tell me, is that where the term 'Beer Baron' came from?"

She interrupted him with, "That's ale actually, not beer. There is a difference. Beer is more popular in America and Germany, but it is true we make more ale than anyone in England, Scotland, Ireland, Germany and any of the other countries in Europe. So, tell me, were you impressed by 'the young Lord-To-Be's description of us?"

"No," he replied a bit more loudly than he intended. It was at that point he realized everyone in the room was intently watching this verbal duel between a person they knew quite well and what they saw only as this recent brash arrival from America.

So be it, he thought. It will be a contest which I would not have chosen, but I certainly have no intention of losing.

Her face was placid, but her green eyes were blazing with an intense fire as she followed with, "Not impressed then, can mean you have not met my father."

Matt knew his eyes had turned their frozen shade of ice blue. He had been made aware it always happened in situations like this, when he was very determined to do whatever was required for victory. He also knew he was entering that place where his very soul and heart turned to glacial entities and he used only those words which he knew would hurt the most. "Oh really?" he lowered his voice to a near whisper causing all those nearby to lean ever so slightly in his direction. All of them now realized this was a prize fight between two experienced heavy weights and one or both was going to get bloodied. "Really," he repeated for emphasis, "the Bank my father heads could easily buy your little breweries without breaking a sweat. Empire National is so large...why," he added a laughing tone to his voice, "it wouldn't even notice the purchase. Now, are you impressed?"

She looked at him for a moment, started to turn away, stopped and flung her reply over her shoulder in his direction. "No, but then I haven't met your father either. I am certain he must be more mature than the boy he has sent to England. And by the way...we are not for sale." A collective intake of breath went though the onlookers, followed by the escape of a collective sigh from all of them.

Matt realized for the first time in his young life that he had never before met anyone with the exception of his father, who was if not more than his match, certainly his equal. Though she was still only about nineteen, Joanna was every inch a lady, but one with sharp teeth and claws who definitely knew how to use them to best effect. He knew if he let her walk away it would end any chance he would have of getting to know her. There was not a single doubt in his mind about whether or not he badly wanted to know this maddening creature better. A quiet voice in his head was pleading with him not to allow her to walk out of his life.

So it was that Matt surprised everyone including himself when he said, "Joanna, please wait. I am sorry and I want to ask you something." She turned back, her arms crossed on her chest; still obviously angry.

"What?" she said in a voice which could have easily cut through tempered steel.

"I am really quite sorry," he dumbly repeated himself, suddenly realizing he was completely surrendering the field of battle to her and astonished at himself for being able to do it. And, to top even that, before a roomful of people who would have it all over University the next day. He saw her eyes soften just a bit, and then she surprised him with a question, "So tell me, is that an expression of regret for your attitude or a fair warning about your reputation?"

She uncrossed her arms when he replied with a simple, "More than a little of each, I am afraid."

He saw that more than a hint of a smile now shadowed the corners of her mouth. He was so relieved in knowing some of the tension had passed that he could not resist smiling at her and was completely delighted to find her smiling broadly back at him. It was a radiant smile which he hoped to see often. "So," she said through the smile, "what was it you wanted to ask?"

Matt's mind went instantly blank. So my boy, you have nearly avoided disaster. You have gotten her turned around and you have made her smile. OK genius. What now? Come on boy think! Surely you're not going to blow it at this point.

Her smile was fading. His tortured mind could only think of one thing and it was really dumb. The thing his father had sent him over to do. It was a hell of a reach but at least it was something....

"If," he asked, "or *when* England is attacked by Germany, can England hold out?"

For a moment he could sense total consternation on her face; the first time he had seen any emotion short of absolute control on her part. Then her face changed completely and true laughter rang forth from her lovely mouth. Matt thought it to be the most enchanting sound he had ever heard. A sound both musical and magical. He was sure he could become a jester if that sound was the reward given one playing the part of fool.

When her laughter finally died away she looked at him and said, "Mathew Weldon, I have to award you high credit indeed for the worst yet most original pickup line I have ever heard."

He replied, "No, Miss Barton, I am serious and would very much like your honest opinion. Frankly I can't imagine *you* ever giving any opinion other than an honest one."

She smiled at him again and moved toward him until only a few inches separated them. When she spoke again it was to quietly ask a question of her own. "An honest opinion from me for an honest answer from you in return. Would that be a fair arrangement in your estimation?"

He thought for a moment, wondering what her questions might be but decided what she was proposing was completely fair. He answered in a voice he knew to be almost a whisper. "Yes, that is an equitable exchange. Regarding anything, that is, except questions relating to our sex lives." It was a tongue in cheek answer. He knew it would have been only a very slightly off color reply around any sophisticated university crowd in America. A very "hip" reply, but he was no longer in America. And no matter her years, this was a capital "L" lady to who he had said it. Matt felt a bit of sweat start on his upper lip.

But she only smiled and said, "I agree primarily because you would be bored with mine, while I am sure yours, from what I hear, would be endlessly entertaining. On your end the bargain would be quite an unfair exchange." The last said laughingly.

He actually found himself blushing and whispered, "Can we forget that codicil which I intended only in jest? I can be such an ass at times."

She was still smiling when she replied, "Yes, we will forget and yes, you can be. I suppose I will just have to get used to it. But I will continue to *hope* for the best."

He too was smiling when he looked her in the eyes and said, "Miss Barton, I will honestly try to do better. I promise you my best behavior." He held up his hand in the Boy Scout oath. The three middle fingers extended.

"Oh, were you a Boy Guide?" she asked.

"No," he laughed. "In America we call them Boy Scouts. Yes, I was a Boy Scout for a few years. I went camping several times and spent two of the longest weeks of my life at a summer camp one year."

Her smile broadened when she said, "What? No girls?"

Matt hung his head and laughed when he admitted, "No girls except across the lake and it was a *very* large lake with the canoes being chained and locked at night. It broke my fourteen year old heart."

She joined his laughter, then moved closer to him. By now their bodies were almost touching and Matt could felt a tiny electric tingle as a result of her nearness.

Her lips were very close to his ear when she whispered, "That's why your father sent you over to England, isn't it? No, not about getting you away from *girls*. If it were that, he would have sent you to Antarctica.

"His bank probably has investments over here and he wants to know if he should divest them. Yes, Mathew, we really do need to talk, but not this evening. My most pressing duty tonight is that of playing hostess. Together we have partially fulfilled one of the primary duties of a good hostess; we have most certainly provided entertainment for my guests. Undoubtedly far beyond their highest expectations. Still, I must see out the rest of the evening in my role. I will send you a note suggesting a time we can get together for a serious chat about your question. Will that be acceptable?"

As much as he hated to see her walk away, he nodded and simply said, "Yes, I will look forward to that."

Walking away, she turned again and said in a voice with warmth he had not heard from her before, "Mathew, it really has been a pleasure after all."

He smiled and said simply, "Yes Joanna, for me too."

The balance of the evening seemed to pass with surprising ease. He found the other guests drawn to him in groups of three or four asking him questions about himself. They wanted to know where in America he was from and where he had been going to university. Most of them seemed to know about Yale and the quality inherent in an education there. One had even applied and been accepted but the situation between England and Germany was the deciding factor in his decision not to go.

And a few of the girls, the pretty ones interestingly enough, asked if his father really owned a large bank. No, he patiently explained, his family had started the bank nearly a hundred and fifty years ago, but they really didn't own it as it was now a publicly traded entity. But yes, his father headed the Bank as his ancestors had since the day it began. A few of the young ladies looked as if they understood his explanation, while others simply looked confused by his use of the term "publicly traded entity."

Matt understood this sudden interest in him. Joanna had given him her seal of acceptance. When she had turned back around, then walked to him and whispered in his ear, the other guests' opinions had been changed to the point that several of the girls were openly flirting with him.

Normally Matt knew he would be having an incredible night from here on, but not one of them held an attraction close to that he felt for Joanna. Each time he glanced at her he saw a woman who was, at one and the same time, the embodiment of total female sexuality as well as ethereal femininity. He knew only that he had never met anyone like her and doubted he might ever meet her like again.

He noticed Trusdale seemed to have disappeared, which meant he was left to his own devices to get back tonight. Oh well, he thought, a short walk to the Underground and another short walk to my rooms. I really should have brought the MG. Would have been a nice drive back with the top down. Any night without rain or fog in London should be celebrated. As far as rain and fog. Well...he was getting used to them.

Shortly before eleven, guests began to leave and Joanna stationed herself near the door so she could thank them for coming and wish them each a good night. As he watched her, he was aware of one certainty, she was a girl who was so far outside his realm of experience that the two of them could be no more different if they had come together from two different planets light years away from each other, yet he was strongly attracted to her.

Matt reclaimed his coat and throwing it over his shoulders walked up to her. He gave her a smile which she willingly returned and extended her hand. Taking it he laid his other hand atop hers.

"Well Mathew, I really am grateful you came after all. I am afraid our young 'Lord-To-Be' left some time ago. Will you be able to make your way back on your own?"

Matt was still smiling when he said, "Yes Joanna, I have learned my way around town pretty well by now. The Underground has become an old friend. I have a little MG, but parking... well, that is always iffy." Then he continued, "Speaking of Larry, I have the feeling there is a bit of bad, shall we say, 'history' between the two of you."

He saw a shadow pass her green eyes, then after a pause she answered, "Bad history. A nice turn of phrase, Mathew. Then, yes, a bad bit of 'history' it is. Perhaps I'll tell you someday when we know each other better."

Matt dropped the smile from his lips and looked for a long moment at her, realizing she was studying him in the same way. Their hands were still together.

"Joanna, at first I was afraid we were going to begin and end badly at our first meeting and never like each other at all. I would have regretted that."

He saw her eyes grow a bit misty before she said, "I believe that would have been a great mistake for both of us but for reasons not yet known; it didn't turn out in that way. I suppose it simply wasn't meant to. I may as well tell you now that I have a belief in Kismet."

"Fate," he said, "until tonight I always laughed at that idea but, you know, I just may have been wrong."

He released her hand and walked into the night.

Chapter 4

THE INVITATION

Two days after meeting Joanna, Matt was in the men's lounge of the Mathematics Building when Larry Trusdale came breezing in. He walked past the table at which Matt was studying without speaking.

Matt quickly stood and grabbed his arm. Trusdale was first stopped, and then forcefully turned until he was facing a grimly smiling Mathew Weldon. "Hello Trusdale. What! Are we no longer best friends? I noticed you simply vanished before the party ended at the Barton place night before last. Didn't things go the way you planned? Were you expecting Joanna to fall into bed with me? I'm wondering, did she refuse you her favors? Was this going to be your sick revenge for her classifying you as considerably less than sexually attractive in her eyes?'"

Trusdale got red in the face and tried to jerk his arm from Matt's grasp but found he couldn't. His mouth hardened into a grimace of hate as he snarled his reply while looking toward the other young men in the room. "Listen, just because Joanna Barton didn't think you were so hot, does not mean that she didn't get bedded by me. No, old boy, quite the opposite. She simply couldn't get enough of Laurence Trusdale. After the first time, she begged for it. After a while it was really pathetic the way she...."

Before he could finish the sentence, Matt hit him with a vicious body block as hard as any he had ever delivered on the football field at Yale or the Rugby fields here in England. This immediately drove Trusdale rapidly across the room with a solid thud into the plastered wall. The line of ancient and stately oil paintings that had hung there for over two hundred years in perfect alignment now hung in total disarray.

The other young men were completely silent, several sitting open mouthed with surprise. This was not the sort of thing which happened at King's College and certainly not to the Trusdales of England. The on-lookers were surprised by the unexpected suddenness of what they had seen, yet several wanted to cheer Matt's explosive reaction to Trusdale's sexual claim.

Matt released his hold on the now shocked Trusdale and stepped back. His erstwhile friend remained upright for a moment and then slid like a stain down the wall and sat partially upright, gasping for breath.

"Well Trusdale," Matt began, "the first thing I want to let you know is I am now certain you are nothing short of a lying bastard. Even though I met Joanna for the first time two nights ago, I am sure she is far too much a lady to have anything of that nature to do with scum such as you. The potential title you may someday carry would not matter in the least to her. She is far nobler than you will ever be. If you feel up to standing, we can have this out right now. If not we can meet at your pleasure, which will in fact be my pleasure. How about it old boy? Care for a touch of fisticuffs? I will even add 'Please.'"

Trusdale could only gasp out a strained, "NO!"

Matt had been expecting a refusal all the while hoping Trusdale would take him up on his offer. He had never met anyone more in need of a good trouncing in his life. Funny, he thought, that number should have included myself for a very long time. What is there about meeting Joanna Barton that makes me want to change that? I don't really know her and yet here I am defending her.

"Very well then Trusdale. I will give you a bit of advice in order to avoid my deciding to reopen this matter.

"First, never repeat the lie you just told and secondly don't go complaining to anyone about your introduction to the wall. There are enough men here who heard what you said about the young lady to put the lie to anything you might say and I am sure they are more than honorable enough to speak out for her reputation in this matter. Finally, if I should be jumped by three or four toughs some dark night,...well old sod, I will certainly come looking for you and you will have a bad limp and no sex life for a long time afterward. Do you understand?"

The look on Trusdale's face bordered on sheer terror and he could only dumbly mouth the word "Yes" to show he understood Matt's question.

Matt saw bystanders' heads being nodded and suddenly understood most of them probably did not like Trusdale at all and would delight in an opportunity to prove it by supporting Matt in whatever he said about this confrontation.

Matt turned and walked back to his table and the complicated mathematics problem he had been working on. Two students he knew to be fourth year men walked by and one of them paused and quietly said, "Good show old boy. Let me know if you have any problems as a result of this incident. I saw and heard the whole thing. I will back you up. Most of us here will be glad to do so."

~ ~ ~ ~

The following afternoon Matt found a pale ivory envelope in his mail box. It was addressed simply to "Mathew Weldon – King's College" and the reverse flap bore the engraving "J. S. B."

The enclosed note was written in a flawless hand of such quality that Matt was reminded of the engraved calligraphy on his prep school invitations for his graduation from Andover. The note read:

Dear Mr. Weldon,

You showed an interest in meeting with me to examine questions you have regarding England's preparedness in the event of a conflict. I will be glad to meet with you next Saturday to open this discussion if that will be convenient. In the event you have never seen a brewery, we could combine our discussion with a tour of our family's main brewery which is not very distant the Tower of London. Just ask anyone the location of Old Oast House Brewery if you are in need of directions. Would 9:30 in the morning be acceptable?

I am also certain I owe you more than simply a word of thanks for defending my reputation in the matter concerning a certain Lord's despicable son. In this particular instance, your behavior was totally correct and while I do not usually condone violence, this is a case where it was completely and thoroughly warranted. I find myself, selfishly perhaps, approving of your actions.

I believe you Americans have a saying, "Not in a million years." Well in the kind of activity implied with the particular individual in question, "Not even once in a hundred million years." Therefore, I will again say, thank you.

I await your reply about scheduling our conversation.

Joanna Barton
#37 Eaton Square
London
P.S. This is not a date. This is a discussion and tour. Perhaps we might call it a visit.

Matt reread the letter twice before he could completely accept that Joanna was saying she would be happy to meet with him and, in spite of her post script, touring her family's brewery certainly sounded like almost a 'date' to him. To be with a girl who had impressed him so much at their first meeting, even if it had begun under initially unpleasant circumstances, was a promising beginning. Besides, her note had thanked him for later defending her reputation.

He had done it as a completely reflexive reaction which he still did not fully understand. It never occurred to him that she would be told about it, even though with so many witnesses he should have known she was bound to hear.

For probably the first time in his life, he realized that many of the things he did had consequences which reached farther than the act itself. How had he gone so many years without this understanding? He made a silent promise to consider the scope of his actions and decisions in the future, to anticipate what consequences might occur on some future day.

He could clearly remember the fascination he had as a small child with the circles made when he threw rocks into the lake at the house on Long Island. The circles always became larger and larger as they moved away from the center until they washed onto the far shores. He now understood that actions and decisions behaved in the same way. His actions could touch and affect others whose shores were distant from his own.

Matt smiled as he sat at his desk and began writing his reply to Joanna's note by telling her that he would be delighted to meet with her at the brewery. He joked that his only contact with ale was his, upon several embarrassing occasions, excess consumption of its close cousin, beer, on fall days following many of the football games he had played for Yale.

He closed his note by thanking her for arranging his tour of the family brewery and telling her he was looking forward to it.

Chapter 5

THE BREWERY TOUR

L ondon was a very large city where Matt had quickly found parking to be a problem in almost any part of the downtown area. He had purchased a slot in a garage near the college for his newly acquired Green 1937 MG 18/80 roadster convertible.

The beautiful machine had belonged to a British Army officer recently shipped to Singapore with his unit. He bought it at what to him was a bargain price as the car only had a little over 10,000 miles on the odometer and even that rich leather smell still emanated from the seats. It was wonderful to drive with the top down, but he quickly learned how impractical a ragtop was in England where it could rain at any moment with little or no warning. Soggy trousers had been his reward for walking away and leaving the top down if he was parked anywhere except in the covered garage.

Since today's "visit" was on a Saturday traffic was lighter. He found a parking spot near the Brewery after following detailed instructions given to him by one of the men in his Literature class. The directions had proven completely reliable. The biggest challenge was remembering to drive on the left and look to the right before turning. It was so alien to him that he had already had a few horn-blowing near-misses along with shouted words and raised fists he judicially chose to ignore.

After a short walk he came to a stone fronted building which appeared to be an ancient Pub set into a block-long stone wall. Carved above the door and faintly legible was the name "BARTON" and the date "1577." In much larger white painted letters set higher on each side of the wall was the name "Old Oast House Brewery."

His watch told him he was almost ten minutes early, so he walked down the block. At the end he saw the same wall continued beyond a gate down the next block with identical white lettering. Further along, the following block was also enclosed by a similar wall and gate. Matt whistled quietly to himself realizing this was no small family business that the Bartons owned; it encompassed three complete city blocks.

He returned to the antique wood double doorway set into the face of the stone building. Two windows, one set on each side of the door, looked out on the street and were hung with white Irish lace curtains. The building retained the look of a cozy old public house. Matt almost expected to hear conversation, toasts and the clank of glasses from inside. He was about to knock when the door was opened by Joanna who smiled and invited him in.

The room he entered was like a museum representing an indeterminate period of history. Matt would have guessed between sixteen hundred and eighteen hundred. The bar, very aged and scratched, was made from exceedingly dark wood. The electric lighting was hidden and subdued which added to the aura of belonging in an age long past. The tables and chairs were scraped, chipped and scratched. The floors were also of very old wood and were heavily stained and scuffed.

Matt looked at Joanna, spread his arms wide while taking in the room and said, "Wow, this is really amazing. It's like stepping through a door leading back into the past. I almost expect Will Shakespeare to step in off the street to enjoy a pint with some of his actors. I mean, this is completely unexpected, Joanna."

She smiled at his words, obviously pleased. "Thank you Mathew. Everything here is period authentic. It is sadly not, however, original. When we became exclusively a brewery and the family closed the pub back in 1708, all the original furnishings were disposed of. We are pretty sure they were sold to another pub or perhaps multiple pubs. They may still be in use somewhere in London or the surrounding area but there are no records to tell us. I like to think they are still around and were not broken up for fire wood. It was restored, as nearly as we could ascertain, to the look it would have had in that era. This was all re-created during the late reign of Queen Victoria. We really didn't intend it to be a museum. It is not open to the public. It exists only to remind us of our heritage. This old Pub is here to stress to us that we are producing a product which is to be enjoyed by regular people, in places such as this. I can never completely express how important quality is to the Bartons."

Matt felt she was advising him about more than just the ale they made with her last statement. He was sure she was pointing out to him that her family, and by implication herself, did not accept second-best in anything. He was forced to look away from her green eyes for a moment because he found them nearly hypnotic.

"So Joanna," he began, "did the early Bartons have a pub first and then become brewers or in what order did the progression occur?"

"Well Mathew...."

He interrupted her with, "Please...look, first I have been calling you Joanna. Is that okay or would Miss Barton be more acceptable?"

She nodded her head 'yes' and followed with, "Please do call me Joanna. That is not too familiar at all."

"Then," he said, "Call me Matt. Almost everyone does."

Her eyes found his as she answered, "I know. But can we say I am different from most people. I really like the name Mathew and unless you strongly object, I would like very much to be allowed to call you that."

He was convinced that she had just complimented him in some way he could not yet fully grasp, so he answered with a simple, "Mathew it is then. That is fine. It is my name after all. It is a family name. My father is Mathew Donnelly Weldon III or simply Trey to his friends, so I was christened Mathew Donnelly Weldon IV. 'Matt' seemed a more acceptable alternative than 'Ivy.'"

Her eyes glazed over for a moment then lighted with recognition, "Oh, I get it. The fourth is IV or IVY. Oh my yes. That is clever. But I still will use Mathew."

"So Mathew, from the 1500's until the 1700's there were no big brew houses. Pubs which succeeded and thrived did their own brewing. Back in those days the ale had a short life, a few days at best. After that it soured and turned rank. So there was a constant struggle to keep good product. For a long time the Bartons were both Publicans and Brewers. By trial and error the old Publican Brewers learned to extend the life of the brew. Wooden casks were sealed which was a big step along the way and the proper use of hops to preserve the ale made it feasible to ship the brew over an ever larger area as the brewing process was perfected.."

"Putting a substantial head on a glass of ale came from that horse and wagon era. The roads were very rough and it was the constant shaking and banging around of the wooden casks that introduced tiny air bubbles into the ale which took the form of a head when the brew was poured. Even today a good head atop the glass is accepted as one of the signs of outstanding ale."

"Joanna, may I interrupt you for a moment? There is something that has bothered me for over a week now and I really need to say it."

"By all means, Mathew. This can all wait." She sat down in one of the old chairs and Matt sat across from her. There was a guarded look of curiosity in her eyes.

He was not sure of how to express what he needed to say in spite of having considered it for days, so he just stumbled ahead.

"The night I first met you I was an insufferable bore with unforgivable manners and I really want to thank you for being so forgiving and especially for agreeing to see me today. I really want to say I am sorry."

The corners of her green eyes lifted with a smile which contained, Matt sensed, a touch of relief.

"No Mathew, I owe you an apology. I completely mistrusted your reason for being there with Larry Trusdale. I had heard from other young ladies that you were quite the practiced seducer. The young Lord-To-Be and I previously had a confrontation of a very personal nature. He could not take no for an answer and tried to be forceful. Well, I believe you are somewhat aware of the situation and I do thank you for what you did.

"Unfortunately, I assumed he had brought you along thinking you would seduce me and in some warped way he would feel revenged. Because I believed that, I was determined to put both of you in your places. I was really quite beastly to you and you had no idea of why my behavior was aimed at you. I now understand that your response to me was in actuality quite predictable given my attitude towards you."

"No, Joanna. I wish I could see the matter in that light but I cannot. Everything you say about our meeting is correct, but the problem I have with myself is how I reacted to the situation in question. I was like a little boy who had just had his favorite toy taken away or had his toe stepped on. I was both childish and churlish; the 'my daddy is bigger than your daddy' was... well, simply unforgiveable."

She gave a short laugh before telling him, "Yes, that one really made me mad. I don't doubt that your Bank ... umm... Empire National is large and probably could buy us if we were for sale, but you can, after all, only buy what is for sale. A situation Larry Trusdale does not understand at all and may never. Some people in England think that a title gives them a license to be crude, overbearing and simply take whatever they want.

"As a business, we are very financially sound and further more we love what we do. I dare say you feel that way about banking."

Her last remark made Matt once again come to grips with a question that he had refused to face since that day his father had told him he *was* going to England and the reason he was going. Did he intend to be involved in the future of the Bank or was he going to break with that tradition? Since he did not want to think too much on that topic and possibly spoil a day he had been looking forward to, he decided a change of topic was in order.

"Look Joanna, rather than go any further with 'my fault your fault,' will it be acceptable to you if we simply say that we misunderstood each other and carry forward with how ale is brewed? It will be, after all, much more fun than flailing our egos, which in my case, certainly got the better of me."

Joanna smiled so broadly that Matt would have sworn the lighting in the room had increased and her eyes had become a brighter green; if that was even possible.

"Agreed! Let's go out the side door to the plant and I'll take you through the process from brewing to shipping."

He followed her through several huge rooms, finally stopping in one with wooden floors. Joanna described its purpose to him.

"In this room, barley is spread on the floor and water is sprayed on it. This allows a germination process to begin. This short growth period softens it and produces enzymes which digest the starch in the grain and turn it into sugar. This is then heated in kilns which halts the growth process in very short order."

She took him into the next room and showed him the large kilns. Even though they were not in operation on a Saturday, Matt could still feel the heat the steel gave off.

"Joanna," he asked, "what must it be like working in here when these kilns are in full operation?"

"Well Matt, there is no denying it is a hot job. There is simply no other way to do this except with heat. The workers are all well cared for. Salt tablets help and water breaks are frequent. The men all look out for each other and we have medical staff in a small clinic on site. Many of our workers are second and third generation employees. We also have an age limitation of 35 in this area. Past that, they move to a less demanding part of the operation though many try to find ways to stay longer. You see, each of our workers gets two pints of free ale each day. These fellows get an extra pint."

She moved him into a room stacked almost to the ceiling with large bags. Each was marked with what appeared to his eyes to be a form of hieroglyphics. Joanna noticed he was looking at the bags with a slightly cocked head; obviously he was trying to understand the markings on the bags.

"Yes Mathew, we have a complicated coding system which identifies several factors about each lot of the malt, which will be required when using it to make ale. We not only want the ale to be consistent in taste but also in color. The coding helps bring out those, as well as other desirable characteristics in the brew.

"After this process, the dried material and resident husk is a form of malt and it is stored until needed. Let's go to the next room where we turn the dried material into mash."

Matt followed her into another large room filled with a slightly sour odor, which he found at first unpleasant.

"Making ale requires large quantities of pure water and here you see the reason why. First we needed it to sprout the barley and now we need it to spray on the milled malt and grain husk residue to make the wort.

"Wort is the end result of malt and the grain husks combined when exposed to heat. Enzymes in the barley now convert the starch into sugar. We filter out the sugary mixture from the rest and this is the part we call wort. Some roasted barley is added to achieve a rich color and better flavor. The wort is boiled and at that point hops are added for additional flavor and to preserve the brew. After it is cooled, the wort is transferred to the next stage in another area. Shall we go there?"

Matt was by now completely intrigued by not only his guide and her complete understanding of the intricacies of making ale, but the science and art required to produce it.

The next room was filled with miles of copper piping and huge upright containers which tapered at the bottom and were rounded on top with the copper pipes running in and out of them.

Joanna pointed up to one of the huge copper vessels. "This is a fermenting tank. Here the wort has yeast added to it. The yeast converts the sugar in the wort into alcohol and carbon dioxide which gives the ale a full flavor. After the fermentation process, the final step is to transfer the ale to kegs or bottles and ship them out. All of that is done here and we have our own trucks and boxcars to move the ale. We also have repair shops to care for the trucks."

Matt and Joanna remained standing beneath one of the big fermenting tanks. After a short pause, Joanna looked him squarely in the eyes and said, "Of course the most important thing in producing great beer or ale is the quality of the ingredients you begin with. Quality ale starts long in advance of the actual brewing process. Before the hops arrive here. If you sow quality seed in rich ground, the chances are much better you will grow superior barley. It follows, if you begin with the very best barley and know what you are doing, the ale will always be exceptional. We at the Old Oast House Breweries have known that basic fact for many generations. It is, truly, in our blood."

Matt once again had the feeling she was speaking not only about brewing ale, but also about her family's philosophy of life and lineage, which she had fully adopted as her own. He also knew that with her, it went deeper than simply the brewing of ale.

It made him painfully aware that his father had tried to pass similar ideals and values along to him. How often had Trey spoken to him about standards such as duty, honor and respect? He had been told many times about how the management of any great institution required all three of these virtues and many more. He had emphasized that if personal gain was possible along with them, then gain was acceptable. If not, personal gain should no longer be a part of the equation. He wished he had listened more carefully, for he was beginning to understand how important those guide posts could be in life.

Listening to her talk, he began to comprehend how shallow his life had been and how, by pleasing only himself, he had undoubtedly cheated others. He had always placed his personal gain over the losses others suffered. It was a most uncomfortable realization and he broke away from her gaze to look at the big tank they were standing under. He had the fleeting feeling Joanna could clearly sense his discomfort.

He suspected that she could very nearly read his inner-most thoughts and know the sudden tumult of feelings he was having. It was not a comforting realization that someone who barely knew him might be able to read his thoughts so clearly. The only thing he could do to break this connection was to ask her, "And how many gallons can each of these tanks hold?"

Those brilliantly green eyes paused, a question in them, and shifted from his to look at the tank above them before she answered, "This one will hold two hundred fifty thousand pints, but we have larger ones in another building. We can see those later if you wish."

Matt grinned impishly at Joanna before telling her, "No, I think this is all I can drink. Let's save the big ones for really thirsty Englishmen."

His reply brought a laugh from his enchanting, yet somehow disturbing, guide. It was the second laugh he had heard from her and was as wonderful as the one he had heard at the party almost two weeks ago.

"Joanna, did know your laugh is really fantastic? It is the kind of laugh one would expect from royalty. A princess perhaps."

She looked back at him; a look of surprise on her face. Those entrancing green eyes of hers searched his before she told him, "Mathew Weldon, I can see why the girls say you are such a dangerous young man to be with, but don't try your wiles on me. You will be disappointed. I am immune to blarney as is my entire family."

Matt was surprised by her answer. "No Joanna. As hard as you may find it to believe, I am serious. No blarney; which by the way, I had always thought to be a castle in Ireland. But that completely aside, you do have a marvelous laugh. I noticed it at your party and promised myself to hear you laugh as often as I could arrange it. At the time I even thought if we had lived in the middle Ages, I would have gladly been a jester just to make you laugh. I think what I am trying to say is, I would like for us to be friends if you would not object. Would you allow me to share your laughs?"

He reached his hand out. She hesitated, but after searching his eyes finally took his hand and shook it.

"Very well Mathew. Friends, but friends **only**. You will find I am the most loyal of friends as long as you can leave it at that. Remember you have a reputation for being a Lothario and I have no interest in having a lover for a short while, then seeing him move on to another conquest. I knew long ago that for me it would be *one* man. It is a decision I will never change. The right man and that one *forever*. So we will be friends and nothing more. Will you agree to that?"

Matt hesitated, but finally gave his answer. "Yes, Joanna I agree, but it will be a learning experience for me. You see I have never been *just* friends with a woman. Friends with guys yes, but never women. You have my past relations with women pegged correctly. I cannot and will not deny it. I suppose by your definition I have been a cad. Even, God forbid, in the same league as Trusdale, though I do hate to think so."

Joanna smiled at him. "Mathew, it will be very easy. Just think of me as a *guy*. Look, I have never been a friend to a man the way I am offering to be your friend. We both probably need this sort of relationship. I know I have never felt I could do it. Men have always wanted to have that other kind of relationship with me. Not one of them ever gave me the chance to be a friend with no other strings attached. What you will get from our friendship is the best tour guide in all of London and I will have a very nice looking young man, who, I truly believe has real potential as a human being, to be my escort. Will that work for you?"

Without hesitation this time, Matt replied with a grin, "We have a deal. It sounds like fun. The hard part will be thinking of you as a guy. That part will really challenge my imagination to its limits. If I should ever get out of line just hit me over my thick skull with the nearest heavy object."

She paused for only a moment before saying, "What and break the nearest heavy object?" It was the third time he had heard her laugh and this time he joined her.

Matt was still watching her beautiful face when she glanced downward and he realized he was still holding her hand from the handshake. The knowledge made him blush. Had he ever blushed before? He didn't know, but he spoke up to cover his embarrassment.

"Sorry Joanna. You'll probably need that hand back. Do I owe you any rental for its use?"

She flashed him a smile and, in a breathless voice answered, "No, but if you had kept it a moment longer you probably would have." He knew he was going to have to watch out because she was every bit as witty as he and any double entendre would not be overlooked.

"Mathew, I know you wanted to ask me about whether or not this little island of ours could stand up to Germany if war comes. My short answer is, pardon the profanity, 'Hell yes.' We British simply don't lose wars. Well, I suppose we did lose one you to 'Yanks.' But that was a long time ago and the rumor over here is we gave it less than our best.

"The Vikings had a go at us, but they finally decided it was better to be lovers than fighters. They settled down and became part of the community.

"But for a more detailed answer I want you to meet my father. I mentioned your quest to him and he is always in on Saturday...and well, he has very good contacts, some of whose information he will share with you if you would like. Shall I introduce you?"

Matt found he was admiring not only Joanna's beauty, but her intelligence and straightforwardness as well. She truly did think very much like a man. No subterfuge, just a completely straight on approach to any situation.

"If you think it will not be too great an intrusion. I promise not to take too much of his time."

"No Mathew," she replied while tilting her head a bit sideways as if studying him from another angle. "But it is thoughtful of you to look at it that way. I am beginning to think you just might be worth my time after all. Follow me. It's a bit of a walk."

Matt followed her back through the old pub and out the front door which she locked behind them. The wall down the third block enclosed a bottling plant and corporate offices. The wall stood apart from a number of large brick buildings contained within it.

Joanna pointed out the bottling plant, clinic, dining facilities, a large garage for the company trucks and the three story corporate office. He followed her up three flights of stairs and stopped outside a door which had a simple "Owen S. Barton" in gold leaf on the wood.

Joanna knocked lightly on the door and was greeted with a booming, "Come in Joanna," which seemed to fill the entire upper floor.

From the sound and volume of the voice, Matt wondered if he was about to meet a man or an ogre. Joanna was smiling at him in a way which said, "Don't worry, it's just my father." He knew whoever had fathered such a beautiful woman couldn't be all that bad.

Joanna opened the door to the most cluttered office he had ever seen. Until now Matt had thought tenured university professors were lacking in organizational skills. Now he knew they were a picture of neatness by comparison.

His first impression of Owen Barton was that of a large man until Matt realized Owen was not as tall as he was. Yet Joanna's father managed to project a substantially larger image. It was when he rose from his deck and kissed his daughter on the cheek that Matt decided he really stood no more than five foot ten inches. It was the voice which had made him visualize such a large man. The voice and the tremendous amount of smoke in the room at first hid his true size.

Only while he kissed his daughter was the battered old pipe removed from his mouth. The rest of the time it poured smoke like an over-worked chimney. A thick blanket of smoke filled the room despite two open windows behind him.

"Well," her father began in a cheerful voice. "You must be Mathew Weldon. Joanna said she was going to bring you around today for a tour and a talk. I expect you have had your tour. What did you think of our little brewery?"

Matt glanced at Joanna before saying, "Well Mr. Barton..."

"No, no my boy, please call me Owen or you will have me thinking I'm old enough to be a father. Oh, I am old enough to be a father... Well, call me Owen anyway."

Matt could now see where Joanna's quick wit came from. "Well Owen, if this is a little brewery; I must remember a spare pair of shoes if I ever tour a big one. But one thing I know. There is no brewery anywhere which has a more knowledgeable tour guide. This lady of yours knows the family business inside out. She understands every aspect of it and her explanations are so concise, I feel I understand it now to the point I could nearly step in on Monday morning for a job here."

Owen Barton sent more blue smoke into the room before saying with a completely straight face, "Sorry laddie; no openings at present. You'll make a better living staying in university and getting your degree. That's the advice my Da' gave me when I was about your age."

Matt was taken by surprise by what Joanna's father had said and he was trying to find a reply when both Joanna and her father burst out in laughter. When they had finished, Joanna smiled a warm smile and said, "Matt, don't bother trying to top him. It just can't be done. I have had to put up with it ever since I was old enough to walk. He will have his little jokes, but he is really not such a bad sort. He grows on you."

Matt had taken all he could and decided it was time to get in the game. He gave her father his best cold blue eyed stare and said, "Sure. Just like athlete's foot," and followed with his warmest smile.

Owen Barton laughed so hard he dropped his pipe in his lap and had to chase it down before any damage was done. When normalcy was restored and the pipe was back in its accustomed position, he turned to his daughter and said, "This one is really clever. Don't get into a contest to see who is best at it. If you two do that, someone is certain to get hurt."

Joanna looked at Matt for a moment before turning toward her father. "Don't worry Dad. Mathew and I are just friends and we are going to keep it that way. I am going to show him around London sort of like a tour guide and he is going to go to some events with me which will keep unwanted attention away. Isn't that right Mathew?"

It was several moments before Matt was able to say, "Yes Owen, that is our agreement. Of course only if you give your approval. I would not feel comfortable about it if you did not approve." Matt looked from Joanna to her father and back again.

Finally Owen Barton gave a short laugh and with a shake of his head answered Matt. "No lad. Don't expect me to save you. She makes her own decisions; has been since she was a lot younger than she is today. Besides that, she is a true Barton. We may joke around a bit, but at bottom we have good sense and don't make foolish decisions. If Joanna thinks this is a good idea then I know it is…. Now, she said you had some important questions, so why don't we move on to that? What is it you want to know?"

Matt saw Joanna was smiling and nodding her head in agreement with what her father had said. He knew the issue was settled and the two of them would be seeing each other as they had agreed.

"Well Owen, my opening question is, 'if England is attacked by Germany can she resist and survive?'"

Owen added to the thick blanket of smoke while he considered Matt's question, then told him, "Well, my boy, you certainly ask large first questions. May I in turn ask you a question for which I expect an answer as honest as those I will give you? Good then. I understand from Joanna that your father is the head of a large New York Bank. Is this your father or you asking?"

Matt now understood what Joanna meant at the party when she said, "Not impressed can only mean you have not met my father." This man with the huge voice and an office in total disarray was a very clever negotiator who only went forward when he fully understood the ground he stood on.

"In reality, sir, it is both of us who are asking. Yes, I am representing him *and* the Bank. He sent me over to be his eyes, ears and feet on the ground. In the short time I have been here, I find I am becoming quite involved. I have seen the sand bags being stacked in front of buildings like Parliament, St. Paul's and so many others. I see the sacrifices that you English are already making. Well, it makes one understand things that people back in America can't easily grasp."

From behind the dense smoke, Joanna's father broke into what he was saying, "Matt, your father's bank holds investments in England and he needs to know if he should hold them or liquidate, is that right?"

Matt was finding himself in the uncomfortable position of answering questions instead of asking them. To answer would be going further than he felt he should in giving information to this man he had just met.

"Sir, there are some facets of my mission in England that are confidential. I do not expect you to tell me anything that you consider not for public knowledge and I hope you will extend the same courtesy to me."

He could hear more than see Owen Barton shift in his chair before he said, "Yes lad that is fair enough. My answer may be a bit long winded, but I want you to know the why of my answer and not simply the numbers in battleships, tanks, soldiers and aircraft.

"We here on this Island have survived so many dangers that we almost expect them to come along daily. The first big invasion on record was the Romans. There were undoubtedly earlier ones, but the Romans were pretty good record keepers so we know those to be reliable. Our friends up in what would become Scotland kept the Romans so heavily under pressure they finally packed up and went back home. Well, most of them did. A few stayed and became part of the country which they had tried to 'civilize.' The next to arrive were the Vikings who first raided here then later took over part of the country before being shown the door by King Harold. By then many of them also had become part of the resident peoples. In the year 1066, another 'Norman' invasion and conquest, but they also settled down and added to the population of the country. It is worth noting that was also the last invasion of England, over 800 years ago. We intend to keep it that way.

"The point of this is that we have a lot of warrior blood running through our veins. It is easy to see us as an overly polite nation where manners are an important consideration. What few people understand is it really only means we will say 'excuse me' after cutting your throat. Please note, because it is important, after, not before.

"In time, the Spanish had a run at us. Built a huge number of large ships and stocked them with the cream of the Spanish army. There were sea battles and Francis Drake won those by sinking a large number of ships. Then a timely storm blew the rest all over the place and sank many more. Thousands of Spanish sailors and soldiers went to the bottom of the ocean instead of landing in England. Only thirty or so ships ever returned to Spain out of the proud fleet of nearly one hundred and fifty which sailed out.

"Napoleon intended to invade England, but never could. Then he made the mistake of using up his assets in a foolish invasion of Russia. The Tsar's troops didn't defeat him, but the Russian winter did. After that he was finished. Waterloo was an almost predictable end to him. We British like to make much of it, but it was inevitable.

"In England, we long ago faced the obvious fact that we were an island. As an Island we are completely surrounded by water and therefore built a large navy with which to protect ourselves. We enjoy a much larger navy than Hitler's Germany.

"This single fact gives Germany a major problem. They cannot challenge our navy with theirs and have any hope to triumph. They would lose their navy in its entirety and without ships they cannot invade."

Matt perceived a hole in this line of reasoning and interrupted with, "Excuse me sir, but as a licensed pilot before I came to England, I have kept up with the changes in warfare because of aircraft. I think the day of big ship battles has passed away. What is to prevent the German air force from simply sending the British Navy to join the Armada?"

Owen realized his pipe had gone out, pulled an identical Chariton pipe out of his rack, packed it with Dunhill Latakia tobacco and fired it up using a wooden match. After being sure it was burning evenly, he presented his framed answer.

"Yes Matt, things have changed and aircraft are now a strategic factor in any war being fought today. So let's examine that part of the coming chess game. The German air force is currently larger than ours but we will catch up in the important area of fighter planes. I know you have seen the Spitfire. That is the focus of our production. She is the equal of Hitler's Messerschmitt 109, Germany's best fighter plane. In some very important respects, ours is superior. Their bombers are sleek and fairly fast, but with short range and light bomb loads. Ships have proven difficult to bomb when in motion. We will not leave them sitting docked in port. If they were, then they would be sitting ducks. We understand that danger all too well. What Germany would need to do first is take out the RAF and we have some aces up our sleeves to prevent that. Germany will need to bomb RAF fields, facilities and manufacturing out of existence. To do so, they would have to catch our aircraft on the ground and they shall find that not only difficult, but in point of fact, impossible. They indeed start with the advantage of more aircraft, but they will end up with fewer because we are able to bring more into each engagement and that is always the deciding factor. I cannot expand beyond this, but, in the end, England will win the air battle, but it will be costly for us. It will, however, be much more costly for them.

You Americans don't yet fully understand the danger Mr. Hitler represents, but then you have the advantage of those two nice wide oceans to insulate you from the hot winds which will soon blow from Germany and already blow from Japan.

"We English and the Chinese are so close to our enemies that Chinese cities are already burning and ours soon may be. No, strike that. Ours surely will be, it is only a question of when. Germany is determined to totally dominate the European continent and Hitler sees that as just a beginning. He will have to first defeat France then England and Russia. Hitler wants revenge for Germany's defeat in World War I. Even defeating those three would only *almost* make up for World War One."

Matt instantly caught what Joanna's father was inferring. "Sir, do you really believe Adolph Hitler to be so insane he would go to war against us? America I mean? Europe I can understand, but... even then... he seems to have gone out of his way to make a treaty with Russia. Stalin and he are cooperating. They are having exchanges. It does not look as if he wants to threaten Soviet Russia. Just the opposite I would think."

Owen walked over to the window and gazed out of the building to the yard below. He turned back and continued, "Son, Hitler makes and destroys treaties at his convenience." He then walked over to a large globe sitting on the wooden floor below floor-to-ceiling book laden shelves and called Matt to come stand beside him. He pointed to Poland on the map.

"Matt, his plan is to first take Poland but he wants to be sure his back is safe when he does it. You can see Germany is located west of Poland; only an easy drive away. And here is Russia both above and to the east of Poland and also just an easy drive away. You wait. He has probably offered Stalin part of Poland in return for no action on the part of Soviet Russia. Hitler needs Poland for its steel production, coal and armament factories. After Poland comes Belgium and France. If he takes them, he will move against us.

"Both England and France are tied by treaty to Poland. The moment Hitler invades Poland an automatic state of war exists. In reality there is little we can do to aid Poland and Germany *will* win. There will be a short pause while Hitler regroups, then he will move into Belgium. The French and we British will try to stop him. This could become a war like World War I. If so, it will take place primarily in France and Belgium. Perhaps we can stop him there. It depends on tactics. It could become trench warfare but I don't see the German Army making that mistake again. They have become highly mechanized so I expect them to use massed armor and move rapidly. France has this fixed line of defenses which is very impressive, but I ask myself, 'What if the Germans simply go around instead of attacking it head on?' If France is lost, that will in reality leave only England in Hitler's way. We won't be able to defeat him single-handedly, but we will stop him from coming ashore. There will be an air war which we will eventually win.

"In frustration, Hitler will turn against Russia and that will lead to the destruction of his Thousand Year Reich. Russia will be no kinder to Hitler's Armies than it was to Napoleon's. Stalin is no bumbling Tsar. The Germans will be lured deeper and deeper into Russia and when they can no longer supply their army the Soviets will begin to inflict such casualties, the Germans will be forced to begin a retreat as disastrous as the one by Napoleon and France.

"I am also certain that at some point and for some reason, America will be forced into the war. I expect it will first sell to us and later the Russians the war materials needed to first slowdown then stop Hitler's war machine. After America is in, we will reenter Europe so that Germany is forced to fight on two, or if Italy is with Germany three fronts. Hitler cannot do that and survive. That is the way I see it playing out. If war comes.

"I suppose there is a slim chance Hitler could get cold feet and none of this will be necessary. If he listens to his Generals, it probably won't happen, but I believe his ego is far too big for him not to move forward.

"In the meantime, England will need help from your country to carry us through the first year of war. We are going to need assistance with everything from weapons to fuel and foodstuffs to help us keep fighting and yes we will need money. What we don't need is American banks pulling investments out at this critical juncture. We need our people to know that you Americans have confidence in our ability to defend this island of ours and to win in the end.

"Matt, we will really be fighting for more than just ourselves. In fact, as Churchill said better than I can, 'for all civilized peoples everywhere.'" Owen walked back to his chair to relight his pipe which had long ago gone out.

Matt didn't quite know how to respond. This was an enormous amount of information both in the form of hard fact and Owen Barton's opinions of the movement of future events. He knew this would take some time to digest before he could forward it along with any of his own comments to his father. He looked at Joanna who had remained silent during the entire course of this conversation. She smiled and stood as did Matt who walked over to the desk where Owen was now standing. He extended his hand and Owen shook it. He found Joanna's father's hand to be heavily callused, but strong. Matt was certain the man standing before him did far more than just sit behind a desk.

"Sir, I very much appreciate your spending this much time with me. You have enabled me to understand what seems to be coming down the road. Perhaps, not only toward England alone, but most of the world. I hope it does not come to pass, but expect that...yes... we had better be prepared in case it does. I will write my father after I have had time to digest the information you have given me. Would you mind if I contact you again with any follow-up questions which might arise?"

"No Matt. I hope you will." He reached into his desk and pulled out a card which he gave to Matt. "I will be happy to see you at any time and I know you will take good care of Joanna. I have been told you are *more* than capable of doing that. I appreciate what you did. We Bartons are proud of our reputation. Too proud perhaps...but there it is."

Chapter 6

A RAINY EVENING ON THE TOWN

The Wednesday morning following his tour of the Barton family brewery, Matt telephoned Joanna asking if she would be free on Saturday night to attend the BBC Symphony Orchestra's performance with him and listen to two works by Debussy in Queen's Hall and to have dinner with him afterward.

It was his way of thanking her for the tour she had given him on Tuesday afternoon of the, in her words, "Bloody Tower of London." At the time it was, she laughingly told him, "Henry the Eighth's divorce court; where he left his wives a bit shorter. No alimony was required in his ideas about what a divorce should be."

Matt replied with, "Well, I suppose he was only trying to keep a *head* of them."

They had spent lots of time laughing at each other's puns, but for him it had been a most pleasant learning experience and he knew there had never been a more beautiful or learned tour guide. She told him about the centuries of history associated with these brooding stone structures as well as the collection of Royal Jewels that were displayed in the Jewel House. The jewels had caused Joanna to turn toward him at one of the cases which held a royal, diamond studded crown. She looked into his eyes and said in a very sad voice, "I suppose these will have to be put away some place safe when war comes along.... That will be only one of the smaller changes we will see. I try not to think on it too very much. It makes me sad. Can you understand that Mathew?

"Until now things have been pretty peaceful in England during my lifetime. Sure, we had a bad economy just like America, but I must say my family was fortunate. We didn't feel it as severely as many did."

Later the two of them had climbed several flights of old stone steps to stand on the wind-swept battlements topping the walls. They looked out over London to see the Thames flowing by filled with ships headed toward the docks and others heading away, outward bound to the Channel.

It was not cold, but the afternoon wind had brought a touch of chill to the air. Joanna shivered slightly and Matt slipped off his jacket to put it over her shoulders. She pulled it around herself smiling a wan smile in thanks.

"We were finally coming out of those hard times and life seemed headed toward some measure of normalcy. Then along comes this threat from Germany. I wonder if life ever will be truly normal again. What we English used to view as normal at least. Do you think it will, Mathew?"

Her luminous green eyes were begging him to reassure her that yes it would, but he knew if he gave her false reassurances she would know. "I honestly don't know. Like you, I am very afraid it may be too late now. If your dad is right, as he may well be, it probably hinges on what happens over the next five or six months. I believe he is seeing things clearly and has a good perception of the way it is all likely to play out.

"The shame of it is, if the League of Nations had spoken with anything approaching a unified voice in the early nineteen thirties, Germany could have easily been stopped. Even later, Hitler could have been blocked when he occupied Alsace Lorraine. The French could have turned him away with a single battalion of armored infantry, but they didn't act. He has run bluff after bluff and no one has called his hand so now... well, now it is really late in the game and he thinks he holds most of the chips so will deal cards as he wishes.

"Joanna, I so wish I could say war won't come, but I am very afraid it will. I am terribly sorry."

She turned away from him to look over the broad sweep of London. Remaining completely silent for a very long time, it was as if she was trying to memorize each tree, building and street. To capture a picture of it all as it was today, to hold that forever in her mind.

"If they bomb us this will all be changed and I do love it so. All I have left is a sliver of hope they won't."

There was nothing Matt could think of to say. There was no way he could even begin to imagine how he would feel if he were anticipating a disaster befalling New York City like the one she was expecting. He knew he did not have nearly the love for that city that she had for her beloved London.

She turned back to him with a small shadow of a smile. "Well Mathew, the good thing is your America looks as if she will be spared and I'm glad. You, at least won't have to be in it and for that I am thankful."

Later at a fish and chips stand, the conversation had turned to lighter topics as she began to list the places she wanted him to see: the major museums such as the British Museum, art Galleries like the Beaux Art and the Redfern, the Hampstead and the quirky Guggenheim Gallery owned by the equally quirky Peggy Guggenheim from New York. The list was so extensive that Matt was delighted he was finding his studies as easy here in England as he had at Yale. His study of mathematics was the only course difficult enough to require his full attention. Even then it was simply a matter of scheduling sufficient time for working assigned problems through to their correct solutions. Thanks to a mathematics professor at Yale, he had become quite proficient with a slide rule. The professor had convinced him that a slide rule was to Math what the Stradivarius was to a symphony. One might get by without it, but it was so much better with it.

As they talked he told Joanna that Larry Trusdale had gone missing from school and it was quite the mystery to all the chaps he had asked about it. One of Matt's friends from the rugby team who had seen the confrontation had remarked, "Well old chap... perhaps you knocked him out of school. If so he won't be much missed. You didn't know him as long as many of us and he was a right rotter. If he was so embarrassed by his confrontation with you that he has gone...well, no great loss old boy. In fact if that is what happened, we owe you a 'thanks' and several brews."

He was quickly realizing the more time he spent with Joanna the more he wanted to be with her. Matt tried to convince himself that she was, after all, just another stunningly pretty young woman and he had been with many like her, but it was an argument, he was forced to admit, he was rapidly losing. Yes, he had been with many lovely young women but not one of them had been like her. He was finding something a bit 'other worldly' about her. She was sensuous yet angelic. A combination he had never seen in a woman before.

Strangely it was as if she knew what he was thinking nearly as quickly as he did and would often express a thought he was having before he could form it into words. Yet he found this surprising ability of hers in no way unpleasant. Matt had been told a similar trait often presented itself with identical twins. Could such a connection occur between two people who were in no way related by blood? Was there a similar relationship or connection possible between spirits? If there was, he had never read about it. Yet the connection seemed to exist with them.

On his side of the equation, he couldn't read her thoughts but he had found he could often sense exactly what she was *feeling*. The few times they touched Matt felt a small electric tingle and saw in her eyes a reaction that he knew was an awareness of this unusual chemistry between them.

Matt had to keep reminding himself, "We are just friends. We are just friends. She made it crystal clear that is all she will allow. Just enjoy her company and be her friend in return."

He once joked, "Joanna you must be aware that just being your friend is going to require lots of cold showers for me."

In reply she had laughingly said, "But my dear Mathew, you are in England. Any other kind is practically impossible."

Shortly after his arrival from America the differences between his home country and England began to reveal themselves. Naturally, the difference of which side of the road one drove on rapidly became, unless one adapted, painfully apparent.

Then there was the strict differentiation between social classes. Yes, there was some amount of movement between them in England but not to the degree he was used to back home. Here, even the conversation used with a person on your own social level was different than that used with one below you in status. That was one affectation Matt had not wanted to acquire.

The manner of dress was another matter. The English, particularly the upper class, were disposed to continue dressing more formally than was practiced in the States.

During his first few months in England, Matt was glad he had packed several fine wool and silk suits and a very fine tuxedo made especially for him by one of the best tailors in New York. He had only worn it twice but now was glad to have it as nearly everyone of class in London dressed for any evening event. For any symphony or dinner after six o'clock it was de rigueur.

He asked the attendant at the garage to be sure the MG was waxed, full of petrol and ready for him to pick up by six on Saturday evening.

~ ~ ~ ~

On Thursday he stopped in a florist shop not far from his rented townhouse to request the finest white orchid they could find and have it mounted on a Kelly green ribbon. He arranged for delivery to Joanna no later than four o'clock on Saturday with his card.

This was the first evening event the two of them would attend and he wanted it to be up to the standards of the afternoon she had arranged.

Everyone said the best place for food and music was the Café de Paris. When he tried to make reservations he was informed that there was simply no way. They were booked up for months. When he dropped by and offered fifteen pounds, an opening magically appeared at a very good table. Some things were the same in New York and London and, Matt supposed, probably Paris and Berlin as well. His father had once told him that money was the international language, spoken by all.

He had been careful to avoid the word date when inviting Joanna and she had responded by referring to it saying, "I am quite looking forward to our event on Saturday evening."

When he awoke on Saturday, Matt was disappointed to find the skies cloudy and rain falling in sheets. It was a marked change from recent weekdays which had presented only sunny skies and, for London, moderate temperatures. He found that the English easily adapted to weather changes because they were so frequent.

He threw on his overworked Burberry trench coat and Irish wool walking hat which, with the usual black umbrella, prepared him to go the three blocks to the small café he usually haunted for breakfast.

Of all the many changes he had adapted to in England, breakfast had required a major reorientation of what he considered the norm. First, coffee was not of the same quality as back home. It was thinner and not normally served with the offer of cream and had a bitter aftertaste. By now, the British authorities were already rationing sugar so he had purchased a pocket-sized container he carried with him containing his own black market supply of sugar.

Then there were the eggs. Heavens, they tried hard to ruin those. They were always served with tomatoes on top which looked as if they were steamed or stewed. Oh, the looks he got when he requested the eggs minus the tomatoes. His request was usually greeted with an upturned nose and a, "Well, if you really insist sir." Which, by now, he understood to be a way of saying, "You aren't one of us, are you?"

He was certain it was a near identical response a Brit would receive in America, when asking where the tomatoes were for his eggs. The real disappointment would have come, for them, when the chef dumped a slice of uncooked tomato on top of their eggs.

Making up for the tomato problem was the quality of the bread served with any meal. It was consistently excellent and Matt knew this was not the product of a factory turning it out by the truck-load.

After breakfast, sans tomatoes, Matt headed back to the rooms he now considered "Home." How strange, he had realized a few days after moving in to the cozy, brick-faced townhouse, to consider a place where every item of furnishing was included in the rent as "Home." Yet, never before in his young life had he felt more settled than he did here in this rented house in a city that was still, in many ways, strange to him.

This settled feeling was even harder to comprehend considering the unyielding certainty that the country was drifting ever closer toward an unavoidable conflict with Hitler's Germany.

The flights of English Spitfires and Hurricanes with their large blue, white and red roundels painted on the top and bottom of the wings as well as each side of the fuselage behind the cockpit were a continual reminder to him of the inevitable slide toward war and the constant challenge being given the enemy.

They fairly shouted, "Look! Here we are. Come over the Channel if you dare. We English are ready and waiting for you to drop by." Each fighter plane already carried camouflage war paint. The swerving colors of dark green and dark tan on the tops of the wings, back onto the body and the rear control surfaces would break up the aircraft's shape when viewed from above. Each Spitfire was also painted a sky grey-blue on the under-side to make her difficult to see when viewed from below.

Matt considered the Hurricane to be a handsome work-horse of an aircraft but the Spitfire was nothing less than exquisitely beautiful. She seemed to him sleek, graceful and very fast. Every line of her body and wings proclaimed that she was the ultimate predator of the skies. She made Matt think of a killer hawk crossed with an elegant butterfly. The Spitfire seemed to move through the sky as naturally as a bird. This plane belonged in the air.

The talk was that a "Spit" could easily top 300 miles per hour and not break a sweat. No one seemed to even know its top speed. Probably a well kept secret as were production numbers. It was known that all Morris auto manufacturing facilities had been converted over to their production and several other large factories were producing engines and sub-assembly component support.

Hawker Aircraft was in exclusive production of the Spit's older sister, the Hurricane, and was rumored to have already produced over 500 of the sturdy little fighter plane which could be turned out more quickly than the Spitfire because of its' simpler design. It too used a Rolls Royce Merlin engine and was almost as fast as her younger sister though somewhat less agile.

No shots had been fired, but it was apparent that England was already considering itself at war and only time would tell if they had started preparations soon enough to prevent disaster.

Matt spent a few hours of the dreary rain-soaked afternoon reading James Hilton's recent book "Lost Horizon." The premise was one of a Lamasery hidden far away from civilization among the highest mountains of Tibet. A place where people lived to be phenomenally ancient and which existed to keep alive the spark of all knowledge and wisdom. This was being preserved for the coming day when man would be thrown into darkness by an awful war. Four people from the outside world are kidnapped and flown there. They were, at first, unwilling additions to the population of the Lamasery known as "Shangri-La." Matt found their individual reactions to the situation to be interesting but when he finished the book there were three things which bothered him.

First, there was no longer any place remaining on Earth which was so difficult to reach it could remain hidden since the advent of powered flight and secondly, this Hilton fellow was a product of the English University system. Anyone who survived its rigors left well educated but pressed into a particular mold. Unfortunately the ones who became authors usually wished to impress their readers with their erudition. To Matt it was a pity because it made a good yarn difficult for people with a lesser education to read.

Most important of all, Matt was convinced Hilton was an idealist and no group of people could cause more mischief in the world than "Well-Meaning" idealists. When the changes they encouraged failed and lay in ruins at their feet they would look you in the eyes and proclaim with all innocence, "But I meant well," as if that put right the damage done.

If it was something that had been tried time after time with spectacular failure following each attempt they would say, "That is only because it wasn't done correctly. We will do it properly this time."

He had read "Mein Kampf" cover to cover two years earlier and was certain Hitler was a dedicated, if dangerously warped, idealist. It was only the higher degree of fanaticism about his ideals which separated him from most other idealists. Hitler thought that what the world needed was a group of leaders who were realists or practicalists; leaders who would destroy the 'cult' of the individual. Only the group was important. Naturally Hitler thought he alone was qualified to decide which groups were important. Matt returned the volume to the packed, built-in book shelves, which were part of the sitting room furnishings.

The chime of the mantle clock told him it was time to dress for his evening with Joanna. After showering and shaving, he donned his black tuxedo with a white pleated silk shirt and black tie. He was pleased the tuxedo pants and coat were still a perfect fit and his gold cufflinks with the Weldon crest engraved on them still showed just past the point where his jacket sleeve ended. His shoes reflected light almost as if they were made of glass. The only item he did not affect which was usually expected here was a top hat. Matt was very vain about his full head of golden brown hair and felt it unnecessary to cover it with a hat. The umbrella and black raincoat would be the extent of his allowance for the rainy weather.

He could not avoid hoping the weather would not begin this more personal phase of a relationship with Joanna on a bad note. He intended to honor her wishes that they just be friends. But they could do entertaining things together and she was such a joy to be with that he was willing, for the first time, just to let things between them move along at their own speed.

By the time he reached the garage his pant cuffs were slightly damp so he was glad to see the MG's canvas top was up. The man in charge told him he had put a bit of heavy waterproof grease around all the edges of the top to seal it. Matt could see the auto had been well waxed as it glowed in the low light like a jewel. It had also, the manager assured him, been fully fueled.

Matt tipped him forty shillings, backed the car out and drove away into the rain of early evening with the wipers trying to keep his windscreen clear. The street lights and those of on-coming autos made the drenched roads appear as if lit from below. His tires made a high-pitched zinging, thumping sound on the macadam-topped avenues most of which were laid over cobble-stones placed during the time of Julius Caesar.

The sidewalks were alive with crowds of people beneath open black umbrellas which appeared as inky rivers gushing along in moving streams; flowing into and out of the underground stations to join with other dark streams in constant motion. At picture theaters the streams became a trickle as their owners jostled and slowed to purchase tickets; the umbrellas disappearing into the building's entrance.

Matt felt there was something frantic about this rain-soaked night. It was as if the people were all trying to cram as much living into these days of peace as they could, anticipating the coming war storms when they could not. When they knew all the lights would be turned off and death might fall from the sky instead of rain.

He finally made his way out of the Piccadilly Circus area and headed toward the Belgravia district and King's Road. Along the way he was stopped for a few minutes by a convoy of twenty trucks with their back ends covered by wet dark green canvas, each truck filled with soldiers.

~ ~ ~ ~

When Matt passed St. Peter's church he slowed knowing he was almost to the Barton's townhome where he was to pick Joanna up for their evening out. He made a mental note to refer to it as their evening "event;" or the symphony, or dinner, and to avoid "date." The important thing was that she had agreed to go out with him on an evening which he had arranged and despite the damn rain it was going to be fun.

He located #37 Eaton Square, pulled in the drive, circled to get as close to the front door as possible so she would get no wetter than necessary, cut his engine and ran to the front door.

The door opened after a single ring of the bell and Matt was ushered into the entryway by an older woman who was obviously a member of the house staff. She showed him to a sitting room and asked him to make himself comfortable as Miss Barton was running a few minutes late. She asked if he would like anything to drink while he waited.

Matt thanked her but assured her he would not and realized he was still holding a wet umbrella. He told her she could help him by taking that and his coat before it soiled the elaborate Persian carpet he was standing on.

"Yes sir," she answered him. "I will have both waiting for you right next to the front door. The entry there is marble and a wee bit of wet won't harm that."

He thanked her and settled into a chair with a lamp beside it to wait for Joanna. Well, he mused, he was glad that in one way she was quite woman-like. Every girl and woman he had met liked to make an entrance. And, he was sure; hers would be an entrance worth waiting for.

He had, by his watch, been seated for fifteen minutes and was so deeply lost in thought that he was startled when something touched his cheek. He turned to find a black and white cat on the arm of his chair. It had rubbed its face against his cheek. Intensely green eyes stared at him and the cat pantomimed a meow; the pink mouth formed a meow but no sound came out.

It was as strange a cat as Matt had ever seen; compact with neither long or short fur but very thick medium length fur. It seemed to have short legs, an illusion caused by the length of its fur. It wore a black hood from the back of its head to just below the eyes which was shaped like an inverted capital Y. Below that and around behind the cat's head was the whitest fur he had ever seen. The shoulders and front feet were likewise snow white. Then just behind the front feet and shoulders the black fur picked up and covered the body above the hips back to and including the tail, but the back legs from the bottom of the hips down were snowy white.

Matt was convinced not only was he studying the cat, but the cat was studying him. Its green eyes were quite intense and after a few minutes he ran his hand along its back and said, "Well cat. What do you think? Do I pass muster?"

Before he could get an answer, Joanna spoke from the doorway. "Well Mathew, I see you have met Haiku. You should feel highly honored. Until now she has only let me touch her. She allows no one else close."

The cat again rubbed her face on his cheek as if to say "oh, don't listen to her. I'm a dear cat who loves everyone." This time when she opened her mouth he heard a very quiet, "Eoow," followed by a purr as soft as a whisper. She now moved from the arm of the chair to his lap where she proceeded to curl into a ball and continue her satisfied purr. Matt looked helplessly at Joanna who simply smiled in sympathy at his dilemma.

As long as Joanna stood in the hall, Matt could only see her as a backlit outline, but when she walked into the sitting room he was able to see that she was beautifully dressed for their first evening out.

Her dress was undoubtedly from a major French designer and caressed each curve of her wonderful figure with shades of greens and blues which seemed painted by a highly talented watercolorist. Her hair with its striking copper highlights was long and cascaded over her right shoulder. The brilliant green eyes were complemented with a rich shade of deep green eye shadow below her gently arched eyebrows.

The dress flowed over her hips and outlined her long legs ending just short of her ankles and her emerald high-heeled shoes.

Matt realized he was staring and for a moment could think of nothing to say. She was so beautiful he felt like a fifteen year old completely overwhelmed on his first date.

He recovered by telling her, "Joanna I am glad we are just friends because it keeps me from having to say you are a vision. That I have never seen anyone as lovely as you. That until tonight I did not believe such perfection existed. Yep, it's a real relief to know all I have to say is... You look pretty good pal."

She smiled, walked over to his chair, picked Haiku up from his lap, set her gently on the floor and shooed her away. Then she turned back to him.

"Yes, my friend and it relieves me of having to tell you what a handsome devil you are and that any girl should be on her guard whenever she is around you. So much easier to say... you look pretty good. For a Yank that is. At least you will when we brush that white cat fur off your black tux pants and jacket. I think Haiku wanted to leave you a reminder of your first meeting which was actually rather remarkable of her since she is always as far away from strangers as possible."

Matt nodded that he understood, and then questioned her with, "Joanna, I know Haiku is a short poem of Japanese origin and she certainly looks oriental to me. Where ever did you find her?"

A thoughtful look crossed Joanna's face as if she were considering exactly how to answer Matt's question. "Well, it was more like she found me. Last Fall on a night very much like this one, only colder, I was reading here in the sitting room and I kept hearing a scratching sound around the front door. After noticing it for a long time, I finally went to the front door to see what was causing it. I thought perhaps a shrub branch was rubbing against the front of the house. When I opened the door there stood a wet, bedraggled small black and white cat who strolled calmly past me into the house then shook herself to spray water in the entryway.... It was as if she had lived here all of her short life. Please don't think me daft, but I swear I heard a voice in my head saying, 'You may call me Haiku and by the way I am very hungry. I prefer fish but since I have arrived unannounced anything will do. Oh, and with a bit of milk or cream if you please.' I can't explain it in any logical way Mathew, but on my honor that was the way it happened. No voices since but I am the only one who has been allowed to touch her until tonight. When I am here, she sleeps on a pillow next to me. On the occasions when I am at the Manor out in Kent, she sleeps on my bed and she will eat what the staff feeds her. She really does prefer fish. Her next favorite is any type of fowl."

It was as unusual a story as Matt had ever heard. He had the infrequent strange voice in his head, but that only happened those times when he drank far too much or after bedding a girl he was no longer interested in. Those times the voice had advised him to 'Get out of here. Time to move on.' It was a voice he always listened to.

What she described was different from anything he could relate to. "So Joanna, I don't suppose you had been drinking. Had you?" She looked at him as if he were the daft one, but simply shook her head "No."

"Then all I can do is to accept that what you told me is what happened. Who would know Haiku's name better than Haiku and certainly we would expect the cat to know its dining preferences. No reason for surprise in either of those areas. My only observation is this. Haiku was very selective in the person she chose to live with. I admire her sense of superior taste in choosing a home."

Joanna gave Matt a smile which was so warm that he forgot the rain outside and the cat fur on his tux. At that moment all he could comprehend was how magnificent this young woman was, how entrancing he found her and what a lucky cat Haiku was.

Once Haiku's fur had been brushed from his tuxedo, both he and Joanna put on raincoats and rushed out to the MG waiting just down the steps. He saw Joanna was carrying the flower he had sent still in its small box.

He held the umbrella for her until she was settled in and the door was closed. Once on the other side, Matt threw the umbrella behind his seat. Joanna was laughing as she said, "Don't worry Mathew, a little rain won't ruin our evening. We won't allow it to."

He wondered, as they drove away, did she somehow know that had been his worry earlier in the afternoon? He told himself it was only a coincidence... wasn't it?

Joanna shifted her body on the seat until she was facing him and in a soft voice said, "Mathew the orchid you sent is wonderful. I have never seen one this perfect. I was late because I wanted to match it with the right dress. I haven't pinned it on yet because I didn't want to crush it under my raincoat. Will you pin it on when we get to the symphony?"

Matt glanced briefly at her before returning his attention to the rainy road and the traffic.

"It is a beautiful dress; I will be delighted to pin the orchid on for you. You must know the way you look makes it difficult to remember our agreement about friendship. You don't need me to tell you what a beautiful, enchanting creature you are. But it is far more than simply that. I am still trying to define the trait you have and give it a name. So far I have had no luck doing so. You are completely beyond my experience. For awhile I toyed with 'class' but I have known women with class before and what you have goes beyond that. I am at a loss except I know you have an exceptional and very special quality."

Matt could feel her looking at him and there was silence for a while. He was surprised to feel her hand softly touch the side of his face and linger there. He was sure the pleasant electric charge he felt was also affecting her.

When she spoke it was almost a whisper. "I am glad we met and I am glad you are my friend. All the negative things I heard about you are hard to believe Mathew. Even the things you have told me about yourself don't seem to fit with the man sitting next to me tonight. Are you such a great actor? I just don't know which one of you is genuine and which is a façade. I hope the one I am seeing is the real one because that one is a very good man and a very dear friend"

Matt didn't know what to say. This was a different Joanna speaking. Not as reserved as the one he had met and toured London with.

Yet he didn't know how to answer because he didn't know for sure himself. He only knew that he didn't want to hurt or disappoint this beautiful, intelligent, magical and yet, he now felt, fragile creature.

"I don't know the answer to that question yet. I know what I have been and hope I'm not like that any longer. I don't like the guy I once was very much and believe me; I have been reminded of him a lot recently.

"What I *am* certain of is that I would never hurt you. I have never been 'friends' with a woman as I am with you. I have told you that before and it is true. I intend to be your friend. I know it is the only thing which is safe now. You need time to get to know me. To find out if I am worth the time you are giving me. And I need to see if I can be what I find I really want to be. For both of us Joanna.

"Before I left New York, my dad said a new day was dawning in my life. He was talking about my coming over to England for the Bank. He said if I could endure the changes which would occur outside my comfortable existence and begin to view life like a grownup, then I would become a man. Otherwise I would be forever nothing more than a child. Sending me over here, I am sure, was his way of giving me a last chance to grow up. But meeting you, Joanna, has shown me what a selfish person I have been. Oh *yes*, you are beautiful. I knew that the first moment I saw you. But from that moment I have found there is so much more about you. I knew I had to know you. For once in my life I have met a woman...a lady who simply being with... doing things with is enough. So we both know the rules and the reason for them. I know you are comfortable with the rules because in the beginning you laid them out, but know this; at this point I need them as much as you do. Possibly even more."

There was a long pause with the only sound the engine running, the sounds of the tires on the wet street and the swish, swish of the window wipers sweeping back and forth.

"Then Mathew, I will observe them as much as I expect you to. I understand what you are telling me. I know how complicated it is for you right now. You have gone through so many changes in your life in such a short time. Many of which can't be easy adjustments. If it helps, I admire what you are doing and I believe your father is going to find he has a son who is a man to be proud of. You need to write him often and keep him up to date not only about your quest but about yourself."

"That is a correspondence I have already initiated Joanna. But you are right I should, and will, expand it. We are almost at Queen's Hall. So if you don't mind can we just have fun together and let tomorrow stay in abeyance until tomorrow?" She was, he could feel, thinking about what he said before replying in what seemed to him, a bit too gay a voice.

"Yes Mathew, I would like nothing more than just to be here, with you, out for a night in London. No worries, except the rain, with hours to have fun together with my best friend. Did you know I really like Debussy, particularly 'La Mer?' The second piece on the program, 'Images,' I don't believe I have ever heard performed. It will be a new experience for me. Have you heard it?"

He glanced at her profile for a moment, glad to be on a new topic, and answered her question, "No, not the entire piece. It is made up of three parts and at Yale I heard 'Sirenes' which is the last part. I find most of his works restful and this one was. I am sure the BBC Orchestra will be better than ours at Yale. Funny, if I had to choose music to go with a night like this, Debussy would be perfect."

Matt had followed Westbury Avenue and she directed him to turn onto Langham Road then cut through Graham Road to park just a short distance from Queens Hall on Langham Place near the BBC building.

~ ~ ~ ~

They had run, laughing, through the rain from the MG to Queen's Hall with Matt trying to be sure his umbrella stayed over Joanna's head so her hair stayed dry. Only when they were in the lobby and his umbrella was folded and checked along with both their coats, did she hand him the box containing the orchid and turn, smiling toward him.

Matt carefully pinned it to her left shoulder. He noted looks of envy from several passing middle-aged men as he placed the flower.

As they walked further inside he was able to look at the magnificent concert hall he stood in. The design, while dated, was none-the-less very impressive. He turned to Joanna and asked, "This looks Victorian. Is it?"

She smiled approvingly, looked around the marble floored lobby with its sweeping stairs to the next level and told him, "Very good Mathew. You have the correct period in history, definitely Victorian and late Victorian at that. Opened as I recall in the mid eighteen nineties. The architect was a fellow named Knightley. It was actually rather drab when it first opened, but since the big Orchestras moved in it has been redone to much higher standards. Its main advantage was and still is the superb acoustics it enjoys. It is said a whisper from the stage can be heard in the worst seat in the house. I understand Toscanini is conducting tonight, so it should be an outstanding concert."

As she spoke, Matt was appreciating how perfectly dressed she was. He had noticed her beautiful gown of greens and blues before they had left her townhouse. Again he noted how it swept away from one shoulder and she wore his flower, where he had pinned it, on the covered shoulder. There was a cascading river of copper hair flowing over her bare shoulder. Her ears were graced by two emeralds set in white gold and around her pale neck lay a short white gold linked chain supporting an emerald also in white gold surrounded by small white diamonds. On her right hand was a large emerald ring also set in white gold. On most women Matt knew it would have been considered a display of wealth, but Joanna was so beautiful that the jewels were simply overwhelmed by the woman wearing them.

A quick glance around the lobby quickly assured him that Joanna's jewelry could very nearly be considered an understatement when judged against what many of the other women were wearing. It became readily evident that Queen's Hall was as much social event as musical performance and making a statement in one's dress was the norm.

As they moved through the crowded lobby, Joanna was greeting and being greeted by many of the attendees and Matt could not ignore the appreciative looks she was receiving from some of the men, nor the glances and smiles he was getting from women who were with these men. They were the kind of looks he understood and was doing his best to ignore while still being pleasant.

When they were seated Joanna leaned close to his ear and whispered, "It's not entirely your fault, you know. Those looks you were getting tell me a lot. And some of them old enough to be your mother. Simply disgraceful! One would have thought they were looking at a dessert menu."

Matt smiled and turned toward her to whisper his reply. "Yes, I saw them but I also saw lots of hungry looks in your direction that probably had nothing to do with a missed meal either."

Joanna gave a low laugh before telling him, "But what can one expect, they are men and men are simply like that."

Matt faked a little boy hurt look and asked "All men, do you think?"

He could feel her lips touch his ear as she whispered "I hope not. I think I have, just perhaps, found one who's surprising me by being quite different."

The orchestra finished the preconcert cacophony involved in tuning many instruments all at one time. The first violinist walked on stage to be greeted with polite applause. This was followed a few minutes later by Toscanini's entrance greeted by thunderous applause. Then as if on cue, total silence fell on the audience as the conductor tapped his baton on the podium to get the musicians' attention, then raised it and the first notes of "La Mer" floated into the air and over the audience. Three hours passed quickly and pleasantly while observing a master conductor and hearing a first rate orchestra bring the works of a talented composer to full bloom. Matt had seen Toscanini in New York with the NBC Orchestra and was once more convinced that this was a conductor whose acclaim was well deserved. He molded music as easily and gracefully as a great sculptor molded clay. The end result in both forms was great art.

As they made their way through the crowd and down the stairs Joanna laid her hand on his arm and looked up at him. "Mathew, thank you. It was a wonderful concert. 'La Mer' was beautiful but I did enjoy the second piece, 'Images' even more. Both 'Nuages' and 'Fetes' were very good but 'Sirenes' was the finest of the three. It seemed mystical. The program listed 'Images' as an early works of his. 1912. 'La Mer' was earlier, 1905. They both seemed fresher than his later works. More imaginative.

"Oh my dear, I will remember *this* night. It's not yet over, but it is already a very special evening to me. Thank you Mathew."

"No Joanna, I want to thank you. Yes, it is a special night for me too, but only because I am sharing it with you. Toscanini is very good and the music was wonderful, but enjoying it with you was fantastic. That is what has made it memorable for me and, yes, it is far from over."

They reclaimed their raincoats and umbrella and went out into a night now slightly misting but turning foggy. This time they walked to his car.

Because of the thickening fog, Matt was dependent on Joanna for directions. He could not read the street signs but she knew London so well that getting to Café de Paris was as easy as if it had been a clear night. Matt had pre-arranged a parking spot for the MG a short block away and by the time they were there only the thickening fog remained. It haloed the street lights and made people nothing more than soft outlines until they were so close you almost bumped into them.

The Club's entrance was at street level with a lighted sign above a large, rounded striped-canvas awning over the sidewalk, which still dripped water from the recent rain. A liveried doorman held the door open and they descended the steps down to the Club.

The hat check stand was set back into the wall beside the area where the stairs ended so Matt checked their things and located the maître d' to get their table. As he expected, it was the same man Matt had paid to be sure they got preference in seating and service.

He asked them to wait while he cleared "their table." Leaving his position at the podium, he went directly to a table where a young couple were seated, spoke to them in a low voice and they rose, left the table and walked into the bar where two chairs and a tiny table seemed to magically appear.

The table was cleaned in an instant, a fresh cloth laid and a rose in a crystal vase set in the middle. Silverware, crisp white napkins and wine and water glasses were also perfectly placed in two settings; the table perfectly prepared in the space of a few minutes. But when the maître d' returned, he apologized for their wait causing both he and Joanna to laugh and the tuxedo clad gentleman, himself, to smile broadly.

"I have got to know," Matt questioned him, "How did you arrange this legerdemain with such precision that it worked out with a complete lack of fuss? What did you say to them?"

The maître d' understood Matt's question to be a compliment of how well he had done his job in having a table ready in such a few moments.

"Well sir, I simply picked a young couple who had no chance of getting a table tonight or any night and settled them at a very good table with the understanding that it was reserved for an important patron who is a regular. They could use the table until that couple arrived, but they must give it up the moment you came in. They naturally accepted without hesitation. I did not tell them I intended to see they were then accommodated in the bar, but it seemed the fair thing to do."

When he and Joanna were seated, Matt stopped the maître d' and asked him to send a bottle of excellent champagne to the young couple's table, put it on his bill and he hoped, in addition, that if they returned on another night the maître d' would try to accommodate them in some way.

The man smiled at Matt and Joanna before telling them, "Yes sir I intend to do just that as they were good sports and I believe they are very much in love. Even in a place like this, one does try to make allowances for the truly important things in life At least *I* do.."

He looked at Joanna a moment before telling the maître d', "This is a special night for us too and I think we should help make it special for them. Special nights are all too rare."

The maître d' looked at the two of them approvingly and smiled. "Very good sir. Very good indeed."

The Club was packed. The only empty tables were those of couples who packed the small dance floor in front of the eight piece band. They played from a raised stage two feet higher than the area where people dressed in the latest fashions danced. On both sides of this area angled stairs rose to an upper level where additional tables were arranged behind railings overlooking the level on which Matt and Joanna were seated. It looked, Matt thought, exactly like what a Hollywood studio would create for a very large-budget film. Even the stylish way the people dressed would fit perfectly into a moving picture.

"The orchestra is Ken Johnson's 'West Indian Orchestra,'" Joanna told him, "even though most of them have never been any place near the West Indies. Johnson was born in British Guyana but arrived here when he was only about fifteen years old. He is one of the most popular singers in England. One can hear him regularly on BBC broadcasts."

Matt asked about the Café de Paris. He mentioned his thoughts about how much it looked like a movie set. This caused her to laugh before telling him, "Well Mathew, perhaps **you** are the one with second sight. Back in nineteen twenty nine, Ande DuPont made a silent movie using the Club as his primary shooting location. It was titled, 'Piccadilly' and starred an American, Anna May Wong. It was quite the hit in England. Our Charles Laughton was in it, a bit part playing a gluttonous patron. Considering his girth it was almost type casting. The 'Café' has always drawn the famous, infamous, royals, big time gangsters, gamblers and a murderess."

"A *murderess*, Joanna?"

"Yes...the murderess' is a bizarre tale. Her name was Elvira Mullens-Barney. The daughter of Sir John and Lady Mullens was reportedly a strange one from childhood. She actually married an American, one of a trio which performed here called 'Three New Yorkers.' She was twenty three then. Her parents protested the union which probably made her more determined to do it. This was in nineteen twenty eight. Her husband John Barney soon fled back to America and never returned. No one knows if there was a divorce or not, only that she continued to use his name. She then entertained a number of men with, shall we say, rather unusual tastes, one of the mentionable ones being drugs.

"Out of this group she began to focus on one young man and that was Michael Stephen who enjoyed a reputation as being bisexual and engaging in fetishism. Neither of which peccadilloes Elvira objected to.

"Just past midnight on May thirty of nineteen thirty two they left Café de Paris in a cab and returned to her house. A short time later, neighbors reported shouting followed by a gunshot. The police were called to the scene where they found Stephen dead of a gunshot wound to the chest. Elvira was begging him to come back to her and she would do whatever he wanted of her. She was never arrested though she was formally charged with murder. Her defense was headed by Attorney-General Sir Patrick Hastings, a King's Council whose closing address was apparently very effective as she walked out of court a free woman."

Matt was silent for several minutes before commenting on the story. "So it seems as if the class system is still alive and well in jolly old England. Kill who you will as long as they are below your status. Shouldn't that be out of date by now?"

Joanna reached across and laid her hand on his arm. "Yes Matthew it should be, but tell me can you honestly say that money doesn't have the same effect in America? That justice isn't for sale there?" He knew she was right so he simply nodded his head no to acknowledge the fact.

"Besides, there are often higher courts. A short while later she died, strangely enough, in a Paris hotel room of a cocaine overdose. It seems the closing argument didn't sway the final judge."

They ordered a fine Bordeaux put up in 1931 to go with their order of Steak Diane, sautéed potatoes and green peas.

While they waited, the orchestra began playing, "We'll meet again," so Matt led Joanna onto the dance floor and the two started, tentatively at first, moving to the music. Matt was a smooth dancer, but Joanna was on an even higher plain. She moved so effortlessly that he had to look at her to realize he was actually holding her. It was as if she weighed nothing. Did her feet even touch the floor? Was she floating inches above the wooden parquet square dance surface? It seemed as if he were dancing with a shadow or an angel. He only returned to reality when she whispered in his ear, "Mathew the music has ended." He walked somewhat embarrassed, hand in hand with her back to their table.

After eating a superb meal, he and Joanna danced twice more. Once to a sad rendition of "Deep Purple" and finally to a most appropriate, "Two Sleepy People." Matt looked at his watch and saw it was past one in the morning. Even though the Club was still as crowded as when they arrived, he suggested perhaps he should settle their check and take her home. He could see some regret in her eyes when she said, "Oh my, is it really that late? Then yes, I suppose we had better go; wouldn't want the family to misunderstand. Dad would be okay because he has met you, but Mother, well she's Mother. I am sure Mrs. Townsend will be reporting. "

Matt paid the bill and left a good tip. The maître d' stopped them after they had collected their coats and umbrella.

"Sir, the young couple who held your table left some time ago. They didn't wish to disturb you and asked me to thank you. An observation if I may. They carried the empty champagne bottle you gave them when they left. I gather it meant something to them. And a personal word from me. I hope to see you both here as often as you can arrange it. You are a beautiful couple. It has been our pleasure having you with us."

Matt started to reach in his pocket to again tip him but the man simply shook his head "No", and then reached out his hand which Matt gladly shook. Joanna had watched all this silently, but when they reached the top of the long stairs and were on the street she stopped him and after looking in his eyes she told him, "Mathew, what you did for that young couple was very nice. It was a truly magnanimous act of kindness."

He was so completely moved by her words, which he felt were undeserved, that he answered her truthfully. "No Joanna, magnanimous in a strict definition means giving of one's self. It may have been an act of generosity but that only involves money. I hope they enjoyed the champagne and it made their night better but it was not a sacrifice. I hope someday I will find a way to be sincerely magnanimous."

She was silent for a long time only staring into his eyes as if to see the future. When they finally headed through the fog to his car *she* took his hand.

Chapter 7

AUGUST 29, 1939

On Tuesday August 29, Joanna sent Matt one of her by now familiar ivory envelopes which he always looked forward to receiving. He found each contained an invitation to some event which invariably proved either entertaining or educational and often both. He understood the true enjoyment was because each outing allowed them to spend time together. It was strange how being with her made him feel more mature yet, at the same time, like a young child on a trip to the zoo. He now understood what the guys back at Yale had been feeling when they spoke glowingly of spending time with one very special girl. Matt knew he had finally found that one very special person.

Joanna never telephoned him about anything except last minute invitations; invitations she could not send in one of her elegant notes. Perhaps the call would be about something she learned that was occurring the next day or evening. An event she wanted to be sure they did not miss. Once she phoned Matt about a sold-out stage play to which a girl friend of hers had tickets she couldn't use and offered them to Joanna.

They were, by now, a regular item of gossip around King's College and Matt began worrying about the volume of rumors. No matter how often he told the guys in his classes that he and Joanna were nothing more than "Good Friends," he kept getting winks and nods in return. Even the lads who played on the rugby team with him said, "Sure you are. You lucky scoundrel."

He told Joanna about the sort of things he was hearing and the questions he was constantly being asked. "I felt I had to let you know about the whispers," he confided to her. "I wouldn't want your reputation to be damaged because of me. I must admit I can understand it because of the way I behaved toward the girls I knew in the past. I wish I could blame the people who are saying these things, but I can understand why. If I were one of those people, it is exactly what I would be thinking. Unfortunately I can't change my past reputation.

"I am very distressed to be the reason people are thinking the wrong thing about you. It is unfair but understandable. Joanna dear, perhaps

73

considering my past, too well known reputation we might need to, well, see a bit less of each other for your sake."

Joanna suddenly put her hand on his arm and looked at him intently with her luminous green eyes. Finally she said, "Mathew, is it *my* reputation which concerns you or is there something else going on here?"

Matt was confused by her question. "Joanna, I don't understand what you are asking. Could you be a little clearer?"

"Very well... Mathew Weldon, have you tired of us being friends? Would you like to be free of our arrangement? As you have mentioned your reputation, I am very aware ours is not the way you have, shall we politely phrase it, enjoyed relationships in the past. If you need the freedom to pursue that kind of life again, then all I can say is I regret you feel that way, but I can understand."

"Oh God no, Joanna," he laughed in relief. "I love everything we have done together. I would miss seeing you so awfully much. I was only worried about what people might think, and worried to death you might say yes we *should* take a break from each other."

She laughed her wondrous laugh then told him with a smile, "Mathew, it is *my* reputation, after all. The people who know me well enough for me to care what they think, would never think that about me anyway. The rest of the gossipers simply don't matter. Like a pack of hounds they are always sniffing someone's rear. Then there is the simple fact that to me, you are worth it and I refuse to let people like that decide what I do with my life. It is sweet of you to be concerned. Besides, there are still so many things left for us to do."

~ ~ ~ ~

Matt opened this most recent letter to find the following:

Mathew

This is an invitation to spend a three day weekend with me and my family at our home, Barton Hall, in County Kent. My mother wants to meet this "brash young American" she has heard is escorting her daughter - Miss Joanna Shaylee Barton - around London.

You already know Dad, so you two can talk more about how he is seeing the political situation now. However I must confess, it is because I want to show you around our country home myself. You have toured some of the city

I love with me and seen the family business. Now I want you to see my home. I would like to leave by eight thirty on Friday morning if you can arrange that. If so, could you pick me up in that lovely little car of yours at our townhouse? Pack for the weekend because you are definitely staying for three days.

If the weather is good we can drive over with the top down. I would really love that. It is a wonderful drive and if the weather holds I also would love to show you Canterbury and Dover. I confess I have a list which will keep us busy for the weekend. I want you to see what England is like outside of London. What everyone who doesn't live in London calls "the real England."

Love,

Joanna

Matt noticed two changes in her letter. She had never before added "love" above her signature and most significantly she did not point out that this was not a date.

Well Matt old boy, perhaps she is finally deciding you are worth all the time she has given. Now try to live up to your newly acquired status. You are, after all, completely crazy about her. Just don't do anything stupid because of the changes in her letter and we know you can be supremely stupid at times. But you know I think she is right. You do have potential and that is enough for now.

Delighted to see a cloudless sky when the sun came up on Friday morning, Matt walked the few blocks to the garage where his green MG was parked. He and the young attendant folded the tan canvas top down snapping the cover tightly over it. When they were finished, he stored his brown leather overnight bag behind his seat along with a trench coat and his now familiar black umbrella. Because it was still cool he had on a light tan zipper jacket knowing he would be pulling it off once the sun warmed the air.

The little car started easily. Matt loved the throaty growl of the engine and the shine of the varnished wood dash with its chrome-circled black faced instruments. Driving his hot little car almost made up for not flying; almost, but never completely.

Matt normally found himself whistling happily as he followed the familiar route to the Barton townhouse. Today, however, was a bit different. He loved having an entire weekend with Joanna ahead of him, but the idea of meeting her mother, Mary Margaret, was another matter entirely. Owen he knew. Owen he liked because they could talk so easily. Man to man. But Mary Margaret, the way Joanna described her, was a completely different scenario.

It sounded to him as if her mother had perhaps expected Joanna to marry into royalty. Someone with a title or at least someone who would have one in time. He could understand why she might have such an expectation for her daughter. Joanna was what royalty should be but never was. Yet he knew Joanna would never live up to anyone's expectations except her own.

It was not that he was frightened. Not of anyone... well maybe a bit in awe of his father, but, he admitted to himself, he was dreading meeting her. He promised himself to remain casual with Mary Margaret Barton and be as charming toward her as she would allow.

By the time he pulled into the drive at Number 37, it was warm enough to allow Matt to slip out of his jacket and push it down behind his seat atop his overnight bag. Removing the jacket seemed to lighten his dread of meeting Joanna's mother.

He and Joanna were, after all, just friends. It was not as if they had... had done anything beyond that. He had been the perfect gentleman. If only, many times, a reluctant one. She was so incredibly beautiful yet he was determined to honor his promise and damn, it was great just being with her. He was even beginning to feel as if she might be feeling the same way about him. If this was what friendship with a woman was like he wished he had discovered the feeling years ago. Then he remembered he had never met a woman like her to be friends with.

The front door opened and Joanna came skipping down the stairs accompanied by Mrs. Townsend who was carrying a small suitcase for her charge's weekend. Matt took it and stored it next to his behind the seat.

Mrs. Townsend disapprovingly eyed his small MG and looked directly at him while giving orders as strict as the ones he would have received from a top Sergeant. "Now Mr. Weldon, you drive carefully. It is a lovely day but the roads going out to Barton Hall are not the best and with so much military traffic on the roads.... Well, just you be careful. I feel responsible for Joanna. Have for years now, since she was born."

Matt was sure this somewhere past middle-aged lady had indeed been very involved in Joanna's upbringing and cared about her a great deal. He was beginning to like this stern lady because she did.

"Mrs. Townsend, I will try to take care of her as well as you would. I know that may not be possible, but I promise not to take chances on the drive and watch out for her both going out and coming back. I will return her safely to your care Sunday evening."

She headed up the brick steps toward the front door, turned back toward them and with the slightest of smiles said, "Just see you do."

When Matt glanced at her standing on the stairs he saw Haiku in one of the front windows looking out at Joanna. Matt was certain the little cat was already missing her.

Joanna wore a simple pair of tan slacks which stopped just short of her ankles. Brown sandals and a white silken shirt with three-quarter sleeves completed the outfit. On her hand was the emerald ring she had worn to the Symphony and her ears sported small square emeralds. Her wonderful copper hair was put up at the back of her head in a French Twist. It was at once sophisticated and simple. He had never known anyone who could be so many things at once. Today she was a little bit more girlish but not a bit less beautiful. Young, but devastating at the same time. How could someone not quite yet twenty manage all this so naturally, without artifice?

Matt helped her into the car then seated himself and cranked the MG. He simply couldn't resist telling her how great she looked. "You are the most amazing woman I have ever known." he told her. "You are such fun to be with and seem lovelier each time I see you. Even at this early hour you seem to glow."

She gave him that smile which always made his heart speed up and said, "Thank you Mathew. I feel really wonderful this morning. It is a beautiful day and we have a lovely drive ahead of us. Did you know County Kent, where we are going, is known as the Market Basket of England? Much of what we put on our dinner tables comes from there. The soil is so very rich that nearly anything planted will grow. It was no accident the Barton family settled in Kent centuries ago. Both hops and barley grow spectacularly well in that wonderful soil. We grow two crops a year of barley, spring and fall, with fill-in crops of beets to replenish the soil. The fall barley is lower in quality and is sold for animal feed so it is harvested in the winter. The spring crop is harvested in late summer and is the quality used in Beer and Ale. The barley you will see on this trip is at its peak.

"I hope you will come to love the place as much as I do. London is the city I love, but the land around our house in Kent is my soul. No, it is more than that. It is my heart and my soul. Oh Lord, let's go. I don't want to waste a minute of our shared weekend."

~ ~ ~ ~

Once they were out of London Matt began to understand what Joanna meant. The suburbs fell away in his rear view mirror and the land became softly rolling and green. Actually, Matt realized, many shades of green; layer upon layer of hundreds of differing shades. Green leaves on the trees softly blown by winds washing across the hood of his little MG as he pointed it toward the still rising sun. It's golden morning light filtering through the leaves flashing patterns across their faces as they raced through the English countryside. There were also different colors of green from the grasses and myriad shades of green from a variety of crops which were already well developed by this point in the summer. The earth he could see along the edges of the fields was in rich tones of dark brown which spoke to Matt of centuries of care by farmers who loved the land and now were completely a part of it. An everlasting oneness with the soil. An unending circle of decay and renewal. Matt began to grasp how limited his knowledge of life and living really was. He was so grateful for having met this exceptional woman sitting next to him and the changes she had brought to his life.

The houses they passed on the narrow roads were thatched roof farm homes, many gabled and white-washed. The barns were equally well maintained set on land enclosed by stacked stone fences. The occasional cow was fat and certainly well cared for as were the many flocks of sheep. Every farm had chickens roaming freely around the house pecking at the ground.

The small towns they drove through were not greatly changed from the way Matt was sure they had looked one hundred or even two hundred years ago. The most noticeable change seemed to be electric wiring. They were much like the villages in stories read to him by his nannies during the years he was only a small boy wandering through a huge, silent, house. Stories about places he had long ago forgotten until today when they suddenly sprang back to life, no longer part of children's stories.

Joanna was leaning back in her seat with her legs stretched out as far as she could get them. Matt heard her humming something he didn't think he had ever heard. It was a lovely sound and so very soft; a cross between a lullaby and a folk melody. Her eyes were closed and she was smiling.

"Joanna what is that song you are humming? It is truly beautiful but I don't believe I have ever heard it before today."

Her brow wrinkled for a few moments as if deep in thought, then said, "I don't know Mathew. I *really* don't know. It seems I have *always* known it. Probably something I heard early in my childhood. Perhaps something Mother or Mrs. Townsend sang to me a long time ago. I'll have to ask them. *Funny*, before you asked, I had never even wondered about it. The notes have always been inside my head and simply come tumbling out when I am happy. And today I am *very* happy."

Matt smiled at her before saying, "I wish I knew the tune. I would certainly join you in humming it. It is a happy day for both of us."

"Yes Mathew, I understand. I can't figure out the why of it but we do seem to have that effect on each other. In fact, the reason doesn't matter. All that matters is we do and, for however long it lasts, I am grateful."

Matt glanced at Joanna and saw a shadow cloud her eyes. There was suddenly a trace of sadness there. "Speaking for myself, Joanna, I hope it just goes on and on. I can't imagine why it wouldn't. I have been given almost everything one could ask for, but nothing has mattered like our friendship but I sense something is troubling you."

"Mathew it is strange to me how much we have both changed since that first night. I don't think either of us would have believed we could be sitting here side by side wanting nothing more than to be enjoying a few days together. I love being with you and I can hardly believe that 'other you' ever really existed. At least I don't want to. I intend to enjoy every minute we have together, but we both know a war is coming. My Lord, I wish it could be stopped but it can't. My brother Alexander has already been in Singapore for over a year with the 18th Division. They are there to block any advances the Japanese Army might attempt in that direction. He is certain Singapore cannot be taken and writes that it is so well defended any landing would be a disaster for the Japs. He says we have huge cannon pointed out to sea, and jungles and swamps surround the city on the landward side. I wonder why, if it is so impregnable, do we have so many troops stationed there?

"England is also facing Germany as an enemy and the only question is when they will go after Poland which, because of treaties we have, means we will automatically be at war against Hitler and his military.

"And, dear Mathew that will mean you will be going back to America. Your mission over here will be finished. Who knows how long the war will last; probably years. And while I believe in the end we British will win out, there are no guarantees. I do so hate the thought of not seeing you again. I think you know how special you have become to me. If not you would be 'daft as a brush.'"

Matt reached over and touched her arm. "Joanna, you won't find me that easy to be rid of. It would take far more than a little thing like a war to breakup our friendship. I will be here with you as long as you can stand to have me around. There is a saying about 'Hell and High-water.' It means staying the course no matter how bad things get. Well my dear, I will be here for you, for us, through Hell and High-water."

They were silent for a while and Joanna slipped back into humming her haunting song. Matt was lost in thoughts of what he would do in the event things went as she feared. What could he do that would protect her? If worst came to worst could he get her to leave England for America with him?

These thoughts seemed to darken what had been a sunny morning. He noticed several graceful Spitfires on maneuvers in the blue skies above them and a few miles later they found themselves behind a long convoy of olive drab trucks loaded with soldiers. That reduced their speed to ten miles an hour.

As they entered the town of Tonbridge with the convoy still stretched in front of them, Joanna suddenly told him to make a hard-right turn onto Bank Street, then a left onto Castle Street. In front of his car he saw what appeared to be the ruins of a huge castle. He parked and they both sat looking at what had once been a mammoth stone structure.

Matt spoke first. "Wow, this must have really been something when it was complete. Even now it is impressive and half of it must be gone. What was it?"

"Well Mathew, this was not on my list of things to do this weekend, but that convoy was so slow I told you to turn so we could see it. It should have been on my list because it is related to one of the most important events in our history and indirectly to yours. Tonbridge Castle goes back to the eleven hundreds. It was owned by the de Clare family, one of the most powerful families in England; nearly as powerful as the King himself. They were Barons and were granted the castle and large land holdings by William the Conqueror. After he died they rebelled against his son William I. William was killed in a hunting 'accident' and the man who killed him was the son-in-law of Gilbert de Clare. He was so 'sorry' to have killed the King it is said he celebrated for days.

"Later the de Clares led a revolt of the Barons against King John, the brother of Richard the Lion Heart, and forced him to sign the Magna Carta in 1215. Later, Tonbridge Castle was owned by the Archbishop of

Canterbury. What had once been one of the most powerful locations in England had by the fourteen hundreds lost all importance and by the 1800's was little more than ruins. The de Clare family status was much the same."

They spent almost an hour walking at the base of the walls and Matt thought about how strange that a family which had once been so powerful had fallen into ruin as fully as had their castle. Matt noticed a new Union Jack flag flying from the top of one tower of the castle. No doubt an attempt to keep the locals spirits high during this stressful period of uncertainty.

When they were once more in the car, Matt said to Joanna, "You know, it seems curious how some families begin at the top with wealth and power, yet seem only to go downward while others start near the bottom and rise ever higher."

"Mathew, are you thinking," she asked, "of us Bartons? Starting as publicans and building a large company?"

"Yes Joanna but also of my family. They left England and went to America with little more than the clothes on their back. Worked hard and saved what little they could. Fought in all America's wars. Lived through hard times and eventually built a banking empire. The amazing thing is I had to come to England before I fully understood and appreciated how hard it was. Thank you for the history lessons."

He started the car and was ready to pull away when she said something surprising from a woman of her age. "Mathew, I wonder how a person as educated as you can be startled to discover that one has to know where they have been to understand where they are going? I am glad I know you have an unlimited capacity to learn. It is the thing which makes you a brilliant student and a constant surprise to your professors. And what has made me able to *bear* you all this time," the last said with a glowing smile.

He grinned at her as he pulled away. "I have a strong suspicion you are numbered among those teachers. I want you to know I have found the lessons most enjoyable and I hope the classes you are giving me never end."

"Mathew Weldon, you had better remember what is always said about statements like that, 'be careful what you wish for.'"

Joanna began to once more hum the haunting tune which he found so entrancing. He retraced the route which had carried them to the castle and headed toward town.

The main route was along High Street where military construction crews were busy building concrete obstructions. These forced Matt to swerve the MG from side to side to pass around them. Many of the sidewalks had barbed wire entanglements and sandbags were piled high around official buildings considered in need of additional protection. Under spreading trees they saw light anti-aircraft (AA) and anti-tank guns with soldiers lounging around them. Many sat on park benches while others sat on the ground leaning against the gun wheels. All their uniforms were new and recently issued. Most seemed middle aged. He was sure they were members of Local Defense Volunteer forces....

Matt was certain the heavier AA guns were being saved for use around London and other major cities.

Further along they saw concrete pill boxes being constructed on the shore of the Medway River which would defend the town and attempt to stop any river crossing by the enemy. It was clear the English High Command had decided to hold each town and force the Germans to try and take each of them. The Army was in the process of turning every town into a fortified position. A viable strategy because attacking forces always suffered the heaviest casualties. The problem for England in the early stages of an invasion would be the superior experience of the German Army. Initially the British would suffer unnecessary losses until they learned some very painful lessons. If the Germans came over, Matt was convinced they would land in a long arc from Dover to Brighton. Another card the Germans would play would be to land a large number of paratroopers behind British defenses, sowing panic among green troops. For Hitler's army the nearly insurmountable problem was landing *anyone* on English soil. To drop paratroopers, the Germans must first be defeat the RAF. To land by sea, their problem would be to overcome both the Royal Navy and the RAF.

Joanna's father, Owen, had calculated the odds against the German Army pulling off an invasion as very high. Matt now believed he was right. It was going to be an air war against England. A very bloody air war.

Matt was so deeply lost in thought that when Joanna spoke it momentarily startled him.

"I am afraid we will be seeing this kind of work everywhere we go this weekend. Dad says every town and village in the country is undergoing defensive conversions. The entire coast is already bristling with guns mounted in protective concrete emplacements. Soldiers are being trucked all over. The ones we saw today are probably headed to Dover for the big buildup there. Tanks, trucks, artillery, ammunition, food supplies; everything an Army needs. The newspapers and the BBC say we are keeping large numbers of our aircraft flying all the time. We have already seen some overhead today and for the last week I have seen more over London with each passing day.

"I keep hoping it won't, but I know in my heart that war is going to happen. That is why I want you to see everything before... before the attacks start and everything changes...forever. Oh Mathew, whatever shall we do?"

For the first time since he had known her, he reached across and squeezed her hand. "Joanna, we will do what people have always done in dangerous times such as those coming. We will do all that is required of us, we will survive and most importantly *will* come through it all together."

She squeezed his hand back and told him, "Mathew, you have become the best friend anyone could ever have. I only hope I have been half as good a friend to you as you have to me. I know it has not been easy for you. You have been the perfect gentleman in every way and I value that greatly. If you choose to stay here in England, I know we will get through it *together.* Yes... we will do whatever it requires to get on with living. I willingly confess I don't know what I would do without you."

"I have no intention of leaving," he said above the engine's roar. "I will be here as long as you want me to be. Things are going very well between the two of us. I can't imagine *not* being with you. I know it is going well because you haven't had to break a heavy object over my hard head. I admit I have shown more self-control than I knew I was capable of. That has only been a problem every time I look at you. I am sure you know you are, as you English say, absolutely 'smashing.'"

"Mathew, you are not the only one who has felt an attraction. You must have sensed it on my part as well. I have struggled to control my reaction to it because I am going to be certain before I act on any feelings like that. I meant it when I said one man for the rest of my life. Yes, I have always known it would be that way. Since I was a small girl.

"The West Wind whispers things to me when I am in the barley fields. It usually tells me about things such as the coming weather and it is never wrong. When I was small it told me about other things. Things about the life I would live. When Alexander and I played hide and seek, the Wind told me where to hide from him. It would tell me where he was hiding. Alexander could almost never find me but I could always find him. Oh Mathew please don't think me mad. It would break my heart if you did. I had to tell you because I want my best friend to really know me."

Matt kept his eyes on the road lying ahead of them while answering her. "My dear Joanna Shaylee Barton. Ah, yes... Shaylee. Such an unusual name. *Shaylee*. I had never heard it before so I researched it. You know how I am about things I don't know. I always have to find out. What I discovered is, 'Shaylee' is an ancient name. It is both Celtic and Gaelic in origin. So, by the way, is 'Barton.' 'Bar' from the word barley and 'Ton' from a measured or enclosed area. How completely appropriate as your family name. Then your middle name, 'Shaylee' which means 'enchantress' or 'princess of the fields.' Neither definition eliminates the other. Both could apply to one person. I have found you to be both at the same time so I do not doubt for even a single moment the wind may tell you things. I am certainly under a spell and I find it a most wonderful one."

"Thank you Mathew but let me assure you I am *no* witch. I would ask anyone except you if they had made-up the information about my middle name. Coming from you I know it is true. I had not heard it until now. I knew 'Shaylee' was an unusual name but thought no more about it than that. It was just one of my birth names. I did not even know the meaning of 'Barton.' That it was Celtic and Gaelic. I imagine Dad knows. He is the real repository of our family history. But he has never told me about it.

"If there is a spell, Mathew, it is not of my making though I have told the West Wind how fond I am of being with you."

"Joanna, if that is all it takes to make magic, then I need to talk to your West Wind while we are there this weekend. I have one wish in particular," he told her with a wistful smile.

The road became heavily shaded by large overhanging trees which gave the impression they were driving through a tunnel with occasional breaks in its roof. When the overhanging trees ended, fields of golden grain stretched out to the horizon and were alive with rolling movement. The wind blew across their tops gently, making them look much like a golden inland ocean.

Joanna asked him to slow down then turn into a side road at a pair of tall stone obelisks, one rising on each side of the entrance to a long hedge-lined drive at the end of which Matt could see a large stone dwelling. The house had several tall chimneys rising from its slate covered roof and was surrounded by lush green lawns enclosed by six foot rock walls. Beyond the walls there rose a cross-topped steeple and nearby he could see a single massive oak. There were other trees but the oak towered so far above them, they appeared small.

He had often thought his family's estate on Long Island was old but looking at Barton Hall made him revise his thinking. The structure he saw before him was considerably older yet it was somehow more comfortable with itself. This was a house built to live in, while his family's home seemed built to impress others.

"Matt, if you follow the drive it will take you around to the right side of the Hall. The garage and parking is around back."

Matt swung his small car around the side of the house noticing a garden full of large rose bushes in full bloom and hundreds of smaller flowering plants placed around them. In the center of the garden was a fountain with a small pond at its base. A circular path of stones ran around it with benches placed at intervals along the circumference.

It was very much a smaller version of the garden they had on Long Island. His father used it for business gatherings and parties for many of the groups he belonged to. When Matt once asked his father how long the garden had been there, his father told him not long the way he saw it now. His wife, Matt's mother, had replanted an old, abandoned garden into the elaborate one he was looking at.

One of the gardeners had told Matt that his father would come in from a day at the bank on many summer evenings and find his wife still working in the garden. That he would take off his suit coat and vest, hang them over the ancient Italian statue of the goddess Diana and begin working beside her. The gardener told Matt he wished the lady had lived so she could see how pretty it was now. The three gardeners who had helped her still cared for the gardens and all of the plants she had selected, planted and loved.

The day his father told him about the garden, which had been at least seven years ago, Matt had been surprised to hear his father speak that way about, what to him, had only represented a bunch of plants, several decrepit statues, and a pond of expensive Japanese goldfish. Today, seeing this English garden, he understood why his mother's garden still meant so much to his father. In that moment he also knew why his father had spoiled him so much. It was about all of the things that are left behind when someone you have loved is gone. It was a flash of understanding about how lucky he had been to have Trey as his father and what a remarkable woman his mother must have been to be so loved. He realized he had missed much.

Matt walked around his little MG, opened the door for Joanna, helped her out of her seat and told her, "Well, I guess it's time for the suspect to undergo his cross-examination by the prosecution."

Joanna's answer was nearly lost in her laughter. "Oh Mathew, she is not that bad. Well... ok maybe a little bit, but not THAT bad. You must remember I am her only daughter so please forgive her for being protective. After all you are a '*Yank*.'" The last was nearly lost in the gale of her laughter.

~ ~ ~ ~

What neither of them knew was that Owen and Margaret had had a serious talk the night before. Owen was determined this weekend would not be a contentious one and he was aware Margaret could be contentious when she was suspicious of someone.

After they had eaten, he suggested a glass of wine in the garden. She agreed it was a lovely evening and she would love to have a glass of sherry with him. What she didn't tell him was that over the years she had learned this had always been his way of saying there was something they needed to talk about and that something was usually a topic she was probably not going to like.

When they were comfortably seated with their drinks and the small talk was out of the way, Owen looked at her and started telling her what had been troubling him since he learned his daughter was bringing Matt out to the Hall for the weekend.

"Margaret, we need to reach an understanding about this weekend. Our daughter is bringing the only young man I have ever known her to have a real interest in. And believe me he is truly a fine young man in spite of the fact that he is an American. No make that... he is simply a very fine young man, period. We have talked a few times and I really like Matt. He has freely admitted that he was a bit wild and out of control in the past. He makes no excuses for having been that way. I know he has grown up a lot in the past few months. Joanna is the cause of much of that. In addition, the situation we are in over here is having an effect on him. He and Joanna are very well matched to each other. They are both highly intelligent. They have similar tastes in almost everything: music, art and literature. Then there is a fact they haven't faced yet. They are deeply in love with each other. Joanna just needs to be sure he has changed before she admits to herself she loves him. If he proved false to

86

her, she would be crushed. I know she has nothing to worry about because he loves her the way I love you."

His wife was silent for several moments before saying... "Yes Owen, I understand what you are telling me but what do we know about this young man? I mean some people are good about fooling others. We are a pretty well established family and Joanna is our only daughter and she will inherit a good deal."

Owen took a drink of his Port and lit one of his well smoked pipes. When it was fired-up he told her, "Margaret, I like the boy but I *did* check him out. He is fourth generation banking money. Lots of it. He is an only child. His mother died when he was under a year old. He attended the very best schools; in fact has had the best of everything. His grades were outstanding to say the least.

"If America had royalty, he would be the son of a Baron and unlike here in England, a very moneyed Baron. No my dear, it is we who are poor by comparison which will give you an idea of his family's wealth. I believe we can dispense with the idea the lad is a fortune hunter. In fact, he and Joanna locked horns the first night they met. Joanna was really quite rude to him, something she has never done before.

"He was brought to a party at the London house as a guest of Larry Trusdale and Joanna detests Trusdale for some reason. Because he was there as Larry's guest Joanna was rude to him. She later learned she had no reason to do so. The boy had the pluck to treat her in the same fashion. He curtly informed Joanna his father's bank could buy our business and not even notice they had done it. She came back with, 'We are not for sale.' Yet, in the end, the boy apologized to *her*. Actually told her he was sorry for his actions. Later Joanna realized that it was she who should have done that.

"The boy's father pulled him out of University and sent him over here to get an answer to the question, 'Can England hold out and fight off Hitler's Germany?' You see their bank has substantial investments over here and he needed to know whether he should hold them or divest the bank of them. Matt and I spent a good deal of time talking about this situation and he has subsequently advised his father to keep the investments and has even suggested making additional loans available to our country.

"That has nothing to do with these two young people, but I want you to know the whole story. I know you are wondering something else about them and, no, I don't think they have done that. I don't think they will until they are certain about being together for a long time. It won't happen until they are confident about all their feelings. Joanna is very level headed and determined. And as for the lad, I believe he would rather cut off his hand than to ever hurt her. I will tell you that Matt took a boy to task who said something off-color about Joanna. As a matter of fact the boy was so frightened of Matt that he left University. That is as much as I know about what happened, so please don't bring it up while they are here. Joanna just wants a chance to show him around so he can understand better who she is. She wants him to also see Canterbury and Dover. She told me she wants him to see it all while there is still time. Joanna thinks he might go back to America when the war starts. I am sure she is wrong about that. This boy is made of steel. I don't think he will run from anything. He will be in England until it ends. If he goes back to America, it will only be if she is with him. So, my dear, let the weekend take its course. Let them have this time together because who knows how many more weekends they will have to be light-hearted together."

His wife looked at him in silence for several minutes before finally replying, "Owen, if this boy Matt is only half as good a man as you are, then he will be all I could ever wish for our Joanna. However I do want to get to know him so I will be comfortable with this young man who sounds as if he could become our son-in-law. I am sure you are right about him but I must be able to make up my own mind. Rest assured I will not cross-examine the young man. I just want the chance to get to know him."

~ ~ ~ ~

Matt and Joanna were walking toward the back door when it opened and Owen and Margaret came down the steps, both smiling. Owen extended his hand then saw Matt's were loaded with Joanna's and his over-night bags.

"Well, the hand-shake can wait. Would you like me to help with the bags?"

"No, I can handle them, sir, but I wouldn't object if you open the door and show me where to take these."

"Certainly Matt, follow me my boy. These steps are old and uneven so be careful of your footing. I really should have them re-laid."

Owen turned and he and Margaret went back up the stone steps where he held the massive oak door open.

Joanna laughed and said, "Dad is telling the truth Matt. I must have skinned my knees a hundred times as a child tripping up or down them. Dad thinks anything less than a hundred years old shouldn't need repair."

"Now Joanna," Owen said. "You know that is not true. I often have things around the Brewery repaired that are only fifty years or so old."

"Yes Dad, you repair them yourself because no one else knows how. Matt you saw for yourself that we have a very modern facility but Dad does insist on keeping a few old items around which we still use and he really does repair them. I suppose it makes him feel useful."

After making it up the steps without incident Matt followed his hosts down a wide hallway with dark mahogany paneling until they came to a stairway. Each step was covered with a faded Afghan Dhurrie carpet in shades of red, blue and off-white. It was woven during a long-past century in a fine tribal pattern of diamonds and stars. Even though it was worn by thousands of footsteps, its beauty, though faded, was still evident.

At the top of the stairs a small landing and hall mirrored the level below. Owen led him to a large room to the left side of the hall and Matt knew at once it was Joanna's. Everything in his sight was completely feminine and he saw pictures on shelves and dresser-tops of her from the time she was a small, serious faced child. One of the pictures where she was smiling showed her missing two front teeth. Matt was glad to know she was not born the beautiful, poised and sophisticated young woman he knew. He had often thought her nearly ageless.

She and her mother entered the room behind Matt and Owen. He had heard them talking quietly with their heads close together almost conspiratorially. He could catch only an occasional word but the way they both glanced at him, there could be little doubt he was the subject. He had heard them both laughing during the climb; once he had very nearly tripped but caught himself without falling or dropping the luggage. Owen and Margaret left Joanna's room telling them to come down as soon as they had settled their things.

"Mathew just place my bag on the bed. I'll put everything away after lunch. Your room is directly across the hall, so just drop your bag over there. Mom and Dad have waited on us to have lunch as the convoy made us later than expected. Fortunately they prepared a cold lunch. Mother did ask about the delay. She asked nicely but she asked."

Matt had been expecting a question about their delay since he felt certain Mrs. Townsend placed a telephone call to Joanna's mother as soon as they pulled away from 37 Eaton Square. He smiled at Joanna before saying, "So did you tell her we parked and made mad, passionate love?"

Her cheeks turned red, but she laughed as she said, "No Mathew. I will leave replies such as that for you should you decide to make them. Which I certainly hope you will not. A reply like that would probably shorten our weekend drastically. Dad would know you were kidding, but my mother...oh my Lord! No, I told her we were held up by a convoy and turned off to see Tonbridge Castle. Now take your things across the hall and let's get down to lunch."

Matt followed Joanna's instructions, crossed the hall, opened the door and put his bag on the bed which looked to be far more than a hundred years old and a bit short for his six foot body.

He and Joanna retraced their steps down the stairs into the large dining room. Matt was certain this room was directly out of the eighteen hundreds. The furniture was large, dark and heavily carved with grapes and grape leaves. Despite the age of the table, chairs, side board and cabinets, their condition was so good it would have been easy to think them newly made.

Matt was reminded of the furnishings in his father's office at the Bank, also very old but so well cared for that all of it looked nearly new. The leather covered chairs had been so well maintained they were still supple and comfortable. The memory returned Matt to a day in the not too distant past when he had sat in one that he found far less than comfortable. He was certain that day had been the most important if humiliating, day in his life. Certainly until the night he first met Joanna.

Margaret pointed him to a seat next to her daughter. Owen was at the head of the table and his wife was seated across from Matt and Joanna. There was room for ten more people along the table and not one of them would have been crowded.

The table end where they sat was covered with platters full of cold cuts of meat, cheeses, breads and a salad. Margaret smiled as she spoke to Matt and said, "What would you like to drink? We have hot tea, wine, water and our ale."

Matt returned her smile saying, "Well Mrs. Barton, at this time of day hot tea would be my choice and will go very well with sandwiches and salad. This is a really nice layout for lunch. It looks lovely and I must say our trip down has left me with quite a healthy appetite. Joanna and I ran into a very long, slow convoy so we took a side-trip to Tonbridge Castle. We strolled around its walls and Joanna was good enough to give me a history lesson about the Castle and thereby the de Clare family. Theirs is quite a story, as entwined with the history of England, as it is."

"Yes Matt, Kent is a very historic area in our country. By the way, I would like you to call me Margaret. You notice I am already calling you 'Matt.' I know my daughter calls you 'Mathew' because she likes that name better. She is a very determined young lady so I guess you have gotten used to being 'Mathew' by now. We believe she is worth a small eccentricity or two."

"Well Mrs... Margaret, I have been called 'Matt' since I was a small boy but I am Mathew according to my birth certificate and besides I love the sound of the name when Joanna says it. But much like a hound, I will answer to either name so long as you don't use too harsh a tone of voice with me. I will keep an eye out for eccentricities, but so far she is the most normal yet charming person I have ever met. I consider it a privilege to be her friend." Matt noticed Joanna was smiling her "What a lovely thing to say" smile at him, as was her mother.

How alike and yet how different this mother and daughter were. Joanna was over two inches taller than her mother with her striking copper hair and ultra-green eyes. Margaret had brown hair with touches of blonde and Icelandic blue eyes much the color of his. Joanna had told him her mother's family had some Viking blood and Matt could easily believe it. She already impressed him as a woman who maintained great control of her emotions, but one who, if pushed too far, would be an unforgiving adversary.

Owen took a long swallow of the ale in his glass stein then asked Matt, "So you got behind a convoy before you reached Tonbridge. A big one would you say?"

"Yes," Matt answered, "I never reached a spot where I could see the entire length but I would guess more than a hundred Lorries loaded with troops and equipment. Joanna thought it was probably headed for Dover. We also saw engineers building all kinds of defensive works, pill boxes, tank traps and laying barbed wire."

Owen took a sip of ale and responded, "The same sort of things I saw happening in every town I passed through on my way down last evening. Lots of anti-tank positions and some anti-aircraft positions being laid-in along with crews to operate them. If Jerry should make it over, he will find a right hot welcome awaiting him. The longer he waits to try it the warmer the welcome will become. I am still convinced he can't do it. You have heard my reasoning on that topic. Now, having said that, I am still more convinced than ever that war is coming. Hell, even Neville

Chamberlin has finally arrived at the same conclusion. Too late for him now. He is a good man. Smart in his way, but a weak reed who Hitler found easy to bend. He will very soon be the Ex-Prime Minister and Churchill will be at Number 10 Downing Street. No chance the wind can blow him away. He is stubborn enough to carry us past the early period when we will take a thrashing and smart enough to turn it around. Yes. Winston Churchill is the man to run our end of this war. He and your President Roosevelt are friends so that will help. They each had a hand in running their country's Navies during the Great War and I suspect they both have a love for the big ships. They know the importance of ships of war on the great oceans; knowledge Hitler lacks. He thinks only about armies on land. Both America and England are building huge navies. Ships almost beyond counting. The Germans intend to use submarines to break up the transports and will be somewhat successful in the beginning but not for very long. Long range aircraft will soon blunt their effectiveness. Plus a few surprises we have for them in that area.

"Matt, what are your plans when the war starts? You haven't said anything about going back home to America."

Matt looked at Joanna and shook his head "No" before telling Owen what he had already told her on the drive down. "No, England will not that easily be rid of me. Running away is no answer. Germany will find it cannot send me packing only to wait at home until trouble finally arrives over there. I suppose one might put it down to being young and foolish, but I am staying and I will try to find something useful to do. Besides the lease for my 'digs' in London are paid for the next four months. I like it there and refuse to be put out by Hitler and his gang of thugs. Besides Joanna and I have an invitation for another evening at Café de Paris."

An hour later Joanna knocked quietly on his bedroom door and entered with a mischievous smile on her lips while shaking her head. "Another night at Café de Paris? Honestly Mathew, it was all I could do to keep from laughing out loud when you came out with that. You had been doing so well until that moment. What a reason to stay when war comes. I thought I saw Mother's eyes glaze over in disbelief and Dad almost choked on his sandwich.

"Leaving that aside you passed muster with high marks. After lunch, I was helping mother put things away when she said 'Café de Paris indeed; that boy is staying for you. He is far too *good-looking* but by-and-large I think he is an admirable young man. I like him.' I have never heard her render that endorsement before on anyone. First my cat, now my mother. What's next? Will you be charming the impossible Mrs. Townsend?"

"Well Joanna, I think you have just laid the correct odds of that ever happening. Impossible!"

The two of them went down the stairs and out the heavy front door. It was still warm and the skies were a wonderful shade of azure blue with a few fluffy puff ball clouds on the horizon. The sky was criss-crossed with a pattern of contrails made by the exhaust from Spitfires and Hurricanes patrolling the Kentish skies. There were far more of them than he had ever seen flying at one time. It looked as if they were up in squadron strength. Matt walked along-side Joanna as she led him down a long walkway running between neatly trimmed ten foot high hedges to a small cemetery. The area was enclosed by a very old rusted wrought-iron fence and the entrance was through a double-hung iron gate which protested loudly when he opened it.

The headstones stood in silent semi-circles around the base of the massive oak which towered over everything. Joanna and he stood in front of each stone marker while she gave him a brief history of the family member who lay interred below. He saw the stones reached back as far as 1735 and many were so weathered the inscriptions were only shadows of words. She told him the present house was not that old because there had been a fire in the original wooden structure in 1788 and the stone house they had just eaten lunch in was finished in 1793. The small chapel he could see just beyond the fence was built in 1769. It was used for funerals and weddings and, in times of danger and hardship, prayers.

When she had completed the tour and history of all the headstones in the small cemetery, she took him to an area which was grassed but contained no stones. The two of them sat quietly for awhile on a carved stone bench. Finally Joanna spoke in a voice which was almost a whisper. "This is the area where my immediate family will be laid. The area directly in front of us is for my father and mother. The spaces to the left are for my brother and his wife and any children. To the right are for me and my husband and children."

Matt reached over and placing his hand under her chin, turned her face towards him. "Dear Joanna, eventually we must, as Shakespeare said, 'come to dust.' But I hope for us that will be a long time coming. It is best to know it will happen, but to live as if it never will. To be as happy as we can until that time. I am not very religious, but I do believe in something beyond all this. I just don't have an idea of what it is. I guess I can only say that I don't believe in death and the grave ending everything. I will also confess I am in no hurry to discover the answer to that eternal question."

Joanna was still gazing into his eyes. "Mathew, I wonder if you will ever stop amazing me. That may be the best philosophy of life I have ever heard. I have read the works of all the great philosophers from Aristotle to Thomas Aquinas, Descartes to John Locke, but you have in a few words, summed up what it has taken others pages and pages or whole books to say. Knowing I will in time lie here, does not make me sad. Quite the opposite. It is comforting to me. I will be with my family and what could be better. To be with the ones I love and who have loved me. You must know by now family is everything to me."

How strange, he thought, this enchanting young girl is teaching me things about life that all the tutors, teachers and professors never could. They probably tried. I simply wasn't listening.

Joanna led him back out the squeaky gates to the chapel. He pushed open the heavy iron-reinforced oak doors. The chapel was small but had an arched ceiling and beautiful stained glass windows. The sun coming through each window placed intricate, many-colored patterns on the stone floor. All were biblical except one. It was to this one that Joanna led him.

"Mathew, I have loved this one...ever since...since I was a child. I can't remember a time I didn't love it. It's..."

Matt interrupted her. " St. George and the Dragon. He is wearing spotless white armor and riding a white horse. This scene is on the back of the English Gold Sovereign and has been for hundreds of years. He is using a lance to slay the dragon. This one is different from the coin. He and the dragon are in a field of, unless I am mistaken, barley."

"Yes Mathew. It is a field of barley. I have looked at it for years. I don't know if the barley was simply there to represent the Barton family or if there was more to it than that. Dad doesn't know. I do know when I was small St. George was the ideal of who I wanted to marry when I was grown. Little girls believe in fairy tales like that and they always have happy endings. As a child, I always assumed St. George won. Now I know there is always a chance the dragon might slay St. George."

They both stood there without speaking for a long time before Matt broke the silence. "When I was a small boy, one of my nannies read 'Peter Pan' to me. I loved the idea of never growing up. I saw how my father was gone so much. How he worked such long hours. The way people who kept our estate up all worked so hard. Yet as a child everything I wanted was given to me. Every toy. Everything. I suppose I got my wish about not growing up for a very long time. Too long. In a way I was one of the 'Lost Boys.' If I had not performed a stupid, willful stunt, I might have remained like that forever. Thank goodness I did it or I would have wasted my life and worse still, I would never have known you."

She took his hand between hers and looked him in the eyes. "Oh Mathew, I have not once seen you acting as a child. Neither of us knew each other as children. We are different now and it is only *now* that matters. The guy on the horse is not real. He is a myth. He is only pieces of colored glass joined with lead strips. It is pretty to look at, but it is not real. And Peter Pan was nothing more than word pictures on the pages of a book. Neither was real. We were children then and are no longer. What I see in you today is a fine responsible man who I very much love being with. Let's go out and take a walk in the barley. I want you to see it. This is the best time of year for barley. In another two weeks it will be harvested. The West Wind is blowing today and I want you to hear it and see how it moves the barley and there is something I need to tell you."

They left the coolness of the chapel and walked into the sunshine of the warm, late July, afternoon. Joanna held his hand as she led him toward the golden fields which covered the gently rolling hills as far as the eye could see. Joanna guided him along narrow paths which cut through the fields of grain. Her other hand gently caressed the tops of the barley as she walked the path. Finally she stopped and closed her eyes.

"Close your eyes and listen to it Mathew. Can you hear the Wind talking? It talks to the barley as it blows over it. As I told you today, it is the West Wind and that is the only one that whispers as it passes."

Matt closed his eyes and listened. At first the only sound he heard was the sound wind makes when it is blowing, then slowly he began to hear another sound. It was a soft sighing. He was sure it was the sound of the barley moving in the wind and rubbing against its neighbors. But it *was* nearly like whispers. He heard Joanna quietly say, "Yes I will. It is time I told him."

"Mathew, I wanted to bring you down to my home because there is something important that I have to tell you and I wanted to do it here. You know I told you we could be friends until I met the man that I would be with forever. Well my dear Mathew, I have fallen in love and I know he is the man who I *should* be with forever. For that reason I am afraid we can no longer continue as *friends*."

A hole opened beneath Matt's feet. He could barely breathe. This young woman he was so taken with was saying that she was in love with someone else. That he was going to lose the one who meant so much to him. What could he say? Could he even speak? What *should* he say? She had warned him this might happen. Yet how could this be?

"Joanna," he stammered his shock apparent in his loud voice. "I would be lying if I said I was not surprised by the suddenness of this. Are you *sure* about this man? I mean...well, I assume he is in love with you?"

"Mathew that is what I don't yet know. Not for certain anyway. He hasn't told me so. I suppose I will have to ask him."

"Joanna, of course he is. How could he not be? One would have to be a complete *idiot* not to love you."

She paused, gazed directly into his blue eyes and said, "Still I think I **must** ask him. Otherwise I could be making a terrible mistake which would cause me to lose the dearest friend I have ever had.

"So do you Mathew? Do you love me? I do hope so, because I love you so *very* much."

He simply couldn't speak. Instead of answering her question, he enveloped her in his arms and kissed her the way he had wanted to since the first night he had seen her. When they finally ended the kiss, Matt breathlessly told her what he had wanted to say for months, "Joanna, my dearest one.... until I met you I had no idea what the word 'love' meant. I do now. Love means Joanna. It means you. And yes, it means the two of us - forever. And I doubt forever will *even* be long enough." They shared another nearly endless kiss and reluctantly started back toward Barton Hall with their arms around each other's waist and their hips touching. As they walked, Joanna began humming. Both were smiling contentedly and the Wind murmured softly in their ears.

~ ~ ~ ~

When they entered Barton Hall, they were met by Joanna's mother obviously in a high state of agitation. "Your father is in the library listening to the radio. He had a telephone call from one of the military fellows he knows from his Club. It has happened! Germany has invaded Poland. They invaded early this morning. Let's go into the library. The BBC is doing nothing except 'War news.'"

They paused briefly to look longingly into each other's eyes before hand-in-hand following Margaret down the hallway into a room lined with bookshelves rising above storage cabinets built out from the walls. Though a daze, Matt saw the shelves were all packed with books; some of the books were ancient with cracked, heavy leather bindings while others were newly published with paper dust covers. Matt noticed a copy of

Fitzgerald's, "The Great Gatsby." The dust cover's art told him it was probably a first edition. It surprised him to see 'Gatsby' in an English country home.

Owen Barton was sitting in the wing chair in front of a large wood-cabinet radio tuned to the BBC. The announcer was broadcasting the news in one of those voices which was so refined, educated and British that one would have known it could only be the BBC if they were hearing the voice in Timbuktu.

"This is Lionel Marston.... Germany has invaded Poland as of 8:00 AM this morning. Many Polish towns have been bombed and Danzig has fallen under German control. Hitler has welcomed the German residents of Danzig back into the German Reich.

"Hitler said Germany had tried in every way to settle this problem peacefully, but had been answered by an attack on a radio station on German soil by Polish forces this morning and was left with no alternative other than to meet force with force.

"Armed forces in England and France have been fully mobilized in response to Germany's naked aggression against Poland. At Number 10 Downing Street, Prime Minister Chamberlain has announced that Britain and France will honor their treaty with Poland and has set a deadline of forty-eight hours for German withdrawal from Polish soil or a State of War will exist between England, France and Germany.

"In London, preparations for War continue. Queen Mary has visited the Women's Voluntary Services in Westminster today. She was there for over an hour. The evacuation of children from around certain industrial locations of the country to safer areas of rural England has begun.

"All Emergency Services Rescue and Demolition Workers are to report at once to their appointed centers or if no center has been assigned, they are to report to the local fire house.

"France has announced full mobilization and marshal law. In London, the King has signed orders for full mobilization of the British Army, Navy and Air Force.

"Hitler has broadcast that he had no choice than to respond to Poland's use of force. Great Britain and France are inflexibly determined to fulfill to the uttermost, their obligations to the Polish Government.

"Hitler told the Reichstag in Berlin that the German Armed Forces were the strongest and the best Armed Force in the world. Hitler added that if anything should happen to him, Field Marshall Göring and after him, Party Member Hess would lead the country. He thanked Italy for their support, but said he would not request their assistance.

"All employers are asked to arrange for members of their staff who are enrolled in the Civil Defense Services to be released immediately. This applies to both men and women. We will be updating you on the situation as bulletins are received."

The BBC began a program of patriotic music and Owen reached over to turn the volume down.

Matt could not help but notice that Joanna's father seemed to have aged at least ten years since they had lunch together a few hours ago. Matt was surprised because it was exactly what Owen had predicted would happen and now that it had, the man seemed shocked by the reality of it.

"Well," Owen said. "The flag has gone up. This complicates everything. Lots of the lads at the Brewery will be going away. Some of the ladies in administration too. The next week or so will be a real scramble. There is going to be a shortage of workers all over England. I am going to pull records on who has retired that I may be able to get back.

"The big problem is going to be 'kiln' workers. They must all be young men thirty-five and under. The ones we have will be grabbed up by Military Services. I will have to find every man under thirty-five who is rejected by them. I hate to break up our weekend, but I am going to have to head back to town early tomorrow. I have to be ready for Monday morning. We can't shut the place down. England is going to need ale as much as bullets and bombs. My father didn't close down for my War and we bloody well will not close for this one."

Joanna waited for her father to finish before saying, "Dad can I help with any of this? Mathew and I will be glad to go back with you. Maybe we could help you do some of this."

Matt broke in with, "Yes sir. We would both be glad to do anything at all that would make this easier for you."

"No thank you Matt. What I need to do now is figure out who we will be losing to the military. It is mostly going through the personnel listings. I know my workers very well. A few of the younger ones probably won't pass the physicals. No, this is something I need to do solo. Later I will need help with other tasks. For now you two stay here with Margaret and enjoy the rest of the weekend as best you can. I will probably need help from both of you during the next several weeks.

"The Jerry's are going to be busy with the Poles for at least a few weeks. After that..."

"Dad, are you certain? I know the guys at the Brewery pretty well. I think we should go back with you."

"No my dear, in this you two would just be in the way. I will have to really focus on this single task and your trying to help would be a distraction. There will be plenty of times during the coming months when I will need help. Both yours and Matt's if he is willing. Who knows, he may even learn the ale-making business first hand after all. For now stay here and enjoy your weekend."

Matt looked at Joanna and her father before saying, "Owen, if you are sure about this. I suppose it is one way of shaking our fist at the 'Boche'... by 'carrying on.' Like all those signs in the Underground stations are already asking people to do. All of us are going to have to learn to 'remain calm and carry on' no matter what. Simply carrying on without fear is a way of fighting back. Fear is a psychological weapon and not being afraid is how we can defeat that weapon."

"Good lad! Matt, you know ours is a very old house. It has stood against many storms and it will stand up to the one which is coming. It may be shaken but it will not fall. It will be here long after Hitler and his Nazis are dust. The barley will be grown in the rich earth of Kent and our family will continue to care for it."

Margaret excused herself saying she needed to get something ready for them to eat and headed toward the kitchen.

The radio continued with bulletins about the German attack on Poland which contained some updated information but was primarily the same report they had heard earlier, just rephrased. It became clear the German Army was pushing ahead despite some effective counter-attacks by the Polish Army. The German Luftwaffe was completely over-whelming the Polish Air Force's outdated aircraft. German pilots had near total control of the air and were able to attack anything which moved on the ground.

Matt and Joanna were sitting side by side and Owen noticed they were still holding each other's hand.

"Good. I am glad you two finally woke up. It was high time you figured out you were more than 'simply friends.' A blind man could have seen it. I'll break it to Margaret before I leave. Though I suspect she already knows.

"Anyone can see what a good match you two are. I knew it from the first. I knew in time the two of you would realize it."

Chapter 8

DEATH OF A YOUNG MAN

Matt was surprised to find a young RAF Officer waiting for him outside the men's lounge near his Mathematics Classroom. The Officer was wearing the silver wings of a pilot on his blue-grey uniform jacket below which were a large number of award ribbons . The young man cleared his throat to be sure he had been noticed.

"Pardon me; are you Mathew Weldon from America?"

"Yes I am. How may I help you?" Matt sensed there was something troubling this young pilot.

"I am Flight Captain Martin LeGard and I flew with Lord Trusdale's son Larry. He asked me to deliver a letter to several people in the event anything should happen to him and you were on his list. I am sorry to say something has happened and he is dead. His Spitfire was shot down four days ago. I was only able to start delivering his letters yesterday because I had to fly the day after it happened and his family members were first on the list. It's not so easy to get around now-a-days, what?"

Matt was not sure of how to reply to the surprising information the young pilot had given him. Matt had no idea Larry had gone into the service, let alone with the RAF. He had seldom thought about him since he had disappeared from University following their run in. He disliked Laurence Trusdale as much as anyone he had ever met and here he was getting a letter from him three days after he had been shot down flying in defense of England. The only thing he could say with any sincerity was, "I am sorry he was shot down. I am certain he loved England and was doing what he saw as his duty."

The young pilot handed him a pale blue envelope with an RAF crest on the back flap, started to turn away, hesitated, and then turned back to Matt before saying, "There were many of us in the squadron who came to admire him. He was beyond simply brave. He never ran away from a fight and died while saving another of his squadron mates. He jumped into a fight with five 109's who were trying to shoot down his wing man. And he got two of them before his Spit was shot to pieces. His mate was able to limp back to the field. Larry went down with his plane. His body is being sent back to his family in Kent."

Matt looked down at the envelope in his hand. The description the pilot standing in front of him had given of the writer of this letter bore not the slightest similarity to the Larry Trusdale he had known. The change described was so great, he could no longer even capture a mental picture of the immature Larry Trusdale he had humiliated nearly a year ago.

The pilot turned and this time walked slowly away down the long oak wood paneled hall to disappear from sight as the echo of his footsteps faded down the stairs.

Matt carried the letter into the men's lounge and settled into a leather chair beneath the pictures hanging from the very wall into which he had driven young Lawrence Trusdale. The envelope opened easily and he removed the letter which was also on pale blue paper matching the envelope.

Why, Matt wondered, would Trusdale have written a letter to him of all people?

Especially one which was only to be delivered in the event he was killed? The two of them had been far from friends. They had in reality been only enemies. The kind of letter you would write to an adversary in a situation like this would be one which was an "I am dead now because of you" letter.

Well, he thought as he unfolded the letter, might as well read it and be finished with this.

The letter had been typed on a machine with a ribbon which had seen heavy use. Most likely a typewriter used by all the pilots in Trusdale's squadron, with a ribbon which did not get high priority for replacement. It was nearly a shadow of a letter. The words faded specters.

Mathew Weldon - King's College.

Matt,

I know you will be surprised I have written a letter to you which is to be delivered only in the event of my death.

Speaking of surprises; imagine my surprise at being dead! That certainly makes your surprise appear small by comparison. And I am extremely jealous of you. You, at least today, retain the ability to be surprised in this lifetime while I no longer do.

You arrived in England with a reputation as a rake and seducer of the girls, a reputation seemingly well justified in the first few weeks after your arrival. But for reasons which I still do not understand, you seemed to change during the course of a single evening. Or could the change have been the girl? The very thing you were reputed to be so adept with. If Joanna was the reason you changed, the irony would be simply overwhelming. She captivated the seducer. You were right. She would have nothing to do with me.

I understand we were never friends. The most I can say of our relationship is we knew each other and yet, strangely, you had a positive effect on me.

The confrontation we had in the lounge on the day you demonstrated what it felt like to play American football, made me painfully aware of what kind of person I was. That was the day I understood social position was in no way a substitute for fortitude. I was on my ass on the floor, but in reality I was running away from you. I was a coward.

As the son of a Lord, I could have easily found a way to keep from serving in the war when the time came. Yes Matt, I was intelligent enough to know war was coming in short order. So I volunteered for the RAF before it happened. I needed to prove something to myself. That, I have been able to do. I have been frightened, but I have never run away again.

They tell me I am a good pilot. I can't help a bit of bragging right at this juncture. To date I have sent 5 sons of Hitler to hell where they belong. Since you are reading this, I obviously met a better pilot or perhaps the odds simply got the best of me. Either way, I am sorry it has happened because I wanted to take you up on your offer for a bit of fisticuffs after the war was over.

That as it may have been, I remember hearing you say you had flown in America as a civilian so I have one request to make. If you somehow end up in this fight and become a flier do me a favor. Shoot down at least one more of the bastards for Lawrence Arrington Trusdale.

Larry

P.S. After a first rate fight between the two of us, I like to think we might have become friends.

Matt was not at all sure that a fight would have been required. They had both been self-centered S.O.B.s for a long time but had changed. "No Larry, it was not me who changed you. It was you. I regret I never had the chance to know this other you.... Requiescat in pace."

Chapter 9

A PROMISE BROKEN

After the first major German bombing of London on Saturday, September 7, 1940 Matt decided he must try to help out by doing something about reducing German air superiority over England, but he had made a solemn promise to Joanna that he would not. He was in turmoil over even considering breaking his word to her.

On the Monday morning following that heavily concentrated bombing of the city, Matt placed a call to Owen at the Brewery. He held for only a few moments before Owen picked up.

"Hello Matt. Are you alright? No harm from the bombing I hope."

"No Owen, all is fine on my end. All of your people okay?"

"Yes, yes. Nothing even close to the Brewery or our Eaton Square house. They would have to be completely lost to bomb our place down in Kent. Joanna is fine. I talked to her this morning. I do worry about her staying at our place here in London so much. I am sure it is low on the German priority list at present, but they have already shown an ability to make targeting mistakes. Perhaps you can convince her to spend more time in Kent, talk to her about it... will you do that for me Matt?"

"I will, but she can be stubborn. I wonder where she could have gotten that trait?" he said with a chuckle. "I will do my very best to get her to do it. No promises though. I have a problem with one promise I made to her already."

"Son, would that have anything to do with staying out of the war? She told her mother she made you promise not to get involved and naturally Mary Margaret told me. In case you don't already know, you can't keep a secret in a family. Simply impossible."

"Thanks Owen. I came up a bit short on education about family. My dad was always very busy running the Bank and... well... you already know my mother died when I was very young. But...yes, my problem is the promise to Joanna. Could I come by some time and talk with you? I just don't know what I should do."

"Of course my boy. This afternoon after 2:00 anytime will be fine."

"Thank you. I will see you about 3:00 since I have a class that is over at 2:00."

"Very good then, 3:00 it is Matt."

Matt drove slowly through London taking several detours around rubble blocked streets that in the past would have given him a straight route to the Brewery. He was thirty minutes past his three o'clock prediction but was still shown directly into Owen's top floor office.

Light from windows behind Owen made him appear only a darkened shadow from Matt's perspective where he sat in front of the ever disordered desk of Joanna's father. As usual the room lay in its perpetual fog-bank of tobacco smoke.

"So, my boy...you have a problem with the promise you made my daughter. She asked you not to get involved in our war with Germany and you promised not to. Now that is chafing you since the bombs are falling on London. A bit too close to someone you love... right?"

"Yes sir, that is exactly right. I could almost stomach it when they were going after the RAF...not that I liked it...but bombing London! That changed the game and damn it, Sir...I am a pilot. I don't think I can stand by and simply watch any longer...but I made Joanna a promise. I just don't know what to do. I was hoping you could help me. Help me see what I have to do. If I honor the promise, I can't fly and if I fly I have to break the promise."

"Well Matt, you have a very real problem. One you have stated well. First son... I want you to know some things. Things I know for certain. I know you two love each other. I knew that before you two finally admitted it. You see Joanna had never brought a boy to the Brewery before. The way you two looked at each other. It was all there. The very fact she asked you for the promise and that you made it is further proof.

"Promises should be kept **but** sometimes situations change so much a promise *must* be broken. Things have certainly changed drastically in the past few days. It now appears Hitler's Air Force intends to destroy London along with other cities in England. This battle will determine the future course of the war. Remember what I told you on your first visit here? If we win now, we will eventually win the war. Also remember I said that America will be in it. I just don't know how or why. If I am right, you would eventually be in it anyway. Sooner or later you would be drafted. Probably as a pilot. Matt, I don't think this is a question of if you will be in it...more a question of when.

"My daughter is a very bright girl. I know you have seen beyond her beauty by now. If you reason with her, she will come to accept your decision. One caution...better not tell her you are doing it for her...to protect her. That way if anything should happen to you...she won't blame

106

herself. You must make her see it was your decision. I am not sure she could live with herself otherwise. She has already told her mother 'he is the one'...the one she always knew she would find. forever's'. She always has done."

"Matt, just between the two of us, man to man I am sure you understand war is not a game. People die. You may die. No one is immune. I saw lads die in my War who were convinced it wouldn't happen to them. To others yes...but not them. Well it *did*. It almost happened to me several times. I lived, but only by inches. That is how survival is measured in a war. Have you thought about that? "

"No Sir. Not in exactly those terms. I am sure you are right. But...well I know I am a good pilot. That should up my chances of making it through. The Spitfire is a great plane. I think it is better than the German ME109 and that too will give me an edge in a dog-fight. But considering all that...Yes Sir, I know I could die. Anything can happen in a war. I suppose it is really random chance... or perhaps it is Joanna's 'Kismet.' Just simply what fate decides."

"Well Matt, whether it is fate or chance or even God... it happens. Just be very aware by trying to save *something*, you might lose *everything*. Your life. And Joanna might lose *you*. Think about that even more than the promise you made. Have you considered those things?"

"Yes Sir, I have. For several days now it is almost *all* I have thought about. I really feel I have to help out. I want to see if I can get into the RAF. As I said...I am a pilot. I should try to do my bit by flying."

"Very well Matt. I am a member of Boodle's. You are familiar with it?"

"Yes. A men-only Club. On Piccadilly. Very old Club. I know where it is."

"Good!" Matt heard him chuckle quietly between puffs on his old Charatan pipe. "Yes lad, a men-only club. Has been since 1762. They like to brag no woman has ever been inside, though for the life of me I fail to see the importance in that. Women would certainly enliven the old place, What? I often think some of the original members from 1762 may very well still be sitting in the Club Room. I think we should check some of them for a pulse from time to time. I'm the second generation of the Barton family to have membership there.

"Well Matt, a night never passes there without one or two high ranking officers from the RAF coming in. They go from there to the RAF Club which is also on Piccadilly and back again. I can't get us into the RAF Club, but I can sure take you as a guest to my Club. Might help if you talked to one of them. Get the straight scoop, as it were. Good contacts help and these will be very good contacts for you to have. And Son...if you do decide to go in, I will do my best to help make it acceptable with Joanna. Want to meet me at Boodle's at 7:30 tonight?"

"Yes, I would like that very much, Owen. I appreciate your helping me with this. I am sure you have enough to worry about without me adding to it. You were the only one over here I could talk it over with. I couldn't talk to Joanna about it. Not yet. Thank you again and I'll see you at Boodle's at 7:30 tonight."

Matt had to stop his MG only once on his way back. It happened on a street partially blocked by debris from several bomb flattened apartment buildings. Nine large black vans were parked in the only passable part of the street completely blocking it. While he waited he saw men carrying covered stretchers from the ruins. The stretcher bearers were covered head to foot with light grey, powdery dust; they were a mournful looking group. Matt saw tears streaking down several of their grey cheeks.

Black rubber sheets covered the stretchers but Matt occasionally saw arms or legs which were not covered dangling loosely over the sides. Some of the bodies were small and he knew they belonged to children. Many of the victims were extremely small, some must have been babies.

At that moment, sitting in a ruined London street, Matt knew his promise to Joanna was no longer one he *could* keep. As much as he loved her, it was no longer a war he would fight exclusively for her. It was a war he must fight for people like those being carried from the ruins. Those who would never know he had fought it.

~ ~ ~ ~

At 7:20 after driving slowly through Piccadilly Square and turning onto St. James Street, Matt arrived in front of Boodle's. He parked his small green MG two blocks away and by the time he arrived back at Number 28, he saw Owen waiting for him in front of the building. If not for the small brass signs attached beside the doors at each end of a large bay window, the structure could have been mistaken for a large, four story Georgian townhouse. The first floor was painted white while those which rose above it were light brown brick with white painted trim around the windows. The building spoke volumes about age and importance.

Owen led Matt through the door to the right side of the window and into a foyer where he registered him as a guest for the evening.

They climbed up to a clubroom on the second floor and settled into comfortable leather chairs beside a small square dark mahogany table topped with two silver ash trays. Even at this early hour the room was awash with clouds of smoke. Owen took out his pipe and began loading it with tobacco. When the ritual was finished, he carefully fired it up with a wood match.

"So, are you still feeling as you did this afternoon... about joining the RAF and flying for England?"

"Owen, I am even more convinced now that I have to. When I left your office this afternoon I still had some doubt, but on the way back I had to wait for bodies to be removed from a row of apartments which got hit last night. Stretcher after stretcher was being carried to a row of black Mariah hearses. Some of the bodies were children; some of the children were quite small. This is not something that I want to do. Anyone who wants to be in a war is crazy. No...this is now something that I *have* to do. I only hope Joanna can find a way to forgive me."

"Well Son, I believe if you explain it that way to her, she will. Maybe not at that instant, but she will. You know about her feelings for St. George don't you Matt?"

"Yes... but she has told me she does not want me trying to be St. George, that she has outgrown that childhood fantasy. She told me about it the first time she showed me the stained glass windows in the chapel. Why do you ask?"

"Because, despite what she said, you are going to be St. George to her forever now. Once she forgives you, and she will when you explain what forced your decision, you will be St. George fighting the Germanic dragon to save England... and despite what she said... *her*. There is so much about Joanna that is grownup and very sophisticated but also there is some that is still little girl. Always remember that Matt.

"Well now... There is a familiar face. A gentleman with four names."

Matt saw the man Owen was looking at and said. "Winston Leonard Spencer-Churchill. Yes, by now even most Americans back home know who he is. The man with the big cigar. He is the rock that England is standing on."

"Well said young man. Very well said indeed. Would you like to meet him? I have known him for years. Since the first war in fact. I am in the Conservative party which he leads. Stay here a moment and I will bring him over for an introduction. His cigar is a bit strong as is his drink and his language, but not when compared to my pipe and you seem to hold up well there."

Matt watched him walk across the room to the chair Churchill had picked out and was about to settle his bulk into. Owen put his hand on the Prime-Minister's arm and turned him until they were face-to-face.

Churchill's first reaction was to scowl and bite down on his cigar. It was the famous scowl Matt had seen often in newspaper photographs which told the world 'I am not pleased.' None-the-less, when he saw who it was, he actually smiled and shook Owen's hand. Matt realized he had never seen a single photograph of a smile on the man's face. Matt could tell Owen was speaking very quietly to the Prime Minister who looked in his direction and nodded "Yes."

The two men walked over to where he stood and Owen made the formal introduction including all Churchill's titles and honors, then he turned to Churchill and introduced Matt.

"This, Prime Minister is Mister Mathew Donnelly Weldon the Fourth from New York City who has been in England for a year. He is attending King's College and is a good friend of my daughter Joanna."

When Churchill shook his hand Matt found the hand shaking his to be strong but with surprisingly soft skin. He also decided the man did seem to have a lot of the English bulldog about his appearance and his voice tended to reinforce the impression. He growled words as much as pronounced them.

"Ah ha... a friend of Joanna's. That would make you a lucky lad. I met her a few years ago when Clementine and I were out at Owen's place in Kent. An exceedingly lovely young lady. Takes after her mother I would judge. Obviously doesn't get her looks from Owen.

"So my boy, my friend here tells me you are interested in getting into our fight and that further, you are a qualified pilot. Been flying since you were sixteen. Unusual to be a pilot so young but with Owen saying it, I know damn well it must be true. He and I have known each other since the trenches in the last bloody war. He is quite a fellow I can tell you. This man was in some very tight spots and came through them.

"I am meeting some other gentlemen here in a few minutes or I would stay so we could talk longer but...." He reached into his inside coat pocket, took out a card and a small black notebook. He scribbled a note on one page and tore it out to hand to Matt along with the calling card which he had signed on the back.

"You take this out to High Wycombe Abbey. RAF Headquarters. About an hour outside London. I will have my Secretary call out there first thing in the morning and have you put on the pass list. I will also have him call 'Stuffy' err... Hugh Dowding and ask him to spend a few

110

moments with you. He can tell you what we can do for you. He runs Fighter Command. Try to be brief. The Jerrys are keeping him very busy. A word of caution...Better not call him 'Stuffy.' I have known him long enough to do that. Besides I am his boss. No, you should call him 'Sir Hugh'."

Matt saw him look toward three men who had just walked through the door. "Thank you, Sir. 'Sir Hugh' it is. I appreciate your time. I know 'Sir Hugh' is not the only one with heavy responsibilities."

Churchill looked back and smiled again. "Thank you lad. Owen informed me of your quote about the rock that England is standing on. May I steal that from you? It might be a useful quote for someone other than me to use so that it gets quoted in the newspapers during an appropriately dark hour and unfortunately we still have more of those coming up before this war will turn in our favor."

Matt smiled at this man who was indeed carrying England almost solely on his back and said, "What quotation is that sir? The one you just originated?"

Churchill roared a laugh. "Good lad. If the RAF can't use you, we still have room in clandestine operations for a fellow like you. Yes indeed!"

When he had joined his party at another table, Owen remarked, "You know Winston is a really first rate fellow. If he had been in charge a few years earlier, we probably wouldn't be in this mess. I think he took a shine to you. Sending you straight to the top the way he did and then you made him laugh. He isn't able to do that often any longer. In normal times he has quite a sense of humor. Old Winston enjoys a good joke. Particularly if it is on someone else and he is the perpetrator. But since the war, he hardly ever laughs. I suppose there is little left to laugh about. The Brewery always used to be full of laughter and little harmless jokes, but not any longer."

Matt and Owen sat enjoying a Scotch and soda as they discussed the imminent war. About nine o'clock the Germans started coming over in waves. The air-raid sirens started their high pitched wail and shortly thereafter the twenty and forty millimeter cannons began their staccato yammering in response. Bombs began falling at the same time.

Some Club members adjourned to the basement for safety. Matt saw Churchill's group trying to convince him to go down, but he stubbornly shook his head. He raised his voice and they heard him say, "I refuse to hide from the swine. I will take my chances like most Londoners are doing." That effectively ended the discussion of that topic. All of his party remained at the table even though several flinched with each bomb that fell.

Owen gave Matt a running commentary of the areas where the bombs were targeted. Bombers were concentrating primarily on the areas near the docks along the Thames; its concentration of warehouses making it a target rich zone for the German pilots and their bombardiers.

There was a pause in the bombing just before ten o'clock.

"Well Matt, I am going to check on the Brewery before I turn in and you had better make your way to your quarters before the next wave starts up. You have an important appointment tomorrow morning. Call me when you know something so I will know what to say - or not to say to Joanna and Mary Margaret. Naturally I will wait until you talk to Joanna before I say anything. Until you do... I will remain quiet...as if I know nothing. I do not intend to let on until one of them tells me about it. If they thought I had known all along. Oh my sweet Lord, I would catch it."

Churchill was still in his conference when they left.

~ ~ ~ ~

The next morning, smoke rolled over the city and a few fires still raged near the docks. The sky was overcast so everything merged into a grey sameness. Matt wondered how many of the black Mariah hearses had made trips from early evening until the sky lightened this morning and how many more would be needed before dark fell tonight.

Matt headed the MG to highway A-40 toward Uxbridge in a northwesterly direction and turned onto M-40 at Gerard's Cross toward Beaconsfield. The day was still overcast but after Gerard's Cross, the air was no longer acrid with smoke which raised his outlook.

Or, he wondered, could finally taking this step be the reason I feel more at ease with myself? I have known for awhile the promise I gave to Joanna was one I was going to have to break eventually. I was rash to have made it so quickly, no matter how much I love her. I have been tying myself in knots over this. All I can hope now is that she will be able to forgive me. I just need to make it clear I am doing it for England and the people being slaughtered in their homes at night. Owen is right...sure I am also doing it for her, perhaps mostly for her, but I mustn't tell her that. Then if something should happen to me she won't feel guilty. God knows she'd grieve enough without that forever in her mind. That word of hers again. Forever.

He pulled his car up to the curb in the town of High Wycombe to ask directions to the Abbey. The girl in the ladies shop told him of the two turns which would take him to his destination and flirtingly told him she liked his car. Her eyelashes heavy with mascara fluttered as she said, "I take it you are an American. Your voice sounds the way they talk in the American movie pictures. The Abbey's not a girls' school any longer. The Government took it over for the military more than a year ago. The girls are all gone if that's what you are looking for. Pretty strict on the girls they were. 'Course I didn't go to school there, so I can't say for sure."

"No... Miss... Not looking for a girl. If I was I wouldn't go any further than this shop. You are a very pretty young lady. No, I know the Abbey has been taken over by the military. That is why I am going there. I have business with them and you have been very helpful. Thank you very much."

"Barbara Langdon. That's my name. And any time you are passing through stop in if you need more directions. I'm very good at giving them. You are a very nice young man and I will be happy to give you directions anytime. I really do like your little green car. Remember... Barbara Langdon."

As Matt walked out of the shop he was smiling wryly. He thought to himself, you know sometimes I really do miss "Matt the Ratt." Where ever he has gone I am certain moments like this must drive him crazy. He probably thinks this new Mathew Weldon is the crazy one. I hope he understands this appointment at the Abbey is more important than another notch on the bed post. The only bed post notches from now on will be Joanna and me. Doesn't keep me from noticing that Miss Langdon was a rather pretty girl, if a bit forward.

Joanna and he had driven through the town on their way up to Oxford several months earlier. He remembered her short history lecture on what she called Chipping Wycombe. That was the old name for the medium size town. The brick Guildhall on High Street had caught his attention. It was an eighteenth century brick building and a work of architectural beauty.

The town, she told him, was ancient dating from before the Roman occupation in the first century. It had long been a major market town due to its central location between London and Oxford. The "Wycombe" originated from being near the River Wye.

Joanna, his wonderful teacher about most things English, could hold him in rapt attention longer than any instructor he had ever encountered. Then there had never been an instructor who looked like her. When she talked it was as if he were in a mild state of hypnosis. Her green eyes held his and all he wanted to do was look at her and hear that wonderfully rich voice. She seemed the same when he talked. They were joined with each other in a way he could never have believed, each almost enslaved to the other.

He realized, I have nothing I can compare my feelings against. In the years at prep school and in college back in America there was no emotion like the one I feel for Joanna. None of my affairs in England in the short time before I met her was any different. The surprise is these feelings have all developed without our having sex. She has started hinting that sex between us might be okay now, but I am still not acting on her hints. Not yet. I am hesitating and that puzzles me. Where has that other guy gone off to, the one who fell into bed with every girl who was willing? The guy who looked on it as nothing more than a form of "Hello."

Can it be because the "Hello" was always so quickly followed by "Goodbye?" Always my fault but damn, I don't want to tell Joanna goodbye. I have broken some of my old "bad habits" but am I sure that one is broken? Could it happen with her if we had sex? Better not to rush it old boy. Not even as much as I want to be with her that way. But if we did that... might she become just another conquest? Would the magic and the mystery be gone? In a way, it is like breaking this promise to her. I didn't do it until I knew it was right. Follow that path and don't leave it until you are certain the love and fascination will live beyond having sex.

A few miles from town, he took the turn toward the Abbey. A mile down the road he came to a guardhouse manned by heavily armed soldiers. A steel lift-gate prevented further progress.

Two young soldiers came out of the small building, one walking to either side of his car. Matt could see they kept one hand on their weapons. He had no doubt they were loaded. Neither guard smiled.

The one on his side of the automobile spoke after looking it over. "Sir, what is your name and business here?"

"My name is Mathew Weldon. The Prime Minister told me to come here today and see Sir Hugh Dowding. I have an appointment made by the Prime Minister's Office."

The young soldier scowled at him before saying, "The Prime Minister you say? That's a thin story. You better turn around and head back. I really should arrest you now for simply being here, but I'll let you go. I had better not see you out here again."

He turned but before he could walk away, Matt warned him, "You had better look at these before you get into too much trouble. In this case, I am being generous. A Court-Martial wouldn't look very impressive on your record. The duty you have now is probably pretty good. Who knows where they might send you if this gets reported, which I assure you it would."

Matt handed the young man Churchill's signed calling card and hand written note. He watched as the guard turned pale, then politely asked "would the gentleman please wait" while he made a telephone call from inside the small brick guardhouse. Matt saw him talking for only minutes before he returned.

"I am so sorry for the misunderstanding, Sir. We occasionally get crazies out this way. Lads who have been turned down for service who decide they'll just go to the top and get a different answer. Thought you were one of those.

"Another mile along you will come to second security check-point. Be assured you won't have this problem there. You are on their list to be admitted to the Abbey. They will help you park your automobile. You will be provided with escort to Sir Hugh's office. They are expecting you. Hope there is no hard feelings about our misunderstanding."

"No. None at all," Matt replied. "I really didn't consider what your job was all about. I should have explained why I was here more fully. Thank you for your help."

The gate lifted and Matt drove past it to the next security gate which was larger and more heavily guarded than the first. Beyond it he could see the magnificent structure of High Wycombe Abbey.

A three story late Gothic stone structure, it had many arched, cathedral-like windows. The building sat in an area of parks and manicured gardens; a large lake was visible in back of the main building. He observed many other temporary structures had been built in wooded areas around the Abbey. They would be difficult to see from the air. From up there, only the Abbey would be visible and it would appear to be nothing more than a late seventeen hundreds vintage country estate. A target hardly worth noting let alone bombing. It was, however, a jewel of the romantic Gothic style. Matt wondered if Joanna had ever seen it. The RAF had chosen a location off the beaten path which the Germans probably believed was simply an upscale girls' school.

He was stopped at the second check-point with a far more cordial reception. Only one guard walked out to his MG and his weapon was slung over his shoulder. He smiled when he checked Matt's I.D. and had another guard point out where he could park his small green convertible. Sitting among the olive drab command cars and a few large trucks it was a greyhound amid mastiffs. The guard then pointed toward the main entrance atop a flight of stone steps and told Matt to meet him there.

His guide walked him to an office on the third floor with a sign on the door which stated "C in C Fighter Command." Matt observed several individuals dressed in American uniforms in the building before arriving on the third floor. He found the sight of American Officers surprising because his country was still claiming official neutrality.

The young woman at the desk in the outer office of Sir Hugh Dowding was wearing a Women's Army Air Force uniform. She dismissed Matt's escort telling him she would call when he was needed to escort his charge back to his car after his meeting. Matt had chatted with the young WAAF for twenty minutes when several senior grade officers walked out of the inner office and Matt was shown in.

The man who rose from behind the large desk was tall and slim with a neat military moustache. Matt knew from newspaper articles the man was fifty-seven years old and had intended to retire before the War started. He was asked to stay on and command England's fighter wings.

His face carried what would be thought by anyone who didn't know him as a very severe expression. Anyone, that is, who did not know the love he had for the pilots he commanded, the articles said that he called them his "chicks" and he did everything he could to give them an edge when they flew against the Germans.

He shook his visitor's hand while Matt introduced himself, and then followed with, "Sir Hugh, I had the good fortune to be introduced to the Prime Minister last evening and I expressed a desire to fly for the RAF. I am a certified pilot, have been since I was sixteen years old. I have my license and papers here."

He handed them to the man now seated behind his desk, who looked them over.

"Well yes, young man. I see you are *an* American. Really knew that already by listening to your voice. But you are a Yank. You fellows are not in this war. At least not yet. A few of you are over here flying on our side, so it is not unheard of but...."

"Sir Hugh, I have been over here a good while now. Yes sir, I am an American but I have seen what is happening to London. To the people who are being bombed and killed. How can a pilot stand by and let that happen? I can't any longer. The aircraft I flew back home was hot and maneuverable. She wasn't a Spitfire, but close."

"My boy, I have no doubt you are a good pilot, but flying for pleasure and combat flying are two different things entirely. Flying a Spitfire in combat requires a different kind of training. We can't just throw someone in a Spit and send them up. They would not come back and frankly we can afford to lose pilots, but not Spits. Every lad in England wants to fly a Spitfire. Unfortunately what we are short of is the fighter planes. If we put you in line even as qualified as I see you are, it would be a year or more before we could put you in an aero plane.

"Ah, wait just a moment. Your papers say you are qualified in multi-engine aircraft. Is that true?"

Matt wondered what difference that made but answered, "Yes Sir Hugh. My father heads a large bank in New York City so I qualified to fly the Ford Tri-motor. Spent a good number of hours flying the Banks.' Why do you ask Sir?"

"Because my boy, we need fellows who can fly large aircraft. In fact bombers. Our fighters will hold the Germans at bay over here but we must, and have already, begun to punish the Jerrys on their turf. Not as glamorous a job, I grant you, but probably more important in the long view. Please don't tell any of my 'chicks' I said that, but it is true. Are you interested in doing that job-of-work for us?"

So here is a conundrum, Matt thought. You want to fly fighters but the man in charge says that can't happen for a year or more. Flying bombers is a different situation. Sounds like you could start on that right away. Hell, getting in the war is more useful than sitting on your ass.

"Yes, Sir Hugh. The point is to make a difference. To do whatever I can to shorten the war. To try and help end it. What should I do from here?"

"Lad, if you will wait in the outer office a few minutes, I am going to pass you on to Air Marshall Peirse who is in charge of Bomber Command. He is just down the hall. The fellow is a bit severe so don't be put off by that. And remember what I am not *officially* telling you. He needs bomber pilots badly!

"I also want to be honest with you about something else. They are taking heavy losses heavier than is fighter command. Don't think this will be a lark by any means! Think that over while you wait."

Matt sat with the young WAAF for another forty five minutes while waiting to see the Air Marshall. He remembered the American Officers he had seen.

"Excuse me Miss. I noticed several American officers in the hallways. Are they assigned here?"

"I am sorry. I don't know about any of that. Lots of people come and go but I don't remember any American Military. I do see lots of Commonwealth Military. Some of them might have similar uniforms."

So, Matt decided, she certainly answered that question by denying they are American. That means we are working with the British already, but in a very hush-hush way. It's happening, but it's not happening.

A few minutes later, a young RAF Flight Lieutenant walked in and asked if he was Mathew Weldon. When assured he was, the young officer asked Matt to follow him to see the Air Marshall.

This time there was no waiting in an outer office. He was shown directly into an office which was nearly identical to that occupied by Sir Hugh. The only visible difference was the pictures on the wall. Sir Hugh's had featured fighter aircraft and the present office had photographs of large, multi-engine bombers prominently featured.

The man behind the desk did not rise or offer his hand. His visage was of a man who had just eaten something not agreeable to his digestion.

"Sir Hugh called me. Your papers." He said curtly. There was a long pause which, when Matt did not hand them over, was finally followed by, "Let me see your papers. Please."

After a pause, he handed the man his pilot's certification and his qualification listing multi-engine aircraft and the hours he had flown them.

"Humm...not bad. You have more multi-engine hours than boys flying bombing missions for me now. If you want to fly for us I can use you. You will need to pass our physical for the RAF, which is no piece of cake I assure you, but you look in good shape. Pass that and it's a bit of basic training, then we'll send you to a short Officer Training School (OTS) followed by a school on the bomber you'll be flying. I'll be honest. We need you, so we will push to get you in the air as quickly as we can that only because you already know multi-engine aero planes. Rest assured, we won't send you on a mission until you are ready. Also rest assured, we are thinking about not wanting to lose an aircraft because the pilot wasn't competent. The cruel truth is the bomber itself is more valuable than you are." He was not smiling when he made the last pronouncement.

Matt was smiling when he said, "Well, with that kind of encouragement how could a chap ever fail to tell you what an honor it will be to have you as commanding officer?"

The Air Marshall actually cracked a tired smile, rose from his desk, walked around it and shook Matt's hand. "Sorry to be so gruff, lad. I've simply seen too many good lads lost already to tell anyone this is an easy job. And it's true the aircraft itself counts most. We can't build them fast enough. I'm already in the 'stew' for complaining about our *personnel* losses. Some believe *only* losses of aircraft count."

He walked back around his desk and sat, reached into a drawer, pulled out a sheet of paper and wrote a short note which he signed with a flourish. He handed it across to Matt along with his license and qualification papers.

"So lad, take this note to any RAF recruiting location in London. They will get you processed and moving toward a pair of RAF Wings. Good luck to you my boy. I admire your spirit. You are the first candidate sent directly to us by the Prime Minister you know. If you will wait outside we will get an escort to return you to your automobile."

As he drove away Matt's mood was as grey as the sky's. He had finally made the commitment he could no longer avoid.

Yet, he wondered, how will I tell Joanna that I have broken the promise I made and how will she react? Can I use fate, Kismet as she always calls it, to explain the reason I am doing this?

Was it not fate which sent me down a half blocked street where I saw dead adults and children, fatalities of a German bombing, being carried out of the ruins? I hope I do not lose her because of what I am doing. Yet this has now become far bigger than the two of us. Years down the road I may have to ask myself how I lost the woman I loved so deeply and have only one answer, the War and a promise I broke because of it....

~ ~ ~ ~

By Thursday afternoon September 19, 1940 Matt was officially a member of the Royal Air Force. He had spent two days being examined by all manner of doctors, having needles stuck in his arms immunizing him against God alone knew how many diseases. His vision was checked and found to be twenty-twenty. His hearing was checked. His reflexes were examined and pronounced "excellent." He was weighed, measured, probed and poked. Stacks of forms were filled out which he carried from point to point through-out the process.

Matt was listed as an Officer Trainee and was issued uniforms befitting that status. Everything in his kit as issued was new, stiff and scratchy. When he tried them on, the fit of most items was truly dreadful.

He was told to appear at the building on the morning of Wednesday week in uniform for his swearing in ceremony. After that he was officially in the RAF even though it would be three weeks before he would report for basic training.

This gave him time to wrap up school and get his uniforms altered for a decent fit. In addition, he intended to order a first rate uniform from a Bond Street tailor plus several good cotton uniform shirts. A pair of decent shoes was also on his list along with getting a shoemaker to work on his issue shoes. They badly needed to be stretched, as they were over half a size smaller than they were supposed to be.

The German bombing continued night after night starting at dusk and continuing until dawn. Londoners by the thousands crowded into the underground stations and slept there as best they could. The stations were plastered with patriotic posters the most prolific of which were on a red background and stated simply 'Keep Calm - Carry On' in black ink.

The message was both simple and profound. It urged the people of London to carry on with their lives as they had done when there was no War. It was effective. The heavier the bombing became, the more determined Londoners became not to allow Germany to break their spirit. They mourned those who died but always, 'Carried On.'

Matt found Joanna in the women's lounge at King's College after lunch that afternoon. He waited outside until she saw him and walked out of the room to where he stood. He could sense when she looked in his eyes she knew something was wrong. The smile left her face as she asked, "What's troubling you, Mathew? You look so serious. I have only seen this look on your face once. The day you thought you were losing me. That I loved someone else. Before I told you the one I loved was you. Has something happened? Are you going back to America?"

"No Joanna. Nothing such as that, but we do need to talk. I assure you I am not going back and, if it is possible, I love you more with every passing day. I intend us to have that 'forever' you talk about. I can imagine nothing more wonderful than loving you forever."

She smiled, looked around to be sure no one was nearby, and kissed him.

"Come over to the house tonight. Before the Germans start up. You had better be there by seven in the event they decide to start early tonight." He recognized the naughty look she gave him before she said, "And you can stay over if you would feel safer doing that." He felt her hand lightly touching his upper leg.

He spoke in a near whisper when he said, "You little minx. Are you trying to seduce me?"

"Mathew, you *know* I am. We love each other. I know you *want* me. I know you respect me so being together *that* way is not a problem."

"Want you? Yes I want you. Joanna this is not the place to talk about that. The effect you have on me, when we discuss this, is far too obvious to anyone standing near. Clear to them and embarrassing to me. So... we can talk about it tonight. Ok?"

While Matt walked away from Joanna, he could not help but be amazed. How can she read me so easily? The minute she looked into my eyes she could tell something was wrong. She missed what it was, thank goodness, but she knew something was wrong. Now I have to still tell her what it is. Perhaps I should take her to bed first. No. That is not fair. Not fair to her. Not "cricket" at all old chap.

Mrs. Townsend opened the door at #37 Eaton Square on his second rap of the aged brass lion's head knocker.

"Well, good evening Mister Mathew. Come in, Miss Joanna will be down very shortly. Haiku is waiting for you in the sitting room. I have coffee ready if you would fancy a cup while you wait. With a scone if you would like."

"Thank you Mrs. Townsend. I would love a cup of coffee and I certainly will never refuse one of your scones. They are quite simply the best. I look forward to coming over. Your coffee and scones are keeping me going."

Matt saw her smile broadly as she headed for the kitchen. A moment later, Joanna's black and white cat was in his lap purring while looking up at him.

"And good evening to you also Haiku. I am glad to see you. I wore tan trousers this evening in your honor. I know you prefer it when I wear a Tux because your white fur shows up so well on black, but this way you can just cover these to your heart's delight. Have you been taking good care of Joanna?"

Haiku clearly understood his question and answered with an eloquent yet barely audible, "Eyooow."

He was certain the cat had said, "Yes I am. I sleep near her at night to protect her from the bombs. The question is... are you taking good care of her?"

The cat's green eyes, so similar in color to Joanna's, looked into his waiting for an answer.

"I am trying to. But I can't tell her that. She might not see it that way. You know how much I love her. I often think you understand her better than I do. I was in love with her long before she felt it was safe to love me. But still...you have known her longer."

121

He was so focused on Haiku that he jumped when he heard Joanna ask from the doorway. "Mathew I know that she sometimes talks to me. I don't know how she does that, but did she say something to you? You were talking to her as if she did."

"Probably my imagination. I'm a little tired. Been busy the last few days. But yes, I believe I heard her ask if I was taking care of you. She informed me she was doing her part."

Joanna crossed the room and sat at his feet in front of the chair looking up at him quietly for several long minutes. Then she took his hand and said, "So it really is you, Mathew. I thought it was, almost from the beginning, but now I know. It has been so very long."

Matt was confused. What she was *saying* confused him. She was so beautiful. She moved toward him and laid her cheek on his upper leg while continuing to gaze at his face with her hypnotic green eyes.

"I don't understand, Love. What do you mean about it being me and it has been so long?"

"Mathew, I have loved you almost since we met. You weren't the only one who fell hard and fast, but I fought it because of your reputation. I was determined not to be just another girl to you. But you changed and I started to open myself to love you. Now I love you totally. It is as if we are complete together. Joined spirits. Two people who were fated to find each other. As if our lives were destined by Kismet to become one. There is more that I will tell you when I am carrying our first child. Your *first* son."

"So our first will be a son, will it? My father will be pleased. There has always been a male heir to continue the Bank. Are you really so certain it will be a boy?"

"Mathew, I *know* it. I knew I would have our son almost the moment I saw you. It frightened me. I fought against it, but I knew it that first night."

"Okay Joanna, I will tell you what I know. He will be a good-looking boy. A handsome child, because his mother is the most beautiful woman I have ever seen and I love her more than life itself. If I believed in magic, I would think we were enchanted."

She rose and moved the cat from his lap to the floor beside the chair. Joanna then sat in his lap and kissed him. When she pulled away she told him, "Oh yes my love. We both are, but it is not the sort of spell you might mean. It is far older than we are. A spell woven long ago out of love. We were meant to be together. We always will be. Forever."

Matt knew he had never seen her look at him the way she was now. It was a far-away look. He knew she was seeing him, but seeing something else at the same time. It was a look as if she were present and, at the same time, very far away. Almost in another time and place.

I must be tired from all the running around in the last few days, he thought. My eyes must really be tired. Everything is a bit out of focus. Joanna, the room and everything in it. Like a soft fog had settled over everything. Well tired or not, I have to tell...

"Here is your coffee and scone, Mr. Mathew." The sound of Mrs. Townsend's voice caused Matt to turn his head to where she stood in the doorway with a surprised look on her face. Matt smiled at her realizing she had never seen them in a situation this intimate.

She stood sharply defined. There was no fog and when he looked around the room and back at Joanna everything was normal. He must have imagined the fogginess and far-away look on her face. Well no surprise. It has been a hard two days and I have to do something I dread. Better to get it over with. The longer I wait, the more difficult it will be.

Mrs. Townsend delivered the tray with scones and coffee and left the room, heading back down the hall humming as she left. Matt thought the tune sounded a bit like the wedding march. Well, Mrs. Townsend, he thought, it is what I intend to do. It will have to be on hold for a while now. At least until after I have finished flying.

He took a bite of scone and put it on the dessert plate next to his coffee cup on the small table beside the chair. "Joanna, the thing that you noticed this afternoon...well, there is something I must tell you. Please let me tell you all of it before you say anything. Will you do that?"

He could see a look of sadness dawning in her green eyes as she nodded "Yes." He felt she already knew what he was going to say.

"I was driving Monday afternoon and was delayed in a street half blocked by debris from the bombing on Sunday night. The rest of the street was blocked by rescue vans and trucks. The trucks were just leaving when I arrived but the vans remained. Men in groups of two were carrying stretchers, covered by a black rubber sheet. These covered the dead dug out from the ruined blocks of flattened buildings. Many of the dead were children. Joanna, when I saw them, I knew I had to break the promise I made to you the day we both expressed our love to each other. The night we knew England was going to war. I thought on that night it was a promise I could keep. I have fought very hard to keep it because I love you so very much. After what I saw Monday, I know I can't. Too many are dying and I am a pilot. This is bigger than just the two of us now. The world has caught fire and it's going to take everyone's best effort to put it out. If we don't do that there will be no room for love anyway."

With his last words, tears began to line her cheeks.

"I am so sorry my darling. The only way around it was for us to go to America together. To run away from it. I thought about that but I didn't believe you would go. Was I wrong Joanna? Would you have gone to America with me?"

Her cheek was now against his chest but her, "No" came without hesitation. Then she pulled away and looked at him through tear blurred eyes. "Mathew, it simply isn't your fight. You're a 'Yank', an American. These are my people. I couldn't leave but you can. That is what I thought you were going to tell me this afternoon. I had rather lose you that way than see you dead. If you die we are truly lost to each other. Alive we still have a chance. If you go home we still have a 'later.'"

He wiped her tears away with his fingers and smiled what he knew must be a sad excuse for a smile. "Sorry darling...can't. I'm in it too far now. The stop I had to make on that ruined street showed me we are all each other's 'people.' The strange thing is; I don't know the street's name. All the signs were gone. Blown away by the bombing last night.

"I love you far beyond anything I used to believe possible. That won't ever change. It will be there long past any idea I have of 'forever.' More than many others, I have a duty to fulfill. Maybe it is a matter of past sins I am trying to expiate or simply to prove to myself that I am worth your loving me. Whatever the explanation, it must be done.

"I am in the RAF as of today. I have three weeks before I leave. Basic training followed by Officer Training School, then Flight Training. The irony of it is they couldn't have me in a Spitfire in under a year. No... I am going to be a bomber pilot and do to the Germans the very thing which drove me to join the RAF in the first place.. I often think this 'Kismet' thing of yours excels in irony."

"Oh Mathew, please don't say that. I asked for the promise because I love you so much. I know we are meant to be together. I just know it. I don't know what I would do if something happened to you. Our losses of pilots are high. The newspapers are full of statistics and they are dreadful. I don't know how those men keep going up knowing about losses like that."

Matt saw the tears begin again. "Joanna you said we would have a boy. You sounded very sure about that. Are you?"

She smiled though the tears were still there. "Oh yes Mathew. Our child will be a boy."

"Very well. And you know I am determined not to make love with you until we are married don't you? I want it to be a real pledge of our love when it happens. I want our first time to be in the 'old fashioned' way. After the wedding."

"Yes Mathew. And you know I am will...no, more than willing...not to wait, but I understand that is what you want and I am trying to keep my hormones at bay."

"Think about it Joanna. If we make love only after we are married and we are married only after I am no longer flying, then for you to have our son, we will both live through the war."

"Matt your logic makes sense. Yet if I was certain about everything, why did I ask for the promise? I don't see everything and I sure don't know everything that is going to happen. I often wonder if you think I believe I am a minor sorceress or something like that or simply daft and you love me anyway. I am neither. I just have feelings about things. Science can't explain how it happens but they admit it does. Let me ask you a question. A very simple question. Do you love me Mathew?"

"Yes Joanna. I love you."

"How do you know Mathew?"

He was stunned by her simple question. How *did* he know? Then he understood why she asked her question. He just knew. That was all there was to it. And if he could *accept* that knowing he loved her was all the proof he needed about loving her, why should he doubt that her knowing other things was proof enough. And damn it, she was very often right. She knew the weather before it came; often days in advance. It was true she oft-times knew what he was thinking as quickly as the thoughts came to him. "The same way you know things Joanna. I just know."

She pressed her body very tightly to his and kissed him; a lingering kiss full of desire and more than a little sadness. She was no longer crying and when she pulled her lips away she studied his face for a long, quiet time and, for his part, he was completely lost in her wonderful eyes.

"I don't entirely forgive you Mathew. It was a promise and you broke it. I hope one or both of us does not have a price to pay for that. I know you felt a heavy weight on you to do what you did. So be it. We will just have to walk the road that is before us now. The price I have to pay is to die a little bit every time you fly. That is what love costs a woman during a war. You had damn well better let me know when you are going up and that you have returned safely. Every time. Do you *hear* me?"

"Joanna, I am sorry. I know I had to do what I did but I never thought about the full effect on you. I am truly sorry. I will always let you know. It will be a while before I am really flying, but I will talk to you regularly during training and see you often. As often as they will allow."

"Mathew, don't you dare get yourself killed. I waited too long for you to be able to bear losing you after such a short time. I am planning on our being together for a very long time. We are supposed to grow old together."

"That's the same future I have in mind for us, my love."

They had a light dinner together. Later, Joanna turned on the radio and they danced to several slow songs. Joanna looked into his eyes as they danced.

It took Matt back to the rainy night they had attended the Symphony and danced at Café de Paris. He had held her in his arms while they had danced lost in each other's eyes.

It's strange, Matt thought, this is very much what making love to Joanna will be like. Some girls close their eyes while making love and a few look right at you. I am sure Joanna will look me in the eyes the entire time. It will be a new experience in one way. I have had sex lots of times, but with her I will be making love. It was hard for him to remember who that 'callow boy' who sailed over on the Queen Mary had even been. The one who doubted love really existed.

Despite her invitation to spend the night, Matt left at ten and drove slowly back to his "digs," the slits in his black-out head-light covers barely indicating the way. Huge fires from the night's bombing furnished a far more unwelcome form of illumination. Firemen were busy on more blocks of destroyed buildings. The warning sirens wailed mournfully until five in the morning. London had spent another night in the depths of hell. Yet when the sun came up Saturday morning, September 21, 1940, the survivors 'Carried on.'

Chapter 10

LETTERS 1940

Dear Dad,   Sept 22, 1940

The weather in London is unsettled with a lot of
rain. Never before would I have viewed weather like
this as a blessing but it really is because it gives
Jerry difficulty in accurately placing his bombs. I
am sure the American broadcast reporters have been
letting the folks back home know the bomber attacks
have shifted away from the RAF fighter bases and the
aircraft production facilities to the major cities
such as London, Birmingham, Bristol, Plymouth and all
the port cities.

I know this is a serious mistake on the part of the
Germans. I don't know if Göring or Hitler made the
decision but it was a deeply flawed one. If they
think they can break the will of the British people
with this tactic they are seriously deluded. The
Spits and Hurricanes are beginning to rip the German
bomber formations to shreds as they no longer have to
worry about their own bases or a flow of replacement
aircraft.   Before this, the RAF had been running
out of aircraft with which to offset the ones they
were losing. The Brits never experienced a shortage
of pilots. As a fellow in the know told me just the
other day "Every mother's son in England wants to be
a fighter pilot."

He's right about that too. It's the glamorous job to
have these days. He also told me they are short of
pilots who can fly multi-engine bombers. Thanks to
the Bank's good old Ford tri-motor, I guess that
describes me to a 'T.'

Yes Dad, I have joined the RAF.

For the first time in my life I have been faced with something that is bigger than just my selfish desires. It seems apparent now that you have to stand for something or avert your face and hide. These people over here are not in a hiding mood and I am not either. I know I am American and not a Brit but I have begun to wonder how long our country can duck out on this War. There is already a full group of Americans over here called the Eagle Squadron and they fly Spits for the RAF. Some have already died and I'll bet you are not seeing that in the papers back home.

There is something else that I have not been including in my reports about morale over here. It certainly relates to my morale.

I have met a young lady, or to be more accurate, "THE young lady." Her name is Joanna Barton. And what a young lady. With a capitol "L". We were both (well I was, past tense now) going to King's College. She is from a very old family with deep English roots. I'll tell you about the roots at a later time. Let me simply say that I love her more than I knew was possible and when all this is over I intend to marry her, assuming she will still have me and I believe she will.

My final report to you on the question you had is: Yes the Brits can hold out. I am certain of it. I am also certain that America will be in it before too long. Why? Because, as a country, we always put things off as long as we can but in the end we always do what is right and fighting this evil is right.

I seem to remember several of your business associates are Jewish. Ask them what is happening to people of their religion in Germany and then decide what needs doing.

Your son,

Matt

Dear Son,   Wednesday, Oct. 30, 1940

I received your letter today. I must tell you it was a shock to me. When I sent you over to report on certain private matters, I never intended you to become so deeply involved with the matters in question. I understand your interest in the young lady but to join the Royal Air Force? By heavens Matt, was there no other way to impress her?

Yes she must really be something. I can't imagine you joining our Army Air Corps for any of the young ladies you knew over here. My biggest worry until now was that you might get in the way of a German bomb falling out of the sky and I had been considering telling you to get back over here where it is safe.

I must assume (or at least hope) that you gave this a good bit of thought before you did it. I also ask if there is a way to get out of it at this rather late date.

I know you certainly must be a good pilot or your antics would have probably killed you before you even went over there, but combat flying is another thing entirely. The papers over here are full of what is happening in the skies over England and the awful loss of pilots and planes on both sides.

On the original reason for your trip: the Bank has decided to keep its investments in England and we will undoubtedly be extending the additional Line of Credit which has been requested by the English Government to purchase American-made armaments.

Washington is encouraging this of ENB and other major banks

If you must pursue the course of action you seem set on, then do your best but try not to make any missteps. In short, I will give you the advice my father gave me before I left for the Great War, "Now you watch your ass. You hear me boy?"

Your Father,

Trey

Chapter 11

FIRST RAF NIGHT MISSION

On that day in late March of 1941, Matt was glad to know that all the training was finally going to pay off. He and his crew had been together now for three long months. All of them had spent twelve or more hours every day getting used to bomber aircraft and each other. There had been constant practice flights over England, Scotland and across to Ireland and back. He had made takeoffs and landings almost without number. Instructors' only words seemed to be, "Let's do it again 'ay what,'" and "I think you need a bit more practice, Yank." So Matt had repeated them again and again.

They carried out seemingly endless navigation, gunnery and practice runs with dummy bombs to the point they all impatiently looked forward to the real thing: flying a mission with real bombs in the bomb bay over enemy territory instead of the British Isles.

The few times Matt found to give it serious consideration, he thought how strange this is. I am looking forward to being shot at, possibly killed and dropping bombs which *will* kill other people rather than continuing all this relatively safe practice flying! But *only* relatively safe because I know that more than ten percent of all aircrews are killed before their first combat mission; killed in seemingly endless practice flights.

He and his second pilot "Mutt" Stanford, a Scott with a heavy burr accent, had made a cardboard dummy of the instrument panel with blank circles where each control dial was. They made a game of quizzing each other hour after hour by calling out an instrument's name and the other had to quickly point to the correct one. They kept score and by the last time they played Matt won by just two correct answers out of thousands of right ones by each of them. It increased their reflexes and ability to make fast decisions on the aircraft's condition. Matt enjoyed working with Mutt and knew if he should be badly wounded or killed, the crew and aircraft would be in very competent hands.

Their graduation from the Training Squadron had, at long last, brought assignment to an active duty squadron. They were attached to Number Seven Squadron at Upper Hayford, an old highly respected unit formed in September of 1914 which flew in the First War and had never "stood down" in the intervening years.

The bomber assigned to them was a large hulking aircraft whose design name was Short Sterling. Theirs had recently left the production line in Belfast as one of England's first four engine heavy bombers designed to fly to Germany to deliver a large bomb load and return.

Because England had no fighter aircraft which could go round trip with the "Short," their missions would of necessity be flown without escort fighter protection. Each plane could only depend on itself and the other bombers in its formation for defense.

The RAF had previously tried daylight bombing and suffered excessively high losses of planes and crews. At least by now they had given up on that and exclusively switched to night missions. Losses of aircraft had subsequently dropped below twenty percent. As the sorties Matt and his crew would be assigned were to be flown at night their 'Short' was painted in dark grays and black only.

Matt's aircraft was known as "E for Edward." The RAF coded each aircraft of a squadron with a different letter of the alphabet such as C for Charley and Z for Zebra.

Matt found while flying her that though she appeared clumsy with her flat-sided fuselage and raised bubble canopy, she was a sturdy bird which could take a lot of damage and still get her crew back home. She also had oversized control surfaces which made her very responsive in turns or when changes in altitude or attitude were needed. Matt had found she could nearly stay inside the turn radius of a Hurricane fighter. Her ability to do wing-overs was a pleasant surprise to him. She flew much better than he had expected when he first saw her....

On the other side of the coin she was slower than Matt would have preferred and did not perform well at high altitude. Her defensive armament was adequate only in the number of guns she carried. The "Short" had a top turret with twin guns and a rear turret with four. Additionally the mid-body had one gun on each side and there were two in the nose. But, and he knew it was a big but, the guns only fired 303 caliber rounds which were rifle cartridge caliber. This left the Short Sterling under-gunned against the twenty millimeter cannons of the German Messerschmitt fighters. She also carried no belly turret which left her gut open to attack.

The newly appointed C in C of Bomber Command, Sir Arthur Harris, had finally faced up to the undeniable fact that the RAF could not continue a high loss rate. What he wanted was round the clock bombing to break the German spirit, but he had been forced to give up on the idea before the spirit and ability of RAF Bomber Command was broken instead.

Matt heard through the grapevine, unofficial source of all things regarding highly confidential military information, confirmation an Op was definitely on their plate for tonight. The origin of this kind of high priority information was never known but most of the time it was bang-on reliable. The reason, of course, was simply the difficulty of preventing someone overhearing one side of a telephone call or seeing a carelessly placed Operations order. Matt had by now learned that when it came to receiving secret or near secret information first, enlisted men way out-ranked officers.

He dashed off a quick note to Joanna saying he hoped to see her mid-week, next week. Matt was convinced with her ability to have a near psychic understanding of the way his mind worked, she would know he was flying and it would pass the censors without being blacked out....

He was certain the English fighter jockeys would be glad to see the sun set on this day. Messerschmitt fighter planes and Stuka dive bombers had arrived in the early morning hours before the whistles all over England had blown signaling the workers it was shift change in the defense factories. The attacking aircraft each carried a black swastika on their tail and were followed by the German Henkel 111 and Junkers 88 bombers with still more Messerschmitts flying cover above them. Arriving in wave after wave until twilight, they would, as usual, continue until well after midnight. All day English Spitfires and Hurricanes rose to meet them; landed, refueled, rearmed and rose to fight again. As a result, many of the bombers went down aflame, parachutes blossoming everywhere in the daytime English skies. Londoners would sleep poorly tonight due to continued bombing, which was what Hitler intended.

As he watched the steel ballet performance in the blue but cloud-besotted sky, he understood that it was a dance of death. They would circle and dive, rise upward and swoop down. Curving elegantly up toward the sun then turning downward toward the earth they would pull up at the last moment to prevent crashing by turning sharply left or right. After a seeming eternity in this pas de deux, one or the other would prove a more skilled pilot or perhaps only luckier and a young British or German pilot would be shot down. All that remained of the dance would be tangled crisscrossing lines of exhaust fading slowly from the sky.

Matt had always believed himself a very good pilot but seeing this deadly dance, he was no longer certain he was good enough. He knew from reports that some German pilots had been flying for "The

133

Fatherland" since the Spanish Civil War, five years ago now. As a fighter pilot there were only two options, you got *good* or you got *dead*. It was a crash course in survival and those who failed it died.

In the afternoon he tried to get some sleep in the officer's Quonset hut but he was so nervous it was impossible. He knew the tension of flying for the first time into enemy territory had him too revved up to really sleep. A few bunks away Mutt was snoring away at a noise level a Merlin engine on a Spitfire would envy.

He remembered the day not long ago when he was assigned to Seven Squadron. He and his crew were told by the squadron commanding officer to go to their quarters and write wills because their life expectancy was a mere six missions, anything beyond that was a gift. Matt had left everything he personally owned to Joanna including his two automobiles. A major in the squadron was a barrister from London and he assured Matt it was completely legal even though the two were not married. It brought to his mind the letter Larry Trusdale had written him before his death in a Spitfire months ago. Had he really anticipated his death or was it just one of those things one did, never really believing it would happen?

That day he had taken the time to write several letters of his own on the blue RAF stationary using an old typewriter with yet another tired ribbon like the one Trusdale had used. He didn't know whether to think it ironic or somehow appropriate.

He wrote letters to his father at the Bank's address, Fizz and Kong which he sent care of Yale in New Haven and finally one to Joanna. That was, by far, the hardest one. He tried his best to say how much he loved her and that she was the *first* love of his life. The only woman he had ever truly loved. He told her how sorry he was their time had been so short and that he would have gladly spent a long lifetime with her. How much it meant to him hearing her say in the barley field that she loved him. That whole day at Barton Hall would be the thing he hoped to carry with him into eternity. He told her she must go on with her life and not be too sad because each time she walked through the barley he would be there speaking to her through the West Wind. That each time the wind kissed her cheek it would be him and when it touched her lips it would be him. That he would still be with her, as she had wished it, <u>forever</u>. It was the best he could do but he knew nothing would be good enough to express how much he loved her.

He left the letters with the Squadron's Exec with instructions on what to do with them. "Just in case, you understand." The Executive Officer opened his bottom drawer and laid Matt's letters on top of a pile of similar letters and replied, "Oh yes lad, I understand. Just in case."

~ ~ ~ ~

He knew by late afternoon the ground crews would be finishing their checks on "E for Edward." Fuel crews would have filled her tanks with the full load of 2,143 gallons she needed for a round trip to Germany. The armourers would fuse the bombs, load them into the bomb bays and check the machine guns. Their check list ran to hundreds of items, each of which had to be checked off and initialed prior to takeoff.

The crews meanwhile, had an early evening meal which would be their last before the breakfast they would eat on their return the next morning. If they returned.

Then the call went out to the crews to ready for the flight. The crews' first stop in their preparations was to go to the large concrete walled Ready Room where a huge wall map detailed the night's operation. All details were drawn on it showing the route to Germany and back to England. Other details about the mission for them such as: how the flight was going to assemble in the air before it left English airspace, radio frequencies to use, detailed information about flak battery concentrations and expected opposition fighter aircraft were printed on very flimsy paper which would burn with the touch of a flame.

Matt's crew sat together as did the other crews. If the target was considered easy the crews were largely silent. If it was a difficult one the moans and curses were loud, long and very vocal. Tonight they were just that. Berlin. The "Big City." The worst mission one could draw.

After the briefing ended the men loaded into crew vehicles which carried them to various locations on the base to get parachutes, heavy sheepskin coats and pants, heavy woolen sweaters, long woolen underwear and sheepskin lined boots for high altitude flying, plus oxygen masks and tubing, wool-lined caps and flight goggles plus silk escape maps, pistols, and emergency food supplies in case they had to bail out.

Once they were wearing all of this, the weight made moving around not only difficult, but almost comical. Matt could see that all of them were sweating but knew once they reached altitude it would be different. Even with all these layers of heavy clothing each of them would be cold. At altitude it was so cold that to remove your gloves for more than a very few minutes could lead to the loss of fingers or hands and losing oxygen could lead to asphyxia even more quickly. During the run in to the target they would no longer be cold. In fact they would be sweating from fear.

When they reached "E for Edward," Matt got his six crewmembers together in a circle like he had always done with the team before a Yale football game. He looked each man in the eyes and after pausing a moment he told them... "Okay men, this is what we have trained so long to do. Each of us knows his job to the point we could do it in our sleep and I know damn well we can do them perfectly awake. You each have my complete confidence and I hope I have yours. "E for Edward" is a good Bird. She will take us there and she will get us back. Yes, I know Edward is a guy's name but to me aircraft are always she's. Always have been, always will be. In my mind she is " Edwina.

Just go ahead and know that we will be fired at so don't worry about it. God! If we don't get shot at I have probably taken a wrong turn and we could be on our way to Miami Beach."

At this the whole crew exploded in relieved laughter and Matt felt the break in the oppressive tension he was sure each one of them had been feeling until that moment.

When the laughter died down Gordon McGregor, his Scottish born Navigator and Gee Set direction finder operator spoke up with his heavy Scottish burr, "Excuse me Number One, but where this Miami Beach place is you might be taking us to?"

After the laughter once again died, Matt explained that it was a resort town in Florida, which elicited a further question from McGregor about the location of this Florida place.

Matt turned to McGregor and said, "Mac, it is a good thing you finally came down from the Highlands. Florida is in the States - You know - Where I'm from. Remember?"

"Okay fellows, if Mac has no more geography questions you may want to go ahead and have a cigarette. If you do, light 'em up now, 'cause it will be a while before your next one and it's a good idea to take a last leak before we get on board. Empty those kidneys while you can. I know I am going to. Nothing worse than soggy sheepskin."

All of them lit the American-made Lucky Strike cigarettes which were being sent to England in cases by uncountable thousands in the parade of liberty ships convoying across the Atlantic while always at risk of being sunk by German U-Boats.

Matt's crew smoked nervously while talking about anything which came to mind. Women, family, weather. The topics didn't matter. It was their way to get past this period of inactivity and, yes, the constant specter of fear.

Even Matt, who really didn't like tobacco lit up and took the occasional "drag" on it. He and "Mutt" stood smoking quietly a short distance away from the enlisted men so they would not intrude on the men's conversation.

A few minutes later, almost everyone had finished their cigarettes and taken leaks on the grass just off the edge of the tarmac paved dispersal area. Two of his gunners, who were superstitious, had urinated on the tail wheel which was rumored to be good luck. After about twenty minutes the signal came down for the crews to get on board their aircraft.

Matt got his crew's attention and in his worst Gary Cooper imitation said: "Okay, it's time mates. As they always say in the western movies 'let's saddle up and go get the bad guys'."

They pulled themselves up through the various hatches into the Short Sterling and spent time getting their assigned stations ready for the flight. The gunners cycled the cocking levers on each gun to make sure it was ready to fire and moved smoothly in case a jammed round needed clearing.

Matt and his second-pilot Mutt Stanford along with their engineer Pat Quill started their checks prior to the run up of the four big Bristol Hercules II radial engines. Matt knew they could each produce almost 1400 horse power if run full throttle but he hoped he never had to push them that hard.

After checking with each of his individual crewmen on the intercom to be sure of their state of readiness, he gave the go ahead to begin starting the engines.

The three of them in the cockpit, working as a unit, started each engine and adjusted it until the black oily exhaust smoke had thinned to a pale white and the rough, misfiring engine had smoothed out to a loud purr. As each engine reached this state, the trio moved on to the next engine in line until all four were performing at normal levels on all the gauges. From point in the mission on the engineer would watch the gauges and instantly alert the pilots of any variation he could not correct in an engine's performance.

Once the three of them agreed that "E for Edward" was running smoothly and she was ready for takeoff, Matt released the brakes holding her back and she began to roll forward until she moved into her takeoff position on the mile-long runway to sit roaring, swaying and complaining about being held back by her brakes. Over sixty Short Sterlings nearly identical to E for Edward, likewise noisily waited nearly nose to tail for a single green flare to be fired from the control tower allowing them to individually release their brakes freeing the engines enormous pent up power then leap forward and one by one rise upward toward their destiny.

After what seemed an eternity of waiting, Matt finally saw the tower door open and an officer walk out. He raised his arm and a moment later the flare drew a white path into the evening sky which, at its apogee, turned into a brilliant green explosion. Nearly the color, he thought, of Joanna's eyes.

In an instant the lead plane began rolling forward picking up speed until it finally lifted free of the runway and slowly climbed toward the broken clouds and the golden half-moon above them. Before the first plane's wheels had even lifted from the tarmac, the next aircraft was already rolling forward and gathering speed.

Plane after plane rose into the darkened sky until Matt released his brakes and ran up the speed of his engines and "E for Edward" first rolled then, gathering speed raced forward. He adjusted his flaps to increase lift until his bomber became suddenly weightless as she climbed away from the field and followed the large dark shadow in front of her toward the clouds.

Edwards's engines were working ever harder as the plane gained altitude and in a few minutes she was in the clouds. Matt held his speed constant certain that if the pilot above him did the same there was no danger of crashing into each other.

In a few minutes he had broken out on top of the clouds and saw the dramatic sight of over thirty aircraft. Dark silhouettes against the moon-lit sky moved in loose formation with more breaking out of the clouds like huge exotic flying fish rising one at a time out of a silver ocean. As each arrived it took its prearranged position in the formation, slowly circling until they were all there and the formation was complete.

When Matt looked off to the East he could see another large formation of a hundred or more four engine aircraft flying to join them and then to the Northeast yet another of at least a hundred heading toward them. That meant almost three hundred planes were setting out to bomb Berlin on this night.

Less than a year ago the English newspapers bragged if the RAF sent one hundred bombers on a mission and now three hundred were hardly worth mentioning. The same newspapers were writing about soon having thousand-plane raids going forth to bomb Germany.

When all three columns of aircraft had closed on each other the formation morphed into three large flying squares of aircraft and changed course toward the Continent and Germany.

As the clouds began to break up below him Matt could see the cliffs of Dover glowing like a pearl, pale white in the light of the half-moon. The ocean crashing on the shingle beach as white foam: radar towers sharply outlined against the breakers.

Matt clearly saw the planes arrayed all around his and he knew this was a dangerous night to bomb Berlin. All of the specially equipped German night fighters would be up defending their capitol tonight and the moon would make their work far easier. Heavy clouds would make target identification more difficult for the bombers but would also make the odds of "E for Edward" being shot down much lower. Yes, heavy clouds over the target tonight would be nice. The worried look he saw on Mutt's face as he scanned the almost cloudless sky told him they were both having similar thoughts.

Matt was certain that without heavy clouds the only problem for the German pilots would be how many Short Sterlings they could shoot down before their ammunition or fuel ran out.

Why the hell hadn't the RAF figured out some way to extend the range of the Spitfires so they could cover the bombers? Without friendly fighter cover survival ratios much lower than they should be. Just a handful of Spitfires covering each group would save so many of the crews and planes that were being lost. "Well, he silently told himself, they aren't here and you knew the risks when you decided to do this and it's for Joanna so quit worrying and do your job. That's what you told the crew and it goes double for you, old boy.

In a matter of less than three hours, he could see the enemy search lights sending their brilliant fingers up into the velvet darkness searching for bombers. Matt knew being illuminated by three of these lights converging on a bomber was the most dangerous problem a crew faced. The anti-aircraft guns were very likely to blow any plane so pin-pointed out of the air because they were synchronized with the lights.

Only an instant drastic response by the pilot might prevent disaster. Matt had practiced a maneuver called "the corkscrew" several times. It required a rapid drop in altitude while turning the aircraft in a tight circle as it fell, then pulling sharply up and away to the right or left. It worked slightly over sixty percent of the time.

Matt's headset crackled to life with one of his gunners, Fred Howie, calling out a contact. "Number One we have a bogey, a ME 110 night

139

fighter tracking us at three o'clock low. He's too low for me to have a shot at him but he's inching in toward us. He's being careful. I think he believes he can sneak in at this angle without us knowing he's there."

Matt clicked his mike and replied, "Fred, let me know when he turns toward us to start his run. I'll drop the wing on that side sharply down and give you a shot at the bugger. Harry, you man the top turret and see if you can get a few shots in too."

Harry Lacey came right back with, "Okay Skipper. You got it. Just let me know when to fire."

This was interrupted as Fred broke in with, "Okay Skipper, he's starting his turn in."

Matt responded with, "Okay guys, grab onto something. Hold on, here we go! Fire at will."

He had no sooner started his wing-over maneuver than he heard Fred's gun start shooting. He was firing in short rapid bursts. Then the twin guns in the top turret joined in loosing a long burst at the German night fighter. To Matt it sounded like several very large woodpeckers banging away on a tin roof. He could hear the empty shell casings from the roof turret pinging as they hit the floor behind him. The cockpit was filled with the sweet pungent smell of cordite as the guns fired. From that night forward he always thought of the smell of burned gunpowder as the perfume of death.

Both Harvey and Fred were talking to him on the intercom, excitedly telling him they had both put rounds into the German and the plane had pulled away with one of its engines burning. Matt could clearly see the flaming aircraft as it spun down toward the darkness of the earth below. He did not see a parachute....

The rest of the mission passed without further serious threat.

Matt managed to avoid being "pinned" by the lights and he stayed out of the kill zone of the flak guns. His bomb aimer, Pat Quill, did a very good job of placing their explosives on target during which Matt held "E for Edward" steady until they got their drop zone photographs. These were needed to prove their hits were on or near the target. Without them the crew would not get credit for flying the mission from the RAF. After the photos had been taken, Rupert Lucas called up the course corrections from the Gee Set so Matt could get them headed back to England.

It took over four hours for them to follow the sinuous course laid out for their return base at Upper Hayford. The landing he made in the early hours of Wednesday morning was far from perfect. He bounced "E for Edward" off the runway once before he finally got her wheels to stick to the tarmac. But when he looked over at Mutt all he saw was a nod and smile of approval. When he finally had her parked on their hardstand and the engines shut down, Mutt told him it was always difficult landing after such a long, exhausting operation. The hours took a toll and the reflexes were slower. Both the First Pilot and Second Pilot had to use a lot of strength in forcing the big bomber to do what it had to in order to survive. It was the shear strength of their muscles, carried by cables, which physically moved the bombers large control surfaces. These were the big wing and tail flaps which altered direction and altitude. At the end of a maneuver like the corkscrew both the First and Second Pilots' arm and leg muscles were screaming in pain. In combat all they could do was ignore it and continue flying.

A bounce or two could be expected after so many hours of exertion. "Hell, Skipper," he told Matt. "You know what they say. Any landing you can walk away from is a good landing. Well it bloody well goes double after a combat mission. And by the way, that move you made to take out the 110 was 'full of beans'."

Matt recognized Mutt's use of "full of beans" for the compliment his Second Pilot intended it to be, so he returned it with another idiom of his own. "Aw, come on Mutt, you know it was 'easy peasy'."

Mutt laughed and said, "Sure Skipper, you can do that in your sleep but I sure don't want it interrupting my sleep. I fully expected to see a wing come off 'Edward.' Let's get out of here. I think my ass has grown to this seat."

When Matt and his crew had gone through debriefing and eaten what breakfast they could manage, it took what small amount of energy they had left to drag themselves off to their cots. If Mutt snored that morning Matt never knew it.

After the first three missions all crews were given a four-day break from flying in order to give the ground maintenance crews time to install new direction finding equipment in the bombers as well as lengthening the runways by removing some trees which grew too close to the end.

~ ~ ~ ~

Matt traveled down to the Barton place in Kent to spend time with Joanna and her family. Owen had extended the invitation but Matt was sure it came as a request from Joanna to her father.

After a strained lunch with Owen and Mary Margaret, Joanna told Matt she would like to take a walk in the barley fields and asked him to go with her so they could talk. Matt felt she was trying to get him away from her mother's constant, if subtle, probing of his intentions toward her daughter. Both could sense that Mary Margaret was worried they were already sleeping together.

Matt rose and slipped his RAF jacket over his shoulders. Joanna shrugged into a light wool sweater as they headed out. After they were gone Owen finally turned to his wife and said, "Give it a rest dear. After all, it is between the two of them." He raised his heavy black eyebrows and leveled his intense gaze at his wife, "If you remember, my dear, it took **us** a while to sort out what *we* should do; after all, we had our war just as they have their war. It makes every decision so much more complicated."

His wife was not happy about being forced to remember that Owen had left her and gone away to France in 1917 during the worst of the fighting. But, he had never promised her *he* wouldn't go. This American had promised Joanna he would stay out of this war.

"Yes, I know it does make decisions difficult, that much is true. We did have our war and it was not easy." Her voice began rising, "But *this* boy, this *American*, promised he would stay out of the war for her. He broke his promise to our daughter. I can tell she is broken hearted about that. Though she is just as stubborn as you and will never admit it. Why would he break the promise if he loves her as much as he says?"

"Calm down, my dear," he said taking her hand and stroking it to soothe her. "At least part of it was my fault, if you insist on placing blame.

"The boy came to me in obvious distress and told me of his promise. He just didn't know what to do. You see he truly loves Joanna, more than his own life, if you must know. It was the change in Nazi bombing strategy which worried him. When they started bombing civilian areas around England he really began to worry about our safety. In addition there was the death of one of the lads from University which weighed heavily on him. A fellow he had gotten to know pretty well. They were not chums but he *knew* the boy. It was the lad who introduced him to Joanna; Lord Trusdale's son, Lawrence. A lad with a somewhat unsavory reputation which should, I suppose, be forgiven now. He had been shot down near London four days before Matt came to see me.

"We talked for a long while and I finally told him that promises should always be kept if possible but that sometime events were such that we must renege on them. I am afraid that I even arranged his getting into the RAF. I have followed Matt's progress with the fellows I know up the line from him and they assure me, he is a truly superior pilot. They feel if anyone can survive in the air, it will be him. He has already had three bombing runs over Germany and gotten back in one piece. Brought all his lads back in one piece too. Please dear, don't tell Joanna any of this. I intend to let her know that I played a large part in his decision after he has gone back. I really should have already done so but I wanted to know how he was doing. Now I know."

His wife rose and walked over to stand beside his chair. After a moment she leaned down and kissed his cheek; a gentle kiss. Then she whispered in his ear. "You are a dear man. I prayed you back from France. I suppose we shall just have to pray him through this war safely for her sake."

She looked out the window and saw the two of them walking hand in hand down the path toward the barley fields. "Oh Lord," she silently prayed. "Please keep him alive. I think Joanna would die if anything happened to him. I hope they are not sleeping together. That would make it twice as bad for her if anything did happen to him."

What she didn't yet know was, this was a thought that very nearly mirrored what Matt had decided would guide his actions in his love for Joanna.

~ ~ ~ ~

Matt flew 13 more missions for the RAF. After his first mission to Berlin came two missions to Bremen to bomb the docks and a submarine building yard, then a later one to bomb a nearby aircraft factory. Hamburg followed with three missions against naval building facilities, docks and oil storage tanks. Essen, with the Krupp Iron Works, received two visits from "E for Edward." The Germans were especially vigilant and protective of this target. Each raid on Essen cost the RAF more than 17 percent of the aircraft and crews sent on the mission.

By now ground crews had begun to whisper that "E for Edward" was beating the odds. When she returned nearly unscratched from two consecutive missions to Berlin, even officers began to comment on how she seemed to be a "lucky aircraft," a few even used the word "charmed."

Matt even saw a difference in the quality of maintenance on "E for Edward." Repairs to the plane were no longer "slap a patch on her and get it back in the air." Twice the plane was grounded by her crew chief for further repairs.

"E for Edward's" crew no longer worried whether she would be in top condition when she took off on a mission. The ground crew made certain she was. They even painted a beautiful pinup girl on the nose with the name Edwina above her. Matt was pleased because he had called the aircraft that since his final training flights in her.

All fourteen of Matt's missions were flown in "E for Edward" and his crew remained largely unchanged. On a few occasions one or the other would be replaced for a few days when a crewmember was ill or injured. The Short Sterling had been patched to cover bullet and flak holes to the point that her crew called her with affection, the "flying quilt." One of her engines ran a bit noisier than the other three, but the ground crew never found a reason. In spite of her heavy use and hours in the air, she always carried them to the target and back home safely. None of them would have traded her for a brand new bomber.

Many of the ground crewmen who cared for the aircraft at Upper Hayford, referred to the plane as "Lucky Edward." She often came back with holes punched in her, but the crew always came back in one piece.

The same ground crews had watched bomber after bomber fail to return from a mission in those early dawn hours, yet "Lucky Edward" always returned. Often she would come limping home, but she always came back with her crew largely uninjured.

At about this time Matt learned from a young RAF ground officer that a decision had been made to stop bombing German military targets and shift to civilian areas. This decision was based on an extensive report which concluded that only twenty percent of bombs dropped by the RAF were coming within five miles of the assigned target. Because of this, the decision was made that future bombing would be directed exclusively against industrial and civilian targets.

When each mission ended, Matt always managed to get word to Joanna by phone that he was back and safe. As time passed, he could feel her becoming more at ease about his safety.

The last mission Matt flew as a member of the Royal Air Force was against Stuttgart in early December 1941. The flight over was a struggle through heavy clouds and high winds. "E for Edward" was constantly blown about the night time sky. The group was not able to hold anything like a normal formation and was strung out across the angry heavens by the time they reached the coast of Europe.

The aircraft arrived over Stuttgart even more separated and found the area heavily clouded. Flying conditions were so poor the Luftwaffe did not bother to go up for interception so only two aircraft were lost to flak. The squadron dropped their bombs, but had no idea where they had fallen. Matt did not know when he landed from mission number fourteen it was destined to be his last in a RAF uniform.

Chapter 12

DECEMBER 1941

On December 7, 1941 the War and Mathew Weldon's part in it changed dramatically.

The Japanese surprised the world by bombing the American fleet at Pearl Harbor thrusting the United States, as unprepared as it was, into World War II. Japan intended it as a dagger into America's heart.

At 12:30 PM on December 8, President Franklin Roosevelt stood before a joint session of Congress and spoke to them as well as the people of America.

"Mr. Vice President, Members of the Senate, and of the House of Representatives:

"Yesterday, December 7, 1941...a date which will live in infamy...the United States of America was suddenly and deliberately attacked by the naval and air forces of the Empire of Japan.

"The United States was at peace with that nation and, at the solicitation of Japan, was still in conversation with its government and its emperor looking toward the maintenance of peace in the Pacific.

"Indeed, one hour after Japanese air squadrons had commenced bombing in the American island of Oahu, the Japanese ambassador to the United States and his colleague delivered to our Secretary of State a formal reply to a recent American message. And while this reply stated that it seemed useless to continue the diplomatic negotiations, it contained no threat or hint of war or of armed attack.

"It will be recorded that the distance of Hawaii from Japan makes it obvious that the attack was deliberately planned many days or even weeks ago. During the intervening time, the Japanese government has deliberately sought to deceive the United States by false statements and expressions of hope for continued peace.

"Yesterday, the Japanese government also launched an attack against Malaya.

"Last night, Japanese forces attacked Hong Kong.

"Last night, Japanese forces attacked Guam.

"Last night, Japanese forces attacked the Philippine Islands.

"Last night, Japanese forces attacked Wake Island.

"And this morning, Japanese forces attacked Midway Island.

"Japan has, therefore, undertaken a surprise offensive extending throughout the Pacific area. The facts of yesterday and today speak for themselves. The people of the United States have already formed their opinions and well understand the implications to the very life and safety of our nation.

"As commander in chief of the Army and Navy, I have directed that all measures be taken for our defense. But always will our whole nation remember the character of the onslaught against us.

"No matter how long it may take us to overcome this premeditated invasion, the American people in their righteous might will win through to absolute victory.

"I believe that I interpret the will of the Congress and of the people when I assert that we will not only defend ourselves to the uttermost, but will make it very certain that this form of treachery shall never again endanger us.

"Hostilities exist. There is no blinking at the fact that our people, our territory, and our interests are in grave danger.

"With confidence in our armed forces, with the unbounding determination of our people, we will gain the inevitable triumph... so help us God.

"I ask that the Congress declare that since the unprovoked and dastardly attack by Japan on Sunday, December 7, 1941, a state of war has existed between the United States and the Japanese empire."

Three days later, on the 11th of December, Adolph Hitler strode to the front of the Reichstag in Berlin and in a long, rambling speech declared war against the United States. In doing so he united the three great powers which would fight against him in Europe: England, Russia and the United States.

Matt's home country was now a part of the fight he had been involved in for over a year. It would change both England and the direction of the war. In the end it would change the world.

That December, the weather in England was cold with sharp winds and heavy snows. Few missions were flown and losses from the weather were heavier than losses to the enemy.

~ ~ ~ ~

He spent most of the Holiday Season with Joanna and her family and helped them decorate the big house in Kent. The tree in the large front room was a twelve foot high evergreen which they lavished with lights, ornaments and a huge star at the tree's apex. Matt volunteered to stand on the tall ladder to place it. Owen was at the bottom steadying the ladder while he reached out to place the star exactly centered on the top.

When he was satisfied the star was perfect, Matt climbed down. Owen slapped him on the back and said, "Matt, it is going to be a pleasure having you in the family. I've gotten a bit portly to put the star up top. Never once got it as straight as you have done.

"You know even Mary Margaret has decided you and Joanna are the perfect pair. She said you are a wonderful young man. Except," Owen laughed, "she did mention that awful accent you have. I told her if she would forgive your 'Yank' accent, you might forgive her English one."

"Oh great Owen, like I can't get myself in enough trouble? You're going to get me in hot water without me saying a word. What a wonderful father-in-law you are going to make."

"Well Lad, the more trouble I can get you in, the less I'll be in."

By now they were both guffawing so hard that Joanna and Mary Margaret came down the hall from the kitchen to find out what they were laughing about.

Joanna looked at the two of them and asked, "OK you two, what's got you two donkeys braying so hard?"

Before Matt could say a word, Owen answered, "Matt was just telling me the most awfully obscene joke I have ever heard." Matt's face turned red, but he was now laughing so hard it was several minutes before he was able to speak and by then Owen had told Joanna and his wife he was only kidding them. When Matt stopped laughing he said, "Thank you for telling the truth. Yes ladies, it was Owen who told that depraved joke, not me."

By now everyone was laughing. Even Mary Margaret.

When they looked at the tree Joanna's mother judged it, "Perfect. Simply perfect."

She kissed Matt on his cheek. "Well Mathew, you are just going to have to help us with the tree every Christmas. Anyone brave enough to climb that ancient ladder is brave enough to be with Joanna."

Joanna walked over and kissed him. He realized it was the first time she had really kissed him in front of her parents. He knew it was not a spur of the moment thing she had done. The two of them were making a statement. One Joanna had decided it was time they made. The kiss was not a little kiss. She held it long enough to tell her Mother "get used to seeing this." It is real and no longer a "maybe" kind of thing. The two of them were "mated."

147

When she pulled away Joanna looked directly at her Mother and said, "Don't worry Mum, I have no intention of letting him get away. It took me much too long to find him."

Matt took Joanna's hand, looked into her wonderful green eyes and had the feeling they had, somehow, always been together. He didn't understand the feeling, but it was there. It was real. He was certain of one thing, he didn't intend ever to lose her.

Two days before Christmas fresh snow fell. Joanna burst into his room and shook him awake. She was as excited as a young girl. She wore a silk gown which outlined her perfect figure. Matt went from sleepy to fully awake in a matter of moments. When she ran from his bed to the window and threw the curtains back, light streamed in and through the thin silk. He just couldn't tear his gaze from her. When she turned back and saw him unable to look away she smiled seductively.

"You know you can. I have told you that more than once. It can be one of your Christmas presents. Now, it's not something you can unwrap under the tree unless it is very late at night after my parents are long abed. We could make it a joint Christmas present to each other. Do you want to do that?"

"Joanna, of course I *want* to. When you tease me like this, it takes every ounce of will power I have not to. You are the most desirable woman I have ever seen. No one else was even close. If I did not love you the way I do, it would have happened a long time ago. Do you enjoy knowing how badly I want to f...err... make love with you? I am sorry Joanna. The word that almost came out is crude but I hear it far too often flying and around the base. It replaces words that range from a simple 'Oh My', to one of my gunners saying 'Shucks, I missed that ME 109 and the German gentleman flying it.' Of course 'gentleman' also has a three letter substitution... S.O.B."

He was sitting on the edge of the bed. She walked over and sat in his lap to put her arms around his neck and kissed him, eliciting a long groan from Matt.

"Thank you, sweetheart. I've heard the other word. The one you almost used. I know what it means Mathew. In some cases it is the only thing that is happening between two people. Just a physical act...nothing more.

"By the way, the word is believed to have originated in seventeenth century court language. Hard to believe but it is reputed to be a legal term. When two unmarried people were found having sex and taken to court the charge was 'Found Under Carnal Knowledge'. In time only the initials were used in court documents. At least that is what I've heard.

"After we are married, it might be a word we sometime use. It is, in some ways exciting simply because we know we shouldn't use it. Even if *we* sometimes use the word in a high state of arousal, for us I believe it will still be making love. I know that's what it will be for me Mathew. Knowing what doing *that* used to be like for you, I am convinced it will also be different when it is you and me. I believe it always is if the people truly love each other no matter the words used to express it.

"That said, I know why you want us to wait and I will if you insist, but I confess I enjoy teasing you a bit from time to time. I will do that even after we are married. I suppose I just like being naughty where you are concerned. You can expect to get the bills for the sexiest lingerie I can find. I want you to clearly understand waiting is as hard for me as it is for you.

"I can understand why guys talk about wanting a girl so badly they think about ravishing her. I have often thought about ravishing you. It was a thought which horrified me when I first had it. But I have even found myself thinking about how I would go about it. Are you shocked?"

"Yes Joanna, I am 'horribly shocked' and also very glad you told me. In a way it helps to know this is as difficult for you as it is for me. I am also convinced the first time will be so heavenly that we will never want it to end. Good thing the barristers didn't simply refer to it as only 'Under Carnal Knowledge' or everyone would be saying, 'Oh UCK'."

Joanna started laughing and kissed him. "Mathew, you are so wonderfully and originally awful. How do you come up with these things? You can make me laugh at obscenities which should shock a nice English girl. If, of course, that *is* what I still am. I constantly have to rearrange my way of thinking about many things because of you. I am afraid I may now catch myself saying 'Oh Uck' when something goes wrong. You are so clever and I love that about you. You are my 'Yank' and I wonder if I was even living before we met."

"And you, Joanna, are my beautiful, still proper, yet very naughty, British lady and if fighting a war was the price for our meeting, it is well worth it. As much as I hate the war, I love you so very much. I'm sure I was only half living at best. Only existing.

I keep trying to define you. Yet you defy categorizing. I heard a term mentioned once when I was in prep school, in my English Lit. Class. Old Professor Dean was teaching Shakespeare. He introduced the concept that some people have 'old souls' by which I think he believed some people had lived before. It was his explanation for wisdom far above what is considered normal. I sometimes feel that about you. Do you know what I mean?"

"If you mean, Mathew, can I accept the possibility of reincarnation; the answer is yes I can. I sometimes get the feeling a particular thing has happened before. The feelings are fleeting, but I have them. I am always sad afterward because I am unable to remember enough to understand the significance of the event. Tell me honestly Mathew, have you ever had that feeling?"

"Yes I have. A few times recently. Strange you should ask, because I never had the feeling before I met you. Even now, I always put it down to being tired or having eye strain. Something of the sort. The main feeling I have is that we are meant to be together. I really don't know much beyond that. I have never been one to believe in anything that can't be proven or quantified. What I think of as 'spooky stuff'."

She gazed at his face and Matt saw disappointment in her eyes before she said, "I can't prove any of this. It is simply what I feel. Perhaps I read too many 'fairy tales' as a child and they have affected me. Please don't think me daft. This is all really unimportant. *Really Mathew.*

Anyway we had better get dressed. I need to go down to Canterbury for some shopping today. I would like for you to drive me in your lovely little car."

When she left, Matt was sure there had been more she wanted to tell him. "Damn", he thought, "I know my attitude about what she was telling me prevented her from saying more. Why did what she was saying cause me to feel uncomfortable? Was the discomfort caused by what I felt or what she said? Even the idea that things exist beyond what I know has always made me a bit uncomfortable, yet Joanna believes those things can and probably do exist. She believes some events are fated to happen. That the two of us were destined to meet. So, Matt old boy, can you say she is wrong? If you look at the odds of us ever meeting, well they would be staggering. My act of flying down Wall Street, then having to come to England as a result. Going to the party where I met her and *me* actually apologizing to *her* that night. Every event drove the odds against us being together higher, yet here we are now together. I love her and happily accept we will not be exactly the same in all things. Love must trump the differences. Is her certainty about us being together a bad thing? It is the thing I want above all else.

After breakfast Matt brought the MG around to the front steps. Joanna came crunching down the steps bundled against the cold and they headed up the long drive leaving tire marks in the freshly fallen snow. Fields where crops of barley were grown lay fallow and covered in white, awaiting the spring plow; the trees barren and the low skies gray. Very much like Christmas weather back home in New York and throughout most of New England. But this would be a different Christmas Season in America. It would be America's first Christmas of this war. Many sad goodbyes were being said during this Holiday Season. Some by young men who would never live to see another Christmas.

After driving in silence for a while, Matt glanced at Joanna. "Look, about this morning I want to..."

"Oh Mathew, I am sorry. I was prattling on about things that must seem really inane. I don't know why I got started on that topic. Past lives and all that drivel. Please forgive me. It must have been very off-putting."

"My dear Joanna. You have no idea how totally spellbound you have me. From anyone else the word 'off-putting' would sound so strange to my American ears. From you it is sheer poetry. You must know that.

"About what you were saying this morning...I am sorry you didn't feel you could continue with what you were telling me. Dear heart, I never want any thought of yours to go unexpressed because I seem unreceptive. What you think and feel *is* important to me."

He could feel she was looking at him as she considered what he had said to her. She remained completely silent for several minutes.

"Thank you Mathew. The problem is the time was not yet right. Yes, there are things I want to talk about with you, but they need to wait until later. Until we are completely one. After we are married. The timing was premature on my part. Your life is serious enough right now. I don't know what I was thinking. We should just try to have fun, enjoy the holiday and being together. Let's make a pact that we will try not to allow any unhappy thought in our heads."

"Dear lady, my *only* thoughts about you are happy ones. I would really like to know what you were trying to tell me this morning. I believe it was important."

"I will tell you part of it Mathew, but please understand most of what I believe will have to wait. I have always known we would meet. Not *just* that I would meet someone who I would be in love with, but when we met I knew it was you. I know we are meant to be together. I am convinced it was fated to happen and that, from long ago. For us not to be together would be a great loss. I knew when we met, you would love me. I knew we would never love anyone else as we love each other. I also know you must be careful because if anything happens to you. Well… I don't know how I could go on without you."

Once they reached Canterbury, the morning passed in a blur of shopping. Matt had purchased Joanna's present weeks earlier in London, but he purchased a golden swan brooch with diamond eyes for her mother and Joanna guided him to a tobacconist shop where he purchased two pounds of what she assured him was her father's favorite tobacco and a blue Delft tobacco jar to hold it.

Joanna spent her time buying presents for the house staff in Kent and their children, plus a warm woolen scarf and hat for Mrs. Townsend. Matt had already put two twenty pound notes in a box and had it wrapped with red paper and a green ribbon for the woman who had cared for Joanna from childhood. His card said, "Thank you for taking care of 'our' Princess." The back of the card read simply, "Matt." When the shopping was finished and the presents were safely locked in the MG's 'boot,' Joanna led him to the magnificent Cathedral which rose above the heart of the city.

"Mathew, I must show you the Cathedral. Our other trips over here have always been rushed, but today we have time. The Cathedral here is considered the Mother Church of religion in England. It is as beautiful and sacred as any in the world. The French love Notre Dame, well; Canterbury Cathedral is our Notre Dame."

He spent the next three hours in rapt attention as Joanna gave him a lecture on the story of the grand church and its place in English history. He followed her as she took him to each of the biers lining the outer halls of the great building. Their longest stop was at the largest one topped by the reclining figure of a knight in dark armor.

"This is Edward of Woodstock, Prince of Wales, Duke of Cornwall, and Prince of Aquitaine. The eldest son of King Edward III. The man who should have been King. He defeated the French at Crecy and Poitiers. He was a fierce warrior but sickness forced his return to England and he died here a year before his father's death. His son became King Richard the II. His epitaph reads: 'Such as thou art, sometime was I. Such as I am, such shall thou be. I thought little on th'our of Death, so long as I enjoyed breath. But now a wretched captive am I. Deep in the ground, lo here I lie. My beauty great, is quite all gone. My flesh is wasted to the bone.'"

He could barely hear her as she translated the Latin inscription around the bier. Her voice choked with emotion. She sounded near tears. When she was finished, she took Matt's hand and pulled him behind a column where they could not be seen and kissed him passionately. Her body was pressed tightly against his as if she were trying to become part of him. He could feel her trembling like she was afraid of something he could neither sense nor understand. When she pulled away she whispered, "Please Mathew, let's never waste a single minute we are together. Time flies so quickly."

Matt lifted her chin so he could look at her eyes. He had thought from her voice she might be crying but found her green eyes dry and unusually bright, almost wild.

"Joanna, are you all right? You sounded sad and frightened."

"I don't know what it was Mathew. Reading his Epitaph struck something inside me. He was once as alive as we are. He walked the earth, fought battles as you are doing, loved a woman and had children and probably, until near the end, never thought he would be lying here. Everything he was, gone. He probably never considered what the passing of time meant. Oh how quickly a lifetime can pass.

I don't want it to be like that for us. Please be with me as long as time allows and love me for I will *never* stop loving you."

Matt took her hand and led her out to the open cloisters which bordered the Cathedral.

"Joanna, as beautiful as it is inside, the biers can get depressing after awhile. I promise we won't ever take each other for granted. We are going to be together. We will love each other as long as we live. In America there is a saying something is going to happen 'come hell or high water.' Well, I am going to love you always, come hell or high water. I could no more stop loving you than I could live without breathing."

She pulled her coat tighter around her body and Matt saw she was not wearing gloves. He took both her hands and held them against his lips blowing his hot breath on them until they were warm. She looked up into his blue eyes while he was doing it. When her hands were warm he released both and said, "Put your hands in your coat pockets until we get back to the car. We need to keep you warm on a day like this. Haiku would be very angry with me for letting you get chilled this way"

She smiled at him. Her smile which always made him feel his heart was skipping a beat. "Yes Sir Mathew. Your Princess will do as you direct. Thank thee for loving me and protecting me from all harm. Thou art my true love. My Prince and my Knight."

The skies began to drop large dry flakes which fell lazily toward the ground. The low slate colored sky promising much more was to come.

"It's starting to snow so we need to get back to the car and back to the house. I have no idea how the MG will handle a lot of freshly fallen snow.

It is a lightweight. I don't think it was built for really slippery weather. Days like this were made for my Duesenberg, but it's in storage back in America. I hope someday I can show her to you. You are a Princess and so is she. The two of you belong together."

The drive back to Barton Hall was much slower than the drive to Canterbury. For long stretches Matt drove in low gear to avoid sliding and by the time they were back it was dark. His shoulders ached as badly as he could remember, even after flying a round trip to Berlin.

~ ~ ~ ~

The skies cleared by Christmas morning with only a few puffy marshmallow clouds being blown slowly toward the east. By the time Matt was dressed and downstairs, Christmas music was playing on the radio in the sitting room and the aroma of hot chocolate wafted throughout. He found Owen in the sitting room by following the pungent smell of strong Latakia pipe tobacco.

When he entered, Joanna's father turned the volume down and greeted him. "Well, Merry Christmas my boy. I hope you slept well."

"Yes, thank you and Merry Christmas to you too, Owen. It looks to be a lovely day, though to be honest I have been glad of this spell of rotten weather. It has let me spend Christmas with all of you. Without it, this Christmas would have been a poor one indeed. Being with your family has made it the best I've ever had."

"Well Matt, you need to start thinking of us as *your* family now. I know you and Joanna are not married yet. I understand why you aren't, and approve of why you are waiting, but I am sure you will be wed. With America in the war, the direction has changed. The big change came when Hitler went after Russia. Once he gave up on invading us, he naturally turned toward the east and that meant Russia. My best guess is... he was *destined* to make the error Napoleon made with the same results. The country is too damn big for him to swallow it in one gulp like he did France. Winter has stopped him cold. Pardon the bad pun. Your country has been shipping enough to keep us above water and you will soon do the same for the Soviets. Stalin will throw as many men into the German meat grinder as needed until it breaks. In the end, Russia will roll Germany back and around that time, England and America will land in France and begin to liberate the Continent. Then we will have Hitler in a vise and crush him.

"It seems some of you Yanks saw that America would be in it months ago. A friend from the Club let it slip that American officers have been over here for quite a while observing the way we run naval and air missions and they are very interested in our special operations fellows... our commandos."

Matt thought back to his meeting with Owen in his brewery office over two years earlier. He had been impressed with the accuracy of the older man's predictions on that day. While he had not been able to predict the reason America would enter the war, he had said it would happen. It was natural he would look at the European situation. The Japanese attack on Pearl Harbor would have been hard to foresee.

Joanna came in from the hallway and, after wishing Matt a Merry Christmas, told them "That is enough of that, you two. It's Christmas Day. No more war talk today. It is a Holiday and a Holy Day." Joanna placed a silver tray on the side table and poured steaming cocoa into silver mugs. Her mother carried in a matching tray covered with cake slices, breads and cookies.

Matt had brought several wrapped presents down the stairs with him and laid them on a chair. When he and Owen finished talking, Matt picked them up, carried them to the tree and arranged them on the floor under it.

The radio was still tuned to the BBC and softly playing Christmas music. At the end of "The Holly and the Ivy," the announcer's voice told the listeners, "We are going to rebroadcast the Prime Minister's Christmas Message which was originally broadcast from Washington D.C. last evening. As it was early morning our time when the address occurred, we feel it is worth repeating for our people this Christmas Day."

Owen sat his cocoa on a table and turned the radio up. After a short pause, Churchill's familiar bulldog growl filled the room.

"I spend this anniversary and festival far from my country, far from my family, yet I cannot truthfully say that I feel far from home. Whether it be the ties of blood on my mother's side, or the friendships I have developed here over many years of active life, or the commanding sentiment of comradeship in the common cause of great peoples who speak the same language, who kneel at the same altars and, to a very large extent, pursue the same ideals, I cannot feel myself a stranger here in the center and at the summit of the United States. I feel a sense of unity and fraternal association which, added to the kindness of your welcome, convinces me that I have a right to sit at your fireside and share your Christmas joys.

"This is a strange Christmas Eve. Almost the whole world is locked in deadly struggle, and, with the most terrible weapons which science can

155

devise, the nations advance upon each other. Ill would it be for us this Christmastide if we were not sure that no greed for land or wealth of any other people, no vulgar ambition, no morbid lust for material gain at the expense of others, has lead us to the field. Here, in the midst of war, raging and roaring over all the land and seas, creeping nearer to our hearts and homes, here amid all the tumult, we have tonight the peace of the spirit in each cottage home and in every generous heart. Therefore we may cast aside for this night at least the cares and dangers which beset us, and make for the children an evening of happiness in a world of storm. Here, then, for one night only, each home throughout the English-speaking world should be a brightly-lighted island of happiness and peace.

"Let the children have their night of fun and laughter. Let the gifts of Father Christmas delight their play. Let us grown-ups share to the full in their unstinted pleasures before we turn again to the stern task and the formidable years that lie before us, resolve that, by our sacrifice and daring, the same children shall not be robbed of their inheritance or denied their right to live in a free and decent world.

"And so, in God's mercy, a happy Christmas to you all."

The announcer voice from the radio continued, "This message was a rebroadcast of the Prime Minister's Christmas Message. It was broadcast on the occasion of the lighting of the community Christmas tree outside the White House. We at the BBC would like to add our best wishes to those of Prime Minister Churchill. God save the King."

The sounds of Christmas music began once more. The four of them sat quietly listening, each remembering what Churchill had said and examining the meaning it had to them as individuals.

Mary Margaret thought of her only son Alexander, sandy-haired and clever. He had played at soldiers when he was a boy and now he was an officer protecting Singapore. The Japanese were steadily moving in that direction and had been since the 15th. The papers said they would never take the city but she worried because of how quickly they were moving.

Owen worried about his son, but also about Matt and many of the lads who had left the Brewery and were in uniform, scattered all around the globe. Then there was the Brewery. So far the Germans had left it alone and the raids were getting lighter every day. He knew they weren't a target like aircraft-building facilities, but fighting lads needed ale almost as much.

There were several worries on Joanna's mind. Her Mum and Dad. She worried Owen was working long hard hours at the Brewery. Then there was Alexander, her brother. Her partner in childhood games of hide and seek. The boy who wanted to be a barrister of all things. He had worked two summers at the Brewery and wanted no more of it. Joanna wished he loved it as she did, but it was clear he did not. The closest he would come was agreeing to handle their legal affairs.

Then her heart worried about Mathew. She admired his determination to protect her country, her people and, she knew, to protect her. She was sure he would be unharmed. That he would live through the war. The West Wind had told her he would make it. Still there was a shadow that kept her from seeing everything. It just had to turn out well. There was the son she *knew* they would have. Little Mathew Somersby. Joanna was so completely certain; she already knew their son's name.

Mathew sipped his second cup of cocoa and thought of his father. What did his dad think of him now? Very little remained of the childish young man who had crossed the Atlantic Ocean on the Queen Mary in 1939. Joanna and the War had seen to that. Matt knew he had grown up and could hardly recognize the person he had been when he walked down the gang plank onto English soil. Matt's worries were for Kong and Fizz, his roommates at Yale. He was certain Kong would jump into the War at once. It would be totally in character for the big man to get into the fight at the first opportunity. Then there was little Fizz. The guy who avoided fights. The one who hated pain. What would he do? Could he get in if he wanted to? He was smaller than normal. A light-weight. A fifty pound pack would pull him over on his back where he would be as helpless as a turtle.

Finally there was Joanna's family. Owen was spending a lot of time at the Brewery. Even sleeping in his office some nights and Joanna was spending most of her time in London, the primary target of the German bombing. The only one he felt was reasonably safe was Mary Margaret who was spending most of her time in Kent.

Presents were passed around and opened. Matt opened his present from Owen and found a small lighter in gold which was old and dented. It carried the initials OSB and the date 1916. Owen later told Matt the lighter had been given to him by his father when he left for World War I in 1916. Owen had carried it for the year and a half he fought in the trenches of France. Matt understood the value Owen placed on it and what it meant as a gift. Mary Margaret had given him a white Irish wool Aran sweater. It was the sweater worn by fighter pilots under their leather jackets. Matt kissed her on the cheek and assured her it was a welcome addition to his "Flying Kit."

Joanna's mother opened the gold swan brooch Matt had selected for her. She smiled at him, pronounced the gift "breathtaking" and praised his wonderful taste.

Joanna opened her gift from Matt and found an antique white gold Victorian locket on a heavy white gold chain. When she opened it, inside she found a miniature painting of her from her shoulders up and on the other side a painting of Matt in his RAF Uniform of the same dimensions. The front carried her initials. The rear was engraved with "Love...Forever... Mathew." She looked at him lovingly and said "Please put it on me my darling Mathew." He stood behind her and placed it around her slender neck with a kiss.

When Matt opened his present from Joanna he found a heavy sterling silver chain bracelet. The front was deeply engraved "Captain Mathew Weldon" and on the back "Love...Forever...Joanna."

She walked over to him smiling and whispered to him, "Well my love, I adore the present. It is beautiful. You must tell me where you found it and who painted the miniatures so I can make a note in my diary. The pictures inside are exquisite. When the locket is closed, they are kissing. But isn't it quite a coincidence we both chose exactly the same words on the reverse? One could almost think it more than simply a coincidence. Whatever the reason, I love it and I love you... Forever my love."

"I hoped you would and I love the bracelet. Now when I fly you will be with me. Of course you always are; in my heart."

After the presents had been passed out there were still many remaining under the tree. Owen saw Matt looking questioningly at the unopened presents.

"Matt, those are for 'Boxing Day' which comes tomorrow. Those presents are for our people who care for the estate and work the fields to grow our barley. They will pick these up today and open them tomorrow. The employees at the Brewery were given an extra week's pay in their last checks of the year. In America I understand you call it a Christmas bonus."

After a large Christmas lunch, the four of them bundled up and went out to the small stone chapel where they spent time in quiet contemplation and silent prayer. Joanna held Matt's hand while they knelt in the ancient building. As they walked back through the cemetery, they placed large sprigs of red-berried holly atop pristine snow at the base of each stone. Matt could remember how Joanna had told him the history of each of her ancestors on a warmer, pre-war day nearly two summers ago.

Later that evening, Matt heard the door to his room quietly open then felt Joanna slip into his bed. He turned toward her and looked questioningly into her eyes. She placed her lips near his ear and whispered, "No Matt, I told you I will honor your wishes on the topic of when we make love, but for some reason I just need to be near you tonight. Think of it as another Christmas gift to me. I want to sleep next to you tonight. I know we have never done this before, but I promise your virtue will still be intact in the morning." When she heard Matt give a quiet laugh at her final words she relaxed and moved closer.

She turned her back toward him. Without a word Matt laid his arm over her and pulled her against him. She snuggled closer and put her arm over his. They both slept peacefully and well through Christmas night and deep into the next morning. When they awoke, Joanna leaned over and kissed him, her arms around him and soon his arms were around her. After the kiss, Matt told her, "My God, Joanna it is worth waking up just to see you. You are absolutely radiant in the morning. I hope you will give me a kiss like that every morning after we are married. Sleeping with you felt completely natural. Almost as if..."

"...we had done it before. Is that what you were thinking Mathew? If so, it felt the same to me. The way our bodies fit together. The way your arm lay over me. The sound of your breathing. Your warmth. Everything about it seemed so natural. It is going to be easy for us to be together once we are married."

"Yes and it is going to make sleeping in a Quonset hut with a bunch of guys really miserable from now on. I may have to go AWOL and come here to spend my nights sleeping with you."

"No Mathew, we both know that many nights like that would be too much of a temptation. Many nights like that and little Mathew Somersby would be on the way earlier than planned."

Matt smiled and kissed her again. "Well my dearest, keep me advised on the plan for him so I can do my part. A part I am looking forward to with happy anticipation. As for me, nine months and one day after the wedding sounds good as an arrival date, but I understand the exact timing depends on you."

"Don't worry. I will do my part. I will definitely *deliver* us a son."

"OK Joanna. I suppose I deserved the double entendre. Shall we go down and have breakfast? I imagine your mother has noticed the rearrangement of sleeping locations by now. So do we explain nothing happened between us last night or leave her in a state of delicious suspense?"

"Well let's wait and see what Mum says. We need to get dressed. If we go down wearing what we are now...well yes, she would be shocked. She has never seen you in only in a pair of shorts. This is probably not the best day for that to happen.

"By the way, when you call the London house to tell me you are leaving on missions or returning from one, I may not be home. Just leave word with Mrs. Townsend. She will let me know when I get home."

"Ah ha Joanna... you must have another guy you are seeing when I am away."

"Actually there are a lot of men I will be seeing. I have signed up to be a nurse's assistant in the Voluntary Aid Detachment at St. Bart's Hospital. I am scheduled to start January Third. The system is strained to the breaking point and will only get worse. This effort needs me more than the Brewery does. You have been *flying* for England. It is high time I did my bit and got into the War. This is what I can do, so it is what I will do."

Matt kissed her. "Well, it is impossible to be jealous of the guys you will be seeing. I admire you for doing this. It is so like you. I am sure they have warned you what you will be doing is very difficult. I have seen the damage to some of the crewmen who are wounded on missions. There have been times I had to look away. In many ways what you will be doing is more difficult than what I do. Your work is more important than mine. I am bringing death to the enemy. You will be helping to save the lives of our people."

She used her fingertips to push the comma of his hair back up from his forehead. "You are such a wonderful man - even if you are an American. I am so glad you are my wonderful 'Yank.' I do not say this lightly, but we are *perfect* for each other. We had such differences when we first met that it is amazing we are even together, yet look at us. We love each other. It is like we are one person. It is beyond anything I could have believed possible." She kissed him and asked, "OK, which of us gets the first cold shower?"

Matt looked down before answering with a laugh, "I think I may need it worse. At least with me it is more obvious that I need it. I hope it won't be this bad after we are married."

"Oh, don't bet on it Mathew darling. I intend to keep you very interested in playing. Yet, after all, a fellow who had five girls in his bed in one night shouldn't have a problem keeping one little English girl satisfied. Isn't that right Mathew?"

"Oh my dear Lord! I think that five-girl fable is going to haunt me for a long time. I was just kidding."

"Yes. I know you were. But *I'm* not. You said it, so you will just have to live up to it. I want to hear our children calling you "Da"."

When they were both dressed and going down for breakfast, Owen stopped Matt in the hallway. "Laddie, I'm sorry to say a call came in for you about an hour ago from Upper Hayford. They need you back as soon as possible. The fellow said he knew your leave was supposed to last for two more days, but that was cancelled. Breakfast is on the table, so eat then you need to pack and get back. The fellow didn't know why, but he said he was told it was urgent. I don't think he knew anymore than that."

Matt looked at Joanna's face and could clearly see the disappointment in her eyes. He kissed her cheek and told her, "Sorry sweetheart. Orders are orders. Given a choice, I would stay here with you but with the RAF it is not a choice I have. Once this lousy war is over I intend us to be together for the rest of our lives. We have promised each other 'forever.'" Owen walked away smiling broadly.

"Mathew, I am disappointed but maybe they will make it up to you by giving you New Years. Will you ask them?"

As it turned out, Matt was unable to make the request of his superiors there. They had him return early because he was being discharged from the Royal Air Force.

As soon as he was handed his discharge, an American Army Air Force Major swore him into the 8th Air Force as a Captain and gave him orders saying he was to report to headquarters at High Wycombe Abbey the next morning to see General Ira Eaker for assignment. The Major seemed to know nothing about what that assignment would be. Matt thought the Major's manor and uniform simply screamed 'retread,' an officer who had been called back to active duty since Pearl Harbor. His demeanor was more like that of a University professor than a professional soldier.

Matt sat in his quarters and wrote a note to his crew members of "E for Edward." He addressed the note to his second pilot Martin "Mutt" Stanford.

Dear Mutt,

Please read this to the crew for me. It has been an honor flying with you. I wish I could stand before you and personally tell each of you what a wonderful bunch of pirates you are. I have been inducted into the

USAAF 8th Air Force, whatever the hell that is. Because my orders require me to leave immediately, I can only ask Mutt to pass this message along. You have all been like brothers and this misplaced Yank thanks you for that. You are the best. I could never wish for better friends.

I have been assured Mutt will be your new skipper. With him in the first seat, you will have the finest pilot I can imagine. If they can find a second seat man as good as Mutt was for me, you will continue to have a first rate group. I pray God will continue to bless you and "E for Edward" as He has done while I was fortunate enough to be your first pilot.
Your mate,
Matt Weldon
PS – This is for you, Mutt

Thanks for watching my ass pal. You are every bit the pilot I am. I know you are going to be caring for the lads, so I don't need to worry about them. You are also a lucky 'sod' because they are a hell of a good crew. I have enclosed a 'twenty.' Take the boys out for some ale the next time you have a break from flying. I hope our paths cross soon and I know we all hope this damn war ends shortly.
Matt

~ ~ ~ ~

The next morning, Saturday, December 27, 1941, found Matt once again at High Wycombe Abbey which he was soon to come to know by its code name "Pinetree." General Ira Eaker immediately set the young Captain on the almost year-long task of readying England for the arrival of thousands of bombers and fighter aircraft from America along with an endless parade of fliers, support personnel and material.

Those aircraft would require large airfields from which to take off and land and the RAF had agreed to turn existing air bases over to their American allies. It was Matt's job to evaluate the bases, delineate their present readiness and report what would be needed in the way of improvements to bring them up to American standards.

Of course, General Eaker informed him, those standards were still being debated by the Pentagon, but that small technicality shouldn't cause a problem for a bright young fellow who had gone to Yale.

"What I expect Matt, is for us to have the bases ready long before they even agree on those standards. My motto has always been, 'Do it!' then ask forgiveness if you have too. But *only* if you were wrong. I have seldom had to ask forgiveness."

His closing words to Matt were, "Just go out and look at them through the eyes of a pilot. Write your reports as if you were going to be personally assigned to each of the bases. You know what it takes to repair aircraft and keep them flying. We have flight surgeons looking at medical facilities and even Padres looking at chapels. Those areas are covered. Your job is flight issues. Aircraft readiness is your primary area of interest; that plus the crews and anything involved in keeping a maximum number of aircraft in the air. Send your reports directly to me. *Be honest.* I will protect your backside on this. If a base is bad, don't sugar-coat it. I would be surprised if the Brits are offering us their finest bases. I am expecting you to help us avoid nasty surprises from the locations we do take over."

The General gave Matt several binders which contained page after page of minutiae on the building of and specifications for Army Air Force bases suitable for handling heavy bombers.

During the months to come as Matt traveled from base to base, he found General Eaker's assessment to be correct. RAF base quality varied greatly. Bases like Great Yarmouth and Horsham-St. Firth were first rate bomber facilities, while several others were below par; all recently built without the care given those built before the war. At the bottom of his list was Polebrook. Matt spent nearly a month there and was still not certain he had found all the problems to be corrected. His report ran to well over seven hundred pages. Single spaced.

In addition Matt checked out the nearby towns to establish the pubs, churches and potential supply of workers to support the base and do whatever other work was needed. Each report contained an index with this supporting information.

The work allowed Matt to spend time with Joanna on weekends when she was not scheduled to be on duty at St. Bart's. As the weeks passed, it was obvious she was paying a price for the work she was doing. She smiled less and often seemed to be walking the edge of crying. When they went out, Matt saw her drink more than usual. He could tell she was tired and he often suggested they sleep together. Even Mrs. Townsend seemed to understand the need to turn a blind eye to them sharing a room. Except for the kiss before settling in to sleep in his arms, Joanna never brought up any other form of intimacy between them.

Near the end of his assignment, Matt was advised the Army Air Corp was transferring him to pilot a B-17. General Eaker sadly told him he would not receive credit for his flights for the RAF. The General had asked Washington to modify the twenty-five flight rule in this case but the request had been summarily refused. He had shown Matt the letter with the stamp, "Request denied by order of General Marshall. No exceptions to the twenty-five missions rule."

Joanna had remained quite when he told her. She finally looked him in the eyes and said with anger in her voice, "It simply is not fair. You should be given credit for the missions you flew in the RAF. They were all safe back in America while you were over here fighting. Then they arrive and pull you out of the RAF and send you all over the English countryside evaluating bases and locations for them. Now they have the nerve to put you in a bomber and say nothing you have done counts for anything. That you have to fly twenty five missions as if you had just arrived from America. Damn it Mathew it simply is not fair. Not a *bit* of it."

He picked up his new orders two days later. When he read them he had only one comment on his assignment. "Well this will be fun. I hope I don't die of laughter". The he sighed and said "I suppose laughing is better than crying."

Chapter 13

KONG'S LETTER TO RATT

Yale University

New Haven, Connecticut ❖ Founded 1701

December 10, 1941

Dear Ratt,

Well, we are all dancing to the same tune now. A jazzy little ditty written by the Japs, their buddy Adolph Hitler and a few fiends/ friends (like my Freudian slip?) of his in Europe. Looks to be a lively little party and a long one.

I have to tell you, all of us left back here at good old Yale were convinced you had gone off your rocker when we heard you joined the RAF. Well buddy it seems you were just ahead of the curve this time around.

As soon as I finish my courses this semester, I am off for the Marine Corps. I've already signed the papers and passed my preliminary physicals. That means we probably won't be getting together for drinks any time soon. I'll be going to O C S then most likely the Pacific to call on our little yellow friends. I'll remember to give them your regards and tell them if you do get out their way to lock up their women.

Speaking of which, the girls around here seemed to have forgiven you your trespasses. They were constantly asking Fizz and me how you are doing. As hard to believe as it is, they worry about you. Who would-a thunk-it? They actually hope you find someone. Frankly so do old Fizz and I. There really are much worse things which can happen to a guy. Especially now.

Speaking of Fizz, he is <u>already</u> gone. Left yesterday. Very hush-hush. Could only tell me it was basic training in the Army and after that he would be going to OCS then he'd be shipped out west somewhere. That was all I could get out of him. You know, I worry about him more than I do us. His forte has always been brains. The two of us did well enough in that area but ole Fizz always left us behind. He just didn't show off with it. Kept us out of trouble more times than I care to count. It is still hard for me to believe he has volunteered for the Army. I am sure of one thing, whatever he is going to do, he will do it well. I just hope he can keep <u>himself</u> out of trouble.
Your dad called and we talked for a while. He asked what Fizz and I were going to do, then said he was proud of all of us. Yes, that <u>did</u> include you. He had questions about what had caused you to join the RAF. He also

questioned himself for putting you in the position which caused you to do it, but he finally understood it was the only thing a man in your situation could do. Yes Matt, he called you a "man."

It is quite a moment when the day comes that a father finally recognizes that his son has grown into a man. I hope if I make it thru all of the things which are to come, and have a son, I will recognize that very important day with the same clarity as your father. It is, after all, a rite of passage to be celebrated. The beginning of the changing of the guard. One generation into another. With us it has simply been pushed forward a bit earlier than usual.

He said he is writing to let you know that he has donated your Waco to the Army Air Corp for use in the early training stage for fighter plane pilots. I know the army is really short of training planes and they are going to need a lot of them now. The entire country is on a wartime footing and it has only been three days. But what a three days! If you were here you would already see and feel a difference. Ammunition plants were immediately put on a 24 hour a day schedule, as were all armament, aircraft and ship factories. Ford and GM are changing to truck and tank production. All State National Guard Units are now U.S. Army Units. It is amazing and it is just starting. The west coast is in a panic thinking the Japs will invade out there. Hell, none of them would ever get out of Hollywood. They would all be hired to play Japs in the coming flood of war movies.

Your dad has had the Duesy put in storage where she can no doubt dream of all the romantic escapades the two of you had at good old Yale. I am afraid that all of us who come back may have little in common with the boys who went away. The same goes for the rest of our class who are leaving now.

The drinking around here has been very nearly non-stop and is of bacchanalian proportion. The going away parties are being held every single night. The Yale and Harvard teams next year could accurately be called the "4 Fers" because that is all that will be left to play on either team. The team which played in the fall of '41 will be scattered hither and thither around the globe by next fall. I say this with more than a little sadness; those of us who are left alive by then. I can't kid myself about our chances of survival, as I am sure you no longer can. The large majority of us are definitely going straight into harm's way.

I have been reading about the RAF bomber raids over France and Germany. The newspapers try to put a good face on it, but it is clear the losses are heavy. I am somewhat comforted by the knowledge that you are a great pilot (I know beyond a shadow of a doubt, because you told us so often) and you will come through it all in one piece.

I had better cut this short because I have several of those goodbye parties to go to and I have to drink to their health for myself, the Ratt and old Fizz.
Keep 'em flying

Your pal, Kong

Chapter 14

THE 8TH AIR FORCE AND POLEBROOK

Matt found it strangely ironic that the former RAF airfield known as Polebrook, in Northamptonshire, should be the base to which he was assigned. From there, he would fly his missions for the U.S. Army's 8th Air Force.

One of the many British bases he had identified for use by the Eighth, he had written in one part of his extensive report, "A good Officer's Club and Enlisted Men's Club will be absolute necessities because this base is very isolated. It, unlike many older RAF bases, is deficient in many areas. It was thrown up in haste and looks as if it might fall back down. It is no accident the RAF is so willing to turn it over for our use. Only the runways and hard stands where the planes sit between missions are first rate. Most structures were so rapidly built that they will require replacement or substantial reworking. Any work we do will be an improvement.

In addition, our agreement with the RAF to use local labor can only benefit the area's economy, as bringing the base up to our minimal acceptable standards will keep local workers very busy for a long time."

Matt had learned the base was built by the RAF on land belonging to one of the Rothschild estates. Surrounding the base was heavily wooded land, so some tree removal would be required to make landings less dangerous. The base truly was in the middle of nowhere. From the Field to London was over sixty miles, so seeing Joanna required driving two hours on narrow graded country roads. If he hadn't had the MG stored in a small garage just off base it would have been nearly impossible to ever be with her.

Sure there were the usual rural villages such as Polebrook and Ashton, each of which had a pub, but no facilities to handle nearly eight thousand young Americans ranging in age from nineteen up to officers in their mid-forties.

In the now, third year of the air campaign, the English people had grown somewhat more tolerant of the idea that fliers were a bit rowdier breed than the Royal Army and Navy because of the unrelenting stress brought on by their manner of combat. Just as they were becoming more comfortable with this idea, the American Eighth Air Force arrived.

American pilots were each like one of the RAF boys multiplied by ten, so the residents of villages near the bases started the universally repeated saying, "There is only one problem with the American fly boys: they are over-paid, over-sexed and over here." It was heard so often, no one ever pointed out they were complaining of three problems.

Very soon the Americans were replying with "There is only one thing bothering the British: they are under-paid, under-sexed and under Eisenhower.

It seemed to Matt the complaints were made primarily by women over forty and men of nearly every age. The younger English women seemed quite delighted with the situation as their social lives had picked up to a level most had never imagined. And they appeared to grasp what their elders had not: when these boys left on a mission the chances were substantial they would not return.

Losses in aircraft and crews on a single mission often were thirty percent and sometimes as high as forty. He knew the average was over four percent loss per mission when you included the "Milk Runs;" those easy missions that met almost no resistance from the Luftwaffe and little flak coverage. When one calculated the current requirement to finish twenty five missions before they could "Stand Down" from flying, simple grammar school math gave them their theoretical odds of survival at... oh my. Zero!

He had spent months attached to General Ira Eaker's unit while selecting existing RAF bases which could be used, with reasonable modifications, to service the large B-17 and B-24 squadrons arriving in streams from the States. The experience had left no doubt in his mind that this shotgun wedding of boys used to doing things American style and the far more reserved English rural village culture was bound to cause friction. For many of the American boys, it was their first time with complete freedom. Many had lived only at home with their parents so Matt could understand their wildness. Add alcohol and girls to the mix and he was surprised there were not more serious problems. The MP's normal arrest was for drunkenness, fist fights or if a woman was involved in the equation, both!

Back in America, factories were turning out heavy bombers by the hundreds each month and it was a good thing crews were likewise being trained using assembly line techniques, because in daylight bombing the losses would be awful. Yet the Air Corp Generals were convinced that only around-the-clock bombing of German military and production facilities would finally break the back of enemy resistance. It was exactly the same method Germany had used against England which had been a spectacular failure for Hitler and his Air Marshal Hermann Göring. All the bombing of English cities had accomplished was to strengthen the people's resolve not to give in.

Matt had finished his final reports to General Eaker two weeks before his arrival at Polebrook. He would be assigned a B-17 F model as soon as a new flight of aircraft arrived from the States.

While he waited there had been weeks of learning about the bird he would be piloting. The B-17 F's had just begun arriving from the States. For Matt it had been love at first sight and first flight. His old Short Sterling had been serviceable but ugly, especially when she was on the ground. Looking at her, it was difficult to imagine her in the air. The B-17 was different. The moment you saw a B-17 you knew her place was in the air.

The Short was a girl you would spend a night with and the B-17 was like Joanna; a girl you would marry and stay with until the day one of you died.

Luckily his training was far briefer than normal because the Air Force knew he had been flying RAF combat missions. He was told to pack away his RAF Medals as he could not wear them on his US Army Air Force uniform. He was issued sterling silver Army Pilot's wings, so his RAF wings were one of the "casualties" of his new allegiance. He was given no credit for the 14 missions he flew before his move to the USAAF. He would have to fly the full 25 missions. He knew Ira Eaker had done all he could.

Even his shortened training schedule consisted of hours in a classroom, but this time he was learning the B-17 inside and out. Specifications and the theory of what she could, and equally important, what she could not do. Later came days of work inside a Link Trainer. No more than a closed metal box with all the important instruments needed to simulate actual flying; its primary job was to keep a pilot from crashing an expensive bomber. Enough new pilots still did that even after hours of Link Trainer practice.

Finally, there was hour upon hour of real takeoffs and landings. Touch and go landings where as soon as the bomber's wheels were down on the runway, the throttles of the engines were pushed fully forward so the B-17 would roar forward down the runway until she was once more airborne. Then around for another touchdown, over and over.

After weeks of practice he was given his Polebrook assignment, and the Squadron he would be part of. His Rank was now Captain, USAAF. A grade higher than his rank in the RAF. His pay was over three times what it had been flying for England.

All the changes he had originally suggested had been made to Polebrook. The 351st Bomb Group had been assigned there, along with two other squadrons. Matt was never certain if his assignment was due to the vagaries of the military system, or if it was General Eaker playing one of his macabre little jokes. Now part of the 351st, he was stuck with only the small nearby village of Polebrook and its "The King's Arms Pub" plus a fourteenth century church for entertainment. Alternately there was the village of Ashton with a seventh century chapel, school house and the "Three Horse Shoes Pub" for a stiff drink and a meal admittedly better than the chow in the Officer's mess hall.

The base did indeed have a very good Officers Club which poured until 23:30 hours when the Squadron Commander insisted it close. Otherwise pilots might not have been able to pilot, navigators to navigate and bombardiers to bomb.

The Enlisted Men's club closed a half hour earlier or, it was in Matt's mind a certainty, the gunners would have been shooting down B-17s faster than the Luftwaffe. Crews always drank and drank hard so only the oxygen after takeoff allowed many to function on the mission. The base Surgeon always checked the condition of crews but if a man could stand up on his own, he flew. Nights following missions with heavy losses were always the worst. Matt had often seen officers who were the best of friends get into fights over nearly nothing. It was one way of warding off both fear and sorrow; the pain inflicted in the fist fight lessening the other kind of pain. No one stepped in unless it was becoming too damaging to one or the other of them. The hard feelings never lasted past takeoff for the next mission. The fat lip or black eye lasted a few days longer.

Worse than getting in a fight was returning to your Quonset hut barracks and having to face all the empty bunks when a crew didn't return. There were special units of men who removed all the belongings of crew members who were shot down or had been killed during the mission; their bunks stripped down and the mattresses rolled up. It was as if the others missing from the hut somehow wouldn't be noticed. In practice it only made everything worse, as if the ones still alive could ever pretend those gone had never lived inside that corrugated steel half-tube.

Matt had inherited a crew from a pilot who had flown three missions and couldn't fly a fourth. It was the kind of story he had heard often during his time with the RAF. A highly competent pilot goes on a mission

174

so difficult that he becomes incapable of ever flying again. He can function well enough in other capacities but he becomes unable to even be inside a bomber again. The RAF tried to force them to fly by treating them as cowards. It seldom worked but when it did; usually lead to disaster.

The story Matt heard from several members of this young pilot's crew made it easy to understand his breakdown. The crew's B-17 was named "Witchy Bitch" and on that mission was the left-most aircraft in their V formation. The target had been a group of concrete-reinforced submarine pens on the northern coast of France. The weather was clear with only a few high clouds and the flight was attacked by German fighter planes as soon as their covering Spitfires turned back toward England. Both of his waist gunners had been killed by the Messerschmitt's twenty-millimeter cannons, their bodies largely shot to pieces. The middle part of the bomber was full of holes and awash in blood. Still the young pilot continued on to the target where the flight came under fire from heavy flak batteries. During his determined run to the target, the pilot's B-17 was badly damaged by flak but he held her straight and true until the bombs from "Witchy Bitch" were released on target. After she was clear of the flak field the German fighters returned for another attack. One flew in a direct line toward the front of their plane and loosed a burst of canon fire at the canopy. Three shots went through the glass in front of his co-pilot, one almost decapitating him. The pilot was covered with the blood and brain tissue of his co-pilot and still he continued to do his job perfectly and he managed to get what was left of his crew safely back to Polebrook where he made a picture-perfect landing with his badly shot-up aircraft. It was later ruled to be damaged beyond repair.

When the dead crewmembers had been removed, he calmly made his report then walked into the Squadrons C. O.'s office and told him he did not think he could keep flying. After being extensively examined by the Squadron's Flight Surgeon he was passed along to Air Force psychologists who agreed. He was re-assigned as a ground control officer and performed his duties well but his fellow officers noticed the strange vacant expression in his eyes when planes were overhead returning from a mission. It was an unfocused stare which lasted until all the remaining B-17s had landed safely. Then he returned to his duties.

The crew members who became the nucleus of Matt's crew were the Bombardier, Lt. "Karl" Karlson, a tall blond and talkative 20 year old from Augusta, Georgia with a strong southern accent; Lt. David ("call me Dave") Shellhamer as Navigator, from Bloomington, Illinois. Master

Sergeant Tony Angerami, an engineer from Brooklyn, N.Y. Mike Gibson, the radio operator, of St. Louis, Missouri, a Sergeant. For his tail gunner he had another Master Sergeant named Eugene Cords from Long Beach, California. Handling the radio was Sergeant Mike (Tex) Gibson of Midland Texas. Crammed into the ball turret was the small gunner, Marty Andrews from Opelousas, Louisiana.

From the replacement center in 8th Air Force Headquarters at High Wycombe Abbey, his request for two waist-gunners was filled by 18 year old Sergeant Leon Nicholson from Bismarck, North Dakota and 23 year old Sergeant Nelson Sakashiva, a full-blood Navaho from Shiprock, Arizona.

The final addition Matt made to his crew was 1st Lt. John Smithson from Knoxville, Tennessee who had, until recently, been a flight instructor at Briggs Army Air Base at El Paso, Texas. He had constantly requested assignment to a combat squadron for over six months. He told Matt the Army must have gotten tired of his incessant written requests and decided "to let the damn fool go ahead and get himself killed." He was disappointed he had been shipped over as a Co-Pilot instead of Pilot. "But what the hell" he told Matt "at least I'm finally in the War."

Like Matt, he had been in his second year of college. He had been the starting Center of his University of Tennessee football team. Matt knew Smithson had departed U.T. the year before the war started, gone to OCS, then moved on to flight school.

He and Matt liked each other from the first day they met. Matt soon came to the realization that Smithson reminded him a lot of his old friend Kong. Both were big, hardy individuals who saw anything difficult as a challenge to be overcome and almost everything else simply as work to be done. They both shared unique views of what having fun meant, often to the extreme. And for reasons unknown to Matt, both seemed to think one of their jobs was to watch his back. He didn't understand why they did it, but he was grateful they did.

Now that Matt's complete crew was assembled at Polebrook, he called a meeting in the operations center. His excuse for calling the meeting was to advise them of the schedule of flights he and John Smithson had worked out so they could get used to functioning as a unit. Two weeks would be given to flights over the North of England, Scotland and crossings to Ireland and back. There would be gunnery practice, runs on targets dropping dummy bombs and navigation challenges. These involved Matt piloting a course he did not know in advance based only on

176

information his Navigator plotted and passed along to him. The point was to see if they arrived at the destination the navigator had targeted.

It was true Matt wanted his crew to understand what they would be doing before they started combat operations, but he actually used this time to know if he had a crew he could rely on. After the horror of the last mission most of them had flown on "Witchy Bitch," he was not certain they would hold together under stress.

After giving them a copy of the schedule he brought up that topic. "Fellows," he began, "we need to talk about something else. I know most of you had a really bad last mission. Some of you may know I flew 14 missions for the RAF in a Short Sterling. We were flying at night because the Brits had gotten their butts kicked flying in the daytime. Even flying at night was bad. The Krauts adjusted their tactics. I had some bad missions; a few I wondered if we'd get back from. But we did. I had a couple of guys slightly wounded but no one killed. The point is I never had a mission as bad as the "Witchy Bitch" on her last flight.

"Your pilot probably deserves a Medal of Honor, but he won't get one. He won't even get a Purple Heart because he wasn't wounded. Not a scratch on him. Not one you can see on the outside anyhow.

"He did the right thing. Despite everything that was happening he carried on. Two men dead in mid-aircraft and he got the "Witchy Bitch" on target and dropped his bombs as if nothing had happened. Then after leaving the target more attacks by the Krauts in FW 190's and his co-pilot sitting next to him is killed. Still he remains calm and gets what is left of his crew back and safely lands in an airplane that I wonder how he even kept in the air. Goes on to make his report on the mission and then, and only then, lets his C.O. know he can't keep flying.

"Boys, as far as I am concerned, that man is a hero. He did everything that could have been done. He kept it together for the sake of his crew and brought the rest of you back alive.

"You know all of us are volunteers. We volunteered knowing there were much safer ways to serve in the armed forces. We also have the right to not fly. All we have to do is go to our Wing Commander or Base Commanding Officer and say we can't fly any longer.

"If any of you feel that way after your last flight, well... I will go with you to the W.C. or the base C. O. to tell them. It is the crew that counts and every man is important to that crew. You have to want to be there; to be fully a part of the crew and do your part no matter what we are hit with. If a single part of a watch fails; the watch dies. I think you understand what I am saying.

"If any one of you wishes to stop flying simply see me before the day is over."

Not one of the crew requested to be relieved of flying.

Before the two weeks of familiarization hops ended Matt was sure he not only had a crew but was convinced it was a very good crew. They watched out for each other. On one high altitude flight, Leon Nicholson, one of his waist gunners, did not realize the tube to his oxygen mask had frozen. Without oxygen he quickly passed out. He could have died just as quickly, but he had barely hit the floor before the other gunner Nelson Sakashiva was on the intercom calling for help and Mike Gibson ran back from the radio room. It was only moments before the two of them had Nicholson back on oxygen and breathing normally. It became a laughing matter instead of another training death and it brought the crew closer together.

Their B-17F was a true virgin. Newly arrived in England she had never flown a combat mission. Matt, Smithson and their engineer, Tony Angerami, had gone over her with a fine tooth comb because they knew how quickly these planes were being turned out in the American factories.

Their first flight, a two-hour hop over northern England and Scotland made them suspect the altimeter on the pilot's side and it had to be replaced as it would not hold adjustment. The motor which drove the ball turret was unreliable and likewise had to be replaced.

For the next two weeks when he and his crew were not flying, they were checking every part of their ship to make sure she was ready for battle and giving list after list to the ground crew of items to be adjusted, repaired or in a few cases, replaced.

As they neared the end of the familiarization flights all of them knew this *lady* was ready for battle. All she was lacking was a name.

Matt requested and received permission from the Wing's Commanding Officer to take his crew off-base for an evening meeting before they flew their first combat mission together. He emphasized the need for esprit de corps in a newly assembled crew. Particularly in one which had been through what most of this one had. His argument that the "condemned deserved a good meal" seemed to do the trick with the "Old Man." He even allowed him to use one of the Base's big, olive-drab, 6 by 6, two and a half ton trucks for transport into the village.

Matt personally drove the big truck because he knew the road which led to Ashton Village's "Three Horse Shoes Pub" so well. The pub was the place he had most often eaten evening meals back in the days when he was surveying the Royal Air Force base for use by the Eight Air Force.

His crew was laughing and talking as they loaded into the back of the truck for the eight mile trip to the pub. Matt had to be very focused on the road in front of him because the small amount of light from the thin horizontal slit in the "blackout" headlight cover gave only weak illumination to the road ahead. Smithson sat next to him and he could feel the big man tighten up at every turn in the road. Matt laughingly told him, "Relax John. I've only run off this road five times... in clear daylight." He felt John relax as he replied, "Thanks Matt. I feel so much better knowing that. What could possibly happen with you in charge?"

When they finally reached the small village, it was so quiet and dark, one would have thought it abandoned. Blackout curtains kept any light from being seen from a single window of the cottages or handful of stores because even the smallest of villages had air raid wardens who constantly patrolled when darkness fell and drew attention to any window which showed a sliver of light.

Entering the pub instantly proved Ashton was not a deserted village; it was busy and noisy. Over thirty heads turned in the direction of the door as Matt's crew entered. All became totally quiet for a long moment as an uneasy silence descended on everyone there. Then Matt shouted, "At Ease." in his best officer voice. The locals all laughed, then relaxed and went back to talking and drinking.

There was a small side room which was not being used. Matt got permission from the owner who recognized him from his many visits months earlier, to use it for his crew. They pushed three of the old wooden tables together and ordered Ale and Shepherd's Pie for everyone. Matt remembered it was the one food item on the limited menu which was surprisingly good.

Matt made arrangements for the bill to be given to him at the end of the evening. His co-pilot offered to split it, but Matt told him, "No thank you John, the first time we all get leave to go to London I will take you up on that offer, but not tonight. Tonight everyone is my guest. Yes, to a degree this is a crew meeting, but I invited you."

After dinner was finished, the plates were cleared away and everyone was nursing at least their third ale. Matt got their attention by saying "OK guys, now that everyone has their personal tank topped off, there is one more item we need to settle.

"I want every one of us involved in this because we are a crew. It concerns our new bird. She has got to have a name. An identity. All of us have worked together to be sure our lady is ready to go into harm's way and we all need to be satisfied with her name. Anyone have a suggestion?"

His Bombardier spoke up with, "I'll go with anything that is not "Witchy Bitch" or "Witchy Bitch II." Matt waited for a moment before saying "Karl, I think you have spoken for several others in saying that. I'm not really superstitious, but let's give this lady a 'new' name.

"Now guys, don't be shy, the lady still needs a name."

Tony Angerami stood up and in his strong Brooklyn accent kicked off the round of possible names with "New York Lady." Name after name was thrown into the hat until Navigator Dave Shellhamer, looked at him and asked, "OK, Mr. Pilot, you have stood there as all these names have been thrown on the table. It's your turn. What name would you suggest? And don't tell us you don't have one. You can surely come up with something."

Before he knew he had spoken, the single word "Joanna" came out of his mouth. He was surprised because he had intended to leave the naming up to the other nine on the crew. "But listen guys, it really doesn't matter to me."

John Smithson sat his beer down and stood up. "Oh no, Skipper. You have us interested now. Who is this Joanna Lady? The way you said it tells me she isn't your sister or your old maid aunt."

Knowing there was no way to avoid it now, Matt grinned sheepishly and began to tell the short version of how he had met Joanna, how they had toured her family brewery and the time they spent at her family's home in Kent. And, holding his mug of ale aloft, he described the fields of golden barley they grew for making the dark golden drink. What a grand old stone house they had in Kent. The things the two of them had done together before the war came. And finally admitting to them that if he made it through his twenty five missions, he intended to marry 'the Lady.'

It was quiet for several minutes before Smithson finally spoke up. "She sounds like a great girl, Skipper. We would all like to meet her sometime but, "The Joanna?" I don't think that gets it for our plane's name. You said it doesn't matter to you. Is it okay with you if the rest of us come up with a name for our bird?"

Matt knew they would all be flying her and fair was fair. It should be a majority decision. He looked at each of them individually before saying, "Guys you get together and name her. Just one request: don't make it **too** obscene. Otherwise it's okay by me."

When they left on their first combat mission together, three days later, the squadron artist, a young man from San Francisco, had painted each of their names on the outer aluminum skin near their combat position in the plane. On her nose was painted a beautiful green eyed, copper haired lass holding a stein of ale and wearing a Union Jack apron. Above her in white letters outlined in red was the name the crew had given her, "THE MAID OF BARLEY."

~ ~ ~ ~

Matt and his crew flew their first combat mission in "The Maid" on Wednesday, March 31, 1943.

The briefing room was chilly at five hundred hours or, what in their old non-military days had been know as five o'clock in the morning or what they came to laughingly call "dark- O-five hundred". He and his crew stumbled through the slushy mud which lay everywhere along the edges of runways and on what laughingly passed for roads. A combination of mist and light rain had fallen most of the night leaving them all chilled.

At breakfast there was spirited betting that the mission would be scrubbed, but real eggs and bacon told them otherwise. These rarified items were reserved for mornings when missions *were* flown. Matt thought of the words he spoken only a few days in the past, "the condemned man had a hearty meal."

The table in the briefing room at which Matt, his co-pilot John Smithson and the rest of the crew were seated was two rows back from the front and near the end on the left side. Thick cigarette smoke clouded the air because most of the men lit new ones from the butt of the one they had just finished; then another and another. Coughs lay heavy in the air. Tension was always an unwelcome guest at each briefing, but it never failed to be in attendance. The big map on the end wall was completely covered by an olive-drab cloth. The covering was always in place by the time even the earliest crew entered. It was as if they were expected to gasp in surprise when the cloth was pulled away. Yes, the gasp often came but when it did, it was never a happy gasp.

It seemed almost a theatrical performance! The audience was the crews who would fly the mission. They filed in slowly and filled seats at each table, one table per crew. Then the actors assembled: the ground officers, the weather guys, the intelligence guys, the guys who give radio frequencies for the mission, the ones who would lay out the data on assembly points. Finally, from the rear door a shouted, "At-Ten Hutt" made everyone rise sharply to their feet as Wing Commander Major Tom Wilheit strode purposefully to the front of the room and up one step onto the low stage. He looked out over his audience. Matt could almost hear him counting under his breath one thousand and one, one thousand and two, and one thousand and three, the pause for effect. Finally he said, "Good morning gentlemen. Please take your seats." After the rattle of seats being occupied had died down he turned toward the olive drab cloth and continued, "Our target for today is (pause for effect) (jerk the cloth away)(wait for the gasp of recognition) the submarine pens, docking facilities, warehouses and rail lines all at, near or in Rotterdam Harbor."

The map showed the line of flight from Polebrook across England, red lines indicating the route of flight continuing in a northward direction across the water to the Netherlands and Rotterdam, then a different set of green lines showing the different return route back to England. Wilheit paused for a few moments then continued, "This will require a high degree of precision because an error of a few hundred meters will mean that you are either dropping bombs in the water thereby only killing fish or if in the other direction, I need not tell you what you will be killing for you will be bombing the town." A moan went up from the fliers because a miss in that direction would mean killing the Dutch who had suffered while fighting the Germans when they invaded Holland in 1940. It would mean killing enemies of their enemies; the Germans. The Dutch had a very active underground organization which continued to harass the German Military.

Wing Commander Wilheit turned back toward his audience, shoved his hands into his pockets and lowered his voice until the tone was very confidential as if he was speaking to each one personally. "I know. I don't like this anymore than you do. It *is iffy* particularly since the weather at the target is pretty much what we currently have over here. In short the whole thing stinks. But the Brass (which he failed to mention he was a member of) said the sub pens are full and it is a good time to take them out. If we get good hits we could take 10 Nazi subs out of the war.

"I am going to lead this one myself. I can't ask you guys to do something I am not willing to do. I am going to fly Copilot for Tom Slade in 'MeatBall.' We'll lead and drop our load first. Just follow us. There is no secondary target, so it's this or come back with nothing."

Major Wilheit was followed by several of his supporting cast. The weather guy (Meteorologist for the college educated in the audience) used enlarged weather photographs to give a high-brow rehash of what the Wing Commander had already told them. It amounted to clouds at both high and low altitude. There would be breaks here and there but not many. They could also expect some pretty strong winds; head winds going and tail winds coming back. Sheets were passed to the Bombardiers with more wind information and Matt saw a frown on Karlson's face when he looked at it. The bombardier and his Norton bomb sight had to take wind speed into account when calculating bomb drops.

The Intelligence Officer brought the kind of news fliers welcomed. Anti-aircraft fire would be light, fighter cover around the area was thin and the German pilots were second rate. The experienced pilots were all reserved for Berlin and the Ruhr Valley and also were being bled off to the Russian front. Besides, the submarine pens were considered bomb proof by the Germans as they had over 22 feet of steel-reinforced concrete protecting them. "However," he continued, "our engineers believe that enough direct hits will eventually cause them to collapse crushing any submarines inside. Yes, I know. We only have 500 pound bombs, but I can only tell you what the 'experts' say. For all I know they may bounce off like tennis balls hitting a steel wall, but it is the mission we have been assigned so it's the one we will fly. The good thing is it is not heavily defended and it counts just as much toward twenty five as one against Berlin, Schweinfurt or the Ruhr Valley. If nothing else, it is a gift. A true milk run for once."

Matt heard Nelson whisper under his breath to Marty, "I hope the Dutch will see it that way after we drop our bombs."

And so it went until all the actors had played out their roles. The last actor was undoubtedly the most sincere. It was the Chaplin. He asked them to bow their heads. It was not required but everyone in the room, Matt included, bowed their head. They had all heard the saying, "There are no atheists in foxholes." Double that for anyone flying in a B-17.

The crews were dismissed and began to assemble everything they needed for the flight. Each man had a parachute which had been unpacked after that last mission and repacked. They picked up their electrically heated flight suits and sheepskin lined boots, pants, gloves and jackets. Each man was already wearing silk long johns under woolen ones. He also had on a wool-lined skull cap and now carried his oxygen equipment and communications gear. Marty Andrews, their smallest member and Ball Turret Gunner had gone from 146 pounds up to 176 with all his gear. The simple act of walking was difficult. They were all sweating but they knew once they were above twenty thousand feet the bone chilling cold would set in. It would feel as if they were in their underwear. If that.   Only a small area around the Navigator and Bombardier was heated because they couldn't work well in gloves.

When they had collected all their equipment, Matt gathered them near the "Maid" as he had always done with his RAF Crew. Now there were eleven of them including him. It was like his first flight back then with his old crew. The first real combat mission with a new crew is always an unknown. No matter how many hours of practice you have together it is the real thing which counts.

"Good," Matt thought, "I hope this is an easy one. It will give us a chance to check each other out. I already know that Nelson and Mike work well together because they sure took good care of Leon when his oxygen froze up. And I would trust John with all their lives if anything happened to me. Hell, he is as good a pilot as I am. No, maybe a *better* one. Tony is a hell of an engineer. He watches those instruments like a hawk. Stands between my seat and John's and calls out everything we need to know about the engines. He knows enough that if John and I were both down... well, I think he could get the "Maid" back home and put her down. Note to myself, 'Get Tony some time in my seat and in John's. Let him get a feel for this bird. Might come in handy and can't hurt anything. Hell, a third guy able to hold her is a good idea anyway on the long flights."

"OK boys, nearly time to get on board. I don't know about you guys but I'm going to take a piss. This is not a long flight but I sure intend to start out on 'empty.' Figure I'll be near a 'full tank' by the time we get back." After they were finished they climbed in "the Maid" to ready her for takeoff.

They had been on board long enough for the gunners to be sure their guns were all properly greased and the cocking handle moved freely before the crew chief gave them the 'start engines' sign.

Matt started the last engine on his port wing first while Tony constantly updated him on manifold pressure, oil temperature and RPMs. When they were satisfied with the performance of that engine the next was cranked until all four were running up to spec.... It was at this point that Karl stuck his head up from the open space between the pilot and co-pilot's seats which allowed access to the bombardier's position in the nose of the aircraft and said, "Are we there yet, Daddy?"

Matt pushed Carl's head back down through the opening with, "Get back in the cellar where you belong. I'll tell you when we get there. Stay down there and polish your Norton or whatever it is you do with one. I'm not sure I even want to know." He heard laughter from all over the ship. The flare went up from the tower and one by one the aircraft began to leave their hard stands to assemble in takeoff order on the long runway.

When the next flare was fired the B-17s began to roll forward. "MeatBall" was first off the ground and climbed quickly toward the misting clouds. It was so closely timed that a problem with any plane could quickly become a disaster. Matt had decided long ago that his only hope would be to get off the runway and even that would only be possible before he had gathered much speed. It was the greatest fear of every pilot and co-pilot, but one which was never mentioned. The result of a B-17 fully loaded with 1,700 gallons of aviation fuel and 5,000 pounds of high explosives hitting another B-17 with the same load was a fear best not dwelled on for long. But it had happened more than once.

Luckily, this morning everything went as it should. The entire operation proceeded on time and exactly as planned. It was later when they got in the top level of clouds that things went to hell.

Matt learned later that Captain Howard Snider of "Witches Broom" had an engine failure and had to turn back. He reported that he had seen two B-17s collide leaving a cloud bank over the ocean. Both were burning and locked together. He reported no parachutes leaving either plane. It was later found to be "Old Hoss" and "Lovely Lorna." No bodies were ever recovered.

Conditions over Rotterdam were even worse than expected. The clouds were very heavy over the city so locating the docks and pens was nothing short of impossible.

"MeatBall" kept leading the Squadron lower in an attempt to locate the primary target, the Submarine Pens. The squadron was lucky the Germans thought the weather was so bad no one would be flying in it or it would have been a field day for their fighters. The feeble anti-aircraft fire was, at worst, a nuisance.

Incredibly, "MeatBall" started around again. With the clouds and a sharp cross wind Matt was having a hard time imagining them being able to hit the state of New Jersey let alone a Submarine Pen or a Railway yard and docks. Suddenly bombs were falling from "MeatBall" and other planes in the squadron were releasing also.

Matt heard Karlson hollering, "Damn it Captain, they are dropping on the town! They are not even close to the ocean. It's the town. It's Rotterdam. I refuse to drop on the town!" Matt answered him, "I Trust you Karl. We are not dropping. You all heard Karl. We will drop our load in the water on the way back. Shellhammer, you got any idea where we are and how to get us the hell out of here?" The answer came back in a few seconds. "Yes Captain, our direction finding signal is strong from two of the English towers. That gives me a general direction and we should get a triangulation soon which will put us exactly on the mark."

Over two hours later they landed back at Polebrook having released 5000 pounds of high explosives into the ocean through a clear spot in the clouds. Each made a large hole in the ocean which was instantly refilled. It made throwing firecrackers in the water pale by comparison.

That night at the officers club, Matt found the Wing Commander sitting with the Intelligence Officer. They were both drinking rather heavily and he knew Major Wilheit seldom drank. He put his hand on an empty chair. "Do you mind if I join you sir?"

"No, I suppose not Captain Weldon. Sit down. I would ask if you need a drink, but I see you already have one. Something on your mind?"

"Well," Matt said, "yes there is. We seem to have missed the target today. I am afraid we dropped on Rotterdam." The Intelligence Officer abruptly stood up. "Nonsense Captain. The pictures show we hit the Submarine Pens and the docks. Clearly."

"I would love to see the pictures, sir. And the camera that could take them through clouds that thick? Hell, I want one in my bird because half the time I have no idea where my bombs are going. The idea that we can put a 500 pound bomb in a bushel basket from 30,000 feet is good propaganda, but it is Pure Bullshit...Sir!"

The Intelligence Officer jumped to his feet. Matt could see that the fellow was ready to fight. That was, until the he sensed John Smithson standing directly behind him. Matt had seen the big man come over. It had the same effect on the Intelligence Officer that Kong always had in this kind of confrontation. The Intelligence Officer stomped away to the bar, cursing under his breath.

The wing commander lit a cigarette. Matt nodded his thanks to John who smiled and walked back to the table where he sat with Karl and Dave.

"Son," the Commander began, the truth is I have no damn idea where the bombs went. 'Meatball's bombardier said he saw the pens. I took his word for it. I couldn't see shit thru those clouds either. Yes, we probably made a mistake today. I am glad you didn't drop. Lots of others in the wing followed your lead. I am glad they did. I don't know if this is a reward or punishment, but from now on I want *you* to lead the Group on missions. I trust your judgment. And it's not like you are new at this game. You had all those missions with the RAF. I will fly with you sometimes to prove to myself I still have the guts for it. That is all right with you Captain?"

"Sir, it will be an honor. I didn't expect it. And as for having you on board... that will be good for all of us. Having an extra pilot of your quality will be really great."

"Captain Weldon, war is often about mistakes. Today we probably made a bad one. Rotterdam should never have been a target but if it was to be it should have been on a clear day. No clouds.

"You know the Germans made a mistake before we were even in the war. They were winning the Battle of Britain. The RAF was on the ropes. Another week or so and they would have been finished. Then one night a German Bomber accidentally dropped bombs on London. Didn't mean to do it. Hitler had specifically directed them not to bomb London. That opened the door for Churchill to bomb Berlin in return. It was a puny little raid, but Winston knew Hitler couldn't stomach an attack on his Capitol. The Fuhrer shifted the Luftwaffe's target from the RAF to London and the war changed direction."

Oh yes, the war changed direction, Matt thought to himself. And so did my life. I joined the RAF to try and protect Joanna and England. Look at what happened. Today I was on a raid where American bombs were dropped on innocent people. No, my plane didn't drop any and for that I am grateful, but l was there. If not for my bombardier's advice, I probably would have bombed the town too. The good thing is when we pulled away so many followed us....

"Son, what I suppose I am trying to say is that in war mistakes happen. As painful as it may be we simply have to follow orders, do our jobs and pray to God that we are doing the right thing and beg his forgiveness when we are not."

~ ~ ~ ~

Years later Matt learned that the raid on Rotterdam missed the intended targets completely. The bombs fell in residential areas. They killed 320 people and wounded over 400 more. Between 10 and 20 thousand were made homeless. None of this was ever reported in the newspapers or official military reports. It was not until years later that even the Dutch made the knowledge public. They never blamed the Americans. Their blame was heaped on the Germans for being there and making a target of their lovely city.

Mathew Weldon always harbored a more bitter view of his first mission for the 8th Air Force in 'The Maid of Barley" than the forgiving Dutch.

Chapter 15

CLARK GABLE AT POLEBROOK

Less than a month later, Hollywood showed up at Polebrook in the form of Captain Clark Gable USAAF who had been assigned to make a film about being aerial gunners in a combat squadron. It was a natural role for him as he had recently graduated from Gunnery School and was beyond doubt the only gunner anywhere with the rank of Captain.

Matt's first view of him was at a meeting with all the Group's pilots and co-pilots. Major Wilheit stood on the low stage in front of the last mission's briefing map. The man standing beside him wore a trim uniform which carried not only the wings of a flight gunner but also the insignia of a Captain in the United States Army Air Corp, a combination of specialty and rank Matt had never seen before. Like everyone else in the room he had seen the man's face many times before. As a star in the recently released film "Gone with the Wind."

What the Hell, he wondered, is he doing over here? My God! He looks at least fifty. How long has it been? Maybe a year ago that he lost his wife, Carol Lombard, in that plane crash in Nevada. The last I read he was still living in their big old ranch house in Encino and drinking heavily. He finished the film he was working on before her death. Then he tried to join the army as a Private. "Stars & Stripes" and "Life" both reported the Army said no to that idea and sent him to Air Force OCS but I figured it was just a military recruiting publicity stunt. Now he turns up here; Polebrook and the 351st! What's next - Santa Claus dropping bombs out of his sleigh?

The Group Commander instructed the fliers to be seated and began.

"Gentlemen, I am sure the man next to me needs no introduction. Captain Gable has been attached to the 351st to make a film on gunners and gunnery. The assignment has come to him and us from the very top of the command chain, General Hap Arnold. Captain Gable has Captain Andrew McIntyre with him who will be handling the cameras. We will do all we can to assist the Captain in completing his assignment with us. It is worth noting that Captain Gable is a qualified gunner as is Captain

McIntyre. Both passed the gunnery qualifications with high marks. They will be going on missions with the 351st and Captain Gable will fly in either the tail gunner or the top turret gunner position. The Captain wants to fly with different crews and aircraft so he can get varied experiences on film. We will notify the Captains which aircraft they will be flying on the day of the mission. Captain Gable, do you have any comments you would like to make?"

Gable stepped forward and for a moment looked at the fliers in front of him. Matt wondered if he was thinking how young they all looked. He knew that every one of them was at least twenty years Gable's junior.

"Men," he started in that distinctly Clark Gable voice. "I am honored to be allowed to fly with the 351st. I know you are professionals and I will try to live up to the outstanding reputation of the group. Now... not everything we will be filming will be combat flying. As a matter of fact, probably two thirds of our filming will be on the ground. Most of that will involve interviewing those on your crews who are gunners. We are going to talk to them, as a group, later today. I wanted to assure you officers that we are not going to endanger your missions or your aircraft. I believe you will in fact find that McIntyre and I will be an asset when shooting needs to be done. As the Major said, we are both qualified gunners. So when we fly there will be two additional gunners on board if you need us.

"The film will be shown back home so some of your family and friends may have a chance to see you. But, we are not looking for performances, we are looking for reality. We are not shooting a 'war picture,' we are shooting a war. We want the recruits as well as the people back home to see what it is really like over here.

"Thank you and we look forward to working with you." The Wing Commander stepped forward to dismiss them. He stepped down from the stage and caught up with Matt.

"Captain Weldon, I have already informed Captain Gable that he will be working with you to get aircraft assignments for flights whenever he is shooting actual combat footage. I understand you can make no guarantees, but I and the USAAF will appreciate it if you can try not to have him shot down. In my and your case, if he is shot down we might have to become permanent residents in England. The women of America would probably insist we *not* come home. Particularly now that he is single again. So let's keep him alive if that's at all possible."

Matt saw that Gable had walked up behind the Wing Commander and had been listening to at least the end of their conversation. He cleared his throat to get their attention.

"Pardon me, Major, l couldn't help hearing what you said. He looked at Matt for a moment before continuing. "Say, you must be Captain Weldon?" Matt nodded in the affirmative. "Well, I've already heard plenty about you. Rich kid pilot from New York. Daddy heads up a big bank. Flew a bunch of missions for the RAF before we were in the war. Yeah, l heard plenty about you at High Wycombe from General Eaker. He said you were a hot-shot pilot. Told me to look you up. How about that, Kid? They know all about you at headquarters."

Matt picked up on the 'Kid' and decided that he had better let Gable understand he might be younger, but he was in every other way Gable's superior. "Well, we all know about you too. Big Hollywood movie star. 'Gone With the Wind.' They call you 'The King' around Hollywood. Got to be the only guy holding the rank of Captain who can shoot a fifty caliber machine gun in the service. Quite a distinction. Yeah quite!

"But don't worry. I was about to assure the Major I will do my best to protect your ass and to you I am Captain Weldon, not 'Kid.' Is that clear?"

Matt could see Gable burning and made a mental promise to himself to let Gable throw the first punch. Then deck him.

Unexpectedly Gable laughed, "Say... you don't put up with any shit do you?"

Matt found the turnaround so quick he laughed in return before replying, "No more than you, old man."

Gable laughed, stuck out his hand and Matt shook it.

"Well CAPTAIN Weldon, what I really wanted to tell you was I don't need any special protection. Treat me like you would any other gunner in the Group. Assign me where ever you will. Despite my rank. I expect to be treated just like an enlisted man. Sure, I went through OCS but it wasn't my idea. I joined as a Private. Given a choice I would have fought the war as one. The Brass decided I had to be an officer. OK? Good PR for the service. Look, I'm in this just like you. My ass is no more precious than anyone else's. If I'm gonna go, I hope I can take out a few Krauts first. I would like to sit down with you and talk about what I want to do with the film. That be OK with you?"

"Fair enough Captain Gable. Nothing you've said so far is out of line or outside what I can agree to. How about a drink and a talk tonight? There is a decent pub a few miles outside the base and I've got a car. Meet you at the south Gate at nineteen hundred tonight?"

"Sounds good, Ki...Captain Weldon."

Gable was on time and enjoyed the ride over because it was a nice night. A soft gold half-moon was rising and a cool breeze flowed over them. He questioned Matt about how he liked the MG and said he should pick up a car for himself as he expected to be in England for the better part of a year. Then he asked Matt what the gas situation was in England for personally owned automobiles. Matt told him it was very tight, but there were 'ways around it.'

Gable didn't miss a beat, "Like back home, huh? The black market. You can get anything you are willing to pay for. Hell Captain, the black market guys back in America couldn't get a regular job but they are getting rich off this war. It's disgraceful. Not to say I didn't ever buy from them. I did."

Matt and Clark had no sooner entered the "Three Horse Shoes Pub" in Ashton than he began to suspect his choice of this location was really a poor spot for a meeting. Even in a small, out-of-the-way hamlet like this, everyone knew who Clark Gable was. Especially the ladies. What began as a quiet middle of the week crowd soon doubled to what would equal weekend standing-room-only numbers. Fortunately Gable was accustomed to this kind of attention almost any place he went and was quite patient about shaking hands with the men and kissing the ladies on the cheek. Matt sensed that he especially enjoyed kissing the younger ones, but the man seems to sincerely enjoy all of the attention. He played the motion picture actor who is really just a regular guy, very well.

Matt had taken a table as soon as they arrived and ordered one Old Oast House Ale. He noticed Gable had one drink of some sort at the bar. After about twenty minutes, he finally broke away from the people crowded around the bar to join Matt at the table he was holding in the corner near the empty fireplace. At Matt's recommendation they ordered the Shepherd's Pie. Matt ordered second ale while Gable ordered a mixed drink which turned out to be scotch and soda, quickly followed by yet another. He noticed Matt's expression of disapproval when his third drink arrived so quickly on the heels of the second one.

"Hey, don't worry. I never drink the night before I fly. It's an unbreakable rule with me. I'll level with you. I do have a problem with booze at other times. I know it all too well. I never used to. It's in the last year. It's just... well."

When the sentence was left in the air, Matt decided for the good of all the flight crews he would bring up the problem it might cause. Right up front.

"Look, Captain Gable..."

The Captain interrupted him, "Clark...OK...? I can't get used to this damn Captain stuff. It's OK on duty and I understand that... but the rest of the time it's just 'Clark' if you don't mind."

"OK Clark. I understand and to make it fair, 'Matt' will do. As long as it's *just* the two of us. In a group we need to observe all the military formalities."

How long, he wondered, had it been since I was "Ratt" to almost everyone who knew me. Years have passed since I last answered to that name. Now it is always Captain or Captain Weldon. Back with my RAF crew it was usually Number One or Skipper. I wonder where Kong and Fizz are now. Hope they are OK. It's only when I am with Joanna or her family that I am Mathew or Matt. I hope someday I will be just Matt or Mathew to everyone. "The Ratt" died suddenly a long time ago, that first night I saw Joanna and her enchanting green eyes, "the Ratt" was a goner.

"OK Clark. About drinking... I really have to insist that you hold to the rule you have made for yourself. I'm not much of a drinker now, so it is easy for me to lay off the hard stuff. I was a pretty heavy drinker back when I was at Yale. Then I drank way too much, but not since. I was afraid the booze was taking over. Now it's one drink if it's scotch or bourbon or a couple of ales. A little more after a really bad mission with high losses but even then a lot less than most of the other guys. I hate the head I have the next morning. And I don't want anything fogging my mind. I have my crew and a whole lot of other guys to think about. Seeing others drink doesn't bother me...unless it might endanger the crew or the mission. Then it bothers me greatly. My crew knows that. So do the other pilots and crewmen." He looked directly at Gable with the last words. Gable looked away for a moment then returned his eyes to meet the younger man's stare.

"OK Matt. I read you loud and clear.... I am over here to make a movie...err...training film. You have my word about the booze. I can control it. Had to in order to be on the set and get the job done on the last film. 'Somewhere I'll Find You.' Ironic title don't you think? Way too much irony floating around lately."

Matt could tell that Clark was disturbed even getting close to the edges of what was really eating at him. The romance between the man sitting at the table with him and Carol Lombard was already a legend in the closed world of Hollywood and, in a larger sense, America as a whole. Gable even made a film he did not want to make simply to finance his divorce from Ria Langham; the divorce which allowed him to marry Carol. That film was, "Gone with the Wind."

"Clark, I think we both understand why you now hit the hard stuff heavier than you used to. I respect your privacy far too much to get into it. If, however, you find you ever want to talk about It, I will be glad to listen. I have found when it comes to things like this all anyone else can really do is listen. But sometimes having a friendly ear can help.

"I will also tell you that simply being over here may help you. That is if you don't get your ass blown off. On that particular topic, Major Wilheit is right. If anything happened to you we probably couldn't go back home. The women of America would rise up and hang us. I would feel sorry for him. I may not be going back anyway."

Gable broke into his famous grin and told Matt, "Say, you're probably right about that. I suppose we'll just have to keep my ass safe for the two of you. But not too safe OK?" Matt nodded yes then saw Gable's face with a questioning look plastered across it.

"Matt... What you just said, well, it sounds like you're thinking about staying over here. That involve a dame?"

Matt gave Gable an almost shy smile. "No Clark, in this case it involves a lady. Yes, before you ask, she is English. And we are talking about getting married just as soon as I finish my 25 missions. I may stay over here or we may go back to America. That is something we have not really discussed yet. We haven't even... well **you** know. God! She is so beautiful. Before I met her. Well I wasn't at all the guy I am now..."

Gable leaned across the table and lowered his voice. "Yeah you probably acted just like me on that subject. Going to Yale with all those Seven Sisters girls' colleges was probably like Hollywood. You were a good-lookin' guy...oh yeah! A good lookin' guy like you with a rich daddy and all the toys? Don't get me wrong. No jealousy here. Despite the studio bullshit, I had a fairly privileged upbringing. I was *never* a lumberjack. That was something they started in the 'Selling of Clark Gable.' They had to do something since I already had a name. They didn't have to create one. I was born Clark Gable. So they made up stories to turn me into a 'HE MAN.' That stupid poor hardworking lumberjack story among them."

"Yes Clark. You're right. I was mighty loose with the girls in prep school and then in college, oh my God. I went crazy. It was like a candy store. But all that was before..."

"Before you met this one. Right Matt?"

"Yes. Before I met this one."

"Ok Matt, this is from one old dog to a younger one. Keep it that way. Don't mess it up. Any woman who is special enough that a man willingly gives up a candy store for her is 'the one' and that is a once in a lifetime thing."

"Gotcha' Clark... I think we were talking about keeping asses safe but not babying them and all I can tell you is, don't worry. The Luftwaffe will make sure that none of us is kept too safe. They are equal opportunity killers. Privates, Generals, movie stars. All the same in their gun sights."

"Jeez Matt." Gable laughed, "I thought only Hollywood was that tough." He paused for a moment, his eyes serious. "You know some night I might like to talk to you about...well you know. Some night when there won't be a mission the next day. When the weather is so lousy the birds are walking. You know the way Hollywood would do the stage setting. One thing is sure. You will have to drive back **that** night. But not tonight because I need to talk about making a movie which isn't like what Hollywood would make."

By the time the two of them left the pub Matt clearly understood the concept Gable had for his film and felt far more comfortable about the man's ability to function as a working crewmember on a B-17, but still held some concern that his real reason for being in the war might be to join Carol Lombard, the woman he loved, in death. He liked Gable, but intended to watch for any signs that might indicate that what the man told him might not be on the up-and-up. In that event, he intended to pull him off flight duty before anything bad could happen. Matt made a mental note to confidentially ask each pilot he assigned to carry Gable on a mission to report back to him after it was done about Gable's performance and attitude. It was something that the lives of ten other men depended on.

He was sorry Gable had lost Lombard. He could only vaguely comprehend how he would feel or what he would do if he lost Joanna, but knew he had to do everything he could to protect the fliers in the Group. And until he was sure about Gable's reason for joining the AAF, he had to watch him.

When they were in the car on the way back to the base, Gable turned in his direction and said, "You know one of the reasons I didn't want to do 'Gone with the Wind' was because every other film I will ever do is going to be compared to it. I knew it would be that way, but I was so crazy about Carol that I did it anyway. I had to have the money to divorce Ria. She was already bathing in a fortune of Texas Money from a previous marriage, but she wanted to punish me. She knew Carol and I were having an affair, and that was something she had no problem with. But for me to divorce **her**? Oh no!

She claimed she had created me and wanted a return on her investment. Investment, by God, that's what she called me! Well she got it and Carol and I got each other. It cost me but I was the winner. Those were the best years of my life. They were just too damn few of them."

Back at the base, Matt dropped Clark at his Quonset hut and watched him walk somewhat unsteadily away before driving back off base to park his car.

~ ~ ~ ~

The next day Matt watched while Gable carefully set up a shot, getting the background exactly as he wanted it. Then he would bring in the gunner he was interviewing and explain what they would talk about until he knew the gunner was comfortable with his part, his 'lines' as it were and only then would McIntyre start rolling with the shot. Gable was such a good director that often the gunner involved would say, "OK, I'm ready now," thinking what he and Gable were doing was simply a rehearsal, only to find out the shot was finished and 'in the can.'

Over the next week, Gable also interviewed a more limited number of pilots, co-pilots, bombardiers, navigators and engineers to show what the rest of the crew did. He and McIntyre spent endless hours filming inside B-17s. He wanted viewers to see that even though the B-17 looked large from the outside, each crewmember's position was quite restrictive on the inside. He wanted the audience who would view the film to understand that the waist gunners were literally standing back to back and the belly-turret gunner was in his tiny space suspended under the bottom of the B-17 like a sardine in a glass ball. The top turret gunner stood directly between the pilot and copilot and also served as the flight engineer.

Matt knew it was no mistake sending Gable to do the film. That was obvious from the careful way he spent hours doing shots of everything, from where parachutes were located to shots of both empty as well as fully loaded bomb bays and ground crews fueling aircraft. When he returned to the States to put his film together, everything he might need would be available to be spliced in. It was clear to everyone Captain Gable had skill that ranged far beyond performing in front of cameras.

He even received permission to film the briefing for the first mission he would fly. It must have required a very good argument to High

Wycombe Abbey to get permission because that was where the final approval came from. Later when Matt asked how he had pulled it off Gable simply shrugged and replied, "Hell Captain, I simply reminded them that none of this will be seen by anybody for a year or more. By then anything involved will be old news. The target will be dust by then. If not, the 8th Air Force wasn't doing its job very well. I guess they saw it my way."

Captain Dan Stone of "Seventh Inning Stretch" was taking Gable and McIntyre aloft on a mission to Antwerp, Belgium. Matt was informed Gable had six drinks at the "O" Club two nights before the mission, but only one the night before and McIntyre was sitting with him that night. Matt arranged for the Group flight surgeon to check out "Stretch's" crew and found them all fit to fly. That included Gable and McIntyre.

The M.P.s at the door always checked every single pass before allowing anyone into the briefing. No exceptions were made: not even for Clark Gable and his cameraman. The only change Major Wilheit approved beyond a standard briefing was to let McIntyre move from location to location with his camera in order to shoot footage of everything. At one point the cameraman moved a chair to the rear of the room to stand on while shooting. Gable later told Matt it was so the Major would appear to have a stronger jaw line. The public expected that of military officers.

Because flight gear was assigned to specific crew members, Matt had all of Gable's flight gear specially marked in advance of his first flight.

When Gable began collecting his gear the other fliers could hear him laughing loudly because he found every piece of his gear clearly marked "Captain Rhett Butler CSA." Matt stuck his head around the corner of the door and remarked... "Just for you."

Gable grinned broadly. "Say, Captain Weldon, I hope you know this is going back with me when I leave here?"

Matt's answer was easy. "We wouldn't have done it otherwise. Just don't get any holes shot in it. OK? Take care of it and it'll be great for duck hunting on cold mornings when you get back to the States."

Gable came right back with, "Yeah, particularly if you're hunting them at, oh say, twenty thousand feet. I'll bet the only ducks we'll see today will be shooting at us."

Matt had a short reply. "Oh, you can depend on it."

~ ~ ~ ~

On this mission, the 351st had four aircraft turn back with problems before they were near the Continent. The Group's escorting Spitfires pushed as far with the squadron as they dared before turning back to England. Matt knew everyone on the flight dreaded seeing them turn back toward their home bases, because it meant they were now fair game for the Luftwaffe . Sure enough, less than ten minutes later they began diving through the formation.

The tactic the Germans were using was "Slash and Run." Dive at high speed into the formation with guns blazing then run away. It meant they were in the killing zone of the massed firepower from the tightly packed B-17s for only seconds. Even with such a short exposure three of the Messerschmitts and a Focke-Wulf were destroyed in exchange for the two B-17s which had been shot down. Looking out his window Matt saw one of them go; on fire and out of control. Fire began on the starboard wing and quickly spread to the body of the plane. He saw no parachutes.

Soon he heard both the guns in his top turret firing and then his belly turret with its two fifty caliber guns. Next Nelson Sakashiva opened up with his single gun from the left side of the fuselage. That told him the enemy was passing on his left hand side. He looked out the window on his side in time to see the ME109 diving away from them at an opening downward angle. There was a dark line of smoke and burning oil perceptible against the sky from the engine of the German fighter. Matt saw the pilot open his canopy and lazily out step on to the wing. The aircraft started a slow spiral as it moved further away from "The Maid" and the pilot simply slid down the wing into the air. A minute later, his parachute bloomed white against the earth below. It was certain he would be picked up and returned to his base. By the time he was needed again he would have a new plane to fly. It was the advantage the Germans had. If an aircraft of theirs was shot down and the pilot lived, he would fight again. If an American or British aircraft was shot down, they either died or became prisoners of war to stay such until the war ended.

The German aircraft were all pulling away now and every man in each B-17 knew that meant flak would soon have its deadly blossoms opening throughout the sky. The 105mm and 128 mm guns were the worst because they could reach the top of any altitude the B-17 could attain. If the formation flew any lower, then hundreds of additional 88mm canon could also target them.

Matt saw the flak begin opening its hypnotic black blooms half a mile in front of the nose of "the Maid." His eyes swept left and right looking for any space free of the flak explosions that might indicate an area where the pattern was lighter. What he finally saw looked like a narrow path, but it was there. He knew the other pilots would follow his lead, so he adjusted his direction and entered the narrow crease in the anti-aircraft fire. The rest of the 351st followed him. He called on his throat-mike to his bombardier Karl to find their target, either the old G.M. Motor plant or the Ford Motor plant, as soon as he could.

"Now listen up Karl, these gunners aren't dumb. They are going to see this open road and put up a steel 'do not enter sign' pretty quick."

Almost at the same instant the flak gunners began to correct their aim, Karl told him he had the target sighted in the Norden. He was even specific enough to say it was the Ford plant. "Just a couple of minutes and I'll take over." Matt knew Karl would then be flying the "Maid" until he hit the switch that would release all ten of their five hundred pound bombs.

The "Maid" was now constantly buffeted by explosions of flak and Matt was always amazed at what steady nerves and hands bombardiers had to have to be able to make the minute adjustments needed to line up the Nordon so their bombs would fall on target. He felt Karlson take over control of the aircraft and then after a few minutes (which always seemed forever) make the blessed announcement, "Bombs away." Matt felt the aircraft lift sharply higher once lightened of the five thousand pounds of high explosives now falling toward the target below.'

Matt answered with his standard benediction, "Well Hell Karl, it sure took you long enough!"

Karl came back with his now standard reply, "Well, Daddy, if you had got us here earlier we'd be done by now."

Both comments were designed to show they had made it through the first half of the mission in one piece.

Almost every plane in the group survived the bombing and flight back through the remainder of the flak. The lighter-than-expected fighter attacks when the flak had fallen away behind them was a welcome plus.

When they landed at Polebrook, six of the sixty-six who had made the trip to Antwerp did not return. "Old Black Magic" made it back but anyone who saw her condition instantly knew she should not been able to return. The belly gunner was badly wounded. The tail gunner was dead. Matt realized that to say the plane was shot-up was a total understatement. Half her tail surfaces were gone. Matt immediately made a recommendation the rest of the crew be given a fortnight's leave. He requested the pilot and copilot be given the Distinguished Flying

Cross (D.F.C) and the rest of the crew should get the Air Medal with the tail gunner receiving a posthumous D.F.C.

The two weeks off would hopefully settle their nerves enough to fly again. They were also going to need another plane. What was left of "Old Black Magic" could only be used for spare parts and there would be few enough of those. The same could have been said of her crew.

Dan Stone and "Seventh Inning Stretch" got back with a few flak holes, but with the crew largely uninjured. After the debriefings, Dan found Matt and took him aside to fill him in on the one crew member who had a minor injury as well as on his performance.

"Well Captain, as near as I can tell Captain Gable performed well. He was noticeably nervous when we left but when the fighters started coming in everyone said he settled right down. He got some shots at the Jerry's and his cameraman said they had some really good film. The waist gunners said he was cussing like, well like our guys do, when he was shooting. He didn't claim any hits, but he said he thought he scared them a little. On the way back, when there was no shooting, he seemed in a good mood and kept the other gunners laughing at some Hollywood stories. To sum up, he is welcome to fly with us anytime."

"Thanks Captain. That takes a load off my mind. I just wanted to be sure he could fit in as part of a crew. Being from Hollywood and all."

Stone looked at Matt a moment before saying. "Sure, if you say so chief. But if it had been dumb ole me, I would have probably wondered what effect losing Carol Lombard might have had on him. But then I only went to Michigan State while you are a Yale man."

"You are right, Stone. A highly educated guy like me, I would have never worried about that. Not officially anyway," Matt grinned.

"Hey, there is one thing. Gable got mild frost bite on his right hand. His gun jammed so he took off his heavy glove to clear it. He left it off and just had the light glove on that hand for a few minutes. I wouldn't plan on sending him up again for a week or so. I told him to check with the surgeon about it. It might earn him a purple heart. I'll put him in for one if you want me to. I know it's kinda iffy."

"Dan, go ahead and put in the paperwork. Most of us are going to have way too many chances at one. His first flight and he got excited and made an honest mistake for the good of the plane and crew. Yeah, put it in. I'll approve it and get Wilheit to sign off. Let's face it; the Big Brass will love it. What great publicity in the papers back home. Gable probably won't like it though. I'll let him know it's legit and that it's good for the war effort. That will make it OK with him. Yeah, let's do it."

The next day Matt found Gable filming a scene with a tail gunner. The two were standing below the tail gunner's position at the rear of the plane. Matt stood out of the shot and looked up proudly at the huge upright tail carrying the large white letter "J" inside an even larger black triangle to identify it as part of the 351ˢᵗ Bomber Group. He walked over to wait under the shade of the wing while Gable finished his shots with the tail gunner. He was once again impressed with how at ease and natural the man was in situations like this. The young gunner seemed to be sincerely grateful to be included in the film and Gable was smiling that big glowing grin of his at the young man. They finally shook hands and Gable walked over to where Matt was standing. His right hand was covered with a thin white cotton glove. He saw Matt looking at the hand and gave an embarrassed grimace.

"Sure...sure, they told me a million times about frostbite but when your .50 Caliber jams and you've got a decent shot at a bogey, well I guess I got excited and forgot. Problem was I left the heavy one off for several minutes. Just had on the thin one. A lesson learned the hard way as they say, but learned none the less. On the good side, I think I got a round or two into him. He turned sharply away from the flight is all I can report for certain.

"No real damage done to the hand. Be as good as new in a few days. The surgeon did a good job but told me to stand down for a week or so."

Matt smiled. He could tell Gable was jazzed. He remembered the high after he had lived through his first mission. It made it easy to think, for a short while, that the rest of the missions would be the same. The fear came back when the German fighters returned and the flak started opening its deadly black roses in the garden of the sky. The high only existed after the very first flight. That one and the twenty-fifth flight, but few men got to experience the latter.

"Clark, I am glad you didn't get any serious damage to your hand. Other than that, how was your first combat mission? Was it what you expected?"

Clark considered the question then surprised Matt with a question of his own, "Do you mind if we film this? I hadn't thought about doing it, but this might make a great segment in the film. Clark Gable's first mission, while that first flight is still fresh? Would you mind?"

"No Clark, not at all. Just tell me what to do and I'll be glad to do it."

Gable sent a sharp whistle in the direction of his cameraman and when he walked over gave him a quick idea of what he wanted to do. Matt heard McIntyre say, "Wow! That's a great idea chief."

"Captain, you'll be playing the part I normally take and asking questions of me. No script, just play it naturally. Just ask any questions you want but start with the one you just asked. Introduce yourself and me then just go ahead. We can cut out anything that doesn't work later. McIntyre will start us off."

McIntyre walked in front of the camera which was mounted on a tripod with a "Clacker," announced the scene number and other data then walked behind the camera and nodded. Matt looked at the camera and began, "I am Captain Mathew Weldon, a pilot of the 351st United States Army Air Force Heavy Bomber Group. I am here with Captain Clark Gable. The Captain is attached to the 351St here at Polebrook, England as a gunner. He has recently completed his first mission with us. Captain, would you share your impressions of that first mission with us?"

"Yes, thank you Captain Weldon." He turned from looking at Matt to full face toward the camera. Matt knew it was a close-up shot.

"Until you have flown on a B-17, you cannot imagine the power pilots like Captain Weldon take into the air. The feeling of the aircraft when you are flying is amazing. You can feel those four huge engines down to your very bones. It reminds you of the power America can bring to bear on her enemies. I was surprised just seeing the large number of aircraft filling the sky around us when we formed up to head to Europe and our target. The aircraft fly in a V formation scientifically designed to give maximum coverage for the Group from all eleven of each plane's fifty caliber machine guns. Each gunner and his weapons are critical to the protection of the formation as a whole.

"The first emotion I had was worry that I might let the rest of the crew down. That was mixed with worry for my personal safety. It is natural when anyone goes into combat that there is a personal kind of worry about that. Nothing wrong with it. But when the time comes, you just do your job. It is what we Americans have always done. You see that is what it is all about; doing your job. You are a part of something bigger than yourself. The crew and beyond the crew, the Wing and past that our country... America... America! That is what will ultimately defeat this evil of Nazi Germany and Imperial Japan.

"Sure you get afraid when it seems every bullet is aimed right at the tip of your nose, but that goes away and you do your job and you get so into the job you don't have time to be afraid any longer. The job gets you through. Don't get me wrong though, you're always glad to be back. Oh yeah. Back on the ground in England feels real good. But so does getting to shoot at the Krauts. We know the job we are doing will shorten this war and get it over with so we can go back to a peaceful civilian life.

"That is pretty much what I felt and saw on my first flight Captain Weldon."

Gable waited a moment and said, "CUT!"

Matt and he shook hands. "Thanks Matt. I think that will be good in the film. You guys are all being really great sports about this. I know in some ways it is a nuisance, but you are all being really helpful."

"Clark, I won't say it's not a change for the Group, but that's not a bad thing. In fact I think it is really good. It breaks the tension.

"Your performance on the mission was quite good. Matter of fact, Captain Stone said you would be a good addition to any crew. Said you kept the guys entertained on the flight back. By the way, he is putting you in for a Purple Heart because of your hand."

"Say... I don't think that is right. No, I made a stupid mistake. It was my fault that I got frostbite. You aren't going to approve it are you Matt?"

"Yes Clark. Matter of fact I am. Sure it was your mistake. I fully agree. But it happened under the stress of combat. Let's say a fellow in the army lets his ass stick up too high and takes one through the keister. Well it was his mistake, but he gets a purple heart. A few more minutes with the gloves off and you lose fingers. Worse still if your oxygen mask freezes up, you die. You don't complain about the Purple Heart then 'cause you can't and you are sure going to get a purple heart then... Posthumously.

"Setting that aside, it will be good P.R. for Uncle Sam in the papers back home. 'Captain Clark Gable awarded Purple Heart for Wound received in Combat.' Look Clark, you happen to be an inspiration for lots of folk back in the States. So take the medal when it comes through. Do it for the folks back home. It's legit. And also do it a little bit for someone who would be proud of you for what you did up there. OK?"

"OK Matt. I get it. You put up a hell of an argument. Good thing you aren't a lawyer. You'd never lose a case. Thanks for reminding me why I'm here. I really am here for two of us. Hers was a pretty high standard for me. I intend to do my best while I am here to live up to it."

They walked side by side in silence. Matt could see that he was deep in thought. Gable finally veered away and headed back toward the flight line while Matt turned off to go over to headquarters.

He stopped and glanced up at the American flag flying outside. After a few moments he went inside the large metal clad building. He had noticed there was a dark cloud bank coming in from the east. The report from the "Weather Boys" had said no one would be flying missions for at least four or five days. It would be good to be able to get away and spend a day or two with Joanna while the weather was bad.

~ ~ ~ ~

During the time the bombers were grounded, repair crews could patch up planes badly in need of help and the fliers could patch up spirits equally in need of repair.

Nine missions down and sixteen to go... God willing.

Matt was able to reach Joanna by telephone at the House at Number 37 Eaton Square. He could tell from the tone of her voice that she was very tired, but she did sound brighter when she knew it was him.

"Heavens Mathew, it is so good to hear your voice. How are you doing dearest?

It was always the way she started any conversation with him. He always had to assure her he was well before they could carry on. "Yes Joanna. I am just fine. But the weather is turning nasty so we won't be flying for several days. I thought I might come down for two days. What does it look like for you?"

"Oh Mathew, that is wonderful. I can swap out with one of the other girls on my shift at the hospital. Is that tomorrow and the next day or day after tomorrow and the next day?"

"Tomorrow and Saturday. I have to be back on Sunday in case the weather breaks early. Let's plan on going out Friday night or Saturday night or both. That is if you can find something you would enjoy doing.

"Sweet Joanna, I am so looking forward to seeing you. I miss you so very much. I have been reminded how precious what we have with each other is, quite often recently."

"You mean being such 'Good Friends.' Oh Mathew, I have tried to make it clear we can be so very much more than *just friends* now."

"Oh God. Joanna. It is hard enough for me not to make love to you without you saying that. I am determined when we finally are together and make love we will be married. I love you with my entire heart, but I want to be finished with my missions. I want us to really do this right, not the way it always was for me before. I do not want anything I did in the past to carry over to us. When it happens I want us to know it is special and forever. You always say 'forever' and that is how it should be."

"Mathew, are you afraid you might feel differently afterward if we did that now?"

"No Joanna. I am afraid you'll find out what a lousy lover I am and say 'forget it.'"

"Mathew you are incorrigible. I've read your reviews remember? They were at least *pretty* good. Most of the girls gave you a 'C'. One C+. We decided to throw out the 2 F's. Remember? And I'm sure you can improve. Particularly with a superior partner."

"Joanna, you wouldn't by any chance be teasing me would you? No not you. You are always far too serious. You have got to learn to make light of things more. We must find something that you can make fun of."

Matt heard her laughing quietly in his ear and asked, "Or have you already found something or someone perhaps? Me?"

"Oh Mathew my love, is our whole life together going to be this much fun? If so we will indeed have an enchanted lifetime. How did I ever doubt you were the one? The West Wind kept telling me *you were.*"

"Boy Joanna, that is one smart wind. It's not full of hot air. Always listen to that wind."

After a few moments of silence he asked, "Are you well? You sounded tired when I first called."

"Yes love, I'm all right but you're right I am tired. Just got in from St. Bart's a short while ago. I did a twelve hour shift today. They are bringing in boys from all over. And God Mathew, some of them are in awful shape. Not just shot. Many are badly burned, usually sailors, or torn up by artillery fire. I hate to say this, but I now know there are worse things than dying. Some of the burn cases well, it's hard to tell they are human. They can't stand to be touched. Even narcotics don't really stop the pain. They simply moan and moan and moan until they die.

"Many of the others are so very brave. They are ruined but they tell me they are doing well. Trying to spare my feelings. Sometime I have to just walk away and cry. It is all such a waste. Sometime we get a German or an Italian in. When you see them in that shape, it is hard to remember we are supposed to hate them. That they are our enemy. Like ours, they are little more than boys.

"So...Yes Mathew, I am very tired and I need to see you so badly. I will sleep tonight and dream of seeing you tomorrow. Good night my love and goodbye for now."

He told her goodnight and hung up. He could hear how tired she was and noticed she sounded rather like a sleepy sad little girl near the end of their call. It reminded him he was not the only one paying a high price for this war.

Matt picked up the papers granting his 48 hour pass and stopped by the O. Club for ale. He saw Smitty and Karl were already at a table and joined them. They were always a quiet pair even though Karl was a joker when flying on a mission. Matt thought it was probably the way he handled stress.

"So boys, what are your plans now that we have some down time?"

The two of them exchanged glances. Then Karl answered him. "Hell Matt, we don't have time for our first choice, going home to the States and if we did we wouldn't come back. So we thought we'd go into London. You know go to the theatre or a library. Perhaps a museum. You *know*... the usual."

Matt laughed until his sides hurt. When he finally got his breath, he looked from one to the other before saying, "Gonna go to London and get laid, huh?"

Karl came right back with, "Sure but only after the theatre or the..."

"OK Karl, I get it. You're both going to try and find classy hookers and actually leave the bedroom a time or two. Well, I appreciate that you are trying to improve your... err... mind."

"Well Matt, you know what they say, 'when the little head is happy, the big head is happy'."

"Good luck boys, but try to see neither head gets a headache. I need both you guys flying, not in the infirmary with anything social. Have you guys seen Clark tonight?"

This time it was Smithson who answered, "No, he left for London late afternoon. I know he wants to shop for a car. Said he was tired of using jeeps. We are supposed to meet him tomorrow night at the Claridge Hotel about six. He said ask you to come by if you aren't busy or at least drop by, if you can, even if you are busy. He wants to meet that lady of yours. In fact we all do."

Clark asked some of the guys from "Seventh Inning Stretch" to be there too. He and Dan Stone seem to have hit it off. How about it, Matt?"

It was several minutes before Matt finally said, "I'm seeing Joanna and we don't get to spend as much time together as we want, but I will ask her if she would mind being around you reprobates for a few minutes. But if anyone forgets she is a lady and gets out of line ...well it'll be pistols at dawn for two and coffee for one." He grinned at John Smithson and continued, "And if they shoot John here, then they'll have me to deal with."

His co-pilot nearly strangled on his drink. "Don't worry Matt. I can hold and shoot a .50 caliber machine gun like most guys can shoot a little bitty dueling pistol and bein' from the south dueling is in my blood. It's simply viewed as a form of light entertainment down under the Spanish moss draped magnolias. But never at sunrise. No one gets up anything like that early down my way. No, we prefer it under a full moon. The ladies in hoopskirts look so much better in soft moonlight. Actually in or out of hoopskirts they look best in moonlight. Now that I think about it definitely out of their hoopskirts. Yesss Sirrr."

By now half of Matt's ale was gracing the table top so he gave up trying to drink any of it. "OK boys, I give up. You are really in a mood tonight. I'm going to get some sleep because I want to leave early in the morning. It's going to be about two hours down to London, if l am lucky. Tell Clark if we don't get there, don't wait. I hope we can, but I will leave it to Joanna. Hell, I get to spend way too much time with you jokers anyway. If I don't see you, have a great time. I would say don't do anything I wouldn't, but that would be way too restrictive... Good night guys."

Chapter 16

"LISBON STORY"

Matt was at the "chow hall" shortly after it opened. The powdered eggs were up to their usual disgusting standard, but the chipped beef with white gravy was at least edible. And they've yet to find a way to mess up the toast. But if I know the military, they are working hard on doing it. Thank God the coffee is pretty good. Coffee, Cigarettes, Booze and pretty dreadful food. I wonder who is getting all that great food the magazines say we are supposed to be eating. I would say the Generals, but I have eaten with them and theirs doesn't seem much better. And we seem to be *winning* the war? Man! Things must really be awful on the other side.

Matt walked out the gate to the small garage where he kept his little MG. Around the small tin building was the usual collection of older autos and farm machinery which the mechanic managed to keep in repair. The cows and sheep scattered along fences leading away from the base watched him. They no doubt wondered why they had lost part of their pasture to these men and the huge noisy birds they crawled inside of and flew away in and perhaps noticed that fewer always came back than had left.

Matt backed the MG out of the garage. The mechanic was up, but still sleepy-eyed. He did wake up enough to put fifteen gallons of precious petrol in the tank, and then gave Matt a slip of greasy paper with two names and addresses in London.

"Lad if you need more petrol see one'a of these two blokes. Ay should be able to fix you up wad enough to get back up ere."

Well, he thought, it's not like the garage in London. No polishing the car 'til it looked like a jewel or greasing around the convertible top to prevent leaks. No one kept the chrome so clean it looked like freshly polished silver, but at least he has fuel for sale and knows where to get more. He does keep the car tuned to perfection. All things considered, not too bad. And there is a war on. I wonder if the petrol is perhaps making its way off the base. Best not to know, then I don't feel guilty about using it.

His auto's radio was able to pick up only one station. Through the static, the song 'Stardust' was playing. It was one of the many songs he remembered as a standard with all of the Big Bands at dances he had taken so many girls to when he was in prep school and later at Yale. The dancers always knew when the band was about to take a break, because they would switch from Swing to either "Stardust" or a song like it. A slow dance so the boys could hold their girls close and tight. Then, when the evening was ending, the band would play "Moon Light Serenade" or "Thanks for the Memory." They always played a song which seemed somehow bitter-sweet. The dancers all knew the music was ending, even if it only meant the dancing was ending. Matt usually was moving on to the seduction of his date, but even to him the last song of the evening by those wonderful orchestras was a bit sad. It was the knowledge that a night of your life was ending which could never be recaptured.

God in heaven...we were all so totally innocent in those days. No responsibilities beyond school. No real understanding there was anything waiting out there beyond what we *wanted* our futures to be. No idea that the old men were carelessly stacking the deck we would be dealt from.

What am I dreaming about? All that was a long time ago. Soft beds and symphonies. Dance bands and dancing. Fine food and flying just for the thrill of it. Classes in English, history and math. Playing football on crisp fall weekends and all the fraternity parties afterward. Leaves falling on lakes in Upstate New York and duck hunting with Dad. Was the world ever really that secure? That safe? Or did we all just want to believe it was? We were too busy having fun to see the storm coming.

My God! America came out of the Depression just to have this damn War come along. But no War, no Joanna. I would still be back in America. Finished with Yale and doing what? Well, probably in the service anyway. Yes- probably flying. Most likely fighters instead of bombers. Still chasing women on leave. A quick tumble with British dames. Just like Karlson and Smitty. But no Joanna. No love and knowing I am doing something worthwhile. I hate doing what I do, but it has to be done. I hope to live through it and I hope there will be enough left of the world I knew so she and I can enjoy it together. If l don't survive? Well I hope I do, but that is up to forces beyond me. Joanna is sure I will. I have to focus on that.

He had to slow several times for convoys of large American-built trucks full of soldiers. He was seeing more and more of them every month. When he was headed on a mission and the weather was clear, he could look down from the air and all of England seemed covered with American-made supplies and war materials. Mile after mile covered with large wooden crates, tanks, trucks and brown or olive-drab tents and buildings. All of the ports were filled with Liberty ships and more anchored off shore waiting to unload.

Roosevelt, Churchill and Stalin had finally reached an agreement that the second-front on the French Coast would come in 1944. Stalin didn't like it. He had pushed for 1943 but had, in the end, agreed on a major attack by the forces of England, Canada, Australia and America somewhere else. Churchill was pushing for an attack against Italy now that the African campaign was won. He said Italy was "The soft underbelly of Europe." The British and American troops from North Africa were available for a limited attack. It wouldn't be in France however. Not in 1943. It simply couldn't be France. Not yet. The buildup for that had to be much larger before the invasion could be launched. The planners knew it must succeed the first time. To be driven out of France and go back would be nearly impossible. If they were pushed out it would take years of preparation before a return could be attempted. There was already talk about upping the number of missions' crews had to fly and the military was considering lengthening terms of enlistment for the Army and Navy personnel in anticipation of a future landing in France.

Yes, he thought to himself, a landing on the coast of France must succeed. The casualties would be high. The Germans have already had three years to prepare their defenses. I have talked to a few fliers who have gone on missions to photograph the coastal emplacements. They aren't allowed to see the photos, but they see the defenses from pretty low altitude and they say they wouldn't want to try to fight past them. They also say the Krauts have defenses in the water to prevent boats from even landing the soldiers ashore. Just getting onto the beaches will be hard enough, but it will be even harder to move inland.

When the landing finally happens, it will be hell on earth. That day will require overwhelming numbers of both men and material to take the expected casualties and keep battering the German positions until they finally collapse. That day will be worse than flying through heavy flak and that has always been my idea of hell, only in the sky. Fire and steel flying everywhere. A random harvest of death. No way of knowing when death will come or to whom. Just an explosion and another plane gone along with eleven men.

I hate to even think of that, times a thousand or ten thousand. This somewhere on the beaches of France. The dead will be bobbing in the water and the beaches running red. That is what they are saying it will be like on that day. Young guys. Younger than I am, who won't live to see the sun set on that deadly day.

Sons and fathers from all over America who will never again see their mothers or wives or girls or their children... Boys who will never dance to the Glen Miller or Harry James bands or Benny Goodman's wonderful "Stardust" again. They will never get to go to college or finish it. Never again go duck hunting or park by a lake with their girls on a Saturday night to neck and maybe more. Never have children. One of them might have cured polio or cancer. Such a damn waste, all of it. Yet it has to be done. No choice. If there ever was a choice it passed a long time ago. Before the first bullet was fired in Poland. Before I left America for England. Before I was out of prep school. That always brings me back to the big "if." If it had been different, I would never have met Joanna. Would I trade all of this not happening for her? No, I suppose I love her enough to see half the world burn and all the death and destruction, even perhaps my own, to have known and loved her.

I never understood how someone could kill and say it was out of love, but now I am doing exactly that. In my case I can't use the 'God and Country' defense. With me it is green-eyed Joanna and the crew I fly with. Nothing much matters beyond that.

Not that God isn't involved. I sure pray enough on a mission, but even then I am asking for our plane to be spared so I can live to be with her. So far we have always made it back. God or random luck or fate? I can't say for certain. But I always say a prayer. Between the RAF and the USAAF I have flown 28 missions. Had a couple of crewmen with minor injuries but no one seriously hurt. At least not so it showed, but I know we are paying for it, a little cut here and a small bruise there. I know I am bleeding and the rest are too. Just on the inside where we can hide it.

On the radio he heard Guy Lombardo performing 'The Way You Look Tonight.' That is an old song I remember from my first year at Yale. Kong, Fizz and I went out to the Band Box. Guy Lombardo was playing there with his orchestra. Kong had a little black Ford run-about which was barely big enough for him and his girl Amy. Fizz and I picked up his date first. She was a pretty little thing and smart as a whip. Dressed all in blue which went with her soft corn-flower blue eyes. I remember she had the blackest hair l had ever seen. It was a sleek velvety black. Then we picked up my date. There was plenty of room for the four of us in the Duesenberg. It was a nice evening so I had the top folded down.

That was during my blond period. My date's name was Suzanne Swift. She was a knock-out with a figure almost beyond belief. Back then it was a girl's body which really counted with me though this girl's face was really beautiful too. But the body? That she had in Spades. The Duesenberg was cruising along with its just under four hundred horse power eight cylinder super charged engine's throaty roar. Burned lots of gas and at ten cents a gallon, she was expensive to operate but her supremacy made her worth every penny. Duesy was such an elegant yet powerful automobile, everyone looked at us as we passed by. We were almost to the Band Box when Suzanne leaned toward me and in as sexy a voice as I've ever heard whispered, "Hey Ratt, I know what you are thinking. Well, you can forget it. I am not that kind of girl despite the way I may look." I found out later, she really meant what she said. Matt found himself laughing into the wind at the vivid memory of that night.

The two of us had a great time dancing. She was a wonderful dancer. Suzanne could do all the newest dance steps and so could I. When we slow danced to "The Way You Look Tonight," simply holding her in my arms was an experience never to be forgotten. That night, the two of us danced until we could hardly stand. She was an incredible partner. We danced to everything from the Lindy Hop, Suzie-Q, Swing, Jive and Jitterbug to Tangos and Waltzes. She knew how to laugh too, a lilting, musical laugh. We were both laughing and dancing. That night it was wonderful just being young and alive, believing we had all the good things in life waiting for us. The band finally played its last song at twelve thirty. It was "Begin the Beguine" and we were all still on the dance floor.

I found myself constantly surprised at how smoothly my big friend Kong could dance. He and Amy danced so well together you forgot Kong's size. Big men can't usually dance as well as he did and Amy matched him step for step. They were wonderful dance partners in spite of how much smaller she was. I knew they were very much in love

Even Fizz was a good slow dancer, though a bit tangle-footed when jitter-bugging. I was certain all six of us were sorry the night was ending. Nights such as that one was are much too rare in a lifetime

We wandered out into the darkness holding hands with our dates. By that time of evening it had grown cooler so we put our jackets over the girl's shoulders and talked for a while about how good the music had been and which Band Leader headed the best orchestra for dancing. We finally said good night to Kong and Amy and watched as his little Ford roadster disappeared into the velvet darkness. Then, under a million distant stars and a golden harvest moon, the four of us walked over to Duesy. Fizz and I put the top up so the girls would be warmer and headed back toward town.

His girl was in a hurry to get back to her dorm. She was worried it was already past curfew so we dropped her off first. Fizz walked her to the door and I saw him lean in for a kiss. They held it for a moment and I heard her say, "Call me," as she ran inside. Fizz was smiling broadly as he came back and climbed into the rear seat alone. I ran him back to Yale. He was whistling happily as he walked toward our building.

I asked Suzanne if she would like to do something else. She smiled and said, "Want to and will are two different things and it's time I was back at my dorm too. Actually I am also late. It has been a lovely evening. I enjoyed it very much, but Matt we are looking for two different things out of life. What you would want to do is something I will only do with someone I love and who loves me.

"You are a beautiful young man. Good looking. Very intelligent. Smooth. And a *very good* dancer. In ancient Greece they would have said you had been favored by all of the gods. In many ways you have been blessed. Yet you are missing something.

"You are like the perfect vase. But like a vase, everything about you is on the outside. You are still empty inside. Perhaps someday you will find something to fill that hollow space, and then you will truly be complete. My wish for you is that it does happen. It will be such an awful waste if it does not. I so hope you find that missing part. And Matt, sex alone can never do it. Love has to be there too."

I drove her back to Vassar. I knew I was sulking because of what she had said about me. I didn't speak another word to her on the way. She got out of the car, then walked around to my side and leaned in. She looked at me for a moment, reached out and gently pushed the comma of hair which always fell down on to my forehead back into place. Then, to my surprise, Suzanne kissed me. And what a kiss it was! A long, passionate, unforgettable kiss. When she finally pulled away I asked her why she did that. If I was such a waste, what was the kiss for?

Her answer shut me up. "That, my dear, is so you will know what you missed. What might have been between us." A slap would have been less painful. She walked slowly away and out of my life. Her hair glowing in the moonlight, almost as if it were sprinkled with stardust.

It has only been recently that I have fully understood what she was telling me that night. Now I finally know. If she had been wrong about me, I would have telephoned her and asked her out again. I also know now she *would* have gone out with me. It was a door she hadn't really closed. I had.

But she wasn't wrong. I never called.

It was not until years later on the night I told Joanna that I was sorry for my behavior that I began to discover something *was* beginning to fill the emptiness. I was becoming more than just a child pretending to be a man. A man Joanna let herself love and who was able to love her in return.

Still I wonder what became of Suzanne Swift and all the other beautiful young girls and fresh faced young men that danced to the Big Bands, went to school, and spent long summer days swimming and sailing, and soft summer nights dancing and laughing and loving. Where did all the dreams they once had go? Where is all that innocence now?

Will there ever be another generation like we were? So naive and young one moment, then London is bombed, or Pearl Harbor, and suddenly we are in a war. And nothing we ever learned in school, on football fields, dance floors and bedrooms had ever prepared us for that. It became learn quickly or die. Become as good as or better than our enemy and that enemy was already very good. Now we were as good and getting better but at a price. One paid in blood, spirit and lost yesterdays. Young men who were no longer young and had only obscene gallows humor at which to laugh and who sought love in many stranger's beds.

As soon as the London suburbs came into sight, Matt stopped at one of the red kiosk telephone boxes and dialed Joanna's number. Mrs. Townsend answered on the second ring. "Hello. Barton residence. How may I assist you?"

"Mrs. Townsend, this is Mathew Weldon. Is Joanna up?"

"Oh Mr. Weldon. I have heard her up but she hasn't been down for breakfast yet. Hold on, I hear her coming down the stairs."

Matt heard Joanna asking who was on the telephone and Mrs. Townsend saying his name. The voice that came back on the telephone was hers. "Good morning Mathew. Where are you dear?"

"Well I'm past Mill Hill on my way in. Probably ten miles out. Maybe a half hour or a bit more. Shall I come on over Joanna or do you need more time to get ready? I can stop and get coffee."

"No! You come right on over. We can have coffee here. I'll ask Mrs. Townsend to make it while I get ready. I don't want us to waste a minute."

"I don't either Joanna. I was hoping I could come over now. I miss you whenever I am away more than 24 hours."

She laughed in his ear. That wonderful voice that still reminded him so much of the classic and husky voice of the Swedish actress Greta Garbo. Such a very sexy voice. "Mathew once we are married you will have to get used to not being away from me that long. I go through withdrawal pangs once you are gone only 12 hours."

He did his really awful Bogart imitation, talking out of one side of his mouth with a slightly slurred New York accent, "OK sweetheart twelve hours it is. By the way sweet-heart we've been invited for drinks tonight by a Hollywood pal of mine. A Captain in the good ole 8th Air Force. A guy named Clark Gable. Do you want to go? I told him it was up to you."

"Matt, is that Clark Gable as in 'Gone with the Wind' Clark Gable? Of course it is. I read he was over here and flying while making a film for the Air Force. I have tickets for a play. It starts at 8:00... oops it starts at 20:00 hours for those of you who think in military time and after that maybe a drink.

"And no argument, you are staying here tonight and tomorrow night. You remember what a real bed is like? And I want you to suffer, knowing I am just down the hall. Worse still, I'm there by your choice. But yes, I would love to meet Mr. Gable if we can fit it in. What time would we be able to meet him?"

"I understand around 6:30 at the Claridge, Joanna. We won't stay long. Will that work with going to the theatre?"

'The Claridge? Yes, definitely he **is** a big movie star. As busy as the Claridge is, only a big star could get in there on less than a month's notice. Tell you what. Hang up the phone and get your rear on over here. We can work it out face to face. I love you. Hurry. I need a kiss from my favorite Yank."

Matt replied with a smile and a simple, "Bye."

The drive through London was always a sad reminder that many of the places he had gone with Joanna were either destroyed or badly damaged.

Queen's Hall, he thought. What a shame. Half blown down, only the facade left. Hollowed out by a German Bomber with incendiary bombs back in '41. I hope they will rebuild it. It was magical hearing Debussy with her that night in '39. The orchestra was wonderful. So was running under the trees dripping with rain and Joanna beside me. Will we ever find a night like that again? Will anyone in the world *ever* have a night like that? Will anyone be left who is young and innocent enough to feel that way? Has that kind of magic between two people been erased from the world?

I think that was the night we knew we loved each other. We hadn't said it yet. Not in so many words, but after that night we both knew. If you could take a single memory into whatever comes after this life, for me it would be that night. She was so very beautiful. And the world was still young.

Later he passed the Cafe' de Paris another iconic reminder of that night. Its striped canvas awning sagged nearly to the ground on the bent metal supports. **Closed**. Since two German bombs had penetrated all five floors of the building above to explode in the basement Club, also in '41. What had become of the young couple to whom we sent a bottle of Champagne? The maître d' had said they seemed deeply in love. Had they survived? Had the love they felt that night?

He was glad to finally get to the Belgravia section of London and turn onto Eton Square. The houses were still quite impressive, but after three years of war were beginning to show signs of wear. White paint was not high on production lists. Colors like olive drab were taking precedence. But Matt was still delighted to see the house. He drove the MG up the drive and set the parking brake because the drive sloped downward to the street. He was not even out of the car before Joanna was down the steps in the rain hugging and kissing him. Her kisses always left him slightly light headed. An intoxicated feeling yet so pleasant.

"Oh Mathew darling, I have been missing you so badly. Whenever are you going to get this dreadful War over so we can be together all the time? Can't you find out where that miserable Hitler is hiding and simply go bomb him? Wouldn't that end it sooner?"

"Joanna ... You must know this is no more fun for me than it is for you. If I knew where the son of a bitch was, believe me he'd be dead before dark.

"The big problem is going to be cleaning up my language after this is all over. It is so bad, l should not be allowed around someone as civilized as you."

"Don't apoligize Mathew. My language has suffered too. The things I see around the hospital have me either praying or cursing most of the time. My vocabulary has certainly expanded in the very worst sense of the word. Let's go into the house. The coffee is ready and we even have a little milk and sugar and, if you can believe it, Mrs. Townsend has made scones just for you. Yes, I think she has been hiding the fact that she secretly likes you too. I know she worries about you. When I said something about that, her reply was, 'Well it takes some of the load off you and Haiku having to worry about him all by yourself, dudn't it?' "

"Joanna we need to get you in out of this rain. I could stand here with you in my arms with it pouring down on us all day, but you are getting soaked." She put her arm through his as they went up the stone steps and inside. He was glad to see her smiling.

Matt had barely settled at the small table in the breakfast nook by the bay window when he felt Haiku rubbing against his ankles. He reached down and sat her on his lap. She looked up at him with her large green eyes and greeted him with a silent, pantomimed, "Meow." He could both feel and hear her whispered purring. Her fur was like thick soft velvet and she had not looked away from his face since he picked her up.

Joanna brought his coffee to the table and smiled at the two of them. "I suppose you know I will have to marry you or my cat... make that our cat... would never forgive me. And damn it you had better stay safe for neither of us would ever love anyone else. You are it and we are depending on you. Do you hear me? Do you Mathew?"

Except for her brother's memorial service, he had seldom seen Joanna cry, but she was crying now. Her wonderful green eyes were clouded with tears. Yet she was smiling. Smiling at him and crying. He sat Haiku gently on the floor and rose to hold her while she cried. When he could feel that she was no longer crying, he held her at arm's length and gently wiped the tears from her eyes and cheeks.

"You two shouldn't worry. I have everything to live for. At least I do now. Until I met you I had no idea what life was about. I thought it was about just playing games. Completely selfish games. But now I know that just being alive with you is wonderful. If I can simply live the rest of my time with you. That is really all I ask out of life now. To be with you for as long as I live."

Joanna turned away and walked to the bay window. She stood silently for a few minutes and when she finally turned back to him she was smiling and her eyes were dry and clear.

"I'm sorry Mathew. Of course nothing is going to happen to you. The West Wind has told me you are going to be all right. And I believe Haiku would know. She fancies herself my 'familiar' and your 'protector' and she is not worried. I would sense it if she were. So let's just have a great two days. Now tell me about this Clark Gable. What do you think about him, hmmm...?"

Together they spent late morning and early afternoon roaming antique shops and old book stores. In one of the antique shops they found a magnificent five carat chrome tourmaline pendant set in white gold which Matt bought for her as an early birthday present. She found a gold Sovereign with St. George and the dragon on one side and Young Queen Victoria on the other.

"Okay now Joanna, l have a reason for your present. Your birthday is coming up in a bit over a week and I may not get back for it. But my birthday is not for months."

"I know *old* man." She laughed, "You are going to be a ripe old 24. No, it is for luck. As long as you have it nothing bad can happen. Just keep it close. Victoria was about your age when that coin was struck, and see, she still looks exactly the same. That surely proves the coin is good luck. The other side is to remind you that you are all the St. George I will ever need."

He held the coin tightly in his hand for several minutes simply smiling down at her then placed it inside his leather wallet.

"Joanna there is something we need to do today. We have talked about it, but have never formally settled it. I wish there was no war on so that we could do it differently. But considering the conditions this will have to do.

"Joanna Shaylee Barton, just as soon as this miserable War ends, will you marry me?"

"Mathew Weldon, just you try to get out of it. Of course I will. It was fated to happen from the day we met. It simply took a while for us to figure it out."

"Well now that that is settled let's find a good jeweler and get an engagement ring to put on your beautiful hand."

They went to Cartier's on New Bond Street. After the better part of an hour, Joanna settled on a platinum band with a simple three quarter carat diamond solitaire. Matt asked several times if she was sure she didn't want something larger. Finally she looked him in the eye and said, "No, Mathew. Maybe for our tenth anniversary, but I don't want you to start out poor. You are only a Captain in the Air Force and we should not spend more than you make. If you were still in the RAF it would have been a much smaller diamond." And he knew that was the end of that discussion. Except for the long unembarrassed kiss she gave him right there at the counter with the older gentleman standing behind it smiling approvingly.

She wanted to wear the ring so they waited the few minutes to have it sized and she was told she could bring it back at any time so they could engrave it to her satisfaction. Matt was delighted to see her constantly glance down at her left hand and the glowing smile on her face was worth many times more than he had paid for the ring.

Matt never worried when he wrote a check about having sufficient funds to cover it. All of the years he had been in England his father had continued to make a monthly deposit into his account. Even during the years he was in the RAF and the Army Air Corp. Even so, Matt was sure it was less than the expenses his father covered for him when he had been in America. His dad must have been part saint not to have thrown him out. He wondered if he could be that patient with a son of his, when he and Joanna had one.

They were back at the Barton house by shortly after 2:30 in the afternoon. Joanna ran through the house until she found Mrs. Townsend. Matt heard the two of them talking excitedly from the kitchen. After spending several minutes together, they came into the sitting room where Haiku was once again purring contentedly on his lap. He stood up as he gently placed her on the now empty chair.

Mrs. Townsend's face was flushed. She stood in the doorway next to Joanna. "Oh Mr. Weldon! I am so pleased you and my young lady are officially engaged. My impression of you has risen since that first rainy night you came to pick her up. I confess I thought you were just another good-looking young man, but you have proved to be worthy of this young lady of ours.

"Then you went to fight for us long before your country was in this war. And I know Mr. Owen thinks you are a special fellow and that is high praise indeed. Joanna has told me the two of you are going to wait until you have completed your mission requirements before marrying. I think that is the right thing to do, but you are to take very good care of yourself. You have a wedding to plan."

Then to Matt's utter amazement, she walked over, stood on her tip toes and kissed him on the cheek. She uttered the single word, "Congratulations," turned and walked back toward the kitchen. Matt thought he heard her sniffling quietly as she walked down the hallway. He sat back down and Joanna came over, sat on his lap, put her arms around his neck and laid her head on his shoulder.

"She likes you a lot. You must know that. She normally thinks Americans are brash and rude, but since the first she has said you have beautiful manners and seem a fine young man. She has never really worried when I am with you. And she is hard to fool where people are concerned.

"I don't think I ever told you much about her. She lost her husband in the Great War. He fell in Belgium during the third battle of Ypres. It was the 2nd of August in 1917.

"They had been married less than a year. When he died she was without means and went to the Brewery asking if there was any job she could do there. My father was young and away at the war also. Grandfather told her there was nothing at the Brewery he could offer. She pleaded with him and told him of her situation. She had neither money, family nor any place to live. She had been 'put out' of her lodgings. I am sure grandfather was touched by her story. He offered her a position caring for the London house with a room to live in. She was just a maid then. Cleaning and dusting. The room was shared with another maid. As the years passed, she came to run the house. Now there is only her and one young girl who works part-time. Today she is more a part of our family than an employee. I believe she looks on me as the child she never had and I readily confess I look upon her as my second mother. I am not sure that when I was very small, I even knew the difference between the two. When we were in town she bathed me and dressed me. Fed me and often put me to bed at night and it was she who always kissed me on the forehead and tucked me in. When I was small she called me her "Little Princess." My brother was her "Little Soldier." So ironic she called him that in light of him being killed in Singapore when the Japs took the city. She hid it well but I could tell his death hit her as hard as it did us.

"I believe our being out at Barton Hall during that time was a blessing for her. She was able to grieve alone here in town. She would have been embarrassed for us to have seen it. I am sure it was as if she had lost a child of her own. Your children are not supposed to die before you. Not even if they are a soldier

"God, how I hate this War, Mathew. We have no choice but to fight it, but I hate it none the less. It makes me so afraid."

By 4:30 the two of them climbed the curving stairs to their rooms on the second floor to get dressed for the evening.

Matt was happy he and Joanna had finally made their engagement official. They had been on the telephone with her parents for nearly an hour. Actually he had spoken with her mother for about three minutes and her father for about five. The rest of the time he had stood quietly next to her while she spent the majority of the time talking with her mother. The two of them must have planned most of the wedding during their conversation. Owen had spent his time trying to talk him into working for him at the Brewery when the war was over. He said the next time he saw Matt he needed to discuss opening a brewery in the U.S. It was something he had planned to do before the war.

Matt showered and dressed in his light tan uniform shirt with a brown tie, his lightweight wool "Pinks" pants. Matt always smiled at the term "Pinks." He thought of the color as a cross between tan and taupe. He slipped on his light wool jacket in OD green with the half belt running at the waist in the back. His wings and flying Medals were above the left hand pocket. The 8th Air Force patch was on the left arm at the shoulder. He would wear his green "Crush Cap" with the large gold American eagle on the front. It was the most distinctive hat in the U.S. Military. The hat immediately identified him as a pilot. It was different from the ones worn by officers in the regular Army.

Army officers raised hell because the hats began life as identical items but the pilots and co-pilots removed the support wire from the sides. This caused the top to flop over on each side rather than stand up. The excuse was that it allowed them to wear their headset when they flew but few actually wore the hat in combat. They needed more warmth than it provided.

All pilots knew it was a damn sharp uniform. Unfortunately many of the men who wore it would not survive to take it home and proudly show their families. For the ones who did, it would hang in the back of the closet to be taken out to show their children when years later they asked, "Were you in the war, Daddy?"

Matt was standing at the bottom of the stairs when Joanna appeared and gave the impression of floating down the steps toward him. He was always astonished by the way she appeared to move so lightly, as if walking on clouds. But then, he knew he tended to see her as somehow angelic. To him she seemed from a place not really of this world. But damn, if she was an angel she was a very provocative and desirable angel.

Oh please, he quietly wished, please let me finish flying my missions quickly. I don't know how much longer I can stay out of bed with her. I am certainly no angel when it comes to that.

He was delighted to see the green chrome tourmaline worn on a white gold chain around her long neck which placed it exactly in the hollow of her throat. She saw he was smiling and touched the drop with her hand; the one with her engagement ring on it. She smiled and winked at him.

"Mathew the drop is spectacular but it is over-shadowed by the ring. A woman gets many birthday presents but only gets engaged once. At least you had better know that is how it will be with us. You have already given me the best day in my life and it's not over yet. And you have managed to do that in the middle of a War. I love you more than you can ever begin to imagine. More than I would have believed it was possible to love anyone. You are and always will be everything to me."

Matt was so captivated by her that he was momentarily speechless. He saw she was wearing the same dress as on the night they had gone to that first "event" he had planned. The night of the Debussy Symphony at Queen's Hall and the dinner at Café de Paris. The first time they had ever held hands and danced.

"God Joanna, I love you and you are so beautiful. You become more so every time I see you. And I love you more deeply with each passing day."

Mrs. Townsend was standing by the door pretending to hear none of what they were telling each other. Holding a light rain coat for Joanna, she handed it to Matt. He slipped it over his love's arms and around her. He was wearing his old Burberry trench coat and carrying his black umbrella.

They went down hand in hand to the MG waiting at the foot of the stone steps. He held the umbrella over the two of them while he opened the door on her side of the little green car. Steady rain had washed the dust off so it now sparkled in the lights from the house as if covered with hundreds of tiny domed crystals.

"Mathew this night seems very much like that one we had when we were just beginning to know we were in love, but afraid to admit it. Tonight is very similar and look at how far we have come. Best of all we still have so much time before us. I pray we both have very long lives with endless nights together both rainy and star filled."

"I don't think even a hundred years with you would be enough Joanna. I can't find the words to tell you how much I love you. The three words by themselves fall miles short of expressing the feeling I have."

She laughed her melodic laugh which seemed the essence of life itself and said, "Don't worry dearest we have a lifetime to find the words. We have the feeling. It will last forever. This enchantment will never fade. For I believe it is eternal."

"Yes, Matt thought, it must be an enchantment. An unbreakable spell we are both under. A spell that neither of us can or will ever want to break. This wonderful green eyed enchantress sitting beside me has woven a spell that has us both willingly and completely ensnared within its web.

The MG moved smoothly down Regent Street then turned onto Brook Street in Mayfair. Soon the Claridge Hotel came into view. He knew people often referred to the fine old hotel as "Buckingham Palace's Extension" because of the number of royal personages who had stayed there during visits to England. The red brick facade was impressive if dated with the English Coat of Arms carved in stone above the entrance. Even at the height of the Blitz, the Claridge never suffered from a lack of fine food.

Matt knew there were well over two hundred sumptuous rooms in the building, all constantly full; now usually occupied by high ranking American officers. It must have required a lot of "pull" for even Clark Gable to have a room here. A doorman ran out with his large umbrella to assist Joanna out of the car. Once she was inside he came back to find Matt was already standing under his own umbrella adjusting his hat.

The doorman gave Matt a small metal tag and said they would only need fifteen minutes notice to get his car back around front when they were ready to leave. The fellow gave him direction to "Coleridge's Bar" just off the Lobby and beyond the main desk.

As soon as they walked into the bar, his copilot John Smithson shouted his name from three large tables pushed together at the far end of the room. He saw members from several crews of the 351st plus Gable and his cameraman in addition to a large coterie of women who were strangers to him.

Gable's back was turned as he entertained the captivated women with a story of some sort and they all leaned in his direction. Matt removed his coat, helped Joanna off with hers and checked them at the small coat-check window along with his umbrella. He and Joanna then walked hand in hand toward the crowded tables as laughter erupted once again. Gable had reached the punch-line of the story he was telling. The women found it particularly amusing. Smithson and Karl both stood when they saw Joanna. Smithson spoke first.

"My God Matt! We are going to have to get the "Maid of Barley" repainted. After seeing her in person, the artist has done her a real disservice." Then he said something that reminded him vividly of his old roommate Kong. "It's such a *shame* she is blind!"

Everyone on his side of the table laughed and Gable finally turned around. The smile which had been on his face froze when he saw the two of them standing there smiling and holding hands. Matt was sure he saw a flash of sadness cross his face, but he was a good actor and it was replaced by the old sparkling 'Gable Grin.' He immediately stood up and took Joanna's other hand. He smiled at her and gave a small bow of his head.

"You can't be anyone except Joanna Barton. Matt has spoken about you. And the fellows are right. The nose art on the "Maid" is way off the mark, but I doubt any painting could ever do you justice. He described you correctly. He said you were a Lady with a capitol L. It is a most apt description."

He turned and looked at everyone at the table. "Gentlemen, take it from a guy who knows one when he sees her. We are in the presence of a Lady. So let's keep it clean while she is here with us and the other ladies."

With perfect timing Joanna let a quiet moment pass, then in a perfect cockney accent said, "An ya'd damn well better listen to tha' bloke, ya' 'ad."

The table exploded in laughter.

Two more chairs were dragged over where Joanna and Matt squeezed in between Gable and Smithy. Gable leaned over and quietly told him, "I already said this once but that was before I met her. Don't you screw this up! Women like her are too damn few and way too far between. I know, I found one and lost her. I doubt I will ever find another. I suspect there is a rule about 'one per customer per lifetime'."

It was obvious Gable was already drinking heavily, but he handled it well enough that most people wouldn't notice. And he had good reason. Would I react any differently in his place? Matt wondered. Probably not.

Smithson and Karl were obviously matched up with the two girls across from them. His copilot was talking to a woman who was probably in her early thirties, had mousey brown hair and a pleasant face. She smiled a lot and laughed at nearly everything. It seemed a bit forced, but then many things were...now.

Karl was talking to a pretty, young English WAAC in uniform. The way the two of them were looking at each other, Matt was sure the WAAC and Karl would be out of uniform before the night was over. He could not blame any of them. You lived as much as you could as fast as you could because...well...because you might not be alive to do it again. Besides, what had his excuse been for doing the same thing when there had been no war on?

He and Joanna sipped slowly at ales while carrying on small talk and after half an hour started letting it be known they had tickets for a play and hated to leave but had to.... They stood and began wishing everyone a good night. Gable had shaken Matt's hand and then took Joanna's. He looked at her and asked when she intended to make an honest man out of

Captain Weldon. She held the hand with her engagement ring on it up for him to see and told him, "We are one step closer today than yesterday."

Gable raised his voice and announced, "Gentlemen, we are in the presence of the luckiest son of a bitch in the entire 8th Air Force. Aw Hell, the luckiest son of a bitch in the whole United States Army, Navy or Marine Corps Captain Mathew Weldon who has just today proven to be much smarter than I ever imagined him to be. He is engaged to Miss Joanna Barton, the real "Maid of Barley." He raised his glass. "Cheers and much happiness to Matt and Joanna!"

Joanna rose up onto her tip-toes and kissed him on the cheek. Matt heard her tell him, "You are quite a gentleman...Captain Butler."

Gable laughed but for the second time that night Matt saw that look of utter sadness cross his face before they walked away from him.

Matt knew that Gable could have his choice of any woman he would meet tonight and he would undoubtedly choose one, but that would never be able to relieve the pain inside him one bit.

The rain had slowed to a light sprinkle. Matt returned the small tag to the doorman who handed it off to a parking attendant and told Matt the car would be around in a few minutes.

"Matt, I thought Mr. Gable was very nice. Not what I would have expected from a big American movie star, but you *are* right. Losing his wife has really crushed him. Men might not notice because he covers it pretty well, but a woman can feel it. There is a huge emptiness inside him. There was a look in his eyes when he first saw us together. It said he had once felt the way we do and he misses that special feeling. He knows it is a feeling he will never be able to recapture. I sense that he blames himself for what happened to her; that he could have prevented it somehow."

Matt was surprised at how close her intuition came to what he knew were the facts about this American tragedy.

"Joanna what you sensed is extremely close to what I know. Carol, his wife, had been telling him he needed to get in the war. Her last words over the telephone before she left to head back to California were, 'You need to get in this man's war, Pappy.' Gable was already forty-two years old, way past draft age. MGM naturally had him under contract and he was due to start a new film. After making 'Gone With The Wind' he was the hottest male film star in the world. He was also in charge of assigning Hollywood's stars to go on fund-raising War Bond drives around the country. He felt he was doing his bit for the war effort but Lombard thought he needed to be in the service. She loved him but felt with so many others going that he should be in it too.

"Carol finally told him she had to do something to make a difference and began pushing him to send her on a 'Bond Drive.' He finally complied with her wishes and assigned her to do a drive in major eastern cities.

"Before she left, she wrote him a series of notes which a friend of hers was to deliver to him; one for each day she was gone. She also asked her "to take care of Clark for me" almost as if she sensed what was going to happen.

"Her mother and agent accompanied her so she could go over scripts of potential future film projects at MGM. They were supposed to return to California by train, but she wanted to get back to her beloved Clark as quickly as possible. She booked three seats on a Trans-World Airline DC-3 flight back to California. It was January 1942.

"The airliner flew into Mount Potosi near the small town of Las Vegas, Nevada. The mountain was covered with snow and the plane burned with great intensity which ignited a forest fire. Clark saw the fire from his plane as he flew into the small airport at Las Vegas to join the search party. He had to have known there was no chance Carol survived.

"Gable had to be physically restrained from climbing the mountain with the rescuers in spite of what he must have understood. It was fortunate he was. The bodies were all badly burned and torn into pieces. The legend is that her head was separated from her body and that one arm and a foot was missing. What they brought him was a bit of her golden hair and the two ruby earrings he had given her when she left on the Bond Tour. He wears them in a locket around his neck. I expect he will still be wearing them on the day he joins her in death.

"He told me a bit about what happened. He only talks about it when he is drinking heavily. The rest of what I know I gathered before I assigned him on his first flight. We decided he is not here to commit suicide per se, but I don't believe he cares if he is killed. He is willing to leave it up to, as you would say, 'Kismet.' He is trying to do what he thinks he should have done while she was alive. I think he believes if he had done what she asked him that she would still be alive today.

"His logic tells him if he had been in the service either she would not have gone east, or if she had, he would not have been home. She would not have flown back. What he misses is that he can't change it. Not if he flew every mission from now 'til doom's day. You can't change what is.

No matter how much you might wish to. All you can do is go on. All that is left for you is to love the 'What Was'. The time you had together"

The very young attendant brought the MG and the doorman saw Joanna to her door and opened it for her while Matt tipped the attendant for retrieving the automobile.

When they drove away she turned toward him and said, "Oh Matt, what happened to them is so sad. I suppose in circumstances like his it is impossible not to go into 'What ifs.' To believe you could have done something which would have changed the final outcome. Which would, somehow, have kept Carol from dying in fire on the side of that frozen lonely mountain?"

She continued to look at him and finally added..."Don't you dare let anything happen to you! I don't think I could handle it at all. Not even close to as well as he is."

"My dear, I have too much to live for now. You have given me that. We shall just have to live as if we are assured forever."

Even as he said the words, Matt knew no one is assured tomorrow let alone forever but he could not bear the thought of telling Joanna. His had become a world which constantly surprised him with the randomness of its cruelty. Still...he couldn't tell *her* that.

Since 1940, Matt had seen more than enough sudden death to know. He also knew not even the greatest of loves could stop it. Death came in many forms. Enemy fighters or the blooming deadly shrapnel flowers. It could be as unexpected as a small error on takeoff or hitting another B-17 while lost in a cloud. There were a thousand ways it could happen but the end result was the same. A loved one dead and those who had loved them feeling their life was over. Best not to dwell on war's vast imponderables.

I am alive now and with the woman I love. Enjoy tonight.

The play they were to see was "The Lisbon Story." A musical spy story by a brilliant young writer and producer of off-beat theatrical performances named Harry Parr Davies. Davies was being viewed as quickly becoming the premier talent in musical theatre. His play was being performed at the Hippodrome Theater on Cranbourne Street in the part of London known as The City of Westminster.

Matt and Joanna had often driven past it in their many rambles around London both before and after the war had started. Even on a misty night it was easy to find. All five stories of the grand Victorian era building were brightly lit and on its facade in brilliantly illuminated ivory letters a full story high shone the legendry theater's name... "HIPPODROME".... In smaller letters it told the world of its current production "The Lisbon Story." Smaller still were the names of the primary stars, "Patricia Burke as Gabrielle Girard and David Farrar as David Warren."

Joanna had told him the musical spy story was set in Lisbon and Paris. One of the songs, "We Must Never Say Goodbye," was quite popular in the dance clubs around town. She told him the reviews of the plot were at best lukewarm but the music was considered by the critics to be quite good. The general public was much warmer toward the musical melodrama as the theatre was sold out most nights.

The large sign was illuminated now that the German raids had slowed to a very few but he knew the lights would be extinguished at any sign of any enemy aircraft activity near London. Thanks to the radar towers spaced along the coast, there would be sufficient warning to take action before the Germans could possibly drop any bombs.

Driving three blocks past the Hippodrome, they were finally able to park in an alley which already had a few cars sitting in it. Only scant minutes were required to walk back and enter the elegantly appointed lobby.

Joanna had acquired excellent tickets which placed them ten rows from the stage in left center of the huge ornate auditorium.

The lights went down, the curtain rose and the play began in Paris shortly before the occupation of France by the German Army. Patricia Burke as Gabrielle was a young French theatrical star in love with David Warren, a spy assigned to the British Foreign Office. Warren was there to get Dr. Pierre Sargon, a nuclear scientist, out of France and to America but was forced to leave for Portugal without Sargon when the Germans marched into Paris. He and Gabrielle sing "Someday We Shall Meet Again."

A few months later Gabrielle escapes from Paris and flees to Lisbon, a neutral city which is a hotbed of espionage. There she meets her lover David again. He and an American partner from the OSS are guarding Pierre's daughter, Lisette Sargon, a theatre actress. Because her father is being held in Paris by the Gestapo, David and his OSS associate plot ways to get him out of France. Lisette agrees to pretend cooperation with the Nazis in order to get access to Dr. Sargon. The song, "Music at Midnight" is sung when Gabrielle and David have a tryst in a darkened café where they met to supposedly discuss Dr. Sargon's rescue. Lisette has also fallen in love with David, but he doesn't know and she does not tell him because she knows he loves Gabrielle.

She sings "For the First Time I Have Fallen in Love" while watching them through the café window, then walks sadly away into the night. The crimson curtain came slowly down as Act One ended.

Matt and Joanna joined the audience in enthusiastic applause for the actors and songs. Hand in hand they walked down the red carpeted stairs to the lobby where Matt purchased crystal flutes of champagne for each to sip during intermission. He noticed that over half the men and many of the women were in uniform. The majority were American or British but he also recognized uniforms from Canada, Australia, Poland, France and India, South Africa, Rhodesia and even a few from Russia. It was a reminder to both of them this was truly a World War. His memory of Bible quotations was weak, but he seemed to remember something from long ago when he was a small boy. He had been sitting with his father in a pew near the front of the great stone church near their estate on Long Island, when he was only six or seven. The minister stood in the raised lectern and read a verse from one of the prophets in the Old Testament.

He was unable to understand it then, yet today it seemed very clear. It was about ignoring a problem until it is too big to be solved without great pain and destruction. Ignoring what is happening until you cannot avoid certain destruction. 'You have sown the wind and now you shall reap the whirlwind.' The minister's sonorous voice echoed clearly in his mind, as if he were hearing it today.

Matt was startled when Joanna asked, "What do you think of the play so far Mathew?"

It took a moment to tear his mind away from that long ago Sunday. "Well, it seems to me this is going to end badly for someone. I mean here we have two women in love with the same guy. I cannot see how we can have a happy ending for everyone involved at least not without a *ménage a trois* and I doubt we will see that on the stage of the Hippodrome."

Joanna actually blushed as she replied, "Mathew Weldon! Here I was thinking you had changed and out of nowhere you come up with that. Though I suppose in your past you probably..."

Now it was Matt who was blushing. "Now hold on a minute. No! No! No! I admit that I had very loose morals but never a threesome." He saw she had the mischievous smile on her face which he always saw there when she was teasing him, and came back with "No, never less than *five* at once Joanna. Why waste perfectly good bed space?"

She looked him right in the eye when she said, "Good, I'll remember that after we are married. I shouldn't ever have to worry about hearing you say, 'Not again, I'm too tired,' should I?"

He nearly strangled on his champagne, "Oh God. I've really gotten myself in trouble now. Can we forget I ever said..."

"*Oh No!* You can count on me remembering what you said and I promise to bring your own words back to haunt you at the worst possible time. Sometimes, my love, you are too clever by far." The house lights flashed and for Matt it was truly a life saver.

The Second Act began with the Nazi Cultural Attaché Karl von Schriner, played by Walter Rilla, trying to get Lisette to return to Paris as his mistress. She refuses until he offers her a theatre she can run and any of the people she wants to be in the theatre's productions including her father (which of course, would get him away from the Gestapo.) David arranges for Gabrielle to plan a big musical production at the theatre in Paris, called "La Comtesse." The plan almost works until von Schriner suspects something and begins to look for Lisette before they can all leave for Portugal. Gabrielle and David sing "We Must Never Say Goodbye" then she impersonates Lisette so father and daughter can go with David first to England and then on to America. When von Schriner recognizes it is Gabrielle not Lisette, he shoots her. As she dies, "The Marseilles" plays. Then there is the sound of bombs falling as British aircraft bomb the theatre to cover the agents' escape.

The musical ended with "The Song of Sunrise" as David, Lisette and her father sail away from Lisbon to England with David looking back toward Portugal, and Lisette and her father looking toward the sunrise, toward England. The audience broke into cheers of "Bravo" and gave the cast three standing ovations.

When Matt looked at Joanna she was clapping but he saw tears running down her face. It was the second time he had seen her cry today. When she felt him looking at her, she stopped clapping and took his hand. She squeezed it gently. "I am sorry Matt. I suppose I must be a bit susceptible to sad endings these days. It seems I am seeing far too many of them. The hospital is one long sad ending. The way she was willing to die so that the man she loved could get away with Lisette and her father. And at the end you could tell she knew Lisette was in love with David. She had let von Schriner make love to her so David, Lisette and her father could get away from Paris. She knew she was going to die fooling von Schriner, but it was her last act of love for David. It was her way of saving him and doing what she had to do for the good of everyone. That is what this war is all about isn't it? Doing what we have to do instead of what we want to do."

Matt got their coats along with his old black umbrella from the coat-check room as they walked out. There was still a little mist but the streets were now filling with heavy fog. It was hard for Matt not to expect horse drawn carriages or imagine bumping into Sherlock Holms and Dr. Watson out on an adventure on a night like this.

After they reached the car, Joanna turned to him as he was cranking the MG. He could see that excited "little girl" look which he loved. It usually meant there was an "Adventure" she wanted them to go on.

"Oh Matt, let's go to the 'Tower' and watch the 'Ceremony of the Keys' Few people go since the War started. The Warders do it each night. The Night Watch receives the keys and locks the Tower. I haven't seen it since I was a little girl. Can we do that?"

He knew if she had said "can we fly to the moon and see if it is really green cheese" he would have tried to find a way to make it happen. In this case he simply said, "Yes," as they drove away.

Matt made his way through Piccadilly Circus. The area would have been packed before the War but on this foggy night had only moderate activity, primarily American soldiers and sailors on leave. However, the pubs and dance clubs wouldn't complain because the Americans spent far more than an equivalent English crowd. All the GI's would be intent on impressing their English girlfriends. The nearby jewelry stores would stay open late to sell rings for the romances certain to bloom on a night like this. Love on a romantically fog-filled London night with regret likely following only in the bright light of the morning.

Matt knew it was one of the reasons he wanted to wait until his missions were finished before they were married and having sex. Too many American boys and English girls had either slept together or rushed to marry so they could. Later, if they had regrets, they would blame it on the War. The Military had tried slowing down the marriage rate with mountains of forms, but a flood of couples either completed them to marry or simply married without permission.

Matt knew in coming years many of them would think, "Hell, I would never have done that if not for the Damn War. I should never have married in such a big hurry." Even as the thought entered their mind, life would be rushing past them like white-water in a mountain stream.

Almost every one of them would stay married, have kids, raise them and then see them grown only to watch them move away for lives of their own. Oh, the family would still gather together for holidays, birthdays and anniversaries. They would be happy about the grandkids when they came along and later the two of them would retire to a warmer climate, warmer yet colder still. Each of them might remember a different someone they could have married if they had waited until later or if there had been no War. Bitter at a decision which seemed so right at the time and with someone who seemed so wonderful. They would get by on little smiles and how well the kids seemed to be doing. Each would be secretly glad they stuck it out because it was for the kids and maybe before the end they would discover that it *had* been love they had after all. Not the fairy-tale kind they had expected when they were young walking in the fog hand-in-hand on a night in London during the War, but the everyday kind of love which lasts even when disillusioned and uncertain.

The thick fog seemed to mirror his thoughts. He noticed, except for instructions on the turns he should make to reach the Tower, Joanna was also in a quiet mood.

They drove past Victoria Embankment and onto Thames Street. The fog was so heavy that if he had not heard the ships' horns he would have never known there was a river nearby. Even when he passed the massive Houses of Parliament and Big Ben, both were merely shadows in the fog. Each street light they drove by was an indefinite halo wavering before them: disappearing when they passed.

"Joanna, you have been very quiet since we left the Hippodrome. Is anything wrong?"

"Wrong? No, not really. Well... I have been thinking about the musical. And about Gable and Lombard. The two keep playing over in my mind. Both are much like an ancient Greek tragedy. You don't want to think things like that happen in real life to real people, but they do. It is so sad. I know it could happen to... well, almost anyone.

"The way Gabrielle died for the man she loved. The fact that Lombard died returning to the man she loved. How Gable may be trying to get himself killed so he can join her in Death. The way David must have felt when he knew for sure Gabrielle was dead.

"I am sure we are supposed to believe he and Lisette end up happily ever after. But would they? David loved Gabrielle, not Lisette. Why would he turn to Lisette? Wouldn't he be simply accepting a substitute for the real thing? And in fact, I think Lombard was such a strong love for Gable that he will never find anyone to replace her. Some loves are like that. I know mine for you is."

Matt understood what she was really telling him and as the Tower of London took shape through the fog, he answered with the only words which came to him. "Sweetheart, we are never going to end up the way the lovers did in 'Lisbon Story.' As for Gable and Lombard, yes, we love as much as that, but to use your word, we are going to have 'Forever.' We need to trust what the West Wind has whispered in your ear. My promise to you is this... I will love you Forever'

"Here we are at the Tower. Let's put these unhappy thoughts aside and go see what this Ceremony of the Keys is all about. I think it is past time you gave me another lesson on what it means to be English. This day has been a special treat. I really enjoy roaming London with you. I have missed doing that. When the War is over I want us to spend lots of time doing that again."

When they got out of the MG, Matt took Joanna's hand and together they walked over the stone bridge which crossed the old moat. They could see neither the bottom of the bridge supports nor the tops of the twin towers guarding the bridge. The fog was so thick it reminded Matt of the heavy clouds he had too often flown through.

When they entered the courtyard, trees and bushes were no more than vague outlines; shadows in a world of fog. Matt felt Joanna shiver, then pull her coat tighter around her slender body so he pulled her close to him.

There were only a few people there: a couple of American Army Paratroopers with young English girls, a Naval Commander with a very pretty WAC and a handful of older civilians.

She leaned toward him and whispered, "The Ceremony of the Keys goes back to the fourteenth century. It is said it has never changed in all that time. The ceremony is performed down to the minute without fail. The Chief Yeoman Warder and the Yeoman Warder 'Watchman' travel the inside of the walls and lock all the main gates of the Tower then return down Water Lane near Traitors Gate. You will have to listen for what happens next."

After a few minutes Matt heard the sound of a gate being locked and heavy keys clanking together. This was followed by the sound of two pair of footsteps in cadence on gravel. The chief Yeoman Warder and the Watchman took form out of the fog. They were dressed in dark Navy blue, almost black with a large red English Crown on the chest and red piping and golden buttons. The uniform was a carry-over from the Tudor era. Matt remembered the uniform's historical period from his visit on a previous day with Joanna before the War.

The Warders were halted by a sentry who challenged them with, "Who comes there?"

The Chief Warder shouted, "The keys."

The Sentry questioned, "Whose keys?"

The Chief Warder replied, "King George's keys."

The sentry answered, "Pass King George's keys. All's well"

Matt saw the party pass through the Bloody Tower archway and at the top of the stairs the Tower Guard presented arms and the Chief Warder raised his hat and proclaimed, "God preserve King George" and the sentry closed with, "Amen."

The Ceremony came to an end and the small crowd began to wander away, dissolving almost as ghosts into the fog.

"Any questions Mathew?

"So, they always do this at this precise time? Every night?"

"For hundreds of years. The only known exception was during the Blitz in 1940. It was in the papers. Some German incendiary bombs fell very close by and knocked the Chief Yeoman Warder and his escort down. They stood back up and dusted themselves off and proceeded with their duties.

"The Officer of the Guard wrote a letter of apology to the King. The King replied in a letter instructing that no one should be punished as the delay was due to enemy action. Other questions?"

"Yes, how the hell do we get out of here if they have locked this place up so tight?"

"Mathew, now it is only symboli.... Oh you! They leave a door unlocked until the people are all gone. Why ever do I take you so seriously?"

"Joanna, it must be because you know what a serious sort I am. And how very much I love to hear you laugh and see you smile. I once told you that had you been a Medieval Princess, I would gladly your Jester have been. But, really, I prefer the way it is between us in this time. Despite the War. And, as with all wars, this one too will end."

They walked out through the gate arm in arm and were swallowed up by the relentless fog.

He and Joanna did not get back to the townhouse until a few minutes after one in the morning after gingerly feeling their way back through the fog. The passionate goodnight kiss she gave him made it difficult to fall asleep.

Why, he asked himself, are you being so determined to wait until you two are married? She has made it clear that you can make love to her now. The lady loves you and you love her and damn Matt, there is a War on. Your intentions are honorable. You are going to get married as soon as.... Yeah that's the problem. You've still got missions to fly. Something bad can still happen and where would she be then? I can't marry her and then not come back from a mission. Got to think of her not me. No marriage, then no sex.

Matt slept in the next morning, a luxury seldom enjoyed since he had left the RAF where he had flown night operations. He had only recently begun daylight bombing with the 8th Air Force which always required him to be up well before sunrise.

He showered, dressed in his civvies and went down the long curving stairway. Sounds of dishes rattling and conversation came from the kitchen.

When he sauntered in, the sight greeting him was a surprise. Joanna was wearing an apron and standing in front of the stove cooking eggs in one pan and bacon in another. Mrs. Townsend sat in a kitchen chair and gave occasional advice on when to turn something. The smell of freshly brewed coffee filled the room. He put his finger to his lips which only Mrs. Townsend could see and tiptoed up behind Joanna. Then when he was close, slapped her on the rear. She spun around with a gasp and as soon as she saw him shouted, "Oh you! That's not polite." She threw her arms around his neck and kissed him while pressing her body against his. When she finally pulled away she looked down and smiled a very pleased grin. At that moment she remembered her cooking instructor was sitting not ten feet away and turned toward her.

Mrs. Townsend smiled a warm smile and told both of them, "I didn't see a thing," glanced to where Haiku was sleeping peacefully in a basket and followed with, "but Haiku is probably shocked."

Matt was finally able to turn toward Mrs. Townsend without embarrassment and said with a laugh, "You have more discretion than anyone I know. The 8th Air Force is an open book when compared to you. I hope you are aware, when Joanna and I are finally able to marry; we are going to want you to go with us. We couldn't get along without you."

"Well, I don't know Mr. Weldon. Who would look after Haiku?"

"You would. This is a package deal and Haiku goes with us. Right, Joanna?"

"Absolutely, and if you're a real good boy the three of us may let you go too. But after what you did just a minute ago...."

"Hey Joanna, you know I'm in the Air Force. Haven't you ever heard of a target of opportunity?"

She laughingly answered, "Yes Mathew, but this target is on the same side you are!"

"Oops. Boy is my navigator in trouble. Besides, what are you doing at the stove?"

"I am learning to cook breakfast for my soon to be husband. I refuse to be one of those wives who can't boil water. I should know how to cook a decent meal... in an emergency of course."

"I don't expect too much from you in the cooking area. I'm an American remember. In America wives only know how to make one thing, particularly at dinner time."

"What is it Mathew? If it is only *one* thing, men must really love it."

"Well I suppose we must. It's reservations at a good restaurant."

Mrs. Townsend exploded with laughter and Haiku woke up peering out of her large green eyes to see what she had missed.

"Well Mathew Weldon, our house will not be run like that, I assure you."

"Of course not, Joanna dearest. Mrs. Townsend will make reservations for us."

"Mathew, you are incorrigible." Now she too was laughing, "I am perfectly capable of dialing a telephone without any help."

When they were seated in front of the breakfast Joanna had cooked, Matt told her, "This is a lovely breakfast. The eggs are great and no tomatoes even, the bacon is just right and the coffee is as good as any I could get in New York. I look forward to having meals like this with you every morning."

"Thank you Mathew, I would love to make breakfast for us when we have our own home. I know it will have to wait until the War ends, but I am so looking forward to it. A place for the two of us. With room for our children. You do want children?"

Matt looked around to make certain Mrs. Townsend had left the kitchen before answering Joanna's question.

"With you? Oh yes. Two or three at least. We will need one boy and you've said that is already arranged. One thing I know, the boy will be a fine looking lad and any girls are certain to be as beautiful as their mother."

Joanna came around the table and sat on his lap. She put her arms around his neck and gazed into his eyes. "Mathew darling, if I have not made this clear enough before, we could start on that now. We love each other. I know you think we should wait until we are married but I *know* you want me that way and I want you so *badly* I sometimes think I will burst into flames."

"Joanna. God, you must know I want that too. You don't want us to make love anymore than I do. But I was so *loose* about that for years it came to be no more than shaking hands for me. I love you so damn much I want it to be different this time. I want it to be *special* for us. The only way I can see it being like that is for us to be married. I am really grateful for cold showers. I need one every time I kiss you. Two cold showers after having you in my lap like this."

She smiled a very naughty smile and wiggled her rear from side to side on his lap. "Oh Mathew, am I making it hard for you? Yes, I feel I am. Should I express my regret for doing this? Hmm...."

Without a word, Matt turned her over his lap and spanked her like a naughty child. An act which unfortunately did not help what he was feeling one bit.

When he finished, Joanna's face was flushed and she was breathing heavily. "Mathew, if you are going to do that anytime I am naughty you will find me being naughty quite often. Particularly if you will consider a request to do it on my *bare* bottom. I find it quite exciting thinking about it."

"Oh my God Joanna, where did that proper English girl go? The one who was so adamant about saying we could only be friends. Never lovers.

"I am going to fly a mission every day so I can get this torture over with. I don't know how much longer I can hold out. I must be completely insane not to do it with you right here in the kitchen. The only reason I don't is because I would hate to shock Haiku. Look Joanna, you said we were going down to Kent and see your parents. If we keep talking about making love, we will never get there.

"Remember what you said when I joined the RAF? You told me we *would* have a child. That he would be a boy. A son. You were so worried back then about me flying. About the things that *could* happen to me.

"You agreed that day if we waited to make love until after my last mission...then for you to be right about a son, nothing bad could happen to me."

"Yes, I remember," she laughed. "I know it is mean of me, but I so enjoy seeing how badly you want me. You certainly must know I am suffering too."

"Please. Joanna. Have mercy on me while I still have a few noble thoughts. When you are like this, my desire for you overwhelms my good intentions."

"OK Mathew. Down to Kent it is. However I can't make any guarantees for the future. I feel like Lady Chatterley."

"Oh God! You haven't read that book have you? D. H Lawrence certainly managed to gain a lot of attention with it. I will say he changed the icy image of English women with his writing. However, all he needed to do was write a one page book saying, 'If you think English women are icy, contact Mathew Weldon and he can dissuade you from that idea. He knows one who is driving him quite mad with desire.'"

"Yes Mathew, I read the book cover to cover. I was trying to learn what to expect from my lover. Namely *you*. The language was crude and her choice for *her* lover left something to be desired but it suggested some very interesting things for us to try."

"Sweetheart that's *enough*! Please... We need to be on our way. I hope you noticed my complete change of topic. Out of mercy for me, let's not return to the old topic for a while. I would really like to relax a little today."

~ ~ ~ ~

The next morning on his drive back to Polebrook, Matt decided to continue to assign his Hollywood gunner and film maker, Clark Gable, to a different B-17 for each mission he flew. There was a partially confirmed rumor to the effect that Hitler had offered a reward to any pilot who could shoot down the plane that Gable crewed on. Rotating him from B-17 to B-17 would reduce the odds of German success. He knew the Germans were successful enough targeting the bombers of the 8th Air Force without his help. Rotating Gable's aircraft had the additional benefit of getting more crew members in his film so the folks back in America had a chance to see them on screen.

After parking his MG at the service station just off base, Matt walked past the security gate, making the first stop his assigned Quonset hut to store his gear in the footlocker at the end of his bunk. While he was folding his wool uniform pants, John Smithson sauntered in looking tired but happy.

"Hey Matt, how are ya' doin? Did you have a good leave? Boy, is that a dumb question. Just looking at that pretty girl of yours would make any guy feel great. You are one lucky S.O.B.. Hell, even Gable would have a hard time finding a woman that beautiful and yours is obviously quite a lady."

"John, the question is how you are? You look more than a little rough around the edges. How's Karl doing? Did you guys get all that 'intellectual stimulation' you were planning in London? Remember you were going to the theatre and art galleries? How did that go? Did you expand your cultural horizons?"

"Yeah Matt, I was deeply immersed in English culture all weekend long. You know what pal? The girl I was with is really nice. She's got six years on me but I like her. I plan on seeing her next leave. Nothing serious can come of it because she has a husband in North Africa fighting Rommel. Her husband is the commander of a British 'Cromwell' tank. But what the hell, we like each other and she is fun to be with. We make each other laugh a lot. In the middle of a war it's good to be able to do that."

"John, have you seen Karl since you got back?" Matt asked his big copilot.

"Oh yeah! We rode back together. Gable bought a big black Bentley and gave us a ride. You think I look rough, wait 'til you see Karl. He is a lot rougher around the edges than I am.

"The WAAC he was with is much younger than my lady. I think she rode him pretty hard around London all weekend. They were constantly on the go. Don't think our bombardier got much sleep. Oh, I think he was in the sack, but not much sleeping happened when he got there. Probably set a record for him for being 'on target.' He was out cold most of the way back.

"The ground crew wanted him to see something about a possible problem with the bomb-sight. He dragged himself over to the 'Maid' to take a look. He'll be lucky to see the 'Maid' let alone a bomb-sight problem."

Later Matt asked his engineer if the enlisted men had a good leave and the answer Tony gave him left him laughing. "Did we have a good leave Captain? Well if you could be an enlisted man for one leave you would want to give up those Captain's bars and be a mere Sergeant. So yeah, we had a great time. 'Course the MP's can be a real nuisance."

Their tenth mission came on Tuesday morning. By then the "Maid's" crew had largely recovered from their leave in London. Early that July morning when the cloth was pulled away from the map, the Colonel's pointer once again tapped the town of Stuttgart.

"Gentlemen, we will be paying a return visit to Stuttgart. Today we want to call on the Porsche tank factory, the Daimler automotive works and the rail yards. The Porsche plant is turning out those Tiger tanks the Russians are finding very hard to knock out. We can give them a hand by destroying the production facilities. We expect determined opposition, so maintain close formation flying."

The briefing droned on for 45 minutes as Matt and his crew took notes on important data such as call signs, radio frequencies and map coordinates. Matt saw Gable and his cameraman filming the presentation and panning around the room for filling shots.

Matt had assigned Gable to fly with the crew of 'Q Ball' on this mission. 'Q Ball' would fly with one less 500 pound bomb to make up for the added weight of the man, his cameraman and his equipment.

As he moved around the room Gable stopped beside Matt, leaned over and whispered, "I don't suppose Joanna has a sister does she?" and chuckled while he moved on followed by his cameraman.

The B-17s all left the ground, but five had to turn back due to "mechanical" failures. Matt knew most of the problems would mysteriously clear up by the time the aircraft were back on the ground. It was something he never understood. Sure, a pilot might get nervous premonitions about a mission. But he would still need to complete twenty five before he could go to duties other than flying. An extra three aircraft had taken off in case they were needed, so the flight was at almost full strength of just under 350 aircraft.

They were initially attacked by over fifty German fighters who rose from the Luftwaffe base at Echterdingen, just south of the targeted city. The 351st squadron lost four aircraft in these attacks and an additional seven from the heavy concentration of flak batteries, a few of which were radar controlled. The formation quickly closed up the openings left by the missing B-17s. Because flight integrity was so well maintained by the remaining aircraft, losses from the German fighters were much lower than expected. And their bombing runs were unusually accurate.

Upon their return to Polebrook and after the debriefing sessions, the written after-raid assessments were quite positive. From the photographs, damage to the Porsche Tank Works looked to be quite extensive. Undoubtedly the number of tanks sent to the Russian front would be reduced for at least several months.

"Q Ball" returned with only very light flak damage. Captain Gable and his cameraman returned with no damage. Gable did tell Matt they shot lots of good combat footage with one scene of a burning German 109 going down and the pilot parachuting out by sliding down the wing. He told Matt it looked almost like a circus stunt. Matt replied saying he had seen a pilot do exactly that once before. To Matt it only meant that pilot would be back in another fighter plane trying to shoot down other B-17s on another day.

At first it surprised him how callous he had become about death. It no longer bothered him as long as the ones dying were Germans. On those days when the fighters were up in force and the flak was heavy, he found himself wishing the enemy were all dead. Those were the nights he had a hard time staying within his self-imposed alcohol limit. The nights when the dreams were bad and he awoke on his cot drenched in sweat.

The weather remained good over the next month so Matt and his crew flew missions to Leipzig, Pilsen and two more to Berlin. Berlin was still a hellish city to bomb. It was clear the Luftwaffe was now using its best pilots and aircraft to protect the German capitol; Hitler's orders, no doubt, though the orders would have come to the Luftwaffe through Göring. Given their continuing high losses, it simply meant the other German cities were beginning to be short-changed on protection.

By now Matt was up to fifteen missions in the "Maid" and Gable was up to six. Not a single pilot on any mission Gable had flown had a complaint about him. They all found him to be a competent gunner and one hell of a story-teller, many about the actresses in Hollywood; all of these were very bawdy tales.

During actual combat his cameraman stayed out of the way, yet got good footage. A few days past the second mission to Berlin, the base C.O. called Matt to his office. Col. Wilheit was there as were two other officers he recognized from his time at High Wycombe Abbey. They had never told him, but he was certain they were involved in 'hush-hush' operations. One graduated from Yale a few years before Matt left for England. The college name was the only information Matt ever heard come out of the man's mouth that he considered even possibly true.

No introductions were made. Col. Wilheit simply looked at the Yale Major and said, "Go ahead please, Major Thomas."

Matt suppressed a laugh. The few times they had spoken at High Wycombe the Major had given him a different name. He wondered how often they changed identities and if they ever got confused about who they were supposed to be this week.

Major 'Thomas' recognized Matt from their meeting at High Wycombe. His cheeks turned a slightly embarrassed red; he cleared his throat and began, "Captain, I know you have been assigning Captain Gable's planes during his tenure here at Polebrook. Washington wants him back in America and orders are being cut for him to return stateside so until that is done we don't want him to fly more missions."

Matt smiled at the Major, "So Major, uh...'Thomas', is it? Yes of course...'Thomas.' So Washington is worried about the bounty on Captain Gable's head. Is that the problem?"

The Major jumped to his feet. "Captain Weldon how did you hear that? That information is highly classified! Restricted to a very select list of people."

"Well Major '**Thomas**,' only a few hundred of us around the base have heard about it. One of the pilots in my squadron who speaks German heard it being discussed weeks ago between two Luftwaffe pilots. They said Hitler wanted an American movie star shot down. We pretty much figured it was Captain Gable. One of our missions to Berlin as I recall. Should I let the Squadron know it is secret? Be glad to pass the word for you if you would like."

Major 'Thomas' sat back down with a relieved look on his face, "Well Captain, it might be Captain Jimmy Stewart they were talking about, he was piloting B-24s out of Tiberham in Norfolk. However, I imagine you are right because Captain Stewart is now assigned to ground ops. But no, let's not go letting the Squadron know they had information before... well no... just let it die. The only important thing is to keep Captain Gable on the ground until he leaves."

Matt looked at the two covert operations men, then directly at Colonel Wilheit before replying with a smile, "I understand, Sir."

He was pleased that they had become upset by his statement that everyone on base knew about the reward put on Gable's head by Germany and that he had said only that he *understood* that they wanted Gable on no more flights. He did not promise he would comply with their wishes. If Gable snuck aboard one more flight before leaving, well who could be blamed for that?

After leaving the Commander's office Matt set off to find Gable but found his cameraman, Andrew McIntyre first. " Captain, can you find Captain Gable and ask him to meet me at the Three Horse Shoes Pub in Ashton at about twenty hundred hours tonight? We need to talk and keep it between you two. Perhaps you should come also but no one else. OK?"

"Sure Captain Weldon. Twenty hundred tonight. That's eight this evening for those of us who still have a civilian mind. Right?"

"Dead on the money, Mac. I'll be glad when the War is over and they return my civilian mind. You know though I'm not real sure the one they issued me is totally G.I. It doesn't seem olive drab through and through."

On the way to the flight line to check on the "Maid," Colonel Wilheit caught up to him. His C.O. was smiling an evil smile. "Useless bunch of bastards, aren't they? Send them on even an easy mission and they would piss their pants but they'll go home and tell everyone they single-handedly won the War. So Captain, are you going to tell Gable or should I do it?" Despite the results of the ill-fated raid on Rotterdam, Matt had found he really liked his C.O. The man did his best to take care of the Squadron and the men in it. He had read the Manual on how things **must** be done, and then thrown it away. He now did them his way.

"No Colonel, I'm going to do it. No need for both of us to get a court martial out this."

"Thanks Son. I really never have looked good in stripes. Takes a tall thin fellow like you to wear those. Seriously though... don't worry too much about a court martial. We still need good pilots. Any proceeding would have to go through me and son that is not going to happen." The last said as he shook Matt's hand followed by a mutual salute.

When Matt arrived at the Three Horse Shoes that evening he found both Clark and Andrew seated at a corner table. The locals had gotten so used to having an American celebrity as a regular visitor in their cozy little pub; they no longer crowded around him. It was clear that he enjoyed being greeted with, "Good evening Captain Gable" or, "Good to see you again." Matt suspected Gable enjoyed knowing he was now simply another fellow who dropped in for a meal and a drink...or two...or three or...? All Matt really cared about was that Gable always seemed sober and clear-eyed when he flew. That was the only thing that counted. How he handled his sorrow over the loss of Carol was his business. His conduct when he flew...well that was *both* of their business.

The two men stood when he walked over to their table. Matt knew Gable understood something was up because of the message his friend had given him about meeting away from the base. As soon as they were all seated, the first words out of his mouth were, "Ok Matt, what kind of trouble are we in? Shoot straight with us."

Matt laughed before saying, "I don't know Clark, what have you done to get in trouble? ...No, don't tell me. I don't want to know. The only thing I do know is the powers-that-be want you back in America. Orders are being cut and you will probably have them in a few days."

Gable's wide brow wrinkled before he spat out the single expletive, "Damn!" He took a long drink of his whiskey before asking, "Any idea why Matt?"

"Matter of fact I do Clark. Have you heard the rumor going around about the reward Hitler personally put on your head for anyone who could shoot you down?"

"Do you mean to say they are pulling me out because of a rumor? In that case, anybody who doesn't want to be here should start one about themselves."

"Not just a rumor any longer. The 'hush-hush' boys have confirmation. They said you are not to go on another flight before you leave. This is no doubt coming from way over their heads."

Gable took another drink before saying, "Double damn, Matt. Not only pulling us out, I assume they are sending Andy with me?" Matt nodded in the affirmative before Gable continued, "But they are grounding us too. Hell, I need more flight footage than I have to do a decent film and damn if I'll use stock footage. I want it to be completely **our** film."

He was ready to take another drink when Matt held his arm down. "Don't get too drunk Captain Gable. That is an order. If you do you will be in no shape to fly with the 'Maid' on her next mission. We need a good gunner even if he is too damn **old** to be doing it. The rumor is you can shoot and I intend to give you the top turret position once we are over enemy territory. It will probably have to be your last flight Clark. I have a feeling they are pushing hard to get you out of here."

He watched as Gable's eyes lit up and that big smile of his flashed across his mouth. "Really Matt? Fly with the 'Maid.' Jesus... I know how much she means to you. Both the plane and Joanna. I only wish...." Matt saw the smile vanish.

"I know Clark. But I believe she knows. You have done things a twenty year old would be proud of. If there ever was a debt, you have paid it. *In spades.* Joanna is a big believer in forever. I can't say she is wrong about that. What I do know is that no one really dies as long as they are loved and remembered."

The three of them sat at the table talking for another two hours. Matt and Andy mostly listened while Clark told stories about things he had done with Carol Lombard during their time together. Hunting, fishing and card games. Often she was the only woman there. He said she could cuss and drink with the best of the guys yet she was still a lady. Even when she told the 'boys' a dirty story she still maintained her aura of class.

He told Matt he had a similar feeling about Joanna. That her class wasn't simply superficial, it was more than that. It went all the way to her heart.

Matt noticed that Gable did not take another drink of his liquor while he told them story after story about his time with Lombard. Most of the stories were told with smiles and laughter, only his closing remark carried a touch of sadness. "You know boys, there will never be another one like her for me, but I am glad for the time we had together."

~ ~ ~ ~

In the darkness of the early hours of Wednesday morning the men were roused by the "wake up crews." Ground crewmen had all worked throughout the night to ready the Squadron's aircraft for the mission.

Matt had left word to load one less five hundred pound bomb in the "Maid's" bomb-bay. They would be carrying out a secret mission. His ground crew all had been told 'The Maid' was carrying Captain Gable and Captain McIntyre on a last flight before they were sent back stateside.

As usual, Matt and "Maid of Barley" were to lead the mission. She would be out in front of the middle V of B-17s as the group headed to Bremen once more. The briefing advised everyone to expect moderate to heavy resistance from the Germans.

Over 400 loaded B-17s were to assemble over southern England in the vicinity of Canterbury before heading north toward the target. They were to bomb three shipyards and the Focke Wulf aircraft factory. Matt's group was to target the Focke Wulf Works along with sixty-six other B-17s.

By 06:00 in the morning, the first of the 351st Squadron's flying fortresses rolled down the mile-long runway and began to claw its way into the grey skies over Polebrook followed by over two hundred more. In total, B-17s from eight wings scattered on fields all over England formed up for the mission.

The aircraft were at three thousand feet when the final "go" signal was radioed to each Squadron. Then the formation had to climb another twenty five thousand feet to get above the heavy clouds that hid the North Sea. The temperature was below -50 degrees centigrade and ice was forming on some of the windows. The bombers had barely reached the coast of Germany when the Luftwaffe pounced.

Matt brought Gable and McIntyre from the middle of the "Maid" where the twin fifty caliber machine guns were mounted, so Gable could man the top turret as promised. He kept his engineer Tony Angerami standing between him and his copilot to watch the gauges and tell him if anything was going wrong with the engines. That meant Gable stood directly behind Tony. He had barely gotten in position to fire the guns when the Germans tore into the formation.

Dropping out of the sun, they started making runs on the high Squadron first by flattening out their dive in front of a B-17 and attacking head on. This tactic was designed to put rounds into the front of the bomber as the vital fliers were all at the front: the two pilots and the bombardier. Even if they missed the crew, the gauges and controls were still vulnerable to their fire. The Messerschmitts and Focke Wulfs would make a single run at the bombers then dive away to hit a lower formation.

Matt heard Gable's twin fifty caliber guns chattering as a lone Focke Wulf made a run at the "Maid." The top turret and nose guns were beginning to make a number of hits on the Focke Wulf. Guns on the German's wings were firing, but luckily his angle had the shots going just over the "Maid." Instead of diving away, this one started to rise with his wings twisting in a slow circle around his fuselage. Gable was cussing fluently and continued to put rounds into the German plane as it rolled away from their starboard wing, then spun sharply toward the ground. McIntyre had filmed the entire scene and was telling his friend, "You got him Clark. You got him. You really nailed him. He's finished." Matt checked with his co-pilot who confirmed that it was a definite shoot-down. He got on the intercom and announced, "I would like to report that Captain Rhett Butler, late of the Confederate Army, has just earned all the money spent to retrain him by the Yankee Air Force by shooting down a Focke Wulf 190. I am sure the good Captain will be buying drinks at the O. Club this evening for the bus drivers and porters who took him on this little jaunt today."

A voice came on the intercom as soon as he finished. "You are damn right," Gable said. "The drinks are on me. At both the O. Club and the Enlisted Men's Club. I will pay for all the drinks. This is one Rebel who will be glad to buy drinks tonight. Funny they had me playing that role. I'm really a damn Yankee."

Fighter attacks continued for nearly a half hour before the German pilots began to pull away from the American bomber formations. Flak was already blooming in the open air in front of them. The large bomber group split into four segments, each with a different target. Flak lessened as the ground gunners were forced to protect four individual areas.

Given that, Matt could see the Focke Wulf plant remained the most heavily protected by the flak-gunners. German High Command was obviously giving priority to aircraft manufacture over everything except tank, cannon and munitions production.

The "Maid" bucked like an unbroken stallion as she moved through the sky. Even moderately distant misses by the flak explosions of big artillery shells could lift the B-17 suddenly upward when they exploded below or push her sharply downward if they exploded above her. It was all Matt and John could do to muscle her into near level flight. Yet that was needed to make a final run into the targeted drop zone. It was a tooth-rattling ride. The fact that Matt's crew looked on the danger of imminent death as well as the discomfort inherent in each flight as just part of their job, was a tribute to both their youth and determination. They had all survived sixteen missions and were feeling the chances were good they might make the required twenty-five.

Just before their final run in to the target, an anti-aircraft round exploded below the "Maid." She was lifted sharply upward and several pieces of shrapnel punched into her belly.

Matt was on the intercom at once. "OK boys, that was a close one. I want to hear from everybody. NOW! Any one hurt or any serious damage to the "Maid?"

One by one his crew checked in. They were all unharmed but the "Maid" had over a dozen holes through her belly in front of the bomb-bay. Metal scraps had gone through the floor and exited the top of the plane. The resultant ragged bottle cap sized holes whistled a high-pitched tune and ensured an unpleasant, even colder than normal flight home.

After five minutes which seem hours, the intercom finally burst to life. It was Karlson's voice with the blessed benediction, "Bombs away. Get us the hell out of here 'Daddy.' Our lovely Lady doesn't need any more holes punched in her."

Matt took control back from his bombardier and turned the B-17 sharply around to point it back toward the relative safety of Polebrook.

Once the "Maid" had pushed her way past the second attack by the German fighters, Gable and his cameraman returned to the waist gunner's area leaving the top turret position to Toni Angerami who would maintain his position as Engineer. Matt could hear the sound of laughter. He was sure from past reports that Gable was entertaining the "troops."

While Gable sat on the floor near the twin fifties, Andy McIntyre noticed a big chunk was missing from both the heel and back of his friend's right boot. Further examination showed a small rip in the back of Gable's high altitude flight jacket.

Once the "Maid" was sitting on her hardstand back at Polebrook, the crew examined the area near where Gable had been standing and found a hole where his right foot would have been. The shrapnel had continued upward and exited the top of the plane.

Matt was reminded of his conversation with Joanna's father before joining the RAF back in 1940. Owen had told him he survived World War I, but sometimes only by inches. Well, Clark Gable had also survived his War. "Only by inches." Or perhaps he had a very special angel looking out for him. Who could say?

That evening's celebration of Gable's kill was dampened by the loss of thirty three aircraft to enemy fighters and flak gunners; a near ten percent loss of all those that started the mission. Three hundred and sixty three crew members were either killed or captured in a single day. Matt hoped what they were accomplishing was worth the cost of so many young lives.

Gable sat at a corner table with Matt, John, Karl, Andy and Colonel Wilheit, nursing the same drink for over an hour as the evening wound down. Matt noticed Gable's mood had changed from highly excited early in the evening when officers from B-17s he had flown with were dropping by to congratulate him on his "kill" to a more pensive one.

When everyone except he and Gable had wandered away, Matt asked how he was doing. The man was silent for several minutes before answering the question. "Funny thing, Matt. I was excited about shooting down the Focke Wulf. Then I understood I didn't just kill a machine. I probably killed a man. I am seeing things differently since I realized that. Sure, I hate what the Germans have done. If Hitler had been in that plane I wouldn't feel this way, but he wasn't. It was some kid who happened to be German. That's different."

"Clark, every one of us on the 'Maid' has, at one time or another, had those same feelings. In time you find a way to make peace with it. We all do. With me it was all the civilians I saw killed in London by those same 'kids.' Just remember the pilot of that FW-190 was shooting at us. In a court of law what you did was self-defense."

"Thanks Matt. That helps. Looks like I'll never be doing it again. When they get me back to the States...well, that is the end of my War. I'll tell you one thing, if I ever make a war movie and play a pilot, it'll be real easy because I've flown with the very best. If there is ever anything I can do for any of you guys... just let me know."

"Clark, when you get back, just finish your documentary. I know it will be a good one. After that make the best films you can for Hollywood.

And... well, you know you won't ever find another one exactly like *her*. Clark, I'm sure she was one of a kind. You have great memories of her. Hold on to them, but she probably wouldn't want you to be alone. Look around when you get back. Sounds like she was as much friend as lover. It's your business of course, but think about it. OK?"

"Sure Matt, it's time I started living again. Something decided I should be alive today. A couple of inches difference in that piece of flak and I wouldn't be. Yeah, I *know* how close it was. I've thought about it a lot. Must be a message of some kind. Maybe Carol wanted me to know she won't stop waiting for me."

"That or you have an angel watching out for you Clark. One who loves you. Maybe both. As you said, you two had wonderful times together. Some people live whole lifetimes and can never say that."

~ ~ ~ ~

Captain Clark Gable and Captain Andrew McIntyre flew out of Polebrook two days later. By September they were back in Hollywood working on the documentary.

Gable was awarded the Distinguished Flying Cross and the Air Medal among others. He later learned it was MGM's badgering of the Pentagon which was actually the reason for his recall. The rest was mere excuse. In 1944 he was promoted to Major. He tried to return to combat but his requests were continually rejected.

In disgust he requested and was granted a discharge. His discharge papers were signed by Captain Ronald Reagan. Gable titled his work "Combat America" and was the narrator.

Chapter 17

LOVE IN THE BARLEY

Matt could never remember seeing Joanna wear white. Her normal style was dresses featuring muted colors, always the ultimate statement of class and with her striking figure never failing to attract attention, especially from men.

Today she was dressed exclusively in white. "My dear, today you are so beautiful it takes my breath away. You should wear white more often. You look wonderful in it. What am I saying?" He laughed, "Everything you wear suits you. You are always perfect."

"Thank you Mathew. You are too, but remember, we are both looking through loving eyes. I hope you will still see me that way when we are seventy. I know I will see you that way. You are everything I am ever going to love. You will *never* have to wonder if I do.

"As far as wearing white for you, I will be wearing white when we are wed. The color a *virgin bride* wears on the day she becomes one with her husband. An old tradition that is not honored much any longer, especially since the War started. We are honoring it; more because you wish it than because I do. I have tried all my wiles to make it otherwise between us. I could be no more truly yours if we were married. You could be no more mine had we married a hundred times. Because you wish it, I will wait until we are married. Anyway, it won't be much longer now."

"No, a few more weeks at most and my twenty five will be history. Joanna, I am going to request assignment at High Wycombe Abbey on either General Doolittle's staff or General Eaker's. If I can land one of those assignments we will be able to be together nights. Do you think your mother and dad would mind letting us use the London House until we can find a place of our own?"

"Mathew, Dad has already made the offer. He not only understands our plans but approves one hundred percent. Mother is only at about ninety eight percent, but for her that is complete approval. She said you were an exceptional young man. Particularly for an American," she said with a grin. "Let's walk to the chapel and look it over with an eye towards the wedding."

The March weather was cool but the warming sun promised higher temperatures as the day passed noon. Joanna threw a white woolen shawl over her shoulders.

Taking his hand in hers, she led him inside. They walked to the front of the small building where they turned so both were looking back toward the doors at the rear of the building. The sunlight pouring through the stained glass windows threw wonderful patterns on the pews and floor.

"Yes Mathew. This is the perfect time of day. About noon. No, now that I think about it, I would like it to be a one o'clock wedding here in the Chapel. We can do a reception in London for many more people and even have one later in New York if you wish. But the wedding itself, small and here. Family only. You do know we have been Anglican for centuries don't you? Are you familiar with the wedding vows we use in the Anglican Church Mathew?"

"Probably pretty close to the ones that are used in America, Episcopalian, I would guess.... The love honor and obey thing... I never thought much about it until I met you, so I'm not very up to date. I do want to get it right. I do not intend to ever do it again. Ours is going to last."

"Forever, Mathew?"

"Yes Joanna. Forever. I promise we will grow very old together."

She kissed him, walked to the pulpit and removed a small black book. "Mathew, this is our Book of Common Prayer. It contains the marriage vows for the Church of England. Let's read them together. That way you will be ready when we make this official. Let me find the page. Oh yes, here it is. The groom goes first. Simply read it out loud and then hand it to me."

"Ok Joanna. Here goes. 'I, state your name,...'"

"MATHEW WELDON! Be serious and do this right."

"Sorry...I, Mathew Donnelly Weldon, take thee, Joanna Shaylee Barton, to be my lawfully wedded Wife, to have and to hold from this day forward, for better for worse, for richer for poorer, in sickness and in health, to love and to cherish, till death us do part, according to God's holy ordinance; and there to I give thee my troth."

Joanna had taken both Matt's hands in hers and was staring lovingly into his eyes. He had to glance away from her for a moment. The small chapel suddenly felt as if it were filled with people. The pews were all empty.

He looked back into Joanna's green eyes. He took her shawl and draped it over her hair so he could see what she would look like as a bride. She was more beautiful than he could have imagined. He took her hand back in his while she read her vows.

"I, Joanna Shaylee Barton, take thee, Mathew Donnelly Weldon, to be my lawfully wedded Husband, to have and to hold from this day forward, for better for worse, for richer for poorer, in sickness and in health, to love, cherish, and to obey, till death do us part, according to God's holy ordinance; and there to I give thee my troth."

Matt found Joanna had taken her engagement ring off and he was now holding it in his hand. She held out her hand and Matt slipped it on her finger. He did not need to be told to kiss the bride. That part he knew without prompting. The kiss was long and very passionate.

"Wow! I can't imagine the actual wedding could be any more real than that. For a moment, Joanna, it felt like the chapel was filled with people and we were really being married."

"We were Mathew. I felt it too. The building was filled. We just couldn't see them. We took our vows in front of God. And, I suppose we could say, a chapel full to overflowing with spirits from the past as witnesses. What could be more holy than that? Our other wedding will be simply a show to make it legal and have a bunch of rice thrown in our hair. Now, for the wedding feast. I have a picnic lunch waiting for us in the barley field."

Hand in hand they walked back into the spring sun light. Joanna laughed a long musical laugh and kissed Matt. When she pulled away she laughed again. Matt had not seen her happy like this since before the War begun. It was as if she was so filled with happiness she could no longer contain it all.

"Oh Mathew, I am simply full of joy. I can't remember when I was this happy. Maybe I never have been. I am feeling so *fey* I just have to let my feelings out or I may explode." Then still laughing... "Come on, I'll race you to the barley." This last said while she was still laughing and already running toward the field. Matt was only a heartbeat later in starting but she was a good runner and he closed the gap between them only slowly. Matt found he too was laughing while chasing her toward the golden field.

Joanna entered an opening in the barley which soon led toward a tree covered with a profusion of white flowers. When they reached the base of the tree, he saw a white table cloth covered with blossoms and more were drifting down onto it and the top of the picnic basket sitting there was likewise sprinkled with them.

Joanna stood in the center of the white table cloth with a rain of alabaster blossoms falling around her. To Matt, who thought her the most beautiful being he had ever seen, it was as if a fairy-tale princess was standing there. Almost something he had once seen in a dream he could barely remember dreaming. Or perhaps it was an enchanted moment from a past lifetime? The thing he was sure of, he would never forget this intoxicating day.

He watched as she removed her white sandals and replaced them with a pair of white high heels she had taken from the picnic basket. He walked slowly to where Joanna stood and took her in his arms. He held her and looked into her eyes.

"Joanna, you are more beautiful than the word can begin to express. I have tried to find a word beyond beauty because that word falls woefully short of what my eyes see when I look at you. If you *are* an 'enchantress' please never lift this spell for it is most wondrous and I would happily live out my life while under it."

She kissed him, a long lingering kiss. At last she pulled away. "If there is a 'spell' it is not of my making, for I am enthralled as well.

"The reason I brought you here is *this* tree. It is a Rowan tree. The 'old ones' believed it was magic; the Mother of all trees and plants. The legend is that an ancient god and goddess made love and from their union came this tree from which all trees and plants descended.

"If I *were* a witch I could not stand here, because witches fear this tree. It destroys evil and strengthens good. The tree flowers every spring and once each three years bears a crop of ruby colored berries. Think about that if you would know magic. How can a tree know three years have passed? It has no clock or calendar. Yet the Rowan faithfully bears its berries each three years. Perhaps the West Wind tells it for it is a very knowing wind.

"The berries are quite wondrous. There are many legends about them. They are said to taste like fine honey and are intoxicants. It is also said that to eat just one is a guarantee you will live to be a hundred years old."

Matt laughed and said to Joanna, "Live to be a hundred? By eating just one? Well that must be some berry. You could get a very high price for each one if that were true. Legend? More like a *fairy-tale*. Far beyond anything from the Brothers Grimm. In America we call stories such as this 'Tall Tales'."

Her green eyes regarded him quietly for several minutes. Finally she asked softly, "Are you *so* sure Mathew? Some people, even those who believe in the magic of the tree, understand age is not always the blessing one might imagine. Old age can be painful because of the changes it brings. We lose so many people on a journey that long. Both friends and those we have loved."

"Regardless of that, I will come back and eat one. When will it be? Three years this fall? Two? Then I can show you it is just a myth. Live to be a hundred. What a fable."

Joanna shook her head slowly, reached into the hamper and pulled out a small white box made from ivory with Viking runes carved into the lid. When she opened the top, Matt saw several dozen small ruby colored berries nestled inside. "No reason to wait. The tree bloomed last fall. Are you sure you want to eat one? Consider carefully my love. There might be truth in the 'fable'."

The berries *were* beautiful. Like the finest pigeon blood rubies. Each was a perfect orb and seemed to glow from some inner light. Yet as perfect as they seemed, Matt hesitated. What if.... The voice in his head said, Hey! Come on. You fly a B-17. The chances you are going to live 'til next week is one in...what... none? And you won't eat a single berry. The worst it can do is kill you and that's probably going to happen anyway. Don't chicken out on me now. I'm curious about how it tastes.

He reached in and removed one from the box. It laid on the palm of his hand a perfect globe of deep ruby. Joanna reached over and held it between her thumb and forefinger. She looked into his blue eyes and asked, "Are you sure my love?"

Her green eyes held his with a questioning look.

"A hundred years with you? Well actually only seventy seven left, yes that would be wonderful."

"Very well Mathew, close your eyes and wish for a hundred years."

Matt closed his eyes and felt her first kiss him then place the berry in his mouth. He let it lay on his tongue a moment before biting into it. His first impression was a momentary bitterness followed by a sweet taste which was a bit honey-like. There were other underlying flavors contained in the berry. Matt opened his eyes to find Joanna smiling at him.

He could not keep from kissing her again. She was so beautiful and desirable. He kissed her and pulled her in to his body. Her arms went around him until they were in an embrace which contained all the pent-up passion they had for each other.

Matt was surprised to find he was slightly light headed. He wondered how he could continue to delay making love with this passionate creature in his arms. When they finally pulled away both were breathing quickly. Joanna was flushed and Matt knew the *same* desire had taken control of them.

Joanna reluctantly pulled her gaze from his and reached into the basket again to pull out two champagne flutes and a Jeroboam of 1938 Godet Champagne. The cork was already partially raised and Joanna pulled it free with a small 'pop' from the bottle.

Matt watched in a passion-fueled daze as she poured each of them a glassful and handed one of the crystal flutes to him.

Joanna gently touched her glass to his, "To us, Mathew. We are now truly joined forever. Time will not dim what we have. There is magic in our love. Do you believe in magic and forever?"

Looking into her eyes Matt was sure she *was* magic. Forever would be every day he could spend with her. "Yes Joanna. I believe. You are magic to me and the love I have for you, that is forever." She touched her glass to his again and they drank. The champagne was cool and soft on his tongue.

He was now feeling even more bemused than when he ate the berry from the Rowan tree. Could the berry have the powers Joanna had described? No, it must be my imagination; that and the champagne. Just old wives tales. Charming but nothing else.

"Joanna, did you ever eat one of the berries from the tree?"

"I tasted one once. Took a small taste out of curiosity. It was like honey, but I didn't want to live a hundred years. In some ways I suppose I am a coward. But not in loving you. Never in loving you. That is the *bravest* thing I have ever done. I was so afraid to love you." She walked forward and kissed him again while pressing her firm body into him. She pulled away and while he watched captivated, slipped her white dress from her shoulders. He saw it drop on top of the white fabric of the table cloth beneath her feet, every movement happening in slow motion.

Underneath all she wore were a white embroidered garter belt and a pair of white stockings with lace tops and the white heels. Even in his entranced state he knew he had never seen any woman who approached such perfection. Most of the young women he had been with in America were beautiful, but she was beyond all of them. Every line of her body was a work of art. No statue or painting could have improved on the vision he now saw before him.

It was as if Aphrodite or Venus had come to earth and was standing there to be admired by this mere mortal. Her copper hair fell in a cascade over one shoulder and was repeated with a small copper V at the junction of her long incomparable legs.

She walked slowly toward him. Matt wanted to say something, but was so beguiled he couldn't find his voice. His mind was saying, no this is not right, not yet, but he was beyond caring what the small voice was saying.

Joanna began to unbutton his shirt. She dropped it on the ground beside her white dress and he still could not break his gaze away from her eyes; those wonderful seductive green eyes which seemed to know him so well. Almost as if they had known each other long before they had met.

"I *am* sorry Mathew, but I want us to make love now. I purposefully left out one other property the berries are supposed to have, they are said to act as a strong aphrodisiac.

"I truly believe nothing bad is going to happen to you in the War, but if it should I do not want to go through life wondering what it would have been like being completely loved by you. I often told you 'one man' and for life and I meant it. You are my one man, Mathew. There will be *no* other. It is time to consummate our wedding"

When she had finished talking, he looked down and found he was likewise naked. Even his shoes were off. She stood with her body pressed to his and her arms around his neck. Their eyes were once again locked, both of them completely enthralled by passion and love.

Matt ran his arms under Joanna and lifted her until she was cradled against his chest. He could feel the wind breathing in from the west as it began to stir the ripening barley.

Whether this was right or wrong was no longer in his mind. They had married each other in the small chapel and, he was sure, in front of the only witnesses which really counted.

He lowered her onto the white cloth lying atop the grassy clearing beneath the tree. The white blossoms continued to fall on and around them and shadows from the sun shining through the branches played across their bodies. The wind whispered its secrets to both of them. Joanna's arms were still around his neck.

For the first time since he met her, Matt was glad of his experience with other women. Even in his intoxicated state, Matt loved her so much he wanted her first experience of sex to be good. He knew he must take his time and be sure she was ready before they joined.

He kissed her and felt her respond. Her body lifted until her breasts were touching his chest. Matt kissed her neck and whispered in her ear of how long he had wanted them to be together like this. How he had dreamed of what it would be like for them. He ran his hands down her sides and up under her back holding her against him. He found her skin to be as smooth as fine silk.

She was moving her hands over his body as if memorizing him by touch. Soon Matt was cupping her breasts in his hands and moved his lips to her nipples. He lightly kissed first one then the other. As he kissed each her breath caught for a moment and that was followed by a sigh and a small moan. One of her hands was behind his head, tangled in his hair. The other had moved down and was caressing him. He could feel her hips rising up under him, pushing against his. He moved one of his hands down over her flat stomach. Then lower. She softly moaned "Oh yes…"

She whispered in his ear, "Now, Matthew. I want you now. Be my husband. This is our wedding day. This is what we were always destined for. Love me. Love me. Here in the barley… now oh please now."

When he entered her it was slowly and gently. She gave a small cry and he stopped for several moments until she relaxed, then he gave another gentle push which she met with an upward lift of her hips toward him. They were kissing and breathing together. She gave another small cry of pain and when Matt stopped, she whispered, "No. It's *all right* darling. I am, now, fully a woman. Fully your woman. Your woman forever."

Matt was looking into her eyes and feeling only the wonderful sensations of making love with his woman. At that moment it was as if he had never made love before.

And, he realized, I never have made *love* before. What I did then went by a much cruder name. And contained only the momentary satisfaction of feeling sexual release and making another conquest. This was what I was looking for but never expected to find.

He felt as if the two of them were adrift on a gently undulating ocean. Rising and falling in perfect harmony with the waves. Their movements choreographed with the movement of the water. A dance set to the music of nature. Then the rolling movement grew stronger and the waves were rising higher.

He could hear Joanna repeating over and over, "Yes…Yes… Oh yesss Mathew."

The sea was in full tempest and Matt knew he could only ride along with it. There was no going back to shore now. The two became one and exploded together.

When Matt finally returned to earth and looked at Joanna she was crying.

"Joanna did I hurt you? I am afraid I lost control near the end."

"No Mathew...well, it hurt some in the beginning but that turned to an incredible feeling of pleasure. I could never describe what it was like. I've known what *loving* you was like. Now I know what it is like when you add having sex to the love. My God, it is beyond wonderful. You had better plan on us doing that a lot because I certainly do. I am crying because now we truly belong to each other. We are one forever"

He smiled down and kissed her gently. "Forever? Such a short time to be with you. I didn't know it at the start; but you are the one I was looking for during all those wasted years before I met you." He rolled over until he lay facing her.

She turned her head so they were looking into each other's eyes. "Yes Mathew, it took a long time for us to find each other but we finally have and we will *never* let each other go. Not in this lifetime and, I believe, beyond. Into the next and the next."

They drank more champagne and dined on cheese with crisp crackers and strawberries; their "wedding feast."

They ate without dressing and Matt could not quit looking at this beautiful woman. He had wondered how she would look nude, but his imagination had failed him totally. She was beyond his ability to fantasize about her. He only wondered how he would be able to keep his hands off her, since they now were, at last, lovers.

Almost as if she had heard his thoughts, she told him, "It's different now Mathew. The other wedding will be just a formality. Only for the family. We are **not** going back to the way things were. Not after what we just did together. I am not giving up being with you that way. I am your new bride and you are my husband and I expect you to be one fully every chance we have."

He knew it was an argument he would lose and worse, one he no longer wanted to win but he had to at least try.

"Joanna, have you really thought this through? Yes, I can take some precautions, but they are not one hundred percent perfect. What if something happened to me and you were..."

"Were what Mathew? Pregnant? Then I would certainly have *our* child. Women are facing that all around the world. It is a fact of the War. It is a risk, but the chances are not all that high it will happen. In a few months at the most, we can repeat the ceremony for the family and start really working on having children and won't that be fun?"

"Joanna, being married to you is going to be both wonderful and difficult. I can't deny you anything. And about this, I would have to be an idiot to try." Matt knew he was in trouble when he saw a seductive look come back into her green eyes.

"Mathew, do you remember what you told me when we saw 'Lisbon Story'? About five girls in one bed? Yes? Well surely you can take care of one English girl on a table cloth a few times."

"You would remember my foolish words now, Joanna. I thought I asked you to forget I ever said that. I was only kidding."

"Well Mathew, I didn't forget and I'm not 'kidding' as you Americans say. The bell has just rung for round two. The question is, are you going to come out of your corner, or are you 'throwing in the towel'?"

He did not throw in the towel and the match ended in a draw. Both were exhausted. Quite an accomplishment considering it was amateur versus seasoned professional.

When they finally walked from the barley field, each of them knew they were even more in love than before.

After everyone was in bed that night, Joanna slipped into Matt's room and they quietly made love again before falling asleep in each other's arms.

Chapter 18

THE LAST MISSION

For the first time since Matt had been flying her, the "Maid" was fighting against him but who could blame her? She had large holes in her starboard wing and both engines on that side were shut-down; two FW 190s having put numerous twenty millimeter rounds into that wing. One of the engines had caught fire, but the flames died quickly when he shut it down. He feathered both propellers so they created less drag, helping him keep her from going into a stall. Still, it was all he could physically do to keep her in trim since her natural inclination was to turn in the direction of her two remaining working engines.

Matt knew if she did stall the chance of him getting her back under control dropped to damn near zero. He was certain if that happened, it was her death knell. She was doomed anyway, but he just didn't want to admit it; most of all not to himself. "The Maid" had somehow come to represent the love he had for Joanna.

Matt knew with only two engines he could never maintain enough air speed to keep up with the group and falling out of formation would only lead to further attacks by German fighter planes and that would end only one way.

The acrid smell of burned cordite from fifty caliber machine gun rounds hung heavily in the air even though he had sent his crew out with their parachutes over five minutes ago. His copilot John Smithson had been the last to hit the silk and he went *only* after Matt had promised him that he would be out in a few minutes. As he watched Smithies' chute blossom open he wondered if he had done the right thing by telling him to bail out.

He watched in alarm as one of the two Focke Wulfs which had methodically shot up "The Maid" peeled away and nosed downward following Smithson's chute. Matt had too often seen German fighter pilots machine gun Americans who were parachuting out of their bombers. Relieved, he saw this German appeared to be flying escort for his copilot. The enemy flier seemed to be making sure that Smithson was able to land safely. It was a show of decency by the enemy which surprised him. The pilot then turned his plane upward toward the limping "Maid of Barley." The yellow nose painted on both of these Focke Wulfs told Matt they were some of the Luftwaffe's best remaining fighter pilots. Many of them had flown since Germany intervened in the Spanish Civil War in the mid 1930's. He wondered if they too might have grown as tired of war and killing as he had. God knew most of them had been at it *far* longer.

Suddenly, another German fighter appeared; this one a Messerschmitt 109 without a yellow nose. The pilot was swinging around in preparation for a final killing run at the "Maid." The only remaining question was if Matt would be alive at the end of this pilot's run. And would he be able to strap on his parachute and get out of her before she broke apart in mid air.

As he tried to get the old girl to take some kind of evasive action, he saw the two yellow noses cut the 109 out of his run. They blocked his line of fire by flying directly at him, forcing the pilot to stop his attack and pull away. It was as if they had threatened one of their own and dared him to fire on this B-17. Matt knew these were the two who had with almost surgical precision damaged "the Maid" to the point she could no longer return to England. It was as if they had said to the other pilot, "Get off, this one is ours." And if that was the message, why were they holding off on the kill? Matt could make no sense of it. He had never seen anything like it in all the missions he had flown.

A few short moments later, one of them pulled along the left side of his limping plane and started giving him hand signals. The German pilot was pointing at his ears and holding up different numbers of fingers with his right hand then putting his thumb and forefinger together and making a twisting motion with them. After the German pilot had repeated this charade several times, Matt understood the message. He was telling Matt to set his radio frequency to one they could talk on. He locked his controls so he could turn and make the adjustments, and then triggered his mike.

What the hell he thought, I have nothing to lose. If they wanted me dead I would have been dead by now. When all is said and done, my life and the plane are all I am risking and the "Maid" will never make it back to England anyway. My crew is, by now, safely on the ground. Probably already prisoners. Hopefully they will live out the War in a POW camp, but they will live out the War. That is more than most can say with assurance. It is *far* more than I am certain of at this moment.

Matt looked over at the German pilot's face, one which appeared years older than his own. The man flew his plane as if it were all he had ever done, simply an extension of his body.

The face that looked back was a world-weary face which had seen far more than it wanted. It was the kind of expression Matt had recently begun to see on his own face in the mirror whenever he shaved. Even Joanna had said she thought he had seen too much War and was glad he would soon be out of it. All that had remained was this mission and one more but now.... Matt's earphones crackled to life.

"Hello American. What is your name?"

The voice which he heard in his ear phones carried a heavy German accent but the English was really quite good. Matt could clearly understand his question.

"Captain Mathew Weldon USAAF," he answered. "And may I know who you are?"

There was a click and a bit of static. "I am Major Hans von Falkenburg. Don't you want to bail out of your aircraft now? We have shot her up rather badly you know. I must say you are a very good pilot, Captain, but there is simply no way she will make it back to England. Best if you leave her now. Plenty of altitude to jump. I assure you from personal experience, parachuting is no disgrace. I have had to jump twice in the last few years."

Matt knew by the silence that the German flying just off his wing tip was awaiting an answer.

"No Major. It's not fear of jumping which is keeping me on board. I don't know exactly how to put it so it will make sense. I got this bird as soon as she got to England. I am the only pilot who has ever flown her and she is named after the English girl I love. The one I intend to marry if I live through all this. Perhaps you have noticed the name on her nose is "Maid of Barley" and she has become more than just an airplane to me; more than just metal and wires and guns and engines. I know I can't get her back to her base. She's going to have to go down somewhere over here, but I would like to try to get her down as gently and intact as I can. That probably does not make any sense to you but it's what I feel I have to try. I want to put her down with some dignity, not just abandon her to crash into the earth alone.

If she starts falling apart I will certainly jump because I do want to get back to the lady she is named for, but so far she is holding together. I really believe she can go to ground with her dignity intact. I would like a chance to help her do that."

After a click and more static the German pilot answered, "Well Captain Weldon, I think it is foolishness, but the kind foolishness only another pilot can understand.

"Yes, our planes do become more than they reasonably should. I lost my old girl, an ME109 almost two years ago. I had flown her for a very long time.

"This Focke Wulf 190 I have now is a better aircraft but I must confess I still miss that old Messerschmitt. She and I were used to each other. Old friends. We forgave each other our faults. Almost a love affair. So, yes I can understand. You are, by the way, a very good pilot. You made our job most difficult today. Both I and Günter, the other 190 pilot, now flying on your right side, were both admiring your skill while trying to line up runs on your plane. Günter, by the way, gave you a high compliment, he wondered if you were a converted fighter plane pilot?"

Matt keyed his mike and responded with a small laugh, "Please tell Günter no, but as a civilian I qualified single engine in a pretty hot little plane I once had. It seems a very long time ago now. I wanted to fly fighters, but that was a glamour job; more applicants for the job than aircraft available."

The major spoke German for a couple of minutes passing along Matt's comments to the pilot just off the right wing of "The Maid."

Matt heard a short reply from the other pilot before the German Major once again spoke to him. "Günter reminded me how lucky we are to have such glamorous jobs," he chuckled. "Lucky we applied early while there were still enough planes so we were able to get one. Günter often has a macabre sense of humor.

"Even though I do believe it is foolish of you, Günter and I will try to help you get her down with, as you say, her dignity. I assume you are going to try to belly her in as that is certainly your best hope.

"First, there is not one of the Luftwaffe fields you could dare use for a wheels down landing. They would be shooting you to pieces as soon as you were in sight.

"You must understand we could not say anything to them in order to prevent it. You are an enemy pilot and besides I am sure there are items on board you will need time to, shall we say 'make unusable.' Isn't that right? Yes Captain, we are aware of the Norden. We have several from crashed aircraft and they are doing us no good at all. But orders are orders and you need to carry yours out. If we didn't obey orders who knows what would happen. We can't have a war without obeying orders. Now can we?"

Matt had forgotten the Norden Bomb Sight and a couple of other items which pilots were constantly reminded should not fall in to German hands.

"Yes Major," he answered, "a landing away from military installations would be for the best."

"Ok Captain. At present we are on a largely unmonitored frequency. When you are down, Günter and I will go to a different frequency to report where you have had the sheer blind luck to be able to set a B-17 down. That is our duty and we will fulfill it. Naturally, it may take a few minutes to get through to the proper level of authority to make this report. Once you are taken prisoner, we will be glad if you could simply not remember the part we may have played in any of this. We would not be awarded Medals for this if you understand my meaning."

Matt was chuckling when he replied, "All I remember is that two FW 190s with yellow noses shot my plane full of holes and did their damndest to kill my young ass and if I was not such a great pilot they would undoubtedly have succeeded."

Matt could hear the German actually laughing, then heard him say, "Yes that about sums the whole incident up and the interviewers will be impressed by the skills of those unnamed pilots who shot down such a superior enemy pilot; we unknown heroes of the third Reich.

"Now I'm going to be off air for a few minutes while Günter and I talk about where you might be able to sit her down."

When he came back, it was to inform Matt that Günter knew a place that should serve his purpose well. It was a farm field which had not been tilled yet. It was full of weeds, almost flat and ran slightly up hill. No trees, only a bit of scrub growth along one edge.

"Captain, Günter is going to fly out front to lead the way. I am staying on your wing to be sure your plane remains sound. Follow him and do your best to match his altitude. Günter is a superior pilot, far better than me and I am pretty damn good. He will lead you in. He will go as low as he dares, and he dares a lot, and I will be talking you down alongside your wing. Just remember your wheels will not be down so you will have to be lower than you are used to before you touch down and this time you will not have the luxury of a 'go around' available to you. This has to be right the first time. Do you understand?"

The difficulty of what he was attempting was made very clear by what the Major had said, but Matt was still determined to try.

"Yes Major von Falkenburg. And whatever happens, I appreciate what you and your friend are doing. I know it is no more in your code of conduct than it is ours. Mores' the pity."

There was a slight pause, then he heard the German quietly echo, "Yes... mores' the pity."

Günter was losing altitude rapidly. Matt's altimeter told him he was under six thousand feet, then a few moments later five thousand feet. Matt watched Günter closely and beyond in the distance saw what he felt was his target. It was flat with a slight uphill slope; landing uphill would help slow him down.

The Major constantly assured him that he was looking good with occasional bits of advice, "down a bit or put on a little altitude.' Matt found he was soon less than five hundred feet and Günter was even lower. By the time the "Maid" was less than two hundred feet, Günter was practically cutting tops off the weeds with his propeller. It was flying which Matt could hardly believe any pilot would attempt and Günter held it so long that he wondered that anyone could have nerves that steady.

He realized he had been following the pilot in front of him so well that his plane was only a few feet from the ground. As Günter began to pull up, he heard the first weeds swishing against the "Maid's" belly and cut his two remaining engines at nearly the same instant their propellers began to slash into the dirt and were bent backward. Seconds later the belly of the "Maid" began to trench the dirt of the field. She was still moving forward at a high speed, but began to slow because of the field's upward angle and the drag of the earth. It was a strange landing because the engines were no longer running. The only noise was created by dirt and scrub vegetation against the aluminum of the airplane's belly. Then there was a loud tearing sound as the belly turret with its two fifty caliber machine guns was ripped away and roughly slid beneath the fuselage. Matt was wildly bumped and jarred, but his lap belt held him firmly in his seat. Empty fifty caliber cartridge cases were flying around the cockpit and he was hit by several; one of which put a cut on his cheek that felt like the wasp sting he remembered from childhood.

He was grateful that the fifty caliber machine gun in the nose hadn't broken loose and come flying backward towards him. Had the designers ever considered that possibility while in the design process? Was a wheels-up landing like this even considered in those calculations?

It seemed forever before "The Maid" slowed, then stopped and rolled over to rest on her right wing tip.

It was not until Matt reached over to set the parking breaks that he realized he had been running through all the motions he would have performed on a normal wheels-down landing. That was when he understood how strong his training had been. He began to laugh a bit hysterically at his trained-animal landing and with a sigh of relief said aloud, "No old boy, I don't think the brakes will be needed."

When he finally stopped laughing, the silence seemed deafening until his earphones crackled to life with a question, "Captain Weldon. Are you all right?"

Matt was startled by the voice, so it was a moment before he could answer. When he finally did, he knew his voice came across as breathless because he realized he had not taken a single breath during the landing.

"Yes Major, I am a bit shaken but otherwise unharmed. Thanks largely to the two of you. Tell Günter that was the best flying I have *ever* seen. I don't know how he held it that low that long. It was completely amazing."

"Very well Captain, I will pass it along to him, but it will just encourage him. He is already an unforgivable show-off.

"Günter cut his teeth in gliders and I think he sometimes forgets the ones we fly now have props. Do you know he occasionally scares even me? Speaking of good flying you did a fine job with yours. From up here, your "Maid" looks in pretty good shape. I think you did her proud with that landing."

"Major von Falkenberg, I am grateful to both of you. I know you didn't have to do that. All I can do is say thank you both, from me and my lady."

The German pilot was quite for a moment. "Captain, you gave us something to do that we can be proud of doing. It has reached the point we are glad of moments like that.

"Well, you have some work to do and we have a report to make about the location of a B-17 that we just saw go down in a field which we think is located at such and such a map coordinate. Understandably our exact information might be a bit off.

"Good luck and after the War, kiss that girl for us. And let's hope nothing like this ever troubles the world again."

Matt keyed his mike saying, "Amen to that Major. Amen to that!"

He watched as the two yellow nosed FW 190s flew over, wiggled their wings in salute and climbed into the sky until they were out of sight.

Even though they were fighting for Germany, Matt wished them well and hoped they survived this War which had seen far too many on both sides die already. He was sure they were the kind the world would need after this finally ended.

He spent a few minutes setting devices to destroy the Norden Device and a few other confidential units, opened his hatch and climbed out. He laid his bare palm against the plane's outer surface for a brief benediction and walked slowly away from the "Maid" for the last time.

A short moment later there were several muted explosions and Matt saw a growing conflagration in the nose of the aircraft as the secret equipment was destroyed. The small grenades burned at such high temperature that the aluminum of the aircraft's skin melted completely away from the nose on one side.

He was so focused watching "The Maid" burn that he didn't notice the large grey painted truck bumping its way to the edge of the field or the seven soldiers who jumped out and started walking quickly in his direction with their rifles pointed at him.

It was only when the one closest to him began shouting, that Matt turned to see a soldier no more than sixteen years old wearing a uniform several sizes too large for him. The language he was using was certainly not complimentary to this American pilot who stood in front of him in the weed covered field.

Matt raised his hands over his head because he did not want this child- soldier to have any excuse to shoot him. The boy had raised his rifle to his shoulder and was pointing it directly at him.

A shout came from an old soldier in the group which had fallen behind. Matt recognized the shouted phrase and its meaning. "Nein Scheisskofp! Nicht Schieβen! Nicht Schieβen!"

Matt knew enough German to know the old soldier had called the young man a "Shit Head," and repeated, "Do not shoot!"

It was obviously an order so the young man lowered his rifle; plainly disappointed. Matt was certain he had intended to shoot him in cold blood. The young soldier did, however, continue to approach him while screaming insults at this downed American flier.

When he was finally standing right in front of Matt, he used the steel plate on his rifle butt to hit him in the stomach. Matt instantly doubled over and fell to the ground gasping for breath. The soldier was still screaming at him and before Matt was able to react, he felt a vicious kick to his left hip by the boy's heavy boot. The pain was so intense he thought he would pass out. He believed his hip was broken.

Through the fog of the pain he vaguely heard the old soldier telling the young man, "Zuruckschieben....Ich werde dich erschienβen."

268

In pained fog, Matt had no idea the man who had called the boy a shithead had now told the boy soldier who had just kicked him, "**Move back... or I will shoot you**!" All Matt knew was the boy turned very pale and quickly moved away from where he lay. If he could have observed the old soldier he would have seen the rifle raised to his shoulder. Matt could see the rifle of the young man lying at the boy's feet. He did know the young man was trembling and terror was plain for all to see; fear printed on his face and deep within his eyes.

When the other six older soldiers finally arrived, Matt was surprised to find they were in their fifties and one looked at least sixty five. They all needed shaves and their uniforms looked as if they had been heavily used, the pants frayed at the bottom of the cuffs.

The soldier who had shouted orders to the boy soldier looked down at Matt and asked in heavily accented English, "American flier?"

Matt groaned out a simple, "Yes, American."

The German said, "Am Hauptfeldwebel Ummm... same as Sergeant Major US Army. Rank from First War. Called up two months ago, same rank this war. You?"

Matt knew that his name, rank and serial number were allowed, so he answered with what this Sergeant had asked for. "I am Captain Mathew Weldon. Pilot U.S. Army Air Corp." Matt remembered he was still wearing his Colt .45 Pistol in a holster on his hip under his high altitude jacket. "Sergeant, I need to surrender my side arm from under my jacket. How shall we do that?"

The Sergeant turned to his unit, spoke for a moment, and then turned back to Matt with the words, "Very slow und careful. You stand?"

Matt was able to slowly though painfully straighten his legs, but didn't know if this was a sign his hip was broken or not. "I don't know Sergeant. I am trying to decide if my hip is broken."

The Sergeant thought for a minute before saying, "Vell, until ve have un idea of das, I vill suggest solution to problem. Round is in chamber or only clip is loaded?"

Matt assured him that only the clip contained rounds; that there was not one in the barrel.

"Das is gut. OK. Vill tell step by step vat to do. Jus do slowly step by step und we vill have no worse day than ve have already. OK? Step one open jacket so I see holster."

Matt slowly pulled his leather flying jacket open until his holster was in plain sight.

"Gut. Sehr gut. Now Captain. Open flap on holster so I see butt of pistol. Ja, excellent. Now for danger part. Slowly pull out... Ach, my man has rifle pointed at back of head so is danger for you. I mean to tell earlier...slowly pull and put on ground far away from you can reach."

Matt followed the instructions the Sergeant had given him to the letter and very slowly. When it was done and the German was holding the pistol, he told Matt he was sorry to have done it that way but being careful was what had gotten him through the last war in one piece.

Two of the other soldiers helped Matt stand up, which he was finally able to do but only in intense pain. The Feldwebel checked his hip with his hands and finally said he didn't believe it was broken but that he was sure it was badly damaged and no doubt hurting like hell. He had something in his canteen that would help for a time but it needed medical care as soon as he could get to a camp.

Chapter 19

GÖRING AND WOLFFCHANDZ

Waffen Schutzstaffel (SS) Captain Frederick Wolffchandz was enjoying a rare treat, a quiet evening in his quarters, reading a book on Roman History and enjoying a glass of schnapps. The scholarly volume covered the wars of Julius Caesar in very descriptive detail. The Captain was, as always, impressed with the military and political brilliance of the man. Caesar always established his utter defeat of one enemy before turning his gaze in the direction of another.

As a graduate student in History at Heidelberg before he was called away to this war, he had studied many other wars beginning at the dawn of recorded history through the most recent war of 1914 – 1918. Forecasting success or failure in any war was very straight-forward if you attended the tactics used by leaders on each side. That remained just as valid when he examined the direction of this war.

Frederick was glad he was able to hide his thoughts behind a face he had long ago trained to never betray his mind. He knew Germany was going to lose this war and he had known it since the day Hitler ordered the attack on Russia. "Der Führer" had attacked two months past the date when German troops had the ability to take Moscow. And, only the capture of that capitol city in rapid fashion would have made victory in Russia even a *distant* possibility.

Of course, long before the imperative of capturing Moscow could be achieved, an unusually brutal winter had set in. The Russians were no longer required to save themselves. 'General Winter' once again saved them by freezing the German Army in its tracks. Men and machines simply couldn't move any further toward achieving Hitler's supreme order to take Moscow.

Russian troops, accustomed to those winters, had the proper clothing. Hitler never considered small necessities like heavy woolen clothing, insulated boots or special machine lubricants. So German soldiers were wasted, freezing to death by the thousands and all the while the Russian army rebuilt its losses to prepare for a spring offensive.

Frederick understood clearly what no one dared say aloud. The attack on Russia was "The Great Blunder," the one overriding mistake which could not be undone and was destined to drag the entire enterprise down in ruin. Knowing the workings of Hitler's mind as he did, the ruin would be total. Hitler would never give up as long as he or a single German soldier was still alive. Adolph Hitler had been allowed by the German people to become the ultimate megalomaniac. Nothing was his fault. Not ever. And if he was not the problem, as he never was, then the German Military and people were and if they all perished, **so be it**.

The field phone in his room jangled rousing him from his unpleasant musing on the future of his country. He put the earpiece to his head, "Ja, this is Captain Wolffchandz."

The voice in his ear was loud, metallic and harsh causing him to hold the phone away from his ear as he heard the voice say, "We have an urgent message from Reichsführer Himmler's office in Berlin which must reach Reichsmarschall Göring at once. They need an answer from him tonight. Berlin orders you to rush the message to him now and if he needs help with the decision; help him with it. They said you would know what they mean, though verdampt if I do."

He put the headpiece back against his ear and answered, "Ja, *I* know; where you have no *need* to. Get the message around to me at once and bring me a Kublewagon at the same time. I'll handle the matter from there."

Ja, Frederick thought as he hung up the phone, I know what they mean by helping him make a decision. Our friend Big Hermann is addicted to morphine and its derivatives because on the day of the Beer Hall Putsch back in '23 when Hitler first tried to grab power, Göring was right up front with him and was shot in the groin by a ricochet; a serious wound. He could easily have died but his wealthy wife smuggled him to Italy, then to Sweden where he was treated for months. During their two year sojourn there, he became an addict and has never been able to break free.

At times he can make perfectly logical decisions but another occasion may find him completely out of touch. At those times his decisions have to be "assisted;" in short, made for him. Afterward the Reichmarshall will, out of embarrassment, inevitably confirm the decision as having been made by him alone.

There was the sound of the small Volkswagen military vehicle arriving outside his door followed by a tentative knock. "Captain Wolffchandz. A message for you to carry to the Reichsmarshall and the requested Kublewagon is here for your use."

He opened his door to be greeted by another of the many young faces which had recently become all too common, in this, the now fifth year of the War. This particular boy could not be even 17 years old. Now the Army was reduced to calling up young boys and old men. The old ones were mostly retreads from World War One. They didn't haunt him as much. They at least knew what war was about; they understood it for the lethal profession it was. These young ones were largely still playing at war. He hoped boys like this could learn it wasn't a game before a bullet taught them that final lesson. The older men had at least enjoyed a share of life. Many had already raised families. These boys hadn't done any of those things and many of them never would. He was saddened to see this becoming a "children's war." He believed the Americans and the British would only inflict the necessary casualties on these young ones but the Russians were another matter. After what the German Armies had done in Russia, there would be no mercy in return. Any living thing which fell in front of a Russian rifle was certainly going to die. One had to hope the Americans and British beat the Russians into Germany or at least most of it. If the Russians were allowed to win the race into Berlin, the city would become a massive butcher shop.

God, he felt such an old man at only twenty six and unmarried. Right now all he wanted to do was live through this war and have a chance to do all those normal things that people used to do. They would do them again on some future day and he wanted more than anything to be alive to be one of them. If he could survive, he wanted nothing beyond returning to his studies in the Department of History then later to teach. Strange, he thought, first you live it, then you teach it. If you survive.

He returned the young boy's salute, took the sealed message, read it and walked over to the small camouflage-painted car. There had been rain earlier so the canvas top was already raised. The car started on his first try and he drove quickly away from the airfield into the forest.

The forest through which he drove was dark and the road narrow. Slits in the caps over the headlights were very thin, so did a poor job of illuminating the road ahead. He kept his speed under ten miles an hour and even then had to keep his concentration sharp on each twist and turn so he didn't suddenly find himself off the lightly graded dirt road. Huge trees rose upward to form an unbroken roof of branches and leaves over him. If he had been able to glance up, there would have been only occasional flashes of a silver-gray clouded sky shining down through the dark canopy above him.

An airplane pilot would have seen only an unbroken landscape of heavy woods: exactly what the people who planned this installation wanted seen from the air. The small airstrip the Captain was driving away from was impossible to spot unless you were almost standing on it. The camouflage was perfect. The road from the airfield to Carinhall was completely tree covered. Carinhall itself, as large and imposing an edifice as it was, had also been cleverly hidden by woods, as invisible as clear air.

Oh yes, there was another "Carinhall" which could be seen. It was several miles away from the site the Captain was driving towards. That Carinhall was likewise hidden just not nearly as cleverly. It lay near a small village on a hillside and was a completely fake Carinhall made from wood, some stone and canvas. Painted to exactly match the real one, it had lights and real military vehicles, anti aircraft guns and spotlights. In short, it was an excellent replica of the real thing. So far it had drawn not a bit of interest from any enemy aircraft. The Reichsmarshall was quite insulted.

The real Carinhall lay less than fifty miles from Berlin, yet not a single bomb had fallen closer than 24 kilometers. And those had been from several American B-17s which had completely missed their aiming points and released the bomb loads far from their intended target.

The Americans were destroying Berlin by day and the British were doing the same by night. Both were paying a heavy price in lost aircraft and fliers, but still they came day after day, night after night. Berlin and every major German city were slowly being reduced to rubble and all the German fighter planes could do was slow them down. German aircraft were being shot down at an alarming rate which neither the factories nor the training facilities could keep pace with.

The Reichsmarshall was extremely offended by the lack of bombs being dropped near his very substantial person. He was, after all, the second most important person in all of Germany; second only to Adolph Hitler and head of the vaunted Luftwaffe, yet the Allies were acting as if he were a nonentity.

He, at least, had ordered bombs dropped with the intent of killing Churchill. They didn't get him but they had at least paid him the tribute of making the attempt. Göring viewed it an insult that they seemed to think so little of his status in Germany that not a single attempt appeared to have been made on his life.

On the other hand, several direct attempts had been made on Hitler's life. True, all the attempts had been heavy-handed and had failed, but at least they tried.

As the Captain drove through the night, he allowed himself a ghost of a smile when he remembered the Reichsmarshall's complaint about the singular lack of an attempt to kill him. On that recent occasion, he had looked thoughtfully serious for a few moments while waiting silently for "great man" to ask his opinion. After a few moments of quiet, the portly figure asked what he thought of the situation.

"Well Herr Reichsmarshall," he began, "you don't hide out. So let's assume they could locate you if they wished." Göring nodded his affirmation granting that to be a fact. "So they could find you to make an attempt?"

Once again the great head nodded yes.

"Then I suggest they do not wish to make an attempt and if that is the case they have a very good reason not to do so. That can only mean you for some reason have more value alive than dead. Now you are the most loyal of Germans, that is well known, but you are also widely known to be a very reasonable man and that seems the most likely answer to our central question. The opposite side may know that when the time for arranging consultations beyond today's situation arises, you would be the one individual who could successfully arrange and chair such consultations.

Göring's large square face broke into a blinding smile. Captain Wolffchandz was convinced the man could not have been happier if Hitler had just awarded him another high sounding title.

"Yes, yes, that must be it." He slapped his big hand on the back of the smaller man not even noticing this caused the younger man to stumble a full step forward.

"Truly brilliant deductive logic, Captain. Naturally, if they don't want me dead there is a good reason and they have an area of cooperation in mind down the road. Perhaps a cease-fire. We might even join up to fight the 'Reds.' That is where the real danger lies for both sides. I've said that very thing, time after time publicly. Stalin and the Communists are simply animals. They know no constraints. They do not understand civilized behavior. Stalin revealed himself when he said, 'The death of one man is a tragedy to his family. The death of millions is simply a statistic.' They have no consideration of the individual only the masses matter to them."

He paused and then continued, "You know Captain, I have just opened a bottle of 1939 vintage red wine that was put up here at Carinhall. It is really excellent. Would you join me in a drink and toast to

275

a day when the guns have gone silent and we can enjoy these forests once again in peace?"

Frederick had joined Göring for the glass of wine and the toast. The wine was indeed excellent. The middle aged Reichsmarshall and the young Captain talked of many things deep into the night and found they enjoyed each other's company. During that evening the Captain decided while in many ways Göring was sophisticated, in others he was almost as innocent as a child. He had been the perfect foil used by Hitler in his rise to the position of supreme power. That power was attained in no small measure through the use of Göring's reputation as a World War One German hero and his family's money.

~ ~ ~ ~

Frederick had been so lost in thought that it came as a surprise to find he had arrived at the two massive stone guard towers protecting the only entrance to Carinhall. Three of Göring's elite paratroopers, the Fallschirmjäger, blocked his entrance and he was again impressed with how well trained and controlled they were in their behavior. In spite of the fact that they frequently saw him as often as two or three times a day, they always performed their duties as if they had never seen him before. It was only after his papers were carefully examined and a clearance call was placed to the residence that he would be greeted in a somewhat more cheerful, *almost* friendly manner.

The singular exception to this careful ritual had been on the one occasion the Reichmarshall had asked the Captain to ride out to his lake for a stroll along the shore with him while he considered a thorny problem. That day the guards had waved them though the gates without a stop. Of course the man he was with was the one who had ordered an H. Göring signature sewn in silver thread on a black band around the bottom of the left sleeve of each of the paratrooper's uniforms.

The one or two times when his pass through the gates was delayed he found himself sweating before laughing at his own ability to be stressed by these very tough gentlemen. He knew if he were in Göring's large shoes, these would be the kind of men he would want guarding his oversized house and with the same high level of care. Not all of big Herman's enemies were flying in American and English bombers in German skies; many were in prestigious offices in Berlin and far more dangerous. Several were trying to remove him from his powerful position in the Nazi pantheon.

After a few moments on the telephone, the Feldwebel paratrooper wearing a camouflaged smock and combat pants came to the door of the stone tower and waved him through after a crisp salute.

The road changed from a roughly graded graveled road to one which was paved and wide enough for two tanks or armored half tracks to easily traverse side by side. Its gentle curve finally revealed the magnificent bulk of Carinhall. It bore no more resemblance to a hunting lodge than the Rhine River did to a small mountain stream. Many of the rooms were lit and Göring was standing outside the huge oaken double doors waiting for him.

As soon as the Captain had parked and was walking up the steps, Göring strode toward him. "Well Captain Wolffchandz, whatever communication has brought you out tonight must indeed be very important. I am certain that the sender thinks so, but as I have given you standing permission to examine the contents, you must agree that it is *really* urgent." He cocked his great head while waiting for a reply.

"Heir Reichsmarshall, it is in effect a matter of life and death and I believe the honor of not only the Luftwaffe, but in reality Germany is at stake here. I hope it is not already too late."

Göring took the thin paper used for all decoded messages from the Captain's hand and both men went into the lighted entry hall.

As soon as Göring had read the contents, he exploded. "Mein Gott! Himmler actually wants to execute the entire crew of an American bomber just because they were shot down on their twenty fourth mission! One mission more and they would have been able to stand down from flying. Yes, it may be good for German morale to say this happened on a next to last mission and it might be a blow to the American Air Force to say they were killed, but that can happen without butchering these men. Himmler says Goebbels agrees with him and since it involves the Luftwaffe he wanted to advise me of their decision. **Their Decision,** he erupted! "By Gott we will put a stop to this and quickly.

"These may be enemy fliers but I will not see them slaughtered like animals. We may be enemies of the British and the Americans but they have done *nothing* like this. The Red Cross has confirmed that all of our boys who went down in England have received very good treatment. You are right Captain, this is uncivilized behavior. I will not have Germany do this. It is totally unacceptable. To announce they were killed is one matter. That can be done. We will simply overlook reporting them to the Red Cross and any letters they write can be misplaced. That would be just bad record keeping on our part, oversights, and things of that nature . We should separate the crew into different camps.

"We first need to get a call through to Berlin telling them.... No, we need to be stronger, warning them that this is a Luftwaffe matter and any action taken before we decide will have consequences reaching to the highest levels. Remind them that this goes against everything that German civilization stands for and would have grave consequences if even a hint of it were to reach our enemies.

"Tell them we have no objection to someone such as Lord Haw Haw announcing on our international broadcast that the aircraft has been shot down with total loss of the crew. That may have some negative effect on the other side's morale. Which, by the way, I seriously doubt, but not a hand is to be laid on them until we get back to Herr Himmler with our decisions.

"Meanwhile, get General Student on the phone. I want him to find the location where they are being held and put plans together to immediately get them under our control. If it requires force we will use it. I intend to authorize him to move in strength and take them. Kurt Student is not a man to be stopped by anything. Nor are our Fallschirmjägers. Ask the armies of Belgium and Greece; they barely slowed my paratroopers down. The Fallschirmjägers ran over both countries in a matter of days when our Army was talking about taking months.

"If we move fast enough with good information, I believe it will be fait accompli before Himmler and Goebbels can react and they would not dare go to Hitler with this. It is too insignificant a matter to be brought before him and he does not like addressing petty matters.

These two roaches hiding in Berlin have been trying to shunt me aside for long enough! This is yet another attempt to grab power by forcing me to give in on something which touches the Luftwaffe. If I do, it shows my lack of resolve. Well, instead they are going to see a naked show of power. Let's see how they like that. By the way, I know the Americans are fond of giving their bombers names. Do we know the name of this one?"

The Captain scanned the message again before replying, "No sir, but I will find out when we have a breather. It sounds like we are going to be very busy for the next few hours."

Hermann Göring walked into the library off the main hall trailed by the young SS Captain. "No my young friend, it is more likely we will be busy all night and into tomorrow morning. I will order coffee and schnapps. When the sun comes up we will breakfast together. You can use the phone on the table near the window and if you run into any road blocks use my name in any way needed. Until further notice you are assigned to me here at Carinhall. Would you have any objection to that?"

There was no hesitation before Captain Wolffchandz came to attention, saluted the big man in front of him and said, "No objection at all Herr Reichsmarshall. It is always an honor to serve you."

Hermann Göring smiled and snapped a casual salute in return. "Good... now let's get to work."

By five the next morning, the young SS Captain had located the pilot of the B-17 who was being held in the small village of Bernshausen. A small home guard unit of the army had him secured in the village jail. The rest of the crew had parachuted down in a relatively small area near an artillery flak unit which quickly captured them and took them to a nearby Luftwaffe base. Those men were, therefore, already under Göring's direct control.

When he heard this from the young Captain, the Reichsmarshall smiled and said, "That is good. That is in fact, *excellent.* Our challenge is much easier now. What remains is the rescue of the pilot and to deliver him safely to a Luftwaffe controlled camp where we can be certain nothing untoward happens to him. Once we have him, I want him in Luft III. It is a huge facility and I trust the Kommandant completely. Like me, he was in the last war. He was on my staff for several years and we still speak quite often. His honor is beyond question. A rare quality in these times."

"Oh... Herr Reichsmarshall... the aircraft was named 'Maid of Barley.' It was partially burned by thermite grenades, but they were still able to read her name. She had the usual scantily dressed female painted on her nose. The Americans seem to like their women skinny and dressed in lingerie. Often in nothing at all. Interestingly, the woman on this American plane had a British Union Jack apron as her covering."

Göring gave the young man a hearty slap on the back along with a broad smile. "Good work Captain. Now, can you put together a reply to the pair of Berlin Roaches? Simply ask how they plan to do their disgraceful deed in such a way it will only appear these fliers died in the crash of their plane. This in case the Geneva Convention people start asking questions. Tell them it will have to be done very carefully. Throw in a few really large words. That alone will slow them down. We just need to be sure we get this pilot while they are still thinking. Neither of them is really very good at that. Plotting...yes. Thinking...no.

"I am calling General Student right away to inform him where our man is being held and have a conversation about what he will need to get the pilot out. It sounds like he is not strongly guarded, but we need to go in totally prepared. I want Student to get this done within 24 hours. Short notice, but that is the man's forte. He has never failed me. There are far too few like him and damn near none in positions of power. We are cursed with a war run by dilettantes and ass kissers. You must forgive me, Captain. I am a man who speaks his mind; a habit which often causes trouble. It is the reason I spend so much time here rather than in Berlin.

"When things die down on the rescue phase, I would like you to put a plan together on how we can have these men alive and well while it appears to the outside world they died in the crash of their B-17. Once we have the pilot safely in our care, get people out there to make the aircraft look as if it crashed. The only reason the roaches wanted him killed was, on their part, an ill advised plan to show me who is really in charge in Germany. What they claimed they wished to accomplish can easily be done without murdering a plane full of young fliers. I believe those two are now so covered in blood, it is their answer to every question.

"Back in my War those two would have been shot for even suggesting something like this. But then those two have become sadists. They enjoy torture and murder.

"So Captain Wolffchandz, would you be too sad if I asked you to leave the vaunted SS and accept a transfer over to the Luftwaffe where you will be working for me directly? You would have to give up that Black Uniform and change to one of Luftwaffe grey.

"I have found you both very intelligent and level headed under pressure. I would like to have you as my aide. My assistant. It is your decision however. This job will not take you often to Berlin. Do you think you could survive living out here in the forest?"

In answer, the young Captain removed the silver death's head from each collar of his uniform jacket and handed them to Göring saying, "I won't need these any longer, Herr Reichsmarshall, but I will, as you suggested, need a new uniform. Grey is a better color. Black shows everything"

Laughing, Göring took the silver insignia in his large hand and walked to the huge fireplace with a smile. He stood there for a moment looking at them laying in his open hand before throwing them into the fire.

He looked at Captain Wolffchandz and smiled before saying, " Good riddance, wouldn't you say? Welcome to the Luftwaffe, Captain."

Chapter 20

LEAVING ENGLAND

Matt drove the borrowed Jeep away from Polebrook. He had been back in England for only a few days. Three in the hospital being checked out following his time in the POW camp in Germany. He had "escaped" during the prisoner transfer from Stalag Luft III to another camp nearer Berlin; almost a year of his life gone. Wasted except for the college level finance courses he was able to finish there. In spite of that, it was time he should have spent with Joanna in England. They could have been married by now.

Many small things he had seen and heard since returning to England spoke to him of everyday life moving slowly toward a prewar normal. Uniforms and attitudes of both fliers and ground personnel were far more relaxed than when he had left on "The Maid's" final flight. Only officers still continued an acceptable level of military disciple in most things.

On that fateful day everything had still been, "Yes Sir! No Sir!" And "I understand Sir!" The preflight briefings were still full of tension and fear which on that day had remained as tangible as the big mission maps hanging on the cold steel corrugated walls of the Quonset hut.

Before Matt drove away, he noticed many enlisted men no longer bothered to salute him or most of the other officers. Not one of the slackers had been dressed down by the slighted officer. He himself certainly hadn't felt any need to correct them. The lack of discipline was an unmistakable signal that in short order almost every one of them would be going back home; included in that number would be many of the officers as well as most of the enlisted men. The War was over and they were not needed over here any longer. At ease!... **Dismissed!** (Thank God!)

In Matt's mind the War had seemed eternal and he never stopped to consider what it would be like when it was over; what would happen after the last act of this apparently endless War if, through a combination of luck and skill, fate decreed he still lived when the last scene ended. He had expected some grand finale. Instead, one day it was simply finished. The cowardly Hitler killed himself as he hid in a bunker somewhere beneath Berlin, and Germany quit fighting. In the meantime, three out of four Allied fliers had died. And for Germany, pilot fatality was statistically even higher, only because they had fewer pilots was the Axis number of killed lower than the number for the Allies.

Untold millions more uniformed soldiers and sailors had lost their lives. The toll on civilian shipping and sailors was horrendous thanks to German U-Boats. The Germans on those U-Boats were themselves nearly all killed. Civilian casualties would never be known with any certainty.

And why had this all come about? Because no country could be bothered to act in the early years when Hitler could have easily been stopped. Had no politician outside of Germany read his book "Mien Kampf"? He had laid it all out for everyone to see as clear as day in that little book of his; the treatment he intended for the Jews clearly defined within its pages. Maybe no one could believe that a single man could be so warped he would want to liquidate an entire group of people because of their religion. In addition, he needed an internal enemy for the country. To envy. To hate. He sold Germany on the idea the 'Rich' Jew had grown rich at the expense of the average German.

Sure, on V.E. Day, they had thrown big parties in London and America. Paris had thrown their party months before when the Germans were pushed out. Civilians and Big Wig politicians were all there along with many young men in uniform. It did make a fellow feel great. For a little while. The soldiers, sailors and airmen got drunk and were kissed by the girls and many even got laid. But the good feelings didn't last long. It started you thinking backward toward a time with too many memories and an overwhelming sadness you hate to remember. There were not enough bottles of liquor or women in the world to avoid that. A fellow was bound to recall others who should have been there celebrating victory, but instead lay cold and dead somewhere; hastily buried in fields in France, Belgium, Italy, North Africa or Germany. The ones who paid the ultimate price and would never be able to celebrate anything again.

A few of all ranks might stay in the military now that Germany had surrendered, but most would not. Those he spoke with told him America was booming and all of them wanted to make up for the years they had lost. How, Matt wondered, was it possible to make up for losses like that even if one were given ten lifetimes to try and do it?

Years ago Matt had read novels about what the writers had called "The Lost Generation" following World War One. Hemmingway and other authors of the period had described how, as ex-soldiers, that war had left them rootless and disillusioned. They no longer felt they had a home to which they could return; so they stayed behind in France, Spain, Italy and England. He had read those books in a world still at peace which on this day seemed eons in the past. They were books he had never been able to understand back in prep school days at Andover and during his over two years in University at Yale. Today, unfortunately, he *could* understand. It was a hard earned knowledge.

The War which Matt had somehow lived through called for great focus on the part of the average GI in order to survive, yet he wondered if the aftermath of this War might cause the men who had survived to withdraw as had the survivors of the previous World War. Or was it possible they might somehow return to a country which was now certain to be changed and pick up whatever shadows perhaps remained of their old lives? Would they go back and enter college on the GI Bill or revert to their old jobs? Would jobs like they had held before the War still exist?

He wasn't at all certain he wanted to go back. Yes, America was the country of his birth, but his fight had really been to defend England. And Joanna. His beautiful, green-eyed Joanna. He'd ask her to marry him as soon as it could be done. He felt sure she would say yes, even though he had been reported as killed almost a year ago.

He was grateful that Kommandant von Lineiner had been honest enough to tell him about it before he counseled him to lag further and further behind while they were making the long march from Stalag - Luft III Camp to Stalag VIIa. That guidance had allowed him to escape earlier than he could have otherwise been liberated. He understood now that von Lineiner was trying to help him escape because the Kommandant was a very honorable man who was very ashamed of the part he had played in a totally dishonorable charade. He assumed his entire crew had been reported killed when in probability they were very much alive and well. Von Lineiner was deeply disturbed that he had been forced to take part in a lie. In fact, the lie had Von Lineiner's name on it. Matt knew the man had been only a bit player in this cruel Kabuki theatre act.

Matt was painfully aware that Joanna would be shocked to see him alive, so he must be prepared to let her recover before asking the question too long delayed, " Joanna will you officially marry me?" He knew she was a very level-headed lady. Because of that, he was convinced once he explained why all of his letters had been destroyed in Berlin for devious propaganda purposes, she would understand. Matt had no doubt the shared story of the rest of their lives would be a happy one. He knew in his heart she would forgive what he, after all, had no control over, or, for that matter, even any knowledge of until just before his "escape" from Germany.

~ ~ ~ ~

The Jeep the motor pool Sergeant assigned him was brand new; undoubtedly one which had been in transit from America when the War in Europe had ended. All the Sergeant needed from Matt was his signature on a single form; far from the strict requirements in nineteen forty three. "No sweat on paperwork anymore," the young man told Matt when asked about the change from what had then seemed a mountain of paperwork. The Sergeant continued, "I don't know what the hell we are gonna do with all of this stuff anyway. Word is, they are pushing hundreds of Jeeps, trucks, tanks and airplanes over the sides of Liberty ships then turning the ships around; back toward home. They already got more of everything than they can use in the Pacific against ole Tojo and the rest of the Japs. Even if they don't get smart and give up and we have to invade Japan itself. We have many times more weapons than we can use and all this stuff is still rolling off production lines back home in endless numbers. There ain't no place to put it all.

"Captain," the fresh faced young man continued, "the Jerrys and the Japs had no idea what they were starting when they came after the good ole U.S. of A. Better Hitler had just gone ahead and shot hisself on that first day and saved everybody all this fuss."

Matt thought how easy it all must seem to this young Sergeant standing there in front of him today. The boy had arrived over here when it was all wrapping up. Now it was really all over. Who could blame him for the way he saw the War? There could be little doubt from his newly starched uniform and brand new shoes, that he had come over only recently from America. Matt knew this boy's attitude would have been different if he had been here in '42 or '43. Even in '44 the War was by no means totally decided. Ask all those young men buried in hastily dug graves in the fields around a frozen little town called Bastogne, when Hitler was finally betting his last remaining stack of chips. No, this young man had missed the "killing years."

Those terrible years when he wouldn't allow himself to make friends with most of the men from the other flight crews for fear they would die on the next mission. And he would have been right because most of them would soon be dead. That or in a POW camp; better for his sanity that when they died they were strangers to him. Just a face he passed with a nod, no name attached. No, he hadn't wanted to know where they were from or about their family or girlfriends or wives or kids. If he spoke to them at all, it was only meaningless small talk in passing.

He had gotten to know things like that only about his own crew. The guys he flew with. Knowing their stories didn't bother him as much because if they all died he would die with them, so there wouldn't be time or need to mourn them. He drank with them and ate with them; they told each other bad jokes and lies about how good they were feeling. The only thing you never told each other was how damn jaw clenching scared you were every time you crawled into the plane and how relieved you were to land back in England after each mission.

You never told each other how short a time it seemed to take to reach enemy territory and what an eternity it was when the enemy Messerschmitts and Focke Wulfs came screaming up toward your B-17 or roaring down out of the sun at you and when the flak started opening its blooms of death across the sky. You never mentioned how you were certain each moment would be your last as you had to fly straight and level for minutes that seemed years while you were on your bomb run on the target and flak exploding all around you. The way your hand shook while you were holding a drink or the uncontrollable tic at the corner of your mouth or eye and the way you wanted to throw-up when your engines fired up on the hardstand before taxiing onto the tarmac for your assigned position in takeoff.

Sure Sergeant, he thought to himself, standing here in your spiffy new uniform like a store window manikin, wearing those perfectly shined shoes and having recently arrived in England, it probably is easy to wonder what all the fuss was about.

But not to me and not to anyone like me who is left from those deadly years when nothing at all was certain except the likelihood of sudden annihilation.

~ ~ ~ ~

Matt drove away from the base with the warmth of a late spring sun on his face and wind blowing through his sandy hair. He no longer felt as young as when he had made this drive so many times in the past. The excitement of looking forward to seeing Joana was as always, still with him, but that was tempered by a sense of loss for the time he had been away from her. Time they could never call back. Matt also knew when he looked in the mirror that he looked older. There were lines beside his mouth and around his eyes that had not been there before he joined the

RAF; most had happened in his time flying "the Maid."

All that is behind me now, he thought. Together we will find a way to pick up the pieces of our lives. There will be a wedding to plan. I know she wants to get married in that little chapel at Barton Hall, a family tradition with the Barton's. I'll have to get Dad to come over, but transportation will take some time to arrange. All in all, it will be easier over here anyway; too many Bartons to transport over there.

Now Matt, don't get ahead of yourself. You haven't officially asked her again yet. Sure, you two had an unofficial wedding but that was a year ago and more. One thing at a time. First tell her as much of what happened as you know. Then give her time to get used to the fact that you are not dead. Do a few things together. Go some places. She was such fun to go places with. Do that again. Is the Symphony performing? Queens Hall was bombed. Where would they be playing now?

He knew they couldn't go to Café de Paris as it had been bombed back in April of '41. Almost a hundred people killed; the bombs hit early in the evening or many more would have died. He'd heard then the maître d who had been so nice and asked them to come back had been one of the casualties. Even if they rebuilt, Matt knew the two of them would never go back. Some things can never and shouldn't ever, be repeated. Their night was one of those. Walking hand in hand with Joanna back to his MG through the fog. No, some things could only be done once in a lifetime. Those things which lead to the love of a lifetime

~ ~ ~ ~

Most of the road traffic was still military, but even that was considerably lighter than when he had traveled to Barton Hall before his final flight The last time he had seen Joanna. They had made love in the barley; a mad fevered passion which had overwhelmed his determination to consummate their love in that way only when they could really be together. Well, he had survived and now they would be truly and completely together. Finally and forever.

The towns fell away behind him. And each town was having the barbed wire barricades torn down. What would England do with that material? Would farmers be given the wire to enclose their fields? So many things would no longer be needed. Gun emplacements along the coast. Temporary airfields. What would happen to them? Would they, in a few years, be simply farmers' fields again? If not, over the years weeds would grow up between the cracked concrete and dead leaves would blow across them in the fall of the year. Snow would coat them in the winter

The wooden buildings would soon collapse in upon themselves and in a few more years, children would ask their fathers what had once been there and their fathers would be forced to remember back to those years. They would recall the distant echo of hundreds of engines revving up in the chill morning air and the thunderous sound as they had rolled down that long-abandoned runway.

How could a father ever really explain that to a child? The way many young men not much older than children had climbed into great flying machines and gone to find their deaths. In a hundred years, even the runways would be gone. The War would fade to no more than a great myth as wars always have. A tale of heroes and villains. Of course, the hero always wins: but as Matt drove along the green springtime roads of Kent, he wondered, do they really? Does St. George slay the dragon or does he find he has, at least in part, become the dragon?

Wars, myths and legends. How quickly, Matt thought, they become intertwined. If Homer had not heard a story which moved him to write a poem about the assault on Troy, which happened hundreds of years before he was born, there would have been no <u>Iliad</u> and the Trojan War would have been lost to the ages. Will my War become the same in a distant eon? In a few hundred years, who could believe over a thousand ships landing men on a small strip of high-cliffed beach in a single day. Thousands of aircraft filling the skies and raining death on the people below. And not simply thousands of warriors as in the Trojan story, but millions. As a myth it would seem impossible. Some future generation might find it easier to believe in dragons than a story that vast. Because, he told himself, the world would have surely moved beyond war, or slipped back into the darkness because of it.

As he neared the turnoff to Barton Hall, he saw a few of the beautiful Spitfires he had loved in what now seemed so long ago. They were still beautiful aircraft that belonged in the air as surely as any bird which had ever flown. He had no doubt it was only pilots finishing their training, who would never be needed unless they were sent to the Pacific to fly against the Japs but even that should end soon. Perhaps a pilot who had lived through it and wanted to get in a flight or two more for the simple pleasure of flying, now that there was no one left to shoot at him. Might as well before you pack away the uniform and the medals and get used to the loose fit of civilian clothes again. No more GI haircuts and bland, assembly line food. No more jeeps and half-ton trucks. No more B-17s named "Maid of Barley." No more bugles before daylight and inspections after dark. No more aircraft dropping out of the sky like geese over a pond in upper New York State on a cold late fall day. All the kind of things you had been around so long they had come to seem normal. So long that anything from before had become a fond, if illusive memory. Everything except, if you were lucky, the girl you loved. Everything for Matt except Joanna.

Ahead, he saw the two tall stone obelisks which marked the turn onto the graveled drive to Barton Hall. His heart was beating faster at the knowledge he would soon see her again.

He drove slowly, gravel crunching under the Jeep's tires. It was a rougher ride than he remembered in his MG. He should have driven it. It was still, he supposed, in that small garage just off the base at Polebrook. But after being parked there for a year, would it even crank? He would check later. He and Joanna could use it and travel anywhere they liked now; the sun on their faces and the wind in their hair. Perhaps drive up to Scotland. Except for flying over, he had never been there. She had told him it was wild and beautiful land. Then there was Ireland. He had landed there once on a training mission, but only long enough to refuel. It would be a wonderful honeymoon trip. She could show him Ireland and Scotland and then he would show her America. That would be a discovery for both of them as he had never been south of Washington D.C. or west of the Mississippi. It was high time he saw other places in his big country. Afterward, a few more courses at King's, then gainful employment. Perhaps with Owen at the Brewery or teaching mathematics. Living in England or America? With Joanna either place would be fine.

He was certain his father had received his telegram by now. He smiled as he remembered his wording, "Rumors of my death greatly exaggerated...stop Will be awhile before I am home...stop Girl to propose to...stop Letter to follow...stop Am in one piece...Matt Weldon IV." He had written a three-page letter on the military typewriter and noticed it had a good ribbon, another indication the War in Europe was over. He posted it airmail, splurging on Special Delivery to the Wall Street office of Empire National.

He came to the turn which carried him around the section of the young barley field on the side by the cemetery and the Chapel, where he parked. He swung his legs out of the Jeep and stood for a moment. He just wanted to take it all in; the sight and soft smell of the young crop swaying before him, the sound of the West Wind blowing over the barley's green tops, bending them with its passage. The barley had been at about this stage when he and Joanna had lain naked among them. A few back-to-back missions later, he had flown mission number twenty four and been shot down. A year. The longest year of my life, he thought. But now I am back and we will go on from here.

Matt entered the barley rows on one of the small paths and found himself running his hands along their tops as Joanna had so often done. The path took him toward the mammoth oak standing sentinel in the center of the Barton family cemetery. He opened one side of the wrought-iron gate and smiled at the familiar squeal. His happy mood turned mournful when he once again saw the temporary marker; the one for her brother Alexander killed in the jungles outside Singapore when the Japanese were attacking the city back in '42. He remembered the Memorial to Alexander's short life held in the stone chapel beyond the gate. Joanna cried and her mother, Mary Margaret, stayed in bed for days afterwards.

But it was Owen he had worried most about. Owen never shed a tear, but Matt could see he was crushed by the death of his only son. Yet, there was this unbreakable rule of how men behaved at times like that. A few days later, Joanna had said to him, "Well Mathew, I suppose it is up to me to carry on the family line." She had paused, then added with a sad little smile, "Up to us, actually."

He was just passing the great oak when he stopped in his tracks. Even though he was still some distance from the house, down the long hedge-lined walkway, he could see Joanna.

She stood in front of the house next to a young man in the uniform of a British Army officer. His arm was around Joanna's waist. In her arms was a very young baby. The officer was looking at her and Matt could hear him laughing. They seemed very happy to be together.

Hardly breathing he stumbled back to the side of the oak to a point where he could not be seen and collapsed on the bench he and Joanna had sat on during those happier days which seemed now so many years ago. Glassy-eyed, he stared at the spot of ground bare of headstones, except the one for her brother. "Well, old boy", he thought, "we know now where you *won't* be buried.... What a stupid thought to have! You have just lost the one woman you finally loved and that is what you think of? My God, Matt!"

Though suddenly shocked, saddened and depressed his mind continued to function with devastating logic. "What was she to have done? Mourn me the rest of her life? I was dead as far as she and anyone

289

outside of Germany knew. We, all of us in the crew, might as well have been killed. At least I would not have seen her with another man and his child." He felt a lone tear streak down his cheek in tribute to the love he now understood was gone.

"Sure, we had quite a love story. Beyond anything I could have believed before I met her. It is only right that she 'carried on.' She looks very happy. Owen will be delighted that there is another generation to carry the line forward. A line which will continue to be totally British, probably the way it should be. I hope he is 'St. George' for her. She deserves a genuine St. George. It is really what she has always wanted. I was at best only a counterfeit playing the part for awhile."

Slowly rising from the bench he noticed there was sharp pain in his left hip; probably caused by the long walk from the Jeep.

"Well," he wondered, "what does one do after something like this?" He began to walk back toward the barley field, feeling his old limp had returned in earnest. He felt old in comparison to five minutes ago.

"Some few put a bullet through their heads. But those are the cowards and if nothing else, the Germans have proven you are not a coward. No, you will simply have to live with this loss".

After walking back through the barley, he arrived at the Jeep and with some effort and much pain was able to step up into the vehicle.

"Oh yes," he thought slumped in the seat, "most often a man gets royally drunk in an effort to forget. I understand it usually doesn't help, but traditions must be upheld. Unfortunately, I will never forget her. The West Wind will *never* let me."

He drove away without looking back over his shoulder even once.

Two hours later, he arrived in London and was able to park not far from "The Clarence," a pub he had gone to with Joanna. Just off Trafalgar Square, it was opposite the Horse Guards' sentry post. One of the oldest pubs in town, it seemed a good location for a "dead man" to start a first-rate drunk.

His first drink was barely on the bar in front of him when a voice called out, "Matt! Captain Mathew Weldon. My God man, they told us you were dead! A year ago at least. Where have you been hiding?"

Coming across the shadowed room was "Mutt" Stanford from his old RAF crew with his hand outstretched. He at first grasped Matt's hand and shook very energetically then pulled away only to throw a first-rate Scottish bear hug around him.

"Funny," Matt thought," the first crew member I see is my old number two from the RAF crew. But maybe my other crew might not be back in England yet. It even took me awhile to convince the Eighth Air Force that I was still alive. Luckily, I had my old AAF ID or who knows how long I would have been held in Europe. They said my pay would catch up with me, but it would take a bit of time. Good thing Dad didn't close my account at Barclay's or I would have been out of luck. I still have over fifteen hundred pounds. Yes... the rest of the "Maid's" crew may well still be in Europe somewhere. I will check tomorrow to see if I can help get them back".

"No Mutt, I did the miracle thing. I rose from the dead. They drove a sprig of holly through my heart. The Nazi's probably mistook me for an Englishman because I hung around so many of you blokes. But with Americans, holly through the heart has the opposite effect. It gives us super powers so I popped up and here I am."

"Now laddie, let's watch that 'you English' rot. You know full well I am a Scot and we Scots take umbrage being called English as much as you Yanks did at being called Colonists."

"So Mutt - what did you do for the rest of the War? Did you keep flying?"

His number two from RAF days took a short drink from the mug of ale in his hand before answering. "Well, after the 'Mighty Eighth' was kind enough to take you off our hands, I was promoted to first pilot of 'E for Edward.' The RAF replacement depot gave us a lad from Bristol as second pilot. Green as the grass he was. Right out of Flight School. They were rushing them through back then as you probably recall."

Oh do I, Matt thought, I remember how they pushed me through those classes. I thought it was because I already had wings in the States. But rushing beginners through training at that speed was criminal. He knew England needed all the help it could get at that point. It cost them many lives, yet England had been saved. The end justified the means; the old standby which allowed Presidents, Prime Ministers, Dictators, Field Marshals and Generals to sleep at night. Churchill was right about "so many owing so much to so few," but it was far from a few who had died. The cost in lives was high indeed.

"Yes Mutt, I remember. It was *so* fast for me all I remember of training is, 'This is a Short Sterling bomber aero plane. It has four engines (count them if you wish.) Let's go inside the Short Sterling. This is the number one pilot's seat. Sit in the seat, Cadet. On the back of the seat is a parachute to be used only to jump out of the Short Sterling in case of emergency. The way things are going you need to remember the location of the parachute. The wings, four engines, dial thingies, landing gear and pilot's seat are just luxuries. The parachute, laddie, is a necessity. Now that you have been properly instructed on the Short Sterling Heavy Bomber, congratulations. Here are your RAF pilot's wings.

"Your first mission to bomb Berlin leaves in half an hour. Come along, I will introduce you to your fine crew-members picked at random off street corners and dark alley ways all over the Empire. You are lucky. Two actually sort of speak and understand English. You can train them on the way to Berlin."

Mutt was laughing so hard his ale sloshed atop of the hard wood bar and they drew disapproving looks from the bartenders. The looks said 'you-two-aren't-going-to-be-any-trouble-now-are-you?' The kind of looks English bartenders specialized in.

Well Matt, he thought, at least you can still tell a pretty good story and make people laugh. Now if you can only find a way to make what just happened with Joanna funny, you can keep from being so damn sad. Well maybe in a hundred years or so I won't care any longer. You know, the hundred years you wished for under the tree that day. Well only seventy five or so left to go. Without her of course.

Matt noticed his friend was no longer laughing. In fact he looked as sad as Matt felt inside. "Hey Mutt what's wrong? You suddenly look like you just lost your best friend."

"No Number One. I have lost all of them. We both have. Our crew of 'E for Edward.' We are the only two left. The rest were killed on a mission to the Ruhr Valley, targeting one of Krupp's big steel mills. I was in hospital. My appendix had ruptured. They had a replacement number one flying and the green kid flying as number two. I was told an ME110 Night Fighter got directly below them. I know they never saw him because they took no evasive action. Two of our other planes saw it and said the pilot just kept flying level. That black painted bastard had all night to line up his shot. He finally opened fire with those up-firing thirty seven millimeter cannons. He must have fired into the bomb-bay which was fully loaded; the plane and everyone on board simply ceased to exist. A brilliant yellow and orange flash in the darkness of night and they were no more. I suppose you could see it as a merciful death in a way. One moment alive the next dead. Like erasing a blackboard of the names written there. I was always afraid I would be trapped in a falling, burning plane. Alive until it crashed to earth. At least the lads were spared that.

"Could be the reason you and I bumped into each other today. We are the only ones left Number One, and someone should drink a toast to them. They were good lads. Now we are the only ones left to do it. Shall we drink to them?" Mutt lifted what was left of his ale and Matt lifted his half glass of Scotch. Both said, "To the boys of 'E for Edward.' You will not be forgotten," and clinked their glasses. Matt saying nearly under his breath, "God bless you all" drained his glass. One of the older bartenders had been holding a glass raised and when he noticed Matt looking at him, nodded with a sad grimace which said he had seen far too many toasts like this.

Mutt watched Matt drink quietly for several minutes. "So Matt, what has you drinking tonight? You never drank much when we flew together. I clearly remember you nursing single ale for hours. Never had more than one in a night. You seem serious about your drinking tonight. In case you don't know, the whiskey will win the bout.... It always does. Take it from a man who has lost that fight often. And the loser of the bout always feels God-awful the next morning."

Matt wanted to ignore his old Number Two's question, but decided a short explanation might be best. The first word out of his mouth was, "Joanna. Mutt do you remember Joanna Barton?"

Mutt laughed wryly, "Remember her? How in the bleeding hell could any healthy man with vision forget her is a better question. Uh oh,... what's happened?"

"Well, I was gone a year. In a Luftwaffe POW camp. Like you, *everyone* believed I was dead. The Germans said I was. Joanna, just like my dad, thought I was killed. I drove out to their country place in Kent today and saw she is with someone else. A young British Officer and they have a baby.

"I left. No need to tell her I am alive and complicate things. Better if I remain dead in her mind. I decided to get rip-roaring drunk. That is the thing to do isn't it?"

Mutt never skipped a beat before replying, "Oh yes. Just the ticket. Take it from an expert. Liberal application of hard alcohol will cure any heartache at least until the hangover goes away. If you don't mind I think I'll tag along. Just as a witness you understand. Wouldn't want to miss this show for the world."

~ ~ ~ ~

The next morning Matt awoke with a raging hangover. His uniform was torn and dirty and he knew he smelled bad. He found he was missing a shoe, the left side of his jaw was sore and swollen and the knuckles on both hands were badly skinned. As his blurred vision cleared, he found it strange that his hotel room had steel bars all the way around it. A large soldier with an arm-band marked MP was shaking him. "OK Captain. Time to wake up, sleepy head. From the looks of you, more beauty sleep would help, but then again it might not. You're kind of a rarity 'round here. We don't normally get officers checkin' in to our flop house. From the looks of you whatever you got into must-a-been a real dilly.

"I heard it took three MP's to pull you loose from six sergeants. They said you was cursing them MPs for all you were worth and tellin' them you didn' need any help. They say there was an RAF-type tangled up with a handful more. The Brit MP's hauled him off too. The story goes he was laughing the whole time.

"We found a clean uniform for you so you need to shower and shave 'cause you got a personal 'point-ment with General Jimmy Doolittle hisself. I heard the General don't stand for no 'fight'n out of his officers and Captain Sir, I bet he aims to relieve you of them bars you'r a-wearin.' Don't worry you'll look real fine as a private," he chuckled. "We got you a uniform with Captain's bars so's he can have the privilege of rippin' them off, personal like."

Matt took a cold shower which helped his headache only a bit. Shaving with a hangover was an adventure which carried a few nicks with it.

The cold water reassured him some things hadn't changed even with the Americans here. What the hell, he thought, have I been here so long I have forgotten I **am** an American?

He was surprised to find the loaner uniform was a good fit. The insignia and small metal-backed bar of award ribbons were all correct. The fit was not quite as perfect as the RAF or USAAF ones he had had tailored in Bond Street, but quite good none-the-less.

Certainly more than adequate for a....What? He thought. Can they Court martial me for a fist fight? Probably, but more than likely General Doolittle will just break me down in rank to Second Lieutenant and kick me the hell out of service. As bad as I feel this morning, I'll probably thank him for doing it. I am surprised it's Doolittle. "Ira" Eaker was my boss when I did all the base survey work before they let me get back to flying. Either he doesn't know about the fight or the Brass wants to be sure no favoritism is shown in this case. Probably the latter. No danger "Jimmy" will show any. They say he is hard as nails. The raid he led on Tokyo back in April of '42 proved that well enough. Roosevelt gave him the Medal of Honor for it. Well deserved, I would say and Ike gave him command of the Eighth about the time I left on my last mission. I've never met the man. Well, I sure am going to meet him today. He found the thought had him sweating.

Two burly MPs escorted Matt out to a Dodge Staff Car painted with the ever-present olive-drab. One of the two seated himself in the back seat next to him. The other settled in the front and cranked the big auto. The MP in the back never spoke a word during the hour long drive. Matt felt his hang-over begin to recede as he watched the familiar sights of London pass by his window. The warmth of the sun soaked his aches away and he began to feel like he might not only live, but eventually feel like himself again one day.

London too had been damaged but given enough time, they would both make a nearly complete recovery. Each would, however, retain empty spaces which would remain for a very long time. Matt knew he would always love London as he would always love Joanna. He knew he had arrived here only a callow young stranger, but the city had helped him grow up and become a part of it. The undeniable reality was a part of him would always be here. It was the place he grew to be a man. He had lived here, loved here and fought for this city and the girl who lived here. He had learned to love the rainy days and foggy nights. Fogs which came at twilight, midnight and dawn. And the girl with the oh-so-green eyes and soft copper hair which fell around her face as they made love on a sunny day in a field of barley beneath a tree of magic. A girl he knew he was destined never to forget. And no, liquor never could or ever would help him forget her.

The driver turned onto the familiar drive leading to the mammoth stone mansion. Matt knew High Wycombe Abbey well from the many trips he had made there so long ago for planning conferences when the 8th Army Air Corps was newly arrived in England and laying out specifications for the bases needed for the soon-to-arrive B-17s and B-25s.

Upon arrival, Matt was summarily escorted to the third floor. The MP had finally proven he could speak by telling the Captain sitting behind a Government Issue desk covered with several telephones that Captain Weldon was here to see General Doolittle. The overly officious Captain pointed to a row of seats and then spoke softly into the intercom. The two of them took seats to await the General's pleasure.

A bit over an hour later the "gate keeper" Captain walked over and announced, "General Doolittle will see Captain Weldon now." He looked down at the MP and continued. "You are to wait here for Captain Weldon's return."

General Doolittle's office was almost as large as the conference room in which Matt had attended meetings at High Wycombe. The General's desk was huge and not at all G.I. Matt could tell it was a Georgian era antique; no doubt a benefit of rank.

Matt came to attention and snapped a smart salute to the General who returned it in a casual, easy manner. He was certain that if a face had ever been created to belong on a hero, Jimmy Doolittle owned the patent on that face.

His sharply chiseled jaw had a deeply cleft chin. He had retained tan from his days in California and had, like Matt, very blue eyes. It was commonly held that a majority of pilots had blue eyes and if true, Jimmy Doolittle fit that mold to a tee.

"So Captain Weldon," the General began with a shadow of a smile. "How are you feeling today?"

Matt maintained his position of attention. "Better than I deserve **Sir**, all things considered. Thank you for asking. **Sir**."

The General threw the word, "At ease" in his direction and Matt relaxed into "Parade Rest." It had been a while since he had observed the strictures of military discipline.

Doolittle stood and indicated a leather chair with one hand, "Why don't you take a seat Captain? Your old boss Ira Eaker asked me to see you today. He didn't want any favoritism shown about this matter."

"Thank you General Doolittle. I do understand the situation. Fighting with enlisted me...they were enlisted men as I recall... is unforgivable. Not remembering the reasons for the fight is even worse. I have no excuse **Sir**. No excuse at all."

Doolittle's carved-in-stone visage cracked into the slightest of smiles as he said, "Well Captain, perhaps I can help you out there. You tangled with four or five tough Regular Army Sergeants, plus one Master Sergeant, three Corporals and assorted Army Privates. The bartenders both said they had been ragging you and the RAF flier about how easy you flyboys had it. How you flew a few hours then returned to the safety of England. Good chow, good beds, good booze and willing broads. How you spent more time boozing and screwing than you did fighting. The word from the bartenders is you got right in the face of the Sergeant who was doing most of the talking and said, 'Yeah and if you weren't such a dumb son-of-a-bitch you might have been a pilot too.' The Sergeant threw the first punch, so the 8th Air Force considers everything from then on to be self-defense. I understand you were giving boxing lessons until several of you ended up in a tangle on the floor, after that it turned into a good old fashioned free-for-all. Early on, the RAF fellow with you decided to get in it to even the odds. The MP's said *he* seemed to be having a high old time. He a friend of yours?"

"Yes General. We flew together once upon a time, as they say, in the RAF. Before the U.S. was in it. At least officially. He was my second pilot in a Short Sterling. A true Scotsman. A fine fellow and a very good pilot.. He and I are the only two left out of that crew."

"That's right Captain, your records did specify you had been an RAF bomber pilot before Pearl Harbor was attacked. Flew fourteen missions for them if memory serves. More than a few air combat medals too. Some really tough missions. Then we came over and pulled you from the RAF to do base location and evaluation duty for the 8th. Ira said you did a 'bang up' job of work for him. He tells me you were the best he ever had doing that and not a single one of your report's recommendations was off the mark. After a year of that you were given a flying assignment and this time you were flying for the 8th Air Force. Some idiot said you had to fly the full twenty-five missions just like a rookie pilot coming from training Stateside. Not at all fair really, but they say you didn't complain. I suppose I wouldn't have either but...well, most would have you know.

"Shot down on your next to last mission. Rotten luck that."

Yes, Matt thought. You will never know what rotten luck or what it has cost me. I should have complained. If they had only credited me with two missions with the RAF counting against my twenty-five...well they didn't and what is, is. The past can't be changed. No matter how I might wish it could.

"In a Luftwaffe POW Camp for nearly a year. Participated in several escape attempts and finally escaped just before the curtain came down in Germany. Quite an admirable record, Captain. Quite a record indeed! You understand we will have to put a reprimand in your records for fighting but **with** cause and justification of course. Now you do understand we can't let you return Stateside as a Captain. It wouldn't be just."

"Certainly General, I do understand."

"I'm glad you do Captain. We really should have made you a Major long ago. You have earned it many times over. Congratulations Major Weldon."

The General walked around the desk and handed a surprised Matt a navy Blue box with a pair of gold lines impressed in its top. It showed some wear around its edges. He shook his hand and said, "I hope you don't mind, this is a pair of my old oak leaves when I was a Major. This should have been done long ago. I can only blame it on the War." He walked back around his desk and stood behind it.

"Major, always remember that bartenders tend to listen to bar side conversations. I am sorry about how you lost your girl. Like so many things in this War it wasn't fair. Probably to either of you.

"Well Major Weldon, Ira and I think you have done more than enough. We are having orders cut to get you back to America ASAP. Medical reports say your hip needs better care than you can get over here. Give us another three days and come back to pick up your orders home and your travel verification. You will be released from active duty in New York. The reason for your release is wounds suffered in combat. A Purple Heart goes with that along with a handful of medals which are all well deserved. You have gone above and beyond many times during your service. All that OK with you?"

"Yes Sir, General Doolittle. Unfortunately nothing to keep me over here any longer. I would like to ask the General for one favor if I may sir."

"Certainly Major. Speak up."

"The fellow on my side of the fight, Martin Stanford, goes by Mutt... Sir if you could put in a good word on his behalf... Well, I certainly would appreciate it General."

"Between you and me Major, it has already been done. What he did proved we have been really good allies in this War, even when the fighting happened in a pub. He won't be punished in any way. The fellow will be released as scheduled with his full rank intact."

They shook hands. General Doolittle wished him good fortune. Matt was driven back to the spot near "The Clarence Pub" where the borrowed Jeep was parked. The same silent MP still said nothing during this trip. Then, as he opened the door for Matt, the big man finally spoke in his laconic Texas drawl. "Well, if this ain't the damndest thing I ever seen. Picked up a Captain at the military jail. Took him out to be busted in rank by General by-God Doolittle hisself and take him back a Major. Whatever you said it must a been somethin' even a Texan wooda been proud of an' we gotta reputation for pretty tall tales."

Matt smiled at him and said, "I've heard about you Texans, Sergeant, but it took a Yankee from New York to pull this one off."

Matt wanted to return the Jeep to have it removed from his responsibility and put back into the vast supply of now surplus military vehicles clogging every American base in England. With only three days remaining before he would leave for America, he had a list of items to do crowding his mind.

The two Privates manning the security gate at the entrance to Polebrook barely glanced at his identity card, snapped a quick salute and waved him through to the base. They paid no attention to the fact his card was now a year out of date, but then it was highly unlikely a Nazi spy would be trying to sneak onto the base now. Matt chuckled to himself. If so, he is really out of touch.

The young supply Sergeant simply stamped the paperwork Matt had signed yesterday with a rubber stamp marked **RETURNED** and initialed it and filled in the time and date.

Matt walked out the gate to the small tin-sided garage where he had left his green MG convertible a little over a year ago now. The mechanic came out to meet him wearing what appeared to be the same grey striped grease-stained coveralls he had worn the last time Matt saw him. Matt shook the man's calloused, grease covered-hand.

"Well Gov'nr, where you been? I wuz b'ginnin' to think ye wuz gone fer good. Still got yer little toy car but ye owez me a bit fer storage, ye does."

Matt paid his bill plus a few pounds extra for the man's honesty in not having sold the car. After a bit of work under the bonnet, the little engine came to life. When the mechanic adjusted the carburetor, the sound was the same throaty purr it had when Matt left on his last mission. The man was able to completely fill the gas tank at a reasonable rate. The year before he'd been lucky to get a few 'black market' gallons at an outrageous price.

Before he drove away, he found his old black umbrella behind the seat along with one of Joanna's scarves. He could still smell just a trace of her perfume on it. A distant echo of an old familiar love song he knew he would never hear again. He tucked it into his pocket. He would decide what to do with it later.

~ ~ ~ ~

Traffic in London was light compared to prewar levels; lighter still than that he had been accustomed to before his capture in the spring of '44. Back then, more than one out of every two motorized vehicles wore olive drab paint and carried passengers dressed in military clothing.

London had survived first the blitz in '40; then in '44 and '45, from Hitler's V-Weapons; those pilotless flying bombs which rained at random on the city. It had survived all of that, but paid a high price. As Matt drove, he came across block after block which had gone untouched, then he would come to large areas which were nothing but rubble. The House of Commons was badly damaged but work was underway to put it back to prewar condition.

Repair work was well underway on St. Paul's Cathedral. A framework of iron support beams topped with catwalks encircled the damaged areas. Workmen were ripping out wall material and the wooden supports beneath. St. Paul's suffered light damage compared to several nearby areas.

There were parts of town that had simply been destroyed in total. It would be years before they were rebuilt and when they were there would be little, if any, resemblance to what had once been.

He drove by several old churches which Joanna had told him were designed by England's best-known architect, Sir Christopher Wren in the late sixteen hundreds. They were little more than dust and ruins.

Areas along the banks of the Thames where he and Joanna had walked on weekends in good weather and likewise several large areas in Southwark were heavily damaged. Southwark which Joanna had taught him to pronounce as a Londoner would, "SUDH-ak," was one of the oldest parts of London. The ruins of nearly everything he could remember from those happy days with her were being pulled down.

He had never considered himself a Londoner, but the extent of the destruction depressed him none-the-less. The city was now a constant reminder of Joanna and the places they had gone. All the things they had once done.

Until the War started, except for his time in classes, she had been his nearly constant companion. Now, like their love, all that was left to him of that time were painful memories and ruins.

Well, he thought, last night did prove one thing. Drinking is no cure for a broken heart. You end up feeling like hell the next day, just as Mutt predicted. You do some really stupid things and can easily end up in jail. This time I was damn lucky. The Brass forgave me my asinine behavior, but that was based on dumb luck and past performance. Don't depend on that in the future, old boy.

Accept the fact she is gone. Lost to me forever. I can't go back and change things. We happened in a world, time and place that have now forever vanished. I am sure Joanna loved me and I know I loved her. Still do for that matter. Probably always will.

I caused what happened when I joined the RAF after I promised not to get in the War. Sure, I thought I did it to protect her. But it was a broken promise which led to everything else that happened. Then she thought I was dead. The German radio broadcast said I was. She couldn't know otherwise. I know she mourned for me. The love was real, so she mourned. I will never know the pain it must have given her.

But she couldn't quit living. I wouldn't have wanted her to. She is young and has a life to live. As she told me when her brother was reported killed, "It is up to me now to carry on the Barton name and line."

Seeing her with a husband and baby was a shock, but I know I did the right thing by walking away without telling her I am alive. That would have made it all the more painful for her. I did the *honorable* thing, but **God**, I will be so glad to get back to America. In England, the temptation to see her again would be simply too great.

He needed to go by his old digs near King's College. His landlady, Mrs. Bellingham, had agreed to let him store his trunks containing most of his civilian things in her cellar when he moved out to enter the RAF.

He was glad to see this area near King's College had largely been spared damage from the heaviest of the bombing. King's College had been completely spared; at least the physical structures were undamaged. Large numbers of young men who had been students when he was there had gone away to a War from which many would never return. The loss to England's future was incalculable.

Matt parked his car along the curb in front of the old brick walkup where he lived over four years ago. He had thought he might be gone a year or so when he walked away. Next door he went to a near identical structure and pulled the bell in the center of the old wooden door; the old fashioned bell was nearly loud enough for the deaf to hear.

Lace curtains which covered the small glass window in the door were parted and the face of Mrs. Bellingham peered out at him. He could see surprise mirrored in her wide eyes. The door was flung open and Matt was pulled inside and dragged into her Victorian era furnished sitting room where he was hugged as if she were his mother.

"Mathew Weldon! Saints be praised. Ye' **are** alive. It is a miracle! Lord Haw Haw said your plane was shot down. E' made a big speech about how close ye' and yer crew were to be finishin' twenty five missions. Rambled on about American bombers being shot down so fast no crew would live to finish the full twenty-five. E' were lyin' the 'ole traitor all that time, wa'nen e'?"

"Yes Ma'am. He was lying. It was all propaganda. Not only am I alive, but so is my entire crew. The Jerry's had us scattered all over Germany in

301

different camps. No more than one of us per Camp. I was told every letter we wrote back was destroyed. I was in a Luftwaffe camp in lower Silesia near the town of Sagan about a hundred miles from Berlin.

"The camp could have been far worse. The ones run by the Army were far worse. Hard as it may be to believe, the Kommandant of the camp was a good man. Quite honorable, actually. Yes, there were some good men even in the German military. If there had been more like this one, there might never have been an Adolph Hitler to trouble the world.

"The food was basic. You could eat it but it was far from good. The last few months it got steadily worse. Let's say dieting was easy. I dropped about twenty pounds in three months."

"Well Mathew, I am relieved to see ye' even if it is that ye' are a wee bit skinny. Ye' look really good to these ole' eyes. If ye' want yur old digs back, they'r open. One of your American Colonels pulled out a week ago. Headed back to Washington, e' was. Said e' would be at that Pentagon place there. Never said, but I know e' was in some kind of hush- hush work. I don't think the name e' used was his and I doubt e' was a Colonel."

"No, but thank you kindly, Mrs. Bellingham. In a few days I'll be headed back myself. Only three more days before I leave. I just have a few things to take care of before then. You were kind enough to store two big trucks full of clothes for me when I moved to the RAF base. I wonder if you still have them. I can understand if you might have disposed of them when my death was announced."

"No sir, Mr. Weldon they've not moved an inch from the day ye' took 'em down there. Never even considered getting rid of 'em. Maybe somethin' told me not to. Ye' wanna get them now or have 'em picked up?"

"Well Ma'am, I plan on having them picked up and shipped to New York. I'll have a freighting service take care of that, if you'll just be kind enough to show them where they are. You were very kind to take care of them for so long. I can't thank you enough for believing in me."

She smiled the kind of smile Matt imagined his mother would have given him if she had lived. "Well if ye' want a place to stay until then, ye' can use yur old rooms. As I said they'r empty and places are not in demand like they were. It'll take a while to fill 'em. It'll get easier as our lads come back. Lots of 'em will be marryin' up then. Why don't I just give ye' a key?"

After a moment's thought, he accepted her offer. It would be more convenient being in London than way out at Polebrook for the next couple of days. There were some places he wanted to revisit before he left for home. There was a gift he had in mind that he needed to buy and make arrangements for delivery. He knew he needed to find out what had become of the "Maid's" crew and arrange to get them to England if they had not already returned

His next stop was King's College. Matt picked up a record of his courses and grades to go with those he had finished while a prisoner at the camp. His POW courses were taught by University level certified professors from several English and American Universities who were also POW's. They had all been air crew members; they were pilots, bombardiers and navigators. These were supplemented by German professors from nearby Universities.

The Army Air Corp had advised him to keep control of the records of those studies as the American colleges and universities were accepting these courses for full credit toward degrees. Two trimesters at Yale at the most and he would be finished with a degree in Finance; *if* he wanted to finish at Yale. Matt was no longer sure Yale meant that much to him. He might finish at NYU by taking night courses.

Yale, he thought. I *loved* Yale in '38, but that was because I wanted to play football and be near the 'Seven Sisters' colleges; my old hunting ground for playmates. Those were good times, but I lost my taste for that lifestyle somewhere along the line. Now I find myself wondering who that lost little boy was. I can't even imagine what he was thinking. Was he? All I can do is accept that was then. Now it's no longer then. That world and those times are gone. So is that spoiled boy. He grew up because of Love and War.

It was fun back then with Kong and Fizz as room-mates. Fizz. Unfortunately he's buried somewhere on a snow-covered mountain in Northern Italy. A frighten kid who became brave enough to win a Medal of Honor while saving others. Dad told me as much as he knew in a letter back in '43.

Big Kong? In a California military hospital. He will recover, but a bullet through his lung.... Well, makes my hip seem nothing but a love tap by comparison. He already had a Purple Heart from Iwo. Then on Okinawa he took the bullet through his chest. If it had been anyone except Kong, he would have died right then and there. They got him to a surgeon barely alive. He lived, but a handful of minutes more and he wouldn't have.

We both ended our War as Majors, but he earned his the hard way. No, I don't believe he'll be back at Yale, certainly not any time soon.

None of us who are left can recapture those days. The War put us on a different path. The times are certainly different. The world? Oh yes, the world is different; we changed it. All of us. I just hope it was worth the cost and it will be a better world. And God, may it never have to be done again! All I want now is peace. That and something worthwhile to do with my life. Now that I will be doing it...alone. No, I am not going to think that way. It will not be easy, but I will live with losing her and move on. Not my choice, but my reality. Maybe in time.... well who knows."

Matt stopped next at an exclusive coin shop where he purchased ten flawless King George VI gold sovereigns as part of a gift. He wrote a draft on his bank while the proprietor wrapped each coin individually before placing them in a purple velvet cloth bag. The coin shop owner was able to direct Matt to a nearby calligrapher as well as a jeweler. He walked to the calligraphy shop and told the lady who owned it what he wished her to execute on a card and an envelope. When she asked about color and weight of paper, Matt asked her to find a good grade of ivory for both. He was quite precise about the wording he wished her to use. When he finished, she showed him a sample of a very rare, fine hand-laid paper which he approved. She promised him it would be ready by noon of the next day.

The jeweler was just closing the door to his shop, but when he saw Matt's uniform he reopened.

"Major, what can I do for you this evening?"

"Well sir, I need a box to package a very special gift."

He laid the velvet bag on the counter. The jeweler unwrapped the gold coins and inspected each one.

"Special indeed, sir. They are all completely mint and as perfect as I have ever seen. What did you have in mind for a container?"

"I would like a very high quality wooden box that will hold the ten coins. Perhaps laid in two rows, five to a row. Glassed over to hold them in place. Also an oval gold plate inset into the top with engraved initials. Could you do that by tomorrow afternoon?"

"I have a very fine Abboyne Burl wood box in the back which should fill the bill. It is old and a beautiful red color wood which means it is heavy and rare. It was purchased containing a sapphire necklace in the partial liquidation of a very old Estate in Kent. They lost their only child, a Son, who flew for the RAF early in the War and were liquidating many fine old items. They had no other heirs to leave things to and were disposing of many items which had been in the Estate for generations. Some of the proceeds were donated to the war effort.

We sold the necklace but the box was not desired by the purchaser. The oval gold plate in the top can be re-engraved to your specifications. The only problem is time. It would require bringing my engraver back to do the top plate while I do the fitting for the coins. It could be done, but would be rather pricey because of the overtime."

"That's acceptable. I have a Captain's pay for a year due me; since I was a prisoner of war my pay continued. I can afford whatever you require; within some bounds, of course."

"I *am* sorry about your German stay, Major. I'm certain that was no picnic. Please know I will do it as economically as possible. It will be ready as you require."

Matt thanked the jeweler but turned before leaving and asked, "Could you tell me the family name... the one the box came from?"

The jeweler paused a moment before answering, "No sir, not without their approval. Transactions such as these are confidential. I would have to have written permission from them. If it is important, I could request that of them."

He thought a moment before saying, "No that's quite all right. I will be gone before you could receive their permission."

As he walked away he thought, how ironic it would be if the box had belonged to Larry Trusdale's family. The box and contents would have, in time, been his and now the box will belong to Joanna. If their story had taken a different turn the box and the necklace might both have been hers.

Musing on the unexpected twists fate could take, Matt returned to his MG and drove away as lights were coming on all over London.

I'm so glad to see the lights again, Matt thought. It has been years since windows shown so much light. The 'black-out' curtains are all packed away and I hope they never have to be brought out again. It has been such a long time that I had almost forgotten what London looks like with the lights on. Nearly five years blacked-out. So many years lost for everyone. People living in the underground stations at night while German bombs fell at random all over town. They'd come up to find buildings and streets centuries old had simply disappeared between sunset and sunrise. Nothing left but ruins to show where buildings stood that I had driven past countless times.

How many buildings in Berlin, Hamburg, Mannheim, Essen and other German cities did I turn into dust? The Eighth Air Force visited destruction on Germany which made that in London look like the work of amateurs. The Germans did make us pay a heavy price for it though.

There were nights I heard "Taps" played when it didn't seem to mean the peaceful end of the day; time to go to sleep. Rather it seemed a requiem for the fliers who had died that day. I was so curious about the song that I learned its words and its history. The words are simple. "Day is done, gone the sun, from the hills, from the lake, from the skies, all is well, safely rest, God is nigh." Such a peaceful song, yet written for War.

During the Civil War, a Union General in the deadly year of 1862 wanted a bugle call which would peacefully end an otherwise bloody day. To tell his troops it was time to bed down and rest up for whatever tomorrow might bring. Later "Taps" was played as soldiers were buried. Even the Confederate South adopted it for their burial details.

For the rest of my life, whenever I hear it, I will remember all those who died in this War. The airmen, soldiers, sailors and civilians. The guilty and the innocent alike. The worst to remember will be the children and babies who had done nothing wrong; nothing to deserve death's cold hand. Their only crime was being born English, German, French, Italian, Russian, Polish, Greek, Chinese or Japanese.

Or Dutch. We bombed the people of Rotterdam and they were never our enemies. When they were invaded they fought the Germans. Then one day an American bombing mission gone awry rained bombs down on them. Thank God "The Maid" didn't drop ours, but others in the formation did. The raid should have been canceled. The cloud cover was too thick. No one could see the target. Yet the lead plane released five thousand pounds of high explosive death on the city and others followed. We did what we had to but were we really any better than the enemy?

After the raid the Squadron Commander told me 'mistakes get made in war.' It didn't make me feel better then, and it still doesn't offer me any solace now. All I can do is be glad my War is over. I can only pray the mistakes made now by the politicians won't prove as deadly.

Matt came out of his reverie to find that he was driving by Old Oast House Brewery. He remembered his trip there in '40. Joanna had shown him the damage from a bomb which had fallen in the open courtyard near the offices. Luckily, it had only blown down part of the wall along the street at night, so all the workers were gone. There was little damage to the office building where he had first met her father Owen, the late spring of 1939. Matt had surmised the bomb was probably hung up in the German plane's bomb bay and was kicked free by a crew member.

He remembered his first visit to the Brewery; their first of many 'non-dates.' He wished he could go back to that day and carry forward once more knowing what he now knew. Yet, if he could it would probably still carry him to this same sad end. Still find him sitting in his little car driving past a closed Brewery with far too many memories.

Joanna's Kismet, Fate. She believed in it so strongly. That and the West Wind whispering to her in the barley fields. Why hadn't it whispered to her that he was still alive? That the Germans lied? Shouldn't a sorceress have known her lover was still living? Forever for the two of them had become such a short time, and without her forever would now be a long, lonely time.

The War and everything he had done. It had been for nothing. He had spent so little time with her in reality. From the time he arrived on the Queen Mary in 1939 until his last mission in '44, their time together couldn't have been more than four months. Five at the very most.

How could I, he wondered, have fallen so completely in love with her in so short a time? Me, the guy no girl had ever put a dent into. I was in love with her from nearly first sight.

Well, I might as well give up trying to rationalize it. Just accept you loved her even though you didn't want to admit it, to yourself or to her. She had to scare it out of you that first weekend she showed you Barton Hall.

With a sad smile he mused, at least I loved a woman truly and fully once in my life, without reservation or conditions and she loved me the same way. The memory of that will have to be *our* Forever. I believe I know now what it was like for Gable when he lost Carol Lombard in that plane crash. You feel there must be some way to undo it. You want her back, but an empty forever has come between you.

Lombard thought Gable should get in the war. But he was well over forty, too old for the draft. Beside he didn't want to leave her. Then when she was killed he moved heaven and earth to get in, to fly.

He lost her and got in the war. What irony. I got in the War and by doing so lost my Joanna; the perfect reversal. You can almost hear the laughter of a dead audience at the comedy of it, as they molder into dust somewhere in a bombed out theatre.

It was late and Matt knew he was dog tired. It had been a long day which started in a military jail with little memory of how he came to be there. Now it was long past dark and he was a Major. A long strange day indeed.

I am glad I accepted the key to my old rooms from Mrs. Bellingham. I know I never want to sleep in another Quonset hut as long as I live. Too many bad dreams lurking there. Maybe a few happy ones but even those are painful now. Dreams of her. Hamlet had it right, "to sleep, perchance to dream, but who knows what dreams might come? Aye there's the rub."

For the first time in a long time Matt slept past eight o'clock the next morning. It felt almost sinful. No more missions to fly or cold early morning inspections to stand in a German P.O.W. camp.

He stripped down and stepped under the shower. The cold water felt like an old friend. How long had it been since he had kidded Joanna about how many cold showers he would need to take from simply being near her? She had smiled innocently and replied, "You are in England, my dear Mathew, and any other kind of shower is nearly impossible." Even now he still had to smile remembering it.

After he dried off, Matt stood in front of the mirror over the small sink and began to shave. The reflection looking back at him made him realize that while he was only twenty six years old, the last six had certainly taken a toll on him. He felt the five years since 1940 had actually aged him the way only twenty or more should. He hoped getting back to America would help, at least to some degree. He would be able to bury himself in work and try to forget the past. The War. Joanna. No, not her. Never her. Though their love had ended in his greatest disappointment.

His hip was hurting. It was always causing him some pain. He believed when he got back home, he would find some relief for it or at least have the pain reduced to a level he could tolerate. But the thing he was sure of, the lines around his mouth and eyes would never go away.

Well old boy, he thought as he considered his reflection, you have been through a real War and you sure as hell look it. I hope mature men are in vogue with the women back home, because damn few of the boys who left will return.

The thought about women back home made him grimace at the face looking back at him in the small mirror. How, he wondered, would he go about seeing women again after Joanna? How could he not compare them to her? If he started with that as his standard, where would he find one who was even close? Damn it Joanna! You are going to make this difficult even being completely out of the picture.

The jail-issued uniform was still scratchy, but due to his reduced weight, the fit was excellent and the Major's oak leaves looked good on his shoulders. If he was not being released so quickly he would have gone to Bond Street to have a uniform made from a softer woolen material.

While brushing his hair, he noticed a small amount of grey at his temples. "Hell, I don't remember that before but I didn't see too many mirrors in the camp in Germany. It must have snuck in while I was there. Maybe it's Government Issue so these Major's Bars look like they belong on my shoulders. You know, maturity and all. Somehow I had always expected the grey would come along after more years had passed; in my late thirties or forties.

Matt had a quick breakfast at the little place down the block where he had once eaten so often before the start of each day's classes at King's. He noticed they now offered tea OR coffee (no doubt added to the menu for all the American soldiers who had flooded into England) and he took coffee.

I may as well get used to having coffee again, he mused silently. Tea won't be on breakfast menus when I get back home. **Home**. Been awhile since I thought of America that way. I had planned all along to stay over here, but things change. Or get changed. The end result is the same. Just imagine eggs without a cooked tomato on top. I'll have to remember to order sausage instead of 'bangers.' I should have asked Joanna why the English call them 'Bangers.' Ah well, like so many things, too late now.

His first item of the day was a return trip to High Wycombe Abbey. When he showed his papers to the guard at the sentry post, he was stopped for only a moment, despite his out-of-date identity card. He was lucky that the duty officer remembered him from his visit of the previous day. The man smiled and said, "You really should get that ID taken care of if you're going to be over very long Major."

Matt thanked him, drove to the Abbey and parked on a graveled area full of olive drab vehicles. His little MG still looked very out of place. It somehow pleased Matt that it did. He returned to the third floor but this time entered a different door. This one marked with the name of his old boss Major General Ira Eaker.

The Gate Keeper here was a strikingly pretty, young member of the Women's Army Corp. She greeted him with a smile and a cheerful "Good morning, Major. What may I do for you?"

Matt laughed aloud and for a moment wished he was the other Matt; the one from his days at Yale. He knew what that Matt would have said. Her eyes said she was giving him an opening for a racy reply and perhaps far more... later. He could still sense things like that.. For a fleeting moment he was tempted...then his heart said, No way. It is far too soon. If you do that it will only make you think about Joanna and what it was like with her. The Lieutenant is quite lovely but....

Instead he said, "Well Lieutenant, I was wondering if I could see the General for a few minutes. I don't have an appointment, but I am sure he will remember me...Captain...err sorry... Major Mathew Weldon."

"Well Major, if you will give me a few minutes I will let the General know you are here. He is on the phone at this moment. Soon as he hangs up, I'll tell him."

The memory of Eaker's phone habits came back to him. "Well, in that case, if he is on more than five or six minutes it means another War has started. I could never keep him on line longer than that."

The Young Lieutenant smiled, turned in his direction and crossed her sleek, long legs before replying to him. "My, my, you really did work for him. I don't think I have ever known him to be on longer than that. If he was it was totally out of the ordinary. Only his face-to-face meetings go longer. He likes to handle a problem and move on. A most efficient man."

Matt had never seen a WAC skirt as short as hers. And he wondered where she had gotten the silk stockings, as silk had all gone into military service when the War started. Parachutes primarily. Were there regulations on skirt lengths for WACs? If so, who could complain in this case? The WAC in question had such beautiful legs, and knew it.

OK pal, enough about her legs, the voice in his head warned him. There must be a magazine or something other than her legs for you to look at.

He found a back issue of "Stars and Stripes" on a small table and spent twenty minutes pretending to be very interested in it. Later he could only remember her exquisite legs.

His next connection to reality was when she said, "General Eaker will see you now. She was noticeably cooler toward him than when he arrived. Perhaps, he decided, I should have brought her a pair of stockings. Well no...we know where that would lead in a very short time. And that it would end in a bed.

General Eaker, on the other hand, seemed genuinely glad to see him again. They shook hands and his old boss said, "Congratulations on the new rank, Major. The promotion was long overdue. It should have been done two years ago. One of a few million things we *should* have done during the War. I would have liked to do it myself, but Doolittle insisted when he saw your record with the 8th. Besides, nothing wrong with having your promotion presented by a Medal of Honor winner. He thought it would be fun to let you think you were headed for a Court Martial instead of a promotion. Tell me, did you sweat a bit?"

"Sweat a bit?" Matt laughed with a grin. "No, I didn't sweat a bit. I sweated BUCKETS. I expected to be broken in rank and kicked out of service with a Dishonorable. I have only been that worried once before."

He silently remembered a green eyed enchantress standing in a field of barley saying, "We can't be friends any longer. I have fallen in love with someone." His heart was breaking until she told him he was the one.

"So... I know we are getting you home in a few days. What brings you here today? Want to be promoted again so soon?"

Matt collected his thoughts and focused only on his reason for being there. "No General Eaker, it's about the rest of my crew from the "Maid of Barley." I know they made it down safely, but have no idea what happened to them later. We were split up all the-hell over Germany. The Kommandant of my Camp told me they were safe and strangely I found him an honorable man. I believe what he said.

"Some would have ended up in the American Zone, some in the British Zone and several in the Russian zone. Would you mind initiating inquiries to locate them and get them back to England as soon as possible? I know we have a lot of boys still in Germany and getting all of them back is a major undertaking, but I really feel responsible for this bunch."

"Sure Matt, I understand. I'll do the best I can. I've got pretty good contacts in Germany. I'll ask them to give your boys priority and have them expedited back over here. I'll say they were part of some secret group or something. One advantage of being a General is people tend not to ask too many questions. They just do the job asked of them. Well, except you. You always asked questions. I liked that about you.

"Tell you what. Spend a few pleasant minutes with Miss Bedows giving her the information about your crew and I'll get on top of it this afternoon. Good enough?"

~ ~ ~ ~

By the time Matt left High Wycombe Abbey he was certain of two things. First he was sure his crew would get back to England as soon as possible. He had always found General Eaker to be a man of his word and a man who got things done promptly.

Secondly he was glad to be leaving England right away or he might have broken down in his resolve not to get involved with another woman so soon. Miss Bedows had brought back the kind of uncontrolled impulses he had not had for over six years. Well, he decided, at least my sex drive is still intact and very much alive.

311

Miss Bedows certainly made him remember, somewhat wistfully, the life he lived before Joanna. But he knew that kind of life, like the world of those days, was now gone beyond recall. A memory only of a life lived by someone who was becoming a stranger to him now.

Mid-day traffic was moving smoothly when he left High Wycombe. It was about twenty five percent military with the remainder civilian autos and trucks with a sprinkling of busses. His first stop was at the jewelers and Matt was pleased with the way the wooden box had been lined in purple velvet with a circular hole for each coin. Each one lay as he instructed with the side featuring St. George slaying the dragon facing up. Glass topped them holding all ten perfectly in place. The coins were perfect. Not a flaw on any of them. The solid gold oval on the box top was now engraved with three initials in old English script. JSB. He complimented the jeweler on his beautiful work and paid the requested amount, which he thought reasonable given the quick turn-around.

"It is a beautiful present, sir. Fit for Royalty."

Matt paused a moment before saying, "Yes it is. She is certainly Royalty as far as I am concerned. The Princess of the Fields."

His next stop was the Calligrapher's Shoppe. She presented him the note he had requested. The old English style lettering was perfect. The front of the note was decorated with a drawing of a sheaf of barley tied in its center so it was shaped like an hourglass. Inside, it simply said, "Congratulations on the birth of your child."

As he had requested, the note was unsigned. The envelope carried the imprimatur 'Joanna Shaylee Barton.' There was a small lump in his throat when he slipped the note in the envelope and closed it inside the wooden box. It felt as if he were closing a coffin containing something very precious and now forever lost to him.

The calligrapher packed it in a small cardboard box and wrapped it in brown paper. She hand-addressed the box according to Matt's instructions and handed it to him.

Mrs. Bellingham had furnished him with the name and address of a liveried and reliable delivery service. Following her instructions, he drove past Big Ben and the Houses of Parliament and crossed Westminster Bridge over the Thames.

Only the English, Matt smiled, could take a river whose name is spelled T-H-A-M-E-S and pronounce it TIMS. Yet that was now the way he pronounced it and would forever more.

He had arrived on the Queen Mary as much a product of America as a dollar bill, a privileged, spoiled, young man. Started that late spring at

312

King's College, a school he at first did not like, played Rugby because it was vaguely like American Football, the game he played at Yale, and soon fell in love with the most English girl he could have found. Yet there was so much more to her than that.

I would have loved her no matter where we met. There was a special connection between us. From the first, it felt as if I had known her before. It was almost like a bond had tied us together even before we met.

Having her gone from my life hurts, but her memory is somehow comforting. Thinking about her is like the memory of a beautiful fall day in upper-state New York spent with Dad on our lake when he would take me duck hunting. The memory of the sky's color as the sun began to rise in the east. The crunch of the leaves under my boots. The trees that lined the lake's edges dropping leaves of yellow, gold, brown, red and magenta into the water where the wind would blow them across the surface like hundreds of small sailboats of fantastic color. The sharp-edged fall air on my face filling my lungs with air so crisp and clean it was a treat simply to breathe. The ducks quacking to each other in flight and the sound their wings made cutting through the morning air.

We were both good shots. Dad had a twelve gauge Browning and I had a sixteen gauge he had given me on my twelfth birthday. His motto was only one shot per duck. If he missed, the duck escaped. Perhaps two out of ten flew away. I was as good a shot, but they were so beautiful I missed many. Purposefully.

He was aware I was doing it, but never complained. He knew I was as good a skeet shooter as he was and shooting skeet and shooting ducks required exactly the same skills. I thought there was simply too little beauty in the world to destroy it without good cause. I need to spend more time with him when I get back. We have lots of time to make up and many things I need to ask him. So very much I need to learn from him. I know that now.

Matt was so deeply lost in thought he drove past the address of the building where the delivery service was located. It required turns around several blocks to get back.

When he arrived the uniformed attendant behind the counter assured him they could deliver the box according to his schedule, but it would be expensive because of Matt's requirement it be sent by either automobile or motorcycle so the delivery would require a trip of several hours. "Not like dropping it at an address in London, don't yak know?"

Matt assured him that price was no problem and wrote a check on his account at Barkley's Bank. The man asked him to wait for a moment and was gone about ten minutes. Matt was sure he was phoning to be sure the check was good. When he returned he was smiling broadly.

"Very good, sir. It is all arranged, the delivery will be exactly as instructed. If our man is asked any questions about the source, he will know nothing. Only that he was told to deliver a package to this address. As I have already forgotten your name, I can be of no help. Rest completely assured the package will be delivered on time with discretion."

As he drove away, Matt considered his progress. I have taken care of "The Maid's" crew as best I can. I am sure General Eaker will request help through all the contacts he has and a General asking for help usually gets it.

Now I have sent the gift to Joanna that I wanted to send. St. George. The love of her childhood. Well, she let me be her St. George for a time. The coins are all perfect as I never could be. I only got around to giving her a few presents. Christmas and her birthdays. The only one she will remember in time will be the small engagement ring. That will end up in a drawer somewhere now that she is married. She will come across it from time-to-time and remember me. I will certainly remember her. At least until forever comes along.

How close we came to being able to really marry. No more than a week or two. One more mission after the one we were on. So damn close. All that is left now are the memories. Like a dream upon awakening. No, not like that. A dream can be forgotten. Joanna never will be. Not for me

The next day Matt returned to High Wycombe; a last trip to a familiar location. The officious Captain behind the desk in General Doolittle's office rose when he entered and, unlike on his last trip, gave Matt a warm smile.

"Ah yes, MAJOR Weldon. It is good to see you again. The General is out on an inspection, but I have some papers for you. They include: copies of all your records plus the necessary papers for you to fly back to the States, a list of flights leaving in the next 72 hours, what bases they are flying out of and where they will land in the U.S. There is also an order from him authorizing you to fly on any one of them. You have our telephone number here in case you have a problem. I will be surprised if you need it. You could kick anyone below two stars off any flight. The General said you had gone way 'above and beyond.' The paperwork is all in here for your separation from service. Any Separation Center in the U.S. can act on them. A list of centers is also in there."

It finally hit Matt that this was the end of his time in the Air Force. Yes it wouldn't be official until he arrived back home, but standing here holding the thick manila envelope full of papers containing the official records of his service during this War, he knew it marked the end of six years of his life. In his mind he relived the drive he and Joanna had taken over to Barton Hall on the Friday Germany invaded Poland. The talk he had with Owen about going into the RAF. Joanna's tearful disappointment about his broken promise to her to stay out of the War. General Eaker pulling him into the 8th Air Force as soon as it arrived in England to select bases for use by the B-17s coming from America. That had allowed him precious days off. Time he could spend with Joanna. Then there was time spent training to fly a B-17 in combat and putting together a crew. His assignment to the 351st Bomb Group flying out of Polebrook. The awful mistake of the mission to Rotterdam. Having Gable fly with them for six months. The day he lost "The Maid." His year at Luft III and last, the discovery that after all this, he had lost Joanna. Finding she was now married to someone else and a mother.

In the end, his side had won the War. Yes, he had helped defeat Germany, but at such a cost. Such a terrible and high cost. It all ran through his mind like a film at high speed. The only exception was the scene of Joanna holding the baby alongside the young British officer. That was a freeze frame which took forever to fade.

He shook the Captain's hand and asked him to thank General Doolittle for him. For everything. The young man held onto his hand, looked Matt directly in his eyes and said, "I envy you. You were in the real War. The only thing I did was sit behind a desk and shuffle people and papers. I tried to keep the General on a schedule. Sure, they figure out medals for people like me. Purple Hearts for paper cuts. They don't really have meaning. I didn't do anything to help win the War. It took guys like you in the planes to do that."

Matt felt some sympathy for the young man, but knew he didn't truly understand what he was wishing for. "I'll tell you what Captain, if you can figure a way to get back to the beginning of it all I'll trade my job and ribbons for yours any day."

He turned and walked away, leaving the young Captain standing by his desk trying to understand what the Major had meant and why he seemed so angry.

Matt limped down two flights of stairs and out through the huge double front doors with their leaded glass inserts. Down the stone steps and over to his MG, he turned around and looked back one last time toward the hulking stone manor house. Before the 8th had moved in, it had been an exclusive girls' school. When they took it over the officers found a small brass bell beside each bed which became the focus of endless bawdy comments and jokes from those who used the beds. The bells had been intended for use by the girls should they need assistance of a matron during the night. The etched message on each bell said simply, "If you are in need of a Mistress during the night, ring the bell."

Looking at the huge building he thought, this is another reminder of the riches England had in an era when it bestrode the world as a titan. In those days they needed no help to fight their enemies. Then Victoria died and the century turned. World War One shook the country and they started the short slide toward this war. After this one they will only be a lovely little island.

The Battle of Brittan was a magnificent effort they can be proud of, but it was exclusively an air war. They could never have defeated Germany in a ground war alone. They required the assistance of both America and Russia to do that.

With Germany's defeat, America and Russia are now the premier powers in the world. The political system the Soviets use won't be able to keep them on top for very long. That system will bankrupt itself.

America? Our system works. Has for a hundred fifty years. The future there depends on education. Too many people don't understand how our system works. Yet they can all vote their vast ignorance. If they ever outnumber those who do know, who understand...then I fear for America. If you ever give government too much control...well we will end up being what we just defeated, Nazi Germany.

As he drove around London, he realized he had spent the last two days doing what Joanna had done on that day years ago when they stood atop the battlements of the Tower of London. He was trying to lock all his memories in his mind. To freeze it as it once was so he would never forget any of it. He had been chasing yesterdays. Chasing what was already gone. All that he had loved

That afternoon Matt booked a room for his last night in England at Claridge's. He remembered it from the night almost two years ago when he and Joanna had met some of his crew and Clark Gable in the bar for drinks. When they first walked in, he had believed Gable was on the verge of tears. It must have been a terrible reminder of how happy he and Carol Lombard had once been. Seeing the two of them coming in hand and hand must have been heart-breaking for him. Joanna had sensed it, because he could remember the gentle kiss she had put on Gable's cheek as they were leaving. As they walked away she had told him, "The poor dear, losing his wife like that. Having lost my brother Alexander as we did, I know how deeply it hurts. No amount of time can ever take that kind of hurt away."

It was getting dark, but after he checked in at Claridge's he had his car brought back around so he could take one last trip to 37 Eaton Place. He parked his car at the curb and walked a short way up the concrete drive toward the house. Stopping in the shadow of one of the trees along the drive, he spent a few moments remembering his time there. His first time he had been with Larry Trusdale who brought him to a party at the house of a girl he didn't know. A girl Trusdale hoped he would seduce and disgrace. That night set everything that had happened since in motion. On that night the house had been gaily lighted but tonight, excepting a single light in Mrs. Townsend's room, the house was dark.

Matt was sure the family was out in Kent at Barton Hall, Joanna with her husband and baby. Then in Joanna's room he saw a curtain move aside. It was Haiku looking down at him. He saw her mouth move in a silent "eeow." He whispered up to the small black and white face in the window, "Take care of her Haiku. It's all up to you now, girl."

He walked slowly back down the drive without looking back and drove away leaving the house and so much more behind him.

Matt wondered what it had all been about. He was leaving without the woman he had done it for. It had become meaningless when he lost her. Yet driving away from the large old English town house, on a nice late spring evening, he knew with certainty that he would never be able to forget any of it. He knew with equal certainty, he neither would nor ever could, return.

317

Chapter 21

SUZANNE

Louis Armstrong and his band featuring the vocal styling of Miss Suzanne Swift, the paper read. Matt looked at the ad in the "Times" twice before he completely understood what he was seeing. Suzanne had been his date on a single spring night that long-ago first year he was at Yale. What was it now? My Lord, could nine years have really passed? What he was looking at was an announcement of entertainment at the Stork Club starting on the nineteenth of December. A Friday night. He had no idea why it had caught his eye. What in heaven's name caused me to notice that? I never pay any attention to what's happening at the clubs. And the starting date is less than a week before Christmas. And of all places in New York, they were going to be at Sherman Billingsley's snooty Stork Club. True enough Sherman has done well for a guy who was, at one time, just a dirt poor Oklahoma moonshiner. To have gone from the life of a low class bootlegger to the owner of this Club, the penultimate symbol of Café Society was quite an accomplishment.

In his Club on any night of the week, power, money, glamour and talent rub elbows. While the El Morocco draws a more sophisticated crowd and Toots Shor's club draws primarily the sporting crowd, Billingsley's Stork Club attracts everyone.

Matt had gone there only twice since he returned from England, then only to listen and dance to the music when one of the big bands from his Yale days was performing. He always took a woman around his own age or a bit younger; though always a woman who still remembered how to dance those dances from the late 1930's. When he was dancing, he could almost relive those carefree days and believe he was once again back in a time which represented America's innocence to him. Before he met his star-crossed love Joanna and before the brutality of the War.

Despite the enjoyment he found in dancing not one of these women held his interest past a second date. He knew the problem lay not with the ladies, but within him. He was not happy alone and yet he never found happiness with his "Lady of the week-end." No matter how lovely she might be.

The biggest difference involved sex. Unlike his Prep School and University years, the point was no longer to bed them. He knew he was trying to find another Joanna Barton. He fully understood the futility of what he was doing, but he just couldn't stop comparing each of them to her.

Every West Wind haunted him by whispering of the love the two of them once had. The undeniable fact was that Joanna had moved on and found another life. Yes, she had believed him dead, but she had moved on with her life. Why couldn't he? Was it because he felt everything that had gone wrong had been caused by the promise he had broken to her.

She was no longer under the spell of their love, so why was he cursed to be? In some ways he *had* moved on. When he was at the Bank everything was Okay. His work kept him busy with loan agreements and consulting with executives from many of the Bank's large corporate customers on their immediate and projected financial requirements. He immersed himself by pouring over the minutia of a client corporation's balance sheets and profit projections. It was second nature for him to be as involved in someone else's business as he was with his family's Bank.

He was also enjoying the task of overseeing the conversion of an old brick warehouse he had bought into living space for himself and to be sold to six other young up-and-comers. Many would, like him, be survivors of the War. Like him, they would also be trying to readjust to peacetime and simply moving forward with their lives in a changed America.

He was retaining two-thirds of the top floor for himself. There was a tent-shaped skylight above his combination living area and kitchen with another over his bedroom and office. The light visible through them throughout the year would be excellent in the daytime and as a bonus he would be able to see the night time sky. The walls in his area had been stripped down to bare brick and were now repainted a stark white. The thick wall between the living space and the bedroom had been completely rebuilt so an open fireplace could be placed within it. When a fire was going it could be seen and felt from either side of the thick wall.

The few women who had seen his place had used words like "chic" and "avant-garde." He viewed his space as light, airy and open, and had already started decorating the white walls with good art. There were three of Georgia O'Keeffe's oversized flower paintings gracing the walls in the living room area while a very large Jackson Pollock abstract hang over his bed. A picture of Fizz, Kong and him from their second year at

Yale hung over his desk. His photographs of Joanna and him were locked away in a desk drawer.

He had Otis Elevator Company replace the large old freight elevator with a pair of regular size elevators so residents would not have to wait to go either up or down.

Since work had begun on his conversion, several other warehouses in the area had sold for similar housing space and prices on the remaining vacant properties were rising. Matt had proposed to the Bank's board of directors that Empire National purchase several solid buildings and do prestige conversions, then sell them. The Bank could handle mortgages for the buyers internally, thereby protecting them from outside costs. That would be good for the purchasers. The savings to them could be a thousand dollars or more; enough to buy a new automobile or furnish their new quarters. New York was booming now that the War had ended and the G.I.'s were getting back into the swing of things. All of America was growing, but New York was the colossus standing at the top of all growth in America. Empire was expanding rapidly and opening many new branches.

Matt had recently moved into his rooms and was getting settled. For the first time since he returned, he had a place. *His* place. Not since he lived in the little walk-up in London near King's College had he felt at home. Certainly never during the almost five years of living in metal Quonset huts or the thin walled wooden barracks of Luft III while a POW in Germany. Anyone comfortable there would have been a masochist.

Their brownstone townhouse, well, that was his dad's and he had never lived at the Estate on the Island long enough for it to feel like home since he was a child. After that it was prep school and Yale.

But the warehouse was his. The building was spacious and solid despite its age. It had the advantage of being in the City which made it convenient for him to get anywhere in a hurry. His main problem was finding places he wanted to go and someone he wanted to go with more than once or twice. It wasn't that the women he had gone with weren't attractive or intelligent. Most were both. But with each of them something always seemed lacking. He was glad he was in New York so there was an endless supply from which to choose.

That brings me back around, he thought, to Suzanne Swift. I remember thinking about her during the War. I was driving in to London and heard a song; one Guy Lombardo's orchestra played the night I danced with her at the Band Stand. Good old Kong and little Fizz were there. We all had dates and danced the whole night away. She was a strikingly beautiful girl, hair the color of moonlight. God, I was so shallow back then or perhaps just innocent of the world. I never looked past her body and face. All I really wanted to do that night was to take her to bed. I was disgracefully young and unforgivably foolish to have been interested in her only for sex. But hell, back then most of us were young and foolish and sex topped most guys' list. She made it clear to me that what I wanted was not going to happen as soon as I picked her up. When the night ended and I was driving her back to Vassar she said something about me being like a vase, good looking, a fine dancer, clever and smooth, but empty inside and then she got out of the Duesenberg walked around, leaned in and kissed me.

I remember how that kiss moved me, but I thought she was kissing me off. Then she ran toward her dorm and I would have sworn her hair had stardust sparkling in it. I came very close to running after her. I should have. But I had such terrible pride then. Hubris, the besetting sin of my youth. Of my generation. If I had gone after her that night... well, who knows?

I wonder how she has been and if she will even remember that single night out of so many that have sped past since? My Lord, almost three thousand nights ago. One kiss out of how many since that night? I am sure neither of us is the same now. Would we recognize the people we were then if we came face to face with them? The years and the War have changed us so much. I have already found that even the ones that didn't go away are different. The mothers, fathers, wives and children all suffered even if their loved one came home safely. I wonder, what effect it has had on her?

Well, Dad always says you never know the answer until you ask the question, so I think I will go to the Stork Club and do just that.

Matt had taken the Duesenberg out of storage as soon as he returned and had it worked on until it was once again in perfect condition. It had new tires and the body was hand-waxed until it glowed with the same deep midnight blue as the day his father gave it to him. The first time he cranked it, he was transported back to the years before the War; the sound of the engine and the feel of a fine hand-built automobile. It had been produced before the "assembly line" became the only way to build a car. She had been lovingly covered with fifteen coats of hand-rubbed paint and wood trim that had all been hand-varnished.

Heads still turned whenever she drove by and young girls still waved at him. He knew she was as close to a "Time Machine" as he would ever find. So many memories rode with him as he drove her.

~ ~ ~ ~

Just for old time's sake he had driven Dusey down to Yale one weekend shortly after he returned from England. The University was much busier than when he, Kong and Fizz were enrolled there. The word he had from a few of the prewar crowd was that Yale, Harvard and all the other Big Universities had become Degree Mills. Uncle Sam was sending so many ex-G.I.s to school that real teaching was no longer possible.

Push them through and stick as much in their heads as feasible in as short a time as was practical; "Here is your degree and the door is over there." The corporations could sort out the truly-learned from the so-so on the job.

The G.I. Bill had turned Universities into another kind of American "assembly line." When the rush caused by returning G.I.s was over, the schools could get back to education.

Temporary housing in the form of surplus Quonset huts had been thrown up to house the new students and their wives, many already with babies or soon to have them. Living in a Quonset hut was something most of the men understood, but the wives found them a bit primitive. On the positive side they were pushing their husbands to finish so they could find a job and buy a house. It was what the women dreamed of at night while their men were up late studying or having nightmares about the War and the things they had seen and done.

He parked in front of his old dorm and climbed the ancient, creaking stairs to the room he had shared with Kong and Fizz. He knocked, but received no answer so pushed the door open. There were small changes but the room remained as it was the last time he'd seen it back when he left in 1939. The old sofa and desks still there. In his memory he heard Kong telling him the life he lived might catch up with him someday. Had his big friend been a seer in his worried prediction? Pushing the door softly closed, he walked slowly back down the stairs. Rooms with too many memories were more bearable when doors were kept tightly closed.

Only "The Old Campus" looked largely unchanged with at least the outsides of Connecticut, Dwight, Street, Vanderbilt, Bingham, and Lindsey-Chittenden residence halls exactly as he remembered them on the day he left for England. He drove past Hewitt Quadrangle where one snowy February day in 1938, Yale's football team had challenged all comers to a snowball fight. All comers ended up being several hundred students. Through sheer stubbornness the team had held its position but his face had stung for two days from being pounded by so many snowballs. They had set up their position in the "L" made by the junction of Commons, Memorial, and Woolsey halls. The tactics were well thought out because no one could get behind them to attack from the rear.

Matt found even the memory of that day left him feeling sad when he remembered Fizz was on the side of the students. Several other friends from that year had gone away to the war, never to return. In his memory of that long-ago day they were all still alive and fighting with snowballs, unable to imagine the hell which was soon to be brought down upon them.

Little Fizz, his friend who hated pain and wanted to be a doctor, died in Northern Italy on another snowy day while saving as many of his unit as he could. The Army had awarded him the Medal of Honor. Well, the hell with that. Fizz's life was worth more than a medal on a ribbon.

The Romans, back when Rome really meant something, put up statues to their dead heroes; something visible that would be remembered for a long time. Except for Fizz's father, himself and Kong, who would remember this brilliant little kid? Well...Maybe at least *one* girl? A remembered kiss from a shy young man in the moonlight. One she had danced the night away with. An unassuming youth who thought kissing a girl was the greatest happiness in the world. His young friend who had always avoided any brawl. Who thought it was better to talk than to fight. He had been afraid of so many things except, in the end, of dying. His body on top of a German hand grenade to save others. An awful waste. Matt knew of all the ones that had been lost: Fizz was the best

When he returned from his trip into the past, he made reservations at the Stork Club for the Friday night that Louie Armstrong and his orchestra were opening. When he phoned and asked for Sherman Billingsley, he announced that the call was from Mathew Weldon of Empire Nation Bank. He did not add the Fourth at the end of his name. The line was silent for only a moment until he heard, "Mathew Weldon, it has been far too long since I saw you. The last time was that charity affair over a year ago here at the Club. The event that night was a fund raiser for wounded soldiers as I recall."

"No Mr. Billingsley, this is his son Matt. Sorry if there was a misunderstanding. At that time I was still in a German P.O.W. Camp. I was a pilot during the War. 8th Air Force. Flying a B-17."

"Matt, of course. Everyone thought you were killed. The "Times" had a short column on your resurrection. Quite a story. Somebody should make a movie out of it. Well how can I help? We haven't bounced any checks at the Bank have we?"

Matt laughed, "No, no, nothing like that. I was wondering if you could get me a good table for Friday night. I love Armstrong and I think his singer and I knew each other during our college years. Sort of an 'old time's sake' kind of thing."

"Consider it done. I'll have a table for you right up front. Should I let her know or do you just want it to be a surprise?"

"Let's not make it a big deal of it. I could be wrong. There may be other Suzanne Swifts, but the picture in the paper sure looks a lot like her."

"OK, that's the way we'll play it. What time do you want a table?"

"I'd like to come about ten if you could arrange that."

"You got it and say hello to your father. He's a hell of a fine gent in my book."

"I'll do that and thanks a lot Mr. Billingsley."

"It's Sherm to you. And you are certainly welcome."

Friday morning Matt ordered two dozen red roses to be delivered to Miss Suzanne Swift, care of the Stork Club, at eight o'clock that night. He instructed the woman on the phone to see that the card said only, "Thanks for the memory – 'Matt the Ratt'."

One of the things he had designed into his top floor living space was a large closet entered through doors at one end of the bathroom just off the bedroom. He had divided the closet into sections, starting with shirts hanging at one end to pants and coats ending with long coats. Once it was arranged to his satisfaction he worried about what that degree of organization said about him. This was not the kind of thing he would have spent time obsessing over a few years ago.

"My God Matt," he said out loud. "You are becoming a regular old maid. Everything has to be just so. Not a single shirt mixed in with the pants or a raincoat in with the sport coats. The ties arranged by color. I am beginning to worry about you, old boy. What I am seeing is not good."

He finally selected a navy blue wool blazer, tan wool pants, a white button down shirt and one of his Yale Club ties. He pulled on a pair of old cordovan leather chukka boots he had worn since prep school and a heavy camel colored wool overcoat.

~ ~ ~ ~

When he backed his Duesy out of the garage, the first small flakes of snow began to fall lazily from the lowering clouds, each becoming a

325

glowing dot as it floated past the streetlights. The first snow of the season in the city, he thought. The store owners will be happy. This is perfect timing for the Christmas season. What is Christmas without snow? Snow and snowball fights.

Except this was dry snow, blown by the wind across streets and sidewalks in sinuous patterns. Christmas shoppers rushed from one store to the next trying to get as much shopping done as possible before closing time. Times Square was busy with crowds of people and bright with lighted neon tubes. Signs were flashing, glowing and huge: a large Camel cigarette sign with a sailor blowing smoke rings, a Pepsi Cola sign fighting for attention with an equally large one for Coca-Cola, flashing signs for a performance by the Andrews Sisters and another for Duffy's Tavern radio show. There was a big sign for "Oklahoma" which had been playing since 1943 and was still drawing large crowds. The snow fell faster and the now larger flakes changed color as they fell past the dazzling neon tubes creating a kaleidoscope of swirling, dancing shades returning to their true white only when they finally reached the street.

By the time he arrived at Number 3 East 53rd Street and the Stork Club, the snow was heavy and the crowd light. There was no wait for a car hop to come park his car. The young man stopped and gave a wolf whistle. Matt was just out of his automobile when the hop said, "Mister, I haven't ever seen one of these before, but it is sexier than any gal in Hollywood. I will take good care parking it 'cause I imagine God would strike me dead if I let anything bad happen to it." He thanked the young man and tipped him a dollar. The boy smiled broadly and as he got in told Matt, "Mister, I feel like I should pay you for letting me drive it."

Matt checked his coat and stopped at the stand to give his name to the tuxedoed maître d' who checked his list and welcomed him. He said that Mr. Billingsley had reserved a fine table for him. Matt noticed the club was only two-thirds full. Just wait until after Christmas. All the nights until New Year's Eve the place will be packed and by New Year's Eve there won't be standing room. It was always full on Sunday because it was the only Club open; the only game in Manhattan.

The maître d' led him to a table just below a small raised stage which was empty at the moment. Only the chairs, musical instruments and drums were there along with two microphones on stands.

He told Matt, "They are on break right now and will return in about fifteen minutes. Mr. Billingsley told me you thought you knew Miss Swift. As per your wishes, no one told her you would be here tonight. I am sure, however, she is the right lady because when your roses arrived she became excited and started looking around the Club. She seemed disappointed not to see you." Matt thanked him and when a waitress arrived ordered a Glendronach Scotch and water with a single cube of ice and bought a pack of Pall Malls from the cigarette girl when she came by his table.

Funny, he thought, the only time I really liked to smoke was after a mission, in the O. Club with the guys or driving the MG with the top down. Most of the guys said "nothing like a cigarette after sex" but it never did much for me. Sex was a great enough high without lighting-up. But in a smoke-filled night club, it becomes practically a form of self defense. Of course the booze probably improves the taste.

Band members started coming on stage followed by Satchmo himself, Louie Armstrong, then came Suzanne Swift.

Matt was not certain how he had expected her to look, but she was even more beautiful than he remembered. Then he realized he was wrong. Tonight she was beautiful in a different way. Then she had been a beautiful young *girl* and now she was a stunningly beautiful woman. Her hair remained the color of the full moon when it rises from the sea on a summer night. And there was a mystical glow to it. Her eyes still the blue-green of a perfect aquamarine. Matt saw a hint of sadness there.

She was wearing a black dress that proved she still had a figure better than almost any he had ever seen. He remembered her exact words, "Hey Ratt, I know what you are thinking. Well you can forget it. I am not that kind of girl despite the way I look."

At that moment Louis picked up his horn and began to play, "A Kiss to Build a Dream On." After the introductory notes Suzanne walked to the microphone and began to sing.

It was the voice he remembered, but fuller, with more depth and feeling. You know Matt old boy; you never even asked her what she was studying at Vassar that whole night. No wonder she thought you were shallow and empty. And tonight you understand how right she was.

It was then he knew the song she was singing was no coincidence. She was looking right at him while singing. Then when she saw him looking back she gave a small "yes" nod with her head.

Throughout the entire set she never looked away from him and he could not look away from her. Either she had told Armstrong he was there before they had gone on stage or he sensed something between them because Louie said there was a song they hadn't planned on doing, but he wanted to do it as the last song in the set. He turned to Suzanne and said, "Lets' do 'If We Never Meet Again,' sweetheart."

Matt had never heard the song before, but when she began to sing, he knew he would never forget it. She sang with such passion the words were burned into his memory.

She sang about people separated never destined to meet again. About roses in winter and the memories they bring. The scent of flowers and the ecstasy of love when they had been together, leaves in the fall and birds singing in the spring reminding them of each other. A love which never dies...forever. Even if they never meet again.

When the set ended the band left the stage, but Suzanne stepped down and walked straight to his table, looked directly into his eyes and said, "Buy a lady a drink mister?" He pulled her chair out and when she was seated said, "That is a question you never need ask. It is my pleasure to buy you a drink. It has been far too long since I saw you Suzanne... a War too long."

They talked until the band started to return. Mostly small talk, but they both talked about their one night together. There were things he desperately wanted to say to her, but the break passed far too quickly so he didn't. Before she went back on stage she said, "We really should talk more Matt. I think we both need that. Our last set is at 12:30, will you stay?"

"Of course I will. It has been so many years. Now that I have found you I have no intention of seeing you disappear into the night like last time. I'll be waiting right here for you."

By the time the last song of the set was finished, the Club was nearly empty and the few remaining Clubbers were paying their bills and leaving. As the final notes of the final song died away, Suzanne walked over to Louie and whispered in his ear. He looked surprised, but said, "Sure Honey. Glad to." He stopped the band and told them, "We have a special request for one more song. I knew it was very good when I wrote it back in '36. It's a special request for a very special lady."

Matt stood as Suzanne walked up to him and whispered, "Dance with me Ratt."

The band started playing "If We Never Meet Again" and the two of them held each other very close as they danced at 1:15 in the morning in the still smoke-filled Stork Club the way they had danced together once on a long ago night in a far younger world.

She laid her head against his shoulder and Matt could sense an empty sadness in Suzanne. It was the same kind of grief he had grown too familiar with since losing Joanna.

They held to each other like the two of them were the only survivors of the sinking of a great doomed ship. They clung tightly together as if they were adrift alone on a great ocean and each had only the other for salvation. As they danced, Matt wondered what had caused this emptiness he felt within her. He knew it was much like the one within him.

When the last notes of the song drifted away and the band members were packing up their instruments, Louie stepped down off the stage and walked to where they stood, still holding hands. Matt turned toward him. "Mister Armstrong, I have been a fan of yours and your wonderful cornet since my college days. I want to thank you for the song you played just for us. I had never heard it until Suzanne sang it earlier this evening, but I will never forget it. Not after tonight."

Louis smiled his big signature smile and said, "It was our pleasure, Son. It was worth doing, just to see *this* lady dancing. I really hope we will be seeing you again." He looked at Suzanne and continued, "I know we all do." He turned, headed back to the stage, packed his cornet in its case and walked out the side door into the falling snow.

"Suzanne, I know it's late but I would really like to spend more time talking. Would that be ok with you? The last time I saw you...well, your evaluation of me was painfully accurate. I was only a shallow young man. I was not worth your time then, but I hope I am now."

"Well Matt, I expect we are both different now. Nine years and a War tend to change people. While we danced I could sense you are very different. There is a touch of sadness about you, a sense of loss.

"I think we should find out who we are now and how we got here. And I'll confess right up front I'm glad we met again. I would invite you to my place, but it's just a little hotel room. Can you suggest some other place?"

"Well, I have a location reasonably close. It's not completely finished yet, in an old warehouse that I bought. I'm having it converted into living quarters; roomy ones with lots of open space. If you would like to see it we can go there and talk."

He saw a touch of doubt shadow her eyes, but only for a moment before she smiled and said, "I would love to see your place Matt and talk about old and new times. Give me a minute to get my things. I'll be right back."

The staff was busy cleaning up for the next day, but he found the Maitre d' and settled his bill. The man told him his car would be waiting for him at the curb. Suzanne came back wearing a grey fox fur-trimmed cape over her dress and carrying a shoulder bag. The maître d' smiled knowingly at the late hour as they walked past his stand and out the door.

It was snowing much harder than when he had arrived at the Club almost three hours ago. Suzanne pulled the hood over her head to protect her hair and drew the cape closer around her body.

Seeing the Duesenberg she laughed and clapped her hands with almost childish delight. It was the way she laughed when they had danced the night away almost two years before his war started. She was breathless when she said, "Oh Matt, you still have her and she is every bit as dreamy tonight as she was then. I am so glad you kept her. She is still mag-damn-nificent. It is like she hasn't aged a day. Just seeing her makes *me* feel younger."

"Suzanne, I wish you hadn't said that about Duesy. I was going to say words like that to describe seeing you tonight. Just looking at you makes me feel I have traveled back to that time and the last too many unhappy years had never happened. Seeing you again, I can almost believe it is 1938 and we are going dancing at The Band Stand. That we will see my friends Kong and Fizz and their dates. Oh God, how I *wish* we were."

Suzanne stood looking into his eyes and he knew he was seeing a similar wistful longing for those happier days in her eyes. "Yes Matt, those were wonderful times. They really were so carefree. I miss them too."

He opened the car door for her and when she was settled, went around and got in on his side. The car had been running so was already warm inside. On the drive to his building they were both quiet, but he kept glancing over at her as if to reassure himself that she was real and not an illusion. Matt could tell she was looking at him in much the same way. He also knew the last few hours were the first time he had not thought about the War or Joanna in a very long time.

They rode the elevator to the top floor and he unlocked the door to his loft. As soon as he turned on the lights he could tell that she liked it. "Oh Matt, this place is really wonderful. I would never have believed a warehouse could have anything like this inside it. It is so you. Even years ago, when you were such an awful rogue, you always had wonderful taste. You designed this didn't you? Of course you did. It shouts 'Class.' Well actually it whispers it."

"I'm glad you like it and yes, the ideas were mine, but I worked with a very good young architect. He turned the ideas into a set of workable plans. Would you like a drink or maybe some coffee, anything at all?"

"Sure. Whatever you are having will be fine."

She took off the cape, laid it over a chair and sat on the large, deep wine colored sofa. Then kicked off her shoes and curled her legs under.

She could smell the scent of coffee before he returned with it on a tray. While she added cream and sugar to her cup Matt told her, "You know Suzanne, I really have thought about the one night we had together a lot lately. What you said about me when the night ended.... Well, you were right on all counts. I was a self-centered, spoiled child and there was nothing of value inside. It took a War and a...ah..."

"The words you are hesitating to say is '*a woman*.' I knew you were different the moment I saw you tonight. It is far more than just that touch of grey at the temples which told me you had been through a lot of changes. Would you tell me about her? Might help a little bit to talk about it."

They talked together for several hours. He told her about how he and Joanna met and came to finally admit they were in love. About Joanna and her family. Their plans to marry. The flying and all the death he saw. How he was shot down and about the two German pilots who shot up his B-17 and after doing that, guided him to a safe landing. His time in the POW Camp and finally, returning to England only to find Joanna with someone else and a baby. How he didn't blame her for continuing with her life because she thought he was dead. About leaving England without telling her he *was* alive.

Suzanne told him how she met and married a tall handsome naval officer in late 1944. She had been volunteering nights at a USO Club and it was there she first met him. They married only a few weeks later. It had to be rushed because he was being shipped out to California and assigned to the heavy cruiser "Indianapolis" which was heading for an island in the Pacific on a mission.

"I received just three letters from him before he was lost when the "Indy" was sunk by a Jap submarine in 1945. It went to the bottom so fast that only 317 of the 1,197 men on board survived. I became a widow so quickly it seemed I had hardly been married.

"I joined Louis' band after meeting him on a USO tour of Army camps they were playing and I was singing for the troops."

"Speaking of singing Suzanne, that song, 'If We Never Meet Again.' It is so different from what I normally associate with Louis' style of music. It is really beautiful. I was so glad I could dance with you again, but it's really quite a sad song. People in love parting never to meet again. It happened so often during the War. You know it almost described the two of us. I am grateful to the good old "New York Times" for running an advertisement with your name in it. If not for that, we might never *have* met again. To top that, I very seldom look at the Entertainment Section. I suppose we were intended to see each other again."

"The funny thing is Matt: the band almost never does that song. It's one of 'Pops' older pieces. I don't think he completely understands how wonderful it is. Or perhaps it is too personal. I can tell he is always a bit sad when he plays it. I know he only did it tonight as a favor for me.

He really *is* as special as people believe. With him it's not an act. He loves everybody from the people at the best table in the house to those in the back row.

"As soon as I saw you tonight everything from that one night we had together came rushing back to me. Just one night but seeing those roses from you and then seeing you reminded me what it felt like to dance in your arms. To kiss you that one time and how hard it was for me to walk away from you. When I got inside the door of the dorm, I turned and looked back hoping you would get out of 'Duesy' and come after me, but all I saw were your tail lights as you drove away. It was all I could do to keep from crying. I just damned everything I could think of instead. Mostly myself for the things I had said to you."

"I wanted to come after you. I knew I should have or I should have at least called later and asked you out again. But it felt so final when you were saying goodbye and God in Heaven knows you had me categorized correctly, but it was very foolish of me to let you walk away.

I knew as soon as I saw you, that you were a very special girl. I believe I also knew deep inside myself that I was not ready for someone like you. Even if I had tried very hard, I would have messed it up. Maybe fate had it end the way it did on that night to give us another chance on this night."

He hung his head as he continued, "That night, I believed you saw me as nothing more than an interesting specimen to be pinned to your collection of insects under the heading 'poisonous spiders.' Worst of all, I knew you had me tagged correctly."

She placed her hand under his chin and lifted his face until they were looking into each other's eyes. In the silence the only sounds were their breathing, the ticking of the bedside clock and the pecking of snowflakes hitting the thick glass of the skylights above their heads.

Her lips met his in a kiss. They had both known it was going to be this way between them from the moment she had walked to his table at the Club.... Each desperately wanting to place their lips on the others. It was a long kiss, as if they were trying to make up for the lost years between them; to erase that long, now sad, space in time. As if to somehow undo all the bad things which had happened since they were last together.

When she finally pulled away, both were silent for a long time. They were breathing heavily. Matt felt as if his heart might come through his chest so he could give it to her as he wished he had done years before.

"Matt. I know it is awful to ask of you, but that doesn't matter to me now. Not after *that* kiss. Can I stay with you tonight and sleep with you? Not the kind of thing a girl is supposed to ask a guy on their second date, but maybe it is decent if the dates and the kisses have been such a long time between. It's not the sex thing, really it's not. I would just like to sleep in the same bed with you. Sleep knowing you are there next to me. Does that make any kind of sense to you at all?"

"I don't believe it matters one bit whether or not it makes sense. It has been a hell of a long time since I slept with a woman, let alone one as beautiful as you. Not just, yes let's do that, but Hell Yes, let's do it. I only wish it were a smaller bed."

At this she laughed, "Oh, don't worry dear 'Ratt.' You will find me more than close enough. I didn't plan on doing this, so I have nothing to sleep in. May I borrow one of your shirts to use for the night?"

Matt walked her to his closet, opened it and said, "Well, if you *insist* on wearing something, take your pick." He closed the bathroom door to give her privacy.

He slipped on a pair of pajama bottoms rather than sleeping in skivvy shorts as he had gotten used to doing when alone and turned down the covers.

A few minutes later the toilet flushed and she walked out wearing one of his white shirts. He would never have guessed that a simple shirt could ever look so good on a woman. Her long legs were perfect. Her skin was the color of slightly aged ivory and he could see the shadows of brown circles at the swell of her breasts thru the material. That familiar small voice in his head was shouting, "Look somewhere else. Don't look there. Come on Matt. This is not the first time you've seen that part of the female anatomy. Just ignore them. You already knew they come in pairs."

Matt answered the small voice with, "Sure! Like you're not looking. Fat chance of that."

He knew the shirt was having its intended effect when she coyly asked, "Is this shirt OK? I just grabbed one at random."

"Good God Suzanne, I am glad you didn't pick one that looks sexy. I might have needed a long run in the snow to cool down."

"Well, I can try on another one if you don't like this or, as you suggested, I could wear nothing at all." Her smile had just a touch of challenge to it.

"OOOH NOOO! No wearing of nothing at all. I like to sleep on my stomach occasionally and I certainly wouldn't be able to do that."

"Braggart," she replied without missing a beat.

She was still wearing her high heels and she pirouetted slowly to allow him to see her body. And he could only think what a beautiful body it was.

Joanna possessed the only figure he had seen which could ever compete with the one presently holding his total attention. At this moment, Suzanne had an unfair advantage. She was the one standing at the end of his bed. And Suzanne **wasn't** married.

She had positioned herself so she stood exactly between his line of vision and a bright floor lamp which allowed him to see every inch of her figure. He no longer had to wonder if she was a true blonde. He could clearly she was. His shirt, made of light weight Egyptian cotton, nearly ceased to exist in front of the strong back lighting.

"Please have mercy on me. I am certain you are aware of the effect you are having. Dressed like that you could excite a statue. Even a dead man."

"No Matt, I draw the line at necrophilia. But a statue...hmmm... that might just work." She laughed then continued, "Not really. I am rather prudish when it comes to sex. Fifteen or twenty positions should keep most people from getting bored. Of course it takes both a borer and a bore-e to work it all out satisfactorily."

"You call that prudish? God, I am only human and if you keep talking like that I can't guarantee you *any* sleep tonight. As much as I know making love with you would be wonderful, I think we should take it a little slower than everything is moving right now. One lesson I have learned is that sex too early clouds things. One tends to confuse really good sex with love. And we both know they are not the same. I confess I want you sexually very badly, or goodly, already. But let's see if we can hold out for at least a little while before we take that step."

"Wow, you really have changed. The old Ratt would have had me on the bed by now and be planning his escape to his next seduction." She sat on the bed next to him and kissed his cheek.

"If it was that Joanna Barton person who brought about this metamorphosis, I am indebted to her. You must have loved her very much to be able to change as you have. But honestly, I am so glad she lost

334

you. Otherwise I wouldn't be sitting here next to you. Whatever the final outcome between us, I will treasure each day we are together. After all it is..."

He picked it up, "'Better to have loved and lost than never to have loved at all.' Do you ever wonder about the wisdom of that? Losing can be damn painful."

"Back then. When we had that first date, dear Ratt, I was afraid you would never really love anyone except yourself. But why should you have? There were so many girls willing to tumble into bed with you. As much as I hated to see you drive away that night, I knew it was for the best. I wanted more than a lover for a few nights."

"Not exactly word for word, but in substance that is what Joanna told me when she was first getting to know me. She had heard about my reputation from other girls she knew. She wanted me to know we could be friends but her lover would be "Forever" and only when they were married."

"She must be quite a Lady. I can see why you fell so hard for her. But I hope you won't spend the rest of your life unhappy because of her loss. To a degree I was more fortunate in the way I lost my 'sailor.' We only had a short time together, so our bonding was not as strong as the two of you. What you had together really amounted to a marriage. But she's gone Matt. When you were a P.O.W. there was no way she could have known you were alive. I am sure she grieved your loss. Then someone came along and she married him. Perhaps only on the rebound. Now you must think of her as dead. Grieve her as you must but move on with living."

"That's what I have done. I did a lot of grieving before I left England. I still feel sadness about it all. Perhaps I always will. She believed in...well she used the term 'Kismet'... Fate. I have accepted that it was just our fate that things happened as they did. As for moving on..., well I think Fate may be a lot like God. The old quote 'What God giveth, He can taketh away'... perhaps what Fate takes away it can replace. Maybe that is why we have found each other again. The odds would have seemed against it."

Suzanne looked at him for only a moment then leaned over, put her arms around his neck and kissed him. It was a kiss that lasted a long time. Each could feel the other's breathing and heartbeats. When the kiss finally ended the embrace continued. Each was completely lost in the eyes of the other.

"Dear Ratt… I know now why so many girls fell so willingly under your spell. Even when they knew what you were like and how it would end. Despite the bad things about you. They could see that you had the soul of a romantic and each one of them hoped to be the one to set it free… or perhaps capture it. I know now that is what made me sad when you drove away that night. I knew I would not be the one to do it."

When he awoke the next morning in bed alone he wondered if she had awakened early and left. Then he heard her singing in the kitchen and he could smell coffee brewing.

When he walked into the kitchen, her back was turned. Since he was barefoot she did not hear him when he walked over to put his arms around her waist. She jumped a bit in surprise, then leaned back into his embrace. He felt her sigh when he kissed her on the side of her slender neck just below the ear. Then she turned in his arms, put her arms around his neck and kissed him. When she pulled away she smiled at him. "Wow, you sure know how to tell a girl 'Good Morning'."

This is quite a woman, he thought silently. No makeup at all and she is gorgeous. Hers is a completely natural beauty. She will still be striking thirty or forty years from now.

"It is a 'good morning' which I enjoyed Suzanne. What would you say to consider making it a tradition?"

She was pouring him a cup of coffee; her hand froze in place. When she had carefully sat the pot down, she turned toward him again, a question in her eyes and on her lips. "What do you mean?"

"Look… this is a pretty big place. You said you are in a little hotel room. I loved having you in bed with me last night. I slept well and it felt so good having you there. Perhaps it was a coincidence, but I often have bad dreams at night. War dreams. I didn't have any last night.

"I guess what I am saying is that I would like to have you here as much as possible. As you saw, this place has a really big closet which would look so much better with your things in it. I know this is very sudden but I would like to have *us* live here.

"What I am asking, very poorly, is… would you please move in with me so that we can find out if we could work as a couple?'"

She looked at him for a moment. He could see in her eyes that she was thinking it over. After several minutes she moved closer. When she finished studying his face she spoke. "Matt, I slept better last night than I have since '45. Just feeling you there was wonderful. Today is Saturday, so I have to be at the Club by six-thirty. Most of the things I have here in New York are clothes and music scores. My other stuff is in storage at my mom's house. If you don't mind helping me load the Duesy up with my clothes then the answer is definitely YES. I would love to tempt fate with you."

~ ~ ~ ~

Monday night when she came in from the Stork Club they made love for the first time. They were both completely swept away with passion. He hoped it would never end and she kept moaning "So good, oh it is so gooood! Yes... oh yeeessss. Oh Matt. Please. Oh God you ARE perfect. We are perfect *together.*"

When it was over they lay still joined. Her arms were around his neck and he was holding her face in his hands looking into her eyes.

"Suzanne, that is as close to heaven as I can image while I am alive. Before the War, I thought nothing could top the thrill of flying. I was wrong. Being with you like that was *worlds* better."

She kissed him almost shyly. "Dear, dear Ratt. I have never felt like I feel with you. I think you have just ruined me for anyone else. I wanted it to go on forever and forever. I could have happily died doing that with you."

"I had a similar thought but I'm glad neither of us died because now we can do it again and again. Frankly I would like to live forever if making love with you can be like that. It was beyond wonderful. You are simply magnificent. Thank you for being so wise the night we first met. It made tonight possible. It was *so* worth waiting for."

He was surprised when she started to quietly cry. He held her tighter and asked "What is wrong sweetheart?"

"As much as you know about women you must know that women don't just cry when they are sad. They can also cry when they are happy and, with you, I am *very* happy."

He was startled at how similar the words were to the ones Joanna had spoken the first time they made love. And, he realized what he and Suzanne had done *was* make love. It had not been just sex. But was it the way he had loved Joanna? Was it enough love to last?

"And dear Matt, I have just realized I can't ever call you 'Ratt' again. I know you haven't really been that guy in a long time. Strangely enough that lost and I believe lonely, arrogant boy will always have a place in my heart. I wish the two of us could have more time back then. It might have cost me a broken heart, but it might also have saved both of us a lot of pain later. It might have kept you from falling in love with her and me

337

from marrying him. We both lost out in those deals but maybe we are finally going to win... together."

He looked into the eyes of the lovely woman in his arms and knew it would have been infinitely better if he could have fallen in love with her. If he could go back to then more like he was now, he would, and he would find a way to love her and to get her to love him. With luck they would be long married by now and probably have a child. Maybe two. But that wasn't what had happened. He had met Joanna and *they* had been in love and nothing he did or wished for could change that. He so wanted to love this wonderful woman looking up at him that much. She still lay in the circle of his arms. He knew that she was as perfect as Joanna. She was no less beautiful and it was exciting when they made love, but some small thing was missing. He loved touching her and being joined with her, but that tiny electric tingle he had felt with Joanna was missing. That little something he had never been able to exactly define.

He was sure he already loved Suzanne, but not as much as Joanna. Not quite as much but he also wanted her there with him. Perhaps in time Joanna would fade and what he felt for Suzanne would grow. He was sure she already loved him and perhaps that was enough after all. Perhaps the magic he felt with Joanna was only his imagination and nothing more. All he was sure of was what he had with Suzanne was close to his feelings for Joanna. And when they made love he could, for a while, forget those bewitching green eyes.

The two of them settled into a pleasant routine. Because she worked evenings at the Stork Club and he worked days at the Bank, they saw enough of each other to be lovers, but not so much that they felt crowded. It gave them adequate time to sort out their feelings for each other. Some evenings he was asleep when she came in, but he always woke up enough to take her in his arms when she got into bed. Even on nights when they did not make love she backed up against him. Matt could no longer imagine sleeping without her being with him. She continued to sleep in one of his shirts and he could not believe a sexier negligee existed.

Suzanne always found breakfast waiting for her when she got up and they usually met for lunch some place near the Bank. When Trey met her at Christmas time, Matt could tell he approved. When he found out she was living with Matt, he was ready to pay for all the wedding expenses. He had to laugh as he reminded his father that according to tradition that was up to the bride's family. Besides it was a bit premature. Nothing was decided yet.

"I want you to listen to me son. I never met this Joanna of yours but she could not be more beautiful than Suzanne or any more of a lady. And she damn sure didn't love you one bit more. This lady loves you beyond anything you could ever deserve. I wish I had someone to look at me like she looks at you. And another fact... your Joanna is married now. So don't mess up and lose this one because of one that is out of reach. If you do you will hate yourself later."

"Well Dad, I don't intend to lose her. I *do* love her. I'm just trying to make sure I love her enough not to cheat her. I know she is good for me. I just want to be certain I'll be as good for her."

Suzanne and Matt put a large Christmas tree in the corner of his living space and decorated it together. It took a while because they made love on the rug in front of the fireplace before they were finished. As they lay there in the glow from the fire, he kissed her gently and told her, "I do love you. Please be patient with me. I want this to work for us as much as you do. God you are so wonderful. I knew that back then, but I think I was a little afraid of you. You seemed to understand me far too well."

"All I can tell you is about now Matt. It may have started *then* but now you have my heart. You are the one who has to decide how it goes between us. For me, I hope we live our lives out together. I hope every Christmas is ours to spend together. I believe we are supposed to, but what I have to hear you say is that you love me at least as much as you did her. I'm not asking for more because I know you had a great love for her. Just love me as much and that will be enough."

New Year's Eve at the Stork Club was just as crowded as Matt had expected, but he was a regular fixture now and Sherman Billingsley held a table for him. It was noisy, smoky and lots of people were getting very drunk.

If he had been far away from the stage he could not even have heard Louis' magical trumpet solos or Suzanne's singing. She took all her breaks sitting with him, but the place was so loud they mostly held hands and looked at each other. Several times he leaned close to her and said, "I LOVE YOU" into her ear. Once she kissed him and said, "I know Matt. But I do adore hearing you saying it."

The band played until after 2:30 in the morning and he could tell she was tired. When they finally got into the car, she surprised him by asking if they could go through Central Park before they went "home." It was the first time he had heard her call it home and he felt a catch in his throat. It sounded so natural to hear her say the simple word. *Home.* For both of

339

them...now. He knew he would not mind hearing her say that... well, forever.

The park was white from a heavy snow-fall the day before. Tree branches and bushes were all bent down toward the frozen earth. The lake was ice covered except for a small area in the center where the geese swam, pale forms against the inky darkness. She asked him to stop near a small bridge arching over the frozen stream which fed its waters into the lake.

When they got out of the car, she took his hand and they climbed to the top of the bridge. Over the trees they could see tall buildings reaching upward toward silvered clouds scuttling toward the River and the great, cold ocean beyond. She was looking up at the juncture where the buildings and the clouds met.

"Do you ever think about time, Matt? I mean how vast the reach of time really is and yet how infinitesimal a portion we are given? You and I met over eight years ago. It seems a long time, but it really isn't. This old earth of ours has been here billions of years. Some few of us are given a hundred years and that is considered a very long time to live. By the time we learn what is really important it's time to leave. And all we were or could have been is lost in time's vastness. The love we have found is blown away like smoke from burning autumn leaves on a windy fall day. Such a short time to love.

"I love you so very much that I wish I could live to love you forever. Do you think that maybe there is a forever for us?"

He turned her face toward his and kissed her gently. "I hope so, but I don't know. I suppose we have to make the time we are given enough. Love as much as we can and then if there is a forever somewhere it is a wonderful bonus. If not, we can at least love each other until the last grain of sand drops to the bottom of the hourglass."

"Take me home Matt. I am tired. Put me to bed and climb in with me. And hold me until I am asleep."

He had a hard time sleeping that night. A new year had started its journey while they stood on the bridge in Central Park. It was 1947. A year and a half since he returned from the War. He had worked hard at the Bank and his father had put him in charge of Commercial Loans. He knew it was only one step away from Bank Presidency.

He had bought the building they were living in and had it re-engineered into residential space. During most of the time he had been very lonely knowing he could never see Joanna again, and then Suzanne had come back into his life.

Now she was sharing his bed and living with him. Tonight she had asked him to take her home and hearing her say that word the way she did filled an empty place in his heart. She had only been with him a short while but he could not even picture the place without her. She belonged there as surely as he did. He loved seeing her simply sitting across from him in the kitchen and sharing a cup of coffee or having a glass of wine in the evening sitting on the floor in front of the fireplace. Making love was better than it had ever been. It had never been quite this good between he and Joanna. So why was he still not sure enough to ask this beautiful, passionate, loving woman to marry him?

He knew his dad was right. If he let her go he would be crazy. She loved him with no restrictions. Well one. She wanted to know he loved her as much as he had Joanna. She didn't ask him to love her more. Only just as much. If she had asked while they were making love he could have told he did. Because then he truly did. It wasn't just sex between the two of them. He knew they truly made love together.

When he and Joanna had made love it had been less spontaneous. The first time, when she had seduced him in the barley field, there had been the worry that someone might see them and he was worried that she might be hurt because he knew she was not experienced. Even later when she became lost in passion, he always contained himself as much as he could.

The other times they were together before he was shot down always seemed rushed. There had never been the time to move slowly into it and fully enjoy being completely together. Never time to let the passion build slowly to the point that neither he nor Joanna could go on living without joining.

Damn, he thought. What keeps me so tied to what is now only a memory? This beautiful, loving woman lying next to me is all any man could ever hope for. Marry her you dumb son of a bitch. Despite what you may think you still feel for Joanna, you will never find a better love than this one. It is time to end the lonely longing for yesterdays that are already gone. Gone into the river of time and swept into the dark ocean of the past.

On Friday, January 3, he took a long lunch hour and went to Tiffany's on Fifth Avenue to buy an engagement ring. It was not the way he had done it in England. There he and Joanna had bought the engagement ring together. That one carried such a small diamond, but it was what she

341

had insisted on. Well, they would never have that tenth anniversary when he could buy her the larger stone she had agreed to. Perhaps the fellow she had married would do that for her. Perhaps he already had.

The salesman showed him many rings, but the one Matt selected was a two carat blue-white diamond which the salesman assured him was as perfect as a diamond could be. He had noticed that Suzanne preferred yellow gold jewelry, so he chose a wide yellow gold band and he guessed at size six. The salesman advised him to bring it back for sizing after he gave it to his lady. If the setting did not suit her, they would be happy to change it. He asked if they could put the ring box inside another box which they did.

When he walked back through the cold late January day he felt better about everything than he had in a long time. He knew that his father had been right at Christmas. He would never find anyone else like her. And he knew she loved him more than he could ever deserve. She was the most open person he had ever known. She asked so very little of him. Just being with him seemed to make her joyously happy. All she had asked of him was to love her in return. As much as he had ever loved anyone. Was that too much for her to expect? And he did love her. He only needed to rid himself of his memory of and love for Joanna.

He drove to the Club at midnight and walked in as Louis and his band were finishing up their last set. Her last song was 'Body and Soul' and, as always, he found that she put so much heart into it you knew she was feeling every word. People referred to women who sang with such feeling as 'Torch Singers'. Of all the ones he had ever heard, she was the best.

Matt noticed she was rather ashen under the spotlights and when she walked over to his table he stood and asked, "Sweetheart, are you feeling good? I've noticed you looking just a bit pale lately. Perhaps we should make an appointment with our family doctor and have him check you out."

She kissed him and put her arms around his neck. "Oh, I'm all right. Just a touch of the winter time blues. When the sun comes back, I'll be just fine. Let's go home now, another night in the salt mines finished. Now I can go crawl in that wonderful bed with you. I don't know how I got by without that to look forward to at the end of each night."

He had left a fire burning when he left to pick her up and he laid another log on as soon as they walked in. She walked over and held her hands toward it. "Sweetheart, thank you for having a fire going. I was chilled and it feels so nice." He took her coat off her shoulders and laid it across a chair. While she enjoyed the fire, Matt walked into the kitchen and uncorked a bottle of chilled champagne. When she heard the cork pop, she walked in and joined him while he poured two glasses.

"Well sir, what is the occasion? It's not my birthday and we know the New Year has passed."

"Yes, New Year's is over and I never thanked you for making it the best in my life. But I should have thanked you then, because you did. In fact every day since you came has been a wonderful day. And the nights. Oh my! I do know it isn't your birthday but I do have this little box for you."

"Matt, what in the world? My goodness a Tiffany's box. What is it?"

"I suppose you will have to open it to find out."

She opened the outer box and when she saw the small blue ring box within, she knew. She stood holding it for a long time before finally opening it and then she looked at it in silence. Her eyes went from the ring to his face and then back to the ring.

Finally he broke the silence. "Should I do this the old fashion way on one knee and say, 'Suzanne Swift I love you. Will you marry me?'"

"No Matt, you don't need to kneel. All you need do is tell me you love me as much as you loved Joanna. You know you don't have to say you love me more. I have never asked you for that and I never would. But I can't be second best. I can't compete for your love with a shadow and a memory. As much as I love you I can't do that. Look me in the eyes and tell me that and I will rejoice in marrying you. I will love you until the day I die. I am going to do that anyway. You already have all of my love. I will have our children and I am sure we can make a very good life together and I am sure I can make you happy. I want that for us."

Matt wanted so badly to say the words she needed to hear but he couldn't say them. He believed that in time he could, but not tonight. Not now. "Suzanne, I do love you. I truly do. You are the best thing that has happened to me in a very long time. Just touching you and being with you makes me happy. Your smiles, laughs and even your tears are things I cherish. I know you want us to begin without that ghost standing between us. If I could undo knowing her I would gladly do that for you. But I did know her and ghosts from the past take time to fade."

"I know they do Matt, but she seems more than a ghost. When you told me about her it was more as if you were bewitched than haunted. I don't believe you will *ever* be free of her. And what if it was not her who has bewitched you? What if you have done that to yourself?

"It is a beautiful ring. It is tasteful and wonderful, exactly what I would expect from you. I would have loved wearing it until I took my last breath on earth still loving you. But I can't accept it Matt. I am so sorry my love. Now let's go to bed. I very badly need you to hold me tonight. And please tell me you love me once more before I go to sleep."

The following Monday when he arrived home from the Bank and unlocked his door, he sensed something was not as it should be. He called her name hoping she had not left for the Club yet. There was no answer. He walked through the bedroom and bathroom and into the closet to change out of his suit into slacks and a sport shirt. He got no further than the door when he saw all of her clothes were missing. Only an empty space remained where her clothes had been. He turned and walked back into the bathroom. Her cosmetics were all gone. By the time he checked the drawers for her underwear, he knew he would find them empty. It was when he turned around and saw the bed was made that he saw a letter and the Tiffany's box on top of it.

The place suddenly felt very empty and hollow. He dreaded opening the envelope even more than he had hated the missions he flew over Berlin in 1943 when the air war was at its very worst.

He didn't want to open the letter, but knew he had to. He finally took it to his desk along with the Tiffany's box, took a deep breath and slit the envelope open. Inside was a single piece of paper with tear stains on it.

"My dearest Matt,

I cannot stay with you here another day but it is breaking my heart to leave. I know the longer I stay with you the harder it will become to do this. There will never be another love in my life like you. My heart is filled with nothing but love of you. Leaving you is the hardest thing I have ever done and yet I know now that you can't love me as much as you did Joanna and as much as I love you I can see that will never change. The sad thing is, I only loved you more when you asked me to marry you. God Matt, I so wanted to say yes. You will never know how much. Years ago when we first met I made a wish for you. I wished that you would someday find someone to fill that empty space inside of you. I should have wished it would be me, but on that night I never expected to see you again. Well, you finally found the girl who filled that empty space and there is not enough room left for me. I hope someday you will find someone and, by then, there will be enough space for her.

Love forever,

Suzanne"

By the time he finished reading the letter, Matt was surprised to find tears freely rolling down both his cheeks. He could not remember shedding a single tear during the War. People died and he refused to act as if he had been affected by it. He had lost Joanna and gotten rip roaring drunk, but he did not shed but a single tear.

Yet he could not bring himself to tell Suzanne that he loved her as much as he loved the girl who was forever out of his life. She had left him and here he was crying over the loss. Why?

All he could think was there had to be some way to get her back. She said she loved him and he knew that was true. He would go to The Stork Club and get her to come back. He knew he must not lose her.

He drove far faster than he should have and only blind luck kept him from getting a ticket or having an accident. He was still wearing his suit and white shirt when he arrived at the Club and he had become such a regular he was given the usual table down front. He was early. The music was not supposed to start for another half hour and he asked the waiter to please let Miss Swift know he would like to speak to her. When she came to his table and sat across from him, he could tell she had been crying. The whites of her wonderful aquamarine eyes were red. She reached across for his hand.

"I am sorry I left that way. I simply couldn't face you and do it. I am such a coward. It took all the courage I had to leave while you were gone. When you asked me to marry you but couldn't say the words I needed, I knew it was time to go. It would only hurt worse to do it as time went by. I couldn't marry you and be second best in your heart. I couldn't go on competing with shadows from yesterday." She was crying and tears were streaming down both her cheeks.

He was having a hard time speaking because of the lump in his throat. "Suzanne, please don't do this. I want you to come back. There must be a way we can work this out. I can't imagine living there without you. I love you."

She looked at him lovingly and caressed his cheek with her hand. "I know you do; as much as you are able to love. I think that back when I first knew you and there were all of those girls, when you went from one to the next you really loved them all. As much as you were able to love each of them. But it just never lasted did it? I said you were a romantic and you are. You, my dearest love, are in love with the idea of love not the day to day reality of it. You said that when you and she first met, Joanna was out of reach. Someone you couldn't possibly have.

"Well, you are more than bright enough to understand what I am telling you. Then, after you lost her, I came along. The girl from years ago that you couldn't have then. This time it was different. This time you could have me. And to keep me all you had to do was say you loved me as much as you did Joanna. You wouldn't or couldn't say it. Why not Matt? You could even have lied and I would have believed you because I love you so completely. I hope what you told me about loving her so much is true because if it is not you have cheated both of us out of a lifetime of love and being together.

"I can't come back. Not the way things are. In time you would drift away and that would kill me. I won't ever forget you, but I can hope in time I will hurt less. I meant what I told you when I said you have my heart and I am filled with you. That will never change. Now you will be *my* ghost... forever."

Matt took the ring from his pocket and opened the small black box. "I am sorry it is ending this way. I hoped for something better. Something happier for both of us. I think we both deserve better. I know you do. I don't know Suzanne, you may be right about me. We may not see ourselves as clearly as someone who loves us does. I only know what I have found in you is a beautiful, talented, loving woman. I will miss you always, but the thought of you staying and being hurt is one I can't bear. I don't know what I will do without you. Thank you for letting me love you, if only for a while. Please take this ring Suzanne. I won't take it back and I will never give it to anyone else. It is yours and no one else will ever wear it. Please."

She looked at him for a moment and saw a single tear roll down his cheek. She extended her left hand and he slipped it on her finger. She stood and said, "Please hold me one last time. Then I've got to pull myself together. We have a show to do. Stay through my first song. It is for us."

Matt ordered his favorite Scotch and soda and a pack of cigarettes while he waited. He had the same empty feeling inside that had been there when he saw Joanna with the English Officer and the baby. It was as if his heart were gone out of him. The single thought he had in his mind was, "What do I do now? And how do I carry on?" Here I am just past my mid-twenties and for the second time in a bit over a year my life has ended. I have really only loved two women and I have lost both of them. I must be a complete fool to have lost Suzanne, but if she is right about me, to have her stay would destroy her. If I let her go now then maybe in time I can think of a way to get her to come back. Maybe I will be able to tell her I love her more than anyone else and mean it.

Louie brought his band out and Susanna walked to the microphone to begin her song. Matt knew it would be, "If We Never Meet Again" and it was.

The spotlight on her hair carried him back to the first night he had seen her. The night they had danced away together in college. And the kiss at the end of the night. How she had run from his car toward her dorm at Vassar. He had been certain that stardust must have fallen from the sky to sparkle on her golden hair.

Matt knew he would never be able to forget the way she teased him by wearing his shirt that first night they slept together. Coffee in the mornings and champagne at night. How much she loved riding with him in "Duesy." New Year's Eve in Central Park when he told her all they could do was love as long as they could. Only a few days ago, but tonight it felt as if it had happened years ago. Suddenly he felt old and tired.

She sang the song with tears running unashamedly down her cheeks. She did not wipe them away. How pale she looked standing in the spotlight. I never did get her to a doctor. I hope she will be okay. Why did I let this happen? She asked so little and gave me so much.

Good job, Matt. Now you have two women who will haunt you and this one is completely your fault. He looked at her one last time, put money on the table and left before the song ended.

He felt he could never return to the Stork Club. In his mind he would always see her there with the tears on her face because of him.

A few days later he heard that Louie Armstrong and his band had left the Stork Club and gone to California to appear in a film and Suzanne Swift had gone with them. He found that one of his Egyptian white cotton shirts was missing. The one she had always worn at night.

Chapter 22

A GAME OF GOLF

Saturday, March 8, 1947, found Matt and his father playing eighteen holes of golf at their club on Long Island. This very early spring day had started with a brushing of frost remaining on the course. They began their round wearing light jackets but by the time both reached the sixth hole the temperature had risen enough so Matt and Trey were playing without them. Spring jonquils were in full bloom around the clubhouse and some of the trees were just beginning to bud out.

Matt finished his round with a respectable 77 but his father finished with a 75. The "old man" as Matt tended to think of him could not hit a drive as far down the fairways as he once had; but his control of the ball was still flawless. If his ball lay within twelve feet of the hole, it was usually one putt from dropping in. Matt still had a hard time believing how seldom his father's putts failed to drop. It was his total mastery of a putter which gave him the edge in a game with nearly any opponent.

It had been a wonderful day to be on the course with the temperature finally reaching the high sixties and a brisk breeze blowing from the West. Matt still could not stop thinking of a West Wind as Joanna's wind and in his mind he saw her standing amid the golden barley blowing in the wind. It was not a vision he enjoyed remembering, but always did. Too many images continued to bring her to mind.

Two years had passed since he returned to America, but he could not forget her and simple things such as a West Wind blowing or seeing a pretty girl with green eyes on the street brought her back added to that were his memories of Suzanne. Both the warehouse and Duesy constantly reminded him of her. The deep ache was still in his heart whenever that happened.

At the end of the round, the two of them retired to the clubhouse bar for a drink. Over the years his father had always sat at a particular table looking out the vast tempered glass wall with an unobstructed view over the last two holes which graced the rolling hills of Long Island. The Weldon family home was less than two miles away on several hundred verdant acres of perfectly manicured property.

Matt could sense that his father had more on his mind than just a post round drink. He decided to initiate the conversation because his father seemed reluctant to do so.

"Dad, I can tell you have something you wanted to talk about today. I had the feeling on the drive over to the Club that this was about more than simply wanting to get away for a round of golf. Is there anything wrong at the Bank or is there something else bothering you?"

His father lifted his Scotch and soda and took a long swallow before looking at Matt. "Well Son, yes there is something, but I wanted to wait until I could show you your old man could still beat you by a few strokes before bringing it up. Actually it is both things you mentioned: the Bank and something not related to the Bank.

"First, about the Bank. You are my son, but putting that important consideration aside, the job you are doing as V.P. of Commercial and Industrial Loans is nothing short of spectacular. You have become more than simply competent in well under a year. You have saved the Bank over six million dollars in loans we would probably have made which would most likely have gone bad. And, because of your advice, we have made several loans anyone else would have turned down which have proven to be very good investments. You look more carefully than any officer before you at the minutiae and it has paid off for us.

"I am delighted to say you returned from the war a different person than the boy who left here for England back in '39. I know the war was an awful experience for you and, well, for me too. For a while I thought I had lost the only child I would ever have and felt very guilty for having sent you there. Thank God you were not dead and came back not only very much alive but in one piece. Well...except for that hip. I know your experiences still haunt you in several ways and, honestly, they may always.

"My own war still haunts me these many years later. It will never completely go away, but as the years pass you will find it does fade.

"When you left Yale and went to England, I never expected you to come back the responsible man sitting here with me today. I am proud to be your father Matt, and I only wish your mother could be alive to see you. I am certain she would say, "Well Trey, I knew all along he would be. I am surprised you thought otherwise. After all he is **our** son."

"I intend in a reasonably short while to give up the Presidency of the Bank and hang on to just the Chairmanship of the Board. This is historically the manner in which power has been transitioned in our family and it is time we started making plans for that looming day.

350

Assuming, of course, you are willing to take on the responsibility of the Presidency of the Bank. Are you ready to do that Matt?"

His father lifted the glass of amber colored Scotch and took another swallow. He looked squarely at his son while awaiting his reply.

Matt was surprised by the question his father had asked. He had long known how his family passed control of the Bank from one generation to another, but he had not expected this question for years to come. His father's expression said he expected an answer today.

He sipped his beer, swallowed, and began "Sorry Dad. This has taken me aback more than a bit. First, I need to say, I hope we are not talking about this coming Monday morning because I don't believe I will be ready for the jump quite that soon."

His father smiled and shook his head, "No."

"Good. You know following in your footsteps as President of Empire is the greatest honor I can imagine in this life and the most demanding job I could ever take on. I know each new Weldon has made the Bank larger and more prestigious, all while watching out for our depositor's and investor's interests year after year for over a hundred and fifty of them. I will do my damndest to follow that tradition and, yes, I understand what a heavy responsibility it is. One lesson I learned in England: nothing is more important than family and family history is sacrosanct. They are lessons learned from the preceding generation and passed to the next. It is the essence of what we Weldon's are. Family is both our past and our future. I will not let you or the Bank down."

His father looked pleased at Matt's reply and reached across the table to pat him on the shoulder. "Matt that is a hell of a good answer. Starting Monday morning, keep handling your Department exactly as you have been, then at four come up to my office so we can review my day. I will go over the day's decisions and why I made them as I did. Marion will make notes so you can refer back to them when and if you have need.

It is the way your grandfather trained me and it worked well. Admittedly, back then we were not as large and he made fewer decisions each day so we usually wrapped everything up by five or so. With us it will go to six, maybe later. Is that OK?"

"It's fine with me Dad. I have the warehouse in town so I'm always only a few minutes from the Bank, but I know you like to go home to the island. Will it work for you?"

He watched as his father gave his question some thought before answering him. "Sure Matt. You're right. I do love that old pile of bricks. Your mother loved it too. You and I were both born there. I know it has always meant more to me than it does to you. Undoubtedly because you really didn't have much family when you lived there and then you were in prep school and on to Yale. It was never home to you in the way it was to me. For me it was always home, both before and after your mother and I were married.

"I still have the brownstone in the city and often use it when I work late anyway. Usually at least twice a week. If I want to go to the island, well Thomas can drive me out. He is a really excellent chauffer and the more I let him drive me the less he has foolish worries about his job. Anything else, Matt?"

Matt considered a moment before replying, "Nothing comes to mind at the moment but a hundred questions will probably pop up later."

His father turned away from Matt to stare from his accustomed place at the great wall of tempered glass. His gaze focused on the hills beyond the course and the club's thirty-six tree lined holes. He was still talking to Matt, "You mentioned the importance of family and ours has a very long history. I have failed completely in my duty to tell you many family details. I must correct that oversight as part of our daily sessions.

"One example comes to mind. Your great grandfather was a founding member of this club not long after the Civil War ended. Back in 1878 if memory serves; shortly after he came back from his war. He also helped found the sailing club out on the point. That was completely appropriate because he had been the captain of an iron clad gun boat on the Mississippi during the siege of Vicksburg. He died shortly after I was born. I wish he had lived longer so I could have known him better.

"And my dad, your grandfather, rode with Teddy Roosevelt in the Spanish American War with the 1st United States Volunteer Infantry. He was friends with both Roosevelt and Bucky O'Neill. O'Neill had been a sheriff in Prescott Arizona as well as a newspaper editor, judge and rail road founder. Dad said the only time he saw Roosevelt show emotion in combat was when O'Neill was killed by a Spanish sniper just before the attack on San Juan Hill. Said Roosevelt cried when they buried O'Neill.

"So you see Matt, like you, each generation of Weldon's, in its turn, has fought their war and survived to return and head the Bank. Perhaps the wars taught us how to be tough, to make decisions under pressure, but most importantly of all to do both with a high sense honor. Our coat of arms in England, long before we came to America, carried a motto at the bottom in Latin. When translated into English, it is most appropriate. It is 'Cum Fortitudine et Honore.' It means..."

Matt interrupted translating, 'With Courage and Honor.' "I know, Dad. I haven't forgotten my Latin quite yet, he laughed, "though I drove my tutors nuts asking why anyone would study a dead language, only to find out later it isn't really so dead after all. A lot of it has hung around in legal documents and on our currency so we see it every day, though we largely don't notice. The founders of America thought it that important and it is still being taught in school so many generations later."

"Speaking of generations son, there is something else I have been putting off talking with you about for too long. I understand you were deeply and truly in love with Joanna Barton. I know you were completely crushed to find out she was married to someone else when you got back to England from your time in the Luftwaffe camp. But that was two years ago. You must be aware you are still trying to find another "her" and are most likely never going to do that. I suspect you know by now that Suzanne was very close to what you wanted and yet you've let her go. Take it from me Son, she completely adored you. I personally think you may have made a mistake. You were much happier while she was with you. For the first time in two years you were smiling and laughing. But that is just my opinion.

"I know you have been out with several women a few times since she left, but I have gotten the idea that none of them have impressed you. Am I wrong Son?"

Uncomfortable with his father's question, he knew the corners of his eyes had closed down in pained thought before he looked back at his father. "No Dad, you *are* right. I have been out with a few ladies and yes, I admit to trying to find one who can make me feel even close to what I felt for Joanna. Yes, letting Suzanne go was probably a mistake... an awful mistake. One I discovered too late. Just know it's not a dead issue. She is still very much on my mind.

"It's not that the ladies aren't attractive. Some have also been intelligent and others have made me laugh, but Joanna was all that and worlds more. She challenged me in ways no one else ever has.... Well, except Suzanne and with her it was different. I don't know how to put it. She was fun, open and very demonstrative. Whereas Joanna was so very damn special, and smart and yes wildly beautiful, but in many ways more reserved. I do understand being with her is *now* a moot point.

"I am looking for a woman who is at least similar in some of the same ways the two of them were. I will just keep looking. I refuse to give up. There just has to be someone out there. I will find her because I must. Don't worry; the idea of being alone long term is not appealing to me."

353

"Son, are you certain you didn't already find her? Just a question to think about. Is it possible you can't see the nose on your face?"

Matt consider for a moment then nodded yes.

His father's scotch was empty so he signaled the bartender for another and ordered additional beer for his son even though Matt's was far from empty.

"Good. Just don't give up on finding someone. I would hate to think you were going to be the last Weldon to ever head up Empire National and without progeny you most certainly will be."

Matt laughed at the seriousness of his father on this topic. He decided to lighten the conversation with his reply. "Well Dad, if I had understood how much this meant to you, I would have flown those missions with a steel jock strap protecting the important parts."

Trey laughed, but shot back an immediate reply. "Well Son, it might have been better if you had been wearing one of those while you were at Yale; before you left."

Matt knew when he had been bested, "Touché."

The club bar was filling with members who had finished mid afternoon rounds. Nearly each of them dropped by their table, obviously to say hello to Trey, but also to shake Matt's hand and exchange pleasantries. He was being included in his father's world and his large circle of friends. What he a few years ago would have thought a phony waste of time, he now found congenial and important. To be assimilated this way felt both warm and fraternal. There was sincerity in the way they were incorporating him into this long-standing friendship. Matt was starting to understand why his father enjoyed being here and knew his father would play golf even if he were not an outstanding player. The game was important, but these old friends were far *more* important. Many of them had their sons by their side. Those close to Matt's age had all returned from the War. Some had been wounded. A few had been fliers. Each had paid their dues to their Country: sadly a number had paid the ultimate price and did not return at all. They were remembered on a plaque in the lobby of the clubhouse.

More than a golf club, this was a place of passage; A continuum of a way of life. These men and others also brought daughters here for swimming, dances on spring and summer nights and tennis. A few of them would bring those young women to learn the game of golf. Their daughters as well as their sons were an affirmation that while generations were constantly passing, family lines and traditions were still being carried forward into this new post-war era.

After most of the men were settled at their favorite tables or in groups around the bar, Matt surprised his father by saying, "So, Dad. Now, let's talk about your love life or *lack* of one.

"I know you loved my mother. That's something I've known since I was old enough to sit the toilet by myself. When I was young I watched you stop in front of her painting in the living room every time you walked by. I also know there are fresh flowers on her grave each and every week and two dozen roses on her birthday as well as your wedding anniversary.

"So let's just accept you have always loved my mother well and faithfully. Just like Joanna for me, there will never be another woman like her for you. But Dad, you and I are far from dead and it's time for us both to live for today, not in the past."

Matt's father was so still and quiet, it seemed he was hardly breathing. He had never seen his father taken so completely unaware by any conversation.

Trey finally took a deep breath followed by a large swallow of his scotch before finding his voice for a reply, "Mathew Weldon, what *exactly* are you saying here? That at my age I should start dating? Huh? If that is what you are advising, how would you suggest I go about it? Perhaps work my way through the secretarial pool at the Bank? Hell boy, most of them are younger than you. No, I don't think that would work out too well. We would have nothing in common. Or would you suggest a match-maker or an advertisement in the "New York Times?" Something along the lines of, 'President of major New York bank looking for young, beautiful lady for dating.' I'll bet that would probably bring quite a few responses. Maybe some we wouldn't want."

Matt watched as his father started laughing. "Oh son, you really had me going there for minute or two. It really is not nice to joke with your old man like that. But I've got to hand it to you, that was a *really* good one."

"No Dad, I am not joking and as for where to look. Well... try your outer office. You might just find the answer to your question there."

His calm-under-all-conditions father stood half way up before bellowing, "What? Have you lost your mind?"

Realizing that everyone in the room had turned and was looking at him he turned toward the bar, spread his hands and very quietly said, "Sorry" and sat back down before continuing in a perturbed but near whisper. "Marion! You are saying I should go out with my Assistant? And here I had been giving you credit for such good sense. I take it all back. You must be a dolt to even suggest something like that."

Matt took a sip of beer and waited a moment before asking, "Are you quite finished?"

His father, still red faced, simply said, "For the moment, but proceed very carefully!"

Matt held his father's gaze without flinching and replied, "As carefully as I can Dad. But like you, there are also things I have left unsaid for way too long. Things a blind man could see. And you don't even wear glasses.

"First, I know in Marion you have the best assistant you could find anywhere. I doubt any executive exists in this country who could even wish for someone as good as she is. And considering she is simply a country girl named Mary Smith from a small failing farm in Oklahoma during the Dust Bowl, what she has become is nothing short of astounding. Yes, I checked up on her because I wanted to know more about her before we talked and everything I learned only heightened my respect for the lady.

"I spoke with the woman who taught her English and mathematics and was the Principal of her school in Oklahoma. She said Mary was the brightest student she *ever* taught. All the teachers hoped she could go on to college, but they weren't able to work out a scholarship. There was this little thing called the 'Depression' going on and the colleges were not admitting students who couldn't pay. When Mary talked about going to New York to find a job, the teachers worked hard to raise $100.00 and gave it to her. When she got to the City, she lived at the YWCA and worked two jobs so she could go to secretarial school. Instructors there also remember her as the brightest and best in her class. The day she interviewed with you was the very first interview they had sent her on and they were very happy about your hiring her.

"Do you know that Marion regularly sends money back to that little Oklahoma school in the middle of nowhere so they can help other worthy students who can't afford college?"

His father sat silently as Matt laid out the history of his assistant and simply shook his head to indicate he had not known a majority of this. He wondered how she could have been with him day in and day out for years and yet he knew so little about who she really was. Yes, he knew she was Mary Smith but he had never once used that name. To him she *was* Marion Tompkins. It was the only way he had ever thought of her. He suddenly realized there was a degree of danger to her reputation and standing at the Bank in what his son was telling him.

"Matt please tell me you haven't told anyone else about the things you have learned about Marion."

"No Dad. The only others who know anything about this are her old teachers in Oklahoma and the lady at the secretarial school. They are all too proud of what she has accomplished to ever hurt her. I assure you it will stay that way. I admire what she has become as much as they do.

"Dad, in Marion you have a most exceptional woman. She is more than just the lady who holds down your outer office. And it is high time you found out more about who she is. She works endless hours to help you do anything that needs to be done. She is always there for you. You may think she is only doing her job but that is because you have never seen her for who she really is. If you had been paying closer attention you would have known that she thinks you are a most wonderful man."

His father interrupted him then. "Matt, I'm over fifty years old and she is much younger. I'm too old and ragged around the edges for her. And I am not so blind that I haven't noticed she is a very attractive woman. But she needs someone closer to her own age. I mean, even if it were possible, it would not be fair to her. And that is assuming you are right about her feelings for me of which I am not fully convinced."

Matt had been ready for this objection and immediately pulled his counter argument. "Okay Dad. Let's go about finding out in a logical yet safe manner. How many fund-raising dinners, award banquets and other evening events do you attend representing the Bank each year?"

Puzzled by his son's question, Trey put the ball back in his son's court with, "Probably in excess of twenty-five. Marion would know for sure. Why?" Then Matt saw him wince at how much he depended on her to run his schedule. With such precision on her part, he never missed anything.

"And you always go alone right?"

His father's reply was instantaneous, "Right, who would I thoughtlessly punish by asking them to go along? These events are normally quite boring and deadly dull. I have to be there for the Bank, but why make someone else suffer with me? I normally leave as soon as I feel I politely can."

Matt gave a hearty laugh, "Oh thanks. So that is undoubtedly going to be part of *my* job description when I become President. You know Dad, you really excel in making a job offer attractive."

Though he could tell his father was a little embarrassed, he continued, "So let me make both a suggestion and an offer regarding these social business affairs. You want me to continue interviewing potential mothers for the next generation of the Weldon Clan. And I would like you to at least get to know who Marion is outside of the Bank. When is your next evening event?"

His father considered for a moment and said, "It's actually one of the better ones. Next Friday the Modern Art Museum is having a dinner-dance and auction to raise money for the new wing. I am on their Board, so naturally I am scheduled to be there."

"So...next Friday? Okay let's do it this way. I will bring one of the young ladies who is a potential candidate and you ask Marion to accompany you. We can, in effect, double date. How about it?"

Matt could see in his father's eyes that he was almost convinced, almost but not quite.

"OK, what could still be holding you back?

"Well, I just worry what people at the Bank will think when the word gets out. And you know it will get out. Me, the President of the Bank, bringing my assistant? I wouldn't want any one misjudging her because of my actions."

"Does that really matter? Look you are widowed. Have been for years. Marion is single and with your present attitude is likely to remain so. She worships the carpet you walk on. You have just been too stuffy and staid to notice. If anyone's eyebrows rise, you can just tell them she will be there to help represent the Bank.

"Dad", He chuckled, "the least you can do is give her a chance to say something to you other than, 'Yes, Mr. Weldon. No, Mister Weldon.' Or, 'I'll get right on it Mr. Weldon.'"

Chapter 23

TREY AND MARION

The next Friday night Matt picked up his date for the evening, Barbara Ann Joiner, a young graphic arts design editor from the group which was producing advertising for his department. A bright, creative young blonde with a quick mind, she was from Atlanta and pronounced her home state as, "JAW-JA." Coming from her, Matt actually found the accent completely charming. He was also convinced by her beauty that she had probably been a cheerleader in high school and college. He made a mental note to ask her and find out if his perception of this pretty, yet very talented girl was correct. He was also sure that at this point she was dedicated only to her career. So, he might have misled his father just a bit by saying she was a 'potential candidate to be mother of a future Weldon generation.'

After he picked her up at her apartment in Duesy they continued to his father's brownstone on the Upper East Side. Trey had arranged a rental limo for the evening with the understanding that his chauffeur would be driving the big Lincoln. Thomas then drove them to a high-rise apartment building not too far from Central Park where Matt and his Georgia girl waited at the curb in the idling car with Thomas while his father went to collect Marion.

Matt noticed his father wore a charcoal grey light weight wool suit with a thin chalk stripe, which he had never seen before, and a pale blue button down collar shirt plus a paisley tie. He was reminded anew what a good looking guy the "old man" was, even at the advanced age of around fifty.

In a few minutes, Thomas jumped out of the front seat to open the back door and Marion slipped in followed by Matt's father who had a slightly stunned look on his face. Matt could not blame him.

This was a Marion Tompkins neither of them had ever seen before. Her hair was down and long, not up on her head as she always wore it at the Bank. Her jet-black hair shone like a black pearl at midnight. Her dress was a simple sheath of black silk which fit her wonderful figure as if every stitch had been taken while she was wearing it. Her nylons, patterned in dark grey led the eye to her simple black pumps with three inch heels. She wore a touch of lavender eye makeup which highlighted her irises; a warm brown with flecks of green in them. Her skin was the glowing tan most women have to spend hours in the sun to ever hope to achieve, yet most never do. No one could have believed her a poor girl from Oklahoma. She looked the very definition of the word "sophisticated."

Matt could nearly forgive himself for what he had almost said about her that dangerous long ago day in his father's office. She was so beautifully striking that all he could manage was, "Wow, Marion! You look spectacular."

She graced him with a smile and simply said, "Thank you Mathew, you look very nice too. Are you going to introduce me to the young lady with you?"

Matt introduced her to Barbara Ann and the two of them chatted pleasantly during the drive to the Museum. He and his dad grunted at the appropriate times.

~ ~ ~ ~

On Tuesday night a little over a month later, Matt was working at his desk in his warehouse library. The building's interior had been in rough shape when he bought it, but the conversion had been completed. It was arranged as spacious quarters for young up and coming business people; those looking for something out of the ordinary in living spaces. He had reserved the largest of them for himself on the top floor. Walls of natural brick were coated stark white. The few friends who had seen it used words such as "modern" and "very avant-garde." He hadn't either in mind when he had the work done. His idea was "spacious and bright." Purchasing the warehouse had proven a bargain because it had been unoccupied for a long time and the owner was under intense pressure to sell. Rental from the other tenants would cover the purchase price prorated plus a bit more, so his quarters cost him nothing.

He was examining information from one of the largest manufacturers of military aircraft that was contracting to build a limited number of new long range jet bombers for evaluation by the Air Force. It was a bit complicated because the Army was presently being separated out of the equation. It was happening at the end of September and the finances involved in the agreement were still muddled guaranteeing the contract was bound to be complicated.

Matt was mentally having a difficult time adjusting to the idea of an independent Air Force because a short three years before he had been flying for the Army Air Corp. It would probably work out for the best but still... best to be very careful with the bank's money.

~ ~ ~ ~

When his phone rang at 9:22 PM, he picked up on the second ring. Before he could even say, "Hello" the voice on the phone said, "Matt it's Marion; I'm at Presbyterian Hospital with your dad. They think he has had a heart attack but he is conscious and completely aware. He had them call me as soon as he arrived and when I got here asked me to call you. As you might expect, he has said don't worry at least five times. Isn't that just like him? He has a heart attack and says don't worry." He could tell Marion was doing more than just worrying by the tone of her voice which was slightly panicky. He could tell she was scared.

"Marion, I will leave here right now and get over there. This time of night I should be at the hospital in less than half an hour. I know you are worried, but stay with him and keep him as calm as you can. Don't let him stress about needing to do this or that. If he starts tell him between you and me we can handle everything until he is back at the helm. Coo in his ear or do whatever you need to do. Just keep him quiet. I am on my way. OK?"

The reply he heard was more like the very much in control Marion, "Yes Matt. You are absolutely right. I will keep him calm if I have to sit on him. Cooing sounds like a good idea. See you in a few. The ER Department by the way."

He bettered his half hour estimate by almost ten minutes and was quickly in the curtained off cubicle with Marion and his father. She was as good as her word; both she and his father were calm. Trey was a bit pale, but greeted his son as if nothing at all was wrong. "Now son, don't worry. I'm sure it's nothing serious. I had a bit of chest pain and called Doc Martin then he insisted on calling an ambulance. Well, the next thing I know I am here and a bunch of people in white smocks are fussing over me, sticking me with needles and drawing blood plus putting this line in my arm and running EKG after EKG. Doc Martin was here a few minutes ago with a fellow he introduced as a heart specialist. I know my condition isn't too bad because that heart specialist was the calmest fellow I think I ever met. I suspect him of being a Harvard grad. Nothing ever excites them. Sometimes it's even hard to tell if they are alive or dead."

In spite of himself Matt was on the edge of laughing and finally said "Oh yeah you are going to be fine. I ever see you in a place like this and you are not kidding around: Then I'll worry. Boy do I feel for the doctors and nurses while *you* are here."

He could not help noticing that Marion was holding his father's hand the entire time the two of them talked and he was certain his father was aware of it too. He also saw his dad smile up at her as if to say, "Don't worry. I am going to be just fine."

Matt found another chair and moved it into the cubicle where he and Marion (still holding Trey's hand) sat for several hours while assorted medical personnel scurried in and out.

At 1:35 in the morning Doctor Martin came in with a very serious young doctor who he introduced as the heart specialist. The young man looked at Matt before saying "You must be Mr. Weldon's son Mathew. Well, the lab tests and EKG's confirm that your father has had a mild myocardial event. In everyday terms, a small heart attack. We believe the amount of damage to the heart is minimal. We do however intend to keep him here a few days so we can do a thorough evaluation just to be certain. If what we are seeing now holds true, medication, exercise and diet should prevent any future recurrence of this type incident. It will be best for Mr. Weldon to see a heart specialist two or three times a year so we can monitor the heart functions as a preventative measure. He turned to his patient then and followed with, "Can we depend on you to do that?"

His father nodded in the affirmative, "I depend on good Doctor Martin here to point me in the right direction on that subject." Looking down at his hand which Marion still held, he said, "Might as well get the best care I can. I still have a lot of things it is way past time I did before I have to check out."

A short while later an attendant rolled a hospital gurney in and, with a nurse's help, transferred him on to it. Marion and Matt followed as the attendant wheeled the gurney out of ER, down a long hall and onto a large elevator. Together they all went up to the fourth floor to room number 427 in an area where Trey could be closely monitored.

By the time he was settled into the bed and the flow of white uniforms had slowed it was well past 3 AM.

Matt could see his father's color had returned to normal but it was obvious he was tired. He was sleepy partially due to the lateness of the hour but the nurse had also let them know that one of his capsules was so he would sleep.

The duty nurse had assured both Matt and Marion that if either or both of them were needed for anything at all, they would be called at home. She suggested they should leave and get some sleep and not to worry because all his vital signs were normal and the staff would be constantly looking in.

Marion had turned to Matt and said, "You go ahead. You will have to fill in for him starting tomorrow morning so you need to get a few hours of sleep. You'll have to be coherent enough to let everyone at the Bank know what has happened tonight. Also let the Bank's board members know your father is expected to fully recover. I am going to wait until he is asleep before I go. I'll see you tomorrow but I may be a little late. I'll probably give you a call in the morning before I get in."

Matt took her hand and gave it a gentle squeeze. "Thank you for taking such good care of him. Not just tonight, but for all these years. Particularly those while I was away. It has only been in the last two years I've gotten to know how really special he is. You have been way ahead of me there. I hope you know he understands how important you have been and *are* in his life. I will talk to you just whenever tomorrow. Don't feel pressured to come in at all."

She blinked away a touch of moisture from her eyes and squeezed Matt's hand in return. "I intend to be in, at least for awhile unless the situation should change. You and I will need to examine what is on his schedule at least for the next week or two. If the doctors can hold him down longer than that I will be astonished. So for now; good night."

He made his way out of the hospital, drove home and, like a college kid fell on to the bed and into a trouble sleep, still in his clothes.

He dreamed he was back in the War again, Group Leader of his flight of twelve B-17 bombers. A single V consisting of four groups of three smaller V's.... Above, below, left and right were more groups of twelve aircraft; hundreds all composing a single enormous V. Each flying in perfect formation so their guns gave maximum covering fire to every other plane in the group. At least that was how it was supposed to work in theory.

Their target was the ball bearing works at Schweinfurt Germany. At the briefing before takeoff the Colonel in charge said if they could destroy this facility the German war machine would soon grind to a halt. He warned them to expect heavy attacks from the Luftwaffe on the way to the target and exceptionally heavy flak from the ground once they were over the target.

German fighter planes had already hit them once but so far none of his group of twelve had been shot down. But Matt knew they had pulled away only because they were getting very close to when the flak guns would to start up. He knew the Luftwaffe would be waiting again on the way back from the target.

Only moments later the group in front of his entered the "Flak Box." The fire was so thick it looked like a garden blooming with hundreds of quickly blooming black roses. A single prick from the thorns of these roses could blow a B-17 to pieces. It was difficult to imagine that a plane could make its way through this menacing sky without bleeding.

He watched as the first group lost two of their B-17s. One lost half a wing and started spiraling down. Several parachutes opened as the crew left her while they were still able to get out.

The other was hit near the bomb bay doors. The shell's explosion set off the bombs and the aircraft became nothing but a look into hell through a hole in the sky. The men on board never had time to know what happened. One moment they were alive and the next... the next it was as if they had never existed at all. All that would remain of their lives was a telegram to the next of kin from the War Department which would start, "Dear Mrs. Jones We regret to inform you that your son Sergeant Paul Jones was killed in action..."

Now his group was flying into the box. The noise from exploding shells was overwhelming and the big bomber was thrown around the sky like a child's toy by near misses from the flak guns. But from the rear of the "Maid," his tail gunner announced that behind their plane, "Miss Behavin'" had two engines on fire and was trying to get out of the flak. There was no way she would ever make it back to England. If she could keep going and get out of the flak; the crew might be able to bail out in the clear and maybe get down safely. Only maybe. Some German fighter pilots liked following parachutes down while machine-gunning the crewmen hanging under them long before they landed.

His top gunner told Matt that "Southern Bell" had been hit in front of the tail so that entire section had been blown away from the wings and body. The only parachute that he saw was the tail gunner's. The rest of the plane was tumbling so fast that no one else could get out. They would probably still be alive until she hit the earth below. It would only be minutes but it would seem a lifetime of terror before they died.

His bombardier was on the horn now telling Matt that he couldn't see the target through the Norden Bomb sight. There was just too much cloud and lots of smoke obscuring the area. He didn't think the first group had dropped their bomb loads even close to the target. He couldn't understand why they were even sent over with this much cloud cover at the target. The mission should have been scrubbed.

All Matt could say in reply was, "Ours not to reason why."

The answer came back from nine of the eleven others on board with him, "Ours is but to do and die."

Only his big copilot John Smithson remained silent.

Before Matt could reply to this, "Easy Aces" off his left wing tip was hit by at least two shells at almost the same instant because it turned into aluminum confetti some of which rained against the "Maid" with a sound like hail on a tin roof. Blood and oil washed his side window until it was largely blown away by the aircraft's speed along with moisture in the high clouds.

The bombardier's inability to find the target made it necessary to go around again; this time with even bloodier results. More aircraft went down in flames and still he couldn't locate the target.

A third pass was made and by now all but three of their group's aircraft had been blown from the sky and still not a single bomb had been dropped.

Finally on their fourth and final trip the target was found and his remaining planes dropped their 5000 pound bomb loads right on target. When they left the black field of flak on this fourth lethal pass only the "Maid" was left and she was riddled with holes.

Most of the other aircraft groups had also been badly mauled and those remaining were stumbling their way back to England. Matt was now flying alone and he could see a sky full of Luftwaffe fighter aircraft rising up to attack "The Maid." His gunners were calling out aircraft from all sides but their voices remained calm and disciplined. "Six planes from twelve o'clock high." "Four bogies from three o'clock low." "Ten coming from eight o'clock...." Their voices started to fade so he wondered if his headset was going bad.

He jerked awake to groggily realize it was 7:45 Wednesday morning and that he had a pounding headache. Still wearing the now completely sweat soaked clothes he had worn to the hospital, he noted the dream had been one of the really bad ones. But then it hadn't actually been a dream, it had been a nightmare. The gunpowder taste of hundreds of fired fifty caliber rounds was in his mouth and he could still smell engine exhaust fumes from the four big Pratt and Whitney Hornet engines.

God, how he wished Suzanne was there. He never had these dreams when she was lying next to him. She had been there such a short time, a few weeks actually but the place had felt more like a real home then. Why did he still miss her so much? There could only be one answer to that question. He knew he had been a fool to let her go. Well, that should tell him something. Was he still certain he didn't love her as much as he had loved Joanna? What he did know for sure was he had wanted no other woman to sleep in his bed since she left. Not even Barbara Ann Joiner though she had been a bit of more of a temptation than the others. He also had known sleeping with her would be a really bad idea as they had official business to do together.

The nights had never been lonely when Suzanne was there. Now they were. He knew with certainty he had better decide what should be done pretty soon or it might be too late. It was clear he needed to find her and do his best to bring her back.

Matt showered, redressed and drove Duesy to the office by eight ten. The guard at the entrance to the underground garage threw a cheerful, "Good morning Mr. Weldon," and waved him through. Once he parked, he boarded the express elevator to the 26th floor.

His assistant from the Corporate Loan Department, Brianna Stanton, was at the desk where Marion would have normally been seated. The brass plate on the door to his father's office which told all visitors this was the office of Mathew Weldon III was replaced temporarily with one which announced the officer within was Mathew Weldon IV. He was in the position until his father' was well enough to return.

Marion had called in early to arrange for the transition to Matt. Then she called around nine and spoke with him to reassure him his father was fine, but had asked her to be there until he was released to go home. He wanted her to be available to help him with any Bank problems which arose because of his absence.

Matt couldn't resist smiling hearing this about his father. The man had been so upset at the idea of a personal relation with his assistant, yet was now asking this of her.

Marion spent an hour on the phone instructing Miss Stanton on where files and schedules were kept and instructing her to call with any question no matter how small. She finally dictated a memo to be given each Bank employee about Trey's medical condition and Matt's new responsibilities.

Chapter 24

A TOUCH OF SHAKESPEARE

A bit over a week later, when Matt studied his schedule for the morning, he found an appointment which stunned him...a nine thirty for a Mr. Owen Barton of Old Oast House Brewery of London, England, along with his Attorney.

He buzzed Miss Stanton and asked, "I see a nine-thirty with a Mr. Barton and his attorney of London. What can you tell me about this?" He heard her rustling papers and she came back. "Well Mr. Weldon, it was an appointment made for your father several weeks ago. Mrs. Tompkins made the appointment. Something about having an interest in purchasing an American brewery that is for sale. Wants to talk about us being involved in the purchase as an intermediary. Said he knew about our bank from Mr. Weldon's son whom he had known during the war. I suppose that must have been you.

"Your father was out of the office, so Mrs. Tompkins made notes to give to your father and she set up the time for them to meet. Is there a problem?"

Matt hesitated before saying, "I hope not. I had better see if I can find the notes. Thank you."

It was already ten after nine and it took five minutes to find the notes in his father's files. He barely had time to scan them, when he heard an out of control woman's voice from the outer office yelling almost hysterically, "No, no, it can't be. That is **not** possible. He is **dead**!"

His door was thrown open so violently it banged back against the wall. Joanna Barton came storming into his office followed by the young English Army officer he had seen her with the day he had driven out to Barton Hall over two years ago. Today the young man wore a fine chalk-striped blue suit, obviously made by a good Bond Street tailor. He seemed sheepishly embarrassed and very confused by Joanna's actions.

Matt stood and walked around his desk. He was unsure of exactly how to react. He knew she was angry, but he had never before seen her like this. The night they met she was angry, but that was a cold anger and she was in complete control. What he saw now was a white-hot anger. Her eyes were the cold green of a jungle cat about to make a kill.

Of all the things he expected, being slapped was at the bottom of his list, but that was what happened. And it was a hard, stinging, head-turning slap.

"You son of a bitch! You low life bastard! You really were 'Matt the Ratt' the entire time I knew you. What was the game? To get me to seduce you? A reversal of the way you played your old game? My God! How could I have been so completely fooled? I have no idea how you arranged to have the Germans say you were dead. But I suppose *you* could get anyone to do almost anything.

"You could have at least been *decent* enough to let me know you were alive. Then you could have had the satisfaction of laughing in my face. You are the most completely despicable person I have ever known. How could I have ever been in love with you?" she spat out.

"Come on Alexander, let's get out of here. There are plenty of other banks in town."

Matt finally found his voice through the shock, "Joanna. Please. Wait a moment."

She was still storming away, so he harshly said the only words he thought might stop her, "So, what happened to 'I will love you...Forever'...Joanna?"

She did abruptly stop just beyond the door in his outer office, seething with fury, her back still toward him. The young man with her was still standing bewildered in Matt's office. Miss Stanton was sitting in her chair as if she were a marble statue; her mouth agape in disbelief.

Matt walked to Joanna and stepped in front of her. "I repeat, I *have* loved you, forever. Please give me a chance to explain as best I can. Will you do that? We were at this point that night years ago when we first met. We both misunderstood what was happening and we were nearly finished before we began. Please give me a chance now, as you did then. Will you do that?"

He looked into her green eyes and saw the fire still raging.

Her answer was short but enough, "Very well, Mathew."

They walked back into his office and pushed the large door closed. The young man still had not moved, as if he was rooted to the carpet. Matt seated Joanna and walked up to the man still standing rigid with shock and offered his hand. "I am Mathew Weldon and you are...?"

The fellow finally regained the use of speech and managed to say, "Alexander, Alexander Barton. I am the attorney for..."

Matt finished for him, "Old Oast House Brewery. Oh, my God! You are Joanna's *brother*. Another dead man come back to life. You were supposed to have died in the fight for Singapore back in 'forty two. I even attended your memorial service out at Barton Hall and was there when they placed your marker."

"Yes... Correct. My unit was very nearly annihilated. I ran out of ammunition for my Sten gun and they took me alive. The few of us left were held for almost a week in a soccer stadium. No water or food. Just a little blessed rainwater to drink. The Japs put us on a ship and sent us to the Philippines. We were put in a filthy prison camp to be slave labor. I was able to escape into the jungle one night and joined a group of rebels. We fought the Jap swine until the Philippines were liberated. I was sent home in early 'forty five and still carry a bit of malaria to remind me of my adventures. That's a very short version of a long and unpleasant story."

After offering Alexander a chair, Matt turned to Joanna and looked deeply into those incredible green eyes. "Now I owe *you* an explanation. On my last flight we were very badly shot up both by flak and two very good German pilots. I am glad they were so good, because they could have killed every one of us. Able to get my crew to bail out, I was determined to get 'The Maid' down in one piece and damned if they didn't help me do it. Led me down to a pasture where I could land her. Those pilots did a 'fly over' to make sure I was in good condition and only then left standing beside the "Maid.".

"I was captured and spent a year in a Luftwaffe camp. Not as bad a place as the one your brother was in, but not exactly a vacation resort.

"Berlin wanted us believed dead for propaganda purposes. So they announced we had all been killed, 'What a shame. Just one mission short of twenty five. See! No one can live to fly twenty five against Germany.'

"They destroyed every one of our letters. Every one of them. I finally escaped just before the War ended."

Joanna interrupted him angrily saying, "Yes, but you could have let me know you were still alive. Why did you let me go on thinking you were killed? How can you say you love me after letting me continue to believe you were dead for two years? Mathew, that simply makes no sense at all!"

"Perhaps it will when you hear the balance of the story. I got back to American lines and they had to have proof of my identity. Many Nazis were using false papers to escape justice. I had to prove I was really Captain Mathew Weldon. That took a few days but once they were sure, they shipped me back to England to be checked out in hospital. I spent several days in one and I know now I should have called you, but I didn't want to give you a shock by using the telephone. So I waited until they released me. Then I got a Jeep and drove out to your place in Kent.

"I parked alongside the barley fields and walked toward the house. I had gotten as far as the big oak in the cemetery and I saw you with this fellow, only then he was in the uniform of a British Army Officer. And you were holding a baby."

Joanna leapt to her feet. The color had left her face and her hand flew to her mouth. "Mathew...you thought! Oh my God. You thought I had married because I believed you dead and that I had a baby. That must have been awful for you. You left without coming to the house because you believed it would be better for me that way.

"I was several weeks pregnant when you left on your last flight. I didn't tell you because I didn't want that on your mind when you were flying. Only that last flight and one more and I could tell you. Then we could have married. There was no disgrace in being pregnant when you married during the War. It was almost expected.

"Oh, dear sweet Mathew. If only you had come down to the house and seen the baby. You would have known he is **your** son. Little Mathew already looks like you.

"Dad was supposed to have come over on this trip, but he had problems at the Brewery. Labor problems. Not all the old crew came back from the War and some of the new ones are trouble. They want to unionize. That is why he sent Alex and me instead. Alex is the firm's lawyer and he would have been with Dad in any event. But I know a lot more about the day to day operations of the Brewery. I know what we need in the way of a brewery which would fit our needs to brew in America.

"Our baby is back in England with the indomitable Mrs. Townsend caring for him. Our son is in excellent hands and it's a good thing because he is a handful. To say he is lively would be a total understatement."

Matt stood speechless. These past two years he had believed one thing and now he found out it had all been wrong. It was as if his world had been turned upside down. He knew Joanna was waiting for him to say something, but what was the right thing to say after two years?

It was at that moment he noticed she was still wearing the small engagement ring they had bought in London on her left hand. "Joanna, I would very much like to buy you a larger ring now. I know it hasn't been ten years yet, but I am making better money than I was then and I promise we can afford it," Matt said with a smile.

She was out of her chair and in his arms before he finished the sentence. She overwhelmed him with a kiss that left him nearly breathless. A kiss full of joy and sorrow for both of them. Amazingly, the small electric tingle he remembered was not a part of this kiss.

Matt knew he must marry her. They had a child together, so it was the right thing to do. He also knew deep within his heart that "Forever" it would be a bitter-sweet union. Now he would always have Suzanne to remember and have to ask himself the question, 'What if?' And if he was so certain Joanna was still the one, why was that question even there?

"Joanna, we need to talk. It has been over two years. I know this has been a shock to both of us, something we had both thought dead (forgive my poor choice of words) but is not. By the way, you have a really effective round house swing," he said rubbing the side of his face. "I thought for a moment I heard angels singing," he said with a wry grin.

"It's going to take a while for us to deal with our emotions. There is much we need to catch up on and plans we have to make. Would it be possible to put the business part of your trip on hold and focus on the personal side of things. If the other is urgent I will do my best to focus on that."

Joanna spent a few silent moments looking into his eyes, then finally took his hand. "No Mathew, you're right. To say it was a 'shock' is an understatement I thought *only* we British were capable of. To me it was more like the earth being torn from its axis. Business is out of the question at this point. We left our return plans open as we didn't know how long it would take to finish our business. What do you suggest we do?"

Matt could tell there had been changes in Joanna. But wasn't that to be expected? It had been almost three years for both of them. Neither had lived in a glass bubble all that time. He had been in the Prisoner of War camp for a year, and then gone to England only to think she was lost to him. When he returned home, he had become deeply immersed in the Bank's business to cover the pain of his loss.

And then there was Suzanne. Today was making him face up to that. For a while with her, he had almost forgotten Joanna. Yet he was never able to tell Suzanne that he loved her as much as he loved the woman who was now standing in front of him.

Joanna? Well, she had believed he was out of her life forever. Dead. He knew she had grieved him. Then there was their baby. She was a mother now. She too had been busy with her family's business. Those were only the things he was sure about. The things he could easily surmise. She had probably been through many smaller changes during that time.

He was determined to marry her, but they had to be alone to talk; to bring their different worlds back into alignment. It had to work for both of them. What was that word? Oh yes, compatibility. They had to be sure they were compatible. Love alone would no longer be enough.

"Where are you staying in town? Can we spend some time together tonight? How about dinner at, say, 7:30, and then enough time for us to catch up on the last two years? I know many things have happened in both our lives."

A quizzical look flashed across her eyes before she answered him. She examined his face thoughtfully, "Of course you are right Mathew. At first I was startled, then furious to find you alive. Especially before I understood what caused you not to let me know. Every other thought was pushed from my mind. I'm sorry I said the things I did. Yes we certainly need to catch up. We mustn't have moments where someone asks, 'And what did your husband do between 1944 when you were parted and 1947 when you were married?' with my only answer being a blank stare.

"We are at the Waldorf-Astoria. And 7:30 will be fine. Alexander, will you forgive us if we don't include you in this evening?"

Still a bit shaken by the events in the past few minutes, he looked from one to the other before smiling and saying, "Not at all Jo. I had heard so much about 'your American' I am delighted that, like me, a few of the reported dead weren't. It's probably a bit premature, but you will be a welcome addition to our stodgy old family. Well, all of us are stodgy, except Dad, he somehow escaped that."

Joanna look at bit startled when her brother spoke his last few words. "Alexander Barton! We are not stodgy. What we are is British; it's not the same thing at all."

For the first time since they had walked through the door, Matt laughed. A long, tension-relieving laugh, which soon proved contagious. A moment later, first Alexander, then Joanna joined in.

While they were still laughing Joanna walked over to Matt, put her arms around his neck and kissed him. Matt was soon found himself responding and the thought took hold, perhaps things will be the way they were after all. Maybe we are largely the same people as before.

After several long minutes, she finally broke the kiss and they looked into each other's eyes. "I say, Mathew Weldon, how is that for 'stodgy old British'? A bit stirring isn't it?"

Matt was always surprised by this green eyed woman; one moment so proper and reserved and the next a willful, very sexy siren. Looking at her now he could remember how completely he had been attracted to her. How had he ever waited so long to make love to her and even then she had to seduce him? He still felt that attraction to her. It was a fact he could not deny. He dared not answer her question about the kiss.

If the only question needing an answer was about her desirability, he would clear the office and make love to her right now on his desk. Unfortunately there were far more pressing questions to be answered. Two people couldn't just make love all the time. He had finally learned that. When he was young sex was only a game; like dancing. Simply fun. But he knew he had only considered it from his selfish viewpoint. Living together required so much more than that once you were grown. It would not be only about the time they spent in bed together. There was so much more about love than sex. And far more about two people building a life together.

When they had been together, she had undoubtedly been way ahead of him in maturity. He remembered the morning when she had been in the kitchen at the town house in London trying to learn to cook so that she could fix breakfast for him once they were married. Had he ever thought that far ahead when they were together or did he think it would all be one long rosy tomorrow where everything simply "worked out" somehow?

Was that why so many in his generation had married so quickly with such little thought of what tomorrow might bring? The romance of the moment out-weighing the reality of what the future would be? Well, there was always the War to use as an excuse. But his War was over now and had been for two years. Perhaps Joanna and he should, as the English like to say, "have done" while the War was raging. It was exclusively his fault they hadn't. If they had he would not be facing all these questions and uncertainties today. But there also would have been no Suzanne in his life to remember.

They kissed again before she and her brother left. He closed the door and sat in his chair for a long time thinking back over the history he and Joanna had shared. Much of it had flooded over him the moment she walked through the door. But it was even stronger now that she was gone.

Matt looked out the window and his mind wondered back. He was sitting at his father's desk remembering a time past. Memories of a foolish boy who had flown past that window in 1939. Looking down from a wonderful little bi-plane and thinking of canyons in Arizona and how that day had changed his life. If not for that who knew what he might have become. Certainly not who he was today.

It had taken him to England to get an answer to a seemingly simple question and the discovery that some things are not as simple as he thought. He had expected to be there for only a few months. He was there for six years. Years in which he fell in love and fought a war. A war he then believed had cost him the love of his life. The one he had fought for and intended to spend his life with. The one he would have died for. Joanna. She had been all he wanted. To be with her forever. Matt had thought for years that she was lost to him and then today she was back in his life. They could be together...forever.

But there was another face he saw. It was Suzanne, standing in a spotlight; her beautiful face pale as she sang with tears running down. Then again another picture of her, when they had both been younger, running from his beautiful Duesenberg. Her golden hair shimmering so that all he could think was, she must have stardust in it. When they had danced together; for the first time in his young life he had wished that a night would never end.

Everything seemed book-ended by Suzanne. The beginning and the end. She would always be there and completely unforgettable.

So, he asked himself, what do I do now? There is Joanna who I spent six years loving and who has borne my child and who I feel I must marry, but there is also Suzanne. Suzanne, who just wanted me to tell her that I loved her as much as I did Joanna. She never asked for more. I loved, but couldn't do what she asked. I love her deeply and could be happy with her. Was she right? Was I in love with yesterday? What did she say? Memories and shadows? What was and what might have been? Was it the "what might have been" that I loved? The memories were good but there were shadows. Yet there is no longer a real choice I can make.

The choice has been made for me. Even if I love Suzanne much more than I have been able to see; it is my responsibility for the child which matters more than anything else. I am the father and Joanna is the mother. In spite of all my questions, there is really no question at all. It is only a matter of details to be settled. All that is left is to be the best father and husband I can be.

~ ~ ~ ~

When his work day finally ended, Matt went to dress for the evening. He was reminded again how empty his place felt without Suzanne. He still didn't understand why she had become so much a part of these rooms so quickly. He had never noticed the echoes when he walked through them before she came or while she was there, but the loneliness had moved in the first day she left. It was as if she had taken more than just herself when she moved out of the rooms that had been "home" to both of them. He knew what it had been between them, but he couldn't bring himself to admit the mistake he made letting her leave. It was suddenly too late.

"If it were not so damned sad it would almost be funny" he thought "I could face German fighter planes and acres of flak. The cold at thirty thousand feet. A German Prisoner of War Camp. Hunger. What I thought was the loss of the one woman I ever expected to love. All of that, but I can't face uttering a single word. Four letters. About another woman. Suzanne. The woman who is out of my life and now it will have to be forever. Can I make the short time I had with her last a lifetime? The feel of her. Her voice whispering in my ear while we lay in bed. The sound of her singing in the Stork Club. What it felt like to hold her in my arms. How can it be these rooms became more her than they are me now? These empty-feeling rooms which she always called 'home.'

Nothing but questions. Questions with no answers. So futile and yet impossible not to ask of myself. They do no good of course. They can change nothing of the reality. Today has decided my entire future. It will just have to work out well. Joanna and I will make it work for the child. For little Mathew. And I love Joanna. If only for the way I did love her. My first love.

I can't know it won't all come back once the two of us are together. That intense passion I felt when we made love. It might still be there just waiting to be released. She is still as beautiful as any woman I have ever seen. I have only known one other who can compare. I have to face the cold reality that Suzanne is beyond reach now. Perhaps she always was. Had it all been dictated by fate long before any of us were born? Are choices only illusions"?

~ ~ ~ ~

He was at the Waldorf-Astoria at exactly seven thirty where she waited for him in the lobby. They had reservations for dinner at the Starlight Room. Since the early spring weather was good the roof was open. Joanna kept glancing casually upward to the sky and he could see she was trying not to appear a tourist.

Matt was delighted to discover the dress was the one she had worn when they had gone to hear Toscanini direct "Sirenes" and "La Mer" on that oh, so rainy and long ago night in London.

The dress remained as he remembered in wonderful shades of greens and blues; a striking sheath with swirling pastel colors which seemed to flow with a life of their own. Even knowing its age, Matt was still taken with the beauty of the gown and the woman wearing it. If she or the gown had aged, it did not show. If anything, both were even more arresting. No one would have believed she had borne a child. Her figure was as wonderful as the first time he had seen her; her long legs still perfection. As good as Betty Grable's, who's pin-up had decorated the walls of thousands of G.I. huts during the War.

She was again wearing the emeralds at her ears and throat. The small engagement ring was still on her finger. She reached across and took his hand smiling, "I am still having a difficult time believing all this has happened Mathew. I have lived with sadness every day since the Germans announced your death. No letters, no nothing to make me think otherwise. Only one thing ever made me wonder.... A gift...."

"A wooden box with ten sovereigns," Matt broke in. "George IV. With your three initials on the top of the box. JSB in old English script. The coins were set St. George slaying the dragon side up. There was a note enclosed. The envelope had your full name on it, the note said only, 'Congratulations on the birth of your child.' It was delivered by courier."

Before he finished there were tears clouding Joanna's green eyes. "Oh Matt, at the time I so hoped it was you who had sent it. I waited for you to call or come and tell me you weren't dead. I wanted you to be alive so desperately, but as the days passed I decided what I wished for was not going to happen. God, it was what I wanted with all my heart. I am sorry about my reaction today, but I truly believed you had let me believe you were dead on purpose. That you had fooled me all along. That you had been Matt the Ratt during all the time we were together. I should have known better. How could I ever think that about you? I should have trusted my instinct and never have questioned our love."

Matt reached across the table, brushed the tear from her cheek and left his hand lying gently alongside it. Joanna covered his hand with hers. She looked at him with softness and love in her eyes.

"Oh Mathew it has been so long since you touched me like that. It brings back many wonderful memories. We were both very young then

376

and so much in love. The War had not started and we thought we had time in front of us. I wish we had married then. Really married. The vows we exchanged in the chapel were special but we should have finalized them. We should have. That was our time."

The champagne he had ordered arrived and he took the magnum from the sommelier. He smiled at the man and dismissed him. He had ordered Armand de Biragnac which he had tasted one night while he flew for the RAF. One of the other pilots had brought it to the O. Club back 1940 for some celebration which now escaped his memory. It was the best champagne he had ever tasted and he had promised himself to order a bottle when the War was over on some very special occasion.

Well, I suppose I could have waited for our wedding, he thought to himself, but tonight is certainly special. It is, I suppose, a very old dream at long last coming true. Joanna is sitting across from me and she is not married. Not yet!

Joanna took a sip from her flute then gave Matt a flashing smile. "My goodness Mathew, was this bottled in heaven? It is wonderful. Exquisite! I see your sense of taste and style has not suffered."

He looked at her, then smiled as he said, "Well I am here with you. What proof would anyone need of my sense of taste beyond that?"

"Years ago I warned you not to try your blarney on a Barton, Mathew. That we were immune to it. Did you forget?"

"What I said is no blarney. Only a simple statement of fact. You are the most beautiful woman here and well you know it. And Blarney is still a Castle in Ireland."

She rewarded him with that wonderful laugh. The one he loved hearing so much he once felt he could live simply to hear it. And they had laughed often until the War. Laughs became more difficult then. Tears replaced most.

"There is so much we need to talk about Mathew. After we finish dinner is there a place you know where we can talk in privacy? It's been over two years now. We need to decide what we should do and when. I have been thinking about that a lot since I saw you this morning."

Reaching across the table, he took her hand and could see she was troubled by looking in her eyes. "Joanna we have found each other again. I believe we were meant to. I am sorry I didn't come to the house that day. If I had we would have been married two years by now."

The band had been playing quietly. Many of the songs they were playing were popular before the War and Joanna turned her hand in the one he had lain over hers so they were holding hands. "Mathew, would you please dance with me? It has been so long since we last danced. Far, far too long."

The song was, "As Time Goes By," from "Casablanca." A war-time song. 1943. As the two of them walked hand in hand out to the dance floor, Matt noticed Joanna still turned men's heads. When he took her in his arms she whispered in his ear, "Yes, and it isn't just the men. The women are still giving you looks too. Most of them wish you were going home with them this evening. But for tonight, we are only with each other. No one else in the whole world exists except us."

Matt remembered their first dance together at Café de Paris in 1939. The War had not yet started. He remembered walking to the dance floor with her, holding hands as they went. They were looking into each other's eyes as they walked and already knew they were in love. The words had not yet been spoken...but they had known. It was a happy night for both of them. Matt had thought that night, just be patient a little longer. That is not much to ask for a lifetime with such a wonderful woman.

Now, while they danced, Matt was surprised to feel a tear run between their cheeks. A single tear from Joanna.... She was holding him very tightly and Matt knew there was sadness in their dancing. But even with that, it was, as always, like dancing with an angel.

Matt remembered that the last time he danced it had been with Suzanne in the Stork Club. The first night after they met again when they danced holding each other as the band played only for the two of them on a smoky dance floor in a closed night club. The night he was once more dancing with and holding the girl with a sprinkling of stardust in her glowing hair. The girl from his first year at Yale, who in one evening had known him better than he had known himself. Who had given him the kiss he had never forgotten, then ran toward her dorm with her hair flashing in the moonlight.

She had stayed with him such a short time, but the rooms in his warehouse felt empty when she left. And, he had found, so did he. As the song ended he felt Joanna gently kiss his neck. It had felt so natural holding her that he hated for the music to end. But he knew all things must and when the last notes had died away they went back to their table.

Matt could tell something was wrong because Joanna ate so little of her dinner. When he asked if it was not satisfactory she replied, "No Mathew. I'm sure the food is fine. I suppose I am not very hungry. It may be the time difference. But if you don't mind I would like to go where we can talk. Alone. There are many things we must discuss. Do you suppose we could take the rest of this heavenly champagne with us?"

Matt settled the bill and had the champagne re-corked. He knew something had changed since she had thrown her arms around him that morning in his office. He had a feeling in his stomach much like the one when he read Suzanne's goodbye note.

They only had a short wait for his Duesenberg to be brought to the front entrance. The top was down as it was a very nice night. Joanna stood on the steps for several minutes just looking at it.

"It is magnificent Mathew. I have never seen an automobile like it before. It is like a beautiful stallion which is born only to race. Born to feel the wind in its mane as it runs. You belong together. Both of you are unlike anything I have ever known before or ever will again."

He drove past Times Square and the Empire State Building. He paused in front of the Chrysler Building which was his favorite while she looked up at it.

"It *is* beautiful Mathew. Your entire city is wonderful. It suits you. You belong here. It is a kingdom filled with palaces and you are its prince... and mine" There was a catch in her voice as she said the last.

"Joanna, I want you to belong here with me. You showed me London and England. Let me show you New York and America. It is a big country. I have not seen very much of it myself and I want to. I want to see it with you. I want to share it with you as you shared England with me."

"That would be wonderful Mathew, but for now show me where you live. I want to be alone with you. We have much to talk about."

When they arrived at his converted warehouse and he had parked in the garage behind the building, Joanna looked up at the three story brick building in surprise. "You live here Mathew? It looks like an industrial plant."

"Well it was a warehouse I bought and converted into living spaces." He unlocked the great oak door and turned on the lights. She walked with him through the lobby to the elevators and together they rode quietly to the top floor and his living quarters.

She walked around looking at the rooms while he got two crystal flutes from his cabinet and poured a glass of champagne for each of them. He found her in his bedroom, standing at the foot of his bed. She took the glass and emptied half of it in one swallow.

"Mathew, it is more severe than I would have expected of you. The pictures in the kitchen area are lovely though. The one over your bed is an explosion of color. Even considering the art, you really should have more color here."

"Well Joanna, after a year in a P.O.W. camp, I find this quite luxurious."

"Oh Mathew, I am so sorry. I didn't think." She finished draining her glass and held it out for more.

He refilled it, but added..."Hey Joanna, slow down. Drinking it like that...well, you could get tipsy in a hurry."

"I have never been drunk in my life, but maybe tonight is the night. Would you take care of me if I did? Get drunk that is?"

Matt gave her his naughty little boy grin, "I don't know. I might be tempted to take advantage of you."

He had expected her to laugh, instead she looked him right in the eyes before saying, "Yes Mathew, and I might want you to." She put her flute on his chest of drawers, walked to him, put her arms around his neck and kissed him. Of all the kisses she had ever given him, there had never been one like it before. This kiss was not a shy young woman's kiss. It was a kiss full of passion and a desire bordering on lust. When she pulled away and he could look in her eyes, he saw a seething green he had never seen there. Both of them were breathing rapidly as if they had made a long hard run up a steep hill.

Matt took her hand and started to lead her to his bed. She took a few steps then pulled away. "No. Not yet Mathew we have to talk first."

Matt took her hand again and led her out of the bedroom and into the kitchen. He seated her at the glass-topped table, found a station playing orchestral music on the radio and turned the volume low.

He looked at her for several minutes. It was as if neither wanted to speak, as if they both dreaded what was coming. Finally Matt broke the brooding silence, "Joanna something is wrong. I could tell during dinner and the drive over. It was as if you had closed something in you which was open. This morning you were the Joanna I knew. Even when you were angry with me. Now you seem somehow different. Are you sorry we have found each other? Is there someone else?"

"No Mathew. There is no one else. I always told you there would only be one man for me. Remember? One man and forever. That was, is, and always will be you. There is room in my heart for only you...and our son. You gave me a wonderful gift when you gave him to me. When I believed you were dead I was glad I was pregnant because it meant you were still alive inside of me."

"Joanna, I am so sorry fate played such a cruel joke on us. I am sorry I didn't come down to the house that day. I am sorry for many things I didn't do which I should have.

"I should have had more faith. At *that* moment I believed it best to let you continue to think of me dead. Because of what I thought I was seeing. You married, with a child."

She took another drink from her glass. "No Matt, what happened was supposed to happen. It was Kismet. If you had a flat tyre it would have slowed you down and Alexander and I would not have been in the yard when you arrived. If you had driven faster we would have still been in the house. Many things could have changed the outcome and brought you to our door. You could have called the London house to be sure I wasn't there.

"Mrs. Townsend would have told you to go down to Kent. She would have called me and I would have been waiting for you. None of those events happened. Why Mathew? I have spent over two years loving a man I believed dead. Mourning a man who was in New York all that time.

"Oh, I have kept busy. Between the baby and the Brewery I have had a busy life indeed. Dad has a difficult job keeping the Company above water. We lost so many workers to the War and most of the replacements are poor quality. Thank God for the ones who returned.

"The baby spends most of his time in London under the care of Mrs. Townsend. It will be a while until he figures out who his real mother is. Right now he probably thinks it is her. I usually put ten hours a day in at the Brewery sometimes more. When I come in I only get to go in and kiss our sleeping son goodnight. I always thought it was also my way of kissing you goodnight. Goodnight to my dear lost love."

Matt poured more champagne into each glass. Then he asked, "But what about your brother? Surely he helps."

Joanna gave a short, sharp laugh filled with irony. "Alexander, well Alexander always wanted to be a Barrister; to wear the powdered wig and black robe and all. He is more than competent in his chosen profession, but not so good at the Brewery. No, that is up to Dad and me. Perhaps this gives you some indication of what our problem is Mathew. Nothing is as it was when you left England for America. I am no longer the same girl.

"Truth be told, you have also changed. You are running a very large bank. At least until your father is back. And, let's face up to it, someday soon it will be your job. Could you give that up? If it were me I know I couldn't. Not anymore than I could give up my family and the Brewery to live in America. So it seems to me we are stuck. One answer is for us to marry despite all this. To live apart a majority of the time, with an ocean separating us. I know we would try so hard to make it work. I know we would, because we love each other.... Just as we both know it wouldn't do."

There were tears running down her cheeks now and still Matt didn't know what to say. He was trying to find a way it could work; a way for them to be together. But she was right. He couldn't leave the Bank and live in England. Not now. That time had passed

"We have only two choices Mathew. We can marry and live apart to eventually watch the love we have die from the separation or keep the love and not have each other. I love you enough to marry you even though I know it is the wrong thing. For both of us. Just as I know there has been someone else for you... I could feel sadness about someone within you while we were dancing. You were dancing with someone else too. Will you tell me about her? Please, I would like to know what happened."

Suddenly it was as if a dam had broken somewhere deep within him. A dam he had struggled to keep in repair. He told Joanna about Suzanne. The story of how they had only one date while he was in his first year at Yale. What she whispered in his ear when he picked her up. The way they danced and the kiss she gave him before running away with the look of stardust on her hair. The entire story came rushing out. Even the way she left after he asked her to marry him. Joanna stood from her chair and walked over to where he sat. She settled into his lap with her arms around his neck and looked into his eyes for a long time.

"My poor Mathew. You really have no *idea* how easy it is to love you. I fought it. Really I did. Because of your reputation. But I loved you long before the day I finally told you.

"I know she must love you desperately. In a few ways you are quite foolish. All you had to do was tell her you loved her as much as you had me and you couldn't do even that. Well Mathew Weldon, I know you love me. Loving her doesn't change what we had and still have between us. That will always be there. Forever...Remember. Whether we are together or not, our love is forever. That is the gift we gave each other long ago. The choice is not between her and me, but between which life you can be happier with. If I thought you could have that life with me, I would fight her tooth and nail to have you. I love you far beyond that much. But we had our time. It has passed. We have gone down different roads now and we have to travel them without each other.

382

"Mathew, I want to dance with you again tonight. I need to feel you holding me in your arms. Finally, I want us to make love together as if we will never see another sunrise and let me fall asleep in your arms.

"Before the War you gave me a promise I had asked for and then you broke it. I understand you felt you had to. I have always known you believed by joining the RAF you were protecting me. I long ago forgave you for breaking that promise even though I spent many nights crying. Love and war. I don't understand how one ever survives the other. Well, the War is over and tonight I want you to make me one last promise.

"Promise me you will find Suzanne and get her to come back to you. Don't stop until you do. And whenever you dance with her, remember us. At least for a moment . For all time, remember our night at Café de Paris, what magic that night was. It seems but a dream now. Will you make me that promise Mathew?

"You and I lost our chance to be together years ago. Don't be a fool and lose your chance with her too. You would regret that the rest of your life. You are so smart in so many ways, why didn't you know you can't weigh or measure love Mathew? It just is. A force of nature lasting beyond forever. Remember us always, but *love* her."

"I'll promise what you ask Joanna. I'll even let you walk out of my life if you will answer just one question for me. I know that at this moment we love each other more than we will ever love *anyone* else, so why in the name of God are we doing this?"

She was still on his lap and put her hand on his cheek, green eyes locked on blue. Streams of tears ran down her cheeks and dropped onto his pant leg. It took all his control not to cry himself. He remembered another woman who had cried standing in a spot light one evening a scant two months past. Was there something about him, he wondered, which made the women he loved leave him?

"This is not about God. He didn't cause what happened between us. We did. There is no guilt. We had the best of intentions. Tell me Mathew, which is the greater sin? Doing the right thing for the wrong reason or the wrong thing for the right reason?"

He tried to think it through, but found no answer. "I don't know, I suppose in the end both are wrong. All I can think of now are all the wonderful gifts you gave me. I grew up because of you. I learned about love and family and responsibility from you. I gave you so little in return."

"Oh Mathew! Never think you gave me so little. You gave me the gift of your love and you gave me our child. So little? You gave me everything. You were, are and always will be my dream come true. Yes my St. George.

And that is why I ask you to find Suzanne. You need a family. You learned how much family matters. I like to think I gave you *that* gift. And Mathew, I know you will make a very good father. You didn't have a mother. It is a wonder you ever grew up at all, but I am glad you did. I would have missed so many things if you had forever remained Peter Pan," she smiled wanly. "Now promise what I asked Mathew. Both parts."

"The part about dancing is easy. It goes even beyond dancing. Know I will never put my arms around a woman without thinking of you. Hell! I don't know what I will be able to do without thinking of you. At night when I dream it is either you or the War. Dreaming of you is always wonderful. Dreaming of the War is awful.

I can't find Suzanne until Dad has recovered. I can't be away from the Bank until then. But when he is back, I will. I don't know what I will say. How can I tell her what she wants to hear? She wants to hear me say that I..."

"Take it from someone who knows you...You do love her. You are the one who has been afraid to face how much. You didn't want to let yourself believe that your first love was less than what you now feel for her. But, my darling, we must live in the now. Oh yes Mathew, then was *so* wonderful. It was a perfect time. A fairy tale romance. A magical spell we were both under. But now the prince and princess have other lives they must live. And we can. No we must. Remember your Shakespeare? Prospero's speech to the audience at the end of the 'Tempest'?"

He reached back in memory to his prep school days. Professor Dean's English Literature class. The old fellow looked much like an actor in a Shakespeare play at the old Globe theatre in London. At the end of the class, his students knew every play nearly by heart.

"As I recall it was, 'Our revels now are ended. These our actors, as I foretold you, were all spirits and are melted into air. Into thin air; and, like the baseless fabric of this vision, the cloud capped towers, the gorgeous palaces, the solemn temples, the great Globe itself. Yea, all which it inherit, shall dissolve, and like this insubstantial pageant faded, leaves not a rack behind. We are such stuff as dreams are made on, and our little lives are rounded by a sleep.'"

Joanna was no longer crying. Her hand was still on his face. It was the way she had looked as she gazed out over London on their day at the

Tower. "I should have known you would know it. You are perfect. How could I have *not* loved you?

"That is it word for word. Now tell me what it means to you. What is Shakespeare telling us, not just about this play, but about life?"

He remembered nearly the same question asked by one of the students of Professor Dean. The old fellow had laid his text on the desktop, nudged his wire-rimmed glasses lower on his nose and began a long dissertation. Matt had been enthralled as the old fellow brought the words to life and explained their meaning. On that day Matt came to understand the genius of William Shakespeare as not only a writer of plays, but as a philosopher.

"The meaning has so many levels we might never reach them all so I will keep it as uncomplicated as I can. On its simplest level, Prospero is telling the audience at the Globe theatre, 'the play is over go home and to sleep.'

"On the next level, it is important to remember Prospero is the magician in the play and he is telling the audience that what they have seen was an illusion created by him. It was only a vision. Nothing was real. Towers, Palaces, Temples even the very actors were created out of air. And have returned to air. Finally that life is, in reality, only a dream.

"At the highest level, Prospero is a philosopher. Nothing is lasting. Even the great globe of the Earth will not last forever. In time it too will dissolve into nothing. We rush around doing all of the things we see as so important, but we are only pretending things are lasting when *nothing* is. We are only distracting ourselves from his final truth, the last words in the speech. 'We are such stuff as dreams are made on, and our little lives are rounded with a sleep.' All of us are insubstantial and must, in the end, die.

"Joanna, there is one other explanation I will give you. This is my interpretation and goes back to the time I first read these play years ago now. It is what *I* thought Shakespeare was saying. All that we believe is 'our lives,' may only be a dream. We may already be in an eternal sleep, where everything is simply the dream within a dream.... If it is, I never want to awaken because you have given me such a beautiful dream. I would happily dream only of you, and of us, through all eternity

"But I have got to ask you. Why did you have me do that? You are English. You learned Shakespeare in the cradle."

"Yes Mathew, but you as usual, have surpassed even me. Oh sure, I knew most of it. As you say 'being English' but in two minutes you expressed it better than a two hour lecture by an Oxford PHD in English literature.

"As for the reason I asked. Well... anytime you wish for the past, our past, please think of Prospero and remember we were like the actors in the play and the world we knew... that time was like the cloud capped towers, the gorgeous palaces, the solemn temples, our world itself was an insubstantial pageant which has faded leaving not a cloud behind. You and I were such stuff as dreams are made of and we know our little lives will be rounded with a sleep. But even in that lasting sleep I will still love and dream of only you.

"They say humans are the only species which knows it will eventually die. Yet we carry on as if we didn't. And that is what you and I must now do. For the curtain on our play has dropped. The actors have left the stage. The audience has gone home. We played our parts well. We can warm ourselves remembering the applause and each other."

Matt saw the tears begin again. She put both arms around his neck and hugged him desperately as would a drowning child. "Oh my God! This is the hardest thing I have ever had to do. Thinking you were dead wasn't this difficult. Death is final. Death gives you no choice. But this...this is like we are both dying and yet will still be alive. I know I am doing the right thing, but it is killing me. I can't imagine how I will do it. I don't believe I can."

Matt knew he had tears in the corners of his eyes. He must have cried before, but when? At the end of another recent tragedy? Suzanne.

Joanna was racked by sobs and he held her tighter. Then he turned her face toward his and they were kissing. These were hungry, yet sad kisses. She pulled away and looked deeply into his eyes.

"Mathew, you are going to have to be strong for both of us. Please my darling. I am sure we have to do this, but I'm not strong enough. You are and I need your strength. Please help me. I know you love me so help me because you love me."

He stood up with her still in his arms, and then carried her into his bedroom to place her gently on his bed. The radio was still playing quietly on the other side of the brick wall. She was still crying silent tears.

He sat next to her and lifted her chin so she could see his face. "No more tears. There is no need. Not any longer. Not between us. It may be hard, but we are stronger than this faded dream. We survived the War and we fought that War together. You were with me every time I flew. The War didn't win. We did. For a while I thought the War had won by costing me you. But I was wrong. I will always have you and you will always have me. The War couldn't end that and now nothing can. You wanted a love to last forever. Well, I don't know where forever is, but I know we will have it."

Matt realized that to keep each other they had to release what they loved the most. It wasn't logical, but then was love? They had lost but now, somehow, they had won.

Joanna kept whispering, "I love you" over and over. He wished the world was such that she would never have to stop saying it. That he would never stop hearing it. He looked at her and said, "And I love you."

Her voice was whispering her love for him near his ear. Its low timbre still reminded him of Greta Garbo's just as it had on the first night they met. If anything Joanna's voice carried even more class, a deeper timbre and more warmth than Garbo's.

Soon they were passionately kissing and undressing each other. The clothes fell intertwined beside the bed. When she lay there naked in the dim light, he could see she was even more beautiful now than she had been when he had last seen her. She was no longer a girl. She was now a woman.

She reached out, took his hand and pulled him over her. Her arms were around his neck and she looked up into his eyes. The tears were gone now. Her arms pulled his face near hers and she whispered softly in his ear, "Mathew I want you to make love with me. Make love as if we were twenty-one again. Make passionate love as we did in the barley when we conceived our child. Make love gently as if we were an old married couple in our forties with a nearly grown child. Make love as if we had grown old together. Make love as if we were condemned to die tomorrow. Make love as if we were never going to die. As if we're going to be together forever. Give us a night which will never end."

Together they made love tenderly with kisses and sighs. They made love desperately as if they were going to die. They made love slowly so they could remember each touch, each caress, and each kiss. Every "I love you." They both cried when they made love the final time because of what they were losing. It was during that last time when Matt realized that making love could break your heart. At last they lay no longer joined. It was early morning. He lay on his side and she backed up to him. They were both completely spent. He softly kissed her neck.

"Hold me please Mathew while we sleep like that first night I slipped into your room. Christmas of '41."

His arms were around her still when he drifted off into a dreamless slumber.

The next morning when he awoke the sun was streaming through his bedroom skylight. It seemed late and he was in bed alone. He smelled the aroma of food and coffee coming from the kitchen. Tossing the covers aside, he grabbed a robe and walked into the large room where the kitchen was. The room was empty. She was not there.

On the table was a plate with eggs, bacon, toast and a cup of black coffee. The coffee was still warm. Under the cup was an envelope. He tore it open to find three words. Stacked one above the other:

Forever

Love

Joanna

~ ~ ~ ~

Still sleepy and tired Matt took a taxi to the Bank, arriving two hours late at his office. From the time he entered the building lobby, he knew the events in his office yesterday had spread through the entire building. It had to be stopped before it got entirely out of hand, so he had Brianna call a meeting of all department heads in the board room at 11:30 that morning. He sat at his father's desk and considered how best to put an end to the speculation which was passing from office to office and floor to floor, before it started having a detrimental effect on everyone's efficiency. In the end, he decided to give an abbreviated presentation of the facts. There were, however, some parts of the story which belonged only to him and Joanna which would go to the grave with him.

A few minutes before eleven, Brianna his assistant knocked lightly on his door. "Excuse me Mr. Weldon, most of the Department Heads are already in the Conference room. I did tell them 11:30, sir. I really did."

Matt shook his head and chuckled softly under his breath. For a normal staff meeting most of the managers would straggle in at the last minute. Amazing what a bit of scandal could accomplish. "Brianna, in the future, please remind me to start the occasional rumor before we have staff meetings. And since I am going to make them wait, sit down. I want you to know what yesterday was about before I tell them."

When he had finished, his assistant sighed and shook her head. "Mr. Weldon, I knew you had traveled to England before the war started. Almost everyone in the Bank does. I knew you had been a pilot. But I didn't know about the young lady or you two being in love. She was certainly a most beautiful woman. It is a wonderful story, but so very, very sad sir. I am sorry it couldn't work out for the two of you. But given the circumstances...."

Yes, Matt reflected, given the circumstances.... Joanna would return to England still loving him and he would stay in America still loving her with nothing keeping them apart except the Atlantic Ocean. No, except nearly everything in the world now.

A buzz of conversation emanated from the conference room but as he entered, total silence immediately descended. Matt slowly walked the length of the large room looking each of them in the eye and speaking to a few. By the time he reached his chair at the head of the long conference table a palpable tension had settled. It proved he was in control and they would have to wait for him to begin. It would also prevent questions when he was done. He stood quietly for a while, simply looking at them; the silence remained unbroken. He finally began.

"Gentlemen, when I was 19 years old and finishing my second year at Yale, my father asked me to go to England for the Bank. It was 1939 and he knew a war was coming. The Bank had German investments which were already in the process of being liquidated. The question was if we should do the same with the ones we held in England.

"My father needed to know if they could hold out when Germany attacked. It was the question he sent me over to answer for him. While I was there I met a beautiful young English girl named Joanna Barton..."

For forty-five minutes, the story of his time in England and the War, washed over the assembled management of Empire National Bank. Matt described his time as a POW but barely touched on his misunderstanding of what he had seen that day in Kent. The biggest omission was the baby. He ended it with Joanna and his decision that what once could have been was no longer possible.

Matt ended the meeting by asking each of them to return to their respective departments and end the rampant speculation regarding the incident.

He was surprised when several managers stopped to express their sympathy about the way things had worked out. When they shook his hand, Matt could tell by their eyes they must have lost something somewhere along the way just as he had. He knew all of them had been in service and that one had served in Australia for two years. He also knew the man had been married when he shipped out. Could he have found and lost someone during his two years away from home?

389

The rest of the day he buried himself in his work. Since he was still in charge of the Industrial and Commercial Loan Department, he met with his staff about several pending loans. He requested more information on two large ones, but gave final approval on a loan to construct a forty story office building. New York was growing rapidly after the War and office space was at a premium. It would be a very good loan for ENB to make.

Matt finished his work day and was glad it had been such a busy one. Now there was nothing to keep him occupied, he felt a chasm in his heart. He was, as Suzanne had said years ago, empty inside.

Joanna was gone. What could be worse than hearing the woman you love say she loves you with all her heart, and will forever, then leave. And worse still, letting her go. Yet she loved you so much she made you promise you would find Suzanne. My Lord! How will I ever get over this?

You always find a solution when problems occur at the Bank, he berated himself. So why couldn't you speak up when Joanna said she would marry you even if she didn't think it would work? Why didn't you simply say we should at least try? Sure there would have been problems. Hers with the Brewery and mine at the Bank. You're good with problems, why didn't you ask about hers? Hey old boy, there is really only one question. Why did you let her go? She was once all you ever wanted and you let her walk away! Why Matt?

~ ~ ~ ~

At the end of the day He took a taxi home dreading the empty rooms. Rooms that asked too many questions of him.

What he couldn't know was that Joanna Barton sat in another taxi just down the block watching him as he got out, paid the driver, limped round-shouldered to the front door of his warehouse, unlocked the heavy oak door and went inside. He had limped most of the day; the old flare up from the damage of that kick to his hip the day he was shot down.

Having waited there nearly an hour, there were tears in her eyes as she watched him go inside. The entire night before had played through her mind numerous times as she waited. Every word, each touch and kiss was locked within her heart. She no longer viewed their situation as she had last night. Today she believed any solution was better than sending him to another woman. One of his two loves had to lose, but why should it be her? They had loved each other longer and they had a child together. Little Mathew should know his father after all. She knew Mathew loved her. And she loved him almost beyond sanity.

She wanted to hear him tell her they mustn't make this mistake. They could surely find a way to be together. They must find a way. She wanted to continue to fall asleep in his arms forever and wake up to his smile and blue eyes. Eyes the color of skies over the barley fields of Kent on a midsummer's day.

She had waited by the telephone in her hotel room for him to call. But he had neither called nor come by to say they were wrong to let each other go after only one night. Perhaps he was relieved. It had been two years. Then, there was Suzanne. Yes, there was Suzanne. The way he talked about her, Joanna knew he loved this other woman too. Mathew had even asked her to marry him. But that was before he learned what he had seen was not true. She was not married and the child he had seen was theirs. *Their* son.

What would she do without this man? How do you give up the dream of a lifetime, now that...? He had been her best friend long before they were lovers. What fun it had been just being with him. He made her laugh often even during the worst days of the War. He was so damn wonderful to be with. And he was beautiful. Until she met him she thought a man could only be handsome, but Mathew was beautiful. His hair was a color she could never easily name but it was nearly the color of the dried barley when it blew in the wind. Hair of a bright golden hue with that one uncontrollable shock which dropped down across his forehead like a shining comma. He was the only man she could or would ever love.

It took every ounce of control she had to not run across the street and ring his bell. Not to beg him to *never* let her go. If not for Suzanne, she would have. Joanna wanted so badly to tell him she had been wrong. That they should try. That together they would find a way to make it work. If not for Suzanne and the promise she made him make last night she would. No she couldn't: at least with Suzanne he would not be alone. He was not to blame for this tragic ending. She blamed herself.

Through her tears she made a wish for both of them. It was the only thing left she *could* do.

Joanna sat there until the lights came on in his third floor windows. Even then, she waited a few minutes looking wishfully upward. Remembering last night. When she could find her voice she asked the cabby to take her back to the Waldorf.

She and her brother flew to England the next day. Like Matt with England, she could never again bring herself to return to America. Nothing was ever done about opening a brewery there.

Chapter 25

THE BROWNSTONE AT EAST 74TH STREET

Matt hung up his suit, kicked off the wingtip cordovans and put on a pair of tan slacks and a blue Oxford cloth shirt. Looking over his closet he thought, "Well, at least not everything is in perfect order any longer. Oh my God! Did I really think that? What irony. Nothing in my life is in perfect order. In the two years I have been back, I have made a fine mess of everything. The only part of my life that is in any semblance of order is my job. But my personal life? Oh, I really excel there. In slightly over two months, I have proposed to two women and both promptly ran away.

Each told me they loved me and seemed to think what they were doing was the best thing for me. I suppose I must find someone who wants what is best for her. No, that wouldn't work either. We would never get to the proposal before she ran away.

Seriously Matt, you have two women who really love you and you love both of them, but short of polygamy you have got to decide on a direction. Fly to England and convince Joanna to change her mind or keep your promise to her and find Suzanne.

Last night for a few minutes I believed Joanna was changing her mind. That she wanted to marry me. I messed up. I should have said let's go back to being friends. Not marry, but not say goodbye to all the good things we had. But when we started making love, the "friends" idea was no longer an option. Only one thing was and it had nothing to do with what friends do together. Well, whatever happens now, we did give each other a night to remember forever. I know I will.

Matt backed his still beautiful old Duesenberg out of the garage. "Only last night, old friend," he told the car, "the Lady who rode with me, said you were a thoroughbred. A racing stallion. Take it from me, this was a lady who knows class. I wish you could have gotten to know her better. Yes, I know..." He said. A catch in his voice. "We both wish it."

Matt drove to the Upper East Side near City College to East 74th Street. The five story brownstone had been designed by Alexander Welch in the Beaux-Arts style in 1898 and finished in 1900. The year of the new century. Two years after his father was born.

He rang the bell and after a short wait heard footsteps coming down. The door was opened by Marion. Matt wondered if she even went to her apartment any longer. She had been watching out for his father for years as his Assistant, now she was with him almost constantly. She had been holding Trey's hand when Matt reached the Hospital and he knew his father had finally reached the realization that the two of them were more than boss and employee. Matt had known for a long time how she felt about Trey.

She kissed him on the cheek and then sadly told him, "I heard Matt. Several of the girls called and told me. I'm sorry. It's a shame really. I've never understood why things that seem so completely right can end in such unhappiness."

Matt took her hand in his. He knew how lucky his dad was. Marion was a lovely woman and completely real. Nothing artificial about her. He didn't know if his dad had popped the question yet, but he knew he would. The man would have to be a greater fool than he was if he didn't.

"Funny Marion, I was asked something like that last night. Which is worse...doing the wrong thing for the right reason or doing the right thing for the wrong reason?"

"What is worse Matt? Doing nothing is worse! At least if you try, you are taking a chance and life is all about taking chances. You may not always win, but at least you give it your best. Then you will never have to look back and wish you had. No regrets if you tried."

Matt looked down at his shoes with a long sigh. "That being the case, I am very afraid there are *going* to be regrets. Probably on both our parts. The sad thing is what no one at the Bank knows. I saw a baby and it is mine. Joanna and I have a son together.

"I really need to talk to Dad. Is he up to doing that tonight?"

Marion was laughing as she told him, "Well Matt, if you consider Trey spending most of the day working in his office on the second floor up to him doing something, then, yes I would say he is swell. Part of what he was doing concerns you. Don't let him know I told you, but you should be prepared. Trey intends to make you the youngest President Empire National has ever had. Matt, I know you will think you're not ready, but you are. You grew up because of the War and you know the Bank almost as well as he does. He intends to continue to hold the title of Chairman of the Board. I am sure it will extend his life to give up the day to day stress of being President. Besides we want time to travel."

"Hold on just a minute Marion. Did I just hear you say we? As in the two of you together? Has my old man finally proved he really is smart enough to ask you to marry him? Oh my God!"

"He asked about noon. When we were at lunch. I love the man dearly, but he has been in banking too long. And it's been so long since your mother died, he has forgotten a lot about women. I wasn't sure if he was proposing marriage or a merger. But he did finally get around to, 'Will you marry me?' So what's a girl who's been in love with her boss forever to do? I said yes. But let him tell you that also. I think he's looking forward to it. After he proposed and I accepted he mumbled something about, 'Damn, the boy was right all along'."

"Marion, I won't let on I know anything about the engagement or the promotion. I do want you to know how glad I am that Dad finally asked you to marry him. I knew sooner or later he would wake up."

"Yes Matt, and you set it up. The Art Museum fund raiser. You and the girl from Atlanta; the blond with that wonderful thick southern accent. One of your 'La Belle de Jour's.' He asked me to go 'as a representative of the bank.' He was so afraid someone would 'misunderstand'."

"Well lady, the way you looked when you came out... all I could think was 'Wow.' You were a knockout. When you two came back to the car, Dad looked like, 'my God and she has been outside my office all this time'."

"You know Matt, you really *are* sweet. Just think, I am going to be married to the Chairman of the board of the Bank and my new son is going to soon be President. Not bad for a gal from a little town in Oklahoma, is it?"

"So what do I call you? Mom, Mother, Marion?"

"Matt, you choose. I am just happy to be in the family or I will be when we are married. Now let's go on up and let him make this official. You know now that I think on it, that day you flew down Wall Street in that little airplane of yours may have been a very good day after all. Look at the good that has came out of that day I only wish you and Joanna..."

"Thank you Marion. Me too."

As they went up the stairs he knew that in some ways Marion was right. His father sending him to England was a life altering occurrence. He had left a shallow young man interested only in his own satisfaction. Spoiled beyond tolerance. Selfish and egotistical. A child with all the toys, yet still wanting more. England and the War changed everything. More than that, Joanna changed me. Love changed us. And now she's gone.

They reached the landing on the second floor and heard the radio in Trey's office. WQXR was broadcasting the evening news.

His dad turned when he heard them and asked, "Matt, did you hear about the big explosion in Texas? No? Well... a French merchant ship was loading ammonium nitrate fertilizer dockside in Texas City and it caught fire. The entire shipload exploded. It was huge. Some people said it was like the A bombs we used in Japan. There are oil, chemical and gas plants burning. The explosion is reported to have blown airplanes to pieces that were circling the area. Some debris was reported to have traveled three miles into the air before falling back to earth. They expect casualties to be in the hundreds. The Monsanto complex is burning and may be a total loss. As they have accounts with us, it would be good to call them first thing tomorrow and offer any assistance we can give."

Matt could imagine the scene in Texas City. It probably looked like a German port city after the B-17s passed over. Nothing but fire, death and destruction everywhere and the survivors wandering around dazed. Everything that was familiar reduced to unrecognizable ruble.

"Sure Dad. My first call in the morning. Well, actually about nine because of the time difference between us and St. Louis. I'll try to reach Ed Queeny since he's President, but if he's busy I'll get Charlie Thomas. He's the one VP that will know the scoop on what we may be able to do."

"Yeah Matt, Thomas is a good bet, probably the best one. Technical directors tend to know everything. Usually in more detail than the President. Just let him know we stand ready to help any way we can."

His father rose from the swivel chair in front of his old roll top desk and walked to the large wooden case Zenith radio. It sat against the wall under a floral stained glass window crafted by Tiffany's in 1899. He clicked the radio off. Matt knew his father considered only news broadcasts worth his time. Hopefully Marion could widen his interests and Matt would bet money she would.

"Matt, come on over and sit down. We need to talk. There are going to be some pretty big changes." Matt saw him look at Marion and wink. "Marion would you make some notes? There is a pad on my desk over here and pencils in the holder at the back." Matt looked away when she bent over to get the pad and to reach way over the desk to get pencils.

Damn, what I thought about her all those years ago was not far off the mark, but I can't have those thoughts about a very nice lady who is about to be my step-mother. Besides she's old enough to be my...older sister? The little voice inside his head clamored for an answer to a question. What...your life isn't complicated enough already? Matt came right back with... complicated? My life? You must have me confused with someone else.

"First of all Matt, I have asked Marion to marry me. I'm not sure she hadn't been drinking heavily, but she said yes."

Marion who hardly ever took a drink turned to Matt and said, "If anybody could be doubted of sobriety it was your father. Had to work up his courage, I suspect."

His father picked up the thread, "Well, if she feels the same tomorrow about marrying an old war horse like me then we have a wedding to plan."

"Dad it's high time you got me a mother."

"It might have done more good when you were in prep school or at Yale, Matt. Maybe then the girls wouldn't have thought you were such a bastard."

Matt said, "DAD!" At the same time Marion shouted, "TREY!"

"Okay, maybe a couple didn't think you were and besides that is all past history. Now I am proud of you. I don't know where they are holding that boy of mine who went to England, but the man they sent back in his place is first rate. I heard about what happened between you and Joanna. Matt I am heartily sorry. I am also sorry I didn't get to meet her, but I know one thing I am grateful for, Son.

"I am very grateful you met her. You had changed for her before the War started. I could read the difference in your letters. Those letters made it clear to me you joined the RAF for her. I wish it could have ended otherwise for the two of you. I really wish it could have.

"Her leaving following so closely on the heels of Suzanne's leaving. Well, I know it's a bitter pill for you. I could never have foreseen Suzanne up and leaving like she did. When we were together at Christmas, I expected you two would have married very soon. I know one thing. I can tell love when I see it. You two were in love and, I believe, deeply in love."

"Dad, I need to tell you a few things about both women. There is something I didn't know about Joanna and me until yesterday. The baby I saw before I left England is mine. Joanna was pregnant before I flew my last mission. She has named him Mathew, but his last name is Barton. The problem we could not solve was how we could marry now. She has to live in England because of the family business and, Dad, I have found I can't leave America. When I was in England, during the War, I thought I could stay, but it's been too long.

"New York is my home. So we were at an impasse; blocked with no way to turn. She would have married me even under those circumstances. She believed, and I think she was right, that the love we had could not survive, living apart like that. That is the gist of a very long night's conversation with a lot of sadness on both sides. But don't think I haven't second guessed myself a lot since. I have."

"Son, it sounds like an impossible problem to solve. One question. What about the boy? Did you two settle that? Are you helping with his support?"

"God, Dad. That went out of my mind. Let me give her time to get back and get over last night and I'll call because the two of us need to make decisions about little Mathew. I not only have a responsibility to help, I want to.

"Funny thing is, I ended up telling her about Susanne. She sensed there had been someone and I told her the whole story. You see, I did ask Suzanne to marry me but she wouldn't unless I could say I loved her as much as I had loved Joanna and I couldn't say it. Not then. I asked her to give me time. Even bought a ring. But she left a few days later.

"Joanna made me promise that I would find Suzanne. I made the promise willingly because I know now that I do love her and I know now I do love her as much as I love Joanna. Suzanne had it pegged. I loved the memory of what Joanna and I had, but I now know that our time has passed.

"So Dad, I have a promise to keep when I have time, but I don't quite know where to start. The last I knew she was going to California with Louis Armstrong's band about a picture they were contracted to be in."

"Matt, I've got some free time right now. Marion and I will find out where she is. Agents, producers and film people all play golf. I know some of them and it's like a college fraternity. Shouldn't take long. That is if you really want to find her. Are you sure you do?"

Matt thought for a moment before answering. "Yes Dad, I do. You know I made Joanna a promise years ago and I was sure it was the right thing to do. But in the end I lost her because of it. In fact, thinking I had lost her brought me Suzanne. I not only want to keep the promise to Joanna, I need to see Suzanne so that I can tell her how much I really do love her. I hope she can forgive me for not doing it earlier."

"I understand Matt. By the way there is something else. Rather important. I know we talked about this a short while ago but we need to speed up the process a bit. You are soon to be President of ENB."

Matt was still not certain how he felt about moving into such a responsible position. Yes, he thought, I was the pilot of a B-17 during the War. In fact I led the Squadron during all of the missions before being shot down in 1944, but this is a different proposition entirely.

Even though Marion had tried to prepare him, the reality of hearing his father speak the words converted the abstract idea into a reality. Was he ready?

"Dad, do you think I am prepared for this?"

"Matt you are far better equipped to take-over than I was. I was back from my war less than thirty one months when my father had a heart attack which he *didn't* survive. I was forced into the Presidency while my Uncle Jonas, who was a Wall Street Attorney, handled the Board for two years. I survived my heart attack, so I will be here if you need me. Any decisions you make that you want to consult with a pretty good older banker about.... Well, you have one in the family. Fair enough?"

"Ok Dad. As long as you don't mind your kid leaning on you. At least in the beginning."

"Good Matt. Now here's what you need to do, Marion please take notes. The first thing is to decide if someone with the Bank already is up to taking over your position as head of C&I loans. It will have to be someone you have real confidence in. Tell them any loan to be approved for over a million dollars during the first six months to a year needs final approval by you. Make sure you have a good Loan Approval Committee for anything over a hundred thousand dollars. Under that, allow your department head to approve all loans. Never second guess him unless he proves unreliable on a number of them.

If he does, call him in to talk and give him time to correct the problems. Let him know that once the allotted time has passed if you do not see very substantial progress, you will have to sack them. Very little you do in business is harder than letting an employee go, but sometimes for the good of the organization it has to be done. A bad employee is like a disease which can, in time, spread throughout the Bank."

"Sure Dad, I know what you mean. I was always very careful when I put crews together in England because one weak link could cost everyone's life. That was as critical as what could happen in the Bank. I have no problem cutting someone loose who needs to go."

"Good... Now I would suggest, after you have settled on your choice for C&I, let them know they will be moving into your slot, but to keep it under their hat until it is announced. Let them know you will make the announcement shortly after your promotion is official. This is a good test of your choice's discretion. You will hear if they leak anything. By the way, keep as much of what you are doing from even Mrs. Stanton. She hasn't been with you long enough to trust her ability to keep secrets." He looked at Marion and smiled. "I was fortunate enough to have Marion. But there are very few women like her in the world."

Marion laid her pad and pencil down, walked softly to the wooden swivel chair where Trey sat, leaned down and kissed his cheek. His father looked up at her and smiled the smile of a much younger man.

"Thank you my dear. What I said is completely true. One of the things I love about you is your innocence about how remarkable you are. I will always be grateful for the first day you walked into my office. Into my life."

She kissed him again. "Cut it out Trey. I am supposed to be taking notes, not crying. And if you take this much farther I shall most certainly be doing that."

Matt had always known the two of them were the perfect pair to work together and now he saw what a wonderfully matched pair they were in a more intimate setting.

They are a damn fine looking couple, he mused. They will get lots of looks when they go out. The way they did at the fund raiser for the Art Museum a couple of months ago.

My Lord, has it been such a short time? So much has happened. Suzanne came into my life stayed with me a few short weeks and was gone; said she loved me too much to stay. Then, out of thin air Joanna comes back; not married, with a child we made together on that golden day we joined in the barley. On that day for the first time I felt everything I wanted or could ever want was within reach. That I would wake up each morning beside an enchanting girl with green eyes. Then, standing in a German field next to a fallen B-17, it all somehow slipped away. Yesterday she was back in my life for a single day and damned if I didn't let her walk away again.

And why did she say she needed to do that? An ocean had come between us. Yet she said I was and forever would be the only love in her heart. Because she loved me, she left and asked me to find the other love in my life. God, I hope I am not damned to end up alone with only memories of loves lost.

Is this simply karma for all the little affairs which meant nothing to me in my youth? All the girls I made love to, then treated with such disdain?

Well, at least Dad has done better. No striking out for him. He has found a love and is smart enough not to let her walk away from him. I am glad to see he has his color back tonight and looks like the man I am used to seeing.

My father, so tall and still very trim, plays a good game of tennis and a top notch game of golf. No riding in carts for him. When we golf together the two of us walk the course. He still has a full head of grey hair and that small grey banker moustache, the same blue eyes I inherited and a disarmingly open smile. Not bad for a guy pushing fifty.

And Marion. She has developed from the rather pretty young woman I once had fleetingly lustful thoughts about when I was young, to the stunningly beautiful and sophisticated woman I saw when I returned from England. The change was so great it was hard to believe she was the same person. She must be all of around 35 now.

Fifteen years difference in age, but I don't think either of them will give that fact much notice. It isn't really a May – December marriage. Perhaps more a June – September one. Pretty good months if one thinks about it.

Later, when he walked into the warehouse, the emptiness seemed to settle heavily back into his heart. Into that space in his heart which had been filled by Joanna in his days in England and again for a few hours last night. Only a night ago he held her in his embrace. "A night to remember forever," she asked of him. Is it to be remembered or be *haunted* by? Ghosts....

Memories and shadows were what Suzanne had said he was in love with. For a few hours yesterday they were gone, but tonight he had memories and shadows where they had both been.

"Now Suzanne too, they are no longer just for Joanna. No. Now I have them for both of you," he said aloud.

Shaylee Princess of the Barley. The green-eyed enchantress I once loved more than my life. The girl who almost made me believe in forever. The girl who gave up St. George to love me. Who said vows with me in the chapel and made love with me in the barley field, beneath a tree imbued with ancient magic.

Suzanne, the girl I thought had stardust in her hair. The girl who asked me where time goes. Who stood with me on a bridge in the falling snow in Central Park on New Year's night. Who called this place home. Who sang me a song about what happens after the last goodbye and danced with me, only on one night when I was young, then again after the War in a smoke-filled night club when everyone else had gone home.

401

The woman with a broken heart because of me. Because of the things I should have been able to tell her. Memories and shadows...and *goodbyes*.

Goodbye. Such a simple little word. I wonder how many hellos and goodbyes we say in a single day, in a lifetime. So automatic. Hello. Good to see you. Goodbye. Hope to see you again soon. Then, when you least expect it, one comes along that *isn't* automatic. A hello when you touch someone's hand and you start dreaming of forever. A hello that starts something you had never expected in your life and after that you are no longer the same. A hello which makes you question everything you were so certain about.

Then, on another day, along comes a goodbye which means being apart for that same forever you dreamed of being together. A love which should have kept you together is suddenly the very thing keeping you apart. The kind of goodbye which breaks two hearts. The kind of goodbye a beautiful golden-haired angel sings to you about with tears in her eyes. A song about never meeting again. What could she have thought when you left before the song ended?

So Matt, old pal, you are so damn smart. Isn't it about time you go and find her and said hello and fight hell and yourself from ever telling her that kind of goodbye again?

You will always have the time you spent with Joanna in England. No one can take that away. You both have that and last night. The night she said we had each other forever and, in the way she sees things, she's right. I love her and I always will and I know she loves me, and for her, I believe I really am forever. To her we are the love which happened in a land somewhere between fairytale and reality in the middle of a war.

One of the first things she told me was that for her it would be "one man, forever." I doubt there ever will be anyone else in her life. We will both go on, but I know I *can* love someone else. I want to continue what Suzanne and I started. Love. I want to hear her say "take me home Matt. I want to fall asleep in your arms for the rest of my life." I should have seen that earlier.

I needed last night to close the book on an old dream. To see "The End" written at the bottom of the last page. It was a wonderful story of love that I'll never forget, but it will for all time remain without a sequel. The story has ended. But I will always cherish the story and the memories I have. A princess and her champion. A Great War and a promise which was broken. Lovers separated by Kismet, yet still loving throughout time.

Now Joanna has her dream. I believe it's what she really wanted. Her beautiful story with a sad ending. And I am left with a reality to live. The prince has returned to his kingdom, taken off his armor, and found he is just a man. She will never have to know that now.

He went into the long closet, hung up his pants and threw his shirt in the cleaning hamper in the corner. As always, he saw the empty coat hanger where Suzanne had left it. Paused for a moment. Slowly shook his head and went to bed alone.

The next day he was in his office before seven.

At noon things had slowed and Suzanne once again entered his thoughts. I know Dad and Marion will be able to get information about where she is in California. If she is still out there. But it will take time. What we need is someone out there who knows their way around. Then it came to him...Gable. Clark Gable.

He phoned his dad. "Hey, I think we can speed this up. Remember Clark Gable flew in my Group at Polebrook? All I need is a phone number for him. At his house and his studio. If you can get that I believe he will help me find her. If anyone out there can, he can."

"Ok. We will get back to you with that in a few minutes. By the way, as soon as you find her, plan on leaving. I can come in and keep the ship in the water while you are gone. And Son...this time please don't come back without her. OK?"

"Thanks Dad. I intend for her name to be Suzanne Weldon. Damn."

"That is a very strange name even if I did use it a lot with your name years ago. What is the problem Matt?"

"I just realized, I have no idea what her middle name is."

"Maybe you can get her to whisper it to you on your wedding night. At least that way there will be one surprise."

"DAD!"

"Gottcha!" His father hung up while Matt was still laughing.

It was only twenty minutes before his father called back.

"OK, I've got some numbers for you. Ready?"

"Sure Dad, shoot."

"The first is Gable's number at his house in Encino. Crestwood 4-1883. His agent is Hal Wallis' sister. She is in Hollywood. Her number is Madison 7-7288. At MGM, Louis B. Mayer's personal number is Hollywood 3-1212. Gable's number at MGM is Hollywood 3-1269. Use Mayer as a last resort. I understand he is very prickly."

"OK, thanks. I'll start calling right away. It's after twelve here, so it's after nine out on the coast. I'll get back to you after I make a useful contact. And Dad... thanks a lot. Thank Marion too. You do know" he joked "she is like finding a real diamond ring in a box of Cracker Jacks?"

"No Son, her ring came from Tiffany's," his father was chuckling when he hung up.

The first call Matt made was to Gable's number at MGM on the chance he was involved in filming a picture. Matt remembered him saying he made a point of being in by 6:30 in the morning so he could get to make-up and review the scenes being shot that day.

The phone was answered on the second ring by a young female voice. She said that Mr. Gable was not in. After a short conversation during which Matt explained how he had come to know Gable during the War, the young lady suggested he could probably catch Mr. Gable at home. She said he had finished his last film a few weeks before and was spending time with his horses and other interests. Matt couldn't help but chuckle as he imagined what those "other interests" might be. The young lady listened as he checked the telephone number he had with her. "Yes," she confirmed, "Crestwood 4-1883. You must be quite well connected. Very few people have that number."

Matt thanked her and dialed Gable's ranch number in Encino. He must still be living in the house he had bought with Carol Lombard. How, Matt wondered, can he do that? I know I couldn't. Everything would remind me of her. Too many ghosts in a place like that.

"Oh," his little voice said, "and you don't have any ghosts you live with. Let's talk about an empty coat hanger in your closet. Let's talk about a girl with stardust in her hair or perhaps a girl with green eyes you were going to spend forever with."

The phone was answered by a woman; her voice familiar. He was certain he had heard it in a movie, but couldn't place it. Matt asked for "Clark." The woman asked who was calling and when he repeated the information he had given the young woman at MGM, he heard a clear undertone of skepticism in this woman's voice. She told him Clark was out with his horses. She took his number at the Bank and at home and said she would give it to him when he came in. She hung up with no goodbye. Matt thought, well, that seems to be a dead end.

Fifteen minutes later Brianna Stanton came through a little breathlessly over the intercom. "Mr. Weldon...I have Clark Gable on the phone for you. At least he says that's who he is and it sure sounds like him."

"Thanks Mrs. Stanton. Yes, it is him. We flew in the War together." He picked up the line. "Hello Clark. Thanks for calling back."

"Hey Matt! I heard you were dead. The Krauts said you and the whole bunch on 'The Maid' were killed."

"Yeah Clark, they told me about that too. Nope, spent a year in camp Luft III. But dead I am not."

"Hell, I'm really glad they didn't get you Kid...err...Matt."

"Come on Gable that was the service. Now you can call me Kid or Matt or what the hell ever you want. The War is over or as much as it ever can be for guys like us."

"You know Matt, that first day when I called you 'Kid.,' you lit into me good. Really pissed me off, young kid like you telling me off. I was ready to take a swing at you, but I got the feeling you wanted me to. Was I wrong?"

"Nope, I was ready for you to do exactly that. I was always pretty good with my fists. But I was not going to start it."

The response came with a laugh "Kid, I knew it. I just knew it. Two things stopped me. First, a guy who gives you the first swing is pretty dangerous and second, I had too hard a time getting in the service to get thrown out for fighting. Later I was pissed at myself because I knew you were right and turned out you were a pretty damn nice guy. Say, did you marry that pretty girl you were engaged to?"

"No, I am sorry to say that didn't work out."

"I...well...I don't know what to say Matt. You two seemed very much in love."

"We were, but the time I was a POW she thought I was dead and when I got back well... there was a misunderstanding. My fault for that. We didn't quit loving each other, but it just wouldn't work. Long story short, she can't leave England and, now, I can't leave America."

"Damn Matt. The War. I know what you mean about it being over 'as much as it can be for guys like us.' You know I always loved acting. Making films. But since the War it's not the same any longer. Now it is just a job. It's not fun the way it used to be. Sorry if Paulette was a bit cool on the phone. She likes to think she is protecting me. Hey... I just keep rattling on. What's happening with you? You heading out this way?"

"Actually I am planning to Clark. There is something I really need your help with. Louis Armstrong is making a film out there at one of the studios and there is a girl with him. A singer. Her name is Suzanne Swift..."

Matt told him the story. All of it and when he had finished Gable was quiet a minute before he answered.

"You are one lucky son-of-a-bitch. In England you have a beauty completely in love with you and you manage to lose her only to come home and have it happen again and you let her get away? OK, I will find out where she is. Won't take long. A couple of phone calls. But this time will you please hold on to this one! The old game warden would say you are exceeding your legal limit on beautiful women. Hey... when you come out you are welcome to stay here."

"Clark, I appreciate the offer but staying in town will more convenient. Besides I think you are occupied."

Gable laughed. "Yeah, I exceeded my limit years ago. Besides she and I are between films and bored."

"Thanks Clark. I appreciate it."

"Nothing to it, Kid. I'll be back to you real soon."

Work kept Matt occupied for the next few hours. A meeting of the Loan Committee in his office had just broken up when Gable called back.

"Hey Matt, I still can't imagine you in an office in New York. Hell Kid, if one of the studios needed somebody to play a pilot of a B-17 you would be perfect for the part. You played it so well in real life, playing it on screen would be a piece of cake for you.

"Anyway. I got what you want. Suzanne Swift. 1630 Lyman Place, Apartment number 9, in the Hollywood Hills. Yeah, she came out here with 'Satchmo' to shoot a film. Something about New Orleans and how Jazz got started and grew. Being done by a company called U/A...United Artists... they've been around a while, but not a real big studio.

"This is a small film with some good Jazz players in it. Your girl came with Armstrong to be in the film, but she's not. They brought Billie Holliday out to do the singing. The studio is paying Suzanne even though she is mostly sitting at home. 'Satchmo' is also playing some gigs out at the Santa Monica Ball Room and she is singing with him there. I can tell you she is disappointed at how things have worked out. All this is from a guy my agent knows over at U/A. This any help Kid?"

"Much more than just a help. It is exactly what I needed. I owe you. If my trip goes well, I want you to call next time you get over to New York so I can introduce you to my new wife. Hard as this may be to believe she is every bit as nice as Joanna and Clark no need to tell me I am lucky"

"I'll call. I want to meet her. Good luck Matt. If I can do anything else give me a call."

Matt called Trey and passed along the information Gable had given him. He knew Marion was listening on another phone when she asked, "Matt, how soon can you be ready to leave?"

"I can leave this evening after work. What do you have in mind?"

"I'll have to call, but I should be able to get you on an American flight to L.A. with a stop in Chicago.

If so you should be there by mid-day tomorrow at the latest."

He heard his dad break in with, "That's great Marion. Get on it right away. Get a car for him. A company called Avis Car Rentals has recently set up to rent autos at airports. I know they are in L.A., see if you can get a number at the airport there. And get them to hold a car for Matt."

Matt found himself laughing into the phone. "Hey Dad, you are either going to have to raise Marion's salary way up or figure out she is about to become far more than your Assistant. Her title is about to be Mrs. Marion Weldon. Remember?"

He heard a laugh followed by a click and a dial-tone.'

Chapter 26

CALIFORNIA

Matt left the newly named LaGuardia Airport at 8:35 in the evening. American was using the DC-3 twin engine aircraft which during his time in England he had called by its military name the C-47 Skytrain. The DC-3, while it looked the same externally was dressed up inside for passenger flights. It had double row seating for twenty-one passengers on day flights or fourteen on night time flights. The reduced number of passengers on the night runs could fully recline for sleeping. Matt reclined and was able to get short naps, but he never really slept as the sound of the engines kept waking him. The twin Wright-Cyclone engines sounded very similar to the ones on the "Maid of Barley" and reminded him of the danger of those years. Would the day ever come when flying would be enjoyable again? Flying at night reminded him too much of all the night missions he had flown for the RAF. Not good memories, especially knowing all but one of his old RAF crew had died years ago.

Matt was certain the train would have been less stressful but it would have taken days rather than hours. He arrived in Los Angles before noon, recovered his suitcase and found the rental auto counter for Avis.

The auto was a very plain blue 1947 Ford. It was a warm day and Matt rolled all the windows down and threw his sport coat in the back seat along with his tie. He understood why the men he saw wore light-weight pants and short sleeved shirts. All he could do to compensate was roll his shirt sleeves up and unbutton his white shirt three buttons down, opening his collar

Lying on the seat next to him was a map the agent at the rental counter had given him on how he could reach 1630 Lyman Place in the Hollywood Hills section of town.

As he drove, Los Angles seemed more movie set than a real city. Palm trees were in concrete dividers centered between the two lanes of traffic and many buildings looked more Egyptian, Moroccan or Aztec than American. He passed a theater which looked as if it came directly from the Forbidden City in China. The exceptions were tall buildings; they would have been at home in any large city in America.

If ever a town had weather perfect for convertibles, he thought, it is Los Angles. And, indeed, it seemed to him every second automobile was and had its top folded down and secured with snap down cover. Cars were as colorful as the flowers which bloomed in nearly every square inch of available earth. In shades of red, green blue orange and even purple.

There was a breeze blowing in from the Pacific. A West Wind. "Of course," Matt whispered. "I suppose I will be haunted by a wind from the west for the rest of my life." As usual, it whispered Joanna's name. Matt whispered back, "That is over. Whisper something else. Whisper Suzanne." The wind continued in a moan....Joanna, Joanna.

Forty five minutes later, he parked the Ford next to the curb in front of a peach and white, U-shaped building. Well, not exactly U shaped as the back side did not curve. It was squared off like the two wings which pointed to the street. One set of apartments at ground level faced an open courtyard which was lush with flowers, palm trees and a fountain in a small pond. Above this was a matching set of apartments which looked down on the courtyard. There were wrought iron stairs up to the second floor apartments, with matching iron railings along the front edge of the second level walkway.

Matt walked up, stopped at the door marked with a bold 9 in black metal and knocked firmly.

There was no answer, so he repeated his knock and was once again greeted with silence. His third knock was ever louder, but this too garnered no response.

Well, I'll be damned. The one thing I never considered. She isn't home. He grumbled to himself, "You practiced a hundred possible conversations, but if she's not home... they do no good. Talking to a closed door won't get her back."

He sat on the top step of her landing considering his next move. A clicking, hissing, sizzling sound came down the street as one of the yellow and white Pacific Electric Transportation System trolleys noisily approached. The wheels clicked at each rail joint and the hiss, sizzle and spark came from the connection of the long overhead steel arm which rode along a spider web of electric wiring above the street. The trolley was marked "V Line – Hollywood Hills."

Matt watched idly as the trolley slowed then stopped a half block down the street from where he sat. Three people got off the trolley. Suzanne was the last to step down.

As she walked toward him, Matt saw she was carrying two large brown bags of groceries. Her eyes looked down to make sure of her footing, so she did not look up until she was on the second metal step leading to her apartment. Matt saw a look of disbelief cross her face and she dropped both grocery bags.

"Oh my God. No! Please, no."

Matt raced down the remaining steps between them and started picking up the cans and boxes which were scattered and rolling across the steps and down to the ground. The bags had split apart so all he could do was set items on the steps as he picked them up.

Suzanne stood there with her hand over her mouth. The color had left her face. She did not move.

Matt found a carton of eggs, only five remained unbroken. "I am sorry Suzanne. I would have phoned, but I was afraid you wouldn't see me and I couldn't have blamed you but I have to talk to you. Face to face."

"Matt. Please leave. I can't do this. I just can't. I left because I couldn't keep just going on day to day. I am sorry you came all this way just to hear this. But *please* go. "

"I'll make a deal with you Suzanne. Let's save as much of your groceries as we can and then talk about your theft."

"Theft! I didn't steal anything from you! I simply couldn't have."

"Oh, but you did Suzanne. Don't worry I have no intention of calling the authorities about it. I just want to hear you say you are guilty, then nothing more needs to be done that involves anyone other than you and me."

"Then you will leave Matt?"

"Suzanne, you have my word, I'll leave if you still want that."

It required several trips to get the jumbled groceries into her little kitchen and a last to clean up the broken eggs and spilled milk.

Matt looked around and knew she must have rented the little apartment furnished. It was not Suzanne at all. Sheet music was scattered on the small kitchen table which had room for only two chairs. The sofa, side chair and coffee table in the living room were worn and had seen years of use.

When everything was stored in the white metal kitchen cabinets and tiny Kelvinator refrigerator, he sat in one of the kitchen chairs and she sat opposite him.

"Alright Matt," she said with a heavy sigh, "what is this about my stealing something from you?"

"You took two things with you when you left that belong to me. The first is a white shirt. Egyptian cotton."

Matt saw her hang her head. "Yes, I took the shirt. I'm sorry I did. You had so many white shirts, I didn't think you would miss it."

"Not miss it Suzanne? It was the most valuable shirt I owned."

"I don't understand. It looked just like all the others."

"Perhaps, but you see it was the shirt you wore every night we were together. I could never put a price on that shirt." He saw that the engagement ring he had finally gotten her to accept was still on her hand.

"Please Matt. *Please* leave." There were tears on her face. "I have cried too much over this since I left. My voice has suffered. I am a singer and it is how I earn a living. We won't work. You know why. I tried until I couldn't try any longer. It hurt too much for me to stay."

"And about that one more thing you took, Suzanne. You also took my heart when you left. The shirt was bad enough but to take my heart.... Well, first about the shirt, you can keep it but only if you wear it when you are with me and secondly, I want you to have my heart but only if you will stay close by with it."

"Matt, we talked about this in New York. I wanted to marry you. You will never know how it hurt to leave. I love you so much, but I just can't be second best. You can't be married to me and always be wishing I was her. I can't be the stand-in for a woman you *can't* have. No! I won't be! No matter how much I love you."

"I would never ask you to be. I do need to tell you a few things that happened after you left. I saw Joanna again. She is not married. Never was. I misunderstood what I saw that day. But you were right. What I was in love with was a time which has passed. I hope you can forgive me for not understanding what you tried so hard to help me see. I know now you and I are the future. I really want to be with you for as long as we live. I want to see you in my shirt every night. I want you to have my heart. All of it. And our children. Please let me take you back to New York. Back home. You see, I discovered something after you left. No place in this wide world is ever going to be home to me unless you are there. And now I know I love you as much or more than anyone else."

Suzanne stared at him for a long moment, then walked around to his side of the little table and he stood up as she took his hand and looked into his eyes. It was a long searching look. "Answer one question for me before I give you an answer."

"That's fair. Ask me."

"*Okay.* Is there room in the Warehouse for a nursery?"

"Certainly. We can take the space on the top floor which was going to be another very small apartment and use it any way we want. It has not been sold or finished out yet so we can hold on to it. Then when we need it we'll make it into a nursery. That way it will be next to our bedroom. Frankly Suzanne, I hope it won't be very long before we convert it."

"Oh, it will be much sooner than you think. About six and a half months now." Matt saw tears running down her cheeks.

"Oh my God Suzanne, you mean you're...you're..." Becoming speechless with joy he swept her into his arms and they shared a long joyful kiss tinged with the salty flavor of her happy tears,

When they finally separated her smile was dazzling through her remaining tears. "Yes my darling, over two months now. I hated to leave you, but I couldn't have stayed any longer or you would have known I was expecting our child. I didn't want you to marry me because I was pregnant with your baby. I only wanted you to marry me because you loved me and really wanted to. *Now I know.*

"I have another question. Before I ask it, I want you to know I will marry you. I have wanted that since the first time you asked me back in New York. The question has nothing to do with our getting married.

"The baby you saw Joanna with before you left England. It was your baby wasn't it?"

"Yes, and it is a boy. Mathew Barton."

"I had to know. Thank you for the truth. It must have been hard for her thinking you were dead and harder still for you when you heard about your child. Are you sure you are willing to lose him to be with me?"

"I would give up everything to be with you. I don't know if he will ever need anything from me, but if he does, I intend to help with his support. I hope you would want me to do that."

"Yes, I would Matt. I know you are an honorable man. And I know now how much you must love me. To have your son in England, away from you. Anything you ever need to do for him, know from this moment on, you have my blessing."

"Now about us, Suzanne. What do we need to do so we can get back to New York? I can't stay away too long. You see Dad had a mild heart attack and I've been running the Bank in his absence."

"Oh no! Is he going to be alright?"

"Yes, he already is. He's handling the Bank while I'm out here. Oh, he's engaged too. My dad is going to marry Marion Tompkins. His Assistant. You met her at Christmas. It's a move I heartily approve of.

"He has me scheduled to take over the Presidency. They want to travel. And I can't wait to see his face when he hears he is going to be a

Granddad. That alone will add years to his life. By the way, the man thinks you are almost as wonderful as I do."

"Well Matt, you already know I think you have a really terrific father. As far as leaving, I will need to let Louie know, but there are plenty of singers around who would love to work with a Jazz group like his. He is such a dear man. So talented, but so down to earth. And so caring about the people he works with. Too few like him around in this business.

"The picture thing didn't go at all the way the way Pops was promised. I am not in it at all He was so mad the studio was not using me in the film, he was ready to walk off. Despite that, I told him the picture was more important than I was. At the time, I was really crushed, but now I am so glad it happened because I don't have to stay. Matt, I don't really like L.A. very much. Not only because of what happened with the film. I like real things and so much out here is make believe. Phony baloney. They make fairy tales and most of them think it's the way real life is. Except the ones who were in the war. They are different.

"The apartment is paid through the end of the month. No signed contract. I took it on a month to month basis. If Louie is okay with it I can leave in a few days. Do you intend to fly back?"

"No, we are going back together. On the train. We will have four lovely days to see a little of America, enjoy good food and make love. We have so much to make up for and only the rest of our lives in which to do it. We mustn't waste a minute."

Suzanne stepped back to him, put her arms around his neck and kissed him. When she pulled away she had that little smile that told him something was coming he should be ready for.

"Well Matt, now you don't have to hope I will get pregnant while we cross America. That's already done. You know, you're not only going to get the title of President of Empire National Bank, but an even more important title, 'Daddy'."

"That night back in college. I really wish I had stopped you from walking away. I wish I had gone after you. Things might have been different... For both of us."

"No Matt. It wasn't supposed to happen then. You followed me this time. That's the important thing. It has all played out as it was intended to. I love you and we were always meant to be together. Even on that first night. But we had to play it out now. That first time you didn't know how to love, you were only a beautiful young boy. You had to go to England and fall in love with Joanna so you could learn what it really meant to love. You grew up over there; the War made you a man. All of it had to

414

happen the way it did so we could be standing here today. So you and I could come to really know each other and ourselves. I had to marry my sailor and lose *him* to find you. We will be happy because we have had enough of misery and loss. But one more time my love. Are you absolutely certain? No doubts left?"

"No doubts Suzanne. Not a one. I love you without reservation. But I do have a question of you. It is something I really need to know. I should have asked long ago."

"It sounds serious. Ok, ask and I will give you an honest answer no matter the question. I promise."

"Ok then. What is your middle name?"

She was laughing; a long musical laugh. Matt had heard her laugh before, but never like this. It was as if some fear she had carried for a long time had suddenly disappeared and was no more substantial than a wisp of smoke. She reached up and kissed his ear and whispered "Marie, it's Suzanne Marie Swift, but the Swift is soon going to be Weldon. Suzanne...Marie...Weldon. I love the sound of it. Speaking of names, we are going to need one for our addition you know."

"Well Suzanne Marie, we can talk about that on our four days back on the train. We'll pick out some boy names and some girl names. As much as I knew I loved you, I find I only knew part of it. I hope you don't mind finding I am head-over-heels in love with you. Remind me I need to call Dad tonight and please call my attention to the time difference. I'm not going to tell him about the baby until we get back. I want both of us to see his face when we tell him. We also will have two weddings to plan; ours plus Dad's and Marion's. And you, my love, need to let your family know.

"I have a suite at the Beverly Hills Hotel. Would it be too forward of me to ask you to stay there with me until we leave?"

She was laughing again when she said, "Only if I can pack that white shirt you came after. I believe you said I could keep it if I promised to wear it only for you. Tonight will be a good night for me to start keeping that promise. I need to call my mom from there tonight. She has been worried. God Matt, she will be so happy. Happy for me...for us. Happier than in a long time."

"Suzanne, she won't be as happy as I am. There is no way you can imagine how much I have missed seeing you in my white shirt. Of course it may end up missing in action for a little while tonight."

That evening after making love, Suzanne turned to Matt and said, "I am supposed to have a practice session with Louie and the band

415

tomorrow. Would you come along so I can ask him about getting another singer and tell him why? He is such a sweet guy, I believe he will understand. I know we need to leave just as soon as we can. Doing it this way should speed up our leaving. Then we can spend those four wonderful days making love across America. Something new for both of us. Crossing America together. I'm feeling really sexy just thinking about it."

Matt gave her his best naughty, over-sexed teenage smile and pulled her to him, kissed her and said, "Well, let's not let a mood like that go to waste. You have no idea how much I have missed being with you. Suzanne, I was a total fool to have ever let you leave."

"No, you are here now and that is all that matters. We have years to be together. A lifetime. And Matt... it is okay to still love Joanna too. I will always have a place in my heart for my sailor as short a time as we had together before... before he was lost. You were with her much longer and she is the mother of your other child. You certainly *should* love her for that. I hope someday I will get to meet your son and her."

After awakening from a dreamless, peaceful sleep, Matt found her still asleep in his arms. No, he thought, there are two of them in my arms. She is pregnant with our child. My God! I am going to be a daddy. A father. Sure, I am a father with Joanna, but I couldn't be there for that. The War saw I was a prisoner when she had our child. I missed out on the birth. And to top that, I believed he was someone else's. I know this one is mine. Ours. This time I will be there. This is a magic beyond my understanding and I just have to see it.

I am glad Joanna made me promise to find Suzanne. If not...I would have never known...Oh, surely I would have come after Suzanne anyway...wouldn't I? Joanna couldn't have known. No surely I would have come anyway.

After a late breakfast, Suzanne directed as he drove out to the Santa Monica Ball Room which was actually built on the Santa Monica Pier. A huge building, it had six minarets spaced around it. The Pacific Ocean rolled underneath to dash its green waters strongly against the support pilings. So, what will happen, Matt asked himself, when a great storm finally hits all this? Hope I am not here to find out.

Suzanne led the way across the vast dance floor and up to the stage where Louie was getting his band organized. He smiled when he saw his singer heading for the stage. Then his smile faded when he saw Matt beside her. He was standing on the floor waiting for them by the time they reached the edge of the stage.

"Hello sweetheart. Are you ok?"

"Sure Pops. This guy with me has just made me a very happy woman. He showed up yesterday at my place. We are getting married Pops. I need to ask you to replace me. Can you do that? Something I haven't told you that I would have had to very soon." She leaned closer and Matt heard her whisper in Louie's ear, "I'm going to have a baby."

Louie's eyes got big, and then he laughed his big, long loud laugh and kissed her cheek and said "That's wonderful darlin'. "He surprised Matt by grabbing his hand and shaking it energetically.

"You got any idea what a lucky guy you are? This is one fine lady you are marrying. You better treat her good or I'll have to bring my cornet upside your head real hard, you hear me?"

"Yes sir, Louie. If I ever treat her less than the lady she is, I would sure deserve it. I know how special Suzanne is and I thank you for taking care of her until we met again."

Louie leaned toward him and told him quietly, "Son, I am so glad you are back. She has been heart-broken since we left New York. I know enough to know she loves you more than anything. More than her singing and that is a mighty lot. She deserves to be happy. The War was hard on her. She is sooo very special. I hope you know."

"I know Pops. It just took a while for me to understand how special."

Louie walked back to the center of the stage and turned back to them.

"Hey, you two still here? You got a big country to cross. Time to get on your way and we got to practice for our show tonight. Come and see us next time we get to the 'big Apple.' We got a special song we'll do for you to dance to. Course by then it won't apply to you two anymore. Jus' be for ole time's sake by then"

That evening Matt called his father and told him they would be leaving Saturday morning on the Atchison, Topeka and Santa Fe's Chief to Chicago then changing to the New York Central into the City, arriving on Tuesday.

"So Dad," he asked, "is everything going OK back there? Any problems?"

"No problems. I am fine and ENB is fine. What's that? Okay... Marion said to give you both her love. We are very happy you are bringing Suzanne back. Now get on back here quick and marry the lady before she comes to her senses."

"That is the plan, Dad. And damn if the same advice doesn't go for you. What either one sees in a pair of old war horses like us is beyond me. We've got a lot of planning to do before the events."

"True Matt, and after that a transition at the Bank to arrange. You know our marriages will have an effect on the Bank. We will have to make it understood our attentions are still focused where they should be. Naturally Marion will see mine is. But you will be even more involved than I will on a day to day basis.

"I have promised Marion that we will travel and I will learn to relax. She seems to think I am worth having around for a long time, and she even has me convinced about that."

"You better be around, Dad, so you can tell me how to make mistakes look good."

"OK Matt, if you ever make one I'll tell you how I handled one just like it. And yes... as smart as you are, you will make a few. I sure have."

"By the way, it's Marie. That's Suzanne's middle name."

"Well Matt, that'll be a big help on the announcements. Whispered it in your ear last night..., right?"

"Well...err...damn close to it Dad."

"OK Son. We'll meet your train at Grand Central Station Tuesday afternoon. Marion and I want to take you two to dinner. Sort of an engagement party just for the four of us, get it?"

"Yep. We are all four engaged. Not totally unheard of for father and son to be engaged at the same time, but probably pretty rare."

"Well Dad, kiss Marion for me. Not that you need an excuse. See you Tuesday."

He told Suzanne about his conversation with Trey. She was quiet for a few minutes and Matt could see she was considering something very seriously.

"Suzanne what's wrong? You know we love each other. That means we share problems and concerns. From now own it's 'us', not 'me' and 'you.' So what is it?"

"It's *my* family. We haven't talked about them but my Mom and Dad divorced while I was in college. Shortly after we met.

"My Dad is a Doctor. He divorced my mother and moved to Chicago then remarried a little later. A nurse he was already involved with before the divorce. I think he only waited until I was gone to make both moves. It crushed Mom. She'd worked hard to put him through Med School. The other thing that hurt her, the nurse was much younger than he was. He could almost have been her father. I don't know what to do about that. Do I invite both?"

"Well sweetheart, in the final analysis, it is up to you. I will abide by your decision. But if you invite both, it will probably be very hard on your

418

mother and if it were me, I wouldn't invite the son-of-a-bitch, not even if I were ill and he was the only doctor in the world."

Suzanne laughed as she threw her arms around his neck, looked him in the eyes and told him, "My, you certainly have a way with words, but you are going to have to stop tip-toeing around difficult decisions or you will never make it as a bank president. But if I understand correctly, you think we should leave him in Chicago with his little nurse. It won't be easy, but I think I can live with that. Yep. In fact, I'm *sure* I can. And Matt... you will never know how special you are and how much I love you."

~ ~ ~ ~

Matt returned the rental car to the airport and took a taxi back to the Beverly Hills Hotel. Suzanne was at the little apartment busy deciding what to pack and carry on the train and boxing the remainder for shipment to New York.

Saturday morning they traveled to Union Station just off busy North Alameda Street. It was another of the city's buildings which seemed more movie set than functioning building. Matt almost expected to see Gary Cooper, John Wayne or his old friend Clark Gable using it as a location for filming a scene in a spy thriller, or perhaps an Alfred Hitchcock production.

Chapter 27

WEDDINGS AND A PHONE CALL

They spent the next four days making both love and plans. Plans for their future, a wedding and a child yet to be born.

Before they arrived in Chicago, they had a list of names for their child. Suzanne told him she assumed if their baby was a boy his name would be Mathew Donnelly Weldon V. After a few moments of silence he told her, "No sweetheart, not unless you really want to name him that. I don't. It would be nice to give him a name that is his alone. Not a left-over from generations before he was born. Let's consider other names for our child should it be a boy."

He did not need to add that his son by Joanna already carried the name Mathew. When she believed he had been killed, she had given their boy his father's name along with her father's middle name.

He and Suzanne considered many names. In the end, both agreed on William. Matt had once told her about his small roommate and explained how "Fizz" had died during the War. She suggested Fitzgerald as a middle name. "William Fitzgerald Weldon," Matt repeated slowly... "Yes, that sounds good. William Weldon. I like it Suzanne. I think Fizz would have considered it an honor. He was a really terrific guy. What he lacked in size he made up for many times over in heart.

"With William as a first name he can be Will, Willie (God forbid), Bill or William. Lots of possibilities there."

Only one girl's name was suggested by Matt, Florence. It had been the name of the mother he had never known. It was no surprise to him that the name Joanna came to his mind and even less surprising he never vocalized the name. For a moment he considered suggesting Carol after the love of Gable's life, then decided it might require too much explanation of a time and place in the past.

Suzanne thought Elizabeth or Margaret would be nice because of her mother and her aunt and Jane or Kathleen simply because she liked the names. She finally suggested Margaret Jane. Margaret Jane Weldon. Matt could only think of Joanna's mother when he heard the name Margaret. That was no reason not to like it. She was, after all, a nice lady with a wonderful daughter. It suddenly all seemed so long ago. Almost another lifetime. But some parts of it had been completely beyond wonderful.

~ ~ ~ ~

They arrived back in New York Tuesday afternoon as planned and found both Trey and Marion waiting for them in the cavernous Grand Central Station lobby. Suzanne kissed Matt's father on the cheek. He was surprised to see his father, a man he considered so reserved, give her a hug and say "I am so glad you are back."

As they walked through the lobby, Suzanne and Marion were whispering to each other and laughing. The four of them were already feeling very much like a family.

In less than a month they were. Mathew Donnelly Weldon wed Suzanne Marie Swift at the Weldon estate on Long Island. It was a perfect April afternoon. The guests included Suzanne's mother, though her father had been 'overlooked' on the guest list. Neither the bride nor groom seemed too upset by the oversight. Both were far too happy and in love to be bothered by anything so trivial.

The following week another wedding occurred at the Weldon estate. This one was for Mathew D. Weldon III and Marion Smith Tompkins. After they were married, Matt heard his father tell his new bride, "Thank you for being so patient with a blind man." He knew Marion understood exactly what his father meant. He saw a single tear track down her cheek as she replied, "Thank you my dear man...for simply everything."

After Matt and Suzanne returned from the four weeks of their honeymoon traveling in the southwestern states, his father retired as President of Empire National Bank. Matt was appointed to follow him and moved into his father's old office.

The nursery on the warehouse's top floor was completed months before it was needed. The room was a gift from his father, thrilled that a new generation of Weldon's was about to be born and telling all his golfing friends that he was going to be a "grandpa."

Each day when Matt arrived home from work, he put on a pair of old tan pants and a plaid shirt to do some painting in the nursery-to-be. Determined to be involved in preparing for the child he and Suzanne were expecting, he knew he was also trying to make up for missing the birth of his son by Joanna.

Painting the walls of the nursery in soft shades of blues and pinks, he thought them a practical choice. The combination would work whether it was a girl or a boy. The room colors were soft and quiet, unlike the stark white walls of the rooms in which he and Suzanne lived; rooms both of them called home. The word still warmed his soul every time she said it. Those rooms which were carved out of a warehouse were special to both of them. It was like the feeling he had once had for the old walkup in London before the War, rooms he associated with his time with Joanna.

Perhaps he loved the warehouse even more because it was where he had held Joanna on their last night together. He had made love with both the women he loved there. It was where he now made love with the one he married who was carrying their child. The question he still could never answer in his mind was which of them he loved more. He only knew which he had married and, in a way, that had become answer enough.

One evening Suzanne came in to look at his work and found him humming the tune he had heard Joanna hum so often in his years in England.

She listened to the sounds for a moment, a questioning look on her face. "Where ever did you hear that? The soft tune you were humming. You are off just a little bit, it is more like this."

Matt closed his eyes and listened to Suzanne hum and was taken back to the first time he heard it from Joanna while driving the MG down to Kent to meet her parents and hear her tell him in a field of waving golden barley that she loved him.

He gave only a partial answer to where he heard the tune. "I heard it in England before the War. Why?"

"Well Matt, if it *is* what I was humming, it is old. Somewhere in the mid fifteen hundreds in England. I learned it in a class I took at Vassar. Part of the syllabus was music from the middle ages. The course covered everything from instruments like the Rebec, Viol and Lute to the human voice when used in Madrigals of the period. The song I was humming is an old lullaby. It originated in Ireland, but was carried across the sea to England. I suppose you might have heard it around King's College while you were there?"

Matt could only answer, "Yes, perhaps that is it." Perhaps, he told himself, that is where Joanna heard it. Then he remembered her saying she had *always* known the tune, long before she could have heard it at King's.

~ ~ ~ ~

In the season of falling leaves, October of 1947, William Fitzgerald Weldon was born. By the time he was a year old, Matt was already talking of sending him to Yale. Suzanne was concerned about far shorter range

423

issues. More practical matters involved in raising a small child. A time their child could sleep all the way through the night. She hoped that would happen very soon because she was running out of new lullabies. Suzanne and their AuPair were both looking forward to the time William could begin learning the art of using a toilet.

Before William's birth, Matt had written a letter to Joanna telling her he wanted to help with any expenses for their son. The last meeting they had still tugged at his heart. Because of that, he kept his letter short and business-like. He was afraid if he did not, he could not constrain his feelings.

When she did not reply, he phoned early one morning from his office. He tried the Brewery first, but was told she was not in. He tried the number he remembered at the London townhouse and found it still worked. Mrs. Townsend answered and recognized who was calling. He could clearly hear the confusion in her voice when he asked to speak to Joanna.

"Well, Mr. Weldon, I...don't know, sir. She is a bit under the weather. Not feeling well. Umm..."

He paused to give her time to think then suggested, "Could you ask if she feels well enough to speak for a few moments. I promise not to keep her long or upset her and thank you for taking care of her. She is so lucky to have you."

"Thank you Mr. Weldon. I'm so sorry...well, that it didn't work out sir. Hold on, let me ask her if she can speak with you."

After a pause he heard Joanna ask the question from the times he was flying, "Mathew, are you all right?"

"Joanna, I am feeling well. The question is how are you? Mrs. Townsend said you were under the weather. What's wrong?"

There was a pause. He heard her sneeze. "Just a cold. Nothing really. I went in to the Brewery, but left early."

"Well, take care of yourself or I'll sic Mrs. Townsend on you." This got a short laugh from her. "Did you get my letter?"

"Yes I did, Mathew. But I didn't know what to make of it. The letter was so very formal. I didn't know if it was written by you or your attorney. Have you changed so much so quickly? I hope not."

"No Joanna. I was afraid if I wrote what I felt... it would hurt both of us too much. I am still very much in..." The rest drifted into silence.

"You don't need to say it Mathew. You know I feel the same. Right now Little Mathew and I are fine. We really don't need anything. If we do you will know right away."

Matt thought he heard a distant 'Eyooow.' "Well Mathew, Haiku said to tell you hello. I think she... well she still misses you."

All he could think of to say was, "Tell her I'll send her my tux pants to sleep on."

In reply he heard a sound somewhere between a laugh and a choked sob. "Joanna, how is your family?"

"They are all fine. The Brewery is running much better. Dad is fine and Mother is really doing well. She is heavily into the grandmother mode. Little Mathew spends lots of time in Kent with her. She's talking 'pony' already, but I'm putting that off for later.

"My brother has married. More than a year ago. His wife is expecting. He wants to stand for election to Parliament next year." There was a long pause before she continued, "I read they have redone Café de Paris and it has reopened. I will never forget our night there. It was magic. I've often wondered what ever happened to that young couple. The ones you sent the champagne to."

Matt could not answer either of her questions. He could only hope the young couple from that night had stayed together and were happy. It was the implied question which bothered him more. What had happened to Joanna and Mathew? The bright promise of their future together?

And, he realized, I'll be damned if I know. Fate gave us more than one chance to make it work. Why didn't we?

When she asked that hidden question, Matt knew it was not over between them and it never could be. All he was sure of when he hung up was what they once had together must now forever remain in the past. Even though he, in so many ways, wished it was otherwise.

Chapter 28

LETTERS 1961

Jan. 8, 1961

Dearest Joanna,

We often talked about time and forever when we were together. Remember? Both have meanings which seem to change as I age. Days and years keep getting shorter now. Rushing by me. Time seemed to move slower when we were together.

It seems such a long time since we last saw each other on a night now forever locked within my heart. That will never grow old. Some might call it foolish. I only know it is there and will be there, well, certainly for as long as I live. It has been thirteen years since we parted. Such a long, yet short time. Does that make any sense?

You once said there were things you wanted to tell me but couldn't. I feel much the same when we talk by phone. So much I mean to tell you, yet I cannot find the words. That all changes when I sit here at my old typewriter at the end of the day. Here I can put down my thoughts and feelings for you.

It is 6:30 and the Bank is quiet and empty. In the silence and echoes all we once had comes back to me. Whenever that happens, I am filled with questions without answers. Questions about our love.

You and I have always been honest with each other. Even when it hurt. It is one of the many things I love about us. I confess it hurt when you told me several years ago, we must never be together again. I also knew you were right. Yes, as much as we would fight it that _would_ happen even now. It would be ecstasy for the two of us and terrible for everyone else involved. And so many others are.

Day to day, I am fine. Happy even. Suzanne and I have a very good life. You _know_ I love her. She and I are well matched. You somehow knew that when we were together that last night. A night full of both pain and love. You were right Joanna, it has truly, for the two of us, become a night to last forever. There never has been, nor ever be, another like it.

William is twelve now. A very bright boy. His grades are excellent. Perhaps his scholarship comes from me but Suzanne is also very intelligent. The part I am certain comes from her is his talent on the piano. She has patiently taught him from the time he was five and now he is a very accomplished pianist. She is a wonderful mother and working quite hard to see he is not at all like I was in my youth. A job she has taken to heart having known me back then.

Have I ever thanked you for changing me? Lord, if not for meeting you, I would have undoubtedly been a worthless human being. Many good things have happened to me but none of them compare with you. You risked giving me your love. The best gift I ever received. Or ever will. The man I am today began the night I met you.

Suzanne and I saw an off Broadway play recently. The Fantastic's. One of those modern productions which has very simple staging with few props. A love musical. You know, boy and girl fall in love. Become separated. Misunderstand each other. (Do things like that ever happen in real life?) And finally find each other then realize they are truly in love. The kind of love which lasts. The play ends happily. (Do things like that etc., etc?) There is a song in the play which moved me deeply. "Try to Remember," if you ever hear it you will know why. It is a song which could have been written about the two of us and our love. While we were together, and now, when we are parted. Oh the dreams I still have of you. The echoes of our past. I wonder if the plays writer also had a great love which somehow failed.

Suzanne, William and I always vacation in different parts of America. We now do this several times a year. It is a wonderful country. A country I had once hoped to show you as you had shared yours with me. England. How I still miss the cold showers and the girl that made me need them.

The question I had that last night we were together still haunts me. How could two people who loved each other so much have walked away from that love? It seems we must have overlooked something that night. I still believe if we could return to that evening, it would end differently.

I now know the answer to one question you asked then. "Which is worse, doing the right thing for the wrong reason or doing the wrong thing for the right reason?" And the answer which came from Dad's assistant (now his wife) that I wish I had known then: "What is worse is to do <u>nothing</u> at all." In walking away from the love we had for each other, that is what we did. Look at where we are today because of it.

You see, Joanna, I am haunted by you. By us together. But I also know that if we had worked it out I would have been haunted equally by Suzanne and I would have never known about her and my son William. I love <u>both</u> of you. You and Suzanne. You were right dearest. One can't weigh or measure love. I simply love you both and probably deserve neither of you. Thank God I have been so fortunate.

Thank you for keeping me up on our son's life. I hope someday to be able to see him face to face. If you ever feel that you could allow… well you know.

I still miss you and I am sure I always will.

With my love, forever,

Mathew Weldon

Mathew Weldon

Jan. 20, 1961

My dearest love,

It always takes a few days after receiving one of your wonderful letters for me to reply. Your letters reassure me in many ways. About both love and time. Yes, it seems to speed up as I age. Yet moments from our time together go on forever. For me it is as real and present as when we were together. Not a single moment has been lost. I am convinced my last thoughts in this life will be of you.

And of love. Oh yes… love. My love for you only grows stronger with the passage of time. People talk of lost loves. Ours was not lost. It still lives with every breath I take. It is the kind of love I wished for when I was not much more than a child. There is an old saying about being careful what you wish for. I know now mine was an incomplete wish. I made a wish for a wonderful hero. One that I would love and who would love me forever. I suppose it was a wish to live… a fairy-tale. But I left out the word "together." I suppose I am still little girl enough to believe wishes are sometimes granted. That wish seems to have been. We will love each other forever… but <u>not</u> as one.

I am glad you, Suzanne and your son are seeing your country as a family. If things could have been different between us, I would have loved seeing America with you and <u>our</u> son. I loved showing you my England but then I enjoyed doing everything with you. We <u>were</u>

enchanted during our time. I confess to having turned us in to a bedtime story for the children of the Barton family. You my love are the brave Prince from across the ocean and I am, shamelessly, the Princess. It is a story of Love and War for children. Dragons and brave knights. A story of lovers separated. The Prince returned to his county to become King. Yet the love lived on between them. Only we two know the real story, but in many ways it is <u>almost</u> that kind of love.

I heard "Try to Remember" and understand why it moved you so. I cried for hours after hearing it. Even now if it enters my head I tear up. I have often heard married couples say such and such a song is "their song." I guess this will forever more be "our song," and it wasn't even written before we parted.

Mathew, our son, is a picture of you. When I see him, I see you, with a British accent of course. Hair perhaps a touch darker except in summer. Then, like yours, it is the color of the golden barley in our fields.

He is fifteen years old and the girls are all over him. One look at him and they go all starry eyed. The way I remember looking at you. I do my best to control the situation and thank God he is a bit reserved. I tell him about what you were like when we first met and how off-putting I found that. But I also tell him what you became. How you changed. I believe he has taken that to heart. He knows our story. All of it. The complete truth, not the version he learned as a child.

Mathew I am sorry you have never met him. That _is_ because of me. I love you too much. What I told you when he was eight has not changed. I would want you if we were together. No, I would _have_ to have you that way. I believe it would be the same for you. We know that would destroy everything. Once that happened between us, neither would give a damn about anything or anyone except each other. We would destroy our worlds to have that. Love is strong and ours is, as I told you, an addiction. We are like two elements which are safe when separated but _explosive_ when together. But know, every day I long for us to be together in that way. Every night I still wish I were lying in your arms. I wish it so much my darling Mathew.

I am glad that Suzanne is there for you. I would not have wanted you to be alone. That last night, I was so convinced we couldn't work out the problems which stood between us. Sitting here today I know I was wrong but that night I didn't want you to be alone.

She was in one picture you sent me with a letter, a few years ago. You, Suzanne and William were all in it. She is _such_ a beautiful woman and the way she was looking at you spoke volumes of how much she loves you.

It was a photograph at once beautiful and heartbreaking. I wished it was a photograph of us Mathew. You will never know how much I wished that. If not for that one night it _would_ have been.

I have reached a point where I cannot continue with this letter. I do not need tell you how much I love you. It is simply a fact of our lives.

Please write when you are able. Yes between us it is more honest than speaking on the telephone. I have noticed that also. It is somehow safer to write the words than to speak them. Be happy Mathew. _For both of us._

All of my love...and, yes, Forever

Joanna

Chapter 29

THE SIGNING

The line to the table where Professor Wolffchandz sat with a stack of his books for signing was a short one, but it *was* a Tuesday night and threatening rain. Matt hoped that was the primary reason for the not-very-large turnout. He also recalled the Professor had titled the book, "A History of Hermann Göring's decisions in World War II" and histories were normally not known to sell in large numbers and the title was not very exciting. Histories written about Nazis other than Hitler himself hadn't done well. It was true people were still fascinated by Adolph Hitler as the ultimate representation of political evil and that alone was enough to still sell books about him, even now, more than twenty years after the war.

It was only a few short minutes before Matt was standing in front of the book's author. He decided to greet him using the German he had learned during his time as a P.O.W. in Stalag Luft III back in the winter of '44 until the early spring of '45. Then he had spoken the language nearly as well as a native Berliner. He had learned it in hopes it would prove useful in an escape.

"Guten abend, Herr Professor Wolffchandz."

The man seated in front of him looked up sharply at Matt, a touch of surprise registering in his grey eyes. When he saw the well-cut business suit and striped tie, he relaxed and returned the greeting in perfect English.

"And a good evening to you sir."

Matt smiled and said in reply, "Sorry about the greeting in German. I had no idea your English would be so perfect, besides... I once prided myself on my German. Of course that was long ago. More than twenty years past. My German has probably gotten rusty. Out of practice."

The Professor smiled in return before telling Matt, "Nein. Und dein Deutsch ist gut zu."

Matt gave both men a small chuckle when he said, "Yes Professor, but not nearly as flawless as your English. So let's use that."

"Excellent." The Professor stood and extended his hand. Matt shook it with warmth which surprised him as the man was a stranger. He had,

435

after all, barely met this man and yet he was already finding something about this graying at the temples, somewhat past middle age professor, which he liked.

"Twenty years ago?" the Professor asked Matt. "That would have been during the War."

"Yes Professor, I had to come down tonight and get a copy of your book. You see, what you have written about Göring fills in some unanswered questions about a time out of my life which has puzzled me all these years."

Professor Wolffchandz had a quizzical look on his face as he asked, "Oh, and how is that Mister... I am sorry. I must have missed your name?"

Matt realized he had not introduced himself and did so. "My name is Mathew Weldon. During the War I piloted an American B-17 named 'The Maid of Barley' from 1943 until mid 1944. Prior to that time, I was a bomber pilot for the RAF.

"Until I saw you on 'Morning in New York' today, I only knew some of the story about the day I was shot down and the strange events which followed. The part I had knowledge of was only because the camp Kommandant was kind enough to tell me what he knew. It may be difficult to believe this, but that was only a few minutes before he advised me of how to 'escape'."

Wolffchandz's eyes grew large behind the steel-rimmed glasses he wore as he exclaimed, "Mien Gott Im Himmel!" The few people waiting in line sensed the Professor's sudden excitement and broke their orderly line to crowd closer to the two men.

Matt found his hand being shaken once again, this time far more enthusiastically as the Professor exclaimed, "I am so very glad to meet you Mathew Weldon. <u>Captain</u> Weldon as I recall. I have thought of you often over the years and quite frequently as I wrote the book. I always hoped you had survived the War. The last information I received was that you simply disappeared when the officers were transferred from Stalag Luft III to a prison near Nuremberg. What happened to you?"

The crowd had been looking and listening to the author and now turned in Matt's direction. He could not help but see that it had grown larger and was attracting even more people by the minute. He noticed them drifting over from other parts of the three-story book store. They all remained silent, as if any sound on their part might end this encounter.

436

Matt decided to make his answer into as good a story as he could and still not embroider the truth.... It might help the sale of the Professor's book tonight.

"Well," he began, "I had been in the camp for almost eleven months on the day we were to be moved. My hip had been badly injured shortly after I got my B-17 'The Maid of Barley' down in a field about 70 miles outside Berlin. She was badly shot-up on one wing. No way could I have flown her back to England. I was able to get my crew out safely; they all parachuted down without incident. Of course I only learned that later.

"The damnedest thing was, the fighter pilots who shot up 'The Maid' with surgical precision and then prevented another German pilot from finishing her off were the same two guys who helped me get her down more or less in one piece. We talked back and forth on the radio as I was taking her down. I was glad to see they were 'Yellow Noses.' They were called that because the noses of their Focke-Wulf fighter planes were painted yellow with another yellow band just before the tail surfaces. I knew they were some of the best remaining pilots Germany had at that point in the War."

The Professor nodded to let Matt know he knew about this.

"One of the two spoke pretty fluent English and at first kept telling me my crew was safely out and under silk, so it was time for me to jump. He said he and his wing man had seen far too much blood and too many aircrews dying in their planes; that a few of the older fighter pilots only tried to shoot a bomber up so it couldn't make it back to England, but could remain in the air long enough for the crew to get out alive."

"That German pilot listened as I told him how much 'The Maid' meant to me, because she was named for the woman in England I loved. I told him I wanted to try and put her down in as close to one piece as I could. He seemed to understand, though he kept saying it was foolish, but that the two of them would ride down with me and keep their eyes on her condition. He made me promise that if he said get out, I would do so. I assured him I would abide by his evaluation and jump if he said to. I wanted to get back to the real girl in one piece, after all.

"Those two pilots were beyond excellent. They flew perfect formation with me; one on each side just past my wing tips. Between the three of us, God alone knows how many military regulations we broke during those few minutes.

"I had already been awarded Army Air Corp medals, but the highest award I ever received was when that German wing man, Major Von Altenburg said, "The other pilot flying with me, Günter, asked me to tell

437

you, 'You are a hell of a good pilot.' He also wants to know if you are a converted fighter pilot." That means a pilot who had once flown fighter planes but had been re-assigned to fly bombers.

"They pointed me toward a piece of reasonably flat ground, probably some farmer's unplowed field and helped me put her down in nearly one piece. They circled above me one time, then wiggled their wings in salute and flew away."

Several people in the crowd actually clapped, then looked embarrassed at having interrupted him.

Matt smiled at the applause and said, "Those two German pilots deserved applause that day. I would have returned their salute with one of my own if I'd had the means to do so. All I could do was say thanks over the radio. I then got busy destroying the Norden Bomb Sight and some other classified equipment that all B-17 pilots were instructed to destroy if a plane went down in one piece. We were issued several devices which looked pretty much like standard army-issue hand grenades, but these were special thermite grenades. Each small metal cylinder burned at extremely high temperatures, so they literally melted the items in question into puddles of unrecognizable metal. I added any papers I thought could be of help to the enemy, so nothing of value remained when I was finished.

"By the time I completed my task and was outside 'The Maid,' less than half an hour had passed. That is when my initial captors arrived bouncing over the field in a dark gray truck with a canvas top. The truck stopped some distance from my burning B-17 and out of the vehicle poured a mix of two young soldiers, not much more than boys really, and five men in their very late fifties and early to mid sixties.

"One of the young ones ran from the truck cursing me as he approached. When he was right in front of me he hit me in the stomach with the steel plate on the butt of his rifle, causing me to fall to the ground. He kicked me hard on my left hip. I thought he had broken it. The pain was that severe. It was only later I learned he had only ruptured the tendons and badly damaged some muscles.

"Luckily a Sergeant in his fifties forced the boy to move away and gave him a dressing down that sounded as painful as my hip felt. The boy had his rifle pointed at me as I lay on the ground; I was sure I was about to be shot. The Sergeant screamed something at the boy which made him back away from me white as a sheet and laid his gun on the ground. He stayed away from both me and the Sergeant from then on.

"The Sergeant had two soldiers help me to the truck and gave me a drink of something from his canteen that was as hard on my throat as the boy's boot had been on my hip, but after a few minutes the pain did subside. The trip to a holding location took the better part of an hour and by then my hip was throbbing to beat the band. The Sergeant seemed to sense it and gave me another drink of whatever it was. That helped reduce the level of pain; at least in my hip. My throat was once again on fire. By then I was flying pretty high.

"I kept reminding myself of the old military mantra, 'Name, Rank and serial number.' You only give the enemy your name, rank and serial number. I never learned the name of the town that I was initially taken to, but they put me in what seemed a regular civilian jail cell and kept me there for two days. No one even asked my name rank or serial number. In fact they didn't ask me anything. Morning and night they brought me food. What I believed to be a regular Army soldier favored me with a single word of English, "Eat." My only companion was the pain in my hip but now the Sergeant was not around to offer both his and my favorite pain killer. I missed both of them. The pain killer most of all.

"Early in the morning of the third day, a force of over fifty men in several armored vehicles arrived armed-to-the-teeth and, after a very noisy conversation with whoever had been holding me, removed me from the jail cell, dragged me outside, threw me into one of the armored half tracks, climbed in beside me, slammed the steel doors and off we went. All of this without a single word to me. I asked several questions which were greeted with a wall of silence so I decided that either no one understood any English at all or something was happening that I clearly did not understand. I was, however certain it was outside normal treatment of captured fliers. Germany could not have afforded this much bother for every flier who was shot down.

"This armored convoy traveled for four hours by my watch until it finally paused while some lengthy conversation passed, then gates were opened and the vehicles proceeded forward a short distance.

"When the back doors were opened, I found myself blinking in the sunlight of an exercise yard or inspection ground of what I later learned was Stalag Loft III.

"It was a very large prisoner of war camp run by the German Luftwaffe, the German Air Force as you know. It was headed by General Hermann Göring, its Supreme Commander.

"Until I heard and saw the Professor on T.V. this morning, I had no idea that Göring had any part in my life what-so-ever and yet it seems he did indeed; that myself and my crew were the rope in a tug of war between him on one side and Heinrich Himmler and Joseph Goebbels on the other. Fortunately for us, Göring won or we would have all been executed."

The crowd was still hanging on Matt's every word but no one standing there had bought a single book. He knew it was time to wrap up his part of the story and hope his audience would be interested enough to want the whole story of Göring's part in World War Two, in which he himself was only a small part. No more than a tiny incident in a huge conflagration.

"But to answer your question Professor, I was in the camp for the better part of a year and involved in two escape attempts which were for me, unsuccessful. However one attempt did allow a large group to escape. Tragically most of the escapees were shot when they were recaptured. In fact, they were slaughtered.

"The Kommandant of the camp, a man named Wilhelm von Lindeiner, as honorable a man as I ever met, was furious. Before commanding the camp he had been a member of Göring's personal staff. If he could have, I believe he would have personally killed the Gestapo who shot the escapees.

"A few months later, when Russia's Second Ukrainian Army of Marshall Ivan Konev was less than twenty miles away and closing toward the Camp, orders came to move us to another location. At that time, Kommandant von Lindeiner had me brought to his office and told me what little he knew about my situation and that of my crew. That all of my letters to my girl in England and to my father in America were sent to Berlin where he felt sure they were destroyed, but was never told why. He also knew the same was being done to all letters from my crew members who had been scattered to camps all over Germany. He said it was obvious to him we were all treated as dead.

"He then suggested if I were to fall out of ranks I could simply disappear from the march the next day. Orders had been issued to the guards, mostly old men like the ones in the party which captured me that they were not to shoot anyone too weak to finish the march. The Kommandant had given the order to honor the Geneva Convention on the treatment of prisoners.

"That was the course of action I followed and with my hip still in pain, it was not an acting job lacking in credibility.

"It was only a few days until I reached American Army Lines. It took awhile to convince them who I was. The Germans had reported me and my crew dead. Each crewmember of the 'Maid' had the same problem. When you are reported to the military as dead, it upsets them greatly when you are not. So much additional paperwork in triplicate to bring you back to life."

"So, Professor, I hope that answers one very small question in your book."

His still rapt audience gave him a round of polite applause, this time with no embarrassment. He heard one man say under his breath, "*Hell* of a story," and an attractive young girl in her early twenties say, "Wow."

He turned to the Professor who had finally sat back down and finished his answer with, "I owe you an apology. I have kept these people from buying your book. I hope you will allow me the honor of buying the next one and that you will inscribe it to 'Matt & Suzanne Weldon'."

Professor Wolffchandz smiled up at Matt and said, "I think a bit more than that is in order," and wrote a long and glowing inscription on the blank cover page, then asked if Matt could sit with him a while. Matt said he would be delighted.

The night manager brought a chair over so Matt was seated next to the professor, then immediately found he was also being asked to sign the book. When he looked at the Professor, he received a warm smile and nod of the head with a simple, "Of course you should."

Almost everyone who purchased a book handed it to Matt after the author had written his inscription. The addition Matt made was a simple and consistent, "Mathew Weldon – pilot of The Maid of Barley 1943 to 1944, POW 1944-1945." Sales remained brisk for well over two hours so more than two hundred and fifty books were sold before the line finally played out.

Matt was surprised to find he had been in the store for over three and a half hours. As the last few customers were presenting books for signature, a harried-looking young man sporting wet hair, a black turtleneck and black slacks walked up to the Professor and introduced himself as Thomas Rolf, the "New York Times" book review editor. In rapid-fire speech he said, "The night manager called me at home saying there was a story happening that would make a good column for the paper as well as a good book review for me. That he was convinced I really must come down. "

The Professor continued his inscription for the buyer standing in front of him, obviously somewhat irritated by the young man's self important attitude. He glanced up and said, "Just a moment please while I finish this."

He completed writing what had been requested, returned the book to its new owner, smiled and said, "Thank you and I hope you enjoy it."

He paused for a moment before turning back to the Times Editor. "Now, young man, how may I help you?"

The newspaper man was quite irritated at the lack of respect from this author (an author, at that, who he had never even heard of.) His reply was chilly when he said, "What can you do for me? No, it's what I can do for you. A book review by me in the 'New York Times' can make or break a famous author, and I certainly have never even heard of you!"

Matt rose to his feet, grabbed the young man by one shoulder and turned him so they were face to face. No more than inches apart, he gave him a look which made the young editor take two steps back.

"I don't know whether the Professor is famous or not. We have only met tonight. I do know he has written a book people should read because it is about things which happened in a tragic War long before you were out of diapers - sonny. It is about the people who caused the War and he was closer to one of those men than nearly anyone else. I am stepping into this, young man, to protect your person. You see, during World War Two, the Professor was a member of the German SS Division. Perhaps you have heard of them? Some of the toughest S.O.B.s, (sorry Professor but it is true,) the world ever saw." Matt turned and gave Wolffchandz a quick wink before looking back at the now pale young man before him. "Now I am certain with a bit more reasonable attitude from you, he would be delighted to see that you get an excellent story, an exclusive which other newspapers around the country would pickup with, of course, your by-line attached."

The young reporter turned to the Professor and started over. "I am sorry. I *was* rude and hope we can begin again. I would like to know about your book and have a chance to sit down with you. Is it true you were SS during the war?"

"Yes Mr. Rolf, I was SS. I wore the uniform of that military unit. In fact, I was an officer in the SS. However, after one year on the Russian Front, I spent the rest of the War as not much more than a glorified messenger between Berlin and Hermann Göring, who was, I am certain you know, head of the Luftwaffe. In effect, I was a delivery boy for top secret messages who wore a black uniform and a silver death's head on my uniform collars. The job gave me constant contact with the second most powerful man in Germany, behind only Adolf Hitler.

"In historical context, it was access to how and why many decisions were made and their effect on the direction of the War. Because we saw each other so often, he did on occasion, discuss his decisions with me."

Matt turned toward the "Times" book review editor and said, "And one of those very minor decisions is the reason I am standing here alive tonight buying the Professor's book."

The young man asked Matt, "I am sorry sir, I didn't get your name and I would love to know what happened."

Matt had no intention of repeating the story he had so recently recounted in detail, so he responded with the short version. "My name is Matthew Weldon IV. I flew a B-17 on raids over Germany and was shot down with my crew on our twenty-fourth mission on a raid over Berlin. Joseph Goebbels and Heinrich Himmler both were determined to have me and my crew shot. It was only the intervention of Göring which prevented our execution. Might I add, it is my guess the Professor had some part in that decision. I've no doubt he has down-played his role to that of a mere message-boy to Hermann Göring. He has certainly shed light on a mystery which has puzzled me for over twenty years."

The reporter had taken notes rapidly as Matt spoke. Then he suddenly stopped and looked up, startled. "Matthew Weldon IV? THE Matthew Weldon IV? Empire National Bank Matthew Weldon IV?"

Matt simply smiled and nodded.

"You flew B-17s in WWII? And were shot down over Germany? And a decision by Hermann Göring saved your life? My God, man. And that is in the Professor's book?"

Matt smiled quizzically at the Professor who nodded his head once again.

By now the young man knew this was a book review he *had* to write for this Sunday's book review section. And he knew the part he would feature as the leading paragraph. He was glad he had reined in his ego and not walked out on these two old warriors. Despite the Professor's attempt to play down his part in the military, the young man sensed this ageing professor had been far tougher than he looked tonight.

Matt turned to Professor Wolffchandz, "Professor, I really hate to leave, but it has gotten late and my wife is probably starting to worry a bit. She knew I was coming tonight, in fact she suggested it, but I really should have called her by now and I haven't. I lost track of time."

The Professor shook his hand and said, "One last question if I may before you go? The plane's name, 'Maid of Barley.' The girl it was named for. Did you two get together?"

"No, Professor. She believed I was dead. Then there were other problems which prevented us from being together. Like so many things during the War, we just couldn't rebuild what we once had. But I am married to a wonderful woman and we have a son. How about you? Have you married?"

Wolffchandz smiled back and replied, "Yes, when I reached full professorial status, I married a young lady from England who was doing research at the University in Medieval German history. We have two beautiful daughters. It seems the ironies from our War never cease."

Matt handed him a card saying, "Please call before you leave town so we can exchange contact information. I would like to keep in touch, because of our common experience on opposite sides of the same coin. There is so much more I would like to know."

Before leaving, he shook hands with the young reporter, gave him a smile in parting and said, "I will look forward to reading your piece in the paper. It is not often that one gets to discover a book with meaning on a Tuesday night." Then he turned and walked out of the store into a slow-falling rain which reminded him of the London he had once known so well.

These many years later he still carried his old black umbrella from those days. It was almost a talisman to him.

Chapter 30

LETTERS 1970

Dear Joanna,   Jan 5, 1970
   1969 has passed away and been replaced by 1970,
the New Year. It happens so quickly now it causes me
to wonder where the years have all gone.
   '69 was a year of notable events over here. Ike
died. His death brought the War back to many of us
here in America. He was always so steady. First as
Supreme Commander of the Allied Forces in the
European Theatre, then as our President. In '69 the
population in the States topped 200 million. An
artificial heart has been implanted in a human
patient: once perfected it may extend many thousands
of lives. Judy Garland died this past year. But you
know that. It happened over there in London. How many
times did we listen to her on the radio during the
war years? Remember "Somewhere Over the Rainbow?"
   Nixon is finally getting his turn as President. He
has promised to try to end the war in Vietnam. He
can't keep that promise fast enough to satisfy the
peace protestors. America's second war since the last
time I saw you. Korea and now Vietnam. We had hoped
ours would end them for good.
   It often seems only yesterday that I was a young
man going down the gang-plank of the Queen Mary.
Setting foot for the first time on English soil. That
young man expected to be there perhaps six months.
Sent by his father to find out if England could
survive a war with Germany. Of course you know the
young man was me and the year was 1939. Over thirty
years ago now.
   Shortly after I arrived, I went to a party in
London and met a most entrancingly beautiful young
woman. She had the most intriguing green eyes I had
ever seen or have seen to this day. I fell under a
wonderful enchantment and soon knew I was deeply in
love with her. She was my first love. To me, she was
the very definition of love itself. And you are
still.

We had a snowy Christmas all through New England this year. It took me back to the Christmas I spent with you and your family at Barton Hall in 1941. I remember your mother saying the tree was perfect and that I should help decorate it every year. I couldn't imagine not doing it from then on. I felt already a member of your family. I remember the kiss you gave me as we stood by the tree and the message it carried. It told your family we were together and would be. It was the best Christmas I have ever had. Being with you made that true.

Even though it did not work out as we would have wished it, I am very grateful I met you and will never regret having loved you. Thank you for loving me in return and for the son we have. I know you have raised him well so I am sure he is a fine young man. He is about the age I was when our War ended in '45.

I see the years we were together as a time of enchantment now. There was a magic about it which, even today, makes those years seem more dream than reality, yet they were real. Even in the middle of the War, simply being with you was always beyond any happiness I could have imagined. Almost like living within a fairy tale which had become reality. You should never ask yourself or doubt for a moment whether I love you still. Simply know you will have my love forever.

Imagine a staid old banker telling you that. For it is what I am now. I wish I could express my feelings for you better but the muse who once sat beside me has been buried under too many business letters.

The first time we made love in the barley field under a mystic tree with intoxicating, ruby berries, (our 'wedding day') seems only a short time ago. Not too surprising because the last night we spent together seems only moments in the past. I know nothing we did together will ever fade from my memory.

I sometimes try to believe we were only two ordinary people who had each fallen in love for the first time and that was the source of the magic we felt. Yet I am never able to convince myself of that. What we had was very rare. There was nothing ordinary about our love for each other.

I understand why you have not wanted me to come to England. Even now, years later, I know you are right about what would happen if I did. Neither of us would wish it, but the desire would be irresistible. And yes, it would destroy too many lives if we let it happen. Like you, my hunger to be one is still there. Only a wide ocean keeps it safely in check.

My William is almost 23. Like **our** Mathew, he has gone into the family business. I am proud of the way he is applying himself to learning banking from the ground up. Because of my War years, I had to jump past several rungs of the ladder when I returned. He started in the mail room and is now in the Investments Department. In a few years he will be ready to take over as President.

I am glad Mathew was ready to take over the Brewery when Owen passed. I know how important it was to have a Barton at the helm. He will do a superb job. He is your (our) child and could never fail at whatever he does. One of my great regrets is that I could not be there for him.

You and I are both heads of our respective families now. I wish I could have come over when your dad passed. But we both understand why that was not possible. He was certainly a great influence on my life during the years I was there. I will never be able to think of your father being gone. In my memory I will always see him sitting in his wonderfully disordered office. Puffing on one of his old Charatan pipes. Sitting in a London-like fog bank of tobacco smoke. Such wonderful memories of a great man.

I am sorry you never met my father. The two men were quite similar in many important ways. I hope someday to be nearly as good a man as they were. I only got to know dad when I came back from the War.

The War and you Joanna. The dividing lines in my life. With you I learned about what a wonderful thing loving and being loved is. The War taught me what a terrible thing hate is. The War was a dividing line in our countries as well. The America I returned to was far different from the one I left. The innocence was all gone. I know England changed because I was there and saw the changes happen.

Thank you for the promise you had me make on that last night we were together. The one I have kept. My only regret is having broken the first one I made you, yet at the time I felt compelled to do so. I know we have <u>both</u> paid for my doing that. I can only blame the results on fate. Kismet. Yet, if I had it to do over again, I am not sure I would change it. We had a great love. Perhaps beyond <u>any</u> other love. It may be that a love like ours also demands great sacrifice…and greatly have we both paid.

It was a love for <u>all</u> times and yes, as close to a forever thing as I can conceive. That last night we were together, you said we would have to be content to warm ourselves with the after-glow of the love we had. I am. The memories I have of you are wonderful. They never dim.

Thank you for insisting I find Suzanne. She and I have been very happy together. We need each other and we love each other. Both of us lost our <u>first</u> loves. It seems Kismet intended her and me to be together. And we are. You and she are the only women I have loved in my entire life.

For years I desperately longed for what we might have had together. That time has finally passed but I have also accepted that what we had was beyond exceptional. During the years we were together, we were like a single being in two bodies. We were joined spirits. I still feel you.

I hope you are well. Tell our son I am proud of him and if either you or he ever needs anything please let me know. I would like to do whatever I can for either of you. Write or call when you are able. I love hearing from you. Your voice is still as beautiful to me as any I have ever heard.

I don't know what you will make of this letter. I intended it to be a short hello, but it has taken on a life of its own. It seems very much a love letter to the past. If that is what it is…well so be it.

Yours and as always, with Love and Forever,

Mathew Weldon

Mathew Weldon

Dearest Mathew   *Feb 4, 1970*

Staid old banker you think? Hardly that, my love. Staid old bankers cannot write letters such as the one I received. You do not need a muse nor have you ever. Your writings have always been inspired. I have read and reread your letter many times. You must have known how badly I needed to read the words you wrote. I miss you so.

Yes, the years have passed very quickly. I will soon be fifty. I was not yet nineteen when we first met.

Oh my, yes. I remember the party and the devilishly handsome young man with clear, sky blue eyes.

The first time I looked in your eyes I was frightened. I saw <u>forever</u> there and I didn't want to. How could it be this man? I had been told you were only interested in women for sex. How then could you be my St. George? The pure knight in white armor I had always dreamed of. Yet in time that is what you became for me.

But on that night I believed we were being introduced only so you could seduce me. I was rude to you because of this misunderstanding on my part. We were nearly over before we began. But you didn't let me walk away. Thanks to you we became friends and, in time, oh so much more, Mathew. We became lovers. We were Friends and lovers. And together we have a son. And, I believe, a love like no other.

As you told me in your letter, never doubt I loved you then, still do and know I will eternally. I love you no less today than I did that wonderful day in the barley or that terrible night when we parted. I cherish even that sad night in my heart.

On that night I made the worst mistake of my life. I have had to live with that throughout these many years. The pain of it has never ended. I know it never will. I lost the life <u>we</u> should have had together.

Thank you for saying great loves may require great sacrifices. Yes my darling Mathew, greatly have we both paid. My only solace is in knowing that my mistake led to a happy future for you. As you pointed out we were like one soul in two bodies. When we danced on the last night we were together I could <u>feel</u> your love for me. I also felt your love for Suzanne. I am glad you are with her. I am glad you two have a son. I am so sorry you lost

449

your daughter. For _both_ of you; I regret Suzanne could have no other children.

Speaking of sons, ours becomes more like you with each passing year. I often need to remind myself he isn't. He looks so like you did that last night in 1947. He has your eyes and sandy brown hair. He even has the same comma of hair over his forehead. The only real difference is his English accent. Both of us love the MG you had delivered as a present on his 17th birthday. He takes great care of it and often drives me places in _his_ little car. Oh the memories that come back. All the places you and I traveled in your wonderful green MG. Those were the happiest days of my life. Being with you made them that.

Yes, much of our time together seems now like a wonderful love story that I read in a misty long ago. It is often hard to believe it actually happened to me. No, to the _two_ of us. Harder still to believe I let it (you) slip away. Kismet gave us two chances. I foolishly allowed the second one to pass by. You once told me about 'come hell or high water.' I should have married you then come hell or high water. Not doing so has cost me more than I could have imagined.

I miss my father very much. He was very loving and understanding. Owen was very fond of you Mathew. After the first time you met he said you seemed a nice young man and asked if I was going to see you again. I told him what I had heard about you. He said he didn't think I should make that decision based on rumors. I will always be grateful the two of us agreed to be friends. Dad saw something very good in you. Because of that I found the love of my life. My happiest six years. Yes Mathew, I will always feel we **were** married. I do until this day. Not according to the church perhaps; but in the eyes of heaven. I believe the words we spoke in the family chapel on the day we created our son in the barley field were as sacred as they could ever have been.

I will never know why we lost everything. Was it fated to end that way? Was it something we did that changed our future? I still feel we were meant to be together.

I miss you every night even these many years later. It is an ache that never goes away yet I would not trade our time together to be rid of the pain which followed.

Thank you for having loved me and for loving me still. It warms my heart my love. It lets me go on.

Forever my dearest one,

Joanna Shaylee Barton

Joanna Shaylee Barton

Dearest Joanna,   Feb.18, 1970

I received your letter of February 4th. We have always been honest with each other about everything. There are some things I need to say to you.

No Joanna my dear, I really am only a staid old banker now. There is little left of the young man you knew. When I see my old uniforms hanging in the closet, it's hard to believe I was the person who once wore them. However it is never hard to remember you. A day never passes I do not think of you. Of us when we were together and how we believed we always would be. We even spoke of growing old. I was certain if I could just survive my "25", we would never have to be apart. You were everything I wanted from life. It was a wish I made to the West Wind. Perhaps like the wish you made, mine may have, somehow, been flawed. My old roommate Kong once warned me my callous treatment of the women I knew before I met you might return to even the score. Perhaps it did. In reality, I do not know the reason for what happened, only the cost to both of us.

Please understand I love Suzanne very much. I am happy being with her. The promise you asked me to make about her was the right one and I have honored it. Not only then but every day since. I am convinced you and I would have been happy but that life is one we were not allowed to live.

You should never blame yourself we are not together. I simply hold the time we did have as a <u>great</u> gift. Joanna please know that each night I still wish I was holding you in my arms. Whenever Suzanne and I dance I am dancing with you also. I am glad I did not have to choose between the two of you. I do not know how I could have ever done that. When I think about it, I laugh remembering what I said the night we attended "Lisbon Story." The only happy ending would have been a 'Ménage a trois.' Great for me but, I am sure, not acceptable to either of you. (The foregoing is only an old joke if you remember. One you used to say you intended to hold me to. Then on an enchanted day in a field of barley and again on a sad night in New York, you did.)

I have said Suzanne and I have a happy life and we do. Largely. This does not mean we have a perfect life. No, there are times we disagree. There have been times we have raised our voices to each other. That happens even if people love deeply. After a while the fairy tale ends. Real life intrudes. If there is a perfect life between two people it is not lived on this earth.

In a way, you and I are lucky. The two of us get to have that perfect life together. Because we are not together. My being married to you would have been perfect. But only in my mind and, yes, my heart. Because we never had to face the day to day reality of it. The hundreds of little differences between us.

Suzanne and I often disagreed over William. She was far stricter with him than I would have been. She was right and I was wrong. If I had had my way he would probably been a copy of me when I was at Yale. Even though I knew she was right we still clashed, often heatedly. There were times we were quite angry when we spoke. You know it is really love if it survives those times. We have. I believe the love you and I had would have also gotten us through those times but we would have had them.

I feel you are blaming yourself we are not together. You must not do that. Until recently I blamed myself. I was wrong. Neither of us was to blame. There is no blame to place. I finally understand what it was about.

Kismet and family. Please follow me on this. You have a love of family and the history of family and

452

tradition. You taught me those values and I learned about my family and our traditions from my father when I returned from the War. Those were the things which decided our fates. Yours and mine. You could not leave England and I could not leave America. Remember that last night together?

You said I had to be in America to become President of Empire National and you had to be in England to help keep Old Oast House on track. Your brother couldn't (or didn't want to) do it. Our Mathew and my William with Suzanne. Think about them and the part they play in all this. Mathew Barton and William Weldon. A Barton to carry on your line and business and a Weldon to carry on mine. No we didn't get what we wished for but were given what we <u>both</u> needed.

Our lineages will carry forward beyond us as will our enterprises. Mathew has both Barton blood as well as Weldon blood. In him we will both live on together. That single fact may be worth the <u>shared pain</u> of our separation. I don't know why this has come to me so belatedly. I only know it must be the reason this all happened. We were intended to carry forward our names and we have. This was not random chance; it was intended to be by a greater power. We were given a great and magical love so this would happen. And so it did. Think on this my dear heart. It may make our separation easier to accept.

The last night we made love you said to think of us as a play which had ended. I now believe we are a play which has not ended. Our time together on the <u>same</u> stage may have but through our sons this play will continue. Hopefully into a far distant and happy future.

Also know I love you as much now as I did those many years ago.

I will <u>always</u> love you,

Mathew

Mathew

Mathew my love,   March 3, 1970

I have spent hours crying about your last letter. These have not been the bitter tears I have often shed over losing you. No these have been tears of a different sort. The kind I shed in the barley field after we made love. On that day I told you I was fully a woman and fully your woman. That remains as true today as it was on that day. Your letter has made my love for you even stronger.

Thanks to you I finally know _why_. Why we met and why we were parted. The answer is in _both_ our sons, our Mathew and your William.

Once I read your letter it was all so very clear to me. Yes, if we had married we might have had additional children but they would have carried the Weldon name. With Barton blood but Weldon's none the less. You are so clever to have seen this. Yes I can believe that it may have been Kismet all the while. Perhaps each step in our journey was planned long before we were born.

Yet Mathew, I do not believe it is the end of _our_ story. I can't explain why but I think there is more to come. Someday. For the first time in a long while I am hopeful about you and me.

I love you sweetheart. Please take care of yourself.

Your once and Forever love,

Joanna Shaylee Barton

Joanna Shaylee Barton

454

Chapter 31

THE RETURN TO ENGLAND

It was late afternoon and Matt's work day had almost drawn to a close. He had now filled the office of Empire National Bank President for twenty eight years.

Late afternoon sun streamed through the windows and washed across his desk, highlighting paintings of all the Bank's past presidents which hung on the wall behind him. His late father's portrait now hung in a prominent place among them.

Sunlight poured through the very windows his father had watched him fly past in 1939. That willful act which began the journey that had changed his life. Or had it?

He was sitting in the same chair his father had used that day and the title on the office door was little changed. Mathew Weldon IV., President & Chairman of the Board. Fate. The great flow of the ocean of time had carried him unerringly to where he was destined to be. Destiny, chance, fate or Joanna's 'Kismet.' What, he wondered, did she think about the paths their lives had taken in the thirty five years since the night they first met or the twenty seven since they parted? He only knew a day never passed he wasn't reminded of her. The memories of what they had and had lost were still painful.

1939 - The year it all began. Except for learning to fly, playing football for Yale and knowing Kong and Fizz, the rest seemed to him empty, wasted time. But then all the sweet swing music from those years came flooding back into his memory. Trumpets, trombones, saxophones, clarinets, piano, bass and the driving sound of the drums. Glen Miller, Tommy Dorsey, Benny Goodman, Harry James, Artie Shaw, Duke Ellington, Guy Lombardo and Count Basie and of course the jazz of Satchmo If we weren't dancing to them we were listening while we studied or parked and made out with our girls. Or danced at USO Clubs for only one night with women we would never see again during a War we would never forget. The college nights we danced away at the Band Box and other clubs. Nights under millions of sparking stars in springtime and blowing, swirling snow in winter. The snowball fights on

Hewitt Quadrangle. And always Dues, his still beautiful midnight blue Duesenberg.

The other car he had loved, the little MG had to be left behind in England when his War was over. A gift to "Mutt" Stanford, his second pilot in the RAF. Just as well... it held too many memories and needed a different owner to make new memories with. The Highlands of Scotland would do that for the little car and for "Mutt."

Duesy had been one constant in his life. He and Suzanne always took the wonderful old automobile out for a drive with any excuse; on every occasion. It was the first car they had ridden in together, to a dance at the Band Box one spring evening.

Come the third weekend in November, he and Suzanne would drive the XJ down to New Haven for the Yale-Harvard Game in the Yale Bowl. Before that Kong and Amy would fly in from Chicago. Then Suzanne and he would pick them up at LaGuardia and, as always, they would drive down together. It was always the start of a bitter-sweet weekend for them,

Duesy, Suzanne and the Bank; the primary constants in his life. Those and his love for Joanna. Both women had ridden with him in Duesy. Suzanne first, in the spring of 1938 and many times since. Joanna only once on a spring evening 1947 on the way to his top floor rooms in the warehouse. The night she said Duesy was "a beautiful racing stallion born to feel the wind in its mane."

Kong and Amy's love had survived the War. As soon as he was out of the hospital, he asked her to marry him. She said yes, and they had married on a lovely April afternoon in 1946. He was Kong's best man. Her Maid of Honor was her room-mate from her years at Wellesley.

The four of them usually get together several times a year around some Yale function. Once or twice a year in the fall at football games. *Always* for the Yale-Harvard game. Many of the players from the '38-'39 teams are there. It is always a long weekend of football, eating, drinking, dancing and remembering.

The dance band play songs from their youth, doing their best, but the Big Bands which defined the college years are largely gone now. Just as well because none of them can dance to every song any longer. Not like they could in those days. Most of the men drink more than they should, giving multiple toasts in remembrance of old friends who didn't return in 1945. He finds it embarrassing to admit; but that's the way it is. Their wives watch out for them and get them safely to a bed in the wee morning hours. For Kong and Matt, the little guy who is never there, Fizz, is *always* there and always missed.

Now, for all of them these are distant yet always poignant memories of a long-ago time and place. Echoes of their youthful innocence and desires.

~ ~ ~ ~

He was wrapping up his last few phone calls when Dianna Roth, his assistant, buzzed him on his intercom. "I am sorry to interrupt your call sir, but you have a caller on the line from England. His voice has an urgent sound to it. The party on the phone gave his name as Mathew Barton. He said to please tell you he was on the line and that you knew him even though the two of you have never spoken or met."

Matt instantly replied, "Yes, Miss Roth. Ask him to hold. I will only be a moment."

Matt got off his previous call in less than a minute and switched to the incoming one. "Hello, this is Mathew Weldon." It was only a moment until he heard his son's voice for the very first time.

"Mr. Weldon, I am Mathew Barton. My mother always told me I am..."

Matt interrupted him, "Yes, you *are* my son. I understand that fully even though the only time I saw you, it was from a distance and you were very small. That was over thirty years ago; summer of 1945 to be exact." Matt had detected stress and sadness in his son's voice.

"Sir, I came across your card from the Bank years ago when I was young and rambling thru the drawers of mother's desk, so I knew where it was to be found. Under the circumstances, I thought I should ring you up. Mother has died and I thought you of all people should be told."

Matt felt as if he had just been punched very hard in the solar plexus. He couldn't seem to draw breath. He heard what his son had told him, but he couldn't comprehend it.... It didn't seem possible that Joanna could have died. She was too young and represented life itself. She had once been everything he ever wanted from the world. How could she be gone? Had every beautiful and magical thing in life gone with her?

He finally found his voice and a bit shakily asked his son, "Forgive my silence. This is a great shock to me.... What happened?"

"It was a stroke, sir. There was no warning. It was very sudden. She seemed in good health until this happened. The stroke came early this evening. Her legs went out from under her and she fell to the floor. She had complained of a terrible headache; then it went away. Thank goodness I had just come in from the Brewery, so I was there with her. We carried her upstairs to her bed and a few minutes later she was gone. We called the doctor, but she passed before he arrived."

"Son, what are the arrangements? When will her service be?"

"Well sir, I am planning on closing the Brewery in tribute to her life and I have just started thinking about all of that. I imagine at least two or three days. We will have a service for her in Barton Hall's chapel."

"Yes Mathew. I will be coming over and I remember the way there. That is, if you do not object."

"No sir. I am sure she would have wanted you here with us at this time. Now that this has happened, I would like to finally meet and talk with you. To be frank sir, I should have called you before this happened but I was never sure of what to say. Should I hold off longer on setting the date for Mother's services?"

"No son. I have been reading about this new aircraft, the Concorde you English and the French have built. They say it can fly the Atlantic in a touch over three hours. I will leave on it tomorrow morning.

"Just to think, back in '42 it took a B-17 crew two days to get across from America. With an overnight stop in Newfoundland for refueling and rest of course. Makes me feel old just remembering those days. Flying was more a test of strength and endurance than skill. But I am rambling. Avoiding the reality of what you have told me.

"Your mother was a very great lady. Perhaps because she *was* your mother, you might not have noticed, but she was. In all the years since I met her, I have never known anyone else like her. This is a very sad day for both of us Mathew, but I will very much look forward to finally meeting you. It should have happened years ago."

There was a silence and Matt wondered if the connection had been broken. Then he heard, "Yes sir, it should have, but I don't think Mother could face seeing you again. Please just know that I will look forward to finally meeting you. One feels at loose ends not knowing their father, no matter how wonderful their mother was."

When he heard his son say this he did not know how to reply. "Well son, as you say we need to talk. I will see you day after tomorrow."

Matt decided he must tell Suzanne about Joanna's death while the two of them were face to face. It was not something he could do over the phone.

As he left, he told Dianna to cancel all his appointments and staff meetings and to please check her phone for possible messages from him sometime before morning. He would be gone for several days, perhaps a week or more and would stay in touch with her by telephone. If anything had to be handled, get his son William in the Loan Department to take care of it. He knew his boy was more than up to any task. Well, he should be. He had a Masters in Business Management and Finance. From Yale of course. A tradition continued. Matt knew only he had temporarily broken with it and that because of the coming war.

When he told Suzanne what had happened and what his plans were for the trip, her reaction quite surprised him. He knew she still harbored more than a little jealousy for the years he and Joanna had been together and deeply in love before he and she had found each other again and married.

It was one of the few times he had heard her use her 'this is the way it is going to be' tone of voice since William had grown up. "Matt, I am going with you. You have always gone out of your way to avoid trips to England. Even about important Bank business. You always managed to find an excuse to send someone else. I know she has become a ghost from yesterday which you still loved and yet couldn't face. Especially since that last time you saw her in New York years ago. Perhaps you don't know this, but both of us have done that. I spent years being afraid of her. I never insisted you go to England yourself because I believed if you saw her again... well, that I might still lose you. I knew if...well Matt I *think* you know. We must face this together just like we have faced everything else in our lives. That was the promise we made each other on the day we married. This will be a last good bye to the past from both of us: to her and to your War and, in a way," there was a catch in her voice as she continued "to my sailor too She deserves to be laid to rest with love and respect for all she gave you during those years. Remember Matt, she is as much a mother to a child of yours as I am."

Matt continued to be amazed by the beautiful woman standing before him. She was now fifty seven years old but to him her beauty only seemed to grow greater with each passing year. He still saw stardust in her hair when they walked on moon lit evenings. The love and passion he felt for her was stronger than ever. He could not deny that what she wanted them to do together was the right thing.

"You are right Suzanne. But then you usually are. Of course I will make reservations for both of us. I want you to be there with me."

They spent most of the evening packing enough for a weeklong trip as Matt had persuaded Suzanne that they should stay a few extra days. When she agreed, she looked him in his eyes and said, "Very well Matt,

459

but only if you will show me as much of England as the time allows and I want you to show me places you went with her.

"I have to come to grips with the love you two shared and it is time for you to quit being hurt by the fact it didn't work out.... The only way to handle ghosts is to face them where they live. As much as we can, I want us to go where you two went back then. I want you to take me to those places. We will make them our places too."

Matt considered her request and knew he could not deny her what she wanted. "As you said, 'we have always faced everything together.' The two of us are also going to do this together."

He wondered what had become of the base at Polebrook and the small villages surrounding it. There were also many other places with no military connection; those which resonated only in his heart, places Joanna had shared with him that Suzanne now wanted to see.

Changes must have occurred in the thirty years since the War ended. My God! How could it have been that long? Where had all those years gone so quickly? It seemed only yesterday when he came back from the War mourning a lost love and today he learned the one he mourned then was now gone forever. That word of hers...Forever.

Years before, Suzanne had questioned him about time on a snowy mid-winter's night. They were standing side-by-side on an arched bridge in softly blowing snow in Central Park. She spoke sadly of how little time we are given and how quickly it is gone. Only a few days later he thought he had lost her forever.

It was now twenty eight years since both that night and the night Joanna was in his arms. On a night in another world, she had given him up so he would be free to go to Suzanne. He knew it was a gift she had given; a sacrifice out of her great love for him. And he knew what it must have cost her because he knew what it cost him. Not just then, but in all the years since. He could still remember the words she said in that old warehouse space.

"It is not a choice between two women Mathew, but a choice between two lives you can live. You and Suzanne will make a better life together than you and I could. At least now. Once...well, that was then. You, my dearest love, know I love you. And no less than the day we first made love in the barley that summer's day years ago. That love has not changed and, for me, never will. But we missed our chance Mathew. The chance we had was years ago and it has slipped away. I know you love me. I know it beyond any doubt. But we have changed and there is no way back to that time for the two of us. We will simply have to go on in this life without each other, but with that love always alive between us.

"I do have one last thing to ask of you. I want you to make love with me tonight. One last night of loving together as if we were both condemned to die tomorrow."

They had talked about their years together in England and danced for a long time. Finally they made love slowly while both cried. Neither would have doubts about their shared love in years to come because of that night. It was the night they both learned making love could be so painfully heartbreaking for two people who *were* in love.

He had awakened the next morning to find her dressed and gone. In the kitchen was the breakfast she had cooked for him and a note with only three words. The three words he could never forget. "Forever...Love...Joanna."

The two of them had talked by phone a few times over the years. Mostly about their son, but when he would ask about coming over to visit "little Mathew," she always had a reason it would not be convenient "at this time."

Over the years since, they had exchanged the occasional letter. Hers always arrived in one of her ivory envelopes with the initials "JSB" on the reverse flap. She always enclosed a picture or two of their son. Matt watched him grow up in a handful of photographs: young Mathew as a three-year-old riding a tricycle, later at his sixth birthday party, when he was twelve in the snow at Christmas. Then there were two photographs of him at sixteen graduating from Secondary School and finally several of his graduation from King's College at twenty one. Joanna stood beside him in one of these. She was smiling the beautiful smile he remembered. It would be easy to believe she was his son's slightly older sister.

Matt always replied with gratitude for the photographs she sent and told her what he was doing at the Bank, what he was reading or plays and symphonies he and Suzanne had been to.

When he funded a new research building for Yale in the name of his late father, he sent her pictures of the building and one photograph of him cutting the ribbon.

They always exchanged cards at Christmas and he still occasionally dreamed of her. The only times the past came up were in letters they wrote in 1961 and 1970. Both knew not writing or talking about it only proved how painfully alive it remained to them. How much in love they still were. How dangerously present it was in both their lives.

461

It was a wound which, like his left hip, never really healed for either of them. And which neither really wanted healed. Both simply continued to cherish the pain and the love that went with it.

There was only one time she allowed him to completely understand why he shouldn't come to England. It happened when their son was turning eight and Matt was pushing harder than usual to come over and see him.

"Joanna, this is simply not fair. You always say he is 'our son.' 'Our' should include you and me; both of us. You always say he *knows* who I am. That little Mathew understands I am his father. He should at least see what I look like. And for me, seeing his picture is not at all the same as being with him. Do you think it is fair to continue keeping us apart?"

There had been a long silence. "No Mathew, it is not fair to *him*."

"Then can I come over?"

"No Mathew. You see it's not our son that I worry about. It's us. And it's Suzanne. It's really about your marriage.

"We have an addiction you and me. We are addicted to each other. That is why I have never let you come over. No matter the promises we would make ourselves, being in the same room would be like a reformed alcoholic taking a single drink. We would sleep together. And one night of making love would never again be enough. Not for either of us ever. You may tell yourself that wouldn't happen, but if you're honest about it, you know it would. We wouldn't be able stop and it would end your marriage." Matt could tell from her voice she was crying, "And the unforgivable thing is, I would be *glad* when it did. It's better this way. Better and yet awful. Awful because I still want that one drink. Please don't ever let me have it. I still depend on you to be the strong one." He had never pushed the issue again because he knew she was right.

Early the next morning, Suzanne and he took a Yellow Cab out to JFK. Even at that early hour the airport was teeming with business travelers. The ticket counters were all crowded and Matt was relieved to see that British Airways had a special counter for passengers on the Concorde.

Once they presented their passports, within five minutes they were holding their tickets. Matt already knew the seating was two side by side positions on each side of the aisle. Suzanne asked if he would mind her taking the window seat and he assured her he had seen enough of the earth from the windows of an aircraft to last him several lifetimes.

After their luggage was checked, they ate a light breakfast at one of the airport restaurants. The food was forgettably bland. My God, he thought, had the cook been trained by the Army Air Corps back in the forties? If so, he should be reaching retirement age soon. It would be a blessing for fliers leaving out of New York City. Back when I was eating food like this every day, I wondered if the food or the Germans would kill me first.

The flight across seemed to pass very quickly. Matt spent his time reviewing report filings for the Bank and reading some of the new banking regulations about lending procedures being issued by the Fed.

Suzanna passed her time reading John Updike's <u>A Month of Sundays</u>. When he asked her about it, she simply answered, "...Well, it is sort of like <u>Peyton Place</u> with a religious twist. It features a very over-sexed pastor who is sent to a recovery facility. The recovery doesn't take. Lots of kinky sex in here."

Matt flashed his teenage, slightly naughty, smile at her. "Well, take note of anything interesting or new and we'll try it."

"Oh, don't worry darling. I will! I hope you are still very athletic."

Matt quickly returned to his reading. She was pleased to see a slight blush appear on his cheeks. She had learned years ago to be as naughty as he was when he slipped briefly into his teenaged persona.

The attractive British Airways stewardess was soon on the intercom announcing their pending arrival at Heathrow Airport. Matt noticed that they all looked to be only slightly over twenty. He wondered if there was an age limit. Was it possible they only flew for a certain number of years? Was there an 'old stewardess' home' they were shipped off to when they reached old age? Say around thirty five?

In their dark navy knee-length skirts and jackets over white blouses and black high-heels, it was as if someone had hand sculpted and dressed one original, then just reproduced that one over and over. Even their short pageboy haircuts were nearly identical. Well, judging by the reactions of the middle aged men as drinks were served during the flight, neither their wardrobes or their figures went unappreciated. Oh well, all things considered it was far more pleasant than having a bunch of hairy guys doing the job. The ladies had charm, but a bunch of men...what a disaster his sex would make of a job like that.

~ ~ ~ ~

He and Suzanne were once again required to present their passports and assure the man behind the counter they were neither bringing fruit or vegetables nor huge amounts of currency into England. Once that was done, they moved on to the automobile rental counter.

He would have loved to rent an MG convertible, but he knew too many memories would ride with them. Even the new models would be a reminder of Joanna, so he requested an Aston Martin V8 convertible and when he asked they assured him that, yes, they had one in British racing green. It was a larger car and Matt knew it would be more comfortable for the two of them and their luggage. Large bags had never been a factor when he had the old MG. When the car was brought up the top was already down.

The weather was beautiful. It was June. The barley would be full grown as it had been the day Joanna had taken him into the field. She asked him to close his eyes and listen to the West Wind whispering to the barley. When she had told him to open his eyes and stood before him naked, he could image nothing more beautiful in heaven or on earth. She was a work of art beyond the statues sculpted by the best Greek or Roman sculptors. His eyes could not get enough of her. She was the most beautiful woman he had seen when she was dressed, but this... The curve of her hips. The swell and rise of her perfect breasts. Her long beautifully shaped legs. The copper-colored V at the bottom of her flat stomach. The glow of her skin in the warm sunlight.

Her arms had circled his neck as she kissed him. Her magnificent green eyes seemed to hold him in a wonderful spell. He felt intoxicated simply looking at her. Her shining copper hair moved with a life and fire of its own. The West Wind sighed and moaned as it blew through the barley fields. It was as though he were seeing it all through a fog. Yet it was a sunny day. Could the berry of the Rowan Tree have really caused him to feel that way? Its white blossoms had fallen all around them. She called it a magical tree and he believed it was. At least on *that* day.

She was totally spellbinding and he had known this was a moment in time that he wished could last for eternity.

When they were finally laying on the white table cloth in the barley together he felt as if he had never done anything like this before. What he had with her was beyond anything a mere mortal could ever know.

He knew it had been her first time. She had cried out at the start and when it was over she had tears running down her cheeks. He asked if he had hurt her. She said not much...well, a little at the beginning. He had wiped her tears away with his hand. Are you sure? Why then, he asked, are you crying? She kissed him almost shyly and told him she was crying because she was now totally his woman and would always be.

They had made vows to each other in the Chapel and now they had made love. No matter what might happen they truly would belong to each other forever. They were one. He loved her so much that it was beyond his ability to find the words to express it. All he could find to say was, "I *will* love you forever." At that moment, years ago, he had held everything he wanted in the entire world inside the circle of his arms.

Today was a warm day and the sun was out. A few clouds drifted lazily across the blue sky above where he was standing. But in his mind all he could see was that day with her.

"Matt dear, where have you gotten off to?" Suzanne's voice brought him back to the present from a great distance and a time long past. She was already seated and the young attendant was impatiently holding open the door on his side of the car.

I have been taken by a muse, he thought, a wonderful, green-eyed muse from years ago. Here I am back in England only an hour and I have slipped back thirty one years in time; I almost wish to see a sky full of Spitfires, Hurricanes and B-17s so I would know that was real. Then what I sadly know is true wouldn't be. Joanna wouldn't be dead.

I must get control of my memories. It is not 1939 and I will never hold her again. She is gone and forever has ended for us. I am cursed to remember; but can never recapture those years. Why does time go so quickly carry so much we love in its passage?

The main roads to downtown London from the airport were wider than he remembered and many new buildings rose above the surviving older ones. As they got nearer to town, Matt could see there were still empty holes in the skyline which had not been there before the war.

Suzanne asked him the occasional question. Usually about the older buildings so he reached back into his memories and told her as much as he could about each one. The roundabouts seemed to especially intrigue her.

"So they use these instead of traffic lights? It seems confusing Matt. How do you know who has the right of way?"

"They work as well as our traffic signals. At least they will if I remember to drive on the left and look to the right otherwise we are going to be very glad I took extra insurance when I rented the car. The last time I was here it was for almost six years and I still had to watch myself. If you see other cars coming straight at me please say something."

Hadn't he once said that to Joanna during their first year? Yes he was sure he had and she had said.....

"Oh, don't worry, Matt. If that happens you will hear me scream." It was Suzanne's voice but what she said to him was almost word for word what the other woman he had loved said to him in a much younger world.

He drove along the Thames on the Victoria Embankment and crossed Westminster Bridge. Then he made a few turns so they could go back across the bridge in the opposite direction. This allowed Suzanne to see the Parliament building and the clock tower of Big Ben directly in front of them.

"Oh Matt, it is truly beautiful. Photographs don't even begin to show how wonderful it is. It is history and art combined. I can see why you loved being here for so many years. I hope we will have time to stop and just wander around after...after...." She let it drift into the wind without finishing.

Matt understood why she couldn't finish. There are times when something you start can't be finished no matter how badly you wish it could. He knew it was true about both the things you say and things you do. Promises you once made which, somehow, forever go unfulfilled.

When he drove past the Bloody Tower he told her, "We will find time to tour the Tower and go on a river cruise down the Thames past the Parliament and Big Ben and on down the river to the Royal Observatory where every day on earth officially begins and ends. In a way it is where time is kept."

And, he thought, where they will tell you time is a constant. Seconds into minutes into hours. The hours into days and the days becoming months. Then years into centuries and centuries into millennia and millennia into eons. But it is all a lie. Some moments can last forever and others flash by so quickly that they are gone before you can touch them. Years become moments too quickly gone and moments become years and last forever. Joanna wanted forever and, in a way, we created it together in that one night. It became our forever. For us that night was beyond time itself. It will last until the sun burns away and only a cold dead cinder remains. Until the last tick of the clock. Until all the stars blink out and only a cold emptiness remains and time finally ends.

I do love Suzanne and I know Joanna was right. She was the one it was best for me to be with. To tell the truth Suzanne and I needed each other. The loss of our other loves made that our reality. She has been the perfect partner. Lover, wife and mother. Our son is much more a tribute to her than me. William is a fine young man. I know the Bank will continue to be in good hands when I am no longer there.

I love her and I am so glad I did not lose her. If not for Joanna I would have. I do not believe there could be a better life than I've had with her. No, not even the one I might have had with Joanna. I know it is only the 'what ifs' that damn me to question myself about 'what might have been' when I should not. I have never been able to accept that what happened was always what was meant to happen. Other possibilities existed somewhere. Perhaps there are parallel times where things happen differently.

The day was passing, so Matt broke his train of thought and turned the car in the direction of Kent and the hotel in downtown Canterbury where he had reserved a suite for two days with an option for a third. After they had checked in and were settled into their rooms, he phoned out to Barton Hall. Following a short conversation with his son he walked into the bedroom where Suzanne had already hung up her dresses and was arranging her other things in two drawers of the chest. Matt knew she was still a woman who could stop men in mid stride. Men years younger than both of them still turned to look at her when she passed. Of course a single scowl from him and they turned back around.

"Well," he said, "Joanna's services are tomorrow afternoon out at Barton Hall. They are scheduled to begin in the chapel at 2:30. I will need to order flowers to be sent out before twelve o'clock and we should set aside at least a few minutes so you can see Canterbury Cathedral."

The next morning they ate breakfast in a small restaurant near the Cathedral. Suzanne looked at her eggs with a puzzled expression before carefully setting the cooked tomato off to the side.

Matt laughed at the small, all too familiar, tableau. He chuckled because her reaction was exactly his first to an English breakfast when newly arrived from America. After they ate, the restaurant owner referred them to a florist down the street. They walked toward it enjoying the cool clear morning.

A small bell on the door of the floral shop announced their arrival and a middle aged woman emerged from the back wearing steel-rimmed glasses which sat half way down her nose. Looking over the tops she asked, "Might I be of some assistance?"

Matt explained the situation and described the flowers he wanted to have delivered for Joanna's funeral. Lilies in an arrangement with one perfect white orchid tied with bright green ribbon. She assured him that while she might be a bit pushed, she could get the job done and delivered on time. He gave her his American Express Card and told her if it was more expensive than her estimate she should simply charge the balance to it.

The two of them walked over to the Cathedral. Inside, he started telling Suzanne the history of this great Church. It was the lecture he had been given thirty-four years ago by Joanna; his guide to much of England's history.

"St. Augustine was sent from Rome by Pope Gregory as a missionary to England in 597 AD. He chose Canterbury as his seat and began building his 'Cathedra' in the town. In the hundreds of years which followed, it grew into the building we are in.

"Thomas Beckett was murdered here in 1170 for stating that his allegiance to the Pope and the Church was stronger than to the King. As time passed Beckett had excommunicated several English Archbishops who supported King Henry over the Church. On the 29th of December, four Knights of Henry's broke in on Beckett while he was at vespers. They stabbed him to death while he was kneeling at the altar. In the days following, miracles were reported to have happened all over England which was considered a sign Henry had caused the death of a saint. It nearly brought the King down."

They walked to the side aisle where the impressive raised tomb he remembered so well was sited. There lay the figure of a knight in full black armor atop the tomb with his hands on his chest held in a prayerful attitude. Matt remembered that now distant December day when Joanna had cried after telling him the story of the Prince who never became King.

"This fellow" he began "was Edward Woodstock – the Black Prince. He was Prince of Wales, Duke of Cornwall and Prince of Aquitaine, the eldest son of Edward III and a great warrior. He was never to ascend the Throne but fathered the next king, Richard II. The first Prince of Wales who failed to become King, he died one year before his father of a disease caught while fighting in France. Despite his importance in English history he has, strangely, been ignored by most English historians." The words he shared were, as well as he could remember them, the ones spoken by Joanna.

It was early and the Cathedral was largely empty so their footsteps echoed hollowly as they walked. He showed her the elaborate stained glass windows while giving her as much history as he could recall from his tour with Joanna on a snowy day before Christmas Eve back in 1941 only two weeks after Pearl Harbor was bombed.

He turned to her to explain how he had first seen the Cathedral in 1941 a short while after America's War started and that Joanna had been his guide.

He did not tell her that Joanna had pulled him behind a marble column and kissed him with great fire and passion or how she had cried. Had she somehow known that they would lose each other? That their time together was slipping away for them?

Matt realized he was using the visit to Canterbury Cathedral to keep his mind busy with a running commentary about the history of the building rather than face the bitter-sweet pain which being back in England and in this ancient building were causing him. He could see in her eyes that Suzanne was aware of the tumult he felt. She *always* was.

They walked slowly back through the morning to the hotel and went up to their suite to change for the funeral. He dressed in a fine dark charcoal grey suit while she wore a dark blue silk skirt and jacket and pale blue blouse.

Matt was always taken with her ability to somehow know exactly what to wear on any occasion. The two women he had loved had both always shown flawless taste. They were very different, yet a single word could describe both. Class. And, he knew, he had the amazing good fortune to have been loved by them and to love them in return.

They drove away from the hotel at 11:30. He knew the drive would take under an hour and that services were scheduled for mid-afternoon. It was a warm, sunny day so Matt drove slowly. The fields were covered with crops growing in lush profusion.

He remembered his first trip with Joanna from London down through Kent to Barton Hall; the drive where his eyes were almost overwhelmed by endless shades and intensities of green. He was lost in love that day and the world was still young and the future remained full of possibilities.

That weekend had been his first introduction to the area she called "the market basket of England." In his mind he could still see her in the little MG with her lustrous copper hair blowing back from her face and flashing in the sun, much like sparks rising from a wildfire.

Matt knew it was memories like these which had caused him to promise himself never to return to England. He had known if he ever returned he would see Joanna everywhere he went and in everything he did. England would always be the two of them young and so in love. Until now he had known if he ever returned, he would go to Joanna and they would surrender to a temptation too great for them to resist. He knew it was stay away or betray his wife's love and he would not do that.

Matt was a little surprised when Suzanne reached over to lay her hand on his leg. Both she and Joanna seemed able to understand what was going on inside him. She squeezed his leg and said... "It's really okay sweetheart. All of us have memories. Some good, some bad, and a few precious ones which are both at the same time."

Matt didn't know how to answer what she had said but he knew that she understood the confusion he was feeling. It was a thing he had come to accept over the years. How strange, Suzanne understands what I feel and Joanna could sense what I thought.

They passed the rest of the drive lost in silence and Matt soon saw the familiar twin obelisks which marked the turn to Barton Hall. The road, which had been graveled the last time, was now hard surfaced. He missed the sound of his tires rolling over the gravel, but at least the great house still looked as it had when he had driven away for the last time on that early summer's day in 1945. That afternoon he had never expected to see the house again. Well, he had long ago accepted that fate often makes our decisions for us.

~ ~ ~ ~

There were about twenty automobiles of different makes and models parked around the front of the house. He parked the Aston Martin as close to the small family cemetery as he could, then they walked to the big front door of the house and rang the bell.

The door was answered by a young lady in her twenties who bore a very startling resemblance to Joanna. Dressed in black, her eyes were green but not with quite the depth of color which Joanna's had always conveyed. But saw a look of recognition dawn in her eyes.

Before Matt could introduce Suzanne or himself the girl blurted out, "You are her American! Her Yank! I have seen pictures of you since I was a little girl. She had photos of you in your RAF Uniform *and* your 8th Air Force Uniform. Other pictures of you and her together. You are Mathew Weldon. I'm Patricia. Patricia Barton. My father was Alexander. I am his youngest. You will meet my brother Martin inside. I am so very pleased to finally meet you in person. You are practically a legend in our entire family. Joanna and Grandfather Owen told us many times about our Cousin Mathew's father. The young American who came over to find out if we could hold out against the German's before the War had started and how you met Aunt Joanna and that you fell in love with each other and the way you stayed here and fought the Germans as a bomber pilot and were shot down on your 24th mission. She told us you were reported dead. And that the Germans put you in a POW camp and burned all your letters so no one would know you were alive.

"That you two met again by accident two years later and you asked her to marry you and how badly she wanted to. But after talking a long time you both decided it wouldn't work. She said you had a bank you were going to have to head and that Grandfather needed her to help run the brewery. The distance had become too great between you. Many of us here today have heard about you since we were small. Aunt Joanna would put us to bed with your story. The story of *her* American. Many of us didn't realize it wasn't just a fairy tale until we were practically grown."

Matt saw Suzanne was looking from Patricia to him and back again. He could not tell how she felt about what she was hearing.

"Aunt Jo said there was another lady you had met. That after the last meeting between you and her that you married the other lady and were very happy. I am sure this must be the lady standing with you. Aunt Jo said the last time she saw you, she was told 'the woman I have met is beautiful and has hair which looks as if it has stardust sprinkled in it.' That description is certainly fitting."

Suzanne was smiling when she reached out and took Patricia's hand. "Thank you for the lovely compliment. I am Suzanne and, yes, Mathew and I married many years ago. I have long suspected your Aunt played more than a small part in that. Thank you for confirming it. I am very pleased to meet you. You are a very lovely young lady and from Matt's description of Joanna, I believe I can see a lot of her in you."

The young woman blushed while smiling a big smile and softly replied, "Thank you. To be compared to Aunt Jo is a great compliment." She waited a moment longer and said..."Let's go inside. Cousin Mathew has been waiting to meet you sir and I will show Mrs. Weldon a painting of Aunt Joanna which was done a few years ago. That is if you would like to see it," she added.

As they went in Matt thought, how like Joanna. How wonderfully like her. She has taken our story of Love and War and turned it into a family legend which will only grow as the years pass. It will now be passed from mother to child possibly for generations. She has made us both nearly immortal now and forever completely linked together. Well, in her honor I will try to live up to my part while I am here.

I suppose my part is that of the young knight who came from across the seas and fell in love with the fair princess. Who loved her and fought the evil dragon for her. Then they were separated by fate and when they

471

met again it was too late for their love. Too late. So the maiden sadly sent him to another love. A beautiful 'fairy tale' of the real story itself yet the facts are all in it... He could almost feel her breath as she whispered softly in his ear, "Continue to be *my* St. George, Mathew. *You always were you know*. I have given us, if not forever, the closest to it I could. Now we will live and love for a very long time indeed."

When they entered the large room where he had listened with Joanna, Owen and Mary Margaret to the BBC announcing the German attack on Poland and what amounted to the beginning of his War, it was again like slipping back in time thirty six years. The room was unchanged since that night. Even the old radio still sat where it had on that fateful night in 1939. At first he could not see a single change, and then he saw there was one.

Patricia had led Suzanne to a wall and hanging above Owens old desk was a large painting of Joanna Barton. Even in the diffused light from the windows Matt nearly expected to see her step down from the painting, walk up to him, put her arms around his neck and kiss him in the hungry way she did while they made love the very last night they were together.

The artist was undeniably talented and the painting was wonderfully accurate. She had a smile on her face which at first glance seemed happy until Matt realized the smile was Delphian, caught half way between happiness and sorrow.

A young man was walking toward him with his hand extended and Matt knew at once it was his son. It could be no one else. He had seen that same face in the mirror every morning from the time he was twenty until he was in his late thirties. Matt extended his hand and they shook while examining the other's eyes, recognizing the undeniable kinship there. Matt spoke first, "Well, I would ask if you are Mathew Barton but I *know* you are. I shaved that face every day until I lost it about twenty years ago. But it looks good on you. I am sorry we are meeting this way, but it is so good to finally meet you...*Son*"

The young man was still grasping Matt's hand when he raised his voice so he could be heard by everyone in the room. "Could I have your attention, please? I wish Mother could be here doing this, but she never could have. I think most of us understand why. This is my father Mathew Weldon from America. Mother and he met in 1939. They were in love. Very deeply in love. Well, no need for me to retell the story most of you have at one time or another heard from Mother since most of us were small and she recounted it far better than I ever could. All I will add to what she said is that I am my mother's only child, born out of two old and

472

honorable families and very proud of that. I am not only a Barton but also a Weldon. Family! Mother taught me nothing is more important than that except love. And if you have both, nothing else that happens in the world really matters." Matt could clearly see almost everyone in the room were Bartons or married to Bartons.

When Mathew finished speaking, they all crowded around Matt to shake his hand and ask questions. By their questions, he could tell that Joanna had been very open about their story but he also knew it had been dressed up and, yes, she had turned it into something midway between myth and fairytale. He was careful to leave it that way.

He only added small details about the big Hollywood star that came to fight in England because of a lost love and of the two German pilots who found the woman in the picture on the nose of the "Maid of Barley" so beautiful that they helped him land it in one piece. And how Clark Gable had found Joanna so striking that he said the painting on the plane paled by comparison and the way he had toasted them on the foggy night they became engaged in 1943.

Later they all walked as a group to the small stone chapel where Joanna's body lay in a mahogany coffin. The entire front wall inside the small building was covered in flower arrangements. One contained a perfect white orchid tied with a green ribbon.

Suzanne slipped something into Matt's hand. When he looked he found it was the sterling silver bracelet Joanna had given him on Christmas day in 1941. She leaned near him and whispered, "I took it from your drawer at home. I thought you might want to give her something from that time. Something that represented both of you and the time you were together. More than simply flowers. Something lasting."

Matt walked to the front of the small church and stood near where she lay for several minutes. He didn't want to look down because he hated to finally accept that she was really gone. He knew equally well that he had to look at her final time. He finally summoned enough will power to look down. It was as if she were only asleep. As if she waited only for his kiss to awaken her. The sleeping Princess awaiting her Prince's kiss.

She remained the great beauty he had loved. The drop with the chrome tourmaline he had given her the day they became engaged was at her throat on the white gold chain. She held a cutting of barley at her breast and on the hand holding it was their engagement ring. The wonderful copper hair cascaded over her shoulder. He laid the bracelet across her wrist.

Matt turned away already feeling tears forming in his eyes. Damn, he thought. Why her? Some few people are so special they should be allowed to live forever. At that moment he heard her voice whisper, *"We will Mathew. Forever."*

He was in a daze as the rest of the service passed and all he could do was remember what she was like when she was alive. He promised himself it was the only way he would ever think of her.

The service moved out to the family cemetery below the great oak and the coffin was placed in the newly turned earth. Each family member dropped a handful of earth on her coffin. Then two young men took up shovels and in a few short minutes her grave was covered. Matt almost felt as if he were under the dark rich earth with her. He prayed for the first time since he had flown in the War. It was a prayer and a blessing for her that he sent up to the heavens.

Their son walked over to him. Matt could tell there was something the boy wanted to say. During the service and the burial Matt could tell his son was quite moved, but he had held up without a quiver. People from other countries talked about the British 'stiff upper lip.' Matt had learned years ago their control didn't mean they didn't care. He was sure that in the entire world he was probably the only one to ever see Joanna cry but he knew she cared deeply about many things.

"Sir, there are things I want you to know. When I was small I asked Mother the kind of questions a small boy would ask about a father he had never met. She never misled me about you even when I was at that young. I once asked her if my father was alive. She said that you had been reported killed in the war but that yes, you were still alive. I asked if the two of you had been married and she said you had nearly married after the war ended but together the two of you had decided it would not work out. She also told me about the day in the Chapel. That in a way you *were* married. That you lived in America where you had returned once the war ended.

"I asked if the two of you had loved each other and she told me both of you had with all your hearts. That it was the War which had torn you apart.

"When I was older I asked her what love was and she told me 'it is doing what is best for someone you love even if it breaks your heart to do it.'

"She said you asked her to marry you and she wanted to but it was not what was best for both of you. Then she said 'You see Mathew, in our family we always do the right thing no matter how hard it may be.'

"When I asked her what you looked like she took me to our family chapel and pointed to the stained glass window of St. George and told me that was the way my father looked to her. I asked again when I was about fifteen and she told me to simply look in the mirror and I would know.

"She always called you her 'American.' She had a very great affection for you. In fact I believe she loved you until the day she died. I know she never took off the little engagement ring you had given her during the war. She is wearing it still.

"When I was about sixteen and starting to date we were talking about girls and being in love (or thinking I was) and she said to me, 'When you find the one you truly love and you are sure you want to spend the rest of your life with, then marry her. Let nothing stop you. Not even a war.' That was what came between you two somehow, wasn't it sir? The war."

What do I say to this son I have just met? Matt thought sadly. Of a woman I had once intended to spend the rest of my life with, but who loved me so much that she pretended it wouldn't work and refused what she must have wanted very badly. There is no way that I can ever express to him the love we once had. I am the only one left to remember what magic she brought into my life. No one left except me knows the West Wind whispered secrets to her or about a cat named Haiku who found her one rainy night. I am the only one who knows what it felt like to hold her while we danced that night at Café de Paris.

So many memories. How could we have loved so much in what now seems such a short space of time? How can I tell this son of ours how much his mother, the first real love of my life, still means to me even today? All these many years later. How do I explain to him that, if not for an accident of war, she would have been my wife? There will never be another like her. She was my first real love

She was right to send me to find Suzanne. The two of us have had a very good life and it has largely been a happy one. As nearly perfect a life as is possible in a real world.

But Joanna's words that last night will forever echo in my mind. "Mathew, we had our wonderful years of love and while I will always continue to love you I am certain you belong to her now. There would be too many difficulties to overcome between the two of us. You are soon to have a bank to preside over and I will have to largely run the Brewery. No, you must go and find her and do whatever it requires to get her to come back to you. The two of you are better suited to each other than we are now. You are both Americans and besides, I know you love her. You and I are not nineteen any longer though I will always be grateful we

475

once were. Mathew my dearest, the world we had then is gone like that film Gable made. 'Gone With the Wind.' Our world, yours and mine, was blown away by War."

"Yes son. It was the War. That awful War. It destroyed a lot of things. We had no choice but to fight that War and win it. But all of us were so young then. We made tragic mistakes in love. Some found a faux-love to hold on to because everything was so desperate and they needed something to anchor their lives. Many of them didn't know if they would see tomorrow (and many didn't) so they lived for today or simply for one night.

"But that was not the way it was for your mother and me. No son, our love was real. As real as the barley growing in the fields all around Barton Hall. Never think otherwise. Through an accident of fate and a misunderstanding we broke each other's hearts and only true love breaks hearts."

Suzanne left the group she had been talking with which included Alexander's son and daughter and walked over to stand beside her husband and take his hand. Matt gave her a smile, but she could tell it was forced. She was still astounded how much his son by Joanna looked like their son William. The two could nearly be identical twins. Of course Mathew Barton was a bit over three years older and their William had hair that was a touch lighter than his father's, but both were the same size and had their father's bluer-than-blue eyes that she had always loved.

In the house she had seen the large oil painting of Joanna. The woman was spectacularly beautiful. She could easily understand why Matt had loved her. She wondered, how did he ever choose me over such a grand beauty? There was an air of sophistication about her and yet the artist had also captured an aura of mystery. Suzanne had never seen eyes as green as Joanna's. They were vivid and even in the painting, so very alive. She also was certain she saw just a touch of sadness in the wonderful green eyes of the woman in the portrait.

What was it that Matt once told her about Joanna's middle name? Oh yes, Shaylee. He had told her it could mean Princess of the Fields but also Enchantress. Well, she could now understand how the woman in the painting could have easily been both. She had been wrong about the spell being of Matt's making. The spell had been cast by the two of them, together.

Suzanne knew she had spent years envying Joanna her time with Matt during the War and the love he had for her. But when she saw the portrait it was all gone. Washed away like the last leaves of fall after a heavy winter rain. She knew it was the only question which had remained unasked between them, which did he love the most? A question which now would never need answering.

Her man simply had two loves in his life. A love in his youth. A love which helped him survive an awful War. And their love. One which had proven its strength through good times and bad. Suzanne knew theirs was the kind of love which could survive anything life could and had thrown at it. How could she have ever thought he could decide which of his loves was truly the greater? She could only know that he had chosen to live out his life with her. And wasn't that all that really mattered?

Still holding Suzanne's hand Matt asked his son, "You said the stroke which took her was very quick. Could you tell if she was in any pain at the end?"

The young man thought for a moment. "No sir, I don't think she was. We got her to her bed and had already called the Doctor. Her eyes were open. She was looking at me so I took her hand. She was gone very quickly, but she looked right at me, smiled and said, 'Forever Mathew,' and she was gone...."

Matt saw a headstone leaned back against the truck of the tree. He knew it would be hers. He walked over to it with Suzanne. The inscription was deeply cut and easy to read. It would last a long time:

JOANNA SHAYLEE BARTON

JUNE 15, 1920 - MAY 18, 1975

WEEP NOT MY LOVE

YOU ARE WITH ME

FOREVER

He stood for a few minutes thinking on the inscription. She must have left specific instructions about the words to be carved into the stone. In coming years, other generations would stand there and wonder at the meaning but Matt knew. He understood because similar words were carved on his heart.

~ ~ ~ ~

For Joanna, he sent a silent prayer out to eternity. "If only I could live two lives. One as I have lived it in this lifetime and another the way I would have wished it to be. That one would be truly forever yours."

After everyone else had gone back to the house, Matt and Suzanne remained behind for awhile near Joanna's grave. They sat on the bench where he and Joanna had sat years before as she recounted the history of her family. She had pointed out her spot on the ground. Now she lay there next to her father and mother and brother next to a still empty spot. One she had said was for.... That long ago day she had said that would be the spot where her husband would lay. Forever. She had always wanted a love to last forever. Then Matt heard the West Wind whispering through the barley and he knew. It would and that love was for both of them.

They rose from the bench and hand in hand walked back toward the house lit from within now that the golden evening was coming on.

Matt's hip had never completely healed since the War and he was once again limping slightly. He closed the gate and paused a moment to look back. Her place was near the base of the giant oak which spread its branches over her.

Chapter 32

THE GREAT OAK

The great oak which towered above the small graveyard was thousands of years old. It had risen above the gently rolling land more than ten centuries before Barton Hall was built and the barley fields had first sprung from the surrounding soil.

It had memories on a level beyond anything the two fragile humans walking away from its trunk and spreading branches could ever comprehend.

Memories of a misty past when men in long robes and dirty white beards worshiped their long forgotten gods around its huge base and tried to perform magic with occasional success; the tree was sure it had recognized the word "Druids" associated with them. They had ceased gathering under its leafy branches many centuries ago.

Later other people had farmed the land and lived in small huts of earth and timber under its spreading canopy. Generations of them being born, living and then dying while scraping their meager existence from the earth which surrounded the ground into which the great oak was forever anchored.

Many years later the fields were carefully ploughed and sculpted and a single crop was cultivated in rolling acre upon acre as the barley was planted and began to thrust its heads skyward and the great stone house had been built. The hedges and gardens were laid-out and a plot of earth around the tree's trunk and under its branches was enclosed with waist high wrought iron fencing.

A small steeple crowned building also of stone and topped with a cross was built just outside the fence and soon upright stones began to appear on the ground around the base of the tree.

People would come out of the building dressed in black with a long box which they would put in the ground then cover with earth; each person dropping a handful of soil on the box. Afterward another upright stone would appear.

The oak, in what seemed only a few days past, remembered a small girl with vivid green eyes and her older brother laughing while playing hide and seek near the upright stones and around the base of its trunk.

The Oak also remembered a woman which it believed was a green eyed, grown-up version of the little girl. She and a stranger had gone into the small stone building and come out again and they had both ran laughing toward the barley fields. The tree had a vague memory of the same man later. It believed it had seen him again; perhaps years after the day he and the woman left the small stone building together. On that day the man had been dressed in a uniform which many young men had worn in those years. The tree was certain it was also the same man it had seen walking from the barley fields a short while later, then stopping, looking toward the big house, turning away and walking back through the fields slowly and sadly shaking his head. It didn't believe it was wrong but the Oak knew it did sometimes get events mixed-up. It had lived so long and had seen so very much in its lifetime that memories were sometimes clouded and confused.

If it was the same man who was here today; he had grown older. But then the tree was often surprised at how quickly these fragile beings aged and then were gone.

The oak often wondered, did they also grow wiser? It seemed they had such a short time to do so. What must it be like to be one of them? Almost as if they were born as the sun rose; grew old in the late afternoon and were gone by sunset. And yet, it pondered, they do seem to accomplish much in their short little lives.

The tree watched as the man turned away from the freshly turned earth he had sat in front of and he and the woman with him walked out of the fence. He turned and looked back for a few moments. Then he turned again and with the woman moved slowly away. He walked toward the path with a hint of a limp. The two of them moved along the path between the tall hedges toward the great stone house which was now fully lit as evening came on.

In its time on earth the tree had learned many things but only one fact seemed immutable. Everything which lived had a beginning and an ending and in-between those two points in time, lay their story.

The West Wind ruffled the tree's branches and leaves. This wind often whispered to the tree of the places it had been and the things it had seen in its travels but today it simply moved silently on. The tree saw it blow across the tops of the fields which surrounded it, making the barley appear as an ocean of gold with gently cresting waves in the golden light of the late afternoon sun.

By then the tree was lost in musing on thoughts of the wind and the sun and the stars and the endless reach of eternity.

Chapter 33

POST SCRIPT

As was his habit, Matt was in his office in the Bank on Monday morning at 7:30. He and Suzanne had returned on the Concord the previous Friday afternoon.

After all these years she still wore one of his white shirts to bed each night. To him it remained far more entrancing than anything else she could have worn and she still had a figure that would have set any teenage boy to dreaming erotic fantasies.

Their first night back she had turned toward him on the bed, a question in her eyes. "Matt, you have been very quiet tonight and you were clearly lost in thought on the flight back. What are you thinking about so deeply?"

"You know...about time passing. Remember that question you asked me late one night, years ago, while we were standing on a bridge in Central Park on a night of falling snow? It was on the night a New Year began. 1947. You questioned me about where time goes?

All I know *is* how quickly it gets away and all the things we have loved which it carried with it: Joanna of course, my father, your mother, our lost little Janie, Fizz and so many of my college friends from before the War. My RAF crew from 'E for Edward.' Your young sailor. All of them and *so* many others, gone now. So many that we knew, and some of them we loved deeply. All too soon gone. Leaving *only* their memories and empty places in our hearts.

"There are so many we loved, and once they are gone, it seems they were gone in the blink of an eye.... 'For we are such stuff as dreams are made on and our little lives are rounded with a sleep.'"

"If I remember correctly, that is from Shakespeare. Isn't it Matt?"

"Yes, my love, 'The Tempest.' The lines spoken by Prospero. About dreams within dreams. The ending of our little plays. Something Joanna made me promise to remember on a now long ago night.

"I am glad we went over together for her funeral. It was bittersweet. The passing of your first love is always sad if it was real. No matter how many years ago that love may have been. You had your Sailor and I had Joanna. You lost your first love earlier than I did. My loss is still too new for me to completely conceive. But I am glad you went with me. It was good we stayed the extra time and went places...well, the kind of places you asked me to take you. I hope it helped you understand how it was.

"We will go back now. I want us to finally get to know our other son. He is *ours* now you know. A gift to both of us from her. She raised him well. He seems a fine young man. Still, he should have parents. The two of us."

"Matt, I want you to know I am not envious of her any longer. I'm glad you loved someone until our time came. She taught you how to love and I am so grateful she did. Seeing the painting of her made a big difference to me. Strangely, I feel almost a kinship with her. We both loved you. In a way we were *both* married to you. We each had your son.

"You and I lost our little girl. I know we always call her 'Janie' but if she had lived we really should have named her Joanna. It is a fine name and I know now she was a fine lady. I hope, in time you will tell me more about her. About the two of you together, actually. I would like to finally tell you about my 'sailor' though it is a much shorter story. But it is time we talked about those things. If not for them, my darling, there would never have been us.

They fell asleep as they had for years with Suzanne spooning against him and his arms around her.

~ ~ ~ ~

Monday morning William knocked on the edge of the door frame to his father's office as he always did. It was his way to ask if Matt was busy. His father waved him in and William folded his lanky frame into one of the leather chairs in front of Matt's desk. They talked for nearly two hours about the occurrences of the past two weeks.

At the end of their talk, Matt asked his son to close the door. When William was once again looking at his father, he saw a look on his face he had never seen before. It was a look at once sad and happy.

"Son, the decisions you made during my absence were all first-rate. I expected no less. You know the history of our family, which is the history of ENB. They are as intertwined as the vines of the lilacs which cover the trees at our old place on Long Island.

"Your mother and I have decided we want more time together. There are places we want to see. I once said I had not seen much of my country and we both want to do that while we can enjoy it together. And we will be going back to England. There are people there *you* need to meet too, but before that I must tell you a story about my time in England before

482

the War started and during the War. I have told you too little about those years. It is hard for me to talk about that time. You know your mother and I went over for a lady's funeral. It is past time you knew about her and her son: your half-brother. If things had turned out differently she might have been your mother. These are things I should have told you long ago. They happened years before your mother and I married. It is a long story and soon I will tell you all of it. This is not the time or the place for that conversation but we will find the time and the place.

"In a year or so you will be named President of the Bank just as I hope you will someday have a son to follow you. I will hang on to the Chairmanship for awhile longer.

"We have many traditions in our family, but one above all. The Bank comes first. Well... the Bank and Family for the two are nearly synonymous. It is not always easy to hold to that tradition. Sometimes it is very painful, but it must be your guiding star.

"I want us to talk about a lot of things. Things we should have talked about some time ago. My fault we haven't, but I will make up that failing. We will be meeting regularly. You need to play more golf, by the way. Think of the course as another office and the clubhouse as a fraternity. You don't have to be a great golfer, just an adequate one. I was never as good as my Dad; in golf and in many other things."

By lunch time Matt began going through the stack of mail in his in-box. He used his green paper memo sheets to indicate the desired handling for each.

About half way down the stack was a large manila envelope with English stamps. He slit it open and a smaller ivory envelope fell onto his desk top along with a small box wrapped in green ribbon. For a few moments he could only stare at it. The envelope lay back-side facing up. The initials engraved into the flap were JSB. Without opening the enclosed envelope he picked up the large envelope it arrived in. It was postmarked Canterbury and dated five days before he and Suzanne had left for England. Four days before Joanna's death.

What a strange coincidence! She wrote this and posted it such a short time before she had the stroke. What could have been on her mind to cause her to write this letter? A letter which came before we returned from her funeral.

Matt finally picked up the small envelope and slit it open.

When he unfolded the sheets of ivory paper, her hand writing was still as precise as the first note he received from her in nineteen thirty nine; the invitation to tour the Brewery. That first small step in the long journey they had taken together. The journey which had so recently ended.

He was reading it with his eyes, but in his mind he heard her voice.

Dearest Mathew,   *May 14, 1975*

The West Wind has been whispering to me recently. It told me to write you this, my final letter. I think I had better do that today. The Wind has told me time is getting short. Because this is a last letter I can say things I have wanted to say to you for years. It can no longer harm anyone if I do so.

By the time you get this, you will have returned from your trip to England and have finally met our son. He is a fine young man and I hope you are as proud of him as I am. You can at last really be his father.

I am sorry you couldn't meet him before but, for the sake of you, myself and Suzanne, it was the only way. I know you are sad but the words engraved on my stone are my words to you.

In all our time together, I only lied to you about one thing. During our first trip out to Barton Hall you were telling me about my middle name: Shaylee. I pretended not to know its meaning so you told me. I already knew. I had for a long while.

You see, there was another Shaylee in our family. She lived in the early fifteen hundreds. A Barton son had traveled to Ireland and fallen in love with her while he was there.... She left her family and returned across the sea to England with him.

Some considered her a witch because her husband's fields produced abundantly and she had five children of whom none died. A rarity during those times. The legend is she had green eyes and copper hair. Her husband was Mathew Barton.

Do you not find it a strange coincidence that I was <u>Shaylee</u> from England and you were <u>Mathew</u> from across the sea?

I want you to understand clearly that I am not a witch. I didn't cast spells and I don't think she did either. I always believed she simply understood nature better than most. I have always had a love for the land and, yes, the West Wind **does** whisper to me. It has talked to me since I was a child, as you know.

Soon you will find it whispering to you. Or have you noticed it already? You will hear it as my voice speaking softly in your ear for I will be in the wind. I will be able to again kiss you as I have wished to these many years... now so quickly flown.

If you and I <u>were once</u> under a spell, it was one each cast on the other. A most loving spell with no evil to be found in it.

The awful thing is I look back on that terrible War with nostalgia. We were <u>together</u> then. That time haunts me and has since our last night together. I had not even returned to England, before I realized the mistake I made in leaving you. At that point, I tried to think only of what would be best for you. I should have considered what was best for us. I made a tragic error that night. I should have stayed with you whatever the cost. I have paid for that mistake every day and night in the long lonely years since. In a way that War cost us everything we loved.

I have not been inside the Brewery in over a year. Our son loves it and he is, in every respect, running it as well as Owen did. Better than I could. The love I had for it is gone. Even my love of family history is gone. All of that seems empty to me now. I am glad I passed both along to our Mathew years ago because all of those things have been burned away by my love for you. It is the only thing which remains. That will never go. It will remain with me after my crossing.

I know I love you as no one else ever has. Yes, even more than Suzanne, though she loves you greatly. You were my first and only love. The love I have for our child is a different kind of love. I love you so much there was no love left for anyone except him.

No one could have ever taken _your_ place in my heart. And that was as I wished it.

Please understand, Mathew, some wishes _do_ get granted. Not right away but in the broad sweep of time. Most of us consider time an enemy. It is not. We only remember what it has taken away. Not what it brings us. It brought you to me and it will bring us together again. And for us, passing centuries will seem as mere moments until we are joined once more.

You made a wish while you were in England. It was the _same_ wish I made sitting in a taxi just down the street from that old warehouse of yours, the day after the most wonderful, most heartbreaking night of my life. Knowing that wish would someday be granted was the only thing which kept me from running to you and begging you _not_ to let me go. I knew then, it was not the end for us. I know it still.

We both wished for a second chance and I _tell_ you we will have it. The second life we both have wished for. Together my Love.

Not soon. You will live to be old and full of wisdom. You will see your son and grandson President of the Bank and our two sons will become like true brothers. In time, my love, we will see each other again. Until then I will wait for you.

This time, my darling Mathew, it truly will be forever with no goodbyes.

I am enclosing a small box for you. It and my ring from you have been my most cherished possessions. It is time you had it my darling. This and my love are my final legacy to you. These and all the memories of our time together.

Yours always,

Shaylee

Matt looked for a long time at the small box which lay on his desk. It was wrapped with a green ribbon. Exactly like the one he remembered on the perfect white orchid he had sent her for their first night out.

He finally removed the ribbon and opened the box. Inside, carefully wrapped in white tissue paper was the locket and chain he had given Joanna back on Christmas Day in 1941.

He opened the locket and looked at the small pictures he had had painted to fit inside. God, he thought, we were so young then. Matt was wearing his RAF uniform. And Joanna was so beautiful, dressed in soft green silk. How in the world, he wondered, did we let it all go so awfully wrong? We were so close. We almost had everything. Together.

He sat looking at the open locket for a long time. Remembering. What seemed to him now another lifetime. In his mind he heard Joanna's voice from that long-ago Christmas telling him how much she loved his present. Her green eyes shining with love. He could clearly remember every word she had spoken that frozen winters day. She had told him when the locket was closed they would be kissing. He closed the locket knowing she had been right. Even about many things he had once doubted.

Matt knew the love they had shared in those years would last beyond them. If only in the stories she had told to the children and perhaps even in ways beyond his understanding. Who could say?

Yet the one question remained unanswered. The question asked of him so many years ago. The one which almost cost him Suzanne.

The question to which he *still* could give no answer: which of his two loves was the greater?

The love he had for the girl with the spellbinding green eyes. The captivating enchantress of his youth. To him she would *always* be the princess of the fields. The girl the west wind whispered its secrets to as it blew through the barley and tousled her beautiful copper hair. A young woman more beautiful than a perfect white orchid. The one he had loved more than his own life. He remembered how she had such devotion for the rich earth of Kent. That same dark earth in which she now lay; her life unceasingly "rounded with a sleep." The unforgettably beguiling Joanna. His first love and guide in so many things. The mother of his first born son and the woman who believed their love *truly* could last forever. Beyond this life; even beyond time itself. Such, Matt at last believed, *was* their love for each other.

Or the one who always seemed to have a touch of star-dust sprinkled in her glowing golden hair. Hair which reminded him of the fall harvest moons of his careless youth. His constant red rose from a snowy winter's night in December of 1946. The breathtakingly beautiful young woman who had given up singing in the spot-light for singing in the shower and bed-time lullabies to their young son. She still sang softly in his ear whenever they danced. The wonderful woman he had built a *happy* life with. The *only* other love of its kind in his life. His graceful Suzanne. Matt was so glad she loved him and they shared *everything* in their lives... together. Both laughter *and* tears He was still deeply in love with her twenty eight years after their wedding day. She was everything to him and by far his best friend. She was all that and so much more and it had all begun on a spring night in 1938 under a million brightly sparkling stars with a single kiss.

Matt no longer questioned the concept of fate. Kismet. Everything happens for a reason. No purpose in questioning that any longer. At least about most things. He *still* questioned the loss of their little girl and, of course, his loss of Joanna and *now* her death. She believed they had only lost each other in this life. Perhaps in another... he could only hope she was right. They deserved another chance. Another life.

The last shots in World War II had been fired over thirty years ago but now, with Joanna's passing, Matt realized his personal war with himself had finally ended. He was sure their love was another casualty of that long ago war and that she had *really* died of a broken heart. Broken hearts and broken promises. Far too many of those in *his* life.

Yet beyond that there still remained the one question which had always been there. Unanswered.

For the first time he finally understood...some questions truly have no answer. Nor do they need one. Love Simply Is. And if it's *real* it lasts.

He glanced at the clock on his desk. The second hand was not moving. He felt a familiar hand caress his cheek as it had on that rainy London night in 1939.

In that crystalline moment suspended in time he found the answer to his questions about so many things when he heard Joanna's voice whisper softly in his ear... *"Next time we will have forever my love."*

Joanna's presence was so strong Matt could not bring himself to believe it had not happened. Even his orderly mind which had always been a non-believer in such possibilities, was convinced she had been standing beside him for a few moments. He was certain she had found a way to return in order to comfort him. To reassure him there *was* going to be another time for them. That death was not an ending to everything but rather was a path leading toward a beginning. Another chance for the precious things that had been lost in the lifetime just ended. That love is stronger than *everything* else: surviving even beyond death. In those few moments Joanna had shown him that the end of one lifetime was only a doorway into another place and time and that nothing is ever lost. Everything continues. Some lives move forward while others travel backward but their stories never end. The pen writing them is never stilled. The page is endless. Only the face of the writer is forever hidden.

He saw the second hand suddenly jump ahead 11 seconds as it resumed its endless quest through time and space...seeking to find that long ago lost world of magic where *all* things become possibilities.

~ ~ ~ ~

Eons later in a place beyond the most distant star yet closer than a lover's kiss in a realm where dreams do come true and love's wishes are granted: there in this mythical land of barley fields and giant oaks the West Wind whispers softly to two people forever young and in love. They often speak of vague memories of other lives they seem to have lived. One, barely remembered, during a Great War. Yet whenever they look in each other's eyes it seems those lives must have been but the stuff of dreams. For them there exists *only* now. Two people in love and wise enough to live as if each moment is all anyone has .

~ THE END? ~

Author's Notes

All of us read from our youth. The ability to read and write sets us apart from all the other creatures with whom we share this remarkable planet. The ability to think and reason is a wonderful gift as is the ability to speak but without the magic of reading and writing the thoughts and concepts would soon be lost.

I have always been intrigued by written fiction. The creation of an alternate world containing fictional characters living out lives of their own often becomes as real to the reader as people they see every day.

How is it done? What process does the writer go through to write a good novel? I will tell you the process which led to "Fields of Gold."

It all began a number of years ago when my wife Candis and I were on vacation in Ireland. We were touring a wonderful old country estate called Mucros House near Killarney in County Kerry. While there we heard a song written by Sting with the name "Fields of Gold;" this version performed by Eva Cassidy. A story began to form in my mind. Later I heard a performance of the piece by the group Celtic Woman and the story expanded. In fact it grew every time I heard the song. Strangely, in the beginning I visualized the story more as a film than a book. In reality every frame of it played in my head. Several years passed before the characters finally ganged up on me and made me sit down to begin the process of telling their story. I must admit only the first half of the book is mine. The second half was written by them. I simply observed and recorded. I had no choice; they refused to live out the ending I had envisioned.

The book spans the period from the late 1930's until the mid 1970's. It is historical fiction and I have tried to keep it as close as possible to the history of those turbulent times. So what you have is love and war. Wars, thank heavens, end but love can go on forever. The song "Fields of Gold" became in my mind Joanna's Theme.

I want to thank Sting for having written the wonderful song and Eva Cassidy (sadly too soon passed) and Celtic Woman for the great performances which inspired me to write the book.

As the book progressed, two other songs became a part of it. The first was "If We Never Meet Again" by the great Louie Armstrong which became Suzanne's Theme. If you have not heard this, it is worth a listen. You can find it on the internet by Louie or to hear the version I first heard on the CD, "A Wonderful World" by Tony Bennett and K.D. Lang.

i

Then you will know how it would sound performed by Suzanne at the old Stork Club on that winter's night in 1946.

The second, "Try to Remember," is a wonderful song from "The Fantasticks" which you may have heard. This wistful score became the background music for the letters Matt and Joanna wrote each other in the years after they parted.

Thank You To:

First I want to express my gratitude to all the men and women who lived those times. The term "the Greatest Generation" is much used but none-the-less completely true. They really were and always will be. In those years America was truly great and your sacrifices made it so.

My wife, who must in fact be a Saint, not only endured all the challenges required in writing this book (all the mood-swings), she was helpful in more ways than I can ever adequately thank her for. I could never have done it without her. She was my editor in residence while I wrote. Without her this book would never have existed.

I want to thank the people who graciously read the manuscript as it was being written, a more difficult task than one might imagine: Gay Bradley, D'ete Sewell, Jerri Bergen, Janis Kouche, Kim Wells, Don (Oso) Contreras, Mimi Gentry, Hal Kent (especially for assistance with British vernacular thanks to his surviving two years in an English boys' school), Carol Stangler, Abby Martin, Angela Ricks, and finally to Dorothy (Dot) Walker who lived those times and was especially helpful in capturing the aura of the '40's.

Additional thanks are owed to Dr. Brad Strickland of the University of North Georgia, Department of English (a talented and oft published author) for his more than generous assistance in preparation of the final manuscript for publication.

The initial design and artwork including the 1937 MG auto, the Castle Gatehouse and the B-17 were by Gerri Bergen of Victory Girl, vintage aviation artwork (www. Victorygirl.com) she is a talented successor to those who painted 'Nose Art" on aircraft from the years of WWI until today.

And finally a thank you to Marsha Richter for the title page art of the hat. By now you probably understand the significance of the two flowers.

Jim Stephens   Oakwood, Georgia   March 15, 2013

Historical Personages

Winston Churchill: Churchill was indeed "The rock England stood on" from the 10th of May, 1940 when, following the resignation of Neville Chamberlain, he became Prime Minister until the end of the War in Europe in early May 1945. England expressed its gratitude by voting him out of office nearly as soon as the war had ended. He left office July 26, 1945. Perhaps out of shame, the Country re-elected him Prime Minister in 1951, an office he held until April 7, 1955. It was Churchill who first tried to warn the United States of the dangers Josef Stalin and Soviet Russia represented to the free world. Franklin Roosevelt ignored the warning, convinced he could get Stalin to do his bidding.

Winston Churchill died at his London home on the morning of January 24, 1965 at age 90. He had survived all the major figures of World War II and, in the intervening years, received the recognition so fully due him.

Franklin Roosevelt (FDR): A unique figure in American history, he was a president both beloved and despised during his lifetime. A Democrat, FDR was elected president in November of 1932 during the "Great Depression." He assumed office in January of 1933 and implemented Government economic policies which can, at kindest, be defined as ultra liberal.

He is often described as saving America during the Depression. Any reasonable examination of the facts would argue that his policies had little if any long-term effect on American economics. It was preparation for World War II which reversed financial circumstances. Before the war began many countries were purchasing huge quantities of military goods and armaments from the United States. For this reason factories had returned to production. The wealth of other nations was fueling America's recovery.

Near the end of the war he made clear his opposition to Churchill's demand that Russia not be allowed to dominate the Countries of Eastern Europe, many of which, like Poland, had suffered greatly under the hand of Nazi Germany and had fought on the Allied side during the war. As a result of FDR's refusal to support Churchill, those Countries continued to suffer under the Soviets. He had completely misread both Stalin's personality and the nature of Communism.

FDR died in Warm Springs Georgia on March 29, 1945 after complaining of "a terrific pain in the back of my head." He did not live to see the war end. He had been unique serving the better part of four terms as President of the United States. A law was passed after his death to prevent any future President serving more than two terms.

Adolph Hitler: Leader of Germany from January of 1933 until April 30, 1945, he was a would-be artist prior to World War I. He was Austrian, not German. The Academy of Fine Arts in Vienna rejected the young Hitler twice as unfit for painting. He worked in watercolor, painting landscapes and street scenes. His rejection by the Academy may have been the beginning of his anti-Semite fixation.

He ignited World War II by attacking Poland in the face of treaties between Poland, England and France which specified if any one of the countries was invaded the other two would come to its defense. Despite advice from his Generals, this WWI Corporal launched an attack on Poland in the morning hours of the first of September 1939. After a warning from England and France giving him forty-eight hours to withdraw, on the third of September both countries declared war on Germany. This date is considered the start of WWII. Six years later Germany lay in ruins. Hitler's dream of absolute hegemony of Europe by Nazi Germany relegated to the "Dust Heap" of twentieth century history. He committed suicide in a bunker near the destroyed Reich Chancellery building in Berlin on April thirtieth 1945. His body was burned along with that of his newly married wife and long-time mistress, Eva Braun.

Joseph Goebbels and his wife Magda poisoned their six children with cyanide before taking their own lives. Heinrich Himmler, Göring's other opponent in the book, also committed suicide when, disguised as a German Sergeant, he was captured by the British.

Hermann Göring: Perhaps the most difficult of all the figures in the Nazi Pantheon to understand. A hero in the German Air Force during WWI, he was the son of a good family. He had also married well. His first wife Carin, a beautiful woman was born in Stockholm. She too was from a wealthy family. Göring fell in love the first time he saw her. On that day he was far from the "Fat Herman" of his later years. They wed in 1923 but she died of heart failure in 1931.

Theirs had been a storybook romance and even though he remarried, he named his great hunting lodge Carinhall. Before and during the war his brother, Albert Göring, brought him lists of Jews to be freed and Herman always signed the lists, each time saying he would never do it again. Then Albert would bring another list and Herman would sign.

Both Goebbels and Himmler constantly tried to replace Göring in Hitler's favor, they never succeeded.

In 1939 Adolph Hitler named Göring as his successor should anything happen. This made him the second most powerful man in Nazi Germany. He was already the man in charge of Germany's Luftwaffe (Air Force) and Fallschirmjäger (Parachutists.)

He honored all fliers; even the enemy. He was in overall charge of POW camps for enemy fliers and it is true that prisoners could take college credit courses in his camps.

He was the highest ranking Nazi to stand in the dock for trial at Nuremberg. There was no doubt of his guilt and Göring was judged so and sentenced to death. The best one can say is he was probably the best of a group of very bad men. He too committed suicide with a cyanide capsule before the date of his execution. Where he obtained the pill remains a mystery. It has been said the Americans who guarded him came to like him.

Friedrich Wilheim von Lindeiner-Wildau: Kommandant of Stalag Luft III during most of WWII, he joined the Luftwaffe in 1939 as a member of Herman Göring's personal staff. He was infuriated that British and American prisoners were shot following "The Great Escape." After a short imprisonment, the British tried him for war crimes. He was facing a possible death sentence, but so many prisoners from Stalag Luft III came forward to testify in his defense that he walked away a free man. He died in 1963 at the age of 82.

Sir Hugh Dowding: Air Chief Marshall RAF Fighter Command during the Battle of Britain, he was the one in charge of those about who Churchill said, "Never in the course of human events have so many owed so much to so few."

In his case, a stern visage covered a good heart. His men affectionately called him "Stuffy." He referred to his pilots as his "dear fighter boys" and his "Chicks" and protected them like a mother hen. His son Derek was one of them. Dowding is credited with first blunting then defeating Germany's air war against England thus preventing the planned invasion. His integrated air defense system and ability to maintain significant fighter aircraft and pilot reserves wore down the German air attacks. It was this defeat which caused Hitler to turn toward an invasion of Russia and his old enemy Joseph Stalin.

He was accused of being very single-minded and lacking in diplomacy and political "savoir faire;" the "failings" often found in many great military leaders who are relegated to the background once their usefulness is over. So it was with Dowding. He was removed from his command on 24 April 1940 and sent to America in charge of the British Air Mission.

He retired from the RAF in July of 1942 and died at his family home in Tunbridge Wells, County Kent on the 17th of February in 1970. He was 87 years old.

Air Marshall Richard E. C. Peirse: A naval pilot who distinguished himself in World War I earning the Distinguished Service Order and the Air Force Cross. He was given a commission as a squadron leader in the newly formed Royal Air Force. Following assignments in Palestine and Transjordan he returned to England and was promoted to air vice-marshal in 1937.

Following the departure of Sir Charles Portal as Commander-in-Chief of Bomber Command in October of 1940, he was given charge of Bomber Command during the extremely difficult period when England had few heavy bombers or well trained pilots. He was then relieved of his command in January 1942 due to the alarming losses being suffered by his bombers.

He retired as an Air Marshal in 1945 and died August 6, 1970 at seventy-seven years of age.

Josef Stalin: The most deadly "Secretary" the world has ever seen. He was born on December 18, 1878 in the town of Gori, part the Russian Empire. He was abused as a child by his alcoholic father and suffered from a birth defect in his foot plus the effects of an accident which caused one arm to be shorter than the other. As a young man he discovered the writing of Vladimir Lenin, converted to Marxism, and became a revolutionary and a member of the Bolsheviks in 1903. He had adopted the name "Stalin" which means steel in Russian.

Nearing the end of World War I he was active in the Revolution of 1917, attacking the provisional government and demanding the end of the war against Germany. He was elected to the Bolshevik Central Committee in October 1917.

Following the Revolution, Lenin appointed Stalin to the post of General Secretary of the Communist Party of the Soviet Union, a post which allowed him to appoint his supporters to powerful posts in the Party.

Lenin suffered a stroke in 1922 and died in 1924 elevating Stalin to the leader of Soviet Russia. Under his leadership and as a direct result of his orders, tens of millions of Russian citizens and foreign residents living there were executed or starved during his "purges." He destroyed many high ranking officers in his own military after being tricked by German intelligence into believing they were traitors; this on the very verge of World War II. He made treaties with Adolph Hitler allowing the invasion of Poland which gave Russia part of that country as a reward.

Once he was attacked by Germany, he allied with The United States and Great Britain out of necessity. He disliked Churchill who understood him far too well. He played FDR by being polite and seeming reasonable. His impression of America was the same as his of FDR; a weak, indecisive country led by a cripple in a wheelchair.

The sop to Roosevelt was his promise to support the idea for a United Nations following the war but only with protections and guarantees of Russia's ability to block decisions it did not like, thus the Security Council of the UN was included in its organization so that a single "no" vote could block any action.

He propagandized Russia as a "workers' paradise" while referring to converts to socialism in other countries as "useful idiots." His first move in the countries occupied at the end of World War II was elimination of the well educated; the Intelligencia. Like Hitler, Stalin had no regard for the individual. They were only a number under his belief system. Individualism was to be eradicated.

On the morning of March 1, 1953 Stalin suffered an apparent stroke. He died on the 5th of March. He is buried in the Kremlin Wall Necropolis. Later investigations have indicated poisoning using a flavorless brand of warferin; a powerful rat killer which induces symptoms like a stroke. Either Lavrentiy Beria or Nikita Khrushchev could have introduced it into his wine on the preceding night. My favorite suspect is Khrushchev who was constantly treated as Stalin's fool, forced to entertain by dancing night after night. It has been reported that Beria later bragged that he had poisoned Stalin. If he was indeed poisoned, the killer had done the people of the Soviet Union a great favor. The killer may have been worried about his own life as Stalin was already planning another great purge when he died.

Sherman Billingsley: Born on March 10, 1896, he was the youngest in a family of six children of parents who settled in Enid Oklahoma during the great 1893 land rush. The children attended a one room schoolhouse. The young boy became a helper to an older brother who was a bootlegger.

Sherman moved to Detroit at age 18 to carry-on the family business but he was soon arrested on Federal alcohol charges. He spent 15 months in prison. When released he moved with his brother to New York City where they bought drug stores as a front for bootlegging. The profits from this were used to start the Stork Club; first as a speakeasy then as a legitimate night club.

He attracted the biggest names in all fields to his club. It has been said Sherman created the concept of "Celebrity." Regular guests included Bing Crosby, Lucille Ball, Charlie Chaplin, the Duke and Duchess of Windsor, the Kennedys, Grace Kelly and Marilyn Monroe to name only a very few

One night Ernest Hemingway wanted to pay his bar bill with a one hundred thousand dollar check he had for the rights to For Whom the Bell Tolls. Hemingway had to wait until closing time but he got his check cashed...

The club began a long slow decline in the nineteen fifties. It closed in 1965 and Sherman Billingsley died in New York City on the third of October 1966. He had already been planning another club.

Louis Armstrong: "Pops, Satch, Satchmo, Louie, Satchel Mouth" Born August 4, 1901. He was born into a very poor family. The grandson of slaves. His youth was spent in abject poverty. His father abandoned his family and young son and daughter. Louis spent most of his time with his grandmother and his uncle Isaac. He attended Fisk School for boys where he learned to read music. As a young man he carried coal to the houses of prostitution in Storyville and listened to the bands playing there. He met Joe "King" Oliver one of the most famous Jazz musicians of that era.

He took up the cornet and developed his style while part of the band in the New Orleans Band for Colored Waifs in the institution where he had been sent for delinquency. Eventually he became the band leader there. He played in many of the city's frequent brass band parades and funerals. Joe "King" Oliver saw such talent in the young man that he became a teacher to him.

In time Louis became in demand in Chicago, New York and the West Coast. He also began writing music. Primarily Jazz but he did write several more introspective pieces such as If We Never Meet Again.

Though married four times; he had no children many people who knew him said he loved the very young and delighted in simply being around them.

He continued to perform almost until his death. He died of a heart attack while asleep on July 6, 1971. He may have been the greatest cornet player ever. His honorary pall bearers included Dizzy Gillespie, Count Basie, Harry James, Ed Sullivan, Frank Sinatra, Johnny Carson, Ella Fitzgerald and Pearl Bailey. What greater tribute could have been paid a good man?

Clark Gable: Born William Clark Gable on February 1, 1901 in Cadiz, Ohio, to a father who was an oil well driller and a mother who died when he was six months old. His father remarried when Gable was two years old and his new mother taught him piano, raised him to be well dressed and well groomed. He always loved automobiles. His father taught him to do "manly things" such as hunting, fishing and hard work. During his high school years he began acting on the stage and later moved on to films and Hollywood.

Though he married a total of five times, his love for Carol Lombard (his third wife) was truly the kind of love legends are made of (and movies are made about.) They were together from 1939 until she was killed in the plane crash in 1942. Her death caused Gable to join the Army Air Corps as an Officer and a gunner; this in spite of his age. He was sent to England to make a film about gunners on B-17 bombers, and did, in fact, fly out of Polebrook. He flew six missions with the 351st before being sent home. Hitler had put a price on Gable's head as stated in the book. I made only one change giving him a seventh mission on the "Maid of Barley." The shrapnel from flack did cut into the heel of his shoe on his last mission (in reality his sixth mission.)

The part of Rhett Butler in "Gone with the Wind" is considered his greatest role. He never topped it. His acting after the war is generally considered inferior to his roles before the war. It was said by his friend, actress Ester Williams, "He was never the same. Something had gone out of him."

His last film was "The Misfits" with Marilyn Monroe and Montgomery Clift. It was also the last film for Monroe and in a quirk of fate was the film Clift was watching on television the night he died in

1966. Gable's acting in this film is considered superior to all his other post-war pictures.

The house on the ranch in Encino, California where he and Lombard had lived was his home until he died on November 16, 1960. The house had remained almost completely unchanged after she died.

His fifth wife Kay had him buried next to Carol Lombard in the Great Mausoleum at Forest Lawn Memorial Park in Glendale, California. The two were at last together again... forever.

---A Final Thought---

About Love: It has been written in many forms that faith, hope, and love are the three greatest of human virtues. Of these love is the strongest and brings us closest to being eternal.